Lethal Memories

Jamil Sherjan & Rob Flemming

Lens & Pen
Cheltenham

ISBN 9781090667007

First Published in the United Kingdom by Lens & Pen in 2019
lensandpenpublishing.co.uk

To my wife Angela, for all her encouragementand support while writing this book.

Jamil

And to Anne for her patience during my timeof preoccupation.

Rob

Contents

Maps

Eastern Mediterranean

Middle East and the route from the Mediterranean through the Suez Canal to the Arabian Sea and to Pakistan

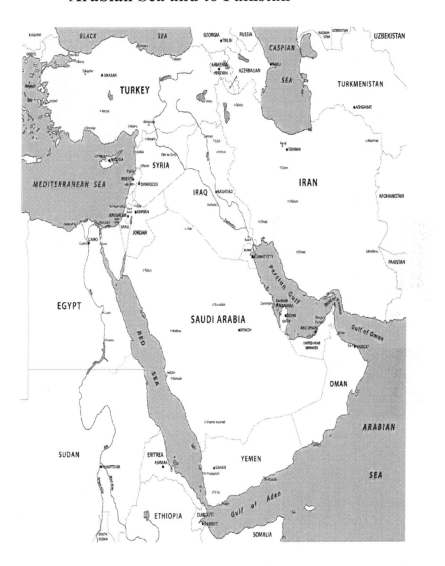

Pakistan

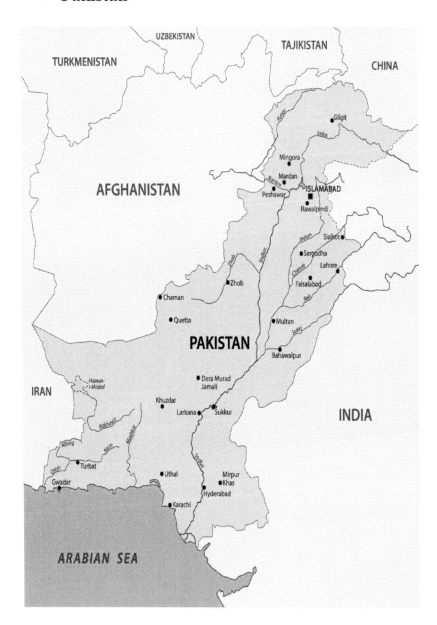

1 ~ Cyprus 1974

Raising herself up on one elbow, Vanessa idly glanced down the beach to the shoreline, where a simplified version of cricket was being played. The basic principle of hitting a moving ball with a swinging bat was adhered to but any further resemblance to the gentlemen's game ended there. John slow-bowled the rubber ball to little Michael who then swung his bat wildly in an attempt to connect. On the whole, he was fairly successful in smacking the ball into the sea for his father to retrieve. When he missed, he invariably spun himself round to trip in the pebble-pocked sand and fall one way or the other. For some bizarre reason he clearly found either outcome hilarious, hooting with laughter at the end of each play.

She lay back on her towel, staring lazily at the clear blue sky and wondered how much longer she dared grill under the sun's glare. One week: that's all they had. But it was one glorious week, one great big adventure. And they still had four more wonderful days in fabulous Cyprus: where the food was delicious, the wine pure nectar, the locals quaintly delightful and the sun shone all day long. It was a far cry from the beaches of southern England where one gambled with the unpredictable British weather. Of course, there were occasional day trips to Calais and even Ostend. Once upon a time, before Michael appeared on the scene, she and John had had decadent weekends in Paris. That was a while ago!

A pebble found its way underneath her bum and Vanessa arched her back to rearrange the towel. As she did so, she was suddenly aware of the number of looks that her manoeuvres were attracting. Although her bikini wasn't that revealing, it did accentuate her natural curves that were naturally being admired by more than a few of the fit males on the sand. And, perhaps, even a few females.

Pissouri Beach was barely 11 minutes drive from forty-seven and a half square miles of the United Kingdom – the Western Sovereign Base Area of Akrotiri. Apparently, more than 12,000 service personnel worked at RAF Akrotiri or at the Episkopi Garrison, which was even nearer. Therefore it was highly likely,

Vanessa decided, that most of her admirers and fellow sunbathers were military. It had been a friend of John's at the bank who had mentioned it to begin with:

'... really, because my brother was stationed at Episkopi, (he's in the army, most people are in the forces over there) and he was talking about a divine little villa called Constantinos (because it's owned by Constantinos Kyriakou, you see), near the square in Pissouri Village, which was ludicrously cheap and yes, it is a bit of a hike down to the beach but worth it when you get there although you really need to take a taxi back but that's fun, so you and Vanessa really ought to go there.'

In imitation, John had rattled the whole thing off in the one sentence. She remembered laughing before he'd even finished; perhaps mainly with delight at the realisation that her normally responsible and careful husband was genuinely suggesting a holiday on Cyprus. And, as per usual, he'd done his research.

'Cyprus was a Crown Colony and granted its independence in 1960, but Her Majesty's Government in Whitehall, true to form, was damned if it didn't keep a couple of footholds on the island. It's all about having a strategic position at the eastern end of the Mediterranean. That allows them to keep an eye, and ear, on the Middle East, the entrance to the Suez Canal and the exit from the Black Sea. So Britain's hung on to Akrotiri in the south west of the island and Dhekelia, sort of on the east coast. That's called ...'

That was as far as he got before Vanessa tuned out, dreaming of sun, sea, sand and sundowners. Now, in real Cyprus time, she was thinking along similar lines. The buzz of conversation on the beach blended smoothly with the hypnotic rhythm of the waves. It gave a bass line to the higher pitch of the seagulls' cries and the laughter coming from the bar at the far end of the beach. Abba's hit song Waterloo added its own melody to nature's music, a little distorted by a few enthusiastic singers. The smell of grilled fish, wafted by a warm breeze, suddenly made Vanessa feel hungry. Lunch was definitely in order. She watched her two men walking happily back up the beach towards her.

'Hey, how does grilled sardines, fresh bread, salad and a cold beer sound?' she called. 'A Coke for you, Mikey?'

'Yay!'

'Sounds good to me.'

The explosion was deafening, a violent ripping noise that sucked the music from the air that was suddenly filled with flying debris. The blast obliterated the shoddily built bar, filling the world with a murderous hail of sharp fragments of wood, nails, shards of hot metal and splinters of glass. Fire broke out as spilled cooking oil ignited, the flames greedily seeking out all that was flammable among the remnants of the shack. Coils of choking black smoke added to the chaos. For one hollow moment, the only sounds were those of grisly impact and the spitting fire. And then came the screams.

'That was a big bang,' Mike said softly. 'There's no more bar.'

'Jesus!'

'We need to get off the beach.'

'John, we need to help.'

'There'll be plenty of people … they know what to do. Bound to be medics …'

His words were cut short by another blast even louder than the first and much closer. Barely 200 yards away, the bomb had been hidden in a metal rubbish bin by the roadside at the top of the beach. The explosion destroyed the bin, sending a rain of nails, ball bearings and deadly shrapnel outwards and upwards. Finding some previously untapped speed of reaction, John threw himself forward, pushing his wife and son to the ground milliseconds after the detonation. He winced, biting his lip as he felt something sharp slice into his back and felt the warmth of hot blood on his skin. And heard the shrill screams.

Ears ringing, covered in a mixture of dust and sand, John Roberts pulled himself up painfully. It took a few moments before he realised it was Vanessa who was screaming. Whitefaced, she sat in the sand staring downwards as she held her left arm with a shaking right hand. Broken spears of white bone stood starkly out from the slow flow of carmine blood and ragged flesh. John felt his gorge rise but managed to repress the muscular contractions in his throat. Crawling across, he carefully put one arm round her shoulders.

'It's going to be all right,' he said quietly, not knowing what else to say.

3

She stared at him with wide-eyed horror, her screams slowing to deep painful moans.

'Mikey?'

They glanced round to find the little boy standing silently beside them, the tears tracking furrows through the dirt on his cheeks.

'Mike, are you hurt? Does anything hurt, Mike?'

He shook his head.

'Are you sure?'

'Yes, Daddy,' he replied, dragging one hand across his face to hide the tears. 'But I didn't like being pushed into the sand 'cos the stony bits were hard. And Mummy's hurt.'

John pulled his son in with his free arm and rested his chin on Mike's head.

'Yes she is but you have to be brave and strong.'

"What's happening John? It hurts and I feel faint.'

Vanessa's voice had dropped to a soft whisper and John could feel the weight of her body dragging against his arm as she started to lose consciousness.

'We're alive thank God. Help's on its way.'

'I'm scared.'

'I know, we all are.' He reached out with one hand to touch her cheek, gentle and reassuring. 'It'll be fine, you'll see,' he said as he let her slowly drop back onto the sand.

All along the beach, there were people sitting motionless, numbed by fear and the gross savagery of it all. Others tried to help those injured by the blasts. The screaming had diminished, replaced by the sounds of distress and loss.

' Mummy's not going to die, is she?' asked Michael, his voice thin and anxious.

'Not today, thank God.'

'Is he asleep!?'

Michael pointed to a young couple higher up the beach, much closer to the wreckage of the bin. She was sitting on the sand with her legs outstretched while he lay at her side, his head gently cradled in her lap. Stroking his hair, she cried softly over him and her tears fell one by one onto his forehead. She'd closed his eyes but she couldn't close the gaping wound in his chest.

*****

Three police officers from the small station on the edge of Pissouri had been the first to arrive. Hearing the explosions and seeing the coils of rising smoke, they feared the worst and came armed but accurately assessing the situation, they called for help. Within half an hour the short stretch of road above the beach was filled with a stream of cars, taxis and ambulances. Doctors and medics from the Royal Army Medical Corps fanned out across the beach. They did what they could, urgently. Some lives were saved, others lost, wounds were cleaned and dressed.

John Roberts was still struggling to staunch the blood from his wife's mangled arm when Lance Corporal 'Needles' McManus arrived, armed with a medical kit. He wore dusty combat fatigues and a weary look that tightened as he saw the damage to Vanessa's arm. Kneeling down in the sand, he nodded to John as he opened his bag.

'OK mate, let me have a look.'

'Thank God you're here. I did the best I could but I couldn't stop the bleeding. I tried ...'

Needles looked at the belt cinched around Vanessa's upper arm. 'You did a good job,' he said, pulling a webbed tourniquet from his bag. 'She's lost a lot of blood but at least you managed to slow it down.'

His fingers kept moving as he talked. Once he had strapped the tourniquet just above Vanessa's elbow and ensured it was secure, Needles removed the belt and held it out for John to take.

'It's better down there,' he grunted, checking the pulse on right wrist at the same time. He leaned over, close to her ear. 'Can you hear me love?' Eyelids flickered open, topaz blue eyes vaguely registering Needles' presence and she nodded her head just a little.

'Going to give you some morphine for the pain and a tetanus injection, clean you up a bit and get you over to a hospital. Do you understand?'

Again the flicker of eyelids, blue focus and a slight nod. Needles wasted no time, extracting vials and syringes, loading up and injecting one after the other. Gauze and saline solution were gently applied to remove the worst of the dirt.

5

'Best I can do out here on the beach, I'm afraid.' He waved at the vehicle line on the roadside, waiting for someone to register. Clocked by another medic, he put one hand on the other with palms down and rocked them from side to side in the air. Getting the thumbs up, Needles turned back to his task, applying two field dressings to the raw stump of arm.

'Where will they take her?' John asked.

'I'm guessing she'll go to Alcatraz but there're a lot of damaged people on this beach. Sorry, that's what we call the hospital down on Cape Zevgari. Proper name's Princess Mary's. That's just off the main base at Akrotiri. But ask the stretcher boys and you can probably ride in the ambi. Otherwise grab one of the cars and follow.'

Finished his work on Vanessa, he leaned back on his heels. 'You OK kid?' Mike nodded silently. 'Right, let's have a look at your back mate.'

'I'm OK I think although …'

'Let me be the judge of that, Sir. If you could turn … that's fine. You've got a fine bit of metal stuck in your back but we can soon fix that. Hold still now.'

John felt the cold metal of large tweezers touch his skin. Then a pause, a sharp tug, a stab of pain and a fresh flow of warm blood.

'You were lucky, hit you right in a love handle and didn't slice any muscle. Clean it up and put in a couple of field stitches; that should do it.'

The medic worked quickly, with calm proficiency. Cleaning the wound, he removed small particles of green paint and stitched the edges of the cut together in two places.

'Tetanus shot,' he said, stabbing the needle into John's shoulder. Get that checked out in about ten days or sooner if it's a problem. Yo Jamie, this one's urgent mate,' he said to one of the two orderlies who'd arrived. 'We've got traumatic amputation with possible extensive fractures, heavy contamination and soft tissue disruption. Father and son ride with you?'

'No problem.'

Kneeling down on the sand, they inched Vanessa carefully onto the stretcher, eliciting only a few cries of pain. Then taking the strain, they lifted her up and started back up the beach towards the ambulance.

'Thank you for your help,' John said. 'I just hope that someone catches the bastards who did this.'

'Don't worry, our lot's going to be crawling all over the place trying to find the murderous slime who did this. You need to go and I need to get on. Good luck.'

Needles watched as father and son walked hand in hand, hurrying to catch up with the orderlies.

'Poor sods,' he muttered, turning back to the beach. 'But not as bad as some. Jesus. Onwards.'

As far as he knew, 17 people had already been confirmed dead and at least 43 were seriously injured. And there was still a long way to go. Needles shouldered his pack, spotted another couple and headed in their direction, hoping for just a minor injury. At two in the afternoon it was still hot, too hot, and there was little shade for anyone who was wounded badly. He picked up a leaflet, left on the ground by a bloodstained towel. The strapline ran:

'A golden sun shines from an azure sky, while cerulean seas lap pristine sands.'

'Some fucking paradise this is,' he spat.

*****

At about one o'clock in the afternoon, Nick Markides was sitting on a stool in a bar called Zephyrus, not far from the Old Port in Limassol. Arrayed on the table in front of him: a slightly scuffed Olympus OM-1 35mm camera on top of a well-used notebook, a half empty glass of Keo beer beside a bowl of olives, a pack of Camel cigarettes, a battered Zippo, an almost full ashtray and a telephone. The last item, a concession made by Kostas (who owned Zephyrus) in recognition of the journalist's need for telecommunications; provided he paid the bills and spent money at the bar. Nick worked as a stringer covering Cyprus and the surrounding region for several foreign national newspapers. His client base included dailies in London, New York, Athens and Berlin, which at first sounded rather impressive. Until he explained that he only got paid if he could provide some news.

'Get a proper job, Nicky,' Kostas was saying. 'If you have to be a journalist, get a job with Cyprus Times or the Mail.'

'Kostas, you know that's crap. News is just slow at the moment, so money's a bit tight. Trust me, something is bound to happen. Makarios will finally get assassinated, Turkey will invade Cyprus properly and EOKA-B's guerrillas will open a Turkish restaurant in Nicosia.'

Kostas snorted.

'Yeah, I know. But something will turn up even if it's only more insane interference from Athens.'

As Nick drained his glass, the phone rang. Kostas picked up.

'Zephyrus. Kostas.' He listened for a moment, then held the receiver out towards Nick. 'I think maybe you are psychic. It's Andreas at Pissouri. There've been two explosions on the beach, some people killed and many injured. The British are already there.'

'Andreas. It's Nick. What happened?'

He moved the camera, opened his notebook and holding the telephone in one hand, Nick scribbled erratic notes with the other. Most of the time he just nodded or spat out an expletive. Kostas watched him, waiting patiently until the call had finished.

'Has anyone assumed responsibility? No. OK. Thanks Andreas, I owe you one. Yeah, I'm going straight to the beach after this, then see if I can get any information out of the Station Commander. No, probably Limassol Hospital, I doubt whether they'll let me into Princess Mary's. Yeah. Then back here and get on the phone. OK, 'bye.'

Nick replaced the handset and looked at Kostas.

'I'm gone. This is seriously bad karma. I'll be back as soon as I can but take any calls, yeah?'

'Be careful.'

'You got it,' Nick replied, gathered up his stuff and was gone.

His battered Land Rover was hardly in the first flush of youth but it suited his temperament somehow; it had attitude. Picking up the Old Paphos Road on the edge of Limassol the way was more or less clear as it ran along the boundary between Cypriot territory and the British enclave. The first roadblock appeared at the point where the road crossed the line from Cyprus into the United Kingdom, just before Kourion. With no one ahead of him, either side of the roadblock, Nick pulled up to the barricade and stopped. On the opposite side of the road, a ragged line of traffic moved slowly through. An ambulance, arriving at the back of the line, was given priority and waved through.

The armed soldier briefly scrutinized Nick's passport and press pass before leaning through the window to stare. A bit longer than necessary, Nick thought, to simply make sure that his face matched the mug shots. There were the usual questions: where had he come from, where was he going to and why. Then there were the usual cautions about entering a hazardous area before he was waved through. He had to run the gauntlet of no less than three more roadblocks before he reached Pissouri Beach.

There was little left to see of the chaos and terror that had dominated the beach only two hours earlier. And yet the signs were all there. The remains of the beach café were still smouldering, tendrils of dark grey smoke rising from the blackened timbers and twisted metal. From time to time yellow flames licked its corpse, turning shattered glass into a mockery of jewels amid the wreckage. Debris from the café and rubbish bin littered the beach. Bloody towels lay on the sand where they'd been when their owners were still healthy and laughing; now they were crimson testaments to mutilation and death. And there were also those things that gave glimpses of lives that had been. A bottle of wine lay on its side uncorked, the leaked liquid now a purple stain in the sand. A nameless paperback that someone had been reading, its cover stripped away by the blast revealing only black print on a page without context.

It didn't require much imagination or experience for a mental picture to form, and Nick had plenty of both. He scribbled a few notes and took a few pictures, even though the beach was empty. He knew which images were really needed if they were to make the cut with any foreign news editor, but there was no one left to photograph.

By the time he'd finished at Pissouri, it was almost three. Exchanging a few words with the guards manning the roadblock told him little more than he knew already. But now at least he did know that Group Captain Rafe Carson was at the Episkopi Garrison. A journey that would normally take no more than half an hour, took almost double that time, thanks to the roadblocks. And then he had to wait for almost 40 minutes before Carson's adjutant invited him in to the Group Captain's office.

Rafe Carson was looking out of the window when the two men entered, but turned at the sound. He was wearing a flight suit rather than a uniform and looked as though he might have just flown a million miles. The angular face showed clear signs of fatigue and the man shrugged his shoulders, stretching the muscles. But the grey-blue eyes were alert and his gaze incisive.

'Nicos Markides, isn't it?'

'It's Nick Markides, Sir,' he said without thinking. 'My mother's English.'

The Group Captain narrowed his eyes.

'Take a seat Nick Markides.' The emphasis heavy on the first name. Transferring eye contact to his adjutant, he said, 'Tom, bring me the telex from Nicosia if you would and see if we have any messages from any of the security details. Oh, and you might as well put a message on the board postponing the polo tournament on Saturday. I don't think we'll have the time or the inclination.'

'Sir!' The adjutant snapped off a salute before leaving the room.

Group Captain Carson lowered himself onto the chair behind the only desk in the office. The two wire trays on the right held a file and a few sets of papers, grouped and held together with heavy-duty paper clips. Noticeably the 'In' tray held more than its sister tray that was marked 'Out'. A simple aquamarine ceramic pot held an assortment of pens and pencils. Together with a pad of lined paper and a diary, that completed the inventory of a place that, seemingly, was little used. Neat but not a priority and dismissed accordingly, thought Nick. The phrase might equally be used, (the word neat being replaced by scruffy), for a slightly irritating Greek Cypriot journalist with an English mother.

'I've read some of your stuff Markides, in The Times I think. Didn't you write that piece about the protests at the Athens Polytechnic in November?' Nick nodded. 'Got a picture of the tank crashing through the gates as well, if I remember.'

'Sadly the picture wasn't mine. An agency photographer, Steve Penney, based in Athens. But copy was mine.'

Rafe Carson pursed his lips and nodded.

'Never mind, it was well written. Bloody mess if you ask me.'

Gratified by the praise, Nick felt the ground underneath him settle and at least start to become firmer.

'Group Captain Carson, I'd like to ask you a few questions about ...'

'The Pissouri Beach bombings. Of course that's why you're here. I can give you some information but, to be blunt, there's not a lot we know ourselves. So far nobody has claimed responsibility for the attack, so at the moment, all we can do is guess. Everyone's appalled, pointing fingers and demanding that we do something. After all, it more or less happened in our back yard; the majority of fatalities are military personnel, as are many of the injured. Cowardly bloody bastards. There were families down there, with kids, for Christ's sake! A lot of good people were killed or injured, and for what? Some grand fucking political principle.'

He paused, took a deep breath and exhaled slowly.

'It's been a long, tough day and it hasn't finished yet. We're fairly certain that the Turkish community had nothing to do with it, neither Turkish Cypriots or from the mainland. Akan Kadir, in Paphos, was outraged that we'd even asked, reminding us that it was invariably the Greeks who were responsible for such outrages. His opinion: EOKA-B terrorists. It's possible. He may be right. They've got a history of bombings and want Cyprus to be Greek; they hate us, the Turks and even Makarios.'

'What does the government in Nicosia say?' Nick asked, taking advantage of Carson drawing breath.

The Group Captain picked up the telex that his adjutant had quietly slipped onto the desk moments earlier.

'This was sent at the behest of President Makarios. He extends 'his deepest sympathy' and denounces the bombings as 'the cowardly acts of criminals and terrorists'. To a degree, he supports Kadir's suggestion that EOKA-B is a possibility but he puts the PFLP as the prime candidate. Because:

'The Popular Front for the Liberation of Palestine is anti-imperialism, anti-zionism, Arab

11

and Palestine nationalists. Many continue to hold Britain responsible for the establishment of the state of Israel and its perceived bias in favour of the Israelis to the detriment of the Palestinians. Therefore, Britain's Sovereign Bases in Cyprus are clear symbols of an imperialistic mindset, the need to have a controlling influence in the region and to provide military support to Israel if needed.'

'After that he goes on to say that Cyprus' Police Force will, um, here it is, 'do its utmost to find the perpetrators and bring them to justice' and 'ensure that every effort is made to assist those investigations made by your officers at RAF Akrotiri.' Could I borrow your notebook quickly?' he asked, stretching his hand out towards Nick.

Nick passed it over, not without a slight qualm. And then watched as the Group Captain calmly tore out not only the notes he had taken while Carson was talking, but also the pages beneath that carried their impression.

Handing the desecrated notebook back, Rafe Carson smiled and said, 'but of course you can't actually go to print with any of that. Wouldn't want to leave you with temptation at your fingertips.'

The words 'you slick bastard' floated through Nick's mind.

'I assume that I can write that officers from RAF Akrotiri are investigating in conjunction with the Police? That it is possible that either EOKA-B or the PFLP might be responsible?'

'You may say the former Mr Markides. That latter can only be speculation and should not be attributed. Tom will give you a few facts and figures that you can use in your report and a quote that may be attributed.'

Recognising that he'd been dismissed, Nick followed the adjutant as he walked into the corridor.

'Thank you for your time, Sir,' he called.

But Group Captain Rafe Carson was writing his own notes. The Ministry of Defence had been informed, as had MI6 and MI5. And as one of their agents had been injured on Pissouri Beach, the CIA was already involved and 'getting personal'. That only left Mossad. Carson was absolutely sure that the Israelis had probably joined the party and were already one step ahead.

*****

By the time Nick left Episkopi Garrison, the sun had slipped down through the sky, its golden beams lending a warm glow to the road ahead. There was little traffic and he was making good time until he hit a short tailback at the roadblock just outside Limassol. At the front of the queue, two men were standing by a red minibus while a third was leaning out through the open driver's door. They appeared to be in animated conversation with a couple of military policemen. It looked as though there were several more people inside the minibus, at least two of which looked like kids. It was fairly clear to Nick that he wasn't going to get back to Zephyrus any time soon. Getting out of the car, he lit a cigarette and sat down on the broad bumper of the Land Rover to watch the show.

The familiar sticker in the rear window of the minibus proclaimed it to be a rental from Star Cars in Limassol. Although they were all speaking English, the men with the bus were certainly not Cypriots but there was a fairly strong accent on the wind. Chandris Line cruise liners stopped en route at Limassol to, or from, Beirut, Nick thought, and Sol Maritime were running ferry services to and from Limassol with Beirut and Latakia. His money was on wealthy tourists, either from Syria or Lebanon.

The taller man was gesticulating, saying that they were all tired, especially the children, and that they wanted to get back to their villa near Limassol before it got dark. From what Nick could gather, they'd arrived on the previous evening and collected the minibus in the morning. They'd driven to Paphos and spent most of the day on the beach at Coral Bay. They were tired, the man reiterated, said that he saw no reason why they should be held up and that they had done nothing wrong. One of the MPs was telling him to calm down and be patient because they'd have to wait until their papers had been checked. It was the same for everybody; these were extremely difficult and serious issues.

A third MP suddenly appeared, carrying a stack of passports. Stopping by the barrier, he spoke briefly to two armed RAF Regiment gunners who followed him as he walked to the minibus. And with their arrival, the dynamic changed from being simply adversarial: the British were enforcing control. Ordered peremptorily from his seat on the minibus, the third man joined his friends on the tarmac. The women and children followed, forming a line 11 people long.

'Bloody hell! They've got something,' Nick murmured, 'or they think they have.'

Casually walking round to the side of the Landy, he opened the door and grabbed his bag. Back on the bumper, he pulled out the camera and notebook, placing one on either side of him. Looking down the side of the cars, he had a reasonably clear shot of the line of tourists by the minibus, the MPs and gunners. Nobody was looking in his direction, each group focusing on the other. Quickly and carefully, Nick took a few pictures, moving as little as possible to avoid drawing attention. No one noticed. Holding the camera by its strap, he lowered the camera gently onto the bag between his feet. Exhaling silently, he realised he'd been holding his breath. He slipped the notebook onto his knee.

The MP was walking the line with their passports, checking faces against photographs, reading out the names to make sure. But his voice was muffled and Nick only managed to get one or two. Abbas? That could be a first or family name. Faridah, Najib, Tarek. The names meant nothing and he stopped trying to write them down. He soon started making notes again.

Shouts from one, maybe two of the men and screams from some of the women. The three men were handcuffed behind their backs and manhandled into two jeeps which were driven back up the road past Nick. In each case the driver was an MP while a gunner rode shotgun. They weren't taking any chances. A moment later, the women and children were hustled back onto the minibus and, driven by a similar team, headed off in the same direction. A gut reaction kicked in: Nick grabbed his gear and jumped into the Land Rover. Wrenching the vehicle round in a brutal two and a half-point turn, he lurched after them with no real plan. He finally gave up the chase when he arrived at the turn to Kolossi. There was no sign of either of the vehicles and no knowing whether they'd gone left to Akrotiri or straight on towards Episkopi. Guessing that he would not be particularly welcome at either, he headed towards Limassol and Zephyros.

He'd get little from the checkpoint guards and he needed a beer and the telephone, in that order.

*****

Ironically, it had been at the Kolossi turn that the vehicles had parted company: the jeeps had headed down the road towards the base. Tarmac and tyres fought each other for dominance as the jeeps bumped down the road. Not designed for comfort, the ride was rough at the best of times. Unable to hold on to anything or brace themselves, the manacled passengers were thrown around the back like washing in a machine.

Najib al-Shami cursed for the hundredth time as his friend's elbow slammed into his ribs.

'For fuck's sake,' he shouted over the noise of the engine. 'Keep your elbow to yourself, Sabir.'

'Fuck your sister! I'm not exactly doing it on purpose. Where are they taking us?'

'I don't know. I think maybe the shithole of the British military base.'

The gunner turned round in his seat.

'Shut the fuck up and stop the Arab shit. You wanna ask a question, speak English.'

Sabir Masri spat the dust out of his mouth from the side.

'Where are we going?'

'Dhekelia.'

'What is Dhekelia?'

'Where you're going!' the gunner said, laughing as he turned back to watch the road ahead.

Alone in the back of the second jeep, Qadir Abbas pondered the same question. As he watched the blurred world go by through the dust, he thought about a lot of things. What were they doing with his Halah and Ali? Why was this happening? They had done nothing wrong. They knew nothing about any bombs or explosions. All they had done was to go to Paphos.

They were friends, the three families and all Palestinians living in Beirut. Not that that had always been the case. They'd met in Beirut. As their name sort of indicated, Najib and Leila al-Shami and their two kids were from Syria; Sabir and Faridah

Masri and their two kids, from Ramallah. Qadir and his family had also come from Ramallah, but he hadn't known Sabir back then. It was only later, through links with the PLO, the Palestine Liberation Front, that they'd all met to begin with. In principle, he and Sabir were members of the Fatah movement but Qadir knew that Najib had connections with the Popular Front and maybe was even an active member of the harder core group. Maybe that's why they'd been arrested; because the British knew, they had intelligence? Why would they know? They weren't bombers, terrorists. Even if they did know about all that stuff, what was wrong with that? The British she-dogs could prove nothing, because there was nothing to prove!

Passing the guard posts, the chain link fences and the barbed wire, the jeeps kept driving. They finally stopped some hundred yards from a large grey helicopter, its main rotor turning lazily around in anticipation of flight. The MPs motioned the three Palestinians out of the jeeps and, then pushing them gently from behind, herded them towards the aircraft. The two gunners walked on either side. An airman stood in the doorway, waiting for his passengers to come within hailing distance.

'Welcome to the Whirlwind, your cattle class carriage to Dhekelia,' he said with a grin. 'No comforts provided.'

He stood back as the MPs hustled their charges through the open door of the helicopter. The men were unceremoniously pushed to the floor against the back panel of the transport area.

'Are you OK?' Qadir asked the other two.

Sabir nodded and Nijab glowered, but neither said a word, lost anyway in the deafening roar as the pilot fed the power in and the rotors spun up to generate the necessary lift. The MPs sat to one side, opposite the door, their faces blank and unreadable. As the airman closed the door, the amount of light dimmed accordingly, only filtering through the grimy squares of windows. The clamour of engines and rotors was now complemented by intense vibration that seemed to violently shake the whole machine.

On the ground outside, the gunners watched as the Westland Whirlwind lifted into the air, turned through 180 degrees and flew eastwards with its five passengers. The downdraft of the rotors had blown up the dust that now hung heavily in the air.

'We're back to Checkpoint Limassol, yeah?'

16

'Yeah, they've got fish heads in charge of security at Episkopi with a few ex-Royals.'

'S'what I thought. Pity, those girls looked sweet.'

'As though you had taste.'

Laughing, the pair split off into the two jeeps and gunned them back up the road to Kolossi.

*****

Unlike the jeeps, the minibus had followed the Old Paphos Road past Kolossi and Kourion until it reached the Episkopi Garrison. Past the boundary fence and its barbed wire, they took a few turns before parking outside a three storey drab white block with a flat roof and peeling paint. It had that vacant look of disuse, disrepair and neglect. A line of darkened sash windows perforated the walls of each floor, the cross rails like bars in the early evening light. Two armed seamen stood in the shade of the doorway, flanking a naval officer holding a clipboard. Leila shuddered even though it was warm in the minibus. Her view through the dusty window had all the trappings of a prison.

A low exchange in English from the front caught her attention. The gunner was on his feet, a physical block to the exits and the military policeman was outside talking to the others. It looked as though he was handing over their passports to the navy man, pausing at one or two as he did so. Navy man looked backwards and beckoned the seamen.

'What is happening?' asked Halah Abbas.

A small rounded little woman, but with a pretty smile, Qadir's wife often looked nervous. With her twitching nose and wide-open brown eyes, she reminded Leila of a large ground squirrel. Today, she looked terrified, hugging her nine-year old son to her bosom for protection.

'I don't know Halah. But I think we're about to find out.'

The navy man, with the clipboard and the passports, had replaced the gunner at the front. At six feet, Pete Simmonds had enough height to see every one of the faces staring at him from behind and over the seats. He could feel the tension and fear that pervaded the confines of the minibus. And he could feel the hate and resentment, see it in some of their eyes. In turn it made him feel sad and angry at the same time. He'd had mates who'd been hurt on Pissouri and what if … he pushed the thoughts out of his mind.

'I am Chief Petty Officer Simmonds of the Royal Navy and I will be in charge of you while you are staying with us here at Episkopi. You are not under arrest but you will be held here securely for your own safety and you will accede to any requests that we make. Rooms have been made available in the barracks here. They haven't been used for a while so the accommodation is fairly basic.'

Why was he sounding so apologetic? Unconsciously, his tone became harder and more business like.

'I need to know which one of you is which. When I call out your name, raise your hand.' Pete flipped open the first book. 'Leena Masri?'

He looked for the hand, and then at the girl who had it raised. Dark hair framed an oval face, almond eyes under thick eyebrows, a nose that perhaps was a little large over full lips. He imagined a wide smile under different circumstances.

'Ayesha al-Shami?'

Pete knew before looking that it would be the girl next to Leena. Overall Ayesha's features were similar but there were slight differences that lent the girl a toughness that was absent in her friend's. The mouth was a little narrower and the nose smaller but the main divergence lay in her eyes. Where Leena's were liquid brown, these were piercing obsidian. Both girls were attractive, sixteen, seventeen? But that one, Ayesha, was dangerous.

'Tarek al-Shami?'

He could see the similarity even though the kid was what – seven years younger. That was some gap. Pete wondered what had happened in between, stopping the parents from having another child sooner.

'Amin Masri?'

Again, a similar age gap between brother and sister. He ran through the rest of the passports, each time appraising the owner's face. Leila al-Shami and Faridah Masri were both handsome women, looks they had clearly passed on to their children. But al-Shami was the stronger force. And then the also rans, Halah and Ali Abbas. They had neither the features nor the edge of the others but still part of the group. If any of them had been involved with the Pissouri bombings, his money was on the al-Shamis. But he wasn't an expert. He knew the three men were on their way to Dhekelia. The question was: would they need to come down to Akrotiri?

'OK we're done. Please come out of the minibus.'

Stepping down to the ground himself, he moved backwards, joining the semicircle of MPs, seamen and gunner. One by one, they came out of the minibus to form a huddle within the hard arms of that semicircle. Leila felt trapped, frustrated and angry.

The Chief Petty Officer led the way into the barracks followed by Her Majesty's guests with the armed seamen fore and aft. Concrete steps echoed to the tramp of feet in the empty building. On the first floor, they turned down an unadorned beige corridor, passing blue-grey flaking doors, kicking up months of accumulated dust and loose cement. About half way down, Pete unlocked a door on his right and, with a light push, it swung inwards. Standing as a barrier to the rest of the corridor behind him, he waved the line of women and children into the hallway.

Once upon a time, this had been family accommodation for military personnel. But that was a while back and since then had scarcely been touched. Enough camp beds had been installed to cope with the unusual influx of people: three in both of the two bedrooms and two in the living room. There was little else in terms of furniture apart from two threadbare green armchairs and a matching sofa.

Gathered together in the living room, they were told that someone would bring them food in a couple of hours. There were blankets on the beds, they were told, and there should be hot water. The front door would be locked and the building guarded; they should not attempt to leave for their own safety. They would all be seen individually in the morning and any questions that they might have would be answered then. And no, there was no information that could be imparted in relation to Messrs al-Shami, Masri and Abbas other than that they should be safely in HMP Dhekelia and would be meeting with intelligence representatives in due course. The door was locked; the women and children were on their own, imprisoned with their thoughts.

*****

They were sitting at a table in the NAAFI's Island Club, mainly drinking beer, although Billy and Chris were trading the odd whiskey chaser. There were five of them: Leading Hands Billy Sullivan and Chris Dalton, Petty Officer Rick Weston, Ratings Steve Marston and Frank Allen. All of them were out in Cyprus with the Royal Naval Reserve; that meant a bit of adventure with mates and a welcome break from the dull monotony of work in England. Of course there were other bonuses like cheap booze, sunshine and the occasional bit of skirt. However, Billy and Rick were due to fly home in the morning; that clearly called for a session in the Island.

Back in civvy street, Billy worked on building sites around London as a brickie while Rick worked a desk in the local borough council offices, pushing paper. Neither was keen to return, thus they were theoretically celebrating the joys of Cyprus and bemoaning the imminent parting of the ways. Normally, a farewell session necessitated drinking copious amounts of alcohol, indulging in tasteless joviality and getting totally pissed. But the conversation was strangely muted, focused mainly on the tragic and violent events at Pissouri. All of them knew at least one or two people who'd been hurt or died in the carnage. By the time they'd had several rounds, the atmosphere had become distinctly maudlin and then Billy began to get angry.

'They're up there, on the second floor of the barracks at the end. I know where they fucking are.' He slammed his fist on the table, shaking the glasses. 'I know where you fucking are!' he shouted.

A few people looked around to see who was causing the commotion but turned back when they saw the low ranking group. Billy saw them back.

'Tossers,' he grunted. Then, much more quietly, he hissed, 'I saw them and they're fucking guilty, I know it. Those cunts are responsible for what happened on the beach. They killed our mates.'

'You don't know that, Billy.'

'I fucking do Marston. And don't argue their case. I heard what Simmonds said, talking to the MP, he said they're BLO or BeefLP terrorists or something.'

'Are you right then?'

'Chris, you know me mate. Am I a bullshitter? I am not. Gospel truth, that's what Simmonds said and he should know because he's fucking intelligence!'

'Jesus!'

'I say we give them some payback, our way and tonight.'

Slowly but surely, each individual was sucked into a vortex of hatred and revenge that could only spiral downwards. Another round of drinks loosened the ratings' tongues: Allen and Marston finally mentioned that they were due to relieve the guards on the barracks at 2200 hours and receive arms. The die was cast.

Half an hour later, Steve Marston and Frank Allen were outside the door to the apartment, both carrying L1A1 Self-Loading Rifles. Rick Weston unlocked the door and the six men strode in, led by Billy Sullivan. Flicking the light switches as they went, they found themselves looking at eight sets of frightened eyes, blinking in the glare.

'Well here we fucking are gentlemen,' said Billy.

'We were trying to sleep,' Faridah said, rubbing her eyes with the back of her hand.

'What do you want?'

Leila's voice sliced across the room, immediately attracting the men's attention. Billy pointed a finger directly at her.

'You'll get yours in a minute darling. Now shut the fuck up.'

Leaning down towards the beds, Billy reached out to grab a handful of Leena's blouse and ripped downwards hard. The thin material ripped easily, revealing firm little breasts barely covered by her floral bikini top below. Leena screamed, Billy smiled.

'Nice,' he murmured.

Faridah flew at him like a wild cat, raking his face with her nails, only to receive a blow from his fist that shattered her nose. And then madness held court.

*****

21

'Both girls and two of the women were repeatedly raped, Sir. The older girl, Ayesha, was cut badly as well. Unbelievably cruel. The bastards sliced her left cheek open so badly, the doc said, that some of the nerves have almost certainly been cut. One of the women, Faridah Masri sustained a broken nose; all of them have substantial bruising on their legs and genitals. Tarek al-Shami, one of the sons, has facial bruising and cuts. The other three are physically unhurt but …'

He left the words hanging in the air.

'Jesus Christ!' Group Captain Rafe Carson shook his head in disbelief. 'First Pissouri and now this. And where are they now Simmonds, the women and children?'

'They're being treated at Princess Mary's. I had them taken there as soon as I found out. The place was a mess, and they were worse. Totally traumatized. And it's not bloody surprising. Funny thing though, the woman who wasn't raped, Halah Abbas, she's almost more traumatized than the others.'

'Are any of them talking?'

'Sir. Leila al-Shami's totally lucid and she's told us what happened in detail. Too much detail. But she's the only one. The worst thing about it is the hatred in her eyes. She stares at you when she's talking, but it's as though you're not there and the eyes just seem to burn. The daughter's got the same look but she's not speaking.'

'And the perpetrators?'

'We've got four of them. At the moment they're under armed security and locked in their barracks.'

'So were the victims of these barbarities,' Rafe Carson snapped.

'Yes Sir. But this time the guards are marines.'

'Who's missing?'

'Leading Hands Sullivan and Dalton. It sounds as though Sullivan was the ringleader.'

'Chief Petty Officer Simmonds,' the Group Captain said in a voice as cold as ice, 'I want them found, now. MPs, Royals and the Regiment, get them all on the case. In addition, we'll need to advise the Cypriot Police and ask for their assistance. Tell them these men are dangerous and possibly armed.'

'We've already got gunners and MPs out. I'll sort out the marines and the police Sir.'

'Thank you Simmonds.'

The Chief Petty Officer saluted and left the office, shutting the door behind him. Group Captain Rafe Carson walked to his favourite spot and looked at the view through the open window. As usual, the sun was shining, gently warming the air over a shimmering green-blue sea. The scent of pine trees wafted by on a light breeze while the thrum of cicadas lent rhythm to the day. Simply, stunning perfection.

'What a bloody mess,' he said as he picked up the phone.

With little preamble, he was patched through to the duty Intelligence Officer and explained what, and who, he wanted.

'Good Morning Group Captain, Tim Sutton.'

He vaguely recognised the name, from somewhere in the past. From the way that Dhekelia communications had patched him through, Rafe Carson did know that Sutton was an expert in intelligence, counter-terrorism, counter-intelligence and interrogation. And probably a few more things about which he'd rather not know. Sutton was a spook.

'They're clean,' Sutton said. 'All three of them. Yes there are connections with certain parties including the PFLP but nothing that's raised any serious concerns. Mossad has two of them as low risk but under surveillance outside Lebanon. Al-Shami's slightly higher up the pecking order but likewise – no real problem.

'As for Pissouri, they're white as snow. Nothing to suggest any involvement, even minor, and apparently they had a tracker on the minibus and it didn't get anywhere close. The vehicle showed clean at your end and their stories all hang together. We're sending them back by Whirlwind this afternoon.'

'I'm not sure whether that's such good news,' the Group Captain replied. And gave him basic details of what had transpired during the night.

'Does the press know?'

'I don't think so. We did have a chap called Nick Markides snooping around yesterday afternoon. Freelances mainly. He's based in Limassol. Obviously no one will be talking to him now

other than our Press Officer. I suppose the Foreign Office will
…'

'I'll be filing a comprehensive report,' Sutton interjected, 'and the relevant details will be passed on to the FO. There'll be a lot of unhappy bunnies in Whitehall tonight. Midnight oil will be burning and cauldrons bubbling. I suspect that they'll give the papers the heads up on Pissouri but bury the aftermath, if you know what I mean.'

'I do Mr Sutton, I do,' Carson said fervently.

'Just Tim will do nicely, Group Captain. Oh, and don't worry about Markides. We'll have a word.'

*****

At 1100 hours on Saturday, 13 July 1974 the sun was well on the way to its zenith. Heat haze blurred the lines that ran either side of the runway and the ground was baked hard after months of drought. Sitting in the window seat on British European Airways flight no 663, Mike Roberts looked vacantly through the window at the parched brown landscape. His father sat next to him, to the left of his Vanessa, ensuring space for her maimed arm. A cauldron of emotional thoughts simmered in his head. He couldn't bear to look at the mother he adored, sedated and almost lifeless and his eyes began to leak every time he looked at her arm. The horror of the beach would creep up on him unawares, particularly in his dreams. He could hear the explosions and screams, see the blood on the sand and his mother clutching her handless raw arm. And he screamed himself awake, finding himself sweating on sodden sheets. It was meant to be a holiday. It wasn't fair.

The engine noise grew louder as the pilot fed in the power and Mike could feel the plane straining at the leash. With the brakes released, the Boeing 707 raced down the runway and then left the ground in a steep climb that forced him back into his seat. When the plane finally levelled out, Mike once again had a view of the coastline with its golden beach and sea that shone with a blue-green iridescence. He'd liked the beach, the sea, the sand and the sounds of music from the bar. Before he really understood what had happened, he'd wanted to go back there to reclaim their holiday idyll. But all that had changed. He hated the people who'd blown up the beach and mutilated his mother. Terrorists his father had called them. Mike wanted to kill them all and swore to himself that he would when he was older.

At 1300 hours an unliveried Jetstream left RAF Akrotiri bound for Beirut with only eleven of its 16 seats occupied. There was little conversation. Tarek sat with his older sister, holding her hand and wishing with all his heart that she would get better. He didn't look at the headscarf she now wore continuously to cover her wounded face. He wished he could push the memories away; they haunted him by day and night. But the nights were the worst: black and white pictures that silently screamed. The plane swung out over the sea before turning back and setting a northeasterly course. Looking out he could see military ships in Limassol port, the airfield of Akrotiri and he hated the people there as hard as his 10 year-old brain would allow. And swore he would kill them all for Ayesha.

Early on 15 July 1974, the military Junta and the National Guard effected a coup d'état, ousting President Makarios. On 20 July, the Turkish war machine invaded Cyprus. The bombings at Pissouri Beach and subsequent horrific attacks at Episkopi were simply lost in a maelstrom of displacement, death and destruction.

2 ~ London 2006

The commuter drones had yet to start the morning's real push towards their London workstations. As the train slid alongside the platform, the windows of the carriage flickered by displaying a line of heads bent forward as if in prayer. Clearly the eager ones were already on the move but Mike Roberts had little difficulty finding a seat. He glanced at his watch. Chiswick Park to Westminster, 26 minutes; five or so minutes to get out and a 16 minute walk to the office. There was time to spare; certainly enough to grab a cardboard cup of coffee from the kiosk at the end of the bridge and ... what? Think?

Mike automatically scanned the people around him. They perched on hard cushioned seats or stood clutching the District Line's yellow scaffolding poles. Most heads were bowed, eyes staring at little screens while thumbs and fingers danced on miniaturised keyboards. Snapshots on the tube.

A girl with narrow lips and pinched face framed by lank blonde hair, whispered urgent words to her male friend in the next seat. He punctuated her sentences with staccato grunts of assent or dismissal. Eastern European certainly; probably Polish or Czech, Mike guessed, in their mid-twenties, living and working in England.

One smartphone stabber looked Japanese, but might have been Korean. He'd jab frenetically at the screen for several seconds, pause ... then sigh or blow despondently. And then repeat the process. Mike had him down for a student or, perhaps more likely, a tourist.

Standing by the doors, the Rasta seemed hardwired into his music, eyes closed and moving to the unheard beats. Until his eyes snapped open, locked on Mike's and gave him a lazy grin before repairing back to 'di muzik'. Rastaman got out at South Kensington, which blew out Mike's idea that he'd been headed for Brixton. Never assume.

Getting onto the train, two suits with very different shapes: one was heavy set and tall, topping Mike's six-feet-something by at least a couple of inches. Bald headed with no neck, barrel chested and broad shouldered; the man was a positive close protection cliché. In contrast, his friend was slim and lithe, wearing an expensive Italian wool tailored suit with an ease that comes from long acquaintance. Russian, Mike thought, definitely Russian. The men's brief exchanges made him grin: at the fact that he'd been right, and at the content of the somewhat one-sided conversation. Given the dressing down being handed out, he was glad that he wasn't in the big man's shoes. But it was good to hear the language again; it had been a while.

As an undergraduate at Cambridge, he'd read Russian and French under the broad umbrella of Modern and Medieval languages. Spending eight months of his third year as a researcher at Ostankino in Moscow had polished Mike's linguistic capability to slick fluency. According to his peers, he'd explored the mechanical dynamics of drinking vodka in the company of several beautiful female Russians, carrying out numerous analyses of cause and effect. Thoroughly enjoyable research but which might have contributed to the attainment of a Two One rather than First Class honours.

He was still smiling at the memories as he bounded up the escalator at Westminster Underground station. Being fit wasn't a chore for Mike Roberts, it was a way of life. Always had been, from the halcyon days at Magdalene and ever since. Of course, now he was the wrong side of 35, the big four-oh edged ever closer and it was becoming a little harder. Even so, he'd still managed two circuits of the three-mile run around Acton Green Common before showering and catching the tube. On average he played squash or tennis a couple of times a week and ran every day. Playing cricket, of course, belonged to those happy rose-tinted student days; now he only followed the sport on TV, watching and ranting like any old fan.

'Bollocks to that,' he said as he paid the man for the coffee.

'You what mate?'

'Not the coffee. Thanks, see ya.'

The biggest difference on the fitness front was, broadly speaking, the absence of hard military training, he thought as he crossed the road and turned to stride past the Houses of Parliament. (Not that walking in Westminster wasn't a form of extreme exercise requiring keen observation skills plus excellent eye and foot coordination. Weaving through static or erratically moving tourists was invariably a challenge.) It had been a while since he'd marched over Pen y Fan in the Brecon Beacons loaded down by a forty-pound Bergen on his back in addition to the rifle and water he was carrying. And all of that, in a way, ran straight after Cambridge. As he walked along Abingdon Street, he ticked off the years in his mind.

Post graduation he'd joined the Army and spent 44 weeks as an Officer Cadet at the Royal Military Academy Sandhurst. On successful completion he was commissioned as a Second Lieutenant in the Light Infantry. The why was not entirely clear. There was no ancestral directive and it certainly wasn't in the genes. Before he retired, his father had been an assistant bank manager and a frustrated academic, a vocational love that continued unabated. His mother was different, possibly and fractionally instrumental in his choice of career. In the years after Cyprus, she'd never once complained or been bitter, stoically enduring all the operations on the remnant of her forearm. When Mike called for justice, Vanessa quietly taught her son forgiveness which he never totally understood. Beloved mother, wife, chef, counsellor and nursemaid but no marching tunes there either.

Perhaps a military seed had been sown in Moscow; the Soviet Union was crumbling and Mikhail Gorbachev was withdrawing its forces from Afghanistan. Rumour had it that the British and Americans were helping the Mujahideen with both training and finance. But closer to home, British troops continued to be embroiled in the Troubles in Ireland and too often the violence crossed over the water to Britain. And Gibraltar. Mike was in the Ostankino Tower when the news came through of the court case involving three Special Air Service soldiers who had shot three members of the Irish Republican Army on the island earlier in the year. And Mike's interest changed to commitment.

'Never thought about it that way before,' Mike muttered to himself as he continued walking, now along Millbank.

Stayed with the Light Infantry for another couple of years before applying to join the SAS. Got through the selection process successfully, but that was tough, mentally and physically. Proud to be a member of 22nd Special Air Service Regiment, continued his training, specialising in counter terrorism and counter revolutionary warfare. Sent overseas as a CT team member on a number of missions in the border areas of Turkey, Iraq, Iran and Syria. Served as 2iC (or second in command) with the raised rank of Captain with a stripped back squadron based on King Abdullah I Airbase in Amman; role was to provide additional training in counter terrorism techniques to selected members of the 71st Special Battalion (Jordan).

Mike's reverie broke as he reached the roundabout. Checking the time, he nodded, satisfied, and turned left towards Lambeth Bridge rather than cross Millbank to Horseferry Road. He walked until he was more or less half way across the bridge before stopping. Little was moving on the flat gunmetal surface of the River Thames as it made its sluggish way down towards the estuary and out into the North Sea. The sky above seemed equally leaden, heavy with a barely undulating layer of grey cloud. The London Eye was a dreary white ellipse staring sullenly sideways across the river to the aging bulk of the Houses of Parliament resting heavily on the Embankment.

The view upriver would be equally torpid and listless grey. Mike didn't bother to turn round to check. He knew that his eyes would track along the Albert Embankment to the geometric stacks of beige and green that housed the Secret Intelligence Service. Some people called the modernistic building Legoland which Mike thought a little simplistic. He preferred the tag – Babylon-on-Thames. It seemed to encompass both the shape and the content so succinctly. Our 'Friends in Babylon'. Then of course, Tower House was only just off the bridge and round the corner on Millbank. The grey grandeur of neo-classical hulk was home to Britain's Security Service whose avowed mission was to keep the country safe. And completed the triangle of intelligence on the banks of Old Father Thames. All hushed behind closed doors, under cloaks with daggers drawn.

'Problem is,' Mike thought, 'we're doing too much of the cloak thing and not enough with the bloody dagger.'

The SAS years and operations had suited his personality perfectly. He'd liked the challenges of on-going training as much as being in the field. True to say that when he was out in Jordan, there was a lot of cloak, travelling around the region in various disguises, watching and listening.

'How to see and not be seen? The best place to hide is not up your own arsehole Roberts. On a recce, when you're following someone, when you need to find out what's going on – you need to be there. And the best place to hide is often in plain view. Which means that you have to learn to fade so far into the background that you are the fucking background!'

Mike grinned, as the bellowing voice in his head took him back to the time when he was a 'pig-ignorant' newbie in the regiment. But that was at the beginning and he'd learned quickly. Jordan had entailed a lot of surveillance but there was also plenty of action. On the way, he'd picked up a rudimentary grasp of Arabic to the point that he could hold his own in a basic conversation. Ironically, it was partially Mike's linguistic skills that steered him away from his beloved regiment. On his return to London …

'As you're probably aware, the Jordanians were seriously impressed with the programme. The General himself asked me to make a point of expressing his personal thanks. Well done Major Roberts.'

Financially speaking, the promotion was a welcome surprise and making the rank of major so soon was no small source of pride. Until he realised that the mandarins in the Foreign Office might have had an ulterior motive.

'Congratulations on your promotion Major … combination of your knowledge gained in the Middle East … understand you've added Arabic to your linguistic quiver … pleased to inform you that you're to join the British Embassy in Cairo as the interim Military Attaché.'

A military attaché's rank was usually at least Lieutenant Colonel; clearly a Major would do for an interim role. No matter, Cairo might be interesting, he'd thought at the time.

The reality was that he found life in the arms of the diplomatic corps to be dull and loveless. The weft of sterile formal functions was woven into the warp of endless tedious meetings, producing a dreary tapestry of monotony. Occasionally he was involved in more sensitive discussions, advising the Ambassador and Egyptian ministers on various matters military, including the supply of arms to Egypt from Britain. On the positive side, he learned to speak Arabic fluently with only the hint of an accent. As well as opening many useful diplomatic doors, his command of the language made him welcome in the coffee houses of Khan el-Khalili. In the maze of Cairo's largest and noisiest souk, money combined with Arabic opened many more doors. With that deeper level of contact and darker flow of information, life had been starting to get a little more interesting. And then he'd been recalled to London.

Summoned to a meeting at the Foreign Office, he remembered sitting in a leather armchair opposite a stern looking secretary who wore no makeup; but who did wear a seemingly constant frown. The double wooden doors to his left were firmly closed. Twenty minutes of silence elapsed. Without any visual or audio prompting, she'd suddenly looked directly at him and smiled.

'They can see you now Major Roberts. Please go in. And use the left door if you would.'

'I'm sorry but ... they would be?'

'You don't know? Of course. They, would be the Permanent Under Secretary for Foreign Affairs, Sir Angus McFadden and Rear-Admiral Sir Reginald Buller.'

That meeting had been 14 months ago. Today's meeting with his boss was in half an hour and Bulldog Buller didn't like his subordinates to be late. Oh no! Mike grinned up into a grey sky that was now leaking badly, shook his head and walked briskly to the end of Lambeth Bridge. Scooting past the roundabout across Millbank, he headed up Horseferry Road for a while before turning off to the office.

That meeting. Opening the door, he'd walked into a spacious room with dark oak panelling, softly lit by a line of large sash windows. An ornate antique desk, supporting a very modern computer screen and keyboard, dominated one end of the room. The other boasted several leather armchairs, of the same mould as the one in the anteroom, in an approximate circle and two of these held Knights of the Realm.

'Good morning Major. I seem to remember the last time we met, we were sending you off to Cairo. Understand you had an interesting time with our Egyptian friends.'

Sir Angus clearly didn't expect a response and didn't wait for one.

'I don't believe you've met Sir Reginald Buller. The Admiral is Director of the Special Arc Force and you have been earmarked as his second in command. Admiral?'

'Sir?' Mike had interposed.

'You were about to ask what the bloody hell the Special Arc Force is? And say that you've never heard of it?' the Admiral interposed in turn.

'Sir.'

'Which isn't surprising since SAF is so new that it's barely out of nappies. Ten months ago the Service didn't exist as an actual entity. Now it does and it has teeth but I need someone who has specific knowledge and expertise. And knows how to use both. I, we, think that person might well be you.' He held up his hand to stop Mike interrupting and continued. 'The Met's in the front line here in London with counter terrorism and firearms units and special branches all over the shop. Round the corner we've got MI5, MI6 is perched over the next bridge and our rural cousins in GCHQ are feeding everyone huge gobbets of global intelligence to add to what they've gleaned for themselves. And despite all those wonderful men and women keeping Britain safe, we're still worrying about what the other bastards are doing.

'There are chinks in the armour and we're never going to plug them all, all of the time. Our objective is stop whoever, and wherever, getting their grubby little hands on the bloody slings and arrows before they can use them.'

'The Middle East as a whole is a major concern,' Sir Angus interjected. 'Iraq has been on fire ever since the invasion and that has spread to other countries in the region. Iran is a major player already and the possibility that it might become a nuclear power is clearly a matter of concern. And that's just the start. Afghanistan is another blasted mess for a multitude of reasons, some of which can be tackled with the right team in place. One of our major concerns is the security of Pakistan's nuclear arsenal, right next door to Afghanistan. Or rather I should say the lack of security. That's a disaster waiting to happen, and one that we need to prevent. Are you following me Major Roberts?'

'Yes Sir.'

'I thought you might. Good man. Naturally you'll be liaising with our intelligence services and a few other agencies overseas, I'm sure. However, the one that always raises a few eyebrows (and hackles) tends to be Mossad. Their people are very good at picking up information early and dealing with the problem, often permanently. Like them or not, the Israelis do have their fingers on the pulse. We have a strong working relationship with Mossad but we want to improve on that with an agent-to-agent liaison. Mossad's Director has already approved the idea. The Admiral can fill you in with contact details in due course.

'One more thing I wanted to mention. I believe you were considering another role with the 22nd? The Special Arc Force is, unofficially, rated among the Special Forces. The Arc tag is intended; it indicates that the team can draw on the resources of the SAS and SBS in particular where and when deemed necessary. You will be maintaining close communications with Hereford and you will have an operational contact. Again, the Admiral will provide details later. Together with answering any of the questions that I'm sure you'll have. Any serious objections to your new post Major Roberts?'

'No Sir.'

'He's all yours Admiral Buller.'

'Thank you, Angus. Welcome aboard Major.'

*****

The Office, as Mike thought of the place, was a handsome redbrick building on a quiet side road. There was no name, number or knocker on the glossy black door. He pushed a sequence of buttons on the entry phone keypad and looked straight ahead.

'Morning Michael. How are we this lovely morning?' said the disembodied voice.

'Damp Helen, and getting damper by the second.'

The lock emitted a barely audible click before the door opened automatically. Mike stepped through the doorway and as he walked across the flagged hallway, heard the door close firmly behind him. The sound of recognisable footsteps on the staircase was shortly followed by the lady's willowy figure.

Unsurprisingly Helen had turned a few heads in her time; most of them had been bitten off and savagely chewed. Too many had assumed that the attractive brunette was simply an office decoration. Field trained, tried and tested, she was known to be an excellent controller and planner in her own right as well as acting as Admiral Buller's personal assistant. 'In more ways than one,' some said mischievously.

'Hi Helen. How's the old man this morning?'

'Irascible as ever. He's waiting for you in the library. Coffee?'

'Please.'

The ground floor was designed along the lines of a comfortable flat which, in effect, it was. There was a bedroom that was sometimes used by agents before a graveyard shift and occasionally by the odd guest. A well-appointed kitchen, gracious dining room, comfortable library, modern bathroom well stocked with luxury toiletries – all were present and correct. But the floors above and one below ground, were manned by SAF staff around the clock and definitely did not have the frills of The Apartment. Ever vigilant, ever calm, they sifted information, talked to contacts, built profiles, acquired details, checked locations; the list went on and on. Only when the evidence was deemed precise and accurate could action be taken; and then any such action had to be cleared and approved.

Mike suspected that the cause of Bully's irascibility was almost certainly sitting somewhere in Whitehall. Highly intelligent and with a wealth of experience, Admiral Buller did not tolerate fools easily; one might comfortably say that he was dubious about most civil servants and considered politicians positively serpentine. On the other hand, he recognised talent when he saw it and gave credit when it was due. Not that anything should be taken for granted but Mike was reasonably comfortable with the knowledge that he certainly rated several notches higher than a civil servant in the man's eyes.

When Mike walked into the library, the Admiral was busy hammering the dottle out of his pipe against a green jade ashtray. He wondered which would break first. Finally deciding that the bowl was clear, the man proceeded to refill the pipe and looked up at his subordinate.

'Bloody civil servants,' he said, bringing a poorly covered grin to Mike's lips. 'Blasted woman's still whingeing on about not wanting to upset the Albanians. She phoned, nagged for 20 minutes and then got upset when I told her to sod off. What does she want us to do, provide them with fucking planes so they can speed up the trafficking process? Idiots! Bugger them all.'

'It might not have been the most politic thing to say, Admiral,' Mike said, now clearly grinning.

His grin was returned. Striking a match on the rough side of the ashtray, Admiral Buller carefully lit his pipe and drew the smoke into his mouth. For a moment he savoured the complex flavours of Borkum Riff tobacco and expelled an aromatic cloud that drifted slowly upwards.

'I really should give this stuff up,' he growled without much credibility. 'But it does go nicely with a good single malt. To business. Where are we with this lot?'

He tapped a finger on the folder that Mike had given him the previous week. It contained summaries of six groups, possible terror cells, three of which were in the capital, two in Birmingham and one in Glasgow.

'To be honest, little change Admiral. They're all still under surveillance but at the moment we don't have enough hard evidence to arrest any of them. Sometimes the whole deal is frustrating as hell. We're expecting activity to happen any time with the top two … if you look in the folder Sir?' (The file was duly opened and given a sideways glance.) 'The Ladies in Birmingham and Woodpecker in Stockwell; we think that they're the most likely to kick off soonest. We're just waiting for a little more before we go in, but they're on the edge. Castle in Brum and the Barracks in Glasgow are both moving up the scale. They could easily go critical in the short term. Your guess is as good as. The last two look as though they could be serious. That's the Waterboatmen near Marble Arch, of all places, and Towers in Hoxton. We've got people out in London with the Met and at Ladywood; Special Branch is covering elsewhere.'

There was a pause as the two men looked at each other in silence. More smoke clouds billowed above Admiral Buller's head before he responded.

'Don't leave it too late Mike,' he advised. 'The last thing we want is the major fuck up we had last year with the London bombings. Yes, it was a tragic disaster in human terms and we're all having to come to terms with that. We, the intelligence services, didn't stop it happening. Khan was fingered by MI5 but not the focus of their attention, so he slips through their net and blows himself up on Edgware Road, taking six people with him. Now we know that he and his buddies went to Pakistan first and hooked up with extremist radicals who may have been al-Qaeda recruiters! Check the links, the connections, think outside the box, look at it sideways and upside down. But don't forget to look inside the bloody thing and shake till it screams. There're an awful lot of people out there who have very nasty ideas. Obviously we need to stop them before the ideas get wings. It's difficult to anticipate? So we react as early as possible and avoid collateral damage.

'Anyway, some good news from the hole. John's managed to get Tracker pretty much ready to fly on filtering email and telephone communications, intel from GCHQ and any other stuff we can get our hands on. I'm hoping Mossad will help with the fine-tuning but initially we can run our own tests. Thought we'd go down to the basement for a preview after we've finished here.'

'Sounds good. If we can drill down individually ...'

He was interrupted by another angrier sound that came from the cradled phone on the writing desk. With surprising speed, Admiral Buller spun out of the high backed Chesterfield, sat down at the desk and picked up the phone, seemingly in one fluid movement.

'Buller. Yes ... Shit ... no. Who have we got on it? ... Fine ... Black Mercedes CL500 Coupe, got it. Registration? Excellent ... I'll feed that back, sierra eight one two, Juliet Juliet Bravo. We're on it ... yes, bye.'

Gently replacing the receiver on its cradle, the Admiral turned back to look at Mike.

'Remember the bits about 'don't leave it too late' and 'react as early as possible'? Well we could be cutting it fucking fine! Looks like the Waterboatmen could be on the move. Apparently they received a delivery this morning which sparked off a lot of movement in the house. Planning stage? That sucks. Looks as though these guys could be locked and loaded. That comes from the surveillance boys who fed it back to the Met's CT unit. Yes, I know. Don't tell me,' said the Admiral. 'Plus there's a tip off that they're planning on going for a lakeland drive this afternoon.'

'As you say, so much for being at the planning stage. By the sound of it, you're planning on coming.'

'In this instance, I think it makes sense. I'll stay with the raiders, you follow the Merc.'

'Fine. I'll phone Paddington Green. Can you get the X5 brought round. A van's not going to be up to the job if they cut and run.'

Mike speed dialled Sergeant Jack Williams.

'Jacko, Mike Roberts.'

'Major Mike, hi. I'm guessing this isn't a social call inviting me for dinner.'

'You got that one right. Might be up for a beer if we crack this one. The Waterboatmen may be on the move. We've got two guys on surveillance there at the moment. They're feeding back to your guys so you need to switch that feed to you. Can't do it at this end. We all need to have immediate intel on any movement either in or outside the house.'

'Mews terrace job, just off the Edgware Road?'

'You got it. It's a cul de sac so any exit has got to be that way. It's going to be a waiting game on Edgware Road until they make their move. When they do, I'm going to be following in the Beemer. I need two firearms with Kevlar and one camera with me.'

'No problem.'

Mike walked into the hall, phone in hand and grabbed his still damp jacket from the rack. The Admiral was already booted and spurred.

'These guys are probably armed. One pistol has already been spotted. Looks like a nine mill Sig but the picture's too grainy to really tell. Once we pick up the Merc, hit the house. So the usual team of raiders, comms in the van and they'll need firearms in the house. We've no idea what we'll find or who's left behind,' he added as he walked out the door in bright sunshine. 'At least it looks as though we've got a nice day for it.'

'Yeah, nice and sunny but bloody cold out there. It's two above outside apparently. See you in a bit.'

'Thanks Jacko, Should be with you in about fifteen. One more thing: after the raiders have secured everything, we'll need uniforms to clear up and forensics. You know the drill.'

When Mike climbed into the driving seat, the engine was already running. He looked at the Admiral in the passenger seat.

'Lights and sounds, Sir, I believe.'

'Lights and sounds indeed, Major.'

An unmarked car with blue lights flashing from every orifice, accompanied by a wailing siren tends to cut through traffic like a hot knife through butter. They were parked and inside an ops room in Paddington Green within fifteen minutes. Sergeant Williams had organized it well: both teams were kitted up, ready and waiting.

'Good job, thanks Jacko,' Mike said as looked round the room. 'You're with me I assume?'

'Wouldn't miss it for the world, Sir.'

Mike nodded at him with a grin and then turned to face the teams.

'Good morning lady, and gentlemen.' He noted the WPC nodding her appreciation. 'Thank you for getting it together so quickly. OK, listen up. You all know what you're doing and how to do it but not what you're dealing with. So I'll give you what we know and a bit more. As far as we can tell there are at least three men and one woman. Two of the guys are thought to be Somalis; the third clearly has Arabic origins, possibly Yemeni. All three wear Western clothes. The woman's Caucasian and has an Eastern European accent but speaks good English. We know that they have at least one handgun; there's no info on any other arms but we don't know, so be ultra careful.

'Earlier this morning a large package was delivered by a private courier. Apparently this resulted in a lot of hands pumping the air and shouting. We know that they have been working on a plan to introduce toxins into London's water supply. That probably means one or more reservoirs. And we have reason to believe that actual supplies arrived today. The package was marked fragile so I think that we can assume glass vials or similar. What we don't know is what's in them or where they're going to be used. If possible don't touch any containers if you encounter them. Leave that to the forensic teams. Gloves and masks are advised. Any questions?' Mike looked around the room, proud of the professionalism on show. 'Let's do this. Good luck people.'

Both vehicles were in place with a clear view of the end of the mews. Two engineers wearing BT overalls twisted complex wires in the box twenty yards from the front door. An hour passed before anything happened. Mike's headset hissed with static and then cleared.

'Two on the move, Major. Looks as though they're going on foot and they're not carrying.'

'I've got 'em. Thanks Ged. Love the overalls.'

'Piss off, Sir.'

The two Somalis strolled casually past between the two vehicles, round the corner and down Edgware Road.

'Ged, have we got anyone on the Road?'

'Yeah mate. Last thing I saw, Tim was smoking shisha outside the Lebanese place. He'll pick them up.'

'They'll probably join him for a pipe or two.'

'Wait up. We've got more movement. The blonde's coming out with two full bin liners. OK, she's dumped them in a commercial bin. Want me to get the uniforms to check them later?'

'Please.'

'No worries. That's her done. She's back inside.'

A full hour elapsed without any movement from the house or sign from the two Somalis.

'Where the fuck are they?' Jacko asked rhetorically. 'You would have …'

Mike raised his hand, stopping the man in mid-sentence.

'Yes Tim.'

'They're on their way back. Should be hitting the mews in about five minutes.'

'You know where they've been?'

'Yes and no. They went to the Maroush, the big Lebanese restaurant on Edgware Road?'

'Where you were a caterpillar sitting on a toadstool smoking shisha?'

'Yeah, I wish. Watching a belly dancer strut her stuff, I suppose. Ged?'

'In one.'

'OK, all I can tell you is that they were there for the duration having coffee and baklava. Most of the time they talked to each other. About ten minutes before they left, one of them took a call on his mobile. There was a lot of nodding from the guy on the phone; nothing from the other one. He simply stared at his mate. Gets off the phone, animated conversation, high fives all round and they're on their way.'

'Good news? Information? Who knows? But could be an instruction to go.'

'Yeah maybe. Good luck Sir.'

'We're ready.'

Mike cut the line.

'They're on their way, gentlemen.'

'Uh uh, they're here.'

Jacko had seen the pair first. All eyes, from the van and the Beemer were on the two Somalis who were walking with a serious bounce in their step. Mike switched channels so that everyone could hear him but said nothing.

One Somali got into the Mercedes and switched on the engine. In the meantime the other had knocked on the door of the house. The Yemeni opened the door, nodded to the man, peered beyond him on both sides, then disappeared back into the house. Moments later he reappeared to hand over some kind of bag, then quickly shut the door. When the man turned to walk to the car, Mike could see what he was carrying. It looked like an old-fashioned classic leather satchel with a long shoulder strap. The sides seemed to bulge as though it was full but was obviously not that heavy.

'OK everyone, we're on our way. Give us fifteen to twenty to get our guys in traffic and then hit the house. And make that fast, no pissing around. The last thing we want is for our two to be warned that they have a tail. Good luck one and all.'

The Mercedes pulled out onto Edgware Road and drove down towards Marble Arch. Mike picked them up as the black saloon turned onto Connaught Street and by the time it turned right on Bayswater Road, he'd positioned the X5 two cars behind.

'They're heading for the M4 at a guess. Down the M3 towards Chertsey and that string of reservoirs?' said Jacko.

'Yeah, you're with me on that one. The question is, which one? There are at least five of them.'

Traffic was as heavy as usual running through Notting Hill and down past Holland Park. It wasn't until they passed Hammersmith that Mike flicked the switch on his radio.

'Admiral, you copy?'

'Yes Mike.'

'We're on the Great West Road, heading west. Our guess is they'll join the M4 at Chiswick Roundabout. All points to one of the reservoirs in the Staines area. I think there are five ... no, Jacko's saying six. Whatever. Someone needs to tell Thames Water to shut down all the pumping stations for the whole group. And do that now. Assuming we're right, these bastards are going to chuck something into the water and we don't know how long we'd have before it takes effect. Last thing we want is to have half of London spitting up its intestines.'

'You got it. And thank you for that lurid description. That done and we're going in. Out.'

'Have fun.'

He glanced in the rear view mirror at the two men sitting behind him.

'John you're firearms right?'

'Yup.'

'That makes you camera, Ian. You've got body worn, yeah? Can't see from here. Shit.'

He braked hard to avoid the Ford Focus that had snapped across him towards a turning on the left. Music blared from the open windows, the young driver rocking to the sounds, oblivious to the world around him.

'Stupid fuck! Ian?'

'Yeah, I'm wearing a body camera. They're good.'

'Brilliant.'

Conscious of the traffic and concentrating on the Mercedes, nobody talked for a while. Driving along Chiswick High Road was slow and the four men watched the people on the pavements. There were those who marched along with purpose; places to go and people to meet. And the others: wandering along with their cares weighing them down or happy thoughts lifting them up. Mike wondered how they would react if they knew that they were only yards away from men carrying guns.

By the time they hit the roundabout, the Mercedes was clearly visible, albeit four cars ahead. It eased out into the maelstrom of traffic and disappeared from view. Mike felt just a twinge of unease as he followed blind; breathed a small sigh of relief when he saw it climbing up the ramp towards the motorway. Once on the M4, he eased into the middle lane, keeping the Mercedes far enough away but in line of sight.

'Ian, back to the camera. When we get to wherever, you and I are out first. Best case scenario, we get close enough to them when they're on the ground with water in full view. You're filming from the moment that happens, or before if you think it makes sense. Jacko, John, second wave. 'Scuse the pun. Watch the play but be close enough to stop these guys in their tracks before they can act. Chances are that at least one of them is carrying. If need be, drop both.'

No response was given, or expected. All four men were on full alert and watching the other car's every move. The M3 route was already well behind them. At Junction Five, the Somalis peeled off with the BMW in its wake, heading for Colnbrook.

'It's the Queen Mother. They're only going for the biggest London's got,' exclaimed Jacko. 'They're either going over the fence or they're using an entrance.'

He worked quietly on a laptop for a moment.

'Two possibilities: Thames Water, but that's going to be gated. Major, there's a sailing club here with direct access to the water. That's got to be it. Whatever they do, there's no chance of us being unobserved.'

After that it all seemed to unfold with terrifying speed, punctuated with sequences in slow motion. Or so it seemed to Mike later on in the day.

The Somalis followed Horton Road and, as predicted, turned onto the road leading to the sailing club. The BMW followed a couple of minutes later, stopping at the end of the clubhouse, a distance away from the Mercedes which had parked at the far end of the car park. The men watched as the pair got out of the Mercedes and began to walk along the waterside and away from the club. The satchel was clearly visible on the man's shoulder; the one closest to the water's edge.

'We go now!' shouted Mike.

Simultaneously, the four men burst from the car and hit the ground running. Mike and Ian to the fore flanked by Jacko and John. Silent they were not and the Somalis weren't deaf. Instinctively, they ran.

'Stop. Armed police. Stop immediately or we will shoot.'

Jacko's stentorian voice rang out loudly in the quiet, away from the hum of the traffic. For a moment, it stopped them in their tracks. Then they turned and ran. One shot was fired above their heads; one stopped while the other, carrying the bag, ran on. The one left behind looked straight at the oncoming force and produced a handgun. But that flew out of his hand as a 9mm bullet hit his right shoulder and threw him backwards. Mike ran past, breathing heavily now, but slowly catching the man in front; and he was slowing himself down by constantly glancing behind at his pursuer.

Finally stopping, he pulled the satchel over his head by the strap, swung it in a violent circle, releasing it at the apex. As it arced through the afternoon sunlight, Mike floored him with a flying rugby tackle. John, hard on his heels, helped secure the man on the ground. And they both looked at the satchel floating on the water.

'Shit,' Mike said before diving into the reservoir.

Despite the sunlight, the dark water was freezing and the swimmer was fully clothed. 'I can do this,' Mike thought as he swam steadily towards the slowly sinking satchel. I can do this. Forward motion seemed agonizingly slow as Mike inched nearer. Close enough for a lunge. Close enough to touch; far enough to push, and for it to drift out of reach. He lunged again and this time managed to hook one end of the strap where it joined the bag – just before it sank beneath the surface. Dragging the bag behind him, he managed to swim back to the bank before his fingers lost all feeling.

'All right Mike. Easy mate, I've got it.'

Jacko took the sodden bag and carefully put it on the ground, well away from the cuffed Somali. Together, he and John hauled the half frozen, soaking man onto dry land.

'Nice dive,' Ian said, 'that'll look good on the silver screen.'

'Sod off,' replied Mike through chattering teeth. Job done, he thought.

The two Somalis were handcuffed to the rollbars fitted to the back of the X5 and Jacko drove home with John riding shotgun. Ian followed behind in the Mercedes with Mike in the passenger seat, shrouded in a silver thermal blanket. They'd turned the heating on full blast and by the time the mini convoy had reached Chiswick, Mike had recovered the feeling in his fingers. After his dip in the reservoir both radio and phone were useless and dead as dodos. Ian passed him his mobile.

'We're done Admiral. Got the bag, although I had to swim for it. I'll fill you in later.'

'Have you opened it?'

'Yeah, there's a large block of styrofoam inside holding four racks of vials. Each one seems to be stoppered by rice paper or something. They're all still firm despite their bath but I'm guessing whoever put this together designed the stoppers to dissolve in water.'

'Bloody hell, good work, Mike. Everyone healthy?'

'Apart from being wet and still fucking cold, I'm fine. Everyone else is good apart from one of the Somalis. We've got them both but that one'll need a medic; Jacko shot him in the shoulder. Man had a gun.'

'On record?'

'Our cameraman Ian says yes.'

'Excellent.'

'And your end? All fine?'

'Uneventful. Our lot popped open the door with a lot of noise and shouting. Found the woman there who screamed a lot when she saw the guns. The WPC carted her off to Paddington Green for questioning. Unfortunately, there was no sign of the Yemeni or whatever he was. Uniforms are still carting stuff out of the house – computers, boxes of files, cash and possibly some more of those vials. We've got a forensics team in and a specialist is on his way from Porton Down to check what might have gone in the water. Thank God you managed to grab that bag.'

'That's it then. We're on our way home. Get me some dry clothes will you Boss?'

'Consider it done.'

As they edged towards the end of the M4 where it drops into the chaos of London traffic, Mike saw the blue lights flashing on the X5 a nanosecond before the wail of the siren hit his eardrums.

'Thank you, Jacko.'

Paddington Green was waiting for them, absorbing the six men with enfolding arms and closing doors. The two Somalis were taken unceremoniously to separate holding cells. Interrogation would come in due course. A medic had been on hand to deal with the bullet wound sustained.

'It went straight through without any lasting damage,' he reported. 'Torn tissue, muscle lacerations and loss of blood, but no bone complications. I've cleaned and disinfected the wound; plugged and bandaged, he'll live. More's the pity some would say.'

The Admiral had been as good as his word. On arrival Mike was given a grey tracksuit, an almost clean pair of trainers and a black bin liner for his wet clothes. It worked. Dried off and reasonably warm, he walked into the ops room he'd left only a few hours previously. To his amazement, both teams were on their feet with Admiral Buller leading the applause. When the clapping subsided, the Admiral indicated that they should all sit.

'You deserved that Mike. However, you can all give yourself a pat on the back. Good job everyone. Excellent work at both locations. I can tell you that Porton Down suspects the vials contain either potassium cyanide or some an anthrax based toxin. Potassium cyanide would have relatively easy to arrange as it's used in gold mining. Plenty of that in Ethiopia next door if Somalia had come up empty. The anthrax theory isn't quite so easy to work out but we'll find out in due course.

'It goes without saying that nothing untoward happened today and we all worked hard in the office. The Home Secretary has put a press blackout on today's events and that's likely to remain until we find out more from our Somalian friends. That's it I think. Thank you everyone.'

Turning to Mike, he said: 'I think you deserve a drink young Major Roberts. Come on, I'll drop you off in Chiswick, it's on my way. How does a large brandy sound?'

'Perfect, thank you Admiral.'

45

*****

Ellie heard the key turn in the lock and looked down the hall to the front door.

'Mike?'

'Hey Ells, I'm back.'

She walked towards him for a welcome kiss but was beaten to the post by a small ball of rough-haired terrier that threw itself as high as it could on his thighs. Mike picked up the wriggling dog to stop it trying to batter itself to death.

'Hi Max. Being stupid as usual I see. Sorry I'm late. Been a long day.'

She kissed him over Max's back, hugging the dog between them.

'Hi big man, good to see you in one piece.'

'Kids?'

She pointed upstairs to the two young kids sitting next to each other on the top step.

'Hi Dad,' they chorused.

'Can we eat now?' little Liz moaned, 'I'm hungry.'

'Me too,' added Mark, demonstrating solidarity with his younger sister.

'Nothing really changes,' observed Mike.

It wasn't until dinner had been cooked, devoured and cleared away that there was an opportunity for further conversation. The kids in bed, the pair sat down in the living room, each with a large glass of wine.

'And?'

'And what?' he replied.

'Come on Mike. I get the vibe.'

'OK, this is how it goes. It started off quietly in the office. Then two Somali terrorists go down to the Queen Mother's very own posthumous reservoir to dump some poison with the intention, and hope, of killing a large number of London's upstanding citizens. My friends and I, including Jacko, decide to disabuse them of this idea. This results in one being shot and both being tucked away in cells at Paddington Green. And en passant, I went swimming in the very cool water. Other than that

I went to the pub with the Admiral for a quick brandy and he kindly dropped me off.'

'For fuck's sake Mike. Are we going back to this?'

'It's my job Ellie. That's what I do.'

She looked at him silently for a while and then nodded.

'I know.' She sighed. 'I just thought that we'd left action man behind.'

'Truce?'

'Truce,' she replied, and snuggled up to his shoulder.

Later, at some time in the early hours, Eleanor Roberts found herself awake, staring into the semi-darkness of the bedroom. A jaundice yellow glow from the streetlight seeped in through a gap in the curtains, the air from the open window cool on her skin. She shivered, spooning into Mike's back for the warmth and the feeling of closeness. For a moment it broke the rhythm of his light snoring and she held her breath, not wanting to wake him.

'Why does it always have to be you?' she whispered.

She really hadn't thought about it when they went to bed, when he made gentle love to her and melted the thoughts away. But they always came back, those thoughts, the ones that gnawed and chewed in her head. With the mental strength that came from years of practice, she pushed them out of her mind. Mike loved the job and he loved her; Ellie didn't want to make him choose between them. Moments later, she drifted off into dreamless sleep.

And Mike left her sleeping, slipping quietly out of the house on his way to the Office. A beam of sunshine lanced through the gap in the curtains, warming her face. Lazily opening her eyes, she threw a languid arm over to his side of the bed. Empty. He'd already left. Turning her head to confirm her assumption, she saw a large piece of paper where his head had been. In big blue letters he'd scrawled: Love You M xx.

*****

'You're early,' Helen's voice remarked from the entry phone.

'Not – morning Michael – or – hallo gorgeous. Just – you're early!'

'My 'umble apologies, Sir. Yer ain't angry wiv this poor fla'er girl are yer?' she said, parodying East End Victorian. 'Get your arse in here, Mike. The Old Man's already here and fizzing. He's in the library, as per yesterday. Coffee?'

'Please,' he said smiling, and pushed the door as it clicked open.

Sir Reginald Buller was standing by the fireplace under his personal white nimbus, pipe in one hand and a slim paper file in the other. His greeting was smoked out rather than spoken. Motioning the younger man to sit in an armchair, he sat down himself in his accustomed Chesterfield.

'We were lucky yesterday, bloody lucky. Fortunately, your quick reactions stopped the stuff that they had with them actually getting into the water supply. Professor Alder, chap from Porton Down who analysed the stuff yesterday afternoon, emailed an initial report last night.'

Sucking hard on his pipe, the Admiral exhaled a jet of smoke towards the ceiling and opened the file.

'According to Alder, and as far as I understand the report, it's essentially a modified form of potassium cyanide. Which is what he'd guessed before he made his tests. There's a lot in here about inorganic cyanides, ions, acids and alkalis which ends up being total bloody double Dutch.' He scanned down the page. 'Something about crystals dissolved in acid 'forming an acidic volatile cyanide suspension, thus overcoming the necessity for internal acidic reagents'.' Throwing the file onto the coffee table, he continued: 'Bottom line is, it's about three times more toxic than the ordinary industrial stuff used in gold mining. However, in his opinion there was nowhere near enough of it in those vials to poison the whole reservoir. But he's not absolutely certain, one, and two, uniforms uncovered three more boxes of vials in the house.'

'Bloody hell!'

'Indeed. One could say, more appositely, that we dashed the poisoned chalice to the ground. Point is Mike, we should have dealt with the bastards beforehand.'

'I agree Sir, but we didn't have all the information. Without sound intelligence we can't act.'

'And I concur. But what if that information was out there? What if there were little whispers in the ether that nobody listened to because there was just too much other noise? Which neatly brings me on to the subject of Tracker. Meant to take you down to John's cave of secrets yesterday, if you remember. I don't think you've actually met him, have you?'

'Not that I'm aware of, Admiral.'

'John Watkins. Ex civil servant, so very diligent and rather serious. He used to work for the MoD as a Senior Information Manager, directly involved in technical surveillance. He was more or less running a team monitoring computers and data, telephony, mobiles and landlines. Then it turned out that he was also a dab hand at systems analysis, so we borrowed him on a sort of sale or return basis. And Tracker's really his baby. Anyway, ready?'

Leaving his beloved pipe dying in the ashtray, Admiral Buller led Mike out of the library, turning right down the corridor. He stopped at the end, turned to the wall and rested the fingertips of his right hand on a small painting of a bowl of apples. A vertical line of light appeared a few feet to the left, which quickly expanded in width; doors parting to allow entry into the lift behind. A simple trompe l'oeil that always amused and surprised the uninitiated. The two men walked in and the Admiral pressed a button among several in an unlabelled line. As the lift descended the doors above closed and once again, there was merely a wall with a painting in the corridor.

The lift softly came to rest and the doors opened onto a brightly lit room, clearly designed as play room for technophiles. One wall was dominated by five huge screens that seemed to be lit from within and positively glowed. A digitised global map was predominantly blue but pockets of other colours – green, yellow, red, black – created splashes of colour. Another screen showed blocks of numbers and symbols scrolling upwards with no obvious purpose or end in sight.

'I see you're admiring our wonderful touch screens gentlemen. Newest of new technology, courtesy of Sartech in South Korea.'

The speaker was a slight but extraordinarily angular man with a shock of grey hair. His face was drawn, the unnaturally white skin taut across his cheekbones and down to the pointed chin. He looked tired.

'Morning John. Apologies for entering your domain without warning.'

'Not a problem Sir Reginald, not a problem.'

'Introductions. Major Michael Roberts meet our systems analyst, engineer and all-round computing wizard, John Watkins. And vice versa.'

What passed for a smile hovered on Watkins' thin lips and he held out a bony hand. Mike shook it tentatively. The fingers felt almost brittle and dry to the touch, like old parchment. But when they made eye contact, he found himself under the scrutiny of a gaze that was both direct and full of life. The black pupils looked capable of boring holes and were surrounded by irises that were not quite blue and not quite lilac.

'I've read your file, Major. You've had an interesting career. I'm pleased to meet the man behind the face.'

'Likewise,' Mike replied, somewhat lamely.

'Be careful of Mr Watkins,' the Admiral interjected. 'He's read all our files and probably all of our emails. Joking apart, John, how are you getting on with Tracker?'

'We're getting there, slowly.'

Watkins waved an arm vaguely in the direction of the twelve operators sitting at individual desks spread around the room. Rapidly switching focus between the two or three flickering screens before him or her, one could feel the concentration emanating from each one. It was like being in the midst of an electrical storm, the staccato sound of fingers tapping erratically on keyboards providing an eerily accurate soundtrack.

'Tracker was originally developed by the Americans but I wanted to improve it and fine-tune the system to suit our requirements. And that's taking longer than I had hoped, even though we're working pretty well round the clock. Just the programming involved is a massive amount of work. On top of that, there are all the refinements that need to be built into the system.'

'I'm sure you're doing a grand job,' Admiral Buller said placatingly. 'I, we all appreciate how hard you're all working. I anticipate that once this is up and running, it will prove to be a vital, indispensable element, contributing to the overall effort.'

He paused before adding: 'So when will it be operational?'

'Oh, it already works to a degree. Just not quite to the degree that we need.'

'Sorry to butt in,' said Mike, 'but I'd be grateful if one of you could fill me in with a bit of background here. What's it meant to do that we haven't got already.'

Admiral Buller pointedly looked at his watch.

'Right. I'll try to keep it simple. There are an awful lot of agencies out there gathering information about an awful lot of things. Thinking about our lot, there's MI6, MI5, Scotland Yard, the Met, Special branches littering the country, GCHQ, web and email servers, surveillance cameras, etcetera, etcetera. Cheltenham alone churns out vast files of information, most of which is, on the face of it totally useless. So what we need to be able to do is efficiently drill down through the dross and pinpoint information that is relevant, concrete and evidential.

'For example, telephone intercepts are not only inadmissible as evidence in a court of law, they're illegal in the first place. But we can use them as pointers to other areas that might yield additional or corroborating information. Tracker enables us to do that by what amounts to electronic triangulation. As we feed in key words, name, places or whatever, Tracker builds up profiles which act as templates to interrogate the flow of information. As that information is refined, Tracker creates sub-profiles and generates more key words in sets that allow us to zero in and give you the whole picture. Which is where you come in I suppose, Major Roberts.

'Tracker also works with intelligent recall, building lists of personal details creating individual files. So it collects telephone numbers and calls, email addresses and emails and so on; also collecting correspondents' details in the same way. As those aggregate into clusters or cells, they form networks that can be displayed visually. And each node in the network can be annotated with whatever details are preferred, provided that they are in the system. In principle, it will have voice recognition ability to the point where Tracker will recognise a voice that is of particular interest, record subsequent conversations, and add the other party to the network automatically.'

He paused for a moment to catch his breath. The Admiral jumped right into the breach of flow.

'That's fascinating John. Mike, any questions before we dash?'

'Yes. Just one. Does it have basic translation capabilities built in or do we have to source physical translators?'

'Yes it does,' Watkins replied, 'but at the moment that's limited to languages that commonly use the Roman alphabet. Languages currently in the immediate pipeline are Arabic, Russian and Urdu. All of those should be on-stream within three months.'

'Excellent. Thank you for your time and expertise Mr Watkins.'

'De nada, Major. And do call me John. Mister makes me sound like a boring schoolmaster.'

Mike had difficulty suppressing the grin.

'No worries. Please call me Mike.'

'For God's sake, will you two stop flirting with each other. Incidentally John, we've got a Mossad chap popping in in a few weeks and he should be able to give us his views on Tracker. Apparently the Israelis have been using it successfully, they say, for a few months. Might be useful for you to have a chat with him, exchange of ideas, best practice and all that. Afraid we have to dash but thanks for your time.'

Admiral Buller strode back to the lift doors with Mike hard on his heels.

'Very worthy and thorough,' he said when they reached the safety of the lift, 'but Watkins can be a crashing bore, given the chance! What else should one expect? Man's wedded to his work, his only other interest being to watch that ultimately dreary game, cricket!'

'Actually, I rather like the cricket myself,' Mike retorted.

'I know,' said the Admiral with a wicked twinkle in his eye. 'By the way, the Israeli chap I mentioned to John? He's also the agent that Mossad's chosen to be your opposite number.'

Emerging from the lift, the two men walked back down the corridor. The Admiral stopped in the hall, at the bottom of the staircase.

'Helen,' he called. He waited for less than five seconds and this time, shouted. 'Helen!'

Heels snapped on the wooden floor and the lady appeared at the top of the stairs.

'I may be many things but deaf I am not Reginald Buller!'

'Sorry, sorry. Um, could you bring down Spiegel's notes, please? We'll be in the library.'

'With pleasure Sir.'

Gleefully, she licked her right forefinger and described a figure one in the air before disappearing.

'Impossible woman,' the Admiral said fondly.

Helen reappeared, leaning over the banisters.

'Do you still want that coffee Mike?'

'Please.'

Helen joined them a few moments later, sitting down on the second Chesterfield. She pushed Mike's cup of coffee towards him over the table, sat back, crossed her well-proportioned and be-nyloned legs. From an A4 envelope she extracted a single sheet of paper and a couple of photographs.

'Not quite my type, but good looking in a stocky sort of way. Short but fit one might say.'

Mike picked up one of the pictures that Helen had tossed onto the table. The man in the photograph was standing somewhere in a rocky dustbowl. Wearing an olive green t-shirt, combat trousers and boots, he looked lean but clearly well muscled. The face was expressionless as the man looked straight to camera, standing with his legs apart and cradling a modified assault rifle. Mike guessed an X95, the ultra compact form of the TAR-21 weapons system developed by Israel Weapon Industries. Designed with Special Forces in mind, the X95 or Micro Tavor was easily modified to a 9mm submachine gun and, as the photograph showed, it was also designed to allow a suppressor to be fitted. All of which also told him that the photograph was very recent.

The other photograph was smaller, a standard head and shoulders, straightforward ID shot. It showed a clean-shaven, pleasant but non-descript face that might interest a few ladies but could equally get lost in the crowd. Only that direct look in the eyes once again gave any indication of the man that lived inside the crop-haired head. Helen's voice pulled him back from his photo inspection.

'Dan 'Danny' Spiegel, born 1966 in Tel Aviv. He's single but has been linked with several named women. Height's five ten, average weight, 79 kilos. Eyes brown, hair dark blonde. Residence listed in Tel Aviv's southern Florentin neighbourhood. Father's Israeli born but mother's English. So he's spent a lot of time over here and knows his way around. He easily passes as being British. Obviously he speaks Hebrew and English, but he's also fluent in Arabic and Farsi.

'Danny Boy is a senior operative with Mossad, but isn't necessarily nailed to one department. His name pops up in connection with Metsada and Kidon operations as well as being a nice regular spy. We're talking sabotage, counter terrorism and assassination among other things. Our Danny is a Bad Boy! He comes with a good pedigree. Before joining Mossad three years ago, he held the rank of Captain in the Mista'arvim counter terrorism unit of the Israel Defence Forces. So he's your man in Mossad Mike. Try saying that after you've had a few drinks.'

Handing the sheet of paper to him, she added: 'For your perusal here, Mike. Just in case you thought of taking it home for bedtime reading.'

'Thank you Helen. In principle, I could see us working well together. When's he over?'

'In about three weeks; in theory he should be arriving in London on the twentieth. He'll be in touch when he's confirmed flights. That's me done. Unless there's anything else?'

'Thank you Helen.'

She smiled graciously, rose elegantly and left the room without a backward glance.

'So, a bite of lunch before you leave?' asked Admiral Buller.

3 ~ From Beirut

Leaning forwards almost protectively over the nargile, Tarek al-Shami carefully spread a layer of tobacco mixed with just a little hashish on the ceramic head. Covering it tightly with a piece of perforated foil, he crowned the pipe with a spoonful of glowing coals and waited. After only a moment a tendril of smoke brought the scent of apples to his nose with a bass note of red Lebanese. Taking a long pull on the hose that coiled so beguilingly, he held the tobacco in his lungs for a second before slowly exhaling a long stream of fragrant smoke into the warm evening air. The second draw on the pipe set the water gently bubbling in the base, laying down a lazy soundtrack to the process.

It was one of his favourite times of the day, when the warm early evening sunshine made the city glow with a dull golden light. The well-appointed apartment, near the village of Mansourieh perched high on the hillside, afforded a panoramic view over across Beirut. He looked out across the multitude of beige building blocks to a ribbon of hazy blue sea; then to the horizon that touched a pink tinged sky, fading up to another, but more delicate, shade of blue. What better way to enjoy the sun's slow descent than sitting comfortably ensconced in the cushions of a wicker chair on the balcony, smoking a pipe or two.

As much as he loved the vibrancy and colour of Beirut, it could also be chaotic, unforgiving and dangerous. In theory, the drive to the American University should have taken approximately half an hour but this morning the trip had taken almost an hour. And the journey home had been no better. Traffic was always heavy in Beirut but in the narrow streets of Hamra it slowed to a crawl, vehicles jammed together in unhappy marriage. Minor accidents were not infrequent; the ensuing arguments as to where the blame lay bringing everyone to a standstill. Most people adhered to the Lebanese philosophy of motion: he who hesitates, waits. And everyone seemed to have lightning reactions when a gap of more than ten centimetres appeared.

But traffic was only part of the problem. The fear of violence floated but a hair's breadth beneath the surface of the collective mind, papered thinly with an outward show of living life to the full.

'Live for the moment, for the next might explode!'

He'd seen it scrawled on a wall, a grim truth that left that sour metallic taste in your mouth. And visual reminders were everywhere. His route to the office took him past the stark 24-storey skeleton of the once luxurious Holiday Inn; desolate and battle scarred, its walls pitted by countless bullets and cratered by rockets. For six months in the early days of the civil war, the Holiday Inn had been home to snipers and drew returning fire like a magnet.

A little further along the road stood the remains of St George's Hotel, one time playground for international glitterati and the jet set. That was before the four-storeyed pink stone building was gutted by fire in the civil war, a war that had finished 15 years ago. But the massive damage to the front of hotel was only a few months old, caused by a truck containing an estimated 1,000 kilos of explosives. The explosion had killed Prime Minister Rafic Hariri and 20 other people, as well as injuring over 200 more.

That had been in February. Before that, in October, there'd been a car bomb that almost killed some politician in West Beirut. And since then there'd been two more bombs: one in New Jdaideh (which was also on Tarek's route) and another in Jounieh, north of the city on the Byblos road. Naturally he wasn't keen to be a victim but ... wrong place, wrong time. One had to be philosophical. But in consequence, checkpoints were appearing spontaneously around the city, armed positions blistering the already scarred skin of Beirut. Although the grey camouflage and automatic weapons of the police were ubiquitous, recently their numbers seemed to have multiplied. In turn, the police been joined by soldiers in the brown and green camouflage of the Lebanese Army.

Tarek took a long pull at the hose of his nargile, drawing the smoke deep into his lungs. Exhaling again with that long stream of smoke, he began to laugh. Perhaps it was the hashish, but it suddenly seemed ironic that he was sitting on the balcony, thinking irritably about bombs and checkpoints in Beirut, when he was considering blowing up far more than a motorcade or a shopping mall. His levity was short lived. He'd been stopped at several checkpoints during the course of the day, and each one took him back 30 years to a checkpoint on Cyprus.

He didn't dwell on the subsequent horrors, of what he'd seen and heard. Ayesha had been his beautiful adult sister who he'd adored, even though she'd always laughed at him. Tarek couldn't, wouldn't go through the mental videos buried deep in his head. What he remembered and relived was a time after they'd returned to the villa. As he had done a thousand times since then, he went through what they'd agreed that day – Ali, Amin and himself – what they'd all promised, and the oath they'd taken.

*****

Afterwards, nobody really talked very much, not on the base or back at the villa. But the raw emotions were molten, white-hot magma that violently erupted through the crust of denial. Occasionally Najib glowed incandescent with anger, verbally lashing out at the vile British dogs for their crimes and then at the women he loved. At times he even shouted that Leila had been at fault, tantalising the men with her sexuality; that his wife and daughter were no more than filthy whores. And almost as soon as the words left his mouth, he would burst into tears and beg their forgiveness. He would punch the wall until his hands were bloody and, in turn, Leila would beg him to stop.

Sabir would suddenly berate Faridah for not defending their honour with greater force. Why had she not protected his beautiful Leena? Then he would either follow Najib's terrible script or simply stare at them both, asking 'why?' over and over again. As for Qadir, he held his wife in his arms, silently thanking Allah for keeping his wife and son safe.

Then the Navy man, Simmonds, had come to the villa to say that they were being flown back to Beirut the following day. He got little thanks for the news, even though it was welcome, and didn't linger. When he'd gone, the deafening silence returned to

57

the villa, an oppressive vacuum that seemed to starve the rooms of air.

Hands clenched in hard fists, Tarek walked out into the garden, drinking in the salty fresh air in big gulps. Skirting the swimming pool, he tramped across the tiled surround and scrubby stony earth to the low wall that marked the end of the property. On the other side, the ground fell away in an arid rock-strewn landslip that finally lost itself in the shallow dunes before the narrow beach. Leaning down, Tarek picked up a few stones from the drift of detritus against the wall. One by one, he hurled them down the slope where they snapped against boulders or raised plumes of dust. As he bent to pick more ammunition, Tarek heard the sounds of shuffling footsteps and saw familiar shoes on either side. He nodded without speaking; it was right that they should be there, together, as they had been before. Nor did Amin or Ali speak with words, showing their allegiance in the throwing of stones. For a while, the three boys communicated by simply throwing rocks at rocks.

'I will kill the shit eating dogs who did this thing,' Tarek hissed finally. 'As Allah is my witness, I will kill them and those like them.'

Amin and Ali looked at each other, and then looked at their friend. What they saw on his contorted face was a look of pure hate.

'How can we kill them?' asked Amin. 'We don't know who they are. Or where they are.'

'You said – we,' Tarek replied, 'then you are with me?'

'Leena is my sister, as Ayesha is yours. Our mothers are their mothers. And we are more than friends. We fight together.'

'Ali?'

The boy nodded slowly.

'We fight together,' he repeated. 'Where you go, I will go also.'

Tarek nodded and scanned the ground for a few seconds before crouching down to pick up a glass jar from the rubbish by the wall. Raising it in the air, he threw it against the stones and the jar shattered with the impact. Leaning down, he inspected the broken glass and chose a long glittering sliver that he carefully held in one hand.

'Maybe we will not find these men themselves. Maybe they will die another way. But we will take the war to their homes. We will make war on the British sailors and avenge our families.'

Ali and Amin watched as Tarek drew the needle sharp point of the shard across the palm of his other hand. They didn't see him wince. A line of red blood appeared. They'd all seen this in films but this was real. Amin held out his hand, followed by Ali a little later. Tarek pulled the glass quickly across the two upheld palms and two more red lines appeared.

As the three pressed their palms together, each one to the other two, Tarek said, 'Now we are more than friends, we are brothers. Maybe not today or tomorrow, but one day we three will strike a mighty blow against these people, I swear, as Allah is my witness.'

'As Allah is my witness, so do I swear,' said Amin.

'I swear also,' said Ali, 'as Allah is my witness.'

'So we are one. Allahu Akbar.'

And the oath was taken.

*****

At least, that was how the film played out in his head, all in black and white, a film noir. Individual frames might have blurred a little over the years but the detail and continuity remained true, the soundtrack crystal clear even now. Through all those tumultuous years, the three men had always kept in close contact even though their paths had radically diverged. Back in the day, that had meant landlines and letters; now it was mobiles, text messaging and email. When they were kids it had been a bit erratic, for obvious reasons, but later they had it taped and they tried to meet up somewhere, at least once a year or more.

Thinking back, had it not been for the Cyprus atrocities, the combination of distance and passage of time might well have conspired to break the threads. But if the horror of what had happened on the island wasn't enough, the afterburn in Beirut added weight and longevity to how the three of them felt. Shit, he'd only been a kid when it all happened, not really understanding either the reality or the implications. He'd thought that when they were home, back in Lebanon with their friends and extended families, that life would return to normal. He'd thought that they could go back to where they were before, how they were before. How naïve. None of them were the same, changed by brutality and bestiality that had branded each one of them. What made it worse was that they were shunned once the news started seeping out, leaked by those who they'd trusted.

Rape had made Leila and Faridah dirty, untouchable sluts with no moral compass. Rape meant that Ayesha and Leena were beyond consideration for marriage, disgusting to both men and women. They were whores and bitches for the dogs in the street. Rape had shamed the men, showing them to be weak without self-respect or honour. Nothing more than the dogs themselves, pimps and whoremongers. Understanding burned the three boys' minds with searing black flames, forging swords of hate and revenge. And the oath they had sworn by the low wall in Cyprus, looking out over the sea was reaffirmed, a sealed compact for an unknown time in an unknown future.

Tarek sucked at the nargile's mouthpiece, inhaling the narcotic smoke slowly and smoothly. The smell and taste of the smoke, the sound of gently bubbling water, the tactile surface and innate beauty of the ornate glass bowl and stem; all harmonized, lending a mellowness to the way he felt. It wasn't lessening the acuity of his thoughts, Tarek mused; more that it smoothed out some of the ruts and ridges in his way of thinking.

The shallow arc of the sun was little more than a yellow smear on the horizon now and the sky above was taking on a darker hue. Looking west, lights were coming on in al-Dahiya al-Janubiya, Beirut's southern suburbs: the Palestinian refugee camp of Shatila, in Ghbayreh and Haret Hreik. The lights might be turned on but the shadows were deepening. Lebanon was not short of men and women who were prepared to fight for their beliefs. Hidden in the shadows and dark corners they planned and conspired: remnants of the Popular Front for the Liberation of Palestine, members of Hezbollah, Hamas and al-Qaeda. Perhaps a few more, here and there. Tarek had at least one or two contacts in every one of the groups and, he told himself happily, most of them held him in high regard. However, he had to admit that without his father's contacts, support and sponsorship, Tarek's network of alliances would have been much more difficult to broker.

With hindsight, Tarek suspected that his father's association with the PLO and PFLP probably dated back to the late sixties. Civil war had broken out in Lebanon less than a year after Cyprus but Najib had kept the family in Beirut. Thanks to his father's influence and connections, they managed to stay alive between the bombs and bullets for almost twelve months before they fled to Cairo. But several more years went by before Tarek discovered that Najib acted as a liaison officer and was responsible for channelling funds to the PFLP from China and the Soviet Union. That had been something of a revelation. The move to Cairo had been more in response to Najib's need for freedom of movement rather than fear of the dangers in Beirut.

Then there was Ayesha. She'd been 21 when she met Abdel Raouf Khoury in one of the narrow alleyways of Khan el-Khalili, the ancient sprawling market in Cairo's medieval quarter. Tarek remembered how she'd described the meeting a few days later: the oppressive heat and humidity, the stench of rotting vegetables blending with rancid cooking oil and sweating dog shit. The sheer press of people that had carried her along, squeezing and pushing her from side to side. Then when there was a little space to breathe, a swarthy young man had appeared out of nowhere. He'd pushed by her so violently that she'd fallen back against the wall, knocking over a rack laden with metal pots. The clatter of metal on metal and metal on stone made him pause, turn. It was hate at first sight, coffee a moment later and then as the days progressed a conflicted relationship began to grow.

A few years older than Ayesha, Abdel Raouf was far more knowledgeable on Palestinian history and keen to educate his attractive new acquaintance. He spoke of Britain's betrayal of Palestine and its support of Israel, of his hate for Israel and of Egyptians pandering to Zionists. In reply, she told him of her hate of the English pigs and why, of bitterness, shame and anger. It was the first time since Cyprus that Ayesha had allowed anyone to see her face; for him she'd removed her hijab. She saw his eyes narrow and face contort; felt his lips on her scarred cheek and heard him say that it only made her look more beautiful. Shared passion and hate grew, entwined together, each one feeding the other. And together, they had gone to Beirut to fight.

'Allah forgive me,' sighed Tarek.

The sky was a darkened dome, dimly lit by a skinny scimitar moon and a handful of stars. With so much on his mind, he had missed his normal observance of maghrib, the evening prayer. Uncoiling from his chair, he flipped a switch on the wall to turn on the balcony's soft lighting and went into the room behind. Approaching a tall but slim chest, Tarek opened the top drawer, took out a small plastic bag of hashish and more tobacco. Given his earlier thoughts, he wasn't surprised to find himself looking at the photograph standing alone on the chest.

A faded colour print, it showed a group of young fighters in the back of an army truck stripped of canvas. Standing in the middle, Abdel Raouf was holding an AK47 high in the air, his mouth open in silent cry. Ayesha was crouching down in front of him with her head uncovered, a smile on her lips and a gun in her hand. It had been taken in 1981; Palestinian warriors on their way to another battle. The Popular Front had trained his sister to shoot, make bombs and use a knife; then sent her out to die for the cause if need be. After a while, it was difficult to say who they were fighting and what the cause, other than survival. Ayesha had survived. Abdel Raouf hadn't been so lucky, vaporised by one of Israel's indiscriminating bombs dropped on Beirut.

'Allahu akbar, Abdel Raouf, allahu akbar.'

He turned away from the picture and walked back to his seat on the balcony to prepare another pipe. Looking west across the city, he wondered where his sister was among the lights and shadows. Maybe she was listening to a refugee in Shatila or, more likely, drinking in a bar with friends in Hamra. Tarek sniffed disapprovingly at the thought. Even now, after all these years, he couldn't quite understand his sister's secular attitude, her lack of faith in Islam and the way in which she flouted its laws. Much as he loved her, sometimes it was actually embarrassing to have to admit that Ayesha was his sister.

He was a Professor of Arabic and Islamic Studies at Beirut's most prestigious university and the faculty's Deputy Director, he thought pompously. Not only that, he'd achieved his Master's degree in Islamic Jurisprudence at the University of Jordan's Faculty of Sharia. Religiously, brother and sister stood at opposite ends of the spectrum. Conversely, when it came to focused mistrust, hatred and revenge – they were in total harmony. He thought she would approve of his current plans, albeit embryonic and provided she let him explain without interrupting!

For a few minutes, Tarek smoked silently to break the ambivalent thought patterns, clearing his mind before moving on to other key human considerations. Another smell lingered in the warm evening air, bringing the scent of lamb roasted with garlic, ginger, fennel and cumin to meld with the smoke. The rhythmic calls of a thousand cicadas lulled the mind further, occasionally broken by the laboured grind of a truck engine or the haunting cry of a tawny owl.

The sharp report snapped him back to full alertness, backing down only a little when Tarek realised that it had been a car backfiring. It had sounded like an explosion, which brought his thoughts back to the ones that he had on his mental drawing board. Since al-Qaeda had the funds and the desire, he'd already floated the principles of his plan with his Lebanese contact, a man who he knew only as Fouad. Tarek had told him of the anticipated targets for a limited but highly destructive bombing campaign. He'd explained how and where he expected to source the explosives; how they would be delivered, deployed and activated. Kerboom! Five days later, he'd received the email:

'Congratulations! You've won today's jackpot. To collect, please move to the next stage and confirm your details once achieved. Good luck.'

To all intents and purposes, the message looked like junk mail and had gone straight into the spam folder. But the email address comprised of a sequence of numbers confirmed its veracity and the identity of the server. Which meant that he had the green light to take his plans to the next level.

Thanks to his position at the university, Tarek was expected to attend international symposiums and conferences relating to Islam and Muslims. Therefore he travelled extensively as a natural part of his work, in addition to his teaching and tutoring responsibilities. The subtext was that his travel arrangements were never questioned, nor did he have to justify his expenses. Over the years he'd made, developed and maintained many useful connections, a percentage of which naturally related to academia. But there were also more than few that were clearly beneficial and of considerable to certain Iranian parties, Hezbollah and al-Qaeda. Thus Tarek had variously been a bagman, intelligence conduit and money launderer. To his surprise, he'd found that he fitted in to all three roles rather well.

Travelling to England for a few days would hardly raise an eyebrow. He'd already booked an early flight with Middle East Airlines leaving Beirut International Airport for Heathrow. That left him three days before flying out on Friday. He was fairly certain that both Ali and Amin would be able to meet him in London, especially once they knew that this was not just a social visit on the back of business. He'd emailed Ali to say he was coming to London but that he'd phone with more details. Tarek made a mental note to phone Ali the following evening – to phone Alan the following evening.

After all these years, he still found it difficult to think of Ali Abbas as Alan Abbot. But Ali had ever been the dark horse. When they were kids, he was always the quietest of the three friends, appeared to be the most reticent, but when he was needed, he'd always been there. On Cyprus, when they'd taken that oath, Ali had seemed to hold back, just that little bit, as though slightly unsure. It had taken Tarek a long time to realise that the man needed to think things through analytically before making a decision. Once taken, that decision was inviolable and action would be taken, but never in haste.

When the war broke out, the Abbas family stayed in Beirut since Qadir couldn't see that they had any other choice. But on the basis that one was safer with some sort of protection, he logically sided with the PLO, picked up his Kalashnikov and became a fighter. Living in a small apartment on the fourth floor of a tower block in Haret Hreik with no air conditioning was dark, humid, grey, dusty and dangerous. Between all the bullets, bombs, rockets and missiles, somehow they all survived but managed little else. When Qadir wasn't at home, Halah and Ali scavenged for food, water and anything they might retrieve from the rubble and sell. When Qadir was at home, he taught his son how to clean and operate the AK47 assault rifle and Czech made CZ52 semi-automatic pistol. And Ali learned how to make bombs; a task for which he showed a distinct aptitude.

One evening in July, Qadir went back to his family having been away for several nights. He was dirty, dusty and hot, his clothes clinging roughly to his skin. Blood seeped from a gash on his arm where he'd caught a piece of flying metal. He badly needed a drink of water, his throat dry and rasping. But when he got to the apartment block, most of it was missing and what was left, still smoking from the Israeli shell that had blown it to hell. Ignoring the dangers of the unstable building, Qadir scrambled up the remains of a staircase praying he'd find them alive.

Little was left of their wretchedly cramped one bedroom apartment. Stepping into the room that had served as their living-stroke-dining room and where Ali had slept, Qadir found himself on the edge of a precipice, looking out over a world of rubble. He'd found Ali and Halah crumpled against the wall behind the wreckage of the bedroom door. A slim thread of blood hung from the corner of Halah's mouth, darkly red against her white dusted skin. The force of the blast must have thrown her against the wall and her neck had broken with the impact. Ali was by her side, covered in dust and motionless apart from his chest which rose and fell slowly with pained breaths. Qadir gathered his son in his arms and cried.

Tarek was sure that the war had refined Ali's anger and hate. But the day his mother died something darker had formed in the boy's soul – the cold desire for deadly revenge. The powerful emotions he'd shared on Cyprus, although genuine, had essentially been reflected through the prism of his friends' pain. Now it was personal.

In the wake of the siege of Beirut, they were evacuated with other members of the PLO by French paratroopers and shipped to Tunisia. In a bar in La Goulette, Qadir persuaded the captain of a fishing boat to take them as far as Sardinia. From there they island hopped to Corsica in a stolen dinghy and managed to stow away on the ferry to Toulon. Tarek had heard the whole story more than once: the long journey up through France, hitching rides, jumping trains and walking until they finally reached the

Port of Calais where they legitimately boarded the ferry to Dover.

Exactly how the pair found themselves living in a bedsit in a slum area in Sparkbrook south of Birmingham was always glossed over. It was as though the journey northward had been simple but Tarek knew that Ali had drawn a blind over the period. A time that had been blighted by bigotry and bureaucracy that only deepened Ali's feelings about the English.

'Too many are ignorant racist pigs who have no soul or belief,' Ali had ranted on more than one occasion. 'And like filthy pigs they have no honour, no self-respect, no manners. Ha! They are worse than pigs!'

The words of the Qu'ran were perfectly clear: the flesh of swine was haram, prohibited eating for Muslims. To Tarek, therefore, Ali's comments served to reassure him that his old friend would never renege on his oath. But the true irony really came at the end of the tale.

As part of his university sandwich course, Ali spent nine months with a relatively small company called Forbes Industries based in South Wales. At the end of his four-year programme, Ali achieved a first class Bachelor of Science degree in Mechanical Engineering and Forbes offered him a fulltime position with the company. Subsequently, it had sponsored him in undertaking master's degrees with Cranfield University: Guided Weapons Systems and Military Electronic Systems Engineering. Forbes Industries produced munitions for the Ministry of Defence with an emphasis on missiles such as the Sea Dart, Seawolf and Sea Skua. Ali was playing with explosives again.

Once he was employed by Forbes, Ali decided to paint out the foreign, Middle Eastern parts of his slightly strange curriculum vitae. Five years in-theatre experience in Lebanon gained while assisting a fighting member of the PFLP – redacted. Practical skills to include: used to handling plastic explosives and detonators, ammonium nitrate/diesel bomb manufacture, field strip, load and fire semi-automatic pistols and assault rifles … – redacted. Name: Ali Abbas – redacted, and replaced with: Alan Abbot. He'd married a pretty girl from Pontypridd called Megan nee Morgan, vaguely supported the Snakes (Aberdare's Rugby

Football Club), drank the odd pint of Felinfoel's Celtic Pride and observed Salat, the five Islamic prayers, unobserved.

Tarek smiled as he recalled Ali-Alan's apparent duplicity, but had no doubts as to his loyalty. Nor had he any doubts about Amin's loyalty or commitment to their pact. Although he did wonder how far his old friend might have fallen for the honeyed embrace of western decadence; whether his overtly hedonistic lifestyle was a blind or, in fact, the new reality. Could one be simultaneously warrior and sybarite?

The scent of cooked lamb and spices still lingered in the air. Further down the hillside, tendrils of smoke curled up from an open grill adding a warm cedar smell. Tarek could hear voices, a man's call and women's laughter. And, softly, very softly, a melody, strains of music, the gentle tapping of a tablah and moving notes, plucked strings on an oud.

Beirut had been like that, both warrior and sybarite. But the former had ever been the stronger of the two. When the madness of the civil war reached an apocalyptic crescendo with the massacres in Karantina and Damour, the Masris sought the safety of Paris. They had friends, Marie and Jean-Paul Clemenceau, who lived near Parc Georges-Brassens in the 15ème arrondissement, Sabir had said. Paris would be safer, especially for Faridah and Leena. They rented a two-bedroom apartment on the Rue de Gergovie, the other side of the railway tracks from Le Parc and a few minutes walk from Gare Montparnasse.

Amin had described it as a: 'dreary little grey-brown street that smelled of smoke and diesel. The apartment, if you can call it that, had peeling wallpaper and walls that wept with damp'.

In the big picture, it hadn't mattered. With a little financial aid from the Clemenceaus, Sabir and Faridah started a small restaurant serving typical Lebanese dishes. It soon gained a strong local Parisien(ne) following, as well as enticing other homesick émigrés from Lebanon. But perhaps the most important achievement of Les Goûts de Beyrouth was not the divine dishes that were carried from the kitchen but the way it brought Leena back to life. She'd barely said one word during the year after she'd been raped, Tarek remembered, and rarely left the house. The angry violence of Beirut's streets had kept her cowed and frightened, hiding behind the curtains in the room she'd shared with her mother. But working first in the kitchen and then serving tables at Les Goûts, Leena slowly emerged like a butterfly from its chrysalis. She'd been a skinny strip of a girl with lank hair and large eyes when they'd left for Paris. Nicely rounded now, thought Tarek. He wondered what the women down the hill looked like. He refocused on Amin.

After getting a reasonable Bachelor's degree in Philosophy, Politics and Economics, Amin spent five years doing a Master's in Management at the Paris School of Business. That was where he'd met the lovely Sophie. Sophie Berthier, daughter of a wealthy industrialist based in Marseille and also Monsieur Berthier's sole heir. Not that he was averse to the flow of money, but Amin swore that he'd fallen in love with her before he knew about all that. Hers was a face carved from alabaster with fine high cheekbones, framed by a tawny mass of untamed hair. The full red mouth pouted in obscene contrast to her pale skin but the grey-green eyes appeared washed out and vapid. Nevertheless, she had a quick wit and a ready smile; Amin adored her. Romain Berthier had serious reservations about his beloved daughter's choice of suitor but grudgingly gave his blessing. Sophie had informed him that he had no choice in the matter. However, to ensure that his new son-in-law would not drag Sophie away to a cave in the Beqaa Valley, Berthier gave the pair a large slice of the business to keep them close. And Sophie, being the perverse minx that she was, decided that she and Amin would open the new operation on her father's behalf on the south coast of England.

International Foods (UK) Ltd offered a global supply chain for a wide range of foodstuffs from fresh fruit to tinned fish, and many other products in between. Its premium service claimed that it would deliver provisions to the client's preferred location, wherever that might be. InterFoods had provided supply-of-provisions support for expeditions in places as remote as the Arctic Circle, the Himalayas and the Sahara Desert. A few specifics – 500gm of Beluga caviar and bottle of Stolichnaya Elit to a hotel suite in Islamabad, 100 tins of chicken soup to Lake Baikal in Siberia – no problem. Interfoods would deliver.

Both Sophie and Amin clearly had a fondness for many of the products that the company imported. Chez Berthier Masri was invariably well provided with the little luxuries of life in which the couple happily indulged. Temperature in the underground stone cellar maintained a constant 54 degrees Fahrenheit with 70 per cent humidity; perfect conditions for the 900 or so bottles of fine wine that were stored in the yellow twilight. Foie gras and caviar were no strangers to the table and the matched pair of 12 gauge Purdeys in the gun cupboard suggested that pheasant and partridge would appear in due season.

Both Amin and Alan had to agree on the viability of the plan, at least in principle, because both were crucial in achieving the outcomes. One pendant question was whether or not Megan and Sophie should be involved. Or at least, whether they should know the basic details. His immediate thought was that, for their own safety, they should be kept out of the loop. And yet he knew that Ayesha would kill him if she found out she'd been kept in the dark.

He checked the curved bowl that held the tobacco on the nargile. There was maybe ten or so minutes of life left in the pipe. For a moment he concentrated on the simple pleasure of smoking, trying to clear his mind of historic details and personnel analysis.

'Enough of the thinking,' he murmured.

Tarek searched his jacket pockets and smiled when his fingers touched the smooth multifaceted beads of the misbaha. Carefully withdrawing the string, he laid the prayer beads across his palm, admiring the warm brown onyx stones, each one with its individual toned or veined quality. Brown onyx from the alabaster deposits of Balochistan. They'd been a gift from the Ashrafia Islamic University when he'd been a guest speaker at a conference held there a few years ago. That was the first time he'd been to Pakistan let alone Lahore. He remembered streets packed with dusty people, gaudily decorated trucks, a kaleidoscope of colour, cacophonous noise and overpowering smells. He remembered the beauty of the Badshahi Mosque, the peace and serenity of the vast sandstone prayer hall with its white marble inlays.

That was also the first time that he'd met Dr Sami Malik. They'd been introduced at a reception held by the Iranian Consulate to which, as a respected friend and ally of the Islamic

Republic, Tarek had been cordially invited. It transpired that Dr Malik worked at Khan Research Laboratories near Kahuta, some 50 kilometres south east of Islamabad. Apparently he joined the facility in the mid 80s, about the time when the team had started producing HEUs, better known as highly enriched uranium; that is, military weapons grade uranium that one puts in a nuclear warhead. Thus Dr Malik was directly involved in the development of Pakistan's nuclear weapons programme, as well as high explosive and thermobaric bombs.

At the time, Tarek's interest had been little more than polite courtesy. That was until he heard that the industrious professor and colleagues were not only selling their expertise but also building weapons to order. Word had it that Sami Malik had become rather fond of acquiring money and that he enjoyed the frisson of danger that came with selling major firepower in a very black market. And of course the two men had kept in touch: both were aware of the other's broad circles of contacts and guessed at more.

Tarek looked at his watch. Assuming his flight was on schedule, Dr Malik would be arriving at Beirut International in just over 16 hours. Allowing time for the taxi ride, he'd arrive at La Paillote in perfect time for lunch. In his email, Tarek had promised two things: lunch at the best seafood restaurant in Beirut and a six-figure business proposition. To a man of Dr Malik's appetites, the offer was irresistible and the affected reticence to add another leg to his journey, short-lived.

Tarek smiled at the thought of seeing his old friend again. Lunch should be interesting, insha'allah. Maybe one last pipe was in order.

4 ~ Many Meetings

'This way, Monsieur al-Shami,' the maître d' said, indicating the route with an outstretched arm. 'It has been a while since we have seen you at La Paillote.'

'Pressures of work, my friend. But you are not so busy?'

'Today, non. At the moment, lunchtimes in the week are a little quiet. But I think that is good for you, n'est ce pas?'

Tarek did not respond but was pleased to see that only a few tables were occupied. He followed the waiter as he threaded his way across to the far corner of the room, finally stopping by a table set for two. Overlooking the sea to one side and bounded by a wall behind, there were no other diners close enough to be of any concern.

'This is good for you I think, Monsieur.'

'It's fine Henri, thank you. A colleague will be joining me shortly, an eminent doctor from Pakistan. He's on the short side, plump and has a moustache. If you could direct him this way when he arrives?'

'But of course, Monsieur al-Shami.'

Tarek watched the waiter float away through the tables and disappear from view. Sitting down on the chair by the wall, he looked out from the window flanked by salt-blasted wooden shutters. The usual picture postcard view of golden sunshine over glittering water was absent. White puffs of clouds skittered in a strong breeze under an ominous slate grey ceiling. Although the temperature was still in the early 60s, somehow it felt cooler and the light breeze held a briny dampness in its wings. The line between sea and sky was merely a monochromatic demarcation. From there, the only differences were the bile green tint, contrasting with the white fringes of angry chop. The lone ship on the horizon, little more than a blurred silhouette, lacking form and definition. Perhaps it was military, an act of aggression by a foreign power – Russia, America or Britain; perhaps a liner full of bored rich westerners, cruising from one tourist purchase to another.

'Kerboom!' he said quietly, raising both hands in mock praise.

A smile flitted across his face. He checked the time: if all were well Malik would be arriving shortly. And as the thought occurred, he saw movement across the restaurant near the entrance. The man had arrived in good time. Tarek saw the maître d' point him the right direction and the good Doctor make his way towards him. He reminded Tarek of a Russian Vanka-Vstanka doll; the one with the lead weight in the bottom that righted itself when pushed over. Except this one was wearing a well-tailored expensive looking suit and carrying a slim document case made from soft black leather. Standing up, Tarek stepped away from the table as Malik approached.

'Doctor Malik, it is truly a pleasure to see you again. How was your flight?'

'Indeed and I am also delighted to be here, isn't it? As to my flight, business class has become far too busy with both travellers and cabin crew, but from Tehran it is not so long to fly.'

'Ah, I did not realise you were coming from Tehran. Anyway …'

Tarek reached out to shake Malik's hand, an action that the man seemed to allow rather than fully reciprocate. As always, Tarek felt a tiny flutter of revulsion at the soft clammy touch of spongy flesh and was quick to drop the connection.

'Please, do sit down. So from Tehran then?'

'Uh huh,' Malik grunted, accompanied by the scraping of chair legs. 'And from here to Dubai.'

'Today?'

'I have a five thirty flight this afternoon.' Malik looked ostentatiously at the gold Rolex Oyster Perpetual on his wrist. 'So I trust we will have plenty of time to talk.'

'I'm sure. Perhaps we should order. I recommend the fish.'

The two men fell silent as they scanned their menus. Dishes of hummus and moutabel accompanied by crudités and olives appeared on the table. A basket of warm flatbread and a jug of iced water arrived. They snacked as they made their decisions. Their orders taken and Malik settled with a large glass of Chateau Kefraya Blanc de Blancs, the conversation continued. They asked about each other's families, broadly enquired about how work was going and opined on the state of the world. But both were aware that the real subject for discussion had yet to be broached.

'So tell me,' Malik finally said, 'you mentioned a proposition, with which perhaps I could assist and that would be mutually beneficial. I believe you were talking of a six figure sum?'

'In principle, funding of that size would be available subject, of course, to approval by the sponsor.'

'And might I be privy to the good name of this sponsor?'

'Forgive me, but at this stage I think it would be wiser not to disclose that information.'

Tarek looked pointedly in the direction of the approaching waiter. Malik nodded, but then sniffed the air like a rodent as the aroma of cooked fish and spices heralded the food.

'Hamour fillet with honey sauce,' the server declared as he carefully placed the dish in front of the Doctor. 'And the samkeh harra for you Sir.'

'That looks good.' Malik made it sound as though he slightly regretted his own choice. 'What is it?'

'Samkeh harra, it means spicy fish. Red snapper baked in the oven with fresh lemon and a tahini sauce with chilli, garlic and coriander, more or less. It's always good. But the hamour is excellent as well,' Tarek added hastily.

They paused while the waiter added a plate of deep yellow saffron rice and another piled with glistening green tabbouleh salad. He dutifully topped up the Doctor's outstretched glass, wished the men 'bon appetit' and headed back towards the kitchen. Clearly hungry, Malik applied himself to his fish with the alacrity of a barracuda, only slowing once in a while to add rice or tabbouleh to his plate. Eating in more leisurely fashion, Tarek savoured the flavours of the dish; inwardly he cringed at his guest's gross table manners and his lack of appreciation of the food. He glanced across at his companion. Fragments of fish nestled in the bush of the man's moustache, the bottom of which was gilded with creamy honey sauce. How revolting, he thought, but struggled to keep the look of disgust from his expression.

'It is good?' he asked, hoping the question would mask his feelings.

'A little bland maybe, but overall the food is very good. And the wine is excellent. A little sin, one of my many weaknesses.'

Malik smiled broadly, revealing a set of gleamingly white teeth of which any Bollywood star would be proud. Bending to the task once more, he quickly devoured the remainder of his fish accompanied by a small mountain of rice and several more spoonfuls of tabbouleh. Pushing back in his chair, he wiped his mouth with a corner of his napkin and belched, loudly. Tarek looked at his plate with a touch of regret, knowing that he needed to sacrifice the remaining third of his own meal. Quietly he placed his knife and fork side by side on the plate, sitting back in imitation.

'You aren't hungry?'

'It's rather a lot for lunch. As good as ever but I think it's enough. For you, a dessert perhaps? Coffee?'

'Coffee would be fine. And perhaps a little baklava for sweetness.'

Again the toothpaste smile. Tarek waved the waiter over and ordered.

'So, to your proposition, Professor. How can I help?'

'Doctor Malik, you're an acknowledged expert in the fields of explosives, weapons development, missiles and so on. I believe you have been directly involved in the development and implementation of Pakistan's uranium enrichment programme.' Tarek noticed the man frown. 'Not that I have any interest in nuclear technology per se, I'm just saying.'

'Mmm.'

They both paused as the waiter served the small cups of black Lebanese coffee. Tarek loved the rich dark smell and inhaled as though it were an exotic perfume. Then watched with wry amusement as Malik intercepted the small plate of baklava, pulling it to his side of the table with childish glee.

'My interest is in explosives,' he continued after the waiter had departed, 'or more accurately, explosive devices. I understand from mutual friends that you are in the business of developing and manufacturing such things for interested parties. For a fee, of course.'

'As you said, my associates and I do assist where feasible and viable. And we have designed and produced a variety of items for friends and clients. Naturally we do consider every opportunity on individual merit but each one clearly has to be evaluated on requirements. In other words, Professor, what do you have in mind?'

'The objective is to obtain a device that would …'

Malik abruptly cut across: 'As the end user, you need to be sure of your objectives and that any device will meet your needs. We do not want any information on how, where or why you intend to use it. Any discussions that you and I have relating to demand and supply are purely on a business basis. My main associate shares my feelings. You might say that we are equal partners, but each with special individual responsibilities. Jointly, the General and I have only two interests in such matters: the first is to provide the item, or items, that meet the specified requirements; the second is the receipt of the agreed financial remuneration. That is all.'

'I understand. I was not, I did not intend to tell you everything that I have in mind. In fact I'm relieved that you don't want to know. This is a covert venture and naturally total secrecy is of paramount importance. The less information imparted, the less danger of a leak. But there can be no leaks, Doctor, as I'm sure you appreciate.'

Another frown crossed Malik's face before he replied and when he did, there was an edge to his voice.

'Professor al-Shami, we are not children and this is not a game. I think it would be fair to say that I have been in this type of discussion more frequently than you have?' He paused, glowering at Tarek across the table. 'Our security is total, our secrecy is total. We do not make mistakes; nor will we tolerate any indiscretions by our clients. And nor do we accept responsibility for the use, or misuse, of items we have supplied in good faith. Do I make myself clear?'

'Of course, Doctor Malik. My apologies if I upset you with my concerns. At no point was I suggesting any criticism of you or your associates.'

Malik raised his hands in mock protest and smiled.

'Let us return to the starting point; what do you have in mind?'

'OK. I'm not sure of the exact dimensions at this stage, but we're looking for something highly explosive that could punch its way through a steel wall. If exploded in a relatively confined

75

space, we would want the explosion to have a devastating effect within that space and beyond. What I'm hoping is that you can design and build such a device, fitted into a cylindrical, sealed container that would then be labelled as bulk canned foodstuffs. The detonator should be able to be armed and fired wirelessly from a distance of up to say, ten miles. Perhaps I'm not saying this quite correctly.'

Malik shook his head. 'Continue'.

'The device would have to be remotely detonated, perhaps triggered by a radio signal or whatever from a mobile phone or something similar. The container itself needs to be portable and the explosive stable, enough to allow long distance transportation, probably by sea. On arrival at the initial destination, it would then be inserted and securely fixed into a much larger container before being deployed. Therefore, given the amount of movement involved, we have to be assured that it will remain dormant until armed. Can you make such a device?'

Doctor Malik slowly masticated the last piece of baklava, washed it down with a sip of coffee and softly belched.

'You are planning World War Three, my friend?' Again the glistening smile but the eyes were lupine. 'Of course, we can do this. It is not such an unusual request and we have built similar devices. One would use a relatively insensitive high explosive which was powerful and had high brisance for the main charge; polymerised RDX or similar for the primary charge. Clearly the more ...'

'My apologies Doctor, but I'm not a physicist or an expert on explosives.'

'A fact of which I am well appraised,' Malik retorted rudely. 'My point here is not to give you rudimentary knowledge, or even expect you to grasp the basic elements of the art, but to state the obvious to the uninitiated!'

Pompous ass. It was common knowledge, among those that were acquainted with the man, that Sami Malik had an overblown and extremely high opinion of himself, took umbrage at the slightest whiff of criticism and invariably became impatient with other lesser (perceived) mortals.

'As I was trying to say ...' Malik continued, 'clearly the destructive effects of an explosion can be measured in direct relation to the volume of explosive used. However, the design and construction of the casing also play an important part in maximising the pressure of detonation and therefore its shattering capabilities. Or 'brisance', a word you obviously haven't come across before.'

'No, ...'

'Quite. I will need the exact maximum dimensions of the outside of the cylinder that will contain the explosive. I will also need the exact internal dimensions of the container into which the device will be inserted. Mobile phone technology, with minor modifications, will provide us with the detonation trigger.'

'But radio waves can't travel through metal, can they?' Tarek asked, in an attempt to show that he was not entirely lacking in scientific knowledge.

'Essentially you're right and cell phones are little more than sophisticated little radios. However, the cell phone converts the radio signal into an electric current that is strong enough to initiate the explosives train. So, dial the number of the receiving phone element attached to the detonator in your cylinder and – boom! The whole system would need rigorous testing before deployment and at varying distances, since you mentioned a potential need range of ten miles. That might be asking a little too much but, we can try.'

'I'm flying to London on Friday and meeting with my colleagues on the south coast; we'll be discussing plans over the weekend. One of them will be able to supply all the measurements and dimensions that you need. His background is in engineering and he's far better placed than I to give you those details. However, I think it's best that direct communications are kept between the two of us, so I'll be forwarding the information.'

'Do you know how to encrypt your email, Professor?'

'Um, no.'

'In that case, it's something to look into. It will mean that we can share private and public keys, passwords, which will allow us to encrypt and decrypt the emails that we exchange. I will arrange for that to be set up. In the meantime, be circumspect as to how you phrase your emails.'

'Something along those lines had occurred to me, in a way. My other colleague owns a company specialising in bespoke food supply. We could talk about the dimensions and details of the proposed device as an innovative new food container and call it newcan, that's with the 'n' and the 'c' capped up and a 'u' in the new.' Tarek scrawled the name on a paper napkin as he spoke. 'NuCan. What do you think?'

'Your choice,' Malik said, sounding unimpressed. 'But that's fine, it will do the job. So I think that almost brings our discussion to an end. Just a couple of things. Do you only want one device or more? Naturally it makes sense to have more than just one and it would be more cost effective.'

'That hasn't been decided yet but I think, assuming we can come to an agreement, that we would want at least four devices.'

'Excellent. Once I have all the information, I can work on the financial structure. I say structure because our fees would cover the design and manufacture, testing and refinements (as and if necessary), delivery and all consultancy work. However, we will offer you a fixed fee without breakdown with the initial payment to be made at the point of actual order. The remainder of the money would be paid in agreed stages. Once finalised and the first payment made, we can take Project NuCan forward. Do you have any other questions?'

'No, I don't think so. Obviously you can't truly evaluate the project until I supply the details. Insha'allah, I'll be able to let you have all you need by the end of next week.'

Once again, Malik looked at the fat Rolex.

'In that case, I think that concludes today's discussion; and it's probably time that I left for the airport.'

Malik pushed himself up from his chair by pressing down on the table. Straightening up, he brushed a few invisible crumbs from his jacket.

'Of course, Doctor. Thank you for taking the time to stop off in Beirut. Your comments have been illuminating and constructive. And I'm confident that together, we can move the project forward fairly quickly. I look forward to our next meeting.'

'Indeed, a most productive conversation and it's always a pleasure to do business so pleasurably. Professor al-Shami, thank you so much for the excellent lunch.'

Tarek watched the taxi leave, taking Malik back to Beirut International.

'Self opinionated little prick,' he muttered. 'But he does know how to make bombs.'

He walked slowly back along the front, joining the Avenue de Paris. Since he'd been in his office for a while before going to La Paillote, it had made sense to leave the car in its parking place outside the faculty rather than drive. Even though it was only a fifteen or so minute walk, Tarek was already beginning to regret the decision. A strong breeze was blowing in from the sea, spitting needles of salt spray and drizzle. It was cold, wet and unpleasant. Hunching his shoulders, he increased his pace and scowled into the wind. But when he reviewed his lunch meeting with Doctor Sami Malik, his mood immediately improved and the scowl became a grin. In the morning, he'd sent a quick message to Alan to say that he'd phone him later; now he was really looking forward to the conversation.

*****

Tarek had spent the remainder of the afternoon in his office, reading through a pile of second year undergraduate papers on: 'Where does the refugee stand? An analysis of refugee status when viewed through the lens of Shari'ah as opposed to that of western legal systems.' He'd set the task, thinking that it might test the students' capacity for objective reasoning and perhaps shed some light on how they viewed camps like Shatila and Bourj al-Barajneh.

He was disappointed. Weighed by the most accurate of scales, the level of interest in the plight of the refugees was still less than feather-light. Of course they brayed on about the values of Shari'ah, that protecting the rights of refugees was intrinsic to its precepts and the principles of aman or safeguarding. Several regurgitated the old idea that perhaps a percentage of zakat, that portion of income that all Muslims are required to give to charity, might be diverted to refugees. Then in usual counterpoint, western legal systems held no safeguards of support or succour for refugees. Added to which there was no spirituality in the western way of thinking, the rules made as applied to secular issues alone.

Several things did leap out at him and every one was negative. All of the students were either Lebanese or from other Arabic countries like Jordan or Syria and none of them were interested in the Palestinian cause. Palestinian refugees were stateless transients, unwanted by Lebanon or the other nations in the region. Palestinians lived in squalor in camps without proper hygiene, where clean drinking water was a precious commodity and electricity frequently failed to spark. Despite the by rote rhetoric in their essays, not one of them would be prepared to go to Shatila to offer help, let alone friendship. Their writings lacked lustre and any new ideas, dull and meaningless.

Admittedly, Tarek hadn't been to the camps either but at least he could stand proudly in the knowledge that he'd helped the cause on a higher level. In essence he was Palestinian, even though he was one of the lucky ones: a powerful position at the university with a good salary, a relatively luxurious lifestyle and, most importantly, Lebanese papers including a passport. The very freedom of movement that those things bestowed made him a useful asset to many proscribed organisations. As Seneca the Younger allegedly wrote – one hand washes the other. With a little financial help from one such organisation, Tarek was about to set foot on the road to revenge.

That last thought had helped him through the otherwise dull afternoon. He'd survived his ordeal-by-reading, rising above his students' prosaic dreary sentences and constructs. The elation he felt at the prospect had allowed his mind to drift in the hellish garden of imagination during the tedium of a staff meeting. His colleagues' arid talk of budgets and figures was eclipsed by a mental video of explosions and pyrotechnics. Nevertheless he felt suffocated by the weight of academia and the sluggish pace of passing time.

Tarek finally managed to escape just before six, inching and hustling through the slow-moving traffic. The rain had stopped an hour or so earlier, but the late afternoon sunshine had been too weak to dry the wet roads. By the time he reached the outer edges of suburbia, the car was streaked with damp, oily dust thrown up by the procession of vehicles in town. He'd left behind the congested roads of the centre and the wet smell of rotting vegetables that always seemed to occur in parts of the southern suburbs. The air was fresher, the traffic had almost disappeared and Tarek could pick up speed. Only minutes later, he'd parked the car underneath the block of apartments, taken the lift up to the fourth floor and was turning his key in the lock. Heaving a sigh of relief, he walked in to the hall, shutting the door behind him, and on into the living room.

Putting his briefcase down by the desk, Tarek shrugged off his jacket and hung it over the back of the chair. It was only then that he noticed the warm breeze on his back and the fact that his airline ticket had been moved from the wire tray and propped up against a half empty water glass. He turned around slowly, wondering who had been in the apartment – or was in the apartment. It had happened once before when an al-Qaeda agent with an overdeveloped sense of melodrama had 'dropped' in to pass on a message. It had scared the shit of him at the time; this time was only a little better. The balcony door was wide open but no one seemed to be there; until he saw a thin stream of smoke rising above one of the wicker chairs and the curve of a head just peeking above the backrest.

'Who are you and what do you want?'

Tarek was faintly alarmed at the unnaturally high-pitched squeak of his voice.

'Just visiting little brother, just visiting.'

'Ayesha?'

She spun the chair on its mounting so she could face him, grinning at his obvious discomfiture.

'As you can see, yes, it's me. But what kind of way is this to greet your only sister? Aren't you pleased?'

'Of course I'm pleased to see you!' he retorted. 'You're incommunicado for two months, disappearing like a ghost with not a mention of where you're going. Then you suddenly turn up on the balcony like some sort of spy in a bad movie. No warning, nothing. So forgive me for being just a little shocked and pissed off,' he added self-righteously.

'Tarek, sometimes you have a wonderful capacity to be a sanctimonious little prick. And this is one of them. I've been waiting for almost an hour; you're usually earlier than this, no? So what to do? I sat on the balcony with a beer, had a cigarette or two and enjoyed the view. And when you finally arrive, you scream like a woman!'

'I did not scream. I was just ... a little unnerved. How would you feel if someone had broken into your house?'

'I have a key, remember?'

Unwinding herself sinuously from the chair, Ayesha walked towards her brother, put her hands on his shoulders and kissed him three times.

'Good evening, Tarek. It's so good to see me after all this time. I wonder where I've been. Get out to the balcony and fix yourself a lung-stopping nargile with a bit of blow. Me, I'm getting another couple of beers from the fridge. And then, we need to talk.'

She left him feeling vaguely stunned, almost disorientated. Ayesha always managed to do that, turn everything upside down, use smoke and mirrors; and you were always found wanting. Shaking his head in mock despair, Tarek collected what he needed from the drawer and went out to the balcony. He had finished preparing the nargile by the time Ayesha returned, blowing softly on the hot coals. Folding herself back into the other wicker chair, she eased the top off a green bottle of Almaza beer and take a deep drink before putting it down on the floor.

'I didn't have any beer in the fridge.'

'You do now.'

'Ayesha, you know the Shari'ah prohibits drinking alcohol and yet you do this against the will of Allah. As Muslims ...'

'Tarek? Shut the fuck up. Remember what I said about being sanctimonious? If he exists (and there's a big question in my mind on that score), I don't think Allah is going to stop me getting into paradise for the sake of a few beers.' She paused to light a cigarette taken from a half empty pack of Cedars. 'You want to know where I've been for the last two months? I spent the first six weeks fighting and hiding in the Gaza Strip with friends. We tried to meet Israeli soldiers and kill them. Then there was no place for me to stay and it took me a week to get back. For a few days, I was staying in Shatila, seeing friends there and around Beirut.

'There's a weird vibe to the place, as though something bad's going to happen but you don't know exactly what or how or when. Like a pressure cooker, it's all building up again and it's going to blow; maybe not this year but if not, it'll happen in the next. Only today I was thinking that I need to see Tarek, find out what he's doing, what he's thinking. So I came to Mansourieh, let myself into the apartment and waited for my baby brother.'

Brother and sister glared at each other, assessing the balance of power and where it lay. Tarek looked at his sister, taking in the scuffed boots, faded jeans and black t-shirt under a well-worn brown leather jacket. Ayesha looked at him with a slight sneer as she assessed the expensive soft leather moccasin style shoes, casual vanilla chinos and the open-necked pastel green polo shirt. Different ways of thinking, different ways of living, different ways of doing maybe, but underneath, essentially the same.

'So you're flying to London on Friday?'

'Yes. I noticed the ticket had been inspected.'

'Don't be so defensive. I didn't 'inspect' it, it was lying on top of the tray on the table, so I looked. But ... why are you going to London?'

'Because I'm attending a conference at the Islamic Cultural Centre which is part of the London mosque. I've been invited to take part in a symposium on Muslim integration and I'm giving a talk on Shari'ah at the School of Oriental and African Studies. It's work, Ayesha, maintaining international relations with other universities and Islamic centres. That's part of what I do, you know that!'

'And of course that means seeing Ali and Amin for a couple of days.'

'Well yes, I had thought of that but ...'

'Thought quite hard by the looks of your diary: today, phone Alan evening; Friday, Alan/Amin (question mark) Heathrow T3; Saturday and Sunday, Christchurch, Dorset/Cardiff, Wales (question mark); Sunday, Monday and Tuesday, London Hilton, Paddington; Wednesday, Heathrow T3. So tell me.'

'What about?'

'Come on Tarek, I'm not stupid, it's all planned out apart from who's picking you up from the airport and whether you're going to Wales or Dorset. When you've attended things in the UK before, you've checked into your hotel and then called to find out if they're around. Meeting up with Ali and Amin isn't purely social, an old friends get together, is it?'

'Yes! Ayesha, this is ridiculous. You need help.'

The three words hung in the air like splinters of white hot metal, radiating cruel meaning in the pregnant silence.

'Ayesha, I'm sorry, I didn't mean ...'

Tarek looked at his sister wordlessly, wishing he could take the words back.

'I don't need help,' she replied softly, her eyes narrowed to black flints. 'I want revenge, payback for what they did. Payback for what the whole fucking country did to Palestine, and is still doing. And don't you dare feel sorry for me!'

She bit her lip, turning to look out over the lights of the city. Anger flared, distorting her face into a mask, the long scar on her tanned cheek standing proud like a bleached bone in the desert.

'The scars of abuse and rape don't fade with time Tarek, nor does hate. Especially not here. When I was in Gaza, I met women, girls, who said they'd been beaten and raped by Israeli soldiers. There were women who told me that soldiers had broken down the doors of their houses by day and night. The soldiers pointed their guns at them, forced them to strip and the women stood there naked, not knowing what would happen next. Sometimes nothing; the soldiers laughed, touched them and spat on them. Some said they were raped by many soldiers, one after the other, taking turns. You know what's funny Tarek? The Israelis say that they don't rape Arabic women because we're disgusting and inferior. I listened to those women and know that a few were telling the truth; the others almost certainly were raped, but by Palestinian men.

'Why? Because, people like you have been telling them for millennia that women are subservient to men. It says so in your beloved Qu'ran. The Surah an-Nisa, Ayat 34; I've heard it quoted so many times, I almost know it by heart. Men are the protectors and maintainers of women because Allah has given them more strength and because they support the women from their property.'

Ayesha held up a cautionary hand willing Tarek to silence.

'If you've been abused or tortured or raped it doesn't make a lot of fucking difference whether it's an Israeli soldier, a Palestinian or a shit-faced British sailor doing the job on you! I remember what happened in Cyprus, to me, mama, Leena and Faridah as clearly as if it were yesterday. Because I'm reminded of it every day, whether it's in Gaza or Shatila, and every time I look in the mirror.'

She paused, reached for the bottle of Almaza and drank deeply before disappearing into the room behind. A moment later she reappeared holding a copy of the Qu'ran that showed all the signs of years of use despite its careful owner. Ayesha held it out to her brother and then pulled it back, out of reach.

'I think that you're planning some sort of revenge for what happened to us on Cyprus, and that's why you want to meet up with Ali and Amin. There was another entry in your diary for today: Dr Sami Malik, 11.20 PakIntAir arr Bey. 12.45 Lunch/La Paillote. From the notation, I'm guessing that Malik's Pakistani and that he's not a medical doctor. So who is he? And why the big deal lunch? That wasn't cheap and I'm thinking that he didn't pay for it. And what he said to you has to be discussed with the others.'

She held out the Qu'ran again and this time Tarek took the book, holding it with both hands, close to his chest.

'What do you want me to say? Ayesha, I'm not ...'

'Not, nothing. Swear to me, on the Qu'ran and in the name of Allah, your all-powerful omniscient God that you are not planning anything. Swear that I'm not on the right lines.'

'Ayesha, I don't ...'

'Swear Tarek.'

The pressure of his fingertips made light dents in the soft cover and Tarek suddenly realised that his hands were shaking. He knew his sister had noticed but he couldn't stop the tremors. Looking up, he saw she'd lit another cigarette, inhaling first and then quietly blowing the smoke into the air in a steady stream. Slow repetition; she was waiting. Unlocking his fingers from the book, he let it drop onto his lap.

'I can't,' he said softly.

'I didn't think you could. And I'm glad.'

Tarek looked at her, nodded and then smiled ruefully.

'You always could read me well,' he said.

'So tell me,' she repeated.

'I will. I mean, I was going to tell you anyway after the meet-up in England. That is, if Ali and Amin buy into the plan.'

'Which is?'

Several seconds elapsed before Tarek answered her question. When he did speak, his voice was soft but the tone, cold and hard.

'Hopefully, to blow up a few of the Royal Navy's ships and send a lot of British sailors to the Fire and the nineteen Guards of Hell.'

'You're serious?' Ayesha looked at Tarek hard, holding eye contact, looking for any hint of dissemblance. 'Oh my God, you are serious!'

'Deadly serious.'

'So I was right about your new friend Dr Malik.'

'Yes. But there really isn't much I can tell you.'

'Tarek! Just tell me what you know.'

'OK. Dr Sami Malik and his colleagues work for the Pakistan government, in defence, weapons and things. I met him in Lahore a few years ago and we've bumped into each other on several occasions since then. Getting to the heart of it, for a fee they can make us bombs that we can disguise, smuggle on board the ships and then detonate from a safe distance. Ali, I mean Alan. You know Ali changed his name?'

'Yeah, you said a while back. Camouflage in deepest Wales.'

'Whatever, they're both vital to the success of the plan. Amin's set up for logistics in terms of transport and information; Alan's role will be to disguise the bombs by putting them in missiles that are then delivered to the ships. But all of that has to be explained to them, discussed and, insha'allah, agreed. That's basically it.'

Having given Ayesha the stripped bare bones of the plan, Tarek physically felt his muscles begin to relax and the tension drain away. He turned to the nargile, only to find that the coals were black and cold. In starting to relight the pipe, his focus changed and he missed seeing Ayesha's shaking head and rolling eyes.

'That sounds like a brilliant idea, and a daringly audacious plan. Provided, of course, that you're either a raving fantasist on a Baron Munchausen scale; or there are one or two choice details that you've forgotten to tell me. I hope it's the latter.'

'Honestly, as Allah (Glory to Him, the Exalted) is the one and only universal God and Muhammad is his prophet (peace be upon him).'

'Yeah, yeah and not to forget the Wise Lord Ahura Mazda and his prophet Zoroaster.'

'Ayesha! Please, do not mock.'

'Pray forgive me, Imam. What you're suggesting sounds like the script for a James Bond film with shitty subtitles. Make me believe you Tarek. Who's the money?'

'Al-Qaeda.'

Suddenly the only sounds on the balcony seemed to be the rasping stridulating songs of the cicadas and two humans' breathing. Tarek sucked hard at the nargile's mouthpiece, thankfully tasting the subtext flavour of hashish. Ayesha lit yet another cigarette, inhaled deeply, then exhaled the smoke through flared nostrils. Brother and sister looked intensely at each other as the name hung in the air between them like a dark flame.

'Al-Qaeda?'

'Al-Qaeda. You know I've helped the organisation with a few things before, mainly financial logistics. I formulated the structure of the idea quite a long time ago, but it only really made sense when I knew Dr Malik was coming to Beirut. Al-Qaeda is not short of funds, it has massive backing; I outlined the ideas to my contact in Beirut. He said he would pass on my request and respond as soon as he could. One week later I received an email that simply said: in principle we would support the projected idea, subject to informed detail and personnel. Al-Qaeda knows Malik, what he can do and he's helped them in the past. So I got in touch and invited him for lunch at La Paillote. On the understanding that an extremely valuable proposition could be on the table, he added an extra stop to his journey.'

'Ya Allah! Tarek, these people are dangerous. I'm sorry but they're Wahhabi fanatics who believe that all non-Muslims should be killed and that religious police should be around every corner enforcing Shari'ah to the letter.'

'Al-Qaeda would be funding the operation. Other than that, no members of the organisation would be involved. I suppose I did suggest that taking responsibility after the fact would give them more international exposure. But that's all, and without their money nothing would be possible.'

'What you're proposing has nothing to do with Islam or any other religion. It doesn't stem from some fatwa on a point of law, issued by some grey bearded imam in an ivory tower. This should be about Palestine and the Palestinians, about what happened on Cyprus and the years of pain. So listen well Tarek, on that basis I want to be involved, and I want to help. And I want to send at least one ship to hell, personally.'

The evening light was soft and warm, adding a glow to her eyes made almost radiant by the film of moisture. Aware of the signs of emotion, she exhaled a stream of smoke, allowing it to drift upwards like a grey gauze mask. But her brother missed neither the passion in her voice nor the emotion in her eyes.

'Insha'allah, so shall it be, Sister.'

She smiled that crooked smile at him, looking tough and vulnerable at the same time. His heart went out to her and he knew that she had to be part of it all, whatever happened.

'I can't go with you to England,' she said, 'not this time at least. There's not enough time to get a visa and maybe it would be difficult anyway.' She sighed and then shrugged, as though she made some kind of internal decision. 'You know what, I'm hungry. You want something to eat?' He did that thing with his eyes that said: whatever. 'I'll put a small mezze together; I saw stuff in the fridge. Phone Ali.'

She went inside and returned moments later with the phone, trailing its long lead behind her. Handing Tarek both phone and diary, she headed for the kitchen.

'Give him my love,' she called over her shoulder before disappearing from view.

Picking up the handset, Tarek punched in the string of numbers that would connect him to a stone-built cottage in a small village in rural Wales. He listened to the double brrrp-brrrp trill of electronic monotones repeat itself slowly, a pause in between each burst. The UK was two hours behind Lebanon so should be about seven pm in the Welsh valleys. Somebody should be there. He heard the click of somebody picking up.

'Alan Abbot speaking.'

'How's wet and windy Wales, my old friend?'

'Hey Tarek, good to hear your voice. FYI, it's a pleasant warm sunny evening over here. There's the smell of mown grass in the air and sheep shit on the ground. What could be better after a day's work and a pint in the pub?'

'Work I understand but the experience of both the pint and the pub is beyond my grasp. How's the family?'

'Anwen's growing up fast. Megan is as beautiful and intelligent as ever but spends too much time with malingerers at the surgery. Ow!'

Tarek heard the sound of a brief exchange and laughter at the other end.

'As you probably guessed, that was Megan punishing me for my disrespect. She sends her love and says she's looking forward to having an intelligent conversation for a change.'

'Give her my love. Ayesha sends her love as well.'

'How is she?'

Tarek could hear the varying subtexts hum in Alan's tone.

'Same old, same old. She's good but spending too much time fighting in the shadows. We had a long talk this evening – she's in the kitchen but she knows I'm calling. As said, we need to talk, the three of us, about old times and moving forwards.'

Alan involuntarily glanced behind himself, checking that no one was there who might have heard Tarek's last few words. He could hear Anwen talking excitedly to Megan in the living room and heard the laughter that followed.

'Alan?'

'Yeah, I'm here. All agreed and understood.' The cheery lilt of his voice dropped off for those few words, replaced by a flatter more business-like tone. Immediately picking up again when he continued, 'we're all looking forward to catching up. We've had an open invitation from Amin and Sophie to go to their mansion on the coast forever. So here's the plan. The three of us are going to drive straight to their place on Friday afternoon. I'm taking a few hours off work so we can get there reasonably early.

'Amin's going to stay at their London apartment on Thursday night and he'll pick you up from Heathrow Friday. If you're on the 7.35 from Beirut, you should arrive at 10.45 GMT; an hour to get through immigration and you're done. Just email him your flight number; I assume you're flying in to Terminal Three but check and let him know. Then you guys'll drive straight down, I guess. I need to back here for work on Monday morning and, we're assuming, you need to be in London. So Amin's planning to drop you off at your hotel on Sunday evening.'

'Alan that's brilliant. Thanks for all of that. I'll obviously fill you in on the rest of the itinerary when I'm there. See you on Friday.'

'Have a good flight and see you then.'

Tarek cut the call. The mezze was already laid out and Ayesha had quietly slipped back into he seat while he was talking.

'I said you sent your love,' he told her, 'and he sent his back.'

'I'd like to be there,' she replied with a wistful tone. 'I'd like to see Leena again too. What happened to those lost years Tarek?'

*****

The flight had been uneventful and fortunately getting through immigration hadn't been too stressful. Obtaining the visa in the first instance had required a stack of papers and answers provided to myriad questions but all that had been in place for a while. Being a frequent flyer between Lebanon and other countries did frequently allow him greater credibility with immigration controls. And since MEA had introduced its Cedar Miles programme around 18 months previously, flying was certainly becoming more comfortable and cost effective.

Amin had been there as promised, whisking him off through the London traffic and down the M3 towards Winchester. Until they reached the New Forest the drive had been fairly dreary albeit dry. Tarek could never understand why so much of England appeared to be composed of a tricolour of grey, green and brown. Here green predominated, broken up by flares of colour from wildflowers at the edge of the road. Dappled sunlight flickered through the leaves above as they drove along verdant tunnels, sometimes skirting past uninterested ponies.

Somewhere, a few miles away from Burley but before Bagnum, Amin turned right down a long leafy drive, bounded by meadowland on both sides. Several hundred yards further on, they drove through a pair of black wrought iron gates and the tarmacked drive gave way to gravel that crunched rather satisfyingly underneath the tyres.

'Home,' said Amin, as they got out of the car.

'Wow!' said Tarek, as he looked up at the imposing stone frontage of a rather fine Georgian country house.

He reminded Amin of an amazed little child looking excitedly at the magic castle. Would the door open to reveal a beautiful princess or an evil black demon? The question was soon answered. Sophie walked out through the doorway, between the stone Doric columns, a smile lighting up her already striking features.

'Tarek, it's so good to see you.'

Skipping lightly over, she put her hands on both his shoulders, kissing him on the cheek three times in the Lebanese fashion.

'Come in, come in,' she said, pulling him by the sleeve. 'There is coffee on the stove, if you want, or perhaps a glass of wine. But, of course, you don't drink. Sometimes I forget, you know, because we are such heathens, no?'

Scrabbling noises on the granite flags of the hallway signalled the approach of the Masri's brace of black Labradors. The pair mobbed Tarek with big slobbery licks and cold wet noses as he bent to stroke their broad heads. Their tails wagged in unison as they pushed ever harder against his legs.

'Khalas! Enough.'

Immediately, the dogs backed off and sat down, looking patiently at Amin for their next instruction.

'Don't mind them, they're just a little over boisterous, particularly when they haven't met people before. On the left, Borak, and she's Jemila,' Amin said, pointing at the two dogs in turn. 'They're youngsters but they're learning fast. Let me take you to your room. Then you can dump your bag, freshen up and come down. Damn, it's good to see you finally here, even if you do look like an emaciated ascetic.' He punched Tarek lightly on the shoulder. 'Sophie, we have to feed this man before he fades away.'

Amin led the way up a wide staircase with a polished and carved balustrade that followed each turn. He showed Tarek into a spacious en suite bedroom decorated with floral wallpaper and dominated by a large double bed, topped by a deep feather duvet. Light streamed in through the bow window that looked out onto manicured lawns and mature trees. Even though the windows were closed, the sound of birdsong rang sweetly and clearly in the fresh air.

'Come down when you're ready,' said Amin, leaving his friend to take in the view.

Lunch was taken in the orangery, attached to the rear of the house, with just the three of them and the dogs. Sophie's idea of a déjeuner léger included a vast platter of crayfish and smoked salmon with brown bread, Caesar Salad with grilled chicken, a crowded cheese platter and a mountain of warm granary rolls. Naturally she apologised for the sparse simplicity on offer.

As the light began to fade and the shadows deepened, Alan drove the blue Volvo estate through the gate and across the gravel, parking it beside Amin's Range Rover. Immediately the area was bathed in a creamy light as soft LED floods came on automatically. As the three of them stepped out of the car, the front door of the house opened releasing Borak and Jemila to welcome the newcomers. Once they were safely inside and the dogs reined in, the door was shut for a merry meeting.

Dinner was served in the dining room, on the mirrored surface of a long walnut table. While the setting was grand, the meal was a less formal affair than one might have expected, although Sophie had made sure that there was no shortage of food. Little toasts spread with melted cheese floated in bowls of French onion soup. The smell of rosemary and garlic heralded succulent roasted spring lamb. Golden Dauphinoise potatoes oozed creamy sauce while grilled vegetables added their greens and reds for colour. The food kept coming and there was no shortage of wine to wash it down.

Nor was there any lack of conversation. There was family news: who was doing what and how well they were doing it; was he still that way and how could she put up with him; and so on and so on. On dit, plus que ça change, ç'est la meme chose. It turned to discussions on world affairs: skipping from country to country like pebbles skimmed over the still surface of a lake, comment and opinion bounced five or six times before sinking beneath the water. They talked about music, films and other pleasures, but of Tarek's plans, there was neither hint nor mention. And finally, when all were sated, the night took them safely to bed where each dreamed their personal dreams.

*****

Warm morning sunshine streamed through the glass panes of the orangery, throwing abstract rectangles of light across the room in patterns of highlights and shadow. The green oak timbers added a mellow tone of strength to the otherwise fragile structure. It was a good place to start the day, calmly but sensuously, lounging in one of the low cushioned seats or lazing on the chaise longue. It was, as Sophie had it, 'chic, civilisé et un peu louche si on veut'. In fact, a perfect place to enjoy breakfast.

Intentionally casual, breakfast had been prepared a little earlier by Armelle, the Masri's occasional maid. In Sophie's lexicon, 'casual' translated to 'elegantly plentiful'. The buttery smell of hot croissants and baguette entwined with the rich dark aroma of freshly made coffee. Champagne flutes stood guard over an open bottle of Laurent-Perrier chilling in an ice bucket. Next to that stood a crystal jug of freshly squeezed orange juice for mimosas or drinking on its own. And, naturellement, there was fresh fruit, fluffed light yellow scrambled eggs …

The conversation had picked up easily from where it had been left the previous night. However the tenor was somewhat lighter in content, leaving behind geopolitics, conflict zones and corruption. At one point, Alan and Amin were debating the relative prowess of rugby teams as demonstrated in the Six Nations Championship earlier in the year.

'Simple really, Wales won the Championship, Grand Slam and the Triple Crown! What did England get? The Calcutta Cup. So you beat Scotland but you still came third from the bottom.'

At another moment, Sophie and Megan were discussing the interwoven subjects of fashion, food and keeping slim. Sophie saw them through the informed consumer's lens; Megan's view was more binocular, being both consumer and a practising doctor.

'You've got a wonderful figure, you eat a balanced diet (on the whole) and you exercise. So why do you need to slim?'

And so it went on for an hour or more until Amin reminded them that time and tide waited for no man. When he'd suggested over dinner that they should take the boat out the following day, their decision was positive and unanimous. Clearly it would be a perfect opportunity for the girls to sunbathe and for the men to discuss some business that had arisen. Family business, he'd said, without saying exactly whose family. There hadn't been any queries.

The boat was moored in the Poole Quay Boat Haven Marina, not far from the Old Town. With Amin in the lead, carrying a large hamper, they threaded their way along a floating walkway past yachts and launches. Towards the end of the pontoon, he stopped and stepped up onto the transom of a sleek, blindingly white power-yacht that positively glistened in the bright sunshine. Putting the hamper on one of the nearby seats, he held out a hand to help Anwen aboard.

'Welcome to the Sirens' Choice,' he said proudly.

The French-built Jeanneau 46 was a dream creation of mahogany, cream leather and stainless steel boasting three cabins and crew quarters under the circular lounge. One by one they climbed aboard, dutifully admiring the elegant boat and complimenting its owners. Sophie happily grabbed a peaked faux naval hat from a shelf, pushed it onto her husband's head and raised one eyebrow in mockery.

'Now mon Capitaine, take us out onto the ocean.'

Taking the helm, Amin fired up the twin Volvo Penta 480hp diesels and slowly backed the boat away from the mooring. Using the combination of engines and bow thruster, Amin turned her easily and slowly steered her past Brownsea Island and out through the gap into Studland Bay. Feeding the power slowly in, he took her up to a cruising speed of 22 knots, sailed down the coastline and beyond, dropping anchor not far from the chalk white stacks of Old Harry Rocks. Armed with thick towels, the women clambered forward onto the sundeck, stripped down to bikinis and lay down in a row for collective sun worship. Meanwhile the three men settled down in the lounge cabin to talk.

'So here we are, Tarek,' said Amin, 'the floor, as they say, is all yours. And I'm guessing that it relates to this.'

His usually cheerful, smiling face was more sombre, serious and determined. He held out his left hand with the palm upwards and ran his right forefinger over the ragged light scar. Involuntarily, both Alan and Tarek turned their left hands over to look at their own scars. Then without prompting or thought, Alan covered Amin's with his and Tarek's followed.

'After all these years, are we still together on this thing?'

'We are,' they said simultaneously.

'Then, insha'allah, we will prevail. Tarek.'

'We have waited a long time for this, as have our mothers, our fathers and our sisters. Now, I believe that we may take up a great sword to avenge the pain and horror. We cannot reclaim the lost years, nor should we wish to bring Halah back from paradise, but we will take a blood payment and the weight of that payment shall be great.'

'You may be a mullah Tarek, but this is not a mosque and there is no need to proselytize. If I could bring back my mother, for me and baba, I would do it in the blink of an eye. We understand and remember the oath that we all took; I, for one, will not be forsworn. Tell us what you have in mind, in plain words.'

Amin grunted his agreement; both men looked at Tarek.

'The basics are like this: I propose that we insert explosive devices in some of the missiles that Alan's company makes for the Royal Navy. Once the adapted missiles are on board specific ships the devices can be remotely detonated.'

Alan and Amin listened, silent and attentive, as Tarek told them of his meeting with Sami Malik and that proposal. The funding he mentioned in passing, glossing over precisely who might be bankrolling the operation at this stage.

'Naturally, this is all still very much on the drawing board and will require a lot more research and planning. Alan, Malik has assured me that he can build devices that are relatively small but with very powerful explosive and he mentioned modified RDX, I think.'

'That's probably HMX, sometimes called octogen. It's one of the most powerful high explosives in production. He's probably using that as the main charge in the explosive train with PETN as the base charge in the detonator. PETN (or pentaerythritol tetranitrate, if you prefer) is a pretty hefty explosive in its own right. It's often the main constituent of plastic explosives like Semtex. Couldn't even guess how Malik's modifying HMX but it would a good choice: it's pretty insensitive, has high shatter capability and one of the highest RE factors in the business. That stands for relative effectiveness which measures the explosive power of a substance in relation to a lump of dynamite. The higher the number, the bigger the bang!'

'Alan, you've got managerial control over production in the facility?'

'More quality control and development. But in principle, I run the whole shooting match on a day to day basis.'

'Fine. So how difficult would it be to insert one of Malik's devices into a missile? On a theoretical level, perfectly possible, but obviously it would depend on the size, shape, weight etcetera. And it would depend the complexity of insertion. Have you got any dimensions?'

'No. That's exactly what I need from you in the first instance. You provide all the dimensions and tolerances; Malik designs and builds accordingly. Presumably, the bigger, the better.'

'Yeah, and the type of bang-bang used as said.' Alan paused for a moment to think but neither of the other two made a sound. 'Sea Dart surface-to-air missiles would probably be the best bet; the Navy has a habit of putting those on all the Type 42 class destroyers. Each one's armed with 24 pounds of high explosive and that would go up when its stowaway blew. The Sea Dart's quite a chunky missile and the wall's quite thick. Diameter's 41.9 centimetres but that's external. To be honest, I'll have to go back, dissect one of the buggers and then I can give you precise measurements. The Dart's guidance system's semi-active radar is all in the cone of the missile. That could be taken out and replaced with your device, Tarek. But they would have to be the same weight and that might affect the final measurements.'

'How long would that take?'

'To a degree, it's a matter of timing. But I should be able to get back to you by the end of the week.'

'There's no actual rush but – the sooner I have that, the sooner I can pass it on to Malik, and the sooner he can evaluate design and production costs. Etcetera, etcetera. It's a chain. So once we have the completed units, you'll need to install them but we need to know where they're going. Do you know destinations or can we track them somehow?'

'Not a problem. Missiles are essentially made to order by volume but allocated to specific ships by the Navy. Each one carries a unique number, freighted to dockside and loaded onto the named vessel. So we know which mother gets which babies. Most of the Sea Darts we supply go to HMNB Devonport, the naval base in Plymouth or the base in Portsmouth. It's about three hours by road from us to both bases.'

'It all sounds good to me. Then we need to know shipping movements, preferably of warship movement in the MENA region. So we're talking the Eastern Med, down through the Gulf of Aden and into the Arabian Sea. Amin, I'm hoping you can help here. I know you have government contracts; what about the Navy?'

'Funny you should mention Portsmouth, Alan. Not at the moment, but I do have a meeting with representatives of the Royal Naval Catering Management team to discuss a Food Supply Contract including international and emergency resupply. That's next week, in Portsmouth. There's a whole book on types of foodstuffs, dry and wet consumables, tinned and bottled goods. The list and permutations are endless. What I can tell you is that approved suppliers under contract are given shipping movements in advance provided there are no security issues involved. That includes ports of call, timescales and destinations with standard requirements for resupply. Emergency stuff is: requested today, react yesterday. Or so I'm told.'

'Excellent,' Tarek exclaimed, clapping with delight.

'Slow down Great One, I need to win the contract first.'

'Yes, but you will, I am sure. They obviously know about your other government contracts so, hopefully, there won't be a problem. Between you and Alan and my own sources, we should be able to cross reference information and triangulate, if that is the right expression.

'From now on, we also need to consider security; an item which naturally arose in my conversation with Dr Malik. I suggested to him, and therefore commend the idea to both of you, that the product under development is a new food container designed for longevity and improved protection for the contents blah blah. Alan, you would obviously be the design and construction consultant; as International Foods, you would be the buyer with a view to franchising, Amin. My role will be to arrange finance for the project, which will be a joint venture between the three of us, and to organise actual production. The name I have suggested is NuCan – that's capital 'n', 'u', capital 'c' – Sami Malik seemed to like it.'

'That works for me,' said Alan with a shrug.

'Yes, it sounds good,' added Amin, 'but ...' He paused for several seconds before continuing. 'You say that part of your role is to 'arrange finance' and you said earlier that you had already spoken to 'certain parties' who had indicated that they would support the project. What you didn't say was who those parties actually are, Tarek. I think we have a right to know, don't you?'

'Al-Qaeda. That was the part that Ayesha wasn't so keen on,' he said calmly.

'For fuck's sake Tarek. They're terrorists, suicide bombers, they're insane Islamic fanatics ...'

'You do know what you're doing?' Alan said, breaking across Amin's rant.

Tarek nodded.

'Yes Alan. Amin, listen to yourself and then think for a moment. In the eyes of the west, what we are planning is no different. Blowing up British ships will be seen as a murderous act of terrorism by violent fundamentalists. We won't be able to stand up and declare to the world that it was an act of revenge for what they did to our families. They won't accept it as a punishment for the injustices perpetrated on Palestine, or on the many other countries that Britain has trampled over in its bloody history. Better that in our hearts, we know that we have achieved our goals; but let al-Qaeda take the blame for what will be perceived as more atrocities.

'As to the actual money, al-Qaeda has seemingly endless funds. As long as Saudi Arabia continues to monetise its oil and gas resources, the dollar stream will continue to flow. Who else would be able to finance and contemplate a venture like this? It's not as though we can arrange a meeting with the Small Terrorists' Loans Department at HSBC or JP Morgan Chase. But with al-Qaeda, we can, have done! Provided we ensure that all the pieces fall into place, it will provide the necessary funds.'

Amin put up both hands in a gesture of defeat, but Alan had another, more fundamental question.

'Have you considered the consequences if it all goes bad Tarek? I'm not changing my mind, there's no question of that, but I have to consider the whole equation. So does Amin. Both of us have built new lives here, with families and homes. I love Megan and Anwen more than I can say and I'd protect them with my life. Amin and Sophie, they may not have kids but they have each other. And I've rarely met two people who have such a strong relationship. Tarek, it's possible that we could all end up in prison for a very long time. Over here, they'd throw away the key and bury us.'

'I know, and I've already factored that into the equation. My intention is to include substantial amounts of money in the overall funding to provide cover for all eventualities. There are precedents for such payments, families being supported after, afterwards. I will ensure that certain payments will be made available, in advance. That aspect will be finalised, and arrangements made, well before NuCan leaves Pakistan.'

'OK. I just needed to know. It's just … Megan has a good job as a GP, she's a senior partner in the practice, but that could all disappear if … you know what I mean.'

'Yes, I do.'

'But there is one more question.'

'Allah preserve me from inquisitive scientists,' Tarek said with a grin.

'Ayesha knows about this?'

The smile fell away at the question, in recognition of the broader implication.

'Yes. I'd intended to tell her once I'd talked to you both, assuming your commitment. A woman's intuition? A guerrilla's innate sense of the coming storm? Who knows but she knew that something was in the wind. More importantly, she wants to play her part and I cannot say she can't. Ayesha has a right. And she has skills and experience in the field that have taught her things that give her strength. I don't know what I'm saying really. But she's involved. I haven't told mama or baba. Najib is too old in his mind and Leila? Leila is still strong but she doesn't want to fight any more. She takes care of him, watches the hillside for signs of Israelis and hopes they don't come.'

The three men sat for a while, each one silent thinking his own thoughts. Tarek thought about Ayesha, wondering what she would have said if she'd been with them on the boat. In the light of Tarek's comments about Ayesha, Amin's thoughts were of Leena and Sophie. Didn't they have a right to know? But what would that achieve? And Alan just thought of Megan and Anwen with love. Their individual reveries were broken by the sound of the door opening.

'Mon Dieu, who has died?' Sophie said with mock solemnity. 'The three men who came from the East with long faces. Smile, it is a sunny day.'

Her cheerfulness was irresistible and they couldn't help but smile.

'It is hot out there. So we girls, nous avons décidé that we need the breeze and so you must take us to Durdle Door perhaps, Amin.'

She dropped herself onto his lap, slinging an arm amorously round his neck, and kissed him loudly on the lips. Tarek looked away, slightly embarrassed at the proximity of so much luscious naked female flesh. Alan smiled benevolently, and slightly lecherously, thinking of Megan making the same move.

'And then we have some lunch, cheri.'

'How could we refuse?' Amin asked rhetorically, returning her kiss.

The decision made, the Sirens' Choice cruised parallel to Dorset's Jurassic Coastline, taking them down to Durdle Door and once again, dropped anchor. The hamper was duly opened, producing rare roast beef sandwiches with just the right amount of horseradish. Little sausage rolls with perfectly divine light pastry ... and so it went on.

For the remainder of the weekend, the six of them simply enjoyed each other's company. Naturally it was de rigueur in the Masri household to relish every meal however lavish or simple. The pool in the garden was duly swum, despite the frigidity of the water. They took a couple of long walks in the forest, accompanied by Borak and Jemila. The dogs sniffed every possible smell, from the damp mustiness of decaying leaves to the intriguing scent of wild mushrooms that they trampled under paw as they raced around. The level of conversation never dropped, invariably punctuated by laughter, covering a vast array of trivia as well as more serious subjects. But NuCan was left undisturbed; for the time being, everything had been discussed as necessary, actions decided upon and there were plenty of thoughts to think. It was only raised one more time, before Alan drove back to Wales with Megan and Anwen; before Amin ferried Tarek to his London hotel. As they stood on the gravel, watching mother and daughter get into the car, Tarek said a few final words.

'We need to keep in touch. But remember, avoid using emotive words and stick to generalities. In other words, avoid specifics and only refer to the project in terms of developing NuCan. We have to assume that there is always the possibility of security people reading our emails or listening in to telephone conversations.'

It was difficult not to smile at Tarek's melodramatics but both friends managed to keep their mouths reasonably well under control. They both understood the risks involved.

'Let me have those dimensions as soon as you can.'

'You know it,' said Alan, climbing in to the car behind the wheel.'

Sophie and the two men watched the car as it disappeared down the lane.

'We should go too,' Amin said.

'Thank you so much, both of you, for a wonderful weekend.'

Sophie gently took Tarek's head in both hands and kissed him on both cheeks. Then without dropping her hands, she leaned away and looked at him, almost with concern.

'De rien, mon frère, it was our pleasure. Listen to me Tarek, take care of yourself and come back. You are always welcome in my house.'

As they drove away, he wondered whether Amin had told her or whether it was just her way. It was how she'd looked at him, called him her brother and the emphasis she had put on the words. Prends soin et reviens; somehow, in French, it was like a prayer.

The next two days were a whirlwind of seminars, discussions, symposiums and meetings. Who would have thought that there were so many words in the English language that actually boiled down to the same thing: talking, listening and sometimes drifting off to some individual intellectual plateau of one's own. Tarek was back in his room in the London Hilton early on Tuesday evening when the phone on the bedside table rang.

'Mr al-Shami, I have an outside call for you from a Mr Masri?'

'Thank you. Put him through, please.'

A click.

'Tarek?' Amin's voiced boomed through the handset. 'How was it all?'

'Good but busy.'

'Excellent. Listen, I'm at the apartment. Let's have dinner together at the Brasserie in the hotel. I've had an email from Alan re NuCan which I've printed out, so you can take it back with you. I'll be with you in … about half an hour. Sound good?'

'Excellent, that's good news. I'll …'

But Amin had already cut the line. Only 20 minutes later there was a knock on the door.

'It's all a bit of a rush I'm afraid. I dashed up so I could give you this, have a bite to eat and then get back to Sophie.'

Amin handed Tarek a large envelope.

'There are detailed diagrams in there, complete with all the dimensions you could possibly need plus a separate specification of the Sea Dart itself. One has to say that whatever else he can do, Alan's also a very fine draughtsman. I've printed everything out but I've also copied the attachments onto a flash drive. That's in there as well. Have a look at the printouts showing the missile but I suggest that you give those back to me and I'll destroy them. I didn't think of it when I printed them out, but it might not be that great if they fall out of your pyjamas if you're stopped. Nobody will notice a flash drive and that makes it easier for you to forward all the stuff rather than rescanning.'

Tarek pulled out several sheets of paper, glancing at them briefly before sliding them back. Dropping the envelope in the bed, he walked over to Amin and hugged him hard.

'Leave it with me and don't worry about destroying the Sea Dart pages, they won't stop an Islamic scholar on his way out of the country. Thank you for bringing these and again, for all your kindness. But there is no need for you to stay. Go back to your lovely Sophie and spend time with her. Go old friend. We will talk soon.'

Amin took his hand.

'Thank you, Tarek. A safe journey. Allahu akbar.'

Giving his friend another hug, he turned and left without looking back.

Sitting down on the bed, Tarek removed the top sheet from the envelope. It was simply a short message from Alan.

'Tarek, have attached scaled drawings of internal parts as well as ones of the proposed NuCan container. The diameter, length and weight are the optimum measurements which cannot be expanded. If necessary the container can be smaller. If this is the case, I suggest a magnetic strip be attached to the side for secure stacking. See fig two on page four. This would also facilitate speed of packing. Suggest that these are forwarded to SM in Pak. If there are any queries from that end, get back to me soonest. Take care and godspeed. Love to Ayesha. AA.'

Tarek emptied the envelope and slowly looked through the meticulously hand-drawn diagrams with their neat notations. They meant very little to him but he knew that what he had in his hand was truly explosive. He smiled and clenched his fist.

'Allahu akbar indeed,' he whispered.

5 ~ A Few More Details

The early morning sunshine streamed into the lounge on the wings of a cool breeze. Somehow it was warm and refreshing at the same time, like skiing under blue skies or sipping iced water after running. A flock of seagulls swirled by in flying argument, hurling abuse at the world as they passed. A black kite's unmistakable piercing cry filled the short vacuum, finishing off with tremulous vibrato and then a reprise. Tarek ducked down to see more easily through the open door, to the rectangle of sky over the balcony. The kite's black silhouette drifted slowly across the false horizon, its forked tail dipping and rising as the magnificent bird rode the air currents. He smiled as he watched, almost feeling a bond with this hunter of the skies.

'So shall I be a hunter of sailors and ships,' he said with a wry grin.

Returning to his desk he picked up Alan's diagrams, marrying them up with the files on the flash drive that protruded from the side of his laptop like a malignant growth. Carefully he sifted out the ones that depicted, or named, the Sea Dart. Amin had been right, but in the wrong way. There was little danger of Tarek being caught with them but sending them electronically to Malik was far too much of a risk. He was well aware that even one tiny lapse might be picked up by one of the many watchers in cyberspace. In addition, Tarek had no intention of giving Malik information on the planned targets and, to be fair, the man had clearly said that he didn't want to know. But ... men with too much information may sometimes get greedy or worse, let their tongues talk to strangers.

To: Dr Malik <smalik@spkrl.com.pk>
From: Professor al-Shami <talshami@gmail.com>
Subject: NuCan Details

Dear Dr Malik
It was a pleasure to see you again last week and my thanks for taking the time to stop off in Beirut.

Further to our discussion in respect of the proposed design and production of the new food container, Mr Abbot MSc has sent me the details that you requested. I have attached his diagrams, annotated to show maximum/minimum dimensions and tolerances. Please note that the weight provided reflects the current unit which NuCan is intended to replace.

Mr Abbot has also suggested the addition of a magnetic strip to be affixed to the unit. However, that is also shown on one of the diagrams.

I hope that they provide you with enough details to enable you to give us an accurate pricing for the project. If you have any questions, please get back to me as soon as possible.

Best wishes   Tarek al-Shami

Making sure that he had indeed appended the files to the email, Tarek reread what he'd typed and clicked send. Within 24 hours, he had a reply.

To: Professor al-Shami <talshami@gmail.com>
From: Dr Malik <smalik@spkrl.com.pk>
Subject: Re: NuCan Details

Dear Professor

In turn, thank you for the excellent luncheon at La Paillote and your interest in our manufacturing capability. Thank you also for your email in respect of your NuCan project and the excellent attachments, which were extremely useful. My compliments to Mr Abbot for his wondrous drawings and the explicit notations; the combination of the two was of great use in our calculations. Once mutual financial arrangements have been finalised, I'm sure that his work will help accelerate the design process.

At this stage I believe it would be helpful and advantageous if you were to visit our facility near Wana. There are quite a few aspects of the project that need to be discussed and agreed. Additionally, my associate feels that it is a professional imperative that you should meet with him before entering into a formal business venture.

Therefore, I suggest to you that perhaps you could fly to Lahore in the next few weeks? Both my associate and I can be available at any time for the whole of June. In order that we might expedite your visit, perhaps you would give me call at you earliest convenience. My home number is (0)423 4336472; mobile (0)343 7728691. I believe +92 is the international dialling code. I look forward to hearing from you imminently.

Your humble servant

Dr Sami Malik

Tarek sipped his coffee ruminatively, leaning against the back of his chair, staring out at blue sky, now decorated with small fluffy white balls of cumulus. The process of travelling from plane to house the previous evening had been agonisingly slow. Like snails drugged by the very boredom of their lives, the line of arrivals inched slowly forward through two separate passport checks. And despite the fact that he had no luggage to collect from the carousel, there was no opportunity for pushing past the throng of people processing through the customs hall. By the time he'd arrived home, it was almost nine o'clock and Tarek had felt drained. This morning however, he felt refreshed, energised by the thought of taking action and shifting up a gear. He was sure that his Director would agree to a sojourn in Pakistan even though he'd only just got back to Beirut.

Lahore was three hours ahead of Beirut so ... 12.10 over there. Tarek carefully dialled the Doctor's home number, heard the electronic clicks of international connectivity and the flat double tone of a phone in a Pakistani echo chamber.

'Malik speaking. And what is your good name?'

'Good morning Dr Malik, it's Tarek al-Shami.'

'Professor, excellent. I assume, therefore, that you have received my email?'

'Indeed. Listen, I'm very happy to come to see you in situ, as it were, in Lahore. I just wondered if you were aware of any Islamic events scheduled for the next few weeks.'

'Every day is an Islamic event, alhamdulillāh. Jamia Ashrafia, the university where you were speaking a few years ago, maybe it has something. Ah, but there is … Al-Mawrid. As an academic, I think that it would be interesting for you to talk to the people at this place, even if they do not have a specific event scheduled. Al-Mawrid is a foundation for Islamic research and education, based in Lahore but has affiliates in some western countries.

'Apparently they have been criticised in the past for some of their ideas, such as the foundation's alleged support of General Zia's Hudood Ordinances back in the 70s. Scurrilous allegations, I suspect but … You would only have been a child at the time. Hudood was 'designed' to align secular Pakistani law and Shari'ah in conformity with the Qu'ran. Most of it was about punishments for extramarital sex and theft but Zia didn't quite hit the mark. A lot of it has been amended since then. But you're an Islamic scholar with in depth knowledge of Shari'ah; maybe they would be interested in a dialogue between you and them. Should I ask them?'

'Absolutely. It sounds ideal.'

'I will talk to them and it will happen. You will have an email with details very soon. Good, very good. Make your travel arrangements for Pakistan; I will do the rest. You will come soon I think?'

'Give me a few days to sort out students and catch up with paperwork. As soon as I have something from Al-Mawrid, I'll get approval from the faculty and book flights. To Lahore, I presume?'

'Indeed. On that note Professor, goodbye, and we will talk again soon.'

It was only a matter of hours before Tarek received an email from one Mr Yasir Marwani.

To: Professor al-Shami <talshami@gmail.com>
From: YasirMarwani <marwani.yas@amfre.org.pk>
Subject: Talking in The Park

Dear Professor
On behalf of the foundation, I am being delighted to extend our invitation to join us for a two-day series of

lectures and discussions on Shari'ah – Understanding, Interpretation and the Law. Talking in The Park is an informal way of discussing issues that affect us all in our daily lives, allowing scholars, students and members of the public to contribute.

As well that we are hoping that you will be finding it interesting and pleasurable, we would be honoured if you would share with us some of your knowledge and insights.

Timings for TiTP have as yet to be formalised, thus we can be flexible and accommodate your travel plans to allow incorporation of your good self. As Dr Malik has given me to understand that you will be in the process of effecting those imminently, I would be grateful if you would advise me accordingly.

I look forward to both hearing from you and meeting your good self in Lahore very soon.

Please accept my most sincere regards. YM

As expected, Professor Mohammed Said Khoury, Director of the Faculty of Arabic and Islamic Studies was perfectly happy for Tarek to go to Pakistan. In fact he actively encouraged his deputy to go; to engage with other academics in discussion on every possible occasion. There were a number of reasons for the Director's laisser-faire attitude and none of them had anything to do with liberalism. The eminent Professor avoided travelling because he found it tedious unless he was doing it for pleasure.

In the modern age, he found academic discussion dull and academics even duller. Reading Rumi's lyrical poetry or listening to the tight riffs of Kamal Mussallam's mean jazz guitar was much more to his taste. And the luscious Sylvie was far better company. More than a mistress, she was a sexual artist who could arouse him with the lightest of touches, torment him to the point of ecstasy and fuck him to a standstill.

Why, therefore, would he want to attend travel thousands of miles just to attend this seminar or that symposium? Particularly since his subordinate invariably produced excellent annotated reports, complete with comment and review, which looked good on his desk. They looked even better collectively, especially when the Board of Trustees queried his requests for more money for the faculty. Thus Professor Khoury not only gave Tarek his blessing but also agreed to cover the cost of his return flight and provide a comfortable subsistence allowance.

*****

Emirates flight 622, from Dubai International descended slowly through the darkness towards Allama Iqbal International. Through the window of the Boeing 777-300ER, Lahore was a vast expanse of blocky shadows striped and starred by the yellows, whites and silver-blues of the lights below. It had been almost 12 hours since he'd left Beirut, stopping in Dubai to change flights and wait for five hours before flying onwards to Pakistan. Used as he was to flying, Tarek was ready to get back onto terra firma, dreaming of a soft mattress and falling into a deep sleep. A blur of beige-grey mixed with green flashed by outside, slowly materialising into shapes of buildings and vehicles. Then the double thump as the wheels hit the runway, the force of braking pushing him forwards into his seat belt. Slumping back as the braking eased and the plane rolled slowly off the runway towards its parking slot.

'Ladies and gentlemen, welcome to Allama Iqbal International Airport, Lahore. Please keep your seat belts on until the plane comes to a standstill and the Captain has turned off the seat belt sign. Local time is 01.50 hours and the temperature outside is a pleasant 21 degrees. Passengers who are not Pak nationals should ensure that they have a completed disembarkation form and passport ready for immigration. On behalf of the Captain and Emirates Airlines, we wish you a pleasant onward journey ....'

Tarek tuned out of the rest of the familiar speech in which the only variables served to remind the traveller of the name of the destination, the time and the weather. He looked out at the bland close-up of the side of glazed building that might have been at any airport in the world. Only the semi-furled flag behind the glass gave any clue to the location: he could see a partial curve of the white crescent against the dark green background.

Despite the hour, the still air was heavy with night heat and Tarek felt beads of sweat forming on his forehead as he

109

disembarked. The frigid air of the terminal soon dissipated the warmth, replacing it with a chill that made him grateful for keeping his jacket out of his main bag. And then, once through the tedious processes of immigration and customs, he was back outside in the warm night, looking for a taxi. There was no shortage of cars, their drivers snoozing at the wheel while others leaned against the side of the vehicle, barely concealing the cigarettes they were smoking in contravention of the law.

'Welcome to Lahore, Sir. Where am I taking your good self tonight?'

'Lahore Palace Hotel please.'

'A very good choice if I say so. In Garden Town, opposite Barkat Market. Is very quiet for Lahore, I think, isn't it?'

The driver turned on the ignition, turning the wheel in anticipation of driving away from the kerb.

'How much is it?'

'You want meter or fixed price offer?'

'Meter,' Tarek muttered, slumping back against the plastic covered seat.

He looked vacantly between the gap in the front seats as the driver flicked the switch on the meter. Leaning forward, he was slightly surprised to see that it was starting at 1,213.64 Pakistani rupees, but too tired to complain. As the cab drove off towards Lahore, Tarek rested his head on the back of the seat, staring up at the ceiling for a moment before closing his eyes. All he could hear was the sound of the engine and the soughing of the air conditioning. He felt the car make the turns, hit the occasional pothole, swerve to avoid something, perhaps a dog or a person. Opening his eyes as they turned left, he looked into the pale orange light, catching glimpses through the trees of the canal running parallel with the road. A road of indolent water, glowing dappled bronze, shown on a strip of old film pulled along by invisible hands through the night. It seemed familiar.

'Where are we?'

'This one is named Canal Bank Road. We are not far from your hotel. Sir, where are you coming from?'

'Beirut, Lebanon.'

'Bey-ruth. Leb-a-non.' The driver savoured the two words, rolling them around in his mouth. 'Ah, you are married?'

Tarek sighed, knowing where the line of questioning was going. Knowing how to stop it, he lied.

'Of course. I have a lovely wife and three beautiful children, alhamdulillāh.'

'You are Muslim? This is good. Allahu akbar.'

He stopped talking and concentrated on driving. They had turned off Canal Bank Road and were heading, more or less, towards Model Town. In Tarek's mind the name conjured up some kind of children's toy, a place of gaudy plastic buildings, cars and trees with green plastic leaves. They finally stopped outside a squat two storey building which looked as though it had seen better days. The word HOTEL was painted in faded green on a white rectangular background. In smaller letters, this time in pastel pink, it read LAHORE PALACE. The journey had taken some 40 minutes even with the lack of traffic and Tarek suspected there might have been a slight detour along the way. The final meter reading winked a figure of 1,834PKR, which seemed a lot of rupees.

'Night price,' the driver explained, 'but for you, cut price. Is nice!'

The words were trite and clearly overused but Tarek was too tired to argue. He paid the man, took his bag from the boot and stumbled into the hotel already half asleep. The receptionist was snoring lightly, his head cushioned by folded arms on the desk. The gentle push on his shoulder caused the man to straighten up as though he'd been burned. Tired eyes peered over glasses rimmed in heavy black plastic, assessing the equally tired man in front of him.

'Mr al-Shami, isn't it? I am being expecting you for some time but now you are here, welcome to the luxurious hotel that is the Lahore Palace. Dr Malik has warned us of your late coming and you must be tired like as I am. Let us check you in chop-chop and then you can sleep in your comfortable bed.'

His words were not idle promises. Processing the paperwork with alacrity, the receptionist picked up Tarek's bag and showed him up to a spacious room with a large double bed.

'Sleep well, Mr al-Shami. I am putting the 'Do Not Disturb' sign on the outside of the door for you, isn't it? May you dream of gazelle-eyed houris.'

Tarek looked at his watch: three fifty in the morning which, in terms of his mental clock still on Beirut time, it was ten to one. It felt later. When he finally climbed into bed, it was as comfortable as promised. Grunting with pleasure, he let his head hit the pillow; his mind switched out the lights and he slept.

Gunned engines, a truck backfiring, screeching brakes, dogs barking, metal wheels grinding on concrete, voices shouting and the hum of conversation: sounds that filtered into Tarek's consciousness as he slowly woke up wondering where he was. It surely wasn't on a quiet mountainside looking down on Beirut. Climbing out of bed, he rubbed his eyes with the back of his hands and drew back the curtains. And Lahore's Garden Town looked back at him through the window. But unlike the crowded characterful streets of Lahore's Old City, this view was more pedestrian and more ordinary. An ordinary street, with ordinary suburban shops and restaurants; even that vile American import, Kentucky Fried Chicken, had a place in the line.

Diesel fumes blended with thrice-used cooking oil, spawning a rank perfume that seeped through the window seals. Carbon dioxide brought a heavy base note to the mix while curry spices provided toxic accents. The sky was the colour of dull grey metal, the sun only leaking though the smog in places. But the heat was there, smearing everything with a wavy haze. It was 11 o'clock, Lahore time and the mercury was rising. The shrill ringing of the hotel phone brought his thoughts back into the room.

'Reception desk, Sir. I have Dr Malik on the phone for you. Shall I put him through?'

'Of course.'

'Professor al-Shami, welcome to Lahore. I hope I have not awakened you.'

'No, I've been awake for a while. I'm just …'

'Excellent. I hope that you are rested and ready for your discussions in the park? Mr Marwani will be in touch very shortly. He will convey you to Model Town, which is not so far from Lahore Palace Hotel, and then take care of you for today and tomorrow.'

'Fine,' Tarek said lamely, feeling as though he had just been run over by a juggernaut.

'Then the day after, in the morning at around ten, we will pick you up from the hotel and go to Allama Iqbal. From there we fly to Wana for about 42 minutes, then drive to our manufacturing facility. So, I think that is it for the moment, unless you have any questions?'

'Um, no, I don't think so. It all sounds … fine.'

'Good. Then I will see you the day after tomorrow. In the meantime, enjoy the al fresco talks and your time in Lahore. By the way, if you haven't had breakfast as yet, the chef does very good Traffic Light scrambled eggs with a perfect balance of tomato, onion and chilli. Very typical.'

The phone went dead as Malik rang off leaving Tarek staring at the handset as though it were some strange unknown object. He felt vaguely disorientated, left in limbo without a defined plan while waiting for the next person to pick him up. As though prompted by his thoughts, the phone rang again.

'Reception desk again, Sir. I have a message from Mr Marwani. He says to offer you his best wishes and that he will come to the hotel to pick you up in half an hour.'

'Half an hour?'

'Yes Sir.'

'I've only just got up. I need to have a shower, get dressed …'
He stopped, realising that there was little point whining to a receptionist. In a more commanding tone of voice, he said: 'Please have some coffee sent to my room. If I am not down by the time that Mr Marwani arrives, please ask him to wait'.

The following 40 plus hours provided an unexpected interlude that allowed Tarek's mind and body to unwind. Model Town Park was a green oasis with manicured lawns, painted with beds of vividly coloured flowers, strung between fine trees whose leafy branches provided welcome shade. The so-called lectures were more like supplications and poetry while the discussions reminded Tarek of university debates. Rather than the combative arguments of warrior scholars, this was an exchange of couplets and verses among the faithful.

Somehow he'd pictured Yasir Marwani as a thin, perhaps slightly stooped, older man with a tendency to pedantry and didacticism. In reality, Yasir was a plump, slicked down little man in his 30s with a huge smile, a temperament to complement

113

it and a fondness for vegetable biryani. He delighted in ridiculing his fellowman while excusing his or her failings by laying the blame at the feet of the politicians and the army. But beneath the jokes and laughter, there lay a cold stream of sadness for the fractured bones of a country he loved.

'You know Mr Tarek, the average Pakistani is really a fine fellow. He is an interesting, fun loving chap who wants life to be beautiful and without the hardships, isn't it? That one there wants to sell his mangoes in the market but the officer says if he wants to sell, he must let the officer dip his beak. Then the owner of the market hears that the officer is dipping his beak everywhere in the market; now he wants to dip his beak as well. So it goes on up the tree to the very top. Now the mango seller has nowhere to go and complains to the politicians: he is a poor man who is being robbed. The politicians tell him they will buy his mango orchard and they give him some money. The seller that was, is now a mango buyer but the politicians have made the price too high and he cannot afford even the ones that have been left to rot. Then the politicians pay the army to protect the market from those who would steal.'

'And where do you stand in all of this?' Tarek had asked.

'Nowhere,' Yasir had replied. 'I don't like mangoes.'

He'd laughed uproariously at his own joke. When they'd parted company on the second day, he made Tarek promise that he would call before he left Lahore. And left him with a warning.

'Be careful Mr Tarek. Dr Malik is a powerful man with powerful friends. There are many people in Pakistan who are dangerous: al-Qaeda, Pakistani Taliban, Lashkar-e-Omar, Jaish-e-Mohammed and many more fundamentalist movements. But there are others who are just as dangerous and in many instances, more powerful. The ISI, you know them, it stands for Inter Services Intelligence, are very dangerous and all Pakistanis are afraid of them. Military Intelligence is also bad. The Americans, the CIA is also here, since many years. And I think Dr Malik knows them all.'

*****

114

A white Toyota Corolla with tinted windows and no number plates pulled up outside the Lahore Palace Hotel at precisely 10.00 hours. The man who got out wore a suit and tie despite the heat. He walked into the hotel and up to the reception desk, putting down his car keys but keeping on the mirror sunglasses. The black hair was oiled back over the man's head, the face devoid of any vestige of emotion and the thin lips formed narrow parallel lines under a sharp nose.

'Tell Professor al-Shami that Dr Malik's car has arrived.'

Everything about the man screamed ISI, from the sunglasses to the Toyota he could see through the glazed door. The receptionist reacted as he would have done if an electric cattle prod had been pushed up his anus. Quickly.

'Yes Sir.'

'Now.'

The receptionist's hand was visibly shaking as he picked up the phone and punched the room number into the system. He could hear it ringing. He breathed a sigh of relief when he heard it stop.

'The front desk, Sir, Dr Malik's car has arrived for you Professor al-Shami.' The words tumbled out as though anxious to leave the man's mouth. Then he looked at his screen and training overtook fear. 'Ah, I presume you are checking out Professor. I'll have your bill waiting for you when you are down …' The words died in his mouth as he saw the man in front of him shaking his head. 'But I believe that has already been taken care of and paid by …' The man was shaking his head again; the receptionist had no words left.

Ready to leave, Tarek had been waiting for the call, walked downstairs and over to the desk.

'Good morning Professor al-Shami. Please, follow me. Dr Malik is waiting in the car.'

'If you could wait one moment. I have to settle my bill.'

'That will not be necessary, Professor. It's all been taken care of, on the house you might say.'

Taking Tarek's arm lightly but firmly, he guided him out to the waiting car and opened the rear door to reveal Sami Malik's slightly bloated, moustachioed face.

'Get in Professor, get in. We have a plane to catch,' he said gleefully, as though they were going on holiday.

Greeting the other man, Tarek eased himself through the door and sat down, joining Malik on the back seat. The car pulled out into traffic that had already slowed down to the speed of an old bicycle. By the time that they reached Canal Bank Road, the brakes had clearly seized and the traffic was bogged down by its own weight. A pall of grey, superheated smog hung over the road, draped between the buildings and over the canal like a stinking shroud, a foul weeping barrier that blocked fresh air and sky.

Overladen ancient trucks nestled against once gaudily-painted buses, crammed with people and more sitting on top. Varicoloured autorickshaws filled the gaps between the larger vehicles, the sound of engines and passengers like chattering starlings. Arguments developed over minor incidents when one vehicle kissed another, the drivers standing in the road bellowing imprecations and shaking their fists. Only mangy stray dogs slipped through the traffic, kicked by those on their feet as they bit rubber tyres and unwary legs. Even though every human being in this vehicular stew recognised the significance of the unmarked white Toyota with its visually impenetrable windows, there was no way to let it through. It took half an hour before the driver could bully his way off Canal Bank Road, feeding into the relative calm of Zahoor Elahi Road.

Twenty minutes later, away from the public gaze, the Toyota pulled off the airport access road and parked near a row of small hangars. A Chinese made Harbin Y-12 Turboprop was waiting for them outside, the door in the body just behind the high wing offering an open welcome. As the two men approached the plane a man stepped out from the doorway, the epaulettes on his white shirt denoting the rank of first officer. Slightly unusually, he snapped off a salute, standing back to let them board; Malik merely nodded.

Usually configured to take 17 passengers, the cabin had been modified to provide a more comfortable flying experience for VIP passengers. Four large seats covered in black leather were arranged in pairs, each facing its opposite number across a polished teak coffee table. Malik waved a languid arm in the air.

'Sit down, Professor,' he said, dropping heavily in a seat himself.

Sitting down opposite his host, Tarek glanced around the cabin, taking in the small bar at one end, next to the door to the flight deck. A rack to the side held a number of international magazines that looked current and a small bookcase displayed several books, including a copy of the Qu'ran, held in place by a polished brass rail. Closing the cabin door, the first officer paused before taking his seat next to the Captain.

'If you would fasten your seatbelts gentlemen, please. We will be leaving in just a few moments.'

Tarek heard the engines being fired up and could see the lower hemisphere of a spinning propeller through the window. The Harbin taxied along the airport roads until it reached the end of the runway. As the Captain fed the power into the Pratt and Whitney Canada PT6A-27s, Tarek could feel the pressure build and the plane vibrate. Brakes released, it rolled down the runway, slowly picking up speed and finally lifting into the air. Gaining height, the plane banked steeply left, overflying Lahore; the city below spread out in a ragged grey-brown patched carpet.

'Consider this Professor, about eight million people live their lives down there, in Lahore. It's the most densely populated city in Pakistan after Karachi. We are crammed into the place like nobody's business but it is a wonderful place, is it not? Historically, culturally and for business, it is probably Pakistan's most important city and certainly one of the wealthiest. But here's the rub, thirty per cent of Lahore is slums where people live side by side in squalor. They exist in tents or shacks made from scraps of wood and corrugated iron. There's rarely any electricity, there are no proper toilets or fresh water and they have no access to real medical care. There are almost two and half million of the poor buggers, for whom daily life is a struggle but they survive.

'Lahore is the capital of Punjab province, so almost half of the people are Punjabi. I am Punjabi. Then there are people from other parts of Pakistan: Pashtuns, Sindhis, Saraikis, Muhajirs and Balochis. Then you can throw in some urbanised Kashmiris, Hazaras and Afghans. On the whole, in Lahore we all get on famously with each one knowing his place. Some are poor and others are not but that is the way of life everywhere. The problem is that not everyone sees or understands this balance and others seek to upset the status quo.'

The flow was stopped by a gentle feminine cough, designed to achieve exactly what it had – temporary silence. Turning, the two men found themselves looking at a twenty something, dark haired and sloe-eyed stewardess wearing a lime green Punjabi suit.

'My apologies for the interruption gentlemen. Please may I offer you some refreshment?'

'Meet the lovely Nargis. In English, it means flower. Our Nargis smells sweet and her beauty admired, as precious as a rare bloom from the Himalayas. But not to be plucked, I'm afraid.' Malik gave her a lewd smile, amused by his own crass humour. 'Johnnie Walker Black Label, please Nargis. With ice. Professor al-Shami?'

'Some water or perhaps fruit juice?'

'May I suggest a soft cocktail of mango and sugarcane juice mixed with just a touch of lime, cardamom, fenugreek and salt? It is very refreshing Sir, and energising. It is beneficial to the heart, brain, kidney and eyes. Something that this behanchood might do well to consider but could never appreciate.'

Malik roared with laughter as Tarek looked from one to the other, slightly bemused.

'That sounds lovely, um, Nargis. Please.'

The girl inclined her head towards him, in semblance of a quiet bow and headed towards the bar.

'Behanchood?'

'It means sister fucker,' Malik explained, still grinning. 'A quaint term of endearment. Nargis knows me well since she's often on this flight. She reminds me that I am but a weak man and putty in her hands. So where were we? Those who seek to disturb the status quo or amend the path of history. Terrorists are everywhere, breeding like flies on carrion and each group has its own agenda. Al-Qaeda, Taliban, Haqqanis, Lashkar-e-Taiba, they're all here, and many more. Some are from Pakistan but many others come from Saudi Arabia, Yemen, Somalia, Sudan, Afghanistan, Iraq, Iran. Even people from Europe come to fight. Often they hate each other, they cheat, betray and they kill; but they all hate the westerners. And you know what is truly ironic, uniquely Pakistani? That these terrorist devils have been supported, financed and cossetted by ISI, MI (the Army Military Intelligence), America's CIA, Britain's MI6 and in some cases, NATO itself! Ah, Nargis comes bringing nectar.'

Placing the glasses carefully on the table, she gave Tarek a winsome smile before leaving. Only to return a moment later with small dishes of shelled raw peanuts and cardamom seeds.

'Please try,' she said, pointing a perfectly manicured finger at Tarek's long glass.

Cautiously obeying, he took an investigative sip of the pale yellow-green liquid, and then a proper mouthful.

'That is absolutely heavenly,' he exclaimed. 'Thank you!'

She smiled at him, putting her hands together and once again giving him that slight bow.

'This is heavenly too,' said Malik, holding up his glass.

Nargis scowled at him before walking towards the rear of the plane. Unsmiling, he sipped his Black Label and watched her walk away.

'All joking apart, don't be fooled by the pretty face and body beautiful, Professor. A highly tuned mind lies behind the stunning looks and that supermodel physique is maintained by training with commandos. She appears on this flight as though she's cabin crew and when there's a foreigner on board. As there is today, and I'm fairly certain that Nargis is listening to our conversation. It has been whispered that she's an operative in ISI's Covert Action Division. I wouldn't be surprised.'

They sipped at their drinks meditatively, looking out of the windows. Apart from the occasional swirl of cloud, the sky was clear and allowing a good view of the ground below. A geometric patchwork quilt spread out beneath them in varied green, brown and beige dulled quadrilaterals. Blotches of trees splashed variegated greens and yellows on a mottled beige canvas. A thick dull grey-green line meandered through the picture, as though some monstrous child had dragged a pencil down that same canvas.

'The River Indus,' Malik said. 'That means we're over half way. I think that's Dera Ismail Khan on the left bank, which means that we've left Punjab and we're now over Khyber-

Pakhtunkhwa Province. A few miles on, we cross over the Gomal River into the Federally Administered Tribal Areas and then down to Wana. I say down, but you're already in the mountains by then and Wana is 1,387 metres above sea level. The good news is that it's not as hot as Lahore.'

It was not long before the land began to rise, slowly at first as though giving itself a springboard to leap upwards to the higher peaks. As the turboprop plane flew above the peaks, the landscape was an arid and rippled brown expanse, streaked by dry riverbeds that might come into flood with meltwater next spring. Now it reminded Tarek of crumpled brown-grey tissue paper, left behind to gather dust. As the plane began to descend, he could see the orchards around the town, what looked like some kind of military base and on the other side of the road, a single grey runway. There had been no warning from either the crew or Nargis, who had not reappeared.

The wheels of the Harbin Y-12 hit the tarmac heavily, the rubber slipping on the sand and dust that covered the ground. It came to a halt, slightly skewed rather than regimentally straight, before the pilot turned the plane on its axis and taxied back up the runway. The first officer came through the cabin and opened the door.

'Welcome to Wana, Sir. You'll be returning this afternoon Doctor?'

'Yes, Warrant Officer Kakar. Thank you.'

Malik stepped out onto the ground with Tarek immediately behind, walking through swirls of tiny dust devils. Just off the runway, a once black Toyota Hilux waited with the engine running. Two bearded soldiers in fatigues squatted in the bed of the truck, AK47s balanced crosswise on their knees. They glanced casually at the two approaching men but said nothing. Two more soldiers were in the front of the pickup, the one in the passenger seat opening the rear door from inside. Once both their civilian passengers were on board, the driver steered the truck onto the runway and accelerated as though he was flying a plane. Without braking, he drove straight off the end onto rough ground, bouncing over rocks and loose shale until he reached the relative smoothness of the perimeter track. There were only a few hundred yards respite before he took the truck off-road once again for an equal distance, before turning right onto the Angoor Adda Road.

'Finally,' Malik said, glaring uselessly at the back of the soldier's head. Turning to Tarek, he said: 'It should take us about an hour to get to the facility, maybe a little less the way this idiot is driving. At least we're unlikely to meet many others on the way. This road goes to the border crossing at Angoor Adda and then on into Afghanistan. If we followed the road, it continues northwest to Ghazni and then north-east to Kabul. To get to the plant, we turn off just before reaching Angoor. Physically, the border is about one kilometre away from where we are but there is no military presence at that point. You can get there, but not by car or truck.'

The nearside front wheel dropped into a deep pothole, throwing the occupants of the Toyota forwards in their seats. As the driver mashed down on the accelerator, the wheel kicked over the lip and back onto level road. All four of them cursed at the jolts that jarred bone and muscle. Billows of dry dust caught in the throats of the soldiers in the open bed and the sound of hacking coughs added to the engine noise.

'A little bit of history as we drive. We think that the original plant was built with American money a few years after the Soviets invaded Afghanistan. At the beginning support for the mujahideen and the Northern Alliance in Afghanistan was financial. Then there were some guns, ammunition, Toyotas and other things but mostly it was lots and lots of dollars. But both the mujahideen in the south and the Northern Alliance, as its fighters spread downwards towards Kabul, they wanted American Stingers, surface-to-air missiles that would bring down the Soviet planes.

'The CIA called it Operation Cyclone and threw millions at the mujahideen every year, especially at the Seven Party Alliance. You may have heard of at least two of the leaders: Hekmatyar who led Hezbi Islami and Lion of Panjshir, Ahmad Shah Massoud who led the Northern Alliance. But funding also ended up in the pockets of groups like the Taliban and, some say al-Qaeda but that is doubtful. In addition, Operation Cyclone channelled billions of dollars to Pakistan to support the country's role in the war effort. A lot of that was used to train and arm

Afghan resistance groups with ISI favouring Hekmatyar while others preferred Massoud.

'The plant was used as a holding facility for all sorts of military hardware, waiting for inward transit to mujahideen units. Weapons were manufactured and adapted here as well, to a certain extent, during the war. When the Soviets withdrew in 1989, the Americans turned off the money tap but left a few members of the CIA. There are still one or two at the military base in Wana. Then Afghanistan turned on itself, the mujahideen tearing at each other like wolves and the plant still had a role. But all this is history. Maybe I am boring you?'

'Absolutely not, it's fascinating. But how long has your operation been here?'

'Alas, the young have little patience with the past,' said Malik with a melodramatic sigh, raising his hands to heaven. 'Professor, you are currently riding in a truck along a road that many international commentators would say is in one of the most dangerous places in the world. Since time immemorial, Waziristan has been home to the Mahsud and Waziri tribes who have constant blood feuds, spending at least part of their lives trying to murder each other. When they're not doing that, they prey upon those who pass through their mountain strongholds. The Afghan-Pak border is porous, here and in many other places, if you know the way through.

'Afghanistan grows more opium and hashish than any other country in the world; plus it produces most of the heroin that finds its way to the west. There is a lot of money to be made and there are few who can resist taking their share of the profits. Heroin helped fund the mujahideen internecine fighting, the Waziris and Mahsouds to survive. At first the Taliban tried to ban the trade but soon realised they were throwing away a lucrative opportunity.

'And there are people like you who, for whatever reason, require a bespoke weapons production service. You know, last year a battle was fought in Wana between Pakistani troops and al-Qaeda? Except it wasn't just al-Qaeda.' Malik described the speech marks with two fingers. 'According to MI, fighters included Arabs, Afghans, Chechens, Tajiks, Uzbeks, Pakistani Talibs, Uighurs and a few Europeans. Interesting, no?'

'Yes, but I don't understand why this plant is based here, in such a dangerous place. It doesn't make sense. Does it?'

'My dear Professor. Of course it makes sense. From an official point of view, the facility doesn't exist; the Pakistani government, together with ISI, MI, army et al, would deny all knowledge of its existence. Where better to hide such a place than in the mountains of the lawless tribal areas? Especially since many of its clients, like al-Qaeda, have a presence here. In fact, they are the reason why running the plant here is so safe – they all have an interest in ensuring that it is secure and well protected. We provide safe transit storage for heroin and opium; offer laboratory time as necessary for refining opium; provide weapons engineering to include design and production of bespoke weaponry; offer a brokerage service for heavy arms. And the Pakistani Army is always happy to provide security to and from the airport from the base at Wana. So we took over the plant about ten years ago, although some of my colleagues have been here for much longer.'

'That's some history lesson Dr Malik.'

'Mm mm. I should have said, of course, that not all of our clients are on some western terrorist list. And one should add the codicil, albeit a somewhat clichéd one: one man's terrorist is another man's freedom fighter. Sometimes that reads: be careful, today's terrorist is tomorrow's President.'

They had been rising constantly as they left Wana, levelling out after some 20 minutes. Ragged barren hill tops, rocks and stones, scrubby bushes and a few trees presented a dreary view. The road itself was reasonable with relatively few ruts and potholes. Well before it started the descent to the border at Angoor Adda, the Toyota turned right onto a stony track running parallel to a shallow stream running through larger rocks and boulders. Although the track was ungraded and rough, it was wide enough to accommodate much heavier vehicles than theirs. Some of the tyre tracks etched into the ruts and mud wet patches signalled the tread of a heavy transport truck. Or perhaps a heavily laden truck, thought Tarek, with missiles in mind.

A little further on, the driver turned left along another, similar track but on either side were signs in Pashto, Urdu and English that read 'Authorised Vehicles Only'. After another couple of kilometres, they were brought to a halt by a heavy duty counterbalanced rising arm barrier. Two men manned the gate, both dressed in dark green military style fatigues and berets with no insignia, both carrying Kalashnikovs. One spoke briefly to the driver and then walked past to stop by the rear door. Malik nodded to him before handing over several documents including Tarek's passport. The guard cast a cursory eye over them all, pausing only to check Tarek's face with his picture. Clearly happy with the papers, the guard put his hand on his heart, gave a slight bow to the Doctor and walked away, calling to his companion. The barrier slowly lifted and the Toyota drove past, through a chicane of broadly spaced concrete blocks.

The road curved round, along a channel hacked though the rock, effectively hiding the plant from the checkpoint behind. Emerging from the manmade ravine, the road dipped gradually downwards to what appeared to be a vast natural rocky bowl. On the far side, a large drab cuboid building seemed to be growing out of the rock face rather than being merely attached. Near the top, a glittering line of tall windows stitched its way around the wall on the visible sides. Below that the face was unrelieved apart from one massive, steel roller door that was firmly closed. A few other, much smaller, buildings stood in rough quadrants at each of the two corners, servants to a greater master.

As the car approached the facility across the empty expanse of the bowl, more details appeared. Utility vehicles in green drab parked in the shade, eclipsed by an ostentatious Toyota Land Cruiser in metallic red. The mirror-glass windows embedded in the walls of the outbuildings allowed no inward sight, reflecting only the barren environment. With no signs or decals to indicate name, function or even instruction, Malik's place of special projects was a faceless anonymity. The glare of harsh sunlight and deep shadows only served to give the place a menacing, inhuman aura. Standing in the heat, beside a hot truck, Tarek shivered.

A previously unnoticed door in the shadows opened and a slim man stepped out. Like the two guards, he was dressed in dark green fatigues but unlike them, had a black plastic nametag over his right breast pocket that said 'KHARAL' in gold lettering.

'Good to see you Sir, and I assume this is Professor al-Shami?'

'Indeed and likewise. Professor, may I introduce my production genius, Captain Ahmed Kharal, technically of the Pakistani Army Corps of Electrical and Mechanical Engineering. Captain, meet our client, Professor Tarek al-Shami.'

'Honoured,' said Kharal, extending his hand.

His handshake was firm and dry, unlike that of his superior.

'It's a pleasure Captain. This must be a strange place to work, so isolated and so … other-worldly. Like being on a different planet.'

Captain Kharal grinned. It was an honest, open and friendly grin; Tarek responded in turn.

'I know what you mean. Fortunately, I'm not here that often and when I am, it's full on for the duration. Doctor Malik has asked me to help him on several occasions and I try to do my unworthy best. This is one such occasion.'

Listening to Kharal's voice, Tarek wondered about his background. The man was clearly Pakistani and spoke perfect English but the accent was American southern slur with a pinch of chilli.

'Come inside, out of the heat.'

Kharal stood back to let the two visitors enter. Following them inside, he closed the heavy door behind him with ease and pressed a button on the wall. There was a soft hissing noise and a thud, as two steel rods slid from the door to the locked position in the wall.

'You'd need a serious bomb to get through that.' He laughed. 'Maybe we should use it to test yours when we've made it. Come.'

Malik mock frowned at the Captain.

'Not only can this upstart play the jester, he has a great capacity for underselling himself to the client and overselling himself to me. I pay a great deal for his foolishness.' Malik continued as the three men walked along the corridor: 'Truthfully, under that comic façade lies a brilliant mind. I have to pay twice for the Captain to come here: one pile of dollars to his Pak Army superiors and another to him. But he's worth every cent.'

At the end of the corridor, Kharal opened an internal door, leading them into a large workshop that positively glinted under bright white lighting. The air was pleasantly cool despite the smell of oil and hot metal.

'When I am in Shawal, this is my home,' he said, 'welcome.'

'Ahmed Kharal, showman, captain and doctor. Oh yes, the word captain belies his true meaning. If I remember rightly, you achieved both your Masters and PhD at the Whiting School of Engineering? Part of John Hopkins University in Baltimore?'

'Correct on both accounts, Doctor.'

'Then got picked up by Raytheon Missile Systems in Tucson, Arizona. Kharal was one of their star researchers among other things.'

'That would account for the accent,' Tarek commented, 'but what made you leave? It sounds as though things were going well for you.'

'I'm Pakistani and, at the end of the day, Pakistan is my home. After 9/11, the government made things rather difficult for people like me. To put it bluntly, the FBI thought that it was anti-American and a security risk for a devious Pak to be at the heart of a company like Raytheon. I was given a one-way ticket, business class to Karachi and a healthy severance pay check. When I arrived back, the Army offered me a job with a commission, free food and clothing and time off for holidays in Waziristan. How could I refuse? Gentlemen, a cup of tea before we talk.'

As if on cue, a boy walked into the workshop with a laden tray. Using a workbench as a table, he laid out three porcelain teacups with saucers, poured black tea from a porcelain teapot and then added a little milk to each one from a porcelain jug. Carefully he presented each one of the men with tea, offering sugar lumps to be picked up with little silver tongs from a porcelain bowl. His job completed, he bowed and departed as quietly as he'd arrived. Kharal picked up the plate of biscuits and held them out.

'Pistachio,' he said, 'they're very good. He makes them himself. Please, sit down.' He pushed a couple of chairs in their direction and leaned against the side of the workbench. 'Professor, please pass my compliments to your colleague. His

126

work was excellent. It was a pleasure to work with such beautiful drawings and precise information. My thanks indeed, it made my life a lot easier as I do hate guesswork. In most scenarios, people say, there has to be a margin for error. In my field I will allow minimal tolerances; I do not believe in or allow error. And before you ask, yes Doctor I have taken your comments into consideration.'

Turning around, Kharal reached across the worktable and retrieved a wooden box. Opening the lid, he lifted out a squat cylinder that looked like a metal hat box and held it out with both hands.

'I expected it to be more, cylindrical, longer somehow,' said Tarek.

'It's all about proportion: in your mind you visualise something cylindrical as a thing of beauty, where the height is greater than the diameter. Not so. Anyway, this has been made to the specifications provided and interpreted accordingly. Ironically, the diameter of the cylinder is almost equivalent to the height. The diagrams showed that they were both 40 centimetres but we have reduced the diameter by two centimetres to allow for the magnetic strip. In addition, that allowed us to place the mobile receiver to the side near the top, which maximises the internal capacity. That works out at just under a cubic metre that we can use for the explosive train. Without going into detail, filling that kind of volume with modified HMX will give you a very big bang Professor.'

'Would it be strong enough to do significant damage to a ship, a destroyer? Or perhaps larger?' asked Tarek.

As the words left his mouth, he realised what he'd done. In just a few words he told them the nature of the proposed target, if not the detail. The strained looks on the faces of the other two men confirmed the thought. For a moment, the only sound in the workshop was that of three men breathing. Kharal cleared his throat.

'The modified HMX takes up less space than its predecessor but is 32 per cent more effective. Using the compression of the cylinder itself within a secondary cylinder will make the brisance, the shattering capability even more effective. Without actually testing the device, I can't give you accurate figures but I am fairly confident in saying that it would cripple a destroyer and cause serious damage to even an aircraft carrier. It would also depend on the actual location of the device. If it was stored together with any other munitions, in all likelihood they would also explode, increasing the damage. If on deck, a percentage would be dissipated but the explosion would still cause enough damage to stop a ship in its tracks. However, let us see what the tests show. Back to pragmatics.

'The casing has been made of a maraging alloy steel containing eight and a half per cent cobalt, three and a third per cent molybdenum. That means the steel has high strength with good malleability but is also brittle in explosive terms. It's similar to the steel often used for missile casings. We have made it fractionally thinner to keep down the weight and allow us a little more leeway with the details. With the naked eye, the line is difficult to see but it does have screw top.'

To prove the point, Kharal placed the cylinder back on the workbench and turned the top against the bottom with very little effort.

'You could use the cylinder as a bulk receptacle for whatever you want. That way NuCan can really be a new can!' He grinned and paused to enjoy his own joke. 'Seriously, it might be a good idea to have a few extra cylinders made to be used as dummies, filled with pistachios, dried apricots or whatever. Actual devices can be topped up in the same way. We have packed this one with sand and plastic to give you the weight you require, but that does need checking. Since we have a lid, the contents can be easily changed, whatever they be.'

'And testing, Captain,' said Malik, 'do we have a time frame for that?'

'We already have all the materials for production and the necessary equipment of course. With a full team of four – they can be brought over within a couple of days – explosive manufacture, machining, electronics … Give me a maximum of six weeks and I say with certainty that we'll have four live devices ready to test. Once you've agreed terms and conditions, we go.'

'What about triggering the devices?' asked Tarek.

'Don't worry, all that will be done at the same time. Since we're using mobile technology, we don't have to manufacture anything from scratch, simply modify units that are in common usage. You press the button on the transmitter and, if you're in range, the receiver says Hi. Bang! But we'll obviously be using those for testing. Catch, here's a transmitter.'

Producing a cheap mobile phone from his pocket, Kharal threw it in a high arc. Tarek watched the phone reach the apex of its ascent and then as it fell. It had been a long time since he fielded at short leg and Tarek fumbled the catch. He stared with horror as the phone clattered harmlessly on the tiled floor.

'Don't worry,' Kharal said laughing, 'nothing is dangerous until it's armed and connected.'

'It was just a reaction,' Tarek said, a hint of embarrassment in his voice. 'I never was much good at cricket. Where are we going to test the devices?'

Kharal looked at Dr Malik, who nodded and said: 'In the Kharan Desert, Balochistan. It's very isolated and used for testing missiles and the occasional nuclear weapon. We have access to the area and, since it's rarely used, it suits our purposes perfectly. Professor, do you have any further questions?'

'None. You, and Captain Kharal, seem to have everything covered. Thank you. The only thing is, I assume we need to discuss ..'

'The financial element of the project?'

'Yes.'

'Which is what we are about to do, Professor. Captain, thank you for your presentation. Excellent work, as ever. I assume the General was watching the show?'

'Of course,' said Kharal, barely supressing his laughter. 'The heroic Pamir Mustagh said he would prefer to watch from the comfort of the conference suite.

'Follow me,' Malik said to Tarek. 'Like many others, Captain Kharal laughs at the General behind his back, but never to his face.'

He pushed a button on the wall and lift doors opened. Inside, he hit the top button on the vertical line of five. Tarek noted that there were three floors above ground, there were also two below. Malik noticed his line of view.

'As I'm sure you have guessed, there is a lot more to the Shawal facility than it appears. You can see from the panel that we have levels underground. What is not so clear is that only half of the plant can be seen from the outside; it continues beyond the rock face and into the mountain to the same depth again on three of the levels. Here we are.' The lift doors opened onto a carpeted corridor that ran along the length of the window line at the front of the building. 'General Mustagh is my close associate in respect of projects such as ours and takes a keen interest, financially and politically.' Malik stopped walking. 'The General is our passport to areas that would otherwise be closed. Through him we get access to test sites in areas like the Kharan which includes secure transport there and back. And, of course, he ensures both secrecy and security. Without him, our ability to test explosive devices would be severely curtailed.' Malik looked at Tarek carefully, saw the slight inclination of the head as evidence of understanding and walked on. 'So now we will discuss the financial aspects.'

Before they reached the end of the corridor, Malik opened a door and led Tarek into a plush suite that would not have disgraced a five star hotel. Light filtered through tinted windows on two sides, illuminating the room with soft natural light. A polished walnut table dominated one end of the room with 14 chairs in the same wood, six along either side and one at both ends. Three places had been prepared with pads, pencils and water glasses; a large jug of iced water completed the tableau. The General was standing beside a flat panel television screen, still glowing dark grey-blue, in a semicircle of leather chairs.

'I watched the presentation with interest myself,' he said, in clear reflection of Malik's comments to Kharal. 'I'm pleased to meet you Professor al-Shami.'

His stride might once have had echoes from the parade ground, but those had long been silenced by over indulgence. Despite having officially retired from service, General Mustagh continued to wear army uniform, complete with insignia. His sleeve below the shoulder was decorated with the lightning bolts and dagger of the Special Services Group commandos, while the winged parachute flew over his right breast pocket. But what really stood out, apart from the belly overhanging his trousers, was the extraordinary array of medals on display. A well as the dense row of ribbons and gongs above his left shirt pocket, his torso was liberally strewn with silver on gold, circled stars. Thus his progress across the thick carpet was accompanied instrumentally by rapid metal clinking.

But his handshake had lost none of its strength and his attitude, still very much that of a military man. It's all in the eyes, Tarek thought as he looked back at the man crushing his hand. In spite of the slack jowls and panda dark eyes, there was that scheming look of determination that had probably deepened and been refined over the years. Gravitating naturally to the table, the three men sat down: the tag team of Malik and Mustagh on one side, Tarek facing them from the other.

'Captain Kharal is a fine officer and an excellent engineer,' General Mustagh began. 'From what I have seen, his work on your project so far seems to be very good. You are pleased?'

'Yes, very pleased. Although what he has shown us is only a dummy ...'

'You will be pleased; you have my personal guarantee. So let us talk of the financial arrangements. We will supply you with eight units complete with remote trigger systems: four to be tested in Pakistan, in the Kharan Desert; four to be delivered to you or your representative at the Port of Karachi or Port Muhammad Bin Qasim, as you prefer. Picking up on Captain Kharal's observation, I suggest that we also supply dummy NuCan containers that you can fill with nuts, fruit or other commodity as you choose. Extra weight can be added to the casing, and especially the base, to ensure that the dummies weigh more or less the same as the actual devices. I happy to enclose those as part of the deal, free and gratis!'

To emphasise his largesse, the General grinned like a wolf ready to bite and banged his fist on the table.

'The price is one million US dollars, to be paid in three instalments. The first payment of $250,000 must be made when you confirm that you wish to, and can, proceed. No further work will carried out until we receive confirmation from the bank that it has received the money. Assuming progression, a further $250,000 to be paid after successful testing and a final payment of $500,000 on delivery.'

General Mustagh leaned forward, resting his forearms on the table and waited for comments. His face was devoid of emotion as he looked at Tarek, knowing that there could only be one answer. Tarek held the other man's eye knowing that he had no choice but equally, unsurprised by the amount demanded. Both men were aware that haggling wasn't an option.

'I am certain that both the total figure and your schedule is acceptable. But, as I'm sure you appreciate General Mustagh, it needs to be ratified by my financiers; you have dealt with the organisation on previous occasions. That done on my return to Beirut, I will then effect transfer of funds once the sample has been checked and pronounced fit for purpose.'

He felt as though he was on a theatre stage, speaking words that had been written by an unknown playwright. It felt exciting and terrifying at the same time: he was making a verbal commitment to spend one million dollars of someone else's money on bombs that he would control. Totally surreal.

'Excellent. In due course, Dr Malik will supply you with a name and contact details for our bank in Zurich. In the first instance, the bank will contact you to establish suitable lines of communication. Do you have any questions?'

Tarek shook his head.

'In that case, I think we are done here. Gentlemen, since I believe that your somewhat uncomfortable transport has been deployed elsewhere, please let me take you back to your flight in comfort. Captain Kharal has already been instructed to put your sample in the back of my Land Cruiser. Shall we?'

•••••

Sitting at a corner table in the Bluebird, a bustling café just off Independence Street in Achrafieh, Tarek watched the world walk by through the window. A few people glanced back, seeing their reflection rather than the blurred images of those inside. The early rain had defiled the clarity of the glass, smearing it with a suspension born of water, oil and dust. From the inside out, Tarek saw the outsiders through fractured prisms that slid lazily down the pane.

Hearing the door open, for the hundredth time he turned and focused expectantly. But not this time. His thoughts skipped back to Pakistan. General Mustagh had provided them with a white-knuckle ride back to Wana, laughing at every corner as he put the Land Cruiser into power-slides that seemed to go on forever. By the time he was safely on the plane, Tarek was starting to regain colour in his cheeks, thankful that he was on the way back home. In Lahore, Dr Malik had dropped him off at the terminal, wished him good luck and disappeared into the distance. Walking through customs with a steel hatbox wrapped in a red, white and blue striped hessian, tied up with old ropes seemed to bother absolutely nobody. Apart from Tarek, who had walked through feeling the cold sweat beading on his forehead and his armpits, uncomfortably hot and moist.

And now he was waiting in a Beirut café for an unknown member of a rabid terrorist organisation who might, or might not, be helpful in giving him a lot of money. Or shoot him out of spite. For the hundredth time, he felt the fingers of fear and the touch of madness. The touch of a real human hand suddenly resting on his shoulder made him start; a jerking motion caused by the psychic electricity of fear.

'Professor al-Shami, how pleasant to finally meet you. Your email was a little vague as to the exact time; I hope you have not been waiting long. You can call me Faisal.'

He held out a slim brown hand. Tarek felt the sinews and muscles flexing as he shook it, feeling the underlying strength. Faisal sat down, the material of the blisteringly white kandura flowing smoothly as he crossed his legs. Dark eyes looked out from the tanned face, framed by the equally white gutra but any feeling of intimidation was allayed by the broad open smile.

'Coffee I think,' said Faisal, catching the eye of a passing waiter. 'Professor?' Tarek nodded. 'Coffee, for three please.' Tarek raised a questioning eyebrow. 'Here he comes; we call him the Bookkeeper.'

Faisal looked pointedly towards the door and Tarek followed the line of view. Limping slightly on his left side, a man wearing a smart dark grey suit was working his way slowly across the café towards their table. From the iron-grey hair but unlined face, Tarek guessed the man to be somewhere in his fifties. Probably a tedious accountant in normal life, with few interests other than money. He was wrong. In his sixties, Haroun al Rachid Quraishi had been an investment banker for many years and his capability for financial manipulation was legendary among those who knew him, or of him. But he was much more than that: fixer, broker, strategist and planner; regarded as indispensable by many in al-Qaeda. More importantly, he had the power to authorise expenditure, and knew how to wield that power very well.

'Professor al-Shami, we have something to discuss I believe.'

Without any other preamble, Quraishi sat down, sipped from the steaming coffee cup and looked at Tarek, waiting for him to speak.

'Thank you for coming at such short notice, Sir,' said Tarek, not entirely certain what to say. 'I'm sure that you are aware of the main details of our project but perhaps you would like me to elaborate.' Quraishi was shaking his head slowly. 'I have the prototype of NuCan the boot of my car which I can show you when we leave.'

Once again, the Bookkeeper was shaking his head. He lifted the cup to his lips, pausing to savour the dark sensuous aroma of the dark coffee before taking another sip. This time he spoke, the voice sonorous but filled with gravel.

'We have already looked at the device in your boot, before we came in to the café. Since it is one of Dr Malik's satanic children,' he said with a smile, 'I am confident that it will perform extremely well when put into service. What I need from you are simply figures.'

Tarek looked at him blankly, stunned and lost for words. Quraishi produced a slim laptop which started up immediately, soundlessly. He tapped quickly on the keyboard, stopped, and looked up.

'You may begin.'

6 ~ Several Threads

Soft yellow light filtered through the green foliage of overhanging trees lending the lazy flow of water a tint of molten gold. A light haze of mayflies speckled the elements, minute gluttons feeding on a banquet of algae and smaller insects, oblivious to the intruder in their midst. The four-pound monofilament line was a silver thread looping languidly through the warm still air, drifting downward to drop the Mohican Mayfly lightly on the water. As piscine lips struck the fly, John Roberts lifted the tip of the split cane rod, maintaining the tension on the line between reel and fish.

Mike watched his father play the trout, slowly reeling him in, inexorably bringing the muscular silver-brown spotted fish closer and closer. And then, slipping the net underneath, he lifted his prize from the water in a spray of diamond droplets. John turned to his son, a happy smile on his face. Mike smiled back. It had been a couple of years since they'd fished together, sharing a rod and taking it in turns. The eight foot two piece Barder had been a present to his father when John retired. At £1,800 it had not been cheap but worth every penny to see the older man's delight. Olive wood, cane and blued nickel silver metalwork, fused together in a thing of beauty to behold and, on the practical side, it was a damned fine fly rod.

'Nice work, Dad,' Mike said, clapping softly. 'At a guess, that fellow should weigh in at almost two pounds?'

'Yep, I think so too. Here.' Passing the trout-heavy net to Mike, John climbed back onto the bank. 'That makes two each. Four trout should be more than enough for lunch, don't you think?'

'Absolutely. I suspect it'll only be you, me, Mum and Ells. I doubt the kids will eat more than a morsel.'

Mike took an iki-jime spike from the creel and thrust it sharply it into the back of the motionless trout's head. He'd learned the technique on a brief sortie in Japan; the quick, humane method of dispatch had the added bonus of improving the taste. That was another thing that he'd passed on to his father. He added the fish to the bag with the other three. Meanwhile,

John had dismantled the rod, returning it to its case and packed the remaining clutter into the creel.

'Shall we?'

'I think so. I hear a gin and tonic calling.'

Side by side, they regained the path leading back through the trees, their footsteps disturbing leaf mould and twigs with their passing. They sent up a sweet damp smell that melded with the faint scent of fresh trout. Behind them they could hear the murmuring eddies of water on their way to join the River Test. Above, hidden in the branches of alder, ash, willow and oak, songbirds sang while rooks held conference. And for a while the men walked silently, revelling in the sights, sounds and smells of the woodland.

'Still enjoying your days of leisure then?'

'I haven't looked back once. At the end, before the end, I was bored with the whole business of banking; and I think it was probably bored with me. Did you know I burned all my ties?' John grinned at Mike's look of shocked surprise. 'I didn't think so. It was my mini rebellion, just for me. It was a few weeks after I retired, left the bank, I took the whole ruddy pile into the garden and threw it on the bonfire. Wonderful feeling and I haven't worn one since. I saw it as symbolically breaking their stranglehold on our lives, mine and Nessa's, sending the last vestiges of regimented drudgery up in smoke.'

'Whoa, where did that come from? I definitely approve. Good for you.'

'Yes, good for me,' he said, almost pensively, 'I sometimes wondered where you got all your fire and drive from. Thought somehow it was from Nessa's side of the family but found that after all, I had a little bit of spark myself.'

'Dad, you've done really well, all your life. OK, it might not have been the most glamorous or exciting job in the world but what you did, you did well. And you've always had a spark there; I just didn't realise the rebel was there as well!'

John paused for a moment, searching his son's face with his eyes.

'You remember Cyprus, Mike? Do you often think about that day, the bomb and all that?'

'Yeah sometimes I do. Occasionally I get this video playing in my head, full of noise and flames. It's weird but sometimes I can actually smell the smoke and hear screams. And in the half-dream I'm there but somehow removed, not involved with it properly. I do remember being scared, not understanding what had happened until much later. There was a huge fire further up the beach. Was that a café or something?'

'A beach bar.'

'Yeah. Mum said something about sardines I think. Neither of you really talked about it afterwards and back then I didn't really know, certainly didn't understand, what had happened. I knew it was very bad and that a lot of people were hurt. And Mum. Obviously I understood she was badly hurt but the fact that her arm had just disappeared didn't compute. Stuff like that doesn't when you're only six. Why do you ask?'

'Umm, I sometimes wondered whether that day on the beach sowed some kind of seed. You know, you're involved in this terror attack when you're a kid and you end up defending the country against terrorists. Your destiny and all that.'

'No,' Mike said, throwing a sideways grin at his father. 'Or maybe! I'm no psychologist, at least not in that way. They do say that what happens to you as kid can affect the rest of your life. From what the medics were saying in the hospital, I did get the shape of it, that bad people called terrorists had bombed the beach because they hated us. And I hated them back unequivocally. I remember swearing to myself on the plane that I was going to kill them all when I grew up. But that was then and I don't believe it influenced my choice of career twenty plus years later. There were other things. Russia for example. Mum's so capable with both arms that now I often forget she's only got one hand. When I look at her, I see my mother; it doesn't make me think of terrorism.'

'But isn't this new job about terrorism and terrorists?'

'Yeah, more or less. But that's nothing to do with Cyprus.'

'It's a bit of a difference though, from when you were in the army?' John persisted.

'At this stage in the game, yes. In this unit, we have more autonomy, working independently as a team on specific targets, you could say. There's a massive amount of research, surveillance, checking and rechecking, sifting through cyber haystacks of information for one tiny threaded needle that might lead to another. Then doing it all over again. Until there's a final tipping point, and someone like me shouts – GO! And then there's no difference.'

They climbed over the wooden stile, weathered grey by the years but still sturdy enough to provide the bridge between soft woodland floor and metalled road. 'The last house on the lane to Rivulet Woods', as John had often directed, was 'home to Mr and Mrs J Roberts.' In this instance, home was a two storey detached stone cottage, capped by a roof of lichened Cornish slate that looked down on a small garden ringed by a riot of early summer flowers. Tendons of ancient wisteria that had long since reached up to the eaves, relieved the gaunt limestone walls. Honeysuckle climbed wantonly around the front porch, exuding a fragrance that perfumed the entrance with sweet promise.

In the kitchen, the trout were laid out in a proud line on the granite top that ran below the leaded windows that looked out onto the garden. Eleanor and Vanessa were sitting on cushioned chairs at one end of the oval wrought iron garden table, chatting amiably. Seeing Mike at the window, his mother played an imaginary fishing rod with hand and arm, then drew a question mark in the air. He held up four fingers; she clapped silently and smiled fondly. Beyond the two women, Mark and Liz were chasing each other through the fruit trees in a manic game which required them to change direction abruptly, resulting in frequent collisions. John came into view, delivering the aforementioned gin and tonics to his wife and daughter-in-law. Mike watched carmined lips form thank you words, saw snippets of unheard conversation and heard laughter in their smiles. A wonderful family idyll that he hoped would continue for many years to come.

'The fish won't gut themselves, young man.'

'You're welcome to help,' Mike responded picking up the long slim filleting knife.

'Deferring to your expertise, I shall busy myself with the salad. One G and T Sir.'

John placed the glass on the granite, far enough away from the fish but close enough to reach. He watched as Mike deftly slipped the knife through the belly of the first trout, running the blade up from the tail to the gills. And then as his son removed the innards of the fish and rinsed the cavity under the tap.

'There's butter on the side over there and fresh fennel from the garden. Next to the Aga.' He sipped his drink. 'Cheers. It's good to see you and the family.'

'Likewise Dad.' Similarly sipping: 'Cheers. I wish it could be more often'.

'Oh we understand, but it would be nice. So is this new job likely to take you overseas much?'

Mike paused, the razor sharp blade held upwards, a poised metal exclamation mark.

'Probably. Security's strong in the UK from MI5 to the regional Specials and they do a pretty good job, in country. The Foreign Office wants our eyes on source countries like Iran, Iraq and Pakistan. That could result in action in the UK or it could mean flying out to wherever to stop the clock. That's an assumption rather than a definite but ...' Mike shrugged. 'The brief is to follow up on international leads which in turn means closer liaison with foreign agencies. That in itself indicates a modicum of travel. Operationally, as and when it happens, there'll be hit and run missions. And for those, I can count on the company of old friends.'

In that frozen moment, his words hanging in the air, Mike thought that his father looked older and more vulnerable. Moisture glistened in the older man's eyes and his lips trembled slightly before he spoke.

'Be careful, Mikey, please do be careful. You're very precious to Nessa and me.' He rubbed his eyes with his fingers, squared his shoulders and smiled. 'Don't mind me. I've been getting older since I retired and I worry more. Not that that changes the sentiment. And I should add that we're very proud of you son. Cheers.'

A soft crystal clink sounded as the two glasses touched in salute and they drank, each one looking at the other. Mike encircled his father's narrow shoulders in a brief big man hug and then held his father at arms' length.

'I love you both, you and Mum. So you two take care of each other. Remember, I'm good at my job and I've got the best guys in the world covering my back.'

'Yeah I know.'

They didn't hear the back door open; thus Vanessa found them standing in the middle of the kitchen, Mike with his hands still on his father's shoulders.

'What's this, a father son bonding session? If so, I want to join in, make it a family affair.' She put her arms around her son's waist. 'What's the old coot been talking about this time?'

'Gossiping about your affair with the Postmaster.'

'Hah! Graham Bracken's even older and uglier than him. Ghastly old lech, leers at me every time I go in there. Let me guess, John was talking work.' Releasing Mike, she peered up at their faces in turn. 'Thought so. May I point out three things to you both: one, our glasses are empty; two, it's your day off young man and work talk is off limits; and three, if those fish don't go on the grill soon, we'll all starve to death.'

Mike kissed the top of her head. 'Yes, ma'am.'

He pushed a dab of butter and a sprig of fennel inside each fish, then seasoned them with a little salt and pepper. He slipped them under the grill, went back to the window and sipped at the remains of his gin and tonic.

'Since they're both having another, d'you want a top up?'

'Yeah, why not. Then one glass of wine with lunch and that should do me. Driving back to London and all that. Going back to Cyprus, did they ever find the people responsible?'

*****

Standing in front of the glossy black door, he could see the reflection of his face smiling back at him. Somehow the door seemed bigger than he thought it would be, wider and taller. The photos he'd seen showed the whole frontage, without close-ups of specifics. Not that it really mattered. He liked the redbrick façade with its unadorned door, the entry phone pad to one side in unassuming brushed steel, without names or numbers. It was all so very – British. He pushed the silver button above the ridged speaker grill and waited.

'Good morning Mr Spiegel. Please, do come in.'

He heard a soft click, saw the door open a fraction, enough to tell him it was open. As he opened it fully and walked through into the flagged stone hall he could hear her heels on the staircase. Peripherally, he noted the paintings on the wall, each one softly lit from above; the crystal chandelier, pendant from the high ceiling and the brass coat stand in the corner. Automatically he looked down the corridor that slipped off from the far side and the closed twin oak doors, hiding the space behind. But his focus was on the lady walking down the stairs and he smiled his appreciation of the view.

The heels rapped a staccato rhythm across the floor as she walked towards him. A slight swing to the hips, down to long legs in finely tailored plum coloured trousers. Narrow waist rising to nicely proportioned breasts in a dark blue satin shirt, open at the collar and far enough down to reveal a hint of cleavage. An attractive face with just enough makeup to enhance the high cheekbones, add colour in the right places. Interesting but …

'Helen O'Connor. Welcome to the Red House.'

Her hand was silky smooth and warm, the grip firm. As they made eye contact, he felt the determination and steel behind the good looks. The smile broadened.

'Hi, Danny Spiegel. Good to meet you.'

'Tell me, do you always smile so much, Danny?'

'Only when I meet very attractive women who also have brains.'

Helen raised one eyebrow, returning his disarming smile with a mock frown. Better looking than the pictures suggested, she admitted to herself, but dangerous.

'Admiral Buller and Major Roberts are in the library.'

Opening one of the twin doors, she walked into the room with him in her wake.

'Danny Spiegel, gentlemen. Your lonely Mossad agent.'

She closed the door behind her with a firm snick as the latch engaged.

'Spiegel, good to have you here. By the sounds of it, our haughty Helen has caught you admiring her with lascivious thoughts.' They grinned at each other like naughty schoolboys. 'Don't worry, it's happened to all of us at one time or another.'

'She's not just the receptionist, I take it.'

'That would be: definitely not just the receptionist. A few years ago she could have given us all a run for our money. Anyway. Meet Major Mike Roberts. Not wanting to waste time, I suggest we go underground.'

Without waiting for an answer, Admiral Buller threw open the doors leaving Mike and Danny to catch up. Unhurriedly, the two men followed, exchanging the usual pleasantries that one does on meeting someone new and on the same level. 'Polite and friendly, but slightly wary' might have run through one's mind. Each man had read the other's file held by their own agency, seen the pictures and done their analysis. There was no need for further background questions; there was simply the here and now.

Mike noted the faded once-black cargos pushed into scuffed Dr Martens 1460s, startling red t-shirt and the well-worn old friend, a black leather biker jacket. Danny clocked the black and yellow-banded rugby shirt, washed out blue jeans and well cared for Timberlands that had seen more than a few years of use. Non-fashion statements that said a lot, and nothing. Both were clean-shaven, although Danny sported designer stubble and wore his dark blonde hair en brosse; Mike's unremarkable brown was more of a soft flop. Eyeball to eyeball, both men comfortably held the other's gaze, confident and aware. Each had the innate capability of accurately assessing the nature of either friend or foe, making split second decisions and taking immediate action. And there was that inexplicable sense of mutual respect.

Seeing the trompe l'oeil play with the lift and the still life painting of apples, Danny commented: 'How quaint!'

'Philistine!' growled the Admiral.

'Wrong tribe Sir,' retorted Danny.

The lift came softly to rest and the doors opened, admitting them to a basement that breathed electricity and light. All twelve ghosts were at their stations as before, Mike noted. The flickering screens and nimble fingers that pecked out staccato rhythms on keyboards with erratic syncopation hadn't changed. And not one of them turned or even acknowledged the presence of the intruders. One more station, a new one, was installed in front of the five screens, its curved console boasting three separate keyboards on different levels. The shadowed man in the high-backed chair looked up at the global map screen on the wall, his fingers resting lightly on the keys. Like a digital organist in an electronic church, he played the keys gently, bringing the screens to life with coloured lines that arced across the global view linking towns and cities, countries and continents.

Danny sighed, almost with pleasure: 'Tracker. The man's playing Tracker.'

The man in the chair turned, changing the glamour from momentary semblance of Phantom of the Opera to simply – John Watkins.

'Playing Tracker?' the Admiral asked, a sliver of criticism sharpening the words.

'Simulation,' said Danny. 'Tracker has a built in simulator that allows the operator to practise using the system with real data but blocks any changes or amendments. Another interesting use of the simulation mode is to let you forecast or guess what might happen 'if'.'

Danny paused as Watkins approached, glanced at Admiral Buller anticipating information but received none. He could feel himself being scrutinized, a specimen examined by a scientist in an inhuman laboratory. Watkins stopped only a few feet away and Danny found himself almost unnerved by the pallor of the man's face and those extraordinary eyes. The thin lips slipped apart, bending into Watkins' best welcoming smile.

'They told me you were coming today, Mr Spiegel. Welcome and, personally, I'm delighted that you're here.' Watkins' smile vanished as he realised that, in his enthusiasm, he'd forgotten the etiquette for greeting visitors. 'So sorry,' he stuttered, 'good morning Sir Reginald, Major. Right, umm ...'

Ignoring both unintentional slight and apology, the Admiral said: 'Morning John, young Spiegel was just saying, you were playing games with Tracker'.

'Simulations, Admiral,' Danny replied in Watkins' defence. 'As I was saying Sir, 'what if' plays can help the operator develop computer models of theoretical terrorist plans, methodology, locations and so on.'

'Absolutely,' Watkins broke in, with a quick grateful nod to Danny. 'We've been trying out some basic simulated exercises, working on country specific concerns. Since you said that one of your prime concerns was the security of nuclear weapons in Pakistan, we introduced some basic parameters such as possible locations, what other countries are interested in the technology, what groups might try to source nuclear materials. It's pretty low level at the moment, but it gets more interesting as one adds more information.'

Watkins moved back to his console, his fingers hovering over one of the keyboards.

'For example, we know that Abdul Qadeer Khan sold specialised equipment, particularly parts for high-speed centrifuges for enriching uranium and instructions, to Libya, Iran and North Korea. Khan was based here.'

A haloed green light appeared, 31 kilometres southeast of Islamabad as the crow flies; red lines arced across the screen to Tripoli, Tehran and Pyongyang. A three-dimensional boxed photograph of Qadeer Khan beamed from the screen, quickly followed by another and then two more below.

'The first is Khan himself and next, Lieutenant General Zulfiqar Khan, who was involved in Pakistan's nuclear bomb tests. Both men made millions of US dollars from the sales. Most of that happened in the 90s. But at the time, Khan also visited Saudi Arabia and Egypt, both in the market for nuclear technology; and then Sudan, Niger and several other African countries rich in uranium.'

Blue and then green lines arced across from Khan's Kahuta base.

'Abdul Qadeer Khan is under house arrest and Zulfiqar Khan has denied allegations that he received money but that doesn't mean they're totally out of the picture. Although there's no actual proof, there is a distinct possibility that they also connected with al-Qaeda and, perhaps the Taliban.' A green haze misted the border between Afghanistan and Pakistan, a similar one over Sudan. Then like electronic missiles, green lines fired off to New York, London, Jeddah and Dubai. 'According to a CIA field agent, Khan got religion after the nuclear tests in the late 90s which might underpin an association with al-Qaeda.'

'These two jokers are even more interesting,' Watkins said, making the two lower photos shine. 'The one on the left is Dr Sami Malik, one of Qadeer Khan's protégés; joined the Kahuta facility back in the mid to late 80s. He has strong connections with Tehran and frequently attends parties at the Embassy in Islamabad and the Consulate in Lahore. His brother-in-arms on the left is General Pamir Mustagh, retired but with more connections than the national grid. In a way, he's linked with Zulfiqar Khan and the testing sites. Although there's no actual evidence, there have been suggestions that these two have taken a more lucrative commercial route, turning out non-nuclear, high grade arms to order. So what we have is ...'

'Is what? Exactly?' asked Admiral Buller tetchily. 'Seems to me that what we have is a lot of coloured lines whizzing around a map like an electronic version of Cat's Cradle. You put up what we already know!'

'Yes, and no,' said Danny. 'What John's showing us is the template, based on what we know and it can be used to try and second guess what might, or will, happen. What happens in real time is the constant feed from field agents of names, addresses, telephone numbers, flights taken to where and when. The operators, your ghosts, feed in relevant keywords that are picked up, phrases that link one point with another. Tracker cross references all this information, builds up files, profiles and then presents itself with questions and suggestions. And gives us answers!

'Let me give you an example of what we've done with the information we have on one of al-Qaeda's more senior players. His cover name is Abu al-Qatari; real name Abu bin Musa al Kassab. We have one address for him in Gaza City, but we also know he uses an apartment in Cairo. Once those basic details were fed into the system, Tracker automatically searched through a mountain range of communications, checked them against border control lists, hotels, banking houses etcetera. Tracker mapped out many of his movements along a given dateline, details of people he was in contact with on the way. Now we're looking at a growing network of people and places which present various levels of security risk. If anything overheats, Tracker red flags the situation, providing an assessment and detailed information.

'At the beginning, our people just threw in anything and everything that we had on file and we overloaded the system. Tracker bogged down under the weight of information that had no pattern. So, we identified key names, stripped the system back to bone and now it's running like a cheetah. I don't know how far you've got but it looks as though you've made good start. Following the Pakistan lines are fine with the links that you have but I think you need to look outside the box.'

'In what way?' asked Watkins, looking for all the world like a German Shorthaired Pointer on point.

'Think of connections that would concern you: possible targets, abnormalities, unusual conversations, odd communications …'

'I think,' said the Admiral, breaking Danny's flow, 'I think that the two of you should continue this meaningful exchange of ideas. Develop the mutual technological attraction that you so clearly enjoy. From a personal point of view, my lungs are crying out for a relaxing smoke and, by the looks of the man, Mike is suffering severe caffeine withdrawal. And although I have absolutely no idea where this is going, you clearly have.

'When you've finished canoodling over systems analysis Danny, we'll probably be in the library. Otherwise ask Helen. Then lunch I think. Major?'

'That's fine Sir. I shouldn't be that long but I would just like to talk John through a few more things …'

The Israeli stopped, realising that he was talking to the Admiral's diminishing rear. He looked at Mike who was just about to follow his superior. Mike shrugged and grinned.

'You don't have to like it. But you can learn how to live with it. Catch you later.'

And then there were two. Looking at John Watkins, Danny wasn't entirely certain that the man even realised that the other two men had left.

'Talking about thinking outside the box, I did think that that's what we were doing but do know what you mean about getting bogged down Mr Spiegel.'

'Sorry, what?'

'Thinking outside the box Mr Spiegel.'

'Right. Call me Danny, please. And can I call you John? Fine. Let's do this.'

'Sorry, do what?'

'Brainstorm.'

Forty minutes later John Watkins had two pages covered with notes, written in neat letters and numbers. A list of key words and phrases stretched down one side, tied into categories that tracked down the other side. A short list of names, each one annotated with basic details including location and links. Then Watkins considered content and metadata, opined on internet protocols and IP addresses, touched on cyber security and hacking. He raised points on the comparative usefulness of SIGINT as opposed to COMINT and the sheer volume of information involved. And by now, Danny was starting to fall by the wayside.

'There's a vast river of content and metadata in flood, flowing through over 1,000 high-capacity cables into the UK all the time. The precise figures are an ascending variable but, working on the basis that each cable has a capacity of ten gigabytes per second and GCHQ taps a quarter of the flow, that provides a throughput of around 20 petabytes of information every day. Allegedly that equates to churning out the British Library's total collection 192 times, every day. Putting the unfamiliar petabyte in an office context, one petabyte of data is equivalent to the contents of 20 million four-drawer filing cabinets filled with text. Extraordinary.

'Of course, the systems at GCHQ automatically harvest only the most interesting information from the flow. Even if that's only one per cent of the total, that would still be 200,000 gigabytes per day. And then they have to be analysed, discarded or filed for further action. It's a massive task, which means that everything takes time and there's often a delay in transmission.'

Danny held up his hand to put the other man on pause.

'John, stop. You're not meant to be one of the rooks waiting for road kills; you're the bloody falcon that drops like a bolt from the sky to nail the tastiest duck on the wing. Tracker needs to be used like a sniper's rifle, not a blunderbuss. Rather than wait to see what drops into your box, interrogate the source, interrogate

GCHQ's databases. How many people have you got on Tracker so far?'

'At the moment?' Watkins punched the numbers on a different keyboard, clicked on a folder, opened an Excel file. 'Seven hundred and sixty three.'

'Does that include people like the two Khans?'

'Yes.'

'Kill them off. Sorry, sign them down as inactive. Don't delete them, put them to sleep. Qadeer Khan's out of the play and, to all intents and purposes, so is Zulfiqar Khan. Neither one has shown up on anyone's radar for years. Go through every name you have up there and check what you have. If it's just a name and some history without recent leads or data, put them to sleep. Names that connect with recent stuff, interesting but assessed as low risk, keep them open on a watching brief. By a watching brief, I mean they need frequent checks but set Tracker to do that on auto with notifications on live.

''Kay. Initially, I'd try to get the numbers right down to, umm, say 60 names. Twelve ghosts get five names apiece; drill into what GCHQ has, mine data, harvest information and append. Look for fragments and then try to connect the dots. Find out the name of the operational officer running agents in your target location. That might be a plural John. Intelligence is unlikely to spit those up easily but MI6 should be comfortable with being the interface. I'm happy to share as long as you reciprocate. I'll ratify that with the Admiral later but I'm sure he'll be cool with that.

'So let's start, right now. You have a VoIP system running from here, like Skype, but your own secure version?'

'Of course.'

'We have Dr Malik on a live watch list because Sami's always so busy going from here to there. He's one fat little slippery eel is our Sami Malik. So far we haven't been able to hook him for anything specific and he manages to claim diplomatic immunity with ease wherever he goes. Let me call Aaron at the Office in Tel Aviv.'

Moments later, Danny was looking at his assistant looking back at him from the computer screen. Aaron Levi blinked at him through round steel rimmed spectacles, unspeaking, seated in front of a bland vanilla wall which could have been in a room anywhere in the world. Leaning forward as though to hear better, his round moon face filled most of the screen.

'Danny?'

'Yo Aaron.'

Aaron's face broke into one big smile, showing the gap in his top row of teeth where an incisor used to sit. He liked to claim that he'd lost it to a Palestinian bullet, a ricochet from a wall in Ramallah.

'Danny, good to see you. How's Legoland doing?'

'Still there I guess, but I'm at the Red House with a techie called John Watkins. He's getting Tracker up and running but he needs to strip back and drip feed.'

'Why does that sound familiar? Rhetorical. What do you need?'

'John's already got the history on Dr Sami Malik with background but no live or recent data. Be a hero, access the file and give me the latest updates.'

Aaron's head bent downwards, giving a glimpse of the bald patch whose area was slowly increasing with the years. Straightening up he looked at another screen to his right; Danny could hear him typing on the unseen keyboard. He turned back within view of the webcam on top of the first screen.

'Be up in a couple of minutes. I've just asked the file to update itself and create a summary report.'

'How's it going over there?' asked Danny, filling in time.

'Busy, as ever. We're picking up on comms and internet through flow but most of it's cheap junk. You know how it is: you know what the needle looks like and you know it's in a haystack ...'

'... but when you're looking at a 1,000 acre farm, you know you need luck,' Danny completed. 'You there yet?'

'It's coming up now.' Aaron twisted the webcam towards the other screen. 'Can you still hear me?'

'No worries. We can see the screen but it's too small to read from this end.'

'If necessary, I'll zoom in. At the moment he's in Lahore but he has been moving around. About a month or so ago he flew to Tehran and was there for several days. That's not too unusual, but from there he went to Beirut. There's no indication who he saw there or why he went. Immigration shows that he flew in to Beirut in the morning but left for Dubai in the afternoon. My money would be that he had a prearranged meeting with someone from Hezbollah, maybe not Hassan Nasrallah himself or Naim Qassem, but someone close to the top. Wait a moment, he ordered a taxi in advance with a fairly new company, Beirut Airport Transfer and was collected from arrivals. The taxi took him to a restaurant in town called La Paillote. That's … looks as though it's on the seafront, north Beirut. You want me to follow up?'

'If we've got a Lebanese in Beirut at the moment, maybe. I think that you're probably right but if so, he's either playing middleman for Tehran or running his own line. Given that Tehran's already supplying 100s of ex-Soviet Katyusha rocket variants and other equipment, what pitch could Malik make? It's possible that he could have another client, from Lebanon or elsewhere and Beirut was simply a useful meeting point. What about Dubai?'

'Nothing useful really. Stayed at the Hyatt Regency for two nights and a Dubai agent walked him to the gold souk in Deira. There's precious little more, excuse the pun, but it appears that he was purchasing gold bullion in kilo bars. Maybe ten or twelve. Small change for a man like Malik. Then back to Lahore. That's it. Does John want Malik's telephone numbers and email address?'

'Ping them over for reference but I doubt if they can use them apart from identifying incoming communications. Listen, let me know if you have anything more. I'll be with these guys for most of the day. I'll be back in the warmth in a couple of days. Thanks Aaron.'

'No problem Boss. Catch you later.'

The VoIP box went black, and then vanished from the screen entirely.

'Less than I thought I'm afraid John, but there are a few starting points.'

'No need to worry, you've given me plenty to think about, and do. As you say, stripping back and all that will give us more than enough work for the moment.'

Danny looked at his watch pointedly, said that he really ought to rejoin Admiral Buller and Mike. Watkins walked him over to the lift, thanked him profusely for his time and assistance. And would it be all right if they kept in touch, it would be so useful. Danny fell into the lift, sighing only once the doors had closed. As it began to ascend, he rested his head against the wood veneer and closed his eyes. At the ground floor, the lift came to a halt with a soft jerk, bringing Danny back to full alert. Doors open, he walked along the corridor and found the two men chatting in the hall.

'Lunch Danny? I suspect you deserve it young man. John Watkins is a fine engineer and technician but he does have an amazing capacity for boring the socks off one. However, I'm sure you've been a great deal of help, so thank you. Right, what do you think Mike, take him to The Speaker?'

'Why not? Five minutes walk to a pub with good cask beers and excellent beef sandwiches. What more could a man ask for?'

'A large glass of Pinot Grigio and a Caesar salad?'

Roars of laughter and derision. The Speaker was indeed only a few minutes away, on the corner of Great Peter Street and Perkin's Rents. The dark green façade and wood framed windows with the name written in gold lettering announced a pub with no frills, in the old way. And as the name might have implied, ignoring the parliamentary reference to nearby Westminster, it was a pub for speaking without music, fruit machines or pendant television screen. Under protest, Danny ordered a rare beef sandwich and a pint of Shepherd Neame's Bishops Finger.

Although there were quite a few people already there, they found a table by the window. The hum of conversation waxed and waned around the small pub, flowing round them in a complex soup of comment, opinion, fact and pure fiction. Two men in suits trying to impress the brunette woman in a suit, her high heels spiking out from her trousers against their flat heeled brogues. A gale of overloud laughter, peeling from two girls by the bar, each bent over with the covert hilarity.

Fragments of sentences overlaid half mentioned phrases, interrupted by coughs or a giggle. But if one listened carefully, information was there to be had.

'According to the Minister, it would be possible to change the order of the bill if it was done at source, before it went to the Commons. Dickheads on the benches wouldn't have a clue. Treasury bonds ...'

'... arrested for selling passports and papers apparently ... seeking residency. Police found a whole stack of them ... yes, in chambers.'

'... Rayworth received £18,000 a month in consultancy fees and never did a bloody thing ... Absolutely not, he was either shooting or sailing or fucking someone else's wife. I saw him myself, all over Janet Hampton in a hotel in Salisbury. Steve Hampton's wife? Salisbury, when he was meant to be sorting the York deal!'

Walls having ears and windows two-way vision, Messrs Buller, Roberts and Spiegel let their own lives rest in the privacy of their minds. They talked inconsequentially about travel and sport, sandwiches and beer. A book, that film, his car, her perfume, some chef who'd won another Michelin star and that ludicrous new installation announced by the Tate. Words ping-ponged across the table, bouncing lightly between the three men, until their short lives expired in the warm air.

Danny heard his phone emit a single tone, dulled by the leather of his jacket. He pressed the power button as he retrieved it, watched the small screen glow up to life and noted a single new text. Danny scanned it quickly, reread it and smiled grimly.

'I think Watkins will be rather pleased,' he said, and passed the cellphone to Admiral Buller.

'Malik guest of IslamLebProf@AUB Tarek al-Shami. Have telno&email. Will send seprt. Marina says u owe her.'

'I think we've just found a nasty little connection,' said Danny.

7 ~ Dominoes

Tarek stared intently at the message, black sans serif letters against the stark white background. The sender's address looked the same: that same string of letters and numbers. He'd never played the Loto Libanais but he knew how it worked with the numbered balls and Tarek felt he was looking at a winning sequence. With the anxious desperation of a Loto player unable to believe that he just might, possibly and incredibly, have won the big prize, Tarek compared the address with the last email that he'd received. They matched, exactly, sequentially and precisely.

> To: Professor al-Shami <talshami@gmail.com>
> From: QQ <ag49iut8zxg68so3@tormail.net>
> Subject: Your Prize

> Congratulations! You've won today's jackpot. To collect, please confirm once you have ordered your gifts and we will transfer the money. Your winnings will cover all of the outgoing capital costs and expenses. Magic bonuses will be held for you on account, to be transferred when the first gift is opened! Please note that hedge plays are only payable in the event of the game being compromised. Good luck!

Even the text was similar, and yet totally different. The first part seemed to make sense, indicating that al-Qaeda would fund all the operational costs. But 'magic bonuses'? Did that mean they'd only pay after the first successful explosion? And 'hedge plays' sounded more like insurance policies rather than payments. Without actual figures, Tarek had no idea what amounts were involved, nor could he solve what seemed to be a cryptic riddle.

He took his coffee out to the balcony and peered into the early morning mist that rose from Beirut River in the valley below. There was a chill in the damp air seeping from a monochrome sky that held little promise of immediate sunshine. And then a single ray of light pierced through the low cloud, a momentary spotlight on the road below before it was switched off again. A mental metaphor made manifest, he thought. The alliterations ground together like the cogs of an ancient machine. It didn't make sense. His initial elation on reading the email had been quenched by the impenetrability of the content; light without definition where shadows held sway.

The meeting with the Bookkeeper had clearly gone well and the figures that Tarek had provided had been provisionally accepted. Now he had an email that confirmed acceptance, he was elated and excited but confused and perhaps slightly afraid. Just knowing that the money was available was a drug far more powerful than hashish; the immense power it bestowed, more intoxicating yet. But he knew that once he set the wheels in motion, there was no going back without punishment, even if there were brakes that could be applied. All the more reason for caution and secrecy. Shivering now with the damp chill, Tarek returned to his laptop.

> To: QQ <ag49iut8zxg68so3@tormail.net>
> From: Professor al-Shami <talshami@gmail.com>
> Subject: Re: Your Prize
>
> Clarification and breakdown? Meet?

Looking at what he'd just sent, Tarek realised that he would have to be more careful. In some subliminal way, he knew that the Tormail address was anonymous and something to do with the deep web. Beyond that he had no idea or understanding of what he saw as arcane cyber skills belonging to a gifted few. He made a mental note to create alternative addresses, perhaps another less obvious address with Gmail and one with Hotmail. Use other computers as well as the one in the apartment; the one in his office at the University was obviously not a sensible option. A cheap pay-as-you-go mobile phone would be useful as well, he thought. But at the moment, what he had in situ would have to suffice.

> To: Amin Masri <amasri@ifl.co.uk>, Alan Abbot <aabbott85@yahoo.co.uk>,

From: Professor al-Shami <talshami@gmail.com>
Subject: NuCan Update

Hi Amin & Alan

Good news. Can confirm that our private bankers have now given their agreement to finance the NuCan food container project.

Following my visit to our manufacturer's production facility, I am pleased to say that they have engineered an inactive prototype to be checked for dimensions and weight etc. Their chief engineer asked me to pass on his compliments to you Alan in respect of the extremely high level of design and drawings; SM/AK seriously impressed. Prototype on its way to you tomorrow to be delivered to the house via courier and should arrive by the end of this week. Tomorrow also, sending further details of perceived responsibilities as previously discussed, now updated; Alan yours to arrive with model NuCan; Amin, yours by airmail packet. Have also suggested meeting in Cambridge next month; details enclosed with letters. Naturally it's important to discuss developments/options well in advance of testing. Please check diaries and confirm.

In passing, believe that your contract tendering meeting is tomorrow Amin? Good luck and hope for a positive outcome.

Best regards Tarek

Rereading what he'd written, he gave a nod of approval and hit the send key. He could hear movement in the kitchen, the sound of coffee being poured into a mug, a throaty but somehow sexy cough. Ayesha had turned up late on the previous evening, declared she was shattered and crashed for the night in the spare room. The cough reminded him of the brief, unexpected encounter in the afternoon with an attractive mature student. She'd said she wanted his comments on the sexual rights of women under Shari'ah Law. He thought they might have had a brief conversation but his memory excluded sound in favour of vision. Her jeans formed a second skin over lithe legs that ended in high-heeled sandals; an equally skin-tight t-shirt followed the contours of her small breasts, down across her flat stomach. It

155

had been difficult not to stare and be slightly aroused; and he'd been caught, seen the brief smile of amused triumph. Then she'd coughed, with that same throatiness that reminded him of Ayesha. Tarek remembered apologising, that it really wasn't his field but perhaps another time, on another subject.

'Khallas, enough!' he said in self-admonishment.

A one-off, pointless conversation, he told himself. He had weightier matters to consider. Another email appeared at the top of the list on his screen.

> To: Professor al-Shami <talshami@gmail.com>
> From: QQ <ag49iut8zxg68so3@tormail.net>
> Subject: Re: Re: Your Prize
>
> Agreed. Café same same as last;
> noon tomorrow. Assume attendance.

'Good,' he said quietly.

Shutting down the system, he watched, waiting for the screen to darken and the lights to fade. As he waited his thoughts drifted back to the woman and he could feel her hand on his arm. He could almost imagine touching the silken skin of her naked thigh underneath the blue denim.

'Tarek, you want more coffee?'

'Damn you,' he muttered softly.

If he remembered rightly, her name was Marina, or something like that.

*****

Aaron Levi had been as good as his word, sending through the information to Danny in an encrypted email. He showed the printout to Mike before passing it on to John Watkins who, in turn and a little later, passed it on to Tristan Smythe-Corton for processing. In a rather offhand way he reminded the pallid three-month old ghost that a corresponding link needed to be made with the system at GCHQ to enable the feed into Tracker. Naturally, Tristan had put the sheet of paper at the bottom of his 'Action' pile in the wire tray to the left of his desk.

Tristan had a very basic mental flow chart for what he called 'robotically processed jobs' or RPJs for short: paper information was taken from the Action tray on the left, moved to the keyboard at centre for inputting, digitising and system processing. From there, the original piece of paper was moved to the 'Completed' tray on the right of the desk which, at varying times of the day, was spirited off in toto for filing, somewhere. Tristan firmly believed that RPJs were beneath him, that they should either be carried out by worker drones or properly automated. Needless to say that he had been recruited from the hive at GCHQ for his analytical abilities rather than dreary logical process or social graces.

Nevertheless, Aaron's email had finally risen to the top of Tristan's pile and he had grudgingly typed the information into the relevant boxes. The ghost checked the details, his eyes flicking from screen to paper and back again, confirming consensus.

Name: Professor Tarek al-Shami. Age: 42 n/c. Weight: 66kg. Height: 1.77m. Eyes: Brown. Hair: Dark Brown. Location: Mansourieh, Mt Lebanon; American University of Beirut. Email: <talshami@gmail.com> & <ptalshami@aub.edu.lb>. Mansourieh Tel: +961 4 533940; AUB dir: +961 1260103 x2; Lb Mob: +961 70 660057. Bank account: Byblos Bank, Hamra Street, Beirut; A/c no 0795859931076; IBAN LB17003900000000795859931076. Car: Honda Civic – black. Reg No: G155812 Liban.

Comments: for backgrounder see attached CV as per HR @ AUB. Also found on lb/LinkedIn – resume. Siblings x1 female: Ayesha al-Shami. NFA but often stays at the Mansourieh apt. Tarek al-Shami is a slim handsome man, definitely attractive to both men and women. He, clearly attracted to women but unsure of himself and does not take the lead even with green light. No known current partner. Hypothetical - possibly attracted to sister in sexual way given over-close relationship with dependency clearly on his side. Might indicate something in background/childhood. Weak area; probably open to sexual manipulation. No indication of gay interest or activity. Does not drink alcohol in accordance with religion but does have reliance on hashish, usually smoked as hash/tobacco mix with nargile. Hashish sourced privately Beqaa Valley. Highly intelligent but prone to lecturing (part of the job!) and dogmatism especially in area of specialisation. Given al-Shami is Prof regarding Shari'ah and Islamic studies, mosque attendance is erratic. Frequent travel on university business; Islamic seminars, conferences etc. 'Religious' ambassador for AUB. Father, Najib al-Shami had proven connections with PLO, PFLP and Hezbollah. NaS now retired; no recent activity. No evidence to suggest that TaS has connections with Palestinian organisations or any fundamentalist groups. Ayesha al-Shami is active and already has open file with Tel Aviv. Only unusual link: Dr Sami Malik, Pakistan nuclear physicist with possible arms sales. Only known joint activity: [social] lunch at La Paillote, Beirut. (See file and connect.)

Current assessment on Tarek al-Shami: low risk with no current evidence for growth.

Confident that all the data provided had been input correctly, Tristan keyed in the codes to allow Tracker to absorb and compute all the information to its own inhuman specification. And then sat back to watch the extraordinary visual vortex that dragged everything away from the front of the screen. At this moment, he always felt that he was feeding some electromechanical cyber monster, looking down a revolving black oesophagus towards the belly of the beast.

He'd been intrigued by the sexual psychobabble that had appeared in the comments section and wondered how the writer had come to her conclusions. It was clearly a woman after all, he supposed. Tristan wondered vaguely who she was, what she was like. He looked at the box at the top of the sheet. It read: 'Ex Marina AgLbRgn'. Lebanese region agent, perhaps? Then Tristan read the words scribbled next to the name: Deus ex Machina.

Tristan Smythe-Corton smiled broadly with delighted appreciation at the word play.

'Ex Marina, Deus ex machina,' he pronounced gleefully. 'Perfect, quite perfect.'

With that, Tristan triumphantly moved the piece of paper from the centre to the right hand side of his desk, placing it ceremoniously into the Completed tray. Promptly forgetting to effect the link with GCHQ's systems, he decided it was time for a cup of tea.

*****

Henry Perkins grimaced as Amin accelerated, flicking out into the fast lane and booted the black Range Rover past a green Audi Quattro, itself running at over 90mph. He tried to concentrate on the details of the passing scenery but saw only a blur of green and brown streaked with grey. Henry Perkins heaved a sigh of relief at the sight of the blue and white sign indicating the slip road that led off the M275 spur, down to Portsmouth's continental ferry terminal roundabout. Only half a mile to go, he thought, only half a mile. Grinning mischievously, Amin picked up the speed again, threading his way through the traffic to finally cut across the nose of a Czech registered articulated flatbed to pick up the slip, braking hard on the way down. Henry Perkins shook his head in despair.

'One of these days you will succeed in killing me. And I will come back and bloody well haunt you.'

'No you won't, you'll be far too busy working out the logistics of transporting celestial vats of milk and honey and making it profitable.'

It was a common enough exchange between the two men and quickly left behind as they switched into workspeak.

'So what do you think? Rubber stamping or more hoops?'

'I think it'll be a bit of both,' replied Amin as he pulled out into the roundabout. 'All the paperwork from the MoD has been completed, we've done the due diligence, they've got the references and we fit the bill. If you think about it, there aren't many companies in the UK, or elsewhere for that matter, that have built up a rep for doing what we've done. Sure some of it might have been gimmicky, but it does prove we can do. The only thing that hasn't been done is for them to make a physical site visit. For my money, I think we should be home and dry.

But, there's always a but. We'll see what they say. Who are we seeing again?'

Amin filtered right, following the signage to HM Naval Base Portsmouth and Portsmouth Historic Dockyard. Crossing Flathouse Road, he pulled up behind a white Ford Transit in the short queue that was moving through Trafalgar Gate.

'Captain John Halliday and Lieutenant Commander Jane Logie.'

The Transit drove onto the base and Amin moved up to the barrier.

'Morning Sir. Do you have a pass?'

'We have a meeting with Captain Halliday and Lieutenant Commander Logie.'

The marine checked his roster.

'Mr Masri and Mr Perkins from International Foods.' He peered at them through Amin's open window, looked back at his roster and ticked off the names. 'Here to improve naval cuisine I hope.' He grinned at his own joke but didn't pause. 'Bear left at the first roundabout and then straight over two more. When you've passed Dock number eight on your right, take the second left and they're on the left. You'll see old Victory berthed up a little further down the road.'

A few minutes later, another marine was checking their reasons for being, this time in the lobby of Victory Buildings. He made a similar culinary joke to the first before handing them over to a stern looking sublieutenant who clearly took her role as a guardian of the higher ranks very seriously. After inspecting the two men with no small degree of suspicion and a terse 'follow me', she led them up the stairs to a door marked Boardroom Two. Sublieutenant Wendell rapped her knuckles on the wood before opening the door and announcing them to the unseen naval officers.

'Mr Masri of InterFoods, I hope?'

Captain John Halliday had a smile on his face and an outstretched hand in welcome. The grip was firm and honest; instinctively Amin liked him immediately.

'Indeed. And this is my works manager, Henry Perkins.'

'In turn, Lieutenant Commander Jane Logie. Jane's my mentor in this instance. She outranks me in knowledge when it comes to MoD contracts. Please.'

Captain Halliday waved vaguely at the long table and attendant seats. Taking his own indication he walked around the end of the table, sat down and waited for the other three to follow suit. They'd barely settled in their seats before the Captain was on his feet bellowing down the corridor for Wendell and coffee.

'Or tea?' he asked, turning his head back towards the room. Getting unspoken negatives, he returned to his seat.

'Gentlemen, welcome to Her Majesty's naval base in Portsmouth and thank you for coming. And thank God it's not raining which is a nice change. After nine months at sea in the Gulf, it's a little strange to be back on terra firma.'

'In command of ship?' Amin asked politely.

'Yes. HMS Monmouth. Doing our bit with Combined Task Force 150 to maintain security on the high seas. We sailed back after the last change of Task Force command in April when Pakistan took the lead. Rear Admiral Shahid Iqbal took over from Commodore Hank Ort who commands the Netherlands Maritime Force. Chubby fella with a double chin and lots of gongs on his chest. Shahid that is. Two and a half million square miles from the Arabian Gulf to the Horn of Africa to patrol.'

'Which would account for the tan?'

'You got it,' said Halliday laughing. 'Anyway, to business.' He opened the folder lying on the table in front of him. The door opened. Sublieutenant Wendell placed cups of coffee, milk and sugar on the table and departed. Captain Halliday didn't miss a beat and kept talking. 'This contract would run under the Overseas Deployable Food Programme for a term of five years with the possibility of two single year on year extensions subject to approval. The anticipated maximum value to be £120,000,000: the cost of food accounting for approximately 30 per cent of that figure and non-food costs such as logistical and sourcing capabilities to account for the remaining 70 per cent. Jane, do you want to go into more detail?'

Up to this point, Lieutenant Commander Jane Logie had maintained a pleasantly plastic smile on her unmade-up but not unattractive face. Being allowed to speak brought life to her eyes and colour to her cheeks as though the on switch had just been pushed.

'Yes Captain, thank you.'

'Ah, let's keep it tight Lieutenant Commander, shall we?'

'Sir. I was just going to add a brief breakdown. Umm, the supply is likely to include, but not specified in advance, fresh, ambient, chilled and frozen products from a range of some 1,000 core lines which number could be variable subject to location and requirement. For example, fresh vegetables and salads might include onions, carrots, spinach, leeks …'

'I think both gentlemen are well aware of what fresh vegetables and salads are. And I'm sure that they don't need to be told the difference between a can of tuna, a lump of cheddar and ten pork sausages!'

'Sir, I was just …'

'Wasn't it your outfit that delivered cans of beef stroganoff and small flasks of vodka to the team of marines that skied across Antarctica last year?' Captain Halliday asked, cutting straight across his subordinate.

'Yes Captain,' Amin replied, smiling at the memory.

'I loved that one. It had definite appeal. Who commissioned that order?'

'I think it was an Admiral. Would it be Sir Reginald Buller?'

'Could be. I thought he'd retired. Although there was a rumour that … never mind. Yes I could see Admiral Buller doing something like that. Anyway. Back to business. Using the Antarctica supply as an initial premise, I presume that you can confirm that you would be able to maintain supply in all reasonable circumstances including to a theatre of war? And that you could react immediately to urgent needs?'

'Due to the nature of the business, InterFoods has teams working on rotation 24/7,' Henry responded, picking up the operational thread. 'We pride ourselves on being able to promise our clients that we will respond to requests at any time of the day or night. Frequently that's simply a case of covering time differences. Ho Nguyen in Hanoi wants to place an order at 09.00 his time? No problem, even though Vietnam is five hours ahead of us and it's a cold and dark four o'clock over here. On a more serious note, we do, and have, covered emergencies and urgent needs. But then some of those were cited in our tender, which I'm sure that both of you have read.'

Lieutenant Commander Logie looked at her superior expectantly, her large eyes almost moist with anticipation; the spaniel aching to go to work. Captain Halliday nodded; Lieutenant Commander Jane Logie smiled her grateful thanks. Captain Halliday yawned.

'So gentlemen, if I could quickly work through your tender with you both, checking details and so forth. Just to cover that last point in a bit more depth, operational requirements can take ships into unforeseen situations, and those ships may be carrying marines who will be deployed on land, possibly in remote areas. In the instance where there is an urgent need for medical resupplies, which is not infrequently the case, you could comply and are happy to have that in your remit?'

'If, Lieutenant Commander, you're asking whether we could drop medical supplies into the middle of a firefight, the answer would be no,' answered Amin. 'I have an aversion to being the target for bullets, RPGs and surface-to-air missiles. But we would get as close as we could. I believe we have mentioned one such instance when we dropped medical supplies by helicopter.'

Logie coloured, looked down at her paperwork. Captain Halliday frowned.

'My apologies Mr Masri, I must have missed that particular item. If then we can continue with the more mundane issues of transport.'

For next 45 plus minutes, they went over company history and finances, equipment, vehicles, production lines and staffing. Logie ran through legislation from equal opportunities to health and safety, not forgetting recruitment processes, holiday pay and maternity leave as subsets. Then she went though a summary, with explanatory paragraphs as necessary, of all of the various forms required by the MoD to ensure compliance with compliance requirements.

'Is there anything that you would like to add Captain Halliday? Or cover anything that I've missed?'

'I think you've covered everything perfectly adequately Lieutenant Commander.'

'Thank you Sir. In that case, as far as I can see, it is unlikely that there will be any objections to your tender gentlemen. The final decision will of course be taken by Whitehall and before that, we will need to make a visit to your main facility which, I believe is not too far from here?'

'It's about half an hour's drive. You're welcome any time but obviously I would like to be there personally for any inspection.'

'Of course. Let me get back to you this afternoon. Once I've checked with compliance, I'll email a few dates and times. Finally do you have any questions that we haven't answered?'

'Just one, I think. Going back to emergency response, I assume that we would be given details of shipping routes, individual ship's scheduled deployment and locations? That would enable us to put our local agents on notice as well as being able to track ships to allow optimum response times.'

Amin was barely aware of the nervous tic that fluttered in the corner of his right eye. Both naval officers were concentrating on other things; neither noticed.

'That information would be made available to you after confirmation of your appointment on an assessed need-to-know basis,' said Logie. 'And we would ask you to sign the Official Secrets Act on behalf of the company, its directors and employees.'

'Thank you.'

'In that case, I think we can call it a day,' announced Captain Halliday, getting to his feet. 'Mr Masri, Mr Perkins. Thank you again for coming today. I believe that this has been a fruitful meeting and I'm sure that we will be meeting in the future. Good luck. But I doubt that you'll need it. I'm sure the mandarins of Whitehall will approve the appointment.'

Amin walked out into the sunshine with Henry Perkins, neither saying a word. But once they were both back in the Range Rover, the two men looked at each other, big grins blossoming on their faces.

'I think that went rather well Boss, don't you?'

'I think it did Henry, I think it did.'

Less than half an hour later, Amin dropped Henry off at the factory before heading off home. His mind was buzzing with information, observations and questions, but there was one thought that rose recurrently to the surface of the cauldron: he hoped that Captain John Halliday would not be commanding any of the ships on their hit list. Twenty minutes later, Amin was turning in through the gates and onto the gravel in front of the house. Sophie was obviously out: her beloved dark blue Mercedes SLK250 convertible was not in its normal nest, nose pointing out of the garage to the side.

As soon as his key hit the lock, he could hear claws sliding on granite as the dogs dashed to be first at the door. Jemila and Borak hurtled past him and around to the garden, barking joyously at their temporary freedom.

'Well, how nice of you to say hello,' Amin shouted after them, smiling fondly.

Their barks of welcome drifted back on the breeze. In the kitchen, he found a note propped up against a tall glass containing a single large sunflower.

Cherie
Suzette phoned to say she was bored and needed someone with whom to have lunch. Since you were at the Navy meeting, I thought, why not? Alors, it is 12.45 now and I am just leaving. We will be at the True Lovers Knot in Tarrant Keyneston. If you are at home by 14.00, come to join us. Otherwise I will see you later. Back by 15.30 latest. Promise! Hope it went well.
Je t'aime   Sophie xxx

Amin glanced at his watch: quarter to two. It wasn't worth driving the 35 plus minutes across to Tarrant Keyneston for the pleasure of listening to Suzette Fullerton moan how bored she was because Trevor was away for two weeks. Trevor was in oil, a consultant of some sort, which meant that he was frequently away. In turn, that meant Suzette was an oil widow with the same frequency. During those periods of separation, she indulged in an on/off affair with an athletic tennis coach ten years her junior, shopped even more indulgently and shared her woes with close friends. That is, anyone who was prepared to listen. As both women were French nationals, Suzette regarded Sophie as her closest confidante and his wife did not have the heart to refuse. Provided that Suzette was paying and she, Sophie, could choose the venue.

In the shared study, he switched on his computer, watching as the wide screen quickly came to life. A well-ordered column of little blue folders lined up on the right while a long row of little icons scrambled for room across the bottom of the screen. Opening up his browser, he clicked through the links to his company email address and into his inbox. Immediately he was presented with the list of unread incoming emails in bold type. He deleted a number without even opening them, knowing they were nothing but unwanted marketing messages; starred a few for later perusal and opened a few more. It wasn't until he got towards the bottom of the list that he spotted Tarek's email, addressed to Alan as well, with the words NuCan Update in the subject line.

'Shit,' he muttered, not really wanting to open it, knowing he must. He was very aware that a part of him had hoped that Tarek's plan would drift away or disappear like dirty water down a drain. Amin clicked on the foreshortened message, enabling the full text to expand into view. He scan-read the message once and then read it properly, more slowly.

'He's got the money and he's got a prototype! It's starting. May Allah protect us all. Allahu akbar!'

*****

He'd got the same table at the Bluebird Café, the one he'd sat at for the first time with two members of al-Qaeda. Then he was asking for funding, now he wasn't sure. Like last time, he looked through the glass of the window, smeared with that ubiquitous oil and dust mix that today had been borne by an overheated wind. Outside, the young covered their eyes with Ray-Bans, Oakleys and other designer sunglasses; a hand or a scarf sufficed to cover noses and mouths. Others, usually older people, had a keffiyeh wrapped round their head covering nose and mouth, eyes squinted, sometimes protected by bushy eyebrows. Tarek missed the door as before, only realising the fact when Faisal sat down on the chair on the opposite side of the table.

166

In an exact replay, the man held out that slim strong brown hand. And once again, Tarek felt the sinews and muscles flexing as he shook that hand. Despite the wind and its dusty cargo, the white kandura remained pristine and flowed just as smoothly as before. The dark eyes looked out from the tanned face, framed by the equally white gutra and the broad smile seemed just the same. Although, perhaps this time, the set of the man's face had a harsher, sterner look. But imagination can be a dangerous friend.

'Professor, you want some coffee?' He signalled to a waiter, looked at Tarek, then ordered two cups of black Lebanese coffee. 'You look well but your heart is perplexed and you send this strange message, asking for 'clarification and breakdown'. You should be happy that the Sheikh has sanctioned your plan.'

'And I am. It's just that I don't know how much money we are getting or when. What are magic bonuses and hedge plays? It doesn't make sense.'

'You must learn to read with understanding. The gifts that you will receive from the good Doctor, those will be paid for in total in the amount that he has requested through you. Operational costs will also be covered both for you and your colleagues. Those have been assessed at $300,000, to be divided equally between the three of you.'

Faisal paused as the waiter approached to serve their coffee. He sipped appreciatively, inhaling the strong but subtle aroma as he drank.

'We understand that each one of you has expenses that need to be covered to ensure success. There may be those that wish to dip their beaks on the way and cannot be swayed. Sometimes there is no other way. So be it. This money will cover all of this and more. If one pot runs dry, then there is another and another to be tapped. Like true brothers, each one of you will help the other in need but no one will hold sway over the others. You understand, Professor?' Tarek simply nodded. 'When will you make the order with the Doctor?'

'The prototype NuCan is on its way to England by courier. Insha'allah, it should arrive there in two days. Once my colleague is happy that it is fit for purpose, he will tell me and I will order four units to be tested with a view to four more for actual use. So maybe in one week.'

167

'As soon as your English friend confirms all is well to you, tell me and funds will be transferred immediately. There should be four separate accounts: one for payment to be made to the Doctor but in your control; the others should be under the control of each individual. I have suggested, and it has been agreed, these accounts will be opened with our friends in Switzerland as soon as possible. I will ensure that our banker makes direct contact by email. His name is Franz Honegger.'

'But when I talked to you before, with the Bookkeeper, I gave you the amounts of money that I believed were needed. Both of my colleagues are taking huge risks. They could lose everything, family, careers, businesses. I promised them that ...'

Faisal held up his hand to stop Tarek's flow. But it wasn't so much the hand that stopped him as much as the look of tempered steel in the other man's eyes. Somehow he had overstepped the mark, misjudged something; he felt the chill of fear and uncertainty again, knowing that this man had the power to stop everything in its tracks. Or even have him killed for his unknown crime.

'When the first gift is opened successfully on a ship, you three will receive another $300,000 between you. As the message implied. Essentially, this money is to cover additional operational expenses as well as providing a contingency fund for each one. Who can foretell what will happen save Allah? If there is a surplus, we will not ask for a return. But all of this money is provided for one purpose, to inflict deep wounds at the heart of the western war machine from within. For us, you are holy warriors fighting a holy war against the western unbelievers and their dissolute, vile ways. You are not paid assassins or mercenaries for hire.' He spat the last sentence out as though it were poison. 'We will not pay you in advance for failure!'

For a second, Faisal's face was a contorted mask filled with anger, which disappeared as quickly as it had been revealed. The blood seemed to have drained from Tarek's face leaving it bone white, pale skin drawn taut over the skull beneath.

'But we do understand the dangers of your endeavour and respect you for your undertaking. It may be that one or all of you will be shaheed and enter into paradise. Or perhaps caught and sent to prison for your efforts. We do not forget our own or leave them to fend for themselves. If something happens to you Professor al-Shami, we will take care of Ayesha and provide for her well.'

What little colour Tarek had regained, vanished on hearing his sister's name spoken by a key local representative of al-Qaeda. Faisal noted the older man's discomfiture but did little to allay the unspoken fears.

'I have met her on one or two occasions. She is beautiful, brave and intelligent, even though she has lost her way. Bismillah, she will find her way back to Islam in time. If you do not return from this road, we will take your sister into our hearts and homes. In the same way, we will provide for the families of your friends in England.'

Faisal looked calmly across the table, waiting for Tarek to speak. Tarek looked back but could not hold his gaze, dropping his own eyes downward to stare at a speck on the table. He looked up again, but past Faisal to a non-descript patch of peeling paper on the wall behind.

'They will ask me how much. How much money will Megan and Anwen receive for losing Alan and everything they've lived for? And Sophie? She adores Amin. She'd lose him, probably the company and the house as well. How much is that worth?'

'Al-Qaeda is not in the business of selling insurance, nor are you buying policies to safeguard the future. Nor do we pay blood debts like the Americans, for what they call collateral damage. You Professor al-Shami are a scholar, a mullah, learned in Shari'ah and Islam; above all people you should understand all that I have said today. No price has been put on those possible eventualities. One thousand American dollars? One million? Suffice it to say that al-Qaeda takes care of its own and will not shirk its responsibilities. Khallas!' Faisal stood up to leave. 'I hope we will hear soon that all is well with NuCan.' And then he was gone, out of the Bluebird Café's front door to slip unnoticed, almost invisibly, into the river of pedestrian traffic that flowed in both directions.

*****

'Al, are you expecting something? There's a FedEx van outside.'

From where Megan was sitting, she had a clear view past her husband and through the drizzle-wet window to the road outside. Still brandishing the knife he'd been using to butter his toast, Alan twisted in his seat for confirmation. They watched the driver disappear into the back of the van, then reappear with a large cardboard box.

'Yeah. It's probably from Tarek. He said he was going to send something when we saw him at Sophie and Amin's house. Some project he's working on with friends.'

As he got up to catch the man at the front door before he rang the bell, Alan prayed Megan wouldn't see the email that Tarek had sent only days earlier. 'Why did I say it was at Amin's house?' he asked himself. He opened the door just as the driver was about to press the button. Indian or Pakistani, Alan guessed. But when he spoke, the accent was hard core Cardiff. That kind of stuff always made Alan smile.

'Hallo. Mr Abbot is it? Mr Alan Abbot?'

'Hi, yes it is. I mean, yes I'm Alan Abbot. I assume that's for me?'

'Yes it is … from Lebanon it says. Bet it's warmer over there than it is here,' he said, handing the box over. 'Probably don't have this bloody rain either.'

'Sometimes they do.'

'Been there have you? Sign here, if you would,' he said handing over the small machine with the little screen and the stylus to scribe. 'In the box if you would. Don't worry,' he added, watching Alan's efforts. 'As long as you've made your mark, it'll do.' Taking the machine back, he looked up at the grey marbled sky through the heavy drizzle. 'Bloody rain. Could do with some sun. Thanks a lot.' And walked smartly back down the path.

'Thank you,' Alan called after him.

Hefting the box with both hands, he guessed it weighed around ten kilos which, if he was remembering correctly, would be about right. The top was covered with taped-on paperwork from LebanonDirectInternational, Middle Eastern Airlines cargo and FedEx, not to mention no less than two green customs labels. Underneath all of that were layers of parcel tape wound around the box like the bandages on an Egyptian mummy. He walked back into the kitchen, dumping it in the corner by the door before rejoining Megan at the breakfast table. Picking up the knife again, he got back to buttering his toast.

'Yes, it is from Tarek.'

'It looks heavy. What is it exactly?'

'Apparently it's some kind of metal container that they want to use for burying artefacts for future generations,' Alan said, improvising at speed. 'A sort of post-millennium pod.'

'D'you want some marmalade on that?' she asked, pushing the jar towards him. 'But why's he sending it all the way over here to you?'

'Thanks,' he said, knifing marmalade straight from the jar. 'For some reason they want it pressure tested and haven't got the facilities over there. I said we could do it over here, at the factory.'

'Will Forbes be happy with that?'

'I checked it with head office before I said yes,' Alan lied convincingly. 'Anwen not up yet?'

'Oh yes. She's in her room isn't she, playing her music as usual. It's early yet for the school bus and there's no point in waiting outside getting wet. You going to open it then?'

'What?'

'Tarek's parcel stupid.'

'No, I'll take it into work, unwrap it there and ask Steven to do the testing. You can see it later if you want.'

'Just interested in everything you do, my love.'

'Sarcasm falls far below your demonstrable level of erudition.'

'There speaks the scientist who believes that everything can be distilled down to a series of numbers. Music is but a series of mathematical phrases? Tell that to your daughter, genius.'

They laughed at each other fondly, enjoying the brief moment of banter.

'You'd better be going hadn't you?' Megan asked.

Alan looked at the kitchen clock: 'I'm gone'.

He drove for two miles before he pulled over into a natural lay-by formed by a five bar farm gate that gave way onto an open field. Opening a penknife, he cut into the tape around the top edges of the box sitting on the passenger's seat. After a few seconds, Alan had cut enough away to see where the top leaves met and the box was soon opened. The container itself was tightly packed with paper wadding and the whole encased in heavy-duty plastic. An envelope was lightly taped to the top, addressed simply to 'Alan'. He glanced at the customs forms on the outside: Food container with peanuts. Trade sample. No Commercial Value. Alan tore them off, glad that Megan hadn't inspected the box for clues. Returning to the envelope, he pulled it away from its mooring, slipped the blade of the knife along the top edge and removed the single page letter.

Dear Alan

Here it is – a full-scale model of the NuCan food container as mentioned in my email. As said, the manufacturers were extremely impressed with your detailed designs and expressed their appreciation in no uncertain terms. I have been assured that they have followed your instructions to the letter. The external dimensions have been followed rigorously to a tolerance of 600 microns (I assume that means something to you!) I was asked to tell you that the casing has been made of a maraging alloy steel containing 8.5% cobalt, 3.33% molybdenum. Apparently it's similar to the steel used for missile casings but a little thinner for technical operational reasons (?). If you unscrew the top of the container you will find it filled with peanuts, but that's only to a depth of about three inches. Beneath that the cylinder has been artificially weighted so that the total combined weight is similar to that of a completed unit. Obviously, the final containers will be filled in their entirety with the contents for which they have been designed. As per your instructions, you'll see that a magnetic strip has been attached to one side; they say that it is very strong and will perform as expected.

In terms of testing/checks or whatever, you know far better than I what you need to do. As soon as you confirm that you are happy with the container and that all is fine, I will give them the go-ahead to manufacture the actual units. Please let me know as soon as possible. Hopefully you won't have any concerns!

Have a word with Amin re a Cambridge meet. Although I'm not especially interested, there's an alumni reunion on the weekend of 8 July which would give me a good excuse to be over there. I would just need to stick my nose in at some point. That would allow us to finalise and catch up. More details and update then.

Love to Megan and Anwen. May Allah protect you. Tarek

Alan stared across the car through the passenger window, to the wooden bars of the gate and the field beyond. The rain rendered the picture in tinted monochrome, dull and dismal. He felt as though suspended in a limbo of time and place where the only reality was surreal. As he touched the plastic covering in the box, Alan sensed the metal below sending fingers of cold dread up to meet his own warm fingertips. A ridiculous notion that he sensibly dismissed. And yet the sensation persisted, borne of the knowledge that what they were about to do was irrevocable if it was carried through to its bitter end.

Pictures flashed across the screen inside his head, as they did from time to time; a gallery of sad horror which he often switched off, not wanting to remember. The sailor standing over Leena, leering as he ripped off her blouse. He could hear the screaming as he watched the repeated rapes. There was the mangled bent and bloodied body of his mother, propped at an impossible angle against the wall. Body parts of friends fragmented by explosions from above, ghoulish paintings on the dusty ground. A long catalogue of violence and inhumanity that, for a while, he allowed to run. He banged his fist against the steering wheel; the price had to be paid. But at what cost, he wondered. Switching back to the now, Alan fired up the engine and drove down the lane.

There was a brief conversation at the security barrier by the low profile Forbes Defence Industries sign. The weather probably hijacked most of the exchange. He parked the Volvo neatly between the lines of his reserved parking space, removed the box from the passenger seat and kicked open the entrance door. Peter Moffitt from HR grabbed it as the door flew inwards, held it open for Alan as he manoeuvred his way through into the corridor.

'Thanks Peter.'

'Let me guess, you've finally bought cake for the office staff?'

'Unlikely. I wouldn't want to encourage their eating habits.'

'Cruel but diplomatic, and thus apt,' he said, swinging past Alan and into the rain.

In the seclusion of his office he tucked the box away, out of sight behind his desk and sat down. Out of habit more than necessity, he switched on his computer and then waited for the inevitable knock on the door. Less than five minutes elapsed before the knock came and the door opened to let Steven Lee walk in with a handful of papers. Sometimes Alan was convinced that his assistant sat by the window watching and waiting for him to arrive.

'Morning Mr Abbot,' he said, pushing back a lock of hair with his spare hand. 'Morning's mail isn't much.' He put the papers on the desk, neatly squaring them off.

'Morning Steven. Are we up to speed on the floor?'

'Yes Sir. As far as I can see we're where we need to be with current orders.'

'Fine. No rush, but can you give me the forward schedules we have for the next three months that have already been confirmed.'

'Anything particular you're looking for Mr Abbot?'

'Not really. I'm just considering overall volumes in terms of capacity. The main areas would be missiles and rockets since there's less automation on those lines. The usual balancing act. You might as well give me ships and points of delivery sheets to go with them. That way I'll have the whole picture.'

'I'll get on to it right away Sir.'

Alan let a good five minutes elapse before he retrieved Tarek's package from behind his desk and took it down the corridor to the first of the factory's three large training rooms. Three full size missiles lay along the far side of the room, each one lying in its own cradle. The cut-away models were exact replicas of the real thing, using the same materials, but designed in a way that allowed trainees to deconstruct the main modular aspects of each one. Alan knew all of them intimately. Less than two metres long, Sea Wolf was the baby of the two surface-to-air missiles and dwarfed by its older brother, a Sea Dart which took centre stage. The third was a Sea Skua short range, anti-ship missile that was carried by the Royal Navy's Lynx helicopters.

Locking the door quietly behind him, Alan carried the box across the room and placed it on a table, immediately in front of the Sea Dart. Without taking breath, he removed the guidance system modules from the front end of the missile and stood back, gauging the vacant space. He took the NuCan container out of the box, carefully cut through the heavy plastic covering and stripped it away. He stared at the metal cylinder, its height equal to its diameter, and guessed at the volume of high explosive capacity. If grins could be phrased in quasi-architectural terms, Alan's might have termed as sardonic brutal.

'You might look like a steel hat box, but you are going to be one very bad motherfucker!'

Lifting the container off the desk, he turned it sideways and inserted it into the gap. Guiding it into the missile's casing, there was precious little room for his fingers to manoeuvre. He suddenly remembered the magnetic strip and quickly withdrew the cylinder from the model. Putting it back on the table, he ran his fingers round the curved vertical surface until he located the slim strip. He held the cylinder up to the outside surface of the Sea Dart, the magnetic strip facing the casing. Alan felt the pull when it was still almost three centimetres away and let it slip through his fingers. The cylinder attached itself like a limpet, the impact producing a loud clang.

'Bloody hell, that was close!'

It was patently clear that the cylinder would fit the space perfectly and the powerful magnet would lock it in place. Once the cylinder was in a missile, Alan realised it would be hellishly difficult to remove without a release key. But then, it hadn't been designed to be removed by human hands. With some difficulty, he managed to break the magnetic lock and, breathing hard, replaced the container in its plastic cover. He paused, pulled back the plastic and twisted the top of the container with both hands. The well-engineered, oiled cap turned easily, without a sound and came off in his hands. Roasted peanuts. He took a handful, flipped a few in his mouth and poured the rest into his shirt pocket. The lid was returned to its rightful place, the plastic pulled closed and the whole, reboxed. A few minutes later, it was back in the corner behind Alan's desk.

Two hours later, he was looking at Royal Navy order sheets, MoD approved, with attached purchase order numbers for Sea Darts or Sea Skuas and Wolves. HMSs Kent, Sutherland, Monmouth, Exeter, Somerset, York, Montrose and Ocean were all listed. Dates, requirements, delivery points at Portsmouth or Devonport. As and when the occasion arose, it would be a simple matter of choosing the most appropriate target, marrying that up with the preferred course and location. Making sure that he knew which ship would receive an extra-explosive missile would be the easy part of the exercise; switching the guidance systems for the container might be a little more complicated. But Alan knew he had time to plan.

By the time he got back to the cottage, smoke was drifting up from the chimney and the lights were on in pretty much every window. Alan parked the Volvo beside Megan's orange four-wheel drive Rav4 that she had insisted was ideal for a doctor driving along Welsh roads. One didn't argue with Megan's strange logic. He carted the NuCan into the kitchen, unpacked and dumped it on the table. Kissing his wife and daughter he asked: 'Anyone want peanuts?' Their interest in the container, now it was in full view and demystified, was as short-lived as he'd expected.

'You want a drink, Al?'

'Yeah, why not? It's almost seven after all. I just need to send a quick email to Tarek. I'll be there in a sec.'

He powered up his laptop on the kitchen table, opened up a new email with 'Testing Today' in the subject line. In the body of the email he wrote: 'NuCan most definitely Can! Perfect fit. Cambridge dates fine with me. Just need location. Alan.' He shut it all down and went through to the living room. He gave Anwen a kiss on the cheek, nibbled his wife's ear, whispered he loved her and took a sip of his whiskey.

It had been a long, frustrating day for all sorts of reasons. Three of his students, in their final undergraduate year, had decided they needed to talk about where a degree in Islamic Studies might actually lead them. One would have thought that they had considered that before taking the course! Tarek resented the implication that it had all been his fault and that now he should wave a magic wand to ensure that all three would be rewarded handsomely and financially on earth. In addition, they felt that there should be some form of assurance that they would also be amply rewarded in paradise for their efforts.

That was the first irritation. The second was his meeting with Professor Said Khoury. Whereas his Faculty Director was perfectly happy for him to go to Cambridge, it was his view that since 'the Professor was taking part in a social gathering of alumni' university funds 'unfortunately do not stretch' to cover any expenses whatsoever. Tarek suggested that he could always drop into the Centre for Islamic Studies in Cambridge and join some discussion. Mohammed Said Khoury had opined that 'some discussion' wasn't quite 'targeted enough to warrant university funding'. Pompous fraud. It wasn't as though he was above occasionally tapping the faculty coffers to cover the InterContinental bills when skiing with Sylvie in Mzaar. Or similar. And it wasn't that Tarek couldn't afford to pay his way, rather that the principle irked.

In an effort to calm himself, to relax and let his mind drift into happy thoughts, he'd awarded himself a hashish hit before smoking his usual nargile. Smoking resin in a chillum hadn't been a huge success, the acrid taste befouling his mouth overcoming any pleasant sensation. Despite the apartment's elevation, the air outside was hot and humid, stagnant and heavy, without a breath of wind to bring relief. The cicadas' cries seemed leaden and lethargic. Even the sound of water bubbling in the base of the nargile was failing in its normal soothing duty.

Walking back into the living room, he flipped up the top of his laptop, powered up and waited. Bring up Firefox, sign in to Gmail and wait. The messages flickered upwards, one after the other. As he saw the names and the foreshortened messages, a spark of excitement began to grow which was soon fanned into a burning flame.

> To: Professor al-Shami <talshami@gmail.com>
> From: Amin Masri <amasri@ifl.co.uk>
> Subject: Re: NuCan Update
>
> Hi Tarek
> The meeting went really well and I'm fairly sure that we've got the contract. They're making a site visit on Thursday next week which should be fine. Once that's done they'll confirm and then we're in! Assuming the contract is awarded, they also confirmed that we will be given information re routes, scheduled stops etc. No problem with your comments – more or less as discussed. See you in Cambridge on 8/9 July.   Amin

> To: Professor al-Shami <talshami@gmail.com>
> From: Alan Abbot <aabbott85@yahoo.co.uk>
> Subject: Testing Today
>
> NuCan most definitely Can! Perfect fit. Cambridge dates fine with me. Just need location. Alan.

'Yes, yes, yes!' Tarek pumped the air with his fist. But the list of new email messages hadn't finished. The next one was from a source and name that initially was unfamiliar. Once realisation dawned, the email fuelled his excitement even more than the previous two.

> To: Professor al-Shami <talshami@gmail.com>
> From: Franz   Honegger
> <frhonegger.dir@krieggessner.com>
> Subject: Private Banking with Krieg Gessner, Zurich
>
> Dear Professor al-Shami & Colleagues

Welcome to Krieg Gessner Banking. As indicated above, my name is Franz Honegger and I am honoured to have you and your colleagues as clients.

Further to instructions from one of our most esteemed clients, I have opened four numbered bank accounts relative to the following names: Tarek al-Shami (x2), Amin Masri, Alan Abbot. As per my additional instructions from the aforementioned client, I have today transferred the following sums of money in US dollars: to al_Shami1, $1m; to al_Shami2, $100k; to Masri1, $100k; to Abbot1, $100k.

Normally I prefer to meet each client in person but have been advised that this is not possible in the current circumstances. Under Swiss legislation it is forbidden to disclose the names of those persons holding numbered accounts, privacy being paramount. However, although individual accounts are referred to solely by number, we are required to verify each individual's identity. To that end, I would be grateful if you and your colleagues would each send a scanned image or pdf of your passports. Naturally, you will only need to send me one scan Professor, rather than one for each account.

Scans should be sent to me at the above address as should any other communications. Once those have been received, accounts should be activated immediately by clicking the link provided in the message of confirmation. Advices on access and security will also be provided at that time.

Prof al-Shami: I would be grateful if you would forward this email to your colleagues with a brief explanatory note if you would like.

Gentlemen, once again I welcome you all to Private Banking with Krieg Gessner and look forward to a long association with each and every one of you. In due course, I hope that it will be possible to meet you here in Zurich. In the meantime, may I offer you my very best wishes with all your endeavours.

Yours sincerely
Franz Honegger
Exec Director, Non-resident Private Banking

For a while, Tarek stared at the screen as though dumbstruck. He didn't know what he had really expected, but it certainly wasn't an email from a private bank in Switzerland informing him that Amin and Alan and he suddenly had numbered accounts filled with American dollars. Stunned, amazed, shocked, elated, excited, frightened – the words came tumbling down in an avalanche of emotion. He walked out to the balcony and stared out over the lights of Beirut. Somehow the humidity had lifted, leaving the hot air charged with electricity. The pungent smell of ozone drifted past, a delicate scarf perfumed by burning metal drawn by an invisible hand and touched by ultraviolet light.

'My God. It's happening!'

Tarek almost ran back to his laptop. Sitting down he reread the message from Franz Honegger, his eyes starting from his head. He clicked carefully on the forward key, inserted Alan and Amin's addresses as recipients. Above the body of Honegger's text, he typed: THE BANK IS OPEN FOR BUSINESS! Allahu akbar. Tarek.

But, there was a but in the back of his mind. What? Then he suddenly realised: the accounts had been opened and monies transferred without confirmation of definite orders! Alan's message had only recently been sent; there was no way that they could have known that NuCan was fine. The second sight of a psychic visionary? Ridiculous, but unnerving all the same. They obviously assumed that it would all be fine and realised that payment would have to be made before production started. He remembered Faisal's comments about Ayesha, imagined the writing appearing on the wall: we know where you live. Tarek shivered, and then shrugged. There was one more message that he had to send.

To: Dr Malik <smalik@spkrl.com.pk>
From: Professor al-Shami <talshami@gmail.com>
Subject: NuCan – Confirmation of Order

Dear Dr Malik

I am delighted to be able to confirm that I am now in a position to progress our project.

My colleague has made the necessary checks in respect of the prototype container and is clearly delighted with your work in turn. The design and fit is perfect for the purpose. I look forward to taking testing onto a higher plane in the not too distant future.

In addition, I am pleased to tell you that funds have now been transferred and verification of accounts should take place within the next three to four days. Once I have received confirmation from the bank that all is in order, I will transfer the first instalment of money to your account as previously agreed.

Best regards

Professor Tarek al-Shami PhD

Tarek clicked the send icon with as much a flourish as possible and then shut all systems down. He returned to the balcony, remade the nargile (heavy on the hashish), lit up and relaxed in his chair to enjoy. Suddenly, the night air was filled with the perfume of success, adventure and retribution. And he grinned maniacally into the darkness.

*****

Looking up at the global screen, Tristan Smythe-Corton heaved a massive sigh of relief. When John Watkins had discovered that GCHQ's systems had not been linked and updated he'd gone ballistic. For God's sake, this al-Shami Lebanese twat was hardly that important. He'd been horrified when Watkins threatened to sack him from his ghost position; he was appalled when it appeared he meant to blacklist him from all government posts. Pleading temporary insanity and a novice's aberration, Smythe-Corton had promised faithfully to immediately rectify the situation. And he had, despite the fact that the Marina girl had rated al-Shami as low risk.

A yellow line was making a delicate arc that began in Beirut and ended in Lahore. He keyed in for graphics; al-Shami at one end and Malik at the other. Excellent, he thought, and thank God. Tracker had caught Tarek's final email of the day. Smythe-Corton wasn't impressed: some project to do with a can! Who gives a shit?

8 ~ Question the If, Consider the But

Perched on her high chair, hair over-dyed to a shiny dark blue-black and eyes decorated with deep blue eye shadow, the diminutive Border Control Officer was the humanoid version of a malevolent crow. Eileen Patterson turned her sharp beady eyes on the slim olive skinned man in front of her window and didn't much like what she saw. To her, he looked distinctly shifty and, after over 15 years peering at people, she knew shifty when she saw it. She looked at the front of the passport, taking in the geometric squiggles at the top which she assumed was Arabic, some kind of tree and then French at the bottom. Far too foreign, she thought. Officer Patterson glanced at the completed landing card, flipped open the passport to the photo page, compared the picture with the face in front of her and silently, grudgingly admitted that they were one and the same. Then she looked past him, to the long queues that stretched away into the distance. It was going to be a long day and she would make each one pay for her pain.

'From Lebanon?'

'Yes.'

'Bay-root?'

'Beyrouth, yes,' he replied, phrasing the name in the French way.

'Bay-root, Lebanon,' said Patterson firmly, making the point.

She started pecking frenetically at her keyboard, flicking the pages, copying detail and form. Checking the expiry date she was disappointed to see that it still had six more years to run before it expired. The multi-entry visa was valid for another 14 months, which was vaguely irritating, as was the fact that it stated he was an academic. Officer Patterson didn't believe in academics or people with fancy titles. In her book, they were all waste-of-space scroungers, getting paid for useless research projects.

'Tarek Al Shammy?'

'Professor,' he said, emphasising the title, 'Tarek al-Shami. Yes.'

'How long are you staying in the United Kingdom Mr Al Shammy?'

'Just a few days. I'm here for a alumni gathering, old students' meet-up.'

Officer Patterson glared at him, wondering whether an 'alum neye gathering' was legal. 'Where will you be staying while you're here?'

'At Christ's College in Cambridge.'

'The university?'

'Yes.'

'And will you be working Mr Al Shammy?'

'No,' he replied, 'my visa only allows me to visit for conferences, seminars and the like. Essentially educational visits one might say and, of course, social visits with friends and old colleagues.'

'So you do understand that you are not allowed to work or to have recourse to public funds?'

'Yes, of course.'

'Just so that you remember is all,' said Officer Eileen Patterson as she date-stamped his passport in the middle of a clean page.

Tarek gratefully retrieved his passport and scuttled off towards customs control and the exit beyond. Horrible woman, he thought. Ghastly, pompous little foreigner, she thought. Who does he think he is anyway, with his alum neyes and his stuck-up Cambridge friends?

Catching the train to Paddington was something that Tarek had done on several occasions; his experience with London's underground was much more limited. As he looked at the grubby map on the curved wall that arched upwards and over his head, he wondered how the English ever found their way around their own city. Looking at the complex network of coloured lines, he tried to imagine how it would look from the air if one could peel back the ground with everything it supported and expose all the tunnels. Miles of deep grooves in the ground, tracks left in the wake of monstrous worms. In fact, it seemed to be a miracle that the whole of London was not sinking due to the subsidence that should have been caused by the system. If London was Beirut, the Israelis would have bombed it out of existence years ago, he thought sourly.

'Paddington,' he said sticking a finger on the name, 'but which Paddington?'

The station seemed to be in several places at once, crossing no less than four different colours and one of them twice. The key to the lines was on the right hand side of the map at the bottom, but looking at that meant taking his finger off Paddington. Making a mental note of the approximate grid placement of Paddington, he searched for Charing Cross.

'Where you goin' luv?'

He looked over his shoulder, and then down, at a little old lady with an impossibly wrinkled face, cloudy blue eyes and a big smile, all capped by a bird's nest of white hair.

'Um, Charing Cross.'

'D'an there, innit.' She pointed to the name on the map with a finger that was just as grubby. 'We're 'ere, right? So you go d'an there where it says Bakerloo Line,' she said, pointing down the platform. Then turned back to the map. 'See, get on the s'afbound train 'n the Bakerloo 'll take ya right d'an t' Charing Cross. Got it?'

'Thank you so much.'

'First time in London?'

'No but I've rarely been on the underground. I'm very grateful for your assistance.'

'Enjoy yerself while yer 'ere but keep yer eyes open on tube. Too many foreign bloody terrists nah. Good luck.'

She paddled past him to disappear among the people further up the platform. Shaking his head in disbelief, Tarek made his way to the Bakerloo Line sign. By the time his final train got into Cambridge it was almost half past three. He took a taxi to Christ's College, checked in to one of the guest rooms and rested for a while. There would be time to revisit a few old haunts, wander the streets and perhaps have something to eat. The truth of the matter was that there was no gathering of alumni for him to join. Tarek had undertaken his PhD with the Faculty of Asian and Middle Eastern Studies, a department within the overarching reach of the University of Cambridge. That wasn't the same as one of the colleges like Trinity or Clare. Not that most people realised that fine degree of differentiation and that suited Tarek's purpose entirely.

*****

Amin picked Alan up at Reading because it had made sense. Megan had dropped Alan off in Cardiff to catch the 08.26 train which got him into Reading at just after ten. The drive up from Bagnum had taken Amin much the same amount of time and Cambridge was two hours up the road further north. Plenty of time for conversation and consideration.

'Why couldn't he have stayed in London?'

'Because he's got this alumni thing happening in Cambridge.'

'But he says he's not bothered about that!'

'True, but for some reason he thinks that it's 'good cover'.' Amin hooked two fingers in the air for the inverted commas.

'So why couldn't he say that he was going to Cambridge but stay in London?'

'Because he's Tarek. And that would be a lie!'

And both men collapsed in gales of laughter. They fell silent as Amin fed the Range Rover into the faster moving traffic on the M4, indicated and accelerated quickly into the middle lane. He settled for a cruising speed of just under 80mph, knowing that there weren't too many speed cameras on that section of the motorway. Given that Amin was driving, that speed was naturally exceeded when overtaking. It wasn't a problem with Alan, unlike Henry Perkins.

'What did you say to Megan?'

'Told her that Tarek had to be at this thing in Cambridge and that he didn't have time to get down to London, let alone Wales. She thinks that it's all about helping Tarek with an archiving project, burying artefacts in the hills for future generations.'

'And she said?'

'Told me I was off my trolley and that it was a total waste of time. You know, she says, 'he tells you to jump and every time you ask, how high. Bloody mad you are Alan Abbot'. And then she happily drives me to the station, sending me off with a 'give my love to the boys'. There's still that question in my mind though, whether I should tell her. Sophie?'

'I haven't told her anything about NuCan, as Tarek calls it. But I think I will, at some point. I'll come back to that in a minute. For fuck's sake!'

Amin hit the brakes hard to avoiding hitting the back of a Downton semi-trailer. Indicating right, he flicked the gearshift down to fourth, pushed out into the fast lane and powered past the long box vehicle. He saw the driver looking down from the window of the tractor unit and gave him the finger as he flew past. A glance in his rear view mirror as he pulled back into the middle lane: the truck driver was flashing his lights in pique. Amin was vanishing in the distance, shaking his head in despair.

'As for this weekend, I said that he'd invited us to join the party in Cambridge and that it was a men only do. All Soph said was: 'maybe I can do something similar with Suzette. You return with scent of parfum, I will find her and scratch out her eyes. Maybe yours too. Have fun. I want to hear all about it when you are back'.'

For a while, neither of them said anything, watching the road, the cars, trucks and vans fly by in their wake. It was one of those days when the canvas of the sky was patterned with streaks of high alto cirrus and occasional cotton-wool balls of white cumulous. Sunshine flashed for a moment, glared and then disappeared, only to repeat the performance further on with slight variations. Amin pulled over to the left lane, picked up the feeder to the M25, driving north towards the turn-off near Bricket Wood.

'Have you been in touch with Honegger, the banker in Switzerland?'

'Yeah, I emailed a scan of my passport as requested. Got his email in reply and followed through with the link.'

'Likewise. So now the three of us have beautiful numbered Swiss bank accounts, preloaded with 100,000 US dollars and our own private bank manager. Ask Uncle Franz for help if needed.'

'Or the great white Sheikh you mean? It's al-Qaeda money and he'll be expecting a good return on his investment. What doesn't make sense is the amount. Tarek implied the figures would be much higher, unless I misunderstood.'

'Yes, that's the impression I had as well,' said Amin, easing out into the fast lane to overtake a slow Fiat 500. 'He mentioned a quarter of a million to me and I think almost double that for you. For me, the amount's not the point. I don't know exactly how much we're worth if I include the company and all our assets, but in the big picture £100,000 is not huge. Realistically, nor is £250,000 if it's not accessible.'

'I think I know where you're going with this,' Alan said, looking across at his friend. 'Not accessible as in we're not available to access it?'

Amin flicked a look back. Neither of them was smiling now.

'This all started over 30 years, but it didn't finish then. I know that. The first ten years were tough and the next ten even tougher. Listen, I know they were much worse for you Alan. I could never …'

'Yeah, it was tough but you don't need to say anything. Go back to what you were saying.'

'OK. What I mean is, that we came out of the tunnel, at the end. I talked to Leena a few weeks ago. Even now she still has the odd nightmare but she's doing well. You know she had a little girl in '98, Fleurette?'

'I remember you telling me. The guy left her shortly afterwards. That right?'

'Mm-mm, Jean-Pierre. He was actually OK but in the end he couldn't handle the depressions, the anger. When Fleurette arrived, he more or less said, 'perhaps now you have someone you can really care about', and left.'

'Where is he now?'

'He kept in touch for a while, sending Leena money every month. He still does occasionally. Last time I heard he was living in Lyon, working as a mechanic in a garage. Anyway, Leena is still running the restaurant, Les Goûts de Beyrouth, dotes on Fleurette and is as happy as she has ever been. I don't want that to stop Alan. Nor do I want Sophie to have nowhere to go, to be alone and hated.'

He stopped talking, staring through the windscreen at the road ahead. One hand crept up to cover his mouth, as though he was trying to stop the words leaking out.

'What are you trying to say?' Alan asked softly.

'Juste que j'ai peur pour l'avenir, Alain. I am afraid for the future. I do not want to be in the prison for years, away from my family. Or worse! And it is the same for you, I'm sure.'

Mother French was breaking into Amin's usually fluent English with the turmoil of emotion. The English words were accented with a French twist and Alan had become Alain. Alan remembered that from Beirut, when they were kids, that the Masris spoke French first and Lebanese second.

'If I'm thinking about Megan and Anwen, it's exactly the same. And you're right, I have a wonderful family that I will protect with my last breath and I don't want them to be without me. I don't want to go to prison either but I'm not planning on getting caught. Al-Qaeda wants the glory: they're welcome to it but that could provide us with a certain amount of cover. But that doesn't mean that we should forgive and forget, Amin. At least, I can't. It goes beyond what happened in Cyprus and the aftermath. This is also about Palestine and Palestinians, what happened to us in Lebanon, what the Israelis did with the support of countries like the US and Britain. I can't forget.'

The pent-up emotions that had flared on Amin's face a moment before had dissipated. When he next spoke, his voice had regained both calm and tone.

'I know. Nor have I forgotten. It's just that life has got muddled over the years and we're both more vulnerable than we were when we only had to worry about ourselves. What I was going to say, before my mouth ran off with my brains, was about telling Sophie. I'm thinking about exit strategies.' He looked at Alan, held his eye for a second before switching back to the road. 'I don't think that we will fail,' he said slowly. 'I'm guessing that one, perhaps two ships will be damaged or sunk before they find out who we are. But in the end, they'll know. If we wait too long or attack too many ships, the chances of getting caught are high.'

'So we limit it to one ship?'

'Maybe. Or perhaps we should make arrangements to leave the country before the first bomb's detonated? Liquidate some assets beforehand and transfer the money overseas? I don't know, but then I'd need to tell Sophie, explain.'

'Do you think she would understand? I'm sure as hell that Megan wouldn't. She'd say, 'You can't change history Alan and revenge is a poisoned chalice. Let history rest and move on'.'

'In France there is a proverb, roughly: 'on dit que la vengeance est un plat mieux si on le mange froid'.'

'If I remember, the misquote that became a proverb: 'it is said that revenge is a dish best eaten cold?'

'Yes. I think Sophie would understand that.'

'There's still time to think. Let's see what Tarek has to say; enough till then.'

*****

Cambridge basked in late morning sunlight that warmed college stones while leaching their soft yellow tones, leaving them withered white. Nevertheless they appreciated Trinity College's gracious buildings as they drove down The Avenue across the River Cam to turn right along the side of New Court. Turning in as instructed, they parked on the near side of the boathouse and walked around the end to the College punts. They saw him before he saw them, at the end of a line of moored punts.

Tarek was lying sprawled on the grass, just in the shade of the overhanging trees. His legs were crossed at the ankle and he was wearing dark green chinos that blended perfectly with the surrounding foliage. The usual polo shirt, today in navy blue and white stripe, had the collar turned up and the dark hair seemed even floppier than normal. To complete the picture, his head was tilted slightly backwards, the eyes gazing up into the cornflower blue sky. Overall he portrayed the perfect cameo of a decadent poet, a Wilde or Yeats perhaps. An impression that could not have been farther from the truth and yet, Tarek had chosen to have a meeting on a punt.

'Do you dream of clouds above or lines of love, oh Prince of Lebanon?' called Amin.

Startled out of his reverie, Tarek jumped as if bitten on the cheek by a horsefly. He looked around accusingly at first, and then smiled when he saw the two men at the far end of the line. He jogged across the grass towards them.

'I'm sorry to drag you both all the way up to Cambridge. Since I was coming to the alumni gathering, it made sense and it's a different location.' He hugged each one in turn. 'Looks as though you've brought lunch,' he said, looking at the wicker hamper Amin was carrying. 'Let's get a punt.'

Tarek jogged round the corner, returning a few minutes later with a long pole. Amin and Alan looked at each other, slight looks of surprise on their faces and shrugged.

'Tarek,' they said in unison. And burst out laughing for the second time that day at the expense of their friend.

He looked from one to the other, not quite knowing what was going on. Then shrugged himself before leading them to their designated punt. Unused to the shallow craft, Amin and Alan installed themselves with caution, watching as he untied them from the mooring. Standing on the flat panel to the rear, Tarek let the pole drop almost vertically by the side of the punt, pushing downwards as his hands climbed up the wood. Tentatively at first, he took them out into the silky slow flowing water; and then more confidently as his hands and arms remembered long unused skills. He found himself smiling vaguely idiotically at the pleasure of it all.

'I thought that it would be more difficult; I haven't done this in years. I always found punting rather soothing.'

'Tarek, either you've been smoking a little too much hash or you're having a psychologically regressive problem, attempting to relive your days as a Cambridge student,' said Alan.

'Or both,' added Amin, 'but you do have to admit that he is doing rather well.'

For a while, the three men watched the world slip by on either side of the river. Past the majestic buildings that were Clare, King's and then Queen's College, before passing under the wooden cat's cradle that was Mathematical Bridge. Green lawns stretched immaculately away from the water's edge to those bastions of educational excellence and profound thinking.

In so many ways, for Tarek, this Cambridge epitomised the elitist world of the British establishment, one of the great seats of learning that had given birth to imperialism and the British belief that they had the right to do with the world what they chose. It suddenly occurred to him that maybe that had been the reason for bringing Alan and Amin to Cambridge, to let them smell one source of the rot, feel the disdain and hate the contempt.

'Beauty befouled,' he said aloud to no one in particular.

He took them upstream a little further before guiding the punt towards the bank near Coe Fen. For lack of a better idea, he pushed the pole down hard into mud of the riverbed, tied them onto that as a mooring.

'Not many punts come down here and nobody will stop, so we have the place to ourselves. I just think that we all have to be careful who is listening or watching.' He handed them each a slip of paper with two lines:

+961 70 380154

tar10sham991@hotmail.com

'Before I left Beirut, I bought a cheap pay-as-you go mobile and set myself up with another email address. Those are the details. I suggest that you use them as an alternative to the usual ones. I think it might be a good idea if you both did the same. And with email I'm trying to use different computers, rather than always the same one. In any electronic communications, refer to NuCan, the container or food container, or similar.'

'Tarek, of course we need to be careful but why would we be under surveillance? And by whom? You're an academic, Alan's a scientist who more or less works for the British government and I'm a legitimate businessman who's just about to enter into a supply agreement with the Ministry of Defence. I can't think of a better cover.'

'But we don't know who's out there Amin and I want to be as sure as I can that no one finds out what we're doing.'

'Of course, you're right. It just creeps me out that whatever I'm doing, wherever, there may be someone peering around the corner. But ...'

'But what?'

'Nothing, I just don't want anything to go wrong or get spooked into thinking it is going wrong. That's it.'

'It won't,' said Tarek confidently, 'this is a good team and we have a good product. Thanks to Alan, we know that a NuCan will physically fit into a Sea Dart and that the weight's fine?'

'Everything's good as far as I can see. It is a tight fit, which is good, but the magnetic strip is almost too strong. It's a matter of being careful and getting it right first time. Once the device attaches itself to the inner wall of the missile, there's no way of removing it other than stripping out the next section and that would be impossible on my own. When you talk to Malik, ask him to make it an electromagnetic strip that can be turned on/off from the opposite side. A simple permanent magnet with a DC temporary release charge would work. But it would be safer to have some sort of release mechanism. But in direct answer to your question, the weight's fine. Reality? I don't think anyone's going to weigh the missile before deployment. Ready to go, a Sea Dart weighs 550 kg; I don't think anyone's going to be lifting one up and saying, 'hang on, this one's a bit heavy'. The odd kilo here or there isn't going to make a difference. But balancing NuCan against the weight of the gyros and guidance system, they certainly feel about the same.'

'OK, I'll email and tell Dr Malik to modify the strip. But otherwise, that's all good. How long does it actually take to make the switch?'

'Seven or eight minutes; maybe less with a bit more practice. But it's more about timing than anything else. There are only two places where it's possible to install the NuCan: while the missile is still on the factory floor or in the storage for pre-delivery. If it's still on the floor, the switch would have to be made right at the end of assembly, but before it's stored. When they're on pre-delivery, there's no reason to enter the facility; anyone accessing storage would have to have a damn good reason for being there. I do not want to get caught with my hands full of explosive baby, saying I'm looking for nappies.' At least that raised smiles, he thought. 'Don't worry, I'll sort it out; there's time.'

'You will know which ships they're going to? And then where the ships themselves are going?' Tarek asked, anxiously persistent.

'Yes, as I told you before. Each missile is uniquely numbered and that number marries up with a specific delivery to a named vessel. This is government stuff Tarek; there has to be an audit trail for every bolt and widget. I'll know the front end to the point of delivery. After that, Amin's information should take over.'

'Right. But before all that, we need to get the devices to you in Wales. All being well, they will provide us with four armed devices, complete with a sort of mobile phone trigger. Or triggers? I don't know. In addition, Captain Kharal suggested that they include a few bottom-weighted containers which can be filled with nuts or spices and be used as dummies.'

'I can't see any use for a lot of dummy units,' said Amin, realising that it was his turn to provide answers. 'They'll take up more space from a shipping point of view and probably attract more attention. Why would you ship peanuts or pepper in steel containers? It doesn't make sense. Stuff like that gets transported in sacks or crates. But oils absolute might just be perfect.'

Both Tarek and Alan looked at him, totally mystified.

'Expensive ingredients for perfume. The essential oils of oud, jasmine, orris, sandalwood and rose. Oud comes from the agarwood tree and costs around $26,000 per kilo. Dried out iris bulbs produce orris and that comes out at even more. Top flight jasmine oil absolute produced from zillions of flowers kicks out at almost $40,000 per kilo. It makes sense to package expensive oils in carefully sealed shiny containers. Most customs officers will think twice before touching those after they've read the customs declarations. As a bonus, all a sniffer dog will smell is oud, jasmine or whatever. The oils should mask any lingering stench of nasty explosive.'

'But wouldn't the price be prohibitive?' asked Tarek.

'No, because we only have to put a little of the oil in the top of each cylinder. Perhaps only a few millilitres to suggest seepage from below. Maybe we use two dummies, which we fill with a less expensive oil that can be used as an example if we're challenged.'

'I think you're right, the oils should disguise any residual smell,' said Alan slowly, thinking as he spoke. 'That's possibly, quite brilliant.'

'Thank you, kind sir,' said Amin, mock bowing as far as he could while sitting cross-legged in a shallow punt.

'They'd have to be cleaned out before insertion. Missiles smelling of perfume would definitely raise a few eyebrows.'

'And get a few comments. Of course, we will need to clean them out.'

'Have you thought about transportation yet?' asked Tarek.

'Yes. As I understand it, the deal includes delivery to a port of our choice?'

'Dr Malik only mentioned Karachi and Port Muhammad Bin Qasim.'

'Fine, either one would do but Port of Karachi allows more options. OK, a wooden, three runner B1210M pallet would take all six containers. That gets shrink wrapped and shipped as a part-container load from Karachi to Jebel Ali as 'machine parts for industrial use'. There may be a little waiting to get the container filled but that isn't a problem. If need be, we can fill the container with other cargo ourselves. Container ships are rarely in a hurry; the average speed used for calculations is only 14 knots.' Amin noticed the blank looks. 'To you landlubbers, that's a fraction over 16 mph. We are talking sloooow; the shipping time is usually ten days or less. Jebel Ali's a free economic zone a few miles down the coast, southwest of Dubai. Nobody gives a damn about what gets shipped in or out, plus we have two large storage units in the zone.

'I can easily get the oils absolute from one of the specialist traders near the old Gold Souk in Deira. Doctor the containers, shrink wrap the whole pallet again and store until required. That's assuming we're looking at storage time. Either way, I'm planning to send the pallet as air cargo from Dubai International to London Heathrow, which will take eight hours. That means I can pick the containers up personally with an InterFoods van and handle any problems with customs.'

'Amin, I thought the deal with the oils sounded good, as I said. On the other hand, isn't it a bit weird for a company dealing in food and beverage, importing ingredients for perfume?'

'Actually it's not that strange. The core business is F and B, but our main usp is that we can supply whatever, whenever and wherever. The MoD navy contract requires us to cover emergency medical supplies; and we were once asked to deliver a crate containing one bottle of Chateau Pétrus, two crystal red wine goblets, a 250gm tin of Imperial Oscietra caviar and two mother of pearl spoons! So why not obscenely expensive oils?'

'Point taken,' Alan said with a grin. 'Incidentally Tarek, do we have test dates yet?'

'Yes we do. Production of the first four units should be completed within four weeks from now. Unless anything changes, I fly to Pakistan in six weeks time for live testing and assuming that goes according to plan, we'll be shipping our four devices from Karachi around the last week in September. That means we could be blowing up ships by November, insha'allah.'

'Delivering Christmas to the Royal Navy early this year,' Alan muttered grimly.

'Allahu akbar,' returned Tarek.

As the three humans fell silent, the void was instantly filled by nature's melodies. Of them all, Amin noticed those sounds most keenly. He recognised the bursts of lilting trills from a nearby blue tit, blending with the seesaw tweets of a coal tit. A wood pigeon cooed softly from a branch somewhere above his head while a parliament of rooks chattered in the distance. He could hear the breeze rustling the leaves of the trees, the susurration of the river and the little slapping sounds of the water against the wooden sides of the punt.

A bright yellow sun shone in a blue sky above, where white clouds drifted in aimless pursuit of other white clouds, merging, mingling, and then separating once more. He smelled the earthy scents of mown grass and cow dung, damp mould and rotting wood, the lighter perfume of apple blossom and wildflowers.

'Tarek?'

'Yes Amin?'

'I need to understand the money Tarek,' Amin said, pacing his words. 'All of this is not about the money, but I need to know what happens if anything does go wrong. And the figures seem to have changed, revised downwards. So tell me what is happening.'

'There will be more money, paid to you, into the same accounts that you now have. After the first bomb ...' He savoured the word for a second, rolling the taste of it round in his mouth. 'After the first bomb has successfully exploded on a ship, a further $300,000 will be paid, $100,000 to each of us as before.'

'That's not enough if something goes wrong, Tarek. There needs to be more, for Sophie if I'm not there. For Megan and Anwen as well.'

'And there will be Amin. I have been assured of that.'

'What does that mean Tarek? In the vulgar terminology of hard cash, what does that fucking mean?'

Amin stared at Tarek with eyes that were hard stones in narrow slits. He saw the haunted look in the older man's eyes and the drawn look of his face. He glanced sideways at Alan; saw the cold impassive face of accepted comprehension.

'You knew?' he asked accusingly.

'No, Amin. But I guessed as much. Al-Qaeda seeks shaheed, martyrs not mercenaries.'

'There won't be any more money, will there Tarek?'

'Yes. But as appropriate and necessary. I have their assurances that if there is a problem, they will take care of our families. Basically they're saying that we have insurance. If one of us is arrested, or hurt perhaps, they will makes sure that there is enough money. I was told: however much it takes, whatever sum is needed, there will be that money and support.'

'And you trust al-Qaeda to do that, Tarek?'

There was a long pause before he answered: 'I think so. I have to, because there is no other choice'.

'At least I know where I stand,' said Amin calmly. 'And there's time to make arrangements. I think I will have to tell Sophie because she needs to know the risks and why this has to be done.'

'But the fewer people ...'

'Sophie will not talk, Tarek. She will listen, get angry, evaluate and then be calm; because she will understand, even if she doesn't totally agree. And it is her right to know. You've already made your decision, told Ayesha. Now I have made mine. What Alan does is his decision and I will not ask him what is in his heart. Khallas!'

Leaning down, he opened the basket at his feet, felt carefully in the bed of straw and produced three small glasses. Saving one for himself, he gave one to each of the other men. Taking the top off the familiar diamond cut bottle, he poured a generous measure of the clear liquid into each glass, topping them up with water from a second bottle.

'Arak Touma, lion's milk from Lebanon, courtesy of Leena and Les Goûts de Beyrouth. She sends her love. So a toast my friends: to family, Palestinians and NuCans.'

As they clinked glasses with each other, each murmured those last few words and sipped in unison. Bzoorat with peanuts, pistachios, almonds and sunflower seeds; hummus and labneh spiked with ginger and strips of flatbreads. All of this and more emerged magically from the depths of the basket.

'Packed by Sophie with her own fair hands,' Amin added. 'She also sends her love.'

They drank and ate without talking, enjoying the food and drink; sitting quietly together on an English river in a punt. And when they'd finished and everything had been packed away, Tarek poled the narrow flat-bottomed boat back downstream towards Trinity College. With renewed expertise, he neatly turned the punt towards the bank, slotting it into a vacant mooring. For perhaps another hour or more they strolled the grounds of Trinity and Kings, admiring the architecture and tracery of windows. They had tea in a very English teashop where that beverage was served in china cups that boasted finely painted roses both inside and out of the cup, resting on similarly ornamented saucers, each one in the shape of a Tudor rose. And they had toasted teacakes with melted butter.

Tarek walked back to the car with them. He was staying one more night at Christ's College, meeting friends for dinner, he said. They were driving back to Bagnum. Alan was going to stay the night at the house; Amin would take him to Southampton to catch the 9.54 to Cardiff. Megan would pick him up from there, he said, but the taxi service would probably cost him dinner. Bidding each other farewell, they agreed to keep in close touch. It would all be fine, they said. Tarek stood by the passenger's door, waiting. Amin turned the key in the ignition.

'Who's going to detonate the first bomb?' asked Alan, calmly and quietly.

'I think it might be Ayesha,' Tarek replied, with equal calm.

Alan nodded. 'That's what you meant, isn't it? When you said she wanted to be involved? Be careful my friend.'

Tarek watched the car turn left, back towards the Avenue and disappear from view. Walking back to Christ's College he wondered how to spend his evening alone.

*****

'Bury him,' said Mike Roberts in voice that was cold and hard. 'Bury the pompous self-opinionated little shit so deep that he'll need a lifetime to dig himself out.'

Not that he knew him that well, personally. After all John Watkins had only met Major Roberts on four or five occasions; each time, the man had listened to what he said, been quietly confident but perfectly friendly. This was different. He'd read the Major's file and Watkins was not stupid. The man in front of him, freezing the very air with arctic anger, was an extremely intelligent and dangerous man. And Watkins was very well aware that his ghost was not the only one in the firing line.

'Let me go through this one more time, and correct me if I miss anything, John.' The voice was heavy with sarcasm and disbelief. 'Sami Malik is already on our radar, not just because of his nuclear background in Pakistan. Intel from several sources suggests that Malik is selling either military hardware, information or both. Danny said as much when he was over and Malik has a high profile on Mossad's radar because he might just be working with Tehran.

'Thanks to Aaron (and his operative in Beirut) we have a line on what might be a rogue Islamist professor who suddenly has lunch with our friend Sami. Marina supplies Aaron with a mass of information that he shares with us. You hand all of this to Smythe-Corton who flips it casually into his in-tray. At the fucking bottom! And all you do is remind him not to forget the GCHQ link?! He finally feeds everything in and forgets the link. Because he 'was thinking about Marina's comments'. That was his excuse? And you slapped him limply on the wrist. Gave him a verbal warning, had a quiet word.'

If sea green was a lighter shade of white, it was probably because John Watkins felt himself sinking under the leading edge of a moving ice floe. He knew better than to even attempt a cry for help by reminding the Major that Smythe-Corton had rectified the link omission.

'Then there's this,' Mike said, waving the piece of paper in his hand. 'Tracker spits up an email from al-Shami to Malik confirming an order for something called NuCan. Money is going to change hands and if Malik's involved, that means a lot of folding green. But this prick doesn't think it's important and holds onto it for almost a week. If you hadn't seen Tracker's Border pick-up ...'

Mike waved both hands in front of his chest, an indication perhaps that the ice was thawing just a little. Watkins suspected that it would be a while before the underlying permafrost would melt.

'The ghosts are your department John. They're your responsibility and I don't want to have to break heads because you're not in control. Get rid of Smythe-Corton now, and that means he leaves the building naked. No mobiles, electronic gizmos, paper, notebooks or anything else that might be useful in any way. Not one fucking paper clip leaves with him. Then you will sit down and look for any other threads that might have been missed. End of.'

'Thank you Major Roberts.'

Mike barely gave the man a second glance as Watkins scuttled out through the open library doors.

'Ouch!' she said, with mock pain.

'You heard, I take it.'

'Most of it.'

Helen went over to the trolley, poured a measure of light amber liquid from a lead crystal decanter into a matching old fashioned tumbler, adding just drizzle of spring water.

'Eight year old Lagavulin single malt from Islay. Care for one?'

'Why not?'

She poured a second drink, took it over to him and perched on the arm of a neighbouring armchair. She sipped, looking at him carefully over the rim of her glass.

'He's actually bloody good at his job,' she said. 'Watkins, I mean. He's trying to get his head around Tracker as a whole and sometimes misses the details. It's early days Mike.'

'You think I was too hard?'

'No I don't. But I do think you could have been a little more tactical in your approach. A little warmth, esprit de corps, goes a long way. Psychologically we are working on the front line but in practical terms this isn't FOB Red House, and this isn't Iraq or Afghanistan. And John Watkins isn't a trooper. End of advisory.'

'Point taken, Colonel. Reprimand accepted.' He smiled at her, took a sip of whisky; she smiled back. 'You're quite the wily old fox, aren't you?'

'I'll settle for foxy lady, it makes me feel younger. However, back to business. What's the bit about border pick-up?'

'Tracker sieved out an entry from a Border Control officer at Heathrow. Woman called Eileen Patterson. Tracker caught it because of the holder name, country of issue and the fact that she'd flagged the carrier as – you'll love this – 'shifty, suggest eyes on'. Nothing would have happened normally. But we've got it because the name's Professor Tarek al-Shami out of Lebanon.'

'OK. What other details have you got?' All business now, Helen grabbed a notebook and pen from the desk.

'Visa is a current business stroke academic multi-entry. The contact address he's given as Christ's College, Cambridge. I know it well.'

'You were at Magdalene, right?'

'Well remembered. Yes and Christ's is only ten minutes walk. I'm sure he got his PhD at Cambridge but it definitely wasn't at one of the colleges. I'd have registered and remembered. Which means it's unlikely that he's there for an alumni ball and jaw. It could be some kind of Islamic symposium. But I'm pretty sure that Christ's College does offer guest accommodation for solo visitors. It's meant to give tourists a flavour of what it's like to live in student digs at a college. A bit of a gimmick, but if it makes money … '

'What's he written for duration of stay?'

'Four days. In theory, he'll be there tomorrow. If he's leaving on Monday, he might even leave Cambridge tomorrow and stay in London overnight.'

'He flew with?' she said, walking briskly over to the desk.

'Middle East Airlines.'

Helen brought the open laptop to life, typed quickly on the keyboard, paused, and then more typing. Neither one broke the silence as she waited.

''Kay. MEA has two flights to Beirut out of Heathrow on Monday. The second one doesn't leave till 2200, getting in at, yuk, 0445 in the morning. My money's on the 0130 which arrives in Beirut at 0805 local time, much more civilized.'

'I'm with you on that one. Can we check the manifest?'

'No problem. I'll see who we have in Cambridge as well. There's bound to be someone lurking around MI6's favourite recruiting city. Even if we miss al-Shami, we might be able to find out why he was there and what he was doing.'

'Yeah. But if there's any link with the Malik deal, we've lost that. What's really bugging me is not knowing what this NuCan project is and who's providing the money. With Malik involved, logically it has to be something to do with munitions of some sort. And that chucks up other questions. It's hardly likely to be a lone wolf operation, so who's al-Shami working for? Who's the end user? And what's the target?

*****

Saturday evening had basked in warm sunlight as Tarek had wandered through the meticulously maintained Victorian park called Christ's Pieces along a path commonly known as Milton's Walk running along Fellows' Garden. Not for the first time, he wondered why it was necessary for Cambridge to have cryptic names for so many locations. The grass had been recently cut, the sweet smell lingering on the air. A few students left over from the summer term were sharing a bottle of wine, laughing over a shared joke. Four girls flowed around him, chattering like starlings as they walked in the opposite direction, dividing and regrouping, seemingly oblivious to his existence.

He'd turned right on King Street, found a Turkish restaurant called Effes and dined frugally on falafel and lamb yoghurt shish. On returning to his room at Christ's College, he had read the first part of an academic paper on 'The Relevance of Medieval Islamic Geometry in Modern Design and Architecture' until he'd got bored and retired early. The following morning, he arose

202

refreshed and went to the breakfast room where he enjoyed a glass of freshly squeezed orange juice, two croissants with organic raspberry jam (naturally made in Cambridge) and two cups of free trade Arabica coffee. It was on the way back to his room that he'd been stopped by one of the porters.

'Excuse me Sir. It's Professor al-Shami, isn't it?'

'Yes?'

'Someone was looking for you yesterday evening, Sir. Said he understood that you might be staying with us here at the College. Of course, I told him that I couldn't possibly divulge personal information of that nature. I just thought you ought to know.'

'You say he was looking for me. Did he say why?'

'He said you were research students together, both doing your Doctorates with one of the faculties he said. He didn't mention which one and I'm afraid I didn't think to ask at the time, Sir. He said you were working on an Islamic paper and he was researching Asian anthropological something or others. I didn't really understand. Would be wonderful to meet up after all this time, he said, and could I call your room.

'Then I told him that I was not aware of anyone by the name of Professor Tarek al-Shami who might or might not being staying with us. Then he asked whether anyone else had asked after you. I told him, as far as I knew, no. I hope that's all right, Sir. We try to ensure privacy for our gentlemen staying at the College.'

'Did he leave a name, or a card?'

'No Sir. He said he might try another time. He spoke to Collins as well, in the Porters' Lodge. Frank said he gave him short shrift as well. He said he thought that the chap looked more of an undergraduate type rather than doctoral. It's not just an age thing, he said, it's a matter of quality.'

'How old do you think he was, err …'

'Benson, Sir. I'd say early 30s tops.'

'Thank you very much, Benson. A case of mistaken identity, I suppose.'

'Perhaps so, Sir.'

It seemed to him that his footsteps on the cobbles were louder than before. And despite the early morning chill, Tarek felt the sheen of sweat on his forehead as he marched the curving walkway around First Court's green lawn. Perhaps he was being watched through one rectangular pane of glass in its wooden frame; one among so many that looked out across quadrangle, blank eyes in the glare of light. Tarek chided himself for being melodramatic but that did nothing to lessen the feeling of disquiet. Questions tumbled around his head, numbered balls in a game of chance that he would have preferred not to play.

How could anyone have known that he was staying in Cambridge, let alone Christ's College? There was no way that anyone could have known, other than the College staff. But then someone could have mentioned his name, in passing. Someone else had recognised it, passed it on. And maybe the unknown visitor been genuine. Dakshi Chakraborty? It might have been. They been quite friendly for a while, each one an odd-man-out in normal Cambridge circles, even within the faculty. Tarek couldn't find the right file in his memory but it was perfectly possible that 'Daks' had been researching things anthropological. There again, why on earth would he be in Cambridge? Why not, thought Tarek, I am!

Deciding that Dakshi Chakraborty was the only rational, albeit surprising, answer was a relief. It allowed him to bury those other questions born of understandable but delusional paranoia. But it reminded him of the constant need for circumspection and caution. Another thought occurred. If the mystery caller had been Chakraborty, this was not the time to renew old acquaintances, especially with someone who enjoyed rooting through other people's brains.

Back in his room, he fired up his laptop and connected to the College wifi system. Searched Google for hotels near Paddington, he could catch a train from there to Heathrow in the morning; reserved a room at the Winchester on Westbourne Terrace, a few minutes walk from the station. Whatever the truth of the matter, it didn't make sense to stay in Cambridge another night and risk a meeting. It made sense to check his emails before he left.

To: Professor al-Shami <talshami@gmail.com>
From: QQ <ag49iut8zxg68so3@tormail.net>
Subject: Opportunity Strikes!

Congratulations! You've been chosen to meet the Main Man in Town this Tuesday. This is a Once Only Offer and it's just for You. @ NooN. Wait outside with the little blue bird and we'll send a cat who'll take you to town. Tell us YeS right back!

Tarek stared at the message, metaphorically scratching his head. As far as he was aware there was absolutely no reason for another meeting with anyone from al-Qaeda. And so soon. His plane wasn't due to arrive in Beirut until Monday evening which meant that he wouldn't get home until nine thirty, maybe ten. Outside the Bluebird at noon; why outside? And who was the Main Man? He realised he had no option, keyed the reply icon, typed 'Yes' and hit send.

*****

Eleven fifty. Ten more minutes to wait before Faisal, or someone else turned up. Leaning up against the wall next to the Bluebird Café, Tarek felt exposed and vulnerable. He thought he'd mentally disposed of the Cambridge incident, having decided it definitely had to have been Chakraborty. But the niggling fear of uncertainty had come back in London.

Walking from Paddington Station to the Winchester Hotel, he'd been alarmed by a woman who'd stopped him the street. She'd grabbed his arm, before asking him in broken English where she could get a bus for Notting Hill Gate. He didn't know and he told her so, but there was a look in her eye that suggested she didn't believe him. But he knew it was nothing. At the airport the following morning he felt certain that he was being watched on several different occasions and by more than just one person. He advised himself to get his head together very quickly, that his fears were totally ridiculous, unfounded and that his paranoia level was red lining.

That level only really started to ease back after take off; passing through immigration and customs at Beirut without a hitch brought it down to normal. Once back in Mansourieh, back in his comfort zone, he felt he was in control again, confident that all would be well. Standing on a side street in Achrafieh wasn't at all comfortable, not least because a cool breeze had sent a sea mist to damp down the dust that succeeded in distributing grime. Plus he was tired, had no idea what to expect and a small part of him wanted to tell al-fucking-Qaeda to just leave him alone to get on with the job. Actually, from his point of view, he thought it was going rather well. And somehow, that final thought made Tarek a little more cheerful.

'Fuck them,' he said.

'Who?' asked Faisal, making Tarek jump.

'Nobody. Sometimes it would be nice if I could see you coming.'

'Then it would not be a surprise. Come.'

Stopping a taxi, Faisal hustled Tarek into the back seat before climbing in himself.

'Zaitunay Bay, but not this side. We need to go out on the long side, the jetty. You know where I mean?'

'No problem. Out just before La Paillote?'

'Yallah!'

The driver wound down the window and spat; winding it up again, he pulled out into the traffic, turning left onto Avenue de l'Independance.

'Today the traffic is bad,' the driver said, 'maybe twenty minutes before we get to Zaitunay.'

'And that's something different for today? It's nothing new for Beirut. It's fine. When we get there, I may need you to wait.'

'That'll cost, my friend.'

'Is not a problem.'

'I could have met you there,' said Tarek.

'No, this way is better. I did not want either of us standing outside, waiting by the quayside. This way, we get there and straight away we go.'

'But go where? And to see who?'

'Patience Professor. All will be revealed in due course.'

There was no further conversation. The driver looked steadfastly forwards through the windscreen, cursing both the traffic and pedestrians alike. When greater emphasis was needed, he wound down the window and shouted abuse directly at the object of his ire. Faisal looked out of the window to the left,

Tarek the one to the right. Faisal tapped out a text on his mobile; Tarek turned to watch. The mist was slowly lifting, leaving behind it a damp city that began to steam as the sun shone through. And as the heat rose, so did the humidity.

After fifteen minutes, they finally turned in towards the old St Georges Hotel, turning left again to parallel the line of the marina as it curved round the bay. Following Faisal's instructions, the driver took the taxi as far as he could along the jetty, parking the car at the end to face the marina itself. Pontoons on the far side grew out from the wharf, each one with lines of attached boats on either side. The masts of the few yachts stood proudly among the lower levels maintained by power launches, hobby boats and other craft. Whatever its designation, whiteness glared from every one. In soothing contrast, the mirrored surface of the water glistened darkly in the sunlight, tie-dyed with the iridescent greens and purples of leaked oil.

As Tarek wondered idly where all people were, the roar of powerful outboard engines heralded a slim speedboat that raced in through the entrance to Zaitunay. Once inside the walls, the driver immediately eased back the throttle, dropping the nose from its previous sharp angle to a more horizontal position, letting the boat idle slowly towards the jetty.

'Our ride,' said Faisal, 'we go.'

In the few seconds that it had taken for Faisal to pay the taxi driver, the boat had been moored. One man had remained in the boat, his left hand resting on the wheel while occasionally blipping the throttle with his right, keeping the engines bubbling in the water. Another man stood on the jetty, his hands crossed loosely in front of him, his legs apart. Taking in the black trainers, jeans and t-shirt, the lean musculature and intelligent alertness, it didn't take Tarek too long to guess what his role might be in the line-up.

'Professor al-Shami, it is a privilege to meet such an honoured scholar. My name is Naseem. In a moment we will go to him on the Rih Albahr but first, a little security measure.'

Standing so his back blocked any view of Tarek, Naseem expertly patted him down, checking for any obvious weapons. He ran his fingers around Tarek's neck, across his chest and back looking for hidden wires. Dipped into his jacket with the light touch of a practised pickpocket. He nodded, satisfied. He helped Tarek clamber down into the boat. Greeted Faisal, exchanging the embrace of old acquaintance but not quite trusted friendship. Faisal climbed into the boat without assistance, closely followed by Naseem who slipped the mooring on his way down.

'Yallah!'

Turning the boat on its beam, the coxswain steered towards the marina entrance, smoothly feeding in the power. Once in the open waters of the Mediterranean, he pushed the throttle further forward taking the speed up to around 50 knots. Bouncing across the chop with its nose held high, the speedboat headed on a north-easterly bearing, quickly leaving Beirut to diminish in its wake. Only minutes later the boat tied up to the side of a sambuk, a large cargo dhow, with the name Rih Albahr written in flowing elegant Arabic calligraphy on the bow. Sea Wind: a good name for a ship, thought Tarek.

Unlike most cargo dhows, the sambuk's superstructure extended forwards from the navigational bridge in a wood-framed canopy, stretching almost to the point where the ship's lines curved in to meet at the bow. Long floor sofas stretched out on the rug-covered deck on either side of a low well-worn wooden table. Lines of kilim floor cushions leant against the bulwarks through the canvas walls. The arrangement was such that, even if all the seats were taken, whoever was steering the ship would still have a clear view from the bridge to the bow and beyond.

Once on board, Faisal found a place to wait but Naseem led Tarek around the leading edge of the Sea Wind's majlis, between two crewmen similarly clad. Tarek noted that both had an AK47 lying within easy reach. But his focus was immediately taken to the burly man sitting on a seat similar in style to the sofas, but this was more sumptuous and only designed to take one person. He seemed familiar, thought Tarek, as though he had met him before, but not face to face. Tarek's mind held no picture of this man but seemed to be able to provide a basic description.

'Welcome to my home on the water Professor al-Shami.'

The voice was melodic, a sonorous velvet that easily carried the length of the ship. It had strength, command and a touch of iron that had forced men to listen and act.

'My name is Abdul Saad Mazari but you may have heard another name, Saad al-Kabuli perhaps.'

The description in Tarek's mind crystallized and took form. He saw the black ghutra flecked with silver wrapped around the man's head like a turban, the loose end resting on one shoulder. Then the faded black kandura, cinched round the waist by a wide black leather belt; the trademark long curved dagger with its white bone handle attached at an angle by a strap over the left hip. The picture he saw was of a younger man, his beard black as his turban, standing against grey rocks, side by side with a tall slim man in a long white kandura and ghutra. But it was still that image of Osama bin Laden and Abdul Saad al-Kabuli that he remembered seeing in his father's 'Book of Photographs ~ With the Mujahideen 1988'. And several years later, he remembered the media calling the man 'one of Osama Bin Laden's most effective lieutenants, al-Kabuli is also regarded as one of al-Qaeda's most intelligent and ruthless leaders'.

'As-salām 'alaykum, I am honoured,' said Tarek, politely inclining his head. 'Yes Sir, I have indeed heard of you, and of your deeds.'

'Wa 'alaykum as-salām. The young professor is teaching the mountain lion to be courteous. Please, sit down. Naseem my friend, call to Yusuf to bring tea for us.'

As Naseem disappeared to do his master's bidding, al-Kabuli sat down in his chair while Tarek took his place, out of deference, some way down a long side sofa.

'Closer Professor, I do not wish to shout.'

As Tarek shuffled towards the bridge house, he was disturbed by the sound of another man entering to the rear on the other side. It was a face he recognised, even though the man had exchanged the expensive suit for a dark brown ghutra and kandura.

'I think you have already met Haroun.' Al-Kabuli brought his hand down heavily on the other man's shoulder, making him visibly wince with discomfort. 'I would trust Haroun with my life, to be alone with my wife and my daughters; with my money, I would trust him to double it but charge me exorbitant fees.'

He roared with laughter at his own joke, slapping his leg exuberantly. The boy Yusuf appeared carrying a tray of glasses and a tall Arabic teapot. He set it down on the table, added sugar to four glasses, poured tea into each one and looked at al-Kabuli for approval. He bowed appreciatively at the smile given, then left as quietly as he'd arrived.

'Naseem, come.'

Naseem took his seat beside the Bookkeeper. Each one of the four took a glass of tea, sipped the hot liquid with care, inhaled the sweet mint bouquet and made noises of appreciation, each in his own way. They were silent, drinking until they had finished their glasses. Yusuf immediately appeared to refill them and then left.

'So why are you here Professor? Because I wished to meet the man who is spending one million, six hundred thousand American dollars of our money, but in a good way. I wish to know more about this man who wishes to kill British seamen and destroy British ships. I want to know who this man is and what is in his heart.'

He stroked the iron-grey silky beard, staring with dark intensity at Tarek. His hooked nose was a promontory overlooking the thick moustache that did little to hide the hard line of a mouth that twisted downwards in repose. His skin was tanned to a fine golden-brown supple leather; the legacy of years of hot suns and winds full of sand, harsh snow-reflected light and temperatures that froze spittle on your lips.

'I met your father once in the mountains, in Afghanistan. He came to speak with the Sheikh, for advice and to share counsel. He stayed with us a while and I think he was a good man, in his heart. He didn't have iron in his soul or blood in his mouth but he served in other ways. There is room under Allah's skies for men like him. But if you are to be the spearhead of jihad, you must have that iron and blood, as do I and Naseem.

'We have a proverb in Afghanistan. Let me tell you, it is this: 'when the mouse steals teeth and claws from the gluemaker and shouts he is a lion, then the cat prepares for dinner'. So I ask myself: is this Tarek al-Shami the mouse or the cat?'

Al-Kabuli gazed at him waiting for his reply. And Tarek talked. He spoke with passion, told his tale of hate, explained the need for retribution and revenge, spread out his plans before them as a merchant shows his wares. He picked up names as items for consideration – Ayesha, Leena, Leila, Faridah and Halah – and said it was for them and family honour. And he spoke of Allah's will, and power and might. Allahu akbar. And not once did his listeners interrupt.

'When are you testing the devices?'

'In six weeks time, in the Kharan Desert?'

'You will be with Dr Malik and General Mustagh? Both of them?'

'Yes.'

'And now you have spoken, told us what is in your head and heart, do you wish to serve al-Qaeda as you have said?'

'As Allah is my witness.'

'Then, you will say to this to them. That you are an authorised emissary from the Sheikh himself in this matter: that al-Qaeda wishes to acquire one nuclear warhead from Pakistan's many and we ask for your help. Tell them that there is plenty more money in al-Qaeda's war chest.' He paused, allowing his words to sink in, and to gauge the reaction. Tarek was pale, saying nothing. 'But this is a big step, my friend. Go home now, smoke your hashish and ponder what has been said. Faisal will ask you for your answer in two days. Today we have finished.'

Al-Kabuli turned to Naseem: 'Take our friend back to Beirut. We will talk again soon, insha'allah.'

And Naseem led him back to the boat.

9 ~ Six Weeks is a Long Time

'The problem with some of these people is that they're over-educated and pampered in universities like Cambridge. No offence Mike.'

'None taken, Sir. I quite agree but it is the culture of the place. Oxford's the same. Some people argue that most of the students bring their silver spoons with them but there are an awful lot at Cambridge to whom that doesn't apply. So, in my opinion, it's a case of nurture over nature.'

Admiral Buller exhaled, sending a cloud of fragrant smoke upwards to join the already hazy sub-ceiling canopy.

'I think you're probably right, but that doesn't make it any better. They're told they're close to genius material, they bloody believe it and then behave as though they're smarter than everyone else! So it doesn't help when some vile spin writer from the Foreign Office writes a piece for The Cambridge Student which endorses that view; then more or less says that being a spy is bloody good fun and it pays well. Here have a read, it isn't long. Pretty much says, all interested students should apply as soon as possible.'

The Admiral pushed the magazine across the table, already open at the appropriate page. While he waited for Mike to scan read the three meagre paragraphs, he buzzed Helen from the console on his desk.

'Can you come down and brief us on Cambridge, please?'

'Give me five and I'm there Sir Reginald.'

'Thank you,' he said to the box. 'And?' he asked, turning back to Mike.

'Hardly impressive. Plus they're still using the old address: PO Box 1300, London SE1 1BD. They might as well say send to: Spies Recruitment, care of MI6, 85 Albert Embankment etcetera.'

'But that's not really the point. What I'm saying is, it's rubbish, gives the wrong message. And now, I don't know whether you've picked up on this one, GCHQ is saying it's going to advertise on video games. For God's sake! No wonder we're ending up with dross like Smythe-Corton. Well done that man who fired him. Of course he should have realised earlier, but John's got a lot on his plate with Tracker. At least he caught on and got rid of the man immediately.'

Hearing the last few sentences, Helen was just about to correct the Admiral when she saw Mike shaking his head. She zipped her mouth with her spare hand and grinned.

'Finding the right staff is a problem,' she said, sounding very serious. 'Cases in point, we have to consider what to do with one redundant naval officer with a bad smoking habit and an ex-army officer with a poor taste in footwear.'

'Bloody women,' said the Admiral.

Mike peered at his Timberlands: 'A man's perfect choice'.

Slipping onto one of the Chesterfields, Helen opened a slim paper file. She glanced at the top piece of paper, then lifted that to see the one underneath and then a third below that. Satisfied that all was in order, she looked at each man in turn.

'Cambridge. Unfortunately the only person the sweepers could get hold of was a post-grad recruit called Rupert Henshaw. The porters would have recognised the others apparently. Nice enough chap but only just out of nappies, training-wise. He talked to two of the porters and both blanked him. The first one,' Helen looked at her notes, 'Hector Benson, gave the impression that al-Shami was staying at Christ's but couldn't say so in keeping with the College dictat on privacy. The second rejected any conversation at all in respect of guests. Henshaw's report indicates that he gave too much away about his cover: told them he'd been at Cambridge with Professor al-Shami. If either porter knew our man by sight, they'd have put two and two together; there must be at least 15 years age difference. My guess is that Benson flagged it to al-Shami and he flees the coop on Sunday morning.

'Henshaw did manage to redeem himself later, admittedly after the bird had flown. At 1100 on Sunday he spoke to a receptionist, Tania Woldovski, who told him that al-Shami had already checked out. Henshaw remarked that it was strange since he was meant to meet him the day before but the Professor had never showed. Did he say where he was going? Ms Woldovski said she had no idea but mentioned, en passant, that she'd seen him the day before. Apparently, the Professor was planning a little punting.

'Henshaw starts to phone the rental companies and strikes lucky on the fourth call. He's playing the 'I have the man's wallet' gambit. The Professor hired a punt for one hour from Trinity College Punts. Trinity man said he went out with two other men. Said he always checks unknowns as they go out on the water, just to make sure they're all right. No recall on what they looked like apart from 'foreign looking, maybe Middle Eastern.'

'So who are the two friends?' asked Mike, somewhat uselessly.

'At the moment, I've no idea but I'm guessing that they're both based here, in England. I checked MEA's manifests and I was right about the time of his flight. Tim nipped down to Heathrow and saw the man go through security. Not that it necessarily means anything, but he got the idea that al-Shami was nervous. Said he kept looking over his shoulder as though he thought he was being watched. Out of curiosity, I asked John to set Tracker searching flights to and from Beirut for the last six months. Including this visit, the Professor has visited our fair isle three times. It's not a lot when you add it all up.'

'It's always a slow burn, you know that,' said Mike. 'Sooner or later, we'll catch up with Professor al-Shami's little friends.'

*****

Amin glanced at the clock on the wall, then tidied his desk, put on his suit jacket and checked by feel to ensure that his tie was straight. He walked across to the window, looked down and across to the main gate. From this distance, the car blocked by the security barrier looked like a dark blue Vauxhall Astra; it felt like the right type of car for civil servants. He watched the barrier rise, the security guard indicating where the car should be parked and watched the Astra pull in between two white lines that weren't bounded by other cars. Then he watched it reverse, correct the angle very slightly to ensure that lines and car were in absolute parallel. And finally, watched a short, rather plump woman get out of the passenger side; a tall, pencil thin man angled out from the driver's. It would have been comical if they weren't here on official business. Amin walked back to his desk and waited.

'Mrs Easton and Mr Lusty are here from the Ministry, Mr Masri.'

Amin keyed the talk button.

'Thanks Connie. I'll come down. Can you page Henry and tell him to come to the conference room down there.'

'Will do Mr Masri.'

Amin walked down the two flights of stairs wondering what on earth they actually wanted to inspect. Warehouses full of stuff, packing equipment, forklift trucks? Metaphorically he slapped himself on the wrist. Of course, none of the above; his money was on health and safety procedures, whether the loos were clean, if nailbrushes were provided by wash basins and other such elements that make vital contributions to the provision of emergency supply. By the time he reached reception, his smile was firmly in place and his hand ready for the shaking.

'Mrs Easton, Mr Lusty, welcome to InterFoods. I'm Amin Masri.'

Her hand was squidgy, warm and unpleasantly damp; his hand was a dry bunch of smooth-barked twigs on a cold day. Her face was bloated, spongy and rather red with one long black hair growing from her chin; his was more on the oiled skeletal side and distinctly sallow.

'Please, do come with me. Would either of you like tea or coffee?'

'Thank you Mr Masri, that's very kind,' said Mrs Easton, in a surprisingly pleasant voice. 'A cup of tea would be nice.'

'Coffee, black, if you don't mind.' Mr Lusty's voice seemed more appropriate: the words came out in way that reminded Amin of an amplified pepper grinder.

'No problem. Connie?'

'Your wish Mr Masri,' she said with a cheerful smile.

The three of them sat at one end of a functional conference table in a functional room unadorned by fripperies. An unmarked white board was fixed to one end wall and an easel stood to attention in one corner, complete with flip chart and coloured felt tip pens, ready for training sessions. A cork noticeboard hung by the door, decorated by a certificate of Employer's Liability Insurance, a small Health and Safety at Work poster and a laminated sheet outlining the procedures to be followed in the event of a fire.

'This shouldn't take long Mr Masri. We are aware that this would not be the only contract between the MoD and International Foods. I appreciate that you have been through all this before but I'm sure that you appreciate in turn, that each contract has to be dealt with independently of any other.'

'Of course Mrs Easton.'

The door opened, letting Connie in to deliver one cup of tea, another of coffee, two spoons, one bowl of sugar and a small jug of milk. As she left, Henry entered and took a seat next to Amin.

'Henry Perkins, our works manager. Please, continue.'

The two officials acknowledged Henry with barely perceptible nods. Mrs Easton continued.

'We are not here to inspect your operation in terms of actual goods, or indeed the various types of storage that you have on site. What we have to establish and approve is your compliance and conformity with employment standards legislation, to include but not excepting Health and Safety at Work, factories, warehousing, both bonded and unbonded ...'

Amin tuned out as Mrs Easton droned on for several more minutes. He was brought back to reality by the sound of Henry's voice.

'Absolutely, that makes total sense.'

'Mr Masri, do have any questions?'

'Ah, no, I don't think so.'

'In which case, I suggest we begin. Mr Lusty?'

'Agreed,' the man ground.

'Fine,' said Henry. 'I suggest that we start with Warehouse One. That's the larger of the two main storage facilities and it's also where all the records are kept in respect of Customs and Excise regs. This way.'

Henry led the pair down the corridor; Amin heaved a sigh of relief. Returning to his office, he sat down at his desk and brought the ultra modern computer back to life with a flick of his fingers across the touch pad. He opened up the folder marked accounts, double clicked on the file named Assets. An Excel worksheet blossomed on his screen, complete with pie and bar charts. He started to read through the detail and weigh up his options. Absorbed with the task, time seemed to pass quickly even though it was over two hours before Henry brought the pair up to his office. Mrs Easton and Mr Lusty sat down on two chairs, set immediately in front of the large ornate wooden desk, a present from his father-in-law Romain Berthier. Henry stood quietly to one side, his face a moulded cliff of inscrutability.

'I'd like to thank you for making Mr Perkins available for our visit. He has been extremely helpful.' (Amin noted her emphasis on the 'He' and the slight pause for reinforcement.) 'I'm delighted to say that neither Mr Lusty nor I can fault anything within your area of operation. Well done!' (Mr Lusty was nodding as his colleague spoke. Amin wasn't sure whether that was in agreement with her sentiments or out of sheer boredom.) 'Therefore, we will be submitting our approval and recommending that International Foods should be awarded the contract as delineated under the Overseas Deployable Food Programme and for Her Majesty's Royal Navy and its extended services as of immediate. I'd say congratulations were in order Mr Masri.'

'Congratulations to both of you,' Mr Lusty ground out.

Standing up to leave, they extended their hands to be shaken by both men. Henry showed them back to reception, returning a few minutes later. Together Henry and Amin walked to the window and watched the pair of civil servants climb back in the Vauxhall Astra.

'Henry, you're an absolute star.'

'Does that mean I get a raise, Boss?'

'It might well do, Henry, it might well do.'

*****

He'd grabbed a cup of coffee from the dispensing machine in the corridor rather than fiddle with filters and jugs in his office. Grimacing at the synthetic taste, Alan wondered why he'd made the exception and put it down to 'having other things on my mind'. Holding the hot plastic gingerly in one hand, he opened the door to his office with the other. Sat down at his desk, powered up his computer, sipped at his coffee again and waited for the inevitable, five-minutes-after-the-boss-arrives tap on the door. It was probably a fraction less than that when Steven Lee's head appeared through the gap giving the illusion of being suspended in mid-air.

'Morning Mr Abbot. Isn't it a lovely one? Nice to see the sun shining again isn't it?'

'Yes Steven. Good Morning.'

Totally missing his boss's lack of enthusiasm, Steven Lee happily continued his cheery chatter.

'I said to the missus, if I wasn't working we could go down to Mewslade Bay, to the beach there. D'you know it? It's a pretty spot just past Swansea. Anyway, I said maybe we could go there on the weekend because this is meant to last for a few days.'

Finally realising Alan's lack of interest, and catching the look on his face, Steven Lee changed tack.

'So, sizeable schedules came through from the MoD this morning and I've patched those through to your computer. Looks like we're going to be pretty busy over the next few months. Forbes should be happy.'

'Any particular trends showing?'

'Not really, it's a fairly even spread. The biggest demand's for Sea Skuas but that's only because there are so many lined up for export.'

'What about delivery dates?'

'Fortunately, there's a fairly good lead time with most of them. Kuwait and South Korea are first in line, with substantial numbers of Skuas requested. But I can't see any problems with production this side of Christmas.'

'That's great, thanks Steven.'

'Give me a shout if there's anything you want me to work through later.'

'Of course.'

Steven hovered for a moment, as though expecting more conversation. Finally concluding that there was nothing more, he raised a hand as if in farewell and left. Alan stared at the slowly closing door, shook his head in mock disbelief and turned to look at the monitor. Opening up the file that Steven had sent through, he keyed in a 'by country' filter and scrolled through the lists.

Brazil, Germany, India, Pakistan, the Republic of Korea, Turkey and United Kingdom; all had orders in for Sea Skuas.

As always, he smiled at the irony of Britain selling missiles to India and Pakistan, considering the volatility of the relationship between the two countries. A newspaper-style cartoon popped into his mind: Musharraf and Kalam facing each other, a missile in one of their hands while the other hands threw money down to a waiting Britannia. Then the greater irony lit up lights: he was waiting for explosive devices being sent from Pakistan to blow up British warships, paid for by Islamic fundamentalists. Divine retribution or insanity born of hatred and greed? This was not the time for philosophical debate; he dismissed the thought as quickly as it had arisen.

With the filter changed from 'by country' to 'by missile; Sea Wolf', the list of countries reduced: Brazil (again), Chile, Indonesia, Malaysia and the United Kingdom. Keeping the 'by missile' filter but replacing 'Sea Wolf' with 'Sea Dart' produced just one client: United Kingdom. Alan double clicked to get: Ministry of Defence – Royal Navy. Clicking again revealed the specifics, by ship's designation, name, the type and number of missiles required and the home port. The first four ships were all Duke Class Type 23 frigates – HMSs Montrose, Richmond, Portland and St Albans. He read through the requirements out of habit rather than interest. The frigates carried surface-to-air Sea Wolf missiles and air-to-surface Sea Skuas for their Lynx helicopters. Varying numbers, mostly for delivery to Portsmouth with a handful for Devonport.

Alan scrolled down to the second category: Type 42, Sheffield Class destroyers, armed with surface-to-air Sea Dart missiles, each carrying a Lynx helicopter armed with Sea Skuas. He looked very carefully at the listed requirements, focusing solely on which ships wanted Darts. HMS Edinburgh – 20; HMS Gloucester – 20; HMS York – 20; HMS Manchester – 20; HMS Nottingham – 20; HMS Liverpool – 16. A total of six ships, all based in Portsmouth. Destroyers like the Edinburgh and Gloucester carried 40 Sea Darts apiece with storage capacity for 15 more. The delivery dates were marked flexible with a back end of mid-December. All they needed was four ships within a given time frame and he had six to play with, each waiting to receive an explosive gift from abroad.

It was as though children were chanting a rhyme, gently tapping fingertips against thighs to keep time; he could hear words in his head:

> Eeny, meeny, miny, moe,
> Catch a sailor by the toe,
> Let him reap what he did sow,
> Eeny, meeny, miny, moe.
>
> Eeny, meeny, miny, moe,
> Twenty sailors in a row,
> One big bang and down they go,
> Eeny, meeny, miny, moe.

'Oh yes,' said Alan softly, his face grim and determined. 'That will do very nicely.'

*****

Tarek shivered in the chill early morning air but wasn't quite ready to go back inside. He hugged the mug of hot coffee with both hands as though hoping that its warmth would somehow transfer. Behind him he could hear the sounds of blast waves, explosions and voiceovers as his laptop looped yet more clips from YouTube. Watching videotape of thermonuclear explosions full of noise, smoke and brilliant flashes of light rolling through, one after the other must have affected his eyes, he thought, made his vision a little blurred. The noise was beginning to irritate.

He walked back inside, switched off the sound and waited for the screen saver to take over the display. He watched as the screen went black, then red pipework started to build, expand horizontally and vertically, bending and twisting. Green pipes intertwined with the red and then orange and blue. He watched as the screen filled with a maze of coloured pipes and then finally disappeared, only to start all over again. As he stared, the words kept coming back, a looping audio clip in his head; as clear now as when al-Kabuli had spoken them two days before.

'Do you wish to serve al-Qaeda as you have said? … an authorised emissary from the Sheikh himself in this matter: that al-Qaeda wishes to acquire one nuclear warhead from Pakistan's many and we ask for your help.'

Tarek knew the damage that bombs and missiles could do, understood their destructive power. He was prepared to use that level of explosive power; was going to use that kind of power in a targeted controlled way, he told himself. But a nuclear warhead? That was in an altogether different league. Rationalise. Analyse the positions of responsibility and accountability. He would simply be the messenger, passing on a request from the Sheikh to Dr Sami Malik. After that, he might convey the answer, whether agreement or rejection. Whatever happened after that would not, could not, be construed in any way to be his responsibility. After all, does one blame the telephone for the conversation of others?

Faisal's email had arrived the previous night with a simple question: and your answer is Yes or No? The clock was ticking and Tarek knew he had to make a decision. Touching the power button to bring the laptop awake, he brought up his inbox, opened Faisal's message and keyed the reply icon. He typed one word – Yes – and then clicked on send. For some reason, he felt a sense of relief.

Relief as in feeling there was nothing more that could be done for a while. Relief as in knowing that, during that time he could think about other things, forget about NuCans for a while. He'd already flagged up the next visit to Pakistan with his Director.

'Pakistan, I can understand,' Professor Khoury had said. 'Pakistan is becoming a totem for Islam and Muslims all over the world. A nexus that should not be ignored. You are going when?'

At the end of the month, for four days, perhaps longer, Tarek had told him. He'd watched as the Director checked his diary, paused at a particular page and held it down with one finger. Although it was upside down, Tarek could read: 'Sylvie/Byblos 01-04/09'. The old goat had obviously promised to take his mistress away for a long weekend. For a minute or two, Tarek had pretended that his trip might overrun just to bait the man. Khoury's facial expression had gone through a cycle that started with patronising beneficence, moved up to agitated panic through to grateful relief.

'Karachi, you said? Invited to the Sindh Madressatul Islam University, of course. I look forward to hearing your thoughts.'

Professor Mohammed Said Khoury, having been distracted by the possibility of having to tell Sylvie that Byblos would have to be cancelled, had been extremely supportive. He actually suggested that flying business class to Pakistan's busiest city should be considered. The cost of the hotel was of less importance than its suitability in terms of proximity to the university. He was delighted that Tarek would be spending more than just a few consecutive days at the faculty with his students in the interim. And perhaps Professor al-Shami might even stand in for some of his official duties? Delighted, Tarek had said.

During this hiatus, as promised, Tarek actually did spend more time in his office at the university. He had discussions with students, conducted tutorials, gave several lectures, marked papers, wrote reports and generally behaved as one might expect a professor to behave. He had lunch with a colleague, spent time with Ayesha and on at least three evenings, went out to dinner. On one hot afternoon, he'd bumped into Marina again. Literally. He'd apologised, she'd said not too worry. Did he have time to talk, she'd asked. Perhaps when he returned from Pakistan, he'd said. Which reminded him that he'd hadn't booked his ticket.

*****

Danny looked down to the dusty street below; a delivery truck had shed its load and the traffic was bottling. In Tel Aviv, it was the sort of situation that always put him on alert, looking for the flash of a knife or the sudden explosion. He relaxed when three policemen appeared.

'Marina's flying solo,' said Aaron.

'Say what?' asked Danny, turning back to look at his assistant.

'Marina in Beirut. Apparently she bumped into her friend, Professor al-Shami, this afternoon. She tried for a conversation but he blanked her.'

'So why are we talking?'

222

'For two reasons. He said that he has too much to do because he is flying out to Karachi, as in Pakistan, in a few days. She did a bit of checking on the students' faculty diary which shows that al-Shami's out of there for possibly one week. No information about why.'

'OK. Throw Tracker at the flight manifests to see if the system can pick out the flight. Then pull up anything else that it's grabbed over the last month re al-Shami. In the meantime I'll try to get Mike Roberts in London on VoIP.'

'You got it,' said Aaron, grinning.

Grabbing a swivel chair, Danny spun himself over to a monitor, brought the system to life and put the call through. Light flared on his screen, moderated and the image crystallized in to a face.

'The handsome Danny Spiegel. How is sunny Tel Aviv this afternoon?'

'Hot and dusty, Helen. You're looking as beautiful as ever. I assume that London's wet and dismal?'

'Actually, it's a pleasant strawberries and cream summer's day. To what do I owe this pleasure?'

'I need to talk to Mike about our man in Beirut. He about?'

'I think you're in luck. Let me go find him.'

For a few moments, Danny had a view of an empty chair and the unadorned wall behind. Bulk blocked the screen, moved backwards and sat down.

'Hey Danny, how's tricks?'

'Good. How're you getting on over there with Tracker?'

'We're getting there,' Mike said slowly. 'You might say we've had a minor personnel problem that set us back a bit, but that's sorted, permanently.'

'Sounds a little drastic?'

'No quite the permanent you'd mean.'

'Ah, you British are so pussy,' said Danny laughing. 'Listen, the main reason for calling – Marina's come through from Beirut to say that al-Shami's flying to Karachi on Friday. Did you know?'

'Shit, no! He was over here a few weeks back, in Cambridge, but we didn't pick it up until it was too late. Looks like he knows people over here but whether that's significant or not, I have no idea.'

'You're picking up both al-Shami's outgoing and incoming mail now, right? Hang on Mike. Yeah, Aaron.'

Aaron's moon face appeared on Mike's screen at a mad angle as the big man leaned down.

'Yo, Major Roberts, good to see you.'

Mike leaned sideways to match and grinned at the grin. 'Likewise.' Aaron disappeared from view but Mike saw him hand a note to Danny.

'Thanks Aaron, keep with it. Yeah, I was saying, email?'

'In principle, yes. Problem is that GCHQ's monitoring is working on a suck-it-and-see basis. In other words, their systems are hoovering up everything that they can without discrimination and we've got Tracker working with detailed filters to target specifics. To misquote what you guys said the other day: we're searching for the eyes of needles in haystacks on a major reproduction drive!'

'Yeah, I know what you mean. Have you picked up on al-Shami's new email addy? That look is saying, oh shit. OK, Aaron says that it looks fairly recent. Take it down: tango, alpha, romeo, numerals one and zero, sierra, hotel, alpha, mike, numerals nine, nine one, at hotmail.com. Feedback?'

'That's – tar10sham991@hotmail.com.'

'You got it. He's on the same IP address at the same location so it's definitely him. He's still using Gmail and the university one, of course. If there are any more email addresses, we haven't seen them yet. Apparently he's also sent stuff on Hotmail from his office. There's only one thing that might be of interest, but that's only because you mentioned possible links in England. It's a maybe.' Danny looked down at his slip of paper. 'We picked it up a couple of days ago. It's from someone called Amin and the address is: alpha, mike, alpha, tango, echo, alpha, lima, at sign, aol.com. So that's amateal@aol.com. Message reads: Contract confirmed! Yeah, all systems go. Al-Shami sent back a two worder: Yes! Congratulations. The IP address shows a London location. Not a lot to go on but worth keeping a note I guess.'

'Thanks Danny. You're right, that's all we can do. Back to Malik, you saw al-Shami's email to him about progressing this NuCan project?'

'Yeah. That came through like a flaming beacon at this end but nothing to do apart from watch and wait. Looking forward to the next episode and Karachi could be it.'

'Our little personnel problem is responsible for us only just having seen it.'

'Ah. Listen Mike, I didn't call because I assumed you'd definitely catch that one, otherwise ...'

'Hey no need to apologise. There's no rule that says you have to spoon-feed. But what you started to say, agreed going to Karachi must mean something's happening that needs al-Shami to actually be on the ground in Pakistan. I think it's safe to assume that money has exchanged hands.'

'That's another thing we sieved. We've seen one or two weird mails to the Professor saying stuff like: congratulations, you've won the jackpot. The last one was about meeting the Main Man in Town. It looks like spam, or some kind of crap marketing. I don't know about the others but he responded to the last one with 'fine'. The message asked for a 'yes' answer. It's probably nothing but, who knows. The emails are coming through Tor. So there's no way of tracing them back to source. You know about Tor, right?'

'The Onion Router, anonymity in the Deep Web for all! Let the Dark Lord come forth.'

'OK smartass. Mock all you like but that shit works. Emails bounce through a hundred relays anywhere in the world before it gets there; no way are you going to track it back. But your point is?'

'That your tormails are almost certainly spam. I think. But can we get some kind of synchronicity between your Tracker system and ours?'

'On the technical front, let me ask Aaron and I'll get back to you. But I also need to check upwards: an actual link would probably need approval and I'm not sure that would be forthcoming. Verbal and written exchanges are cool; cyberwiring could be a megabyte too far. Back to the here and now, I think we need to see what the Professor does in Pakistan. You want to play with your people or you want to use ours?'

'If you've got people in the flow, I'm happy. We haven't got an organised network in Karachi that I can tap into without talking to other agencies.'

'Fine. I also think that we need to put him under light surveillance when he gets back to Beirut. I'm thinking Marina?'

'Offer words on the pillow to one, but a multitude might hear? Maybe. Let's see where Karachi leads.'

'OK, I think we're done. Don't be a stranger.'

'No worries. And, thanks Danny.'

'No problem.'

Danny clicked on disconnect; the screen blinked to black. He swivelled round in his chair and looked at Aaron.

'Get in touch with David Bernstein at the American Consulate in Karachi. Ask him who he's running for us, locally. Tell him we need three.'

*****

Emirates flight 602 touched down at Jinnah International Airport in Karachi at 19.45, 20 minutes ahead of schedule. The lights of the terminal glowed orange in the early evening darkness, reflecting on the wet tarmac. Leaving the plane, Tarek sucked in his breath as the hot humid air enveloped him and squeezed like a wetsuit. The arctic chill of the terminal reversed the process with a brutal immediacy. The crush of people would have seemed to make immigration a long and tedious process. However, the dense line of passive humanity was processed at a smooth, steady pace, like treacle poured from a jug. But once released into the baggage hall, the line fractured into a thousand flying fragments, each searching for bags yet to arrive.

As the carousel began to move, it brought a tumble of red, blue and white hessian bales tied up with string or tightly bandaged by brown parcel tape. Amid these dry rolling rapids, ancient suitcases surfed the flow, crashing against newly-bought-in- Dubai pieces of luggage. Tarek waited stoically, surrounded by a population of Pakistani expats on brief leave from their lives of construction. They plucked bags and bales from the conveyor as crows peck at carrion on the road. Harried businessmen waited anxiously on the edges, slashing ruthlessly through the melee on spotting their precious bags. Tarek was relieved when he saw his own small silver suitcase appear unharmed.

In the arrivals hall, he scanned the vast amorphous collage made from pieces of card and paper, each one bearing the name of one or more passengers.

Mr T J Chugtai; Ahmad Dogar Snr; Muhammad Rajpar; Vinjan ATV Welcomes Gita Shah (Ms); Atlas Sindi Tours – Mr & Mrs Manson, Mr K Pullen, Viktor Menz; Bindi Unar and Blessing Rathore … … And somewhere to the right hand side of the collage, a man in a maroon salwar kameez held up a sign that read: Professor Tarek al-Shami. He watched Tarek's progress across the hall, knowing what he looked like from the pictures shown at his briefing.

'Welcome to Karachi Professor al-Shami. I am Bheyrya. Please, follow me.'

Picking up Tarek's suitcase, he led the way in a long loping stride that had Tarek jogging to keep up the pace. In the car park on level two, Bheyrya unlocked a black Suzuki Potohar 4x4, dropped the suitcase in the back and motioned him to climb into the passenger seat. Neither of them spoke until they had turned right off the terminal road onto Shahrah-e-Faisal and were heading towards the city centre. The traffic was heavy, a slow moving loose-linked belt of vehicles rolling on a five lane carriageway. Bheyrya produced a mobile phone from somewhere and tossed it into Tarek's lap.

'Courtesy of Dr Malik. It's got a prepaid Pak SIM card but it's not meant for calling home or finding a little company for the night. Three people have the number: Dr Malik, Captain Kharal and me, just in case we need to find you or call. Those same three names are on the contacts list, just in case you need to call one of us. The Doctor should be calling in a moment; when it rings, push the green telephone button to connect.'

Past Shaheed-e-Millat Expressway, the traffic started to thin out and Bheyrya picked up speed. Forty miles an hour seemed fast after a walking fifteen. A kaleidoscope of colour fragments whirled through the windscreen and past: white headlights and red brakes, green billboards tinted blue, blue ones tinted red, flashes of orange that burst and winked out into black. Contrasting darkly against the bright lights, buildings merged into one fluid shade that dipped and rose, broke and reformed. The inconstant hum of traffic outside seemed to find myriad ways to play its mechanical symphony, its very density alternating adagios with allegrettos. Inside the car, the air conditioning wheezed asthmatically, producing a thin wash of air on the cool side of lukewarm.

'We have a tail,' Bheyrya observed. 'Don't look backwards,' he ordered, anticipating the reflex action. Twisting the mirror on the windscreen to allow Tarek a rear view, he said: 'the white Toyota in the next lane, about four cars behind'.

'I see it. It's got no plates!'

'ISI. Inter-Services Intelligence,' he added, noticing Tarek's look of confusion. 'Bastards are everywhere, creeping up on you from nowhere. And they're fucking arrogant. They like to put the frighteners on people, especially when they're new in town. Watch, in moment they'll pull alongside.'

Bheyrya twisted the mirror back, checked his rear view. 'Here they come, the motherfuckers,' he muttered.

Tarek saw the far wing mirror go white, followed immediately by the bulk of the Toyota as it drew parallel. He could see the man in the passenger seat looking straight at him, tiny reflections of car window and occupants in the mirror glasses. He registered the gold-badged black beret, the camouflage shirt in duo-tone brown-beige, and the patronising sneer. Bheyrya kept his head facing forwards, saying nothing. The Toyota held position for perhaps half a mile before accelerating away. The Lollywood ghazal sounded lonely and tinny, competing with the AC and the traffic.

'The phone Professor. Answer it.'

Tarek tentatively picked up the phone as though it were alive and vaguely dangerous. He pushed the flashing green button and put the mobile to his ear.

'Hallo?'

'You have arrived. Good. Welcome back to Pakistan, Professor. Please pass the phone to Bheyrya for a moment; then I will talk to you again.'

'Thank you. OK. It's Dr Malik, he wants to talk to you.'

Bheyrya scowled, grabbed the phone from Tarek's hand and put it to his ear.

'Haan, Doctor … Nahin … haan … shaa'yed pandra … haan, OK.'

The conversation went on for a couple more minutes before Bheyrya pushed the phone back towards Tarek: 'For you again'.

'Professor?'

'Yes, hallo Doctor.'

'Apparently you have a little tail.'

'We did have a few minutes ago. But they went past and …'

'Bheyrya told me about the ISI but that's not who I'm talking about. This one is a little less obvious and if he is there, there will probably be one or two more, elsewhere. Do not look for him but you may see him from time to time. He has already passed you twice and then dropped back. Your fan is riding a Honda CD 70 motorcycle, wearing a yellow shirt with thin brown stripes and white trousers.'

'Who is he?' Tarek could almost hear Dr Malik shrug.

'Who knows? Maybe the Americans or the British or even the Iranians. It doesn't matter but … were you expecting someone?'

'No, I wasn't expecting anyone at all! When you mentioned there was someone, I only thought, maybe the Israelis? Because I'm Palestinian and from Lebanon.'

Malik's laughter was brief but loud. 'Ever since Israel tried to destroy our research facility in Kahuta, we haven't really been talking to each other. On the other hand, I wouldn't put it past ISI getting into bed with Mossad and Mossad's probably in cahoots with the CIA people at the consulate. Maybe? But it doesn't matter. Whoever it is, they will find nothing.

'So, tonight you will be staying at Paradise Hotel in Saddar Town. It's bit down at the heels but it's comfortable and it has easy access to Paradise Shopping Centre. You should be there in about ten minutes from now if Bheyrya is right. Check in, go to your room and have a rest for a short while. In one hour, a man will bring you something to eat in your room. He is called Bara Yasir. In English, bara means big. Yasir is very short and seriously strong. It's a joke, but not a joke. You'll understand when you meet him. He will also bring you a package that he will show you. When he leaves, give him 50 dollars. Bheyrya will give you some more instructions before he takes you into the hotel. Once you are there, do not leave. In the morning, early, we will go to the Kharan.'

'Are we flying?'

'Yes. Tomorrow we will have time to talk and drink tea together. Tonight, get some rest. Oh yes, do you have something warm with you? A jacket perhaps?'

'No, will I ...'

'I will organise it. Now, I bid you goodnight Professor, sweet dreams.'

Malik cut the connection; Tarek looked at Bheyrya.

'How far is it to Paradise, Bheyrya?'

'One knife, one bullet or one bomb,' he said, and roared with laughter at his own joke. 'About five minutes now.'

They parked with one tyre in a pothole on the other side of the dusty street from the entrance. Bheyrya led the way between the rank of bikes ranged along the roadside and under the blue-signed Paradise Hotel in letters that might once have been white. The mottled grey and white marbled staircase took them past the first floor balcony lined with mostly darkened shop fronts. Here and there low wattage tungsten lights lent orange illumination to piles of brightly coloured fabrics or stark electronic entrails leaking from perforated grey metal boxes. On the second floor, through a glazed door, an unremarkable man stood behind a tired wooden reception desk.

The Paradise boasted 156 spacious rooms; room 403 was on the fourth floor. Ensuite with a window that overlooked Shambhu Nath Street, number 403 had a large double bed in pride of place, neatly made with clean white sheets and pillows, and a purple coverlet that was perfectly folded to a point half way up the bed. A small table with one chair was placed in front of the window to ensure that if a guest were to sit at table, he or she had the full benefit of daylight as available. The remaining space was minimal but sufficient.

Bheyrya placed Tarek's bag on the bed and a hand on his shoulder.

'Bara Yasir will come soon with food and some clothing that you will need to wear tomorrow, as a disguise. He will show you how to wear this tonight because in the morning you will need to dress yourself alone. A man named Mumtaz will come for you at seven o'clock and you must be ready to leave. He will bring a bag for all your things; your bag is too obvious and they have already seen that it shines like the moon on a dark night. Go with him, do what he tells you without discussion and he will bring you to us. Do you understand, Professor?'

'Yes. And thank you Bheyrya.'

'Alhamdulillah.'

*****

In the street below, Ghous lit another cigarette from the cigarette he'd just finished and looked up at the fourth floor window. After the foreigner and the bad-news sisterfucker had gone into the hotel, he got the room number from the receptionist. And he'd demanded 20 rupees! Twenty rupees for a room number? That was fucking extortion. He leaned forward on the handlebars of the parked motorbike, changing the angle of his back for a moment. He heard footsteps on the stairs, looked at the dimly lit entrance to the Paradise and watched the mean man walk out and over to the Suzuki Potohar. Watched him get in, fire up and drive off. Upstairs the light was still on. Straightening up, Ghous pulled a mobile from his jeans' pocket and speed-dialled Farrukh.

'What's up?'

'The foreign guy checked into 403 and hasn't come out, so maybe he's ours for the night. Unless you say otherwise.'

'Nuh. The back end is dark and shitty. All I've got for company is one big motherfucking rat and his family rooting through the garbage. Nobody's out here. Ghous, you wanna change for a bit?'

'No chance; miss something and the man isn't going to be happy. Tell me if anything happens.'

'You got it. Do we have a change?'

'He said around four o'clock. Maybe.'

'It's going to be a long night.'

Ghous cut the call, put his phone back in his pocket, leaned his forearms back on the handlebars. The street was still buzzing with cars, bikes and people doing their thing, going wherever they were going. The enticing smell of pakora frying in oil was too much of a temptation; walking over to the stall, he paid for a one small portion and a paratha that he used as a plate. He took it back to the bike, sat astride and ate with relish. Once finished, he chewed at the paratha for a while until he got bored, dropping the remains in the dust by his foot.

A very short but muscular man appeared from around the corner past Pakgreen Souvenirs, walking towards him, carrying a thick square parcel under one arm. The other hand held a plastic bag that clearly contained several packets of snack food wrapped in paper.

'When you going to grow up, shit-eating dog fucker?'

The dwarf said nothing, but gave him the finger before turning into the entrance of the Paradise. He disappeared up the stairs leaving Ghous' foul mouth behind him. Ghous looked for something, or somebody else, to amuse him while he watched and waited. Twenty minutes later, he watched the dwarf come down the last few stairs, empty handed now, and out onto Shambhu Nath. Stepping away from the bike, Ghous walked towards him, blocked his path and produced a knife.

'Don't give me the finger, you little cocksucker. I think a little tattoo might help you remember.'

Bara Yasir hit Ghous once, very hard and very quickly, in the testicles.

'Arsehole,' he said, before walking on down the road.

Curled up in a foetal position on the road, all that Ghous could think of was the extreme pain in his balls that made his stomach churn and his eyes water. Someone prodded him in the back with a hard shoe and Ghous heard laughter. He grunted, only to be rewarded with a sharp kick. More laughter, followed by the sound of several pairs of feet moving away. Fucking bastards!

After half an hour the pain eased just enough for him to sit upright and a small part of his mind thought of what would happen if they missed the foreigner leaving. He looked up at the window, heaved a sigh of relief when he saw the light through the glass. He leaned back against the nearest bike, carefully cradling his crotch with his legs spread wide. Ghous sat there for perhaps another hour, maybe more before he found the strength to get off the ground.

At around midnight, he phoned Farrukh. Apart from a few more rats and some poor sod shooting up and overdosing in the alley, nothing was happening. Of course the bastard was dead. It wasn't unusual. Junkies were dumb losers, wasters he said. Ghous told him that nothing was happening on Shambhu Nath either. He didn't even have rats or a junkie to watch, he complained. He didn't tell Farrukh about the dwarf or his balls getting mashed. He did mention that the foreigner had switched off the light, so that was probably that for a few hours. Farrukh was out for the count by two thirty; Ghous nodded off around three.

It was almost seven before he was startled out of his sleep by the sound of a car backfiring. The sun was filtering slowly through the hazy soup of polluted air, a fan of warm rays from a dirty blue sky. His balls still ached from the night before and Ghous got gingerly to his feet. Legs together really wasn't an option quite yet. He glanced at his watch. His eyes flew upwards searching for the foreigner's window: the curtains were closed.

'Thank fuck for that,' he said quietly.

Saddar Town was slowly waking up. One or two cars, a few people, stalls and shops starting the day early. Someone was cooking eggs with onions and chilli, the hint of freshly made roti, the delicate high notes of tea. An ox slowly dragged a box cart through with a cargo of rotting vegetables trailing that sour acrid smell that stings your nose. And then the good stuff came back.

The sound of footsteps on the stairs drew his attention back to the Paradise. Ghous glanced up at the fourth floor window: the curtains were still closed. He sat sideways on his bike, lit his first cigarette and sighed his relief with the accompaniment of a stream of smoke. A tall, smartly dressed man came into view carrying a black holdall. When he stepped out into the sunshine, Ghous could really admire the beautiful cut and quality of the dark blue kameez salwar. Add the well-tanned handsome face and the hooded eyes; the man looked every bit the Lollywood star. He was talking quietly on a mobile phone. A brief conversation.

An equally tall woman followed him out, stylishly slim in a free flowing dark green abaya with a long dupatta in emerald green elegantly draped over one shoulder. The dark green niqab only served to add to the woman's mystery, showing only a pair of ebony eyes that gleamed in the light. Despite the diminishing but still present pain in his balls, Ghous felt a small twinge of lust as he wondered what she looked like without the veil.

To complete the image, a black Mercedes drove up the road and slowed to a halt. A uniformed chauffeur got out, walked around the car and opened the rear door. Ghous was not at all surprised to see the man get in first, followed by the woman. The chauffeur shut the door, walked back to the driver's door and that shut with a satisfying clunk. Ghous watched the Mercedes execute a perfect three-point turn, drive back down Shambhu Nath Street, turn left onto Clarke Street – and then it was gone. If his grin had been any broader it would touched his ears with delight. Ghous almost clapped the end of the show and wondered whether they really were film stars. He pulled out his mobile; speed dialled Farrukh.

'So much for the fucking change of guard at four! No foreigner came out the back way for sure. Some drunk bastard dropped a whisky bottle from a window and shouted 'fuck your mother'. That, plus the rats and the junkie, wraps up my night. You?'

'He hasn't come out the front door either and the curtains are still drawn. But, you are not going to believe this, I think two Pak film stars were having a shag in the Paradise last night. I've just seen them come out and get chauffeured off in a Mercedes.'

'You and your sister, Ghous.'

'I'm telling you man, he looked really smug pleased with himself and she looked stunning and wasted.'

'Hash dreams or chasing the dragon. Which one is it?'

*****

The early morning traffic running east out of Karachi on Shahrah-e-Faisal was running smoothly as the Mercedes pulled out into the flow. The driver accelerated, bringing the car up to a cautious cruising speed of 60kph, with one eye on his rear view mirror. Mumtaz leaned forward, resting one arm on the back of the passenger seat.

'Are we clear, Obaid?'

'There's no sign of a tail. I think they'd have tagged us before Sharah-e-Faisal if they'd realised. Certainly the morons at the Paradise weren't going to call us in. Did you see the one at the front with the idiot grin? I could swear he thought you two were some kind of stars.'

'Yeah I saw him. It must have been you Professor. You look so cute in an abaya, I could go for you myself.' Mumtaz leaned into Tarek's shoulder. 'And that niqab is so sexy!'

Obaid was almost crying with laughter, howling for Mumtaz to stop before he ran the car into the wall; Mumtaz was incapable of speech, laughing in big whoops as he clutched his stomach. Even Tarek was giggling through the material of his veil.

'Can I take this thing off now?' he begged.

'No!' Mumtaz screeched, unable to control himself. Making a big effort he managed to slow the whoops down to a gurgle. 'It's about 15 minutes before we turn off; leave the niqab on until then. The last thing we want is someone spotting you before then. Once we're off Sharah-e-Faisal, we're home free.'

Tarek peered through the narrow slit in his niqab, holding the material away from his mouth and nose. At least that was a relief from the constant irritating movement of the veil as he breathed. How the women who had to wear the damn thing all the time coped was beyond him; he supposed it was just different, a controlled way of life. Alhamdulilah, he was not such a woman. As the car turned off Sharah-e-Faisal, he pulled off the niqab with relief and ran his fingers through his crushed hair. Obaid took them up the road at right angles to the expressway, around the roundabout and back again. As he drove up the overpass across Sharah-e-Faisal, Tarek saw the sign for Jinnah International pointing away to the left.

'I thought we were going to the airport?'

'We are,' said Mumtaz. 'Welcome to Pakistan Air Force Base Faisal.'

He flashed an ID card at the guard on the security gate; he received a smart salute and the barrier lifted. Ignoring what passed for a perimeter road, Obaid drove them straight down a runway past a handful of parked Dassault Mirage III fighter jets, turning left at the end towards three helicopters. He stopped the car by the one nearest the runway; the one with its main rotor turning slowly in big circles.

Standing on the tarmac, Mumtaz pulled Tarek's abaya upwards and over his head.

''I don't think you'll be needing this in the desert,' he said, handing Tarek his new bag. 'Come.'

He walked Tarek over to the open door of the Russian-built Mil Mi-17, helped him climb into the aircraft and walked back to the car. A hand pulled him further in and to one side. Dr Malik waved his hand at Mumtaz on the ground, held out a hand with the thumb pointing up, then reversed it so the thumb pointed down. Mumtaz gave him the thumbs up sign; Malik mock saluted and shut the door.

'Good. You were not followed this morning. And good morning Professor. Please sit down and buckle up.'

Although designed primarily for military use, the cabin of the Mi-17 had been modified to make it slightly more comfortable than if it was used as a troop carrier. Ten ageing armchair simulacrums had been bolted to the floor in two rows of five, allowing each passenger quite a reasonable amount of space. Apart from Malik and Tarek in two front seats, the only other passengers were four technicians sitting quietly behind them. They were not introduced; nor did they expect to be.

'All in,' said the voice over the sound system. 'Once we've completed all our checks, we'll be on our way. Flying time to site should be a shade over an hour and a half, cruising at 260kph. Weather's looking good, we have a tail wind and the current temperature in the Kharan is 32 degrees centigrade. Enjoy the ride, Professor.'

The pilot in the commander's seat turned to look at Tarek, grinned and gave him the thumbs up. Bheyrya's flight suit bore the winged dragon and lightning bolts insignia of Pakistan's elite Special Service Wing. Turning back to the job in hand, Bheyrya pulled in the power from the Klimov TV3-117 gas turbine engines, twisting the throttle grip on the collective. As the rotor blades spun into a blur above the mast, he pulled in the collective helping the lift, bringing the helicopter up to a hover. Pushing the cyclic away from him, the pitch of spinning disk angled forwards and the Mi-17 headed north, northwest in a clatter of turbocharged noise and resultant clouds of brown dust.

The combined noise of the engines and vibrations of the aircraft prevented any normal conversation. Thus, apart from an exchange of one or two shouted comments, each man kept his own counsel. Unpressurised, the Mi-17 was flying at 10,000 feet and Tarek had a clear view to the ground for most of the flight. It seemed a barren, harsh landscape with little relief. As the helicopter descended, all that could be seen below was rock, sand and scrubby plants. Bheyrya brought the helicopter down with a soft bump; the view from the window obliterated by a dense fog of yellow dust from the rotor's downwash. He cut the engines and for the first time in over an hour and a half, Tarek could hear himself think.

One of the technicians came forwards, opened the door and jumped out. Two Toyota Landcruisers stood waiting, a hundred yards from the helipad, their engines idling to keep the air conditioning running. Jumping down from the helicopter, they jogged over to the cars, bent over as though afraid of being hit by the slowing rotors that had already been left behind. The Toyotas took them to a small encampment a few minutes away, consisting of a neat semicircle of huts surrounded by windbreaks and a larger area enclosed by similar fences made of wattle and saltbush.

A light breeze provided mild relief to the almost palpable heat that surrounded Tarek as he was taken to one of the huts by a Balochi attendant. As neither spoke the other's language and with no lingua franca, everything was conducted by sign language or demonstration. A bed with blankets, a flushable toilet, a shower with hot and cold water, in the desert!

'This is one of several camps built in the Kharan some years ago. Welcome to Seedhin 763/2h, or as it's better known in these parts, the Iron Graveyard.'

Tarek turned at the sound of the familiar voice.

'Captain Kharal, hallo. This place is extraordinary. How on earth can you have hot and cold water in such a godforsaken place?'

'Money is a powerful tool. All of this was put together before my time. Here, you'll need this,' he added, holding out a thick tanned sheepskin jacket. 'It gets cold at night in the desert. In the evening, one of the men will build a fire in the pit outside if you want. We will all eat in the enclosure that you saw as you drove in. Dr Malik apologises for leaving you so abruptly when you arrived. He had a few phone calls to make.'

'You said this was called the Iron Graveyard?'

'Ah yes. Come, let me show you why.'

Captain Ahmed Kharal led Tarek away from the encampment until they had an uninterrupted view of the desert. It stretched out before them in a lumpy carpet of saltbush scrub, yellow sand and dirty brown-grey rock. A dust devil twirled at their feet before dancing away to a fade a few yards away. In the middle distance, a group of crescent shaped dunes rose gracefully upwards, their western curves shining orange in the sunlight. In the far distance, to the north, a low range of mountains laid a dark ragged shadow on the horizon. Captain Kharal raised his arm, pointing to them with a single finger.

'What you see is the southernmost edge of the Sulaiman mountains that leads on to the Hindu Kush. But below that edge, in the shadows, lie the Ras Koh Hills in the Chagai District. That is where Pakistan flexed her nuclear muscles for the world to see, only eight years ago I think. Five atomic devices were exploded; a little more powerful than the ones we have for you,' he said laughing. 'Don't worry Professor, your devices will have more than enough bang. So turn around. You asked why the Iron Graveyard. Now you are looking south and that is where we will do your testing tomorrow. Have a look through these.' He held out a powerful pair of binoculars. 'Look south and tell me what you see.'

Tarek held the binoculars up to his eyes, scanning the desert in front if him. At first, all he saw was the desert itself, the sand and rock and saltbush scrub. But after a while he made out what looked like old jeeps, derelict armour personnel carriers and even the occasional desiccated tank.

'You have got to be kidding me? How did they get here?'

'In the 80s, when the Soviets were still in Afghanistan, the Americans provided Pakistan with a lot of support, not just financially but also with equipment. So we borrowed a Chinook and airlifted loads of stuff out here. Somehow, the PAF forgot to give it back and it's still dropping stuff out here for us to play with.'

'But there are tanks out there!'

'True-ish. Most of those came out in bits and we put them together for show. It impresses the generals and the VVIPs they've invited to watch testing. Let's blow some of them up with your devices tomorrow. So now, let's go back to your room.'

The sun was beginning to lose its heat and a fire had already been lit in the firepit. They sat on mats laid around one side, protected from the wind and warmed by the flames. Kharal produced what looked like two mobile phones from a leather pouch. He held one of them out to Tarek.

'This is your remote signalling control and this,' he said holding up the other mobile, 'is replicating the receiver on your device. So, press the button at the top to switch on. OK, good. Now, push the green button, followed by 01 and tell me what you see on the screen.'

'It looks as thought it's calling, sending out a fan signal. Now that's static but flashing on and off.'

'Look at mine.'

A green globe was flashing in synch with Tarek's mobile.

'That means your remote has made the connection with the device. Now push the red button.'

A long tone sounded from the unit in Kharal's hand.

'You have just successfully detonated your first device. Congratulations Professor al-Shami. Bang! OK, I'll reset them both, Give it to me.' He pressed tiny recessed buttons on the rear of both units with the tip of a knife. 'Here. Now do it again.'

Tarek pressed the green button, followed by 01, watched the signal fanning out, searching for the other unit. It locked on, the fan flashing on the one, the globe flashing on the other.

'Now do nothing, just watch.'

After a while the globe froze and faded; the fan blacked out.

'If you don't press the red button within 15 seconds, the device will go back to sleep and return to its safe, dormant state. Once more. This time, I'm going to disable the receiver entirely.' Kharal removed a plate on the back, flipped a switch and replaced the plate. 'What we're doing is emulating the situation where the device is out of range. So go.'

For the third time, Tarek went through the sequence, getting to the point where the unit was sending its signal. For a while, the fan fanned green but finding no connection, it stopped, held the fan solid that went orange before blinking out.

'And that's it. Here,' said Kharal holding out the receiving unit, 'practice a few times with both units before dinner. Tomorrow, we do it for real.'

*****

The sun was a golden orb hanging low above the horizon, just starting its ascent in a perfect blue sky. This morning the wind had dropped a little but the air still had a bite and Tarek was grateful for the warm sheepskin despite the smell. The rich dark scent of coffee drifted up comfortingly like an old friend from the mug that he clutched in both hands. He could feel the afterburn in his mouth from the chilli in the morning's omelette and relished the taste. Somehow it worked well with the sweetness of the heavily sugared coffee.

'How are you this morning Professor?' Malik asked as he approached with Captain Kharal.

'Good thank you.'

'Are you excited?'

Tarek thought for a moment; and he realised he was. He'd been looking forward to the thrill but hadn't understood the feeling. Suddenly he felt a rush of adrenalin.

'You know, I think I am!'

'Good. Let's go look at your toys.'

Malik led the way into the enclosure where four shiny cylinders sat on a solid table. The way they shone and sparkled was surprisingly disarming. Malik walked up to the table; banged the heel of one hand hard on the top of one of the cylinders. He smiled at the look of shock tinged with fear on his client's face.

'Oh yes, Professor, each one of these is very much alive with potentially devastating power. And each one will remain dormant until you use the remote to detonate them.'

'You have both the units?' Kharal asked.

Tarek nodded, taking them from the pockets in the jacket, holding both out to the Captain. Kharal took the receiver.

'That one you will need. This one is now redundant. By the way, the strip on each cylinder is now electromagnetic as requested. See the switch. OK, let's go.'

He waved at the group of waiting technicians and drivers standing by the Landcruisers. The technicians loaded the cylinders in the back of one before climbing on board. Captain Kharal took the wheel of the second Landcruiser, while Tarek took the passenger seat and Malik the rear. With Kharal leading, the two vehicles headed into the desert towards the military detritus, the depressurised tyres easily keeping a hold in the soft sand. The pace was smooth but fast and Tarek found himself enjoying the simple thrill of off-road driving in the desert. The car took the bumps and troughs without any difficulty, sliding at an angle across the shoulders of dunes as Kharal drove with practised ease.

After about twenty minutes, the Captain pulled up next to a large, solid APC with barely a spot of rust. Indicating for Tarek to get out, he walked over to the other car and retrieved one of the cylinders. Turning he walked back to Tarek.

'You can put the first one in. Here.'

Pushed as it was into his chest, Tarek had little option but to take the device from the Captain. He followed him round to the side of the APC where the door had been forced open, held the cylinder's magnetic strip up to the face of the metal inside and pushed the switch as instructed. Immediately, it clamped onto the metal with a loud clank; Tarek's efforts to physically remove it were fruitless. Like a child, he pushed the button again and the cylinder fell into the sand; and like a child, he laughed with delight. Lifting it up, he brushed some residual sand off in an almost proprietorial way before reattaching it to the metal.

'Excellent!' he pronounced.

'You're happy, I'm pleased' said Malik drily.

'The technicians will seed the other three, if you're comfortable with that?'

'That's fine, absolutely fine,' said Tarek, the big grin still on his face.

Captain Kharal went back to the other car to give them instructions. Tarek could see them nodding, listening and nodding again.

'I think you will be pleased with Captain Kharal's work,' said Dr Malik. 'As I said before, he is a very fine engineer and in this instance, I believe that he has truly excelled himself. But, as they say, the truth will be in the exploding.'

He giggled, Tarek smiled and Captain Kharal returned.

'Let's go. They will seed the remaining three and stay out on the range at a clear distance on either side. So there will be a little wait before we are ready to test. All in? Good. I'm ready for more coffee, and a piss.'

The drive back was even more exhilarating than before as the Captain showed off for the hell of it, to Tarek's enjoyment and to Malik's disgust.

'For god's sake, Kharal, this is not funny!' moaned the man in the back as the car flew over the lip of a particularly large dune to hurtle vertically down the other side.

'No, but it is good fun,' said Kharal laughing.

Snacks and soft drinks had been laid out on a table beneath a large gazebo with white canvas walls pulled into the sand on three sides. Chairs had been placed facing outwards on the open side facing south, towards the testing range. Tarek and Malik sat in two of the chairs waiting patiently for Kharal.

'Rather than go back to Karachi, I think it's better if you fly back to Lahore with me and then onto Beirut. Whoever was tailing you in Karachi failed miserably and for them the trail has gone cold. As fetching as you looked in an abaya and niqab, according to Mumtaz, I doubt whether you want to bother to go through that again.' Tarek scowled; Malik grinned. 'I'll take that as a no. If the tail order started in Beirut, they'll pick you up on re-entry whichever way you travel. Flying in from Lahore will only serve to confuse them more. Agreed?'

'Absolutely!'

'Good. Ah, Captain you are back.'

'Yup,' he said, sitting down heavily in the third chair. His mobile chirruped happily. 'Yes? Good. And you are off site but with a clear view? Excellent. So, gentlemen, are we ready?'

Both of them nodded vigorously.

'Each device is numbered. The closest is the one you placed Professor at eight kilometres, the second is at 16, with the third and fourth repeating the sequence. The only difference being, that the second two have been seeded in vehicles which have obstacles between us and them. Dunes basically. I'm fairly certain that that won't make a difference but it's important that we have the information. You are comfortable with the sequence Professor, on the remote?'

'Yes, I'm pretty sure. On, green button, watch fan signal, wait for it to lock on and press red.'

'Almost, you forgot the number?'

'Of course, 01 after green.'

'Yes. But only the first is 01. The second is 02, third 03 and obviously 04 is the fourth. Make sense?'

'Yes.'

'Then go for it,' said Kharal, and picked up a chicken tikka sandwich.

Tarek looked down at the transmitting device, then out to the desert, and then back to the unit. Turning it on he pushed the green button, typed 01 and watched the unit trying to find its mate. The signal locked on and Tarek stared for a moment before pushing the red button. He looked up and out across the desert. Nothing. A huge cloud of black smoke billowed up in the distance, an orange bloom at its heart. A split second later, the blast of the explosion arrived with a deafening aural shockwave.

'It's almost time for you to pay the second instalment of $250,000 Professor al-Shami,' said Dr Malik with a smile.

'If the others are as successful as this one appears to be, I'll be making the transfer within the next few days.'

'Before you promise him your money Professor, let's find out how successful it was on the ground. Doctor?'

'I know what it will look like without dicing with death as you drive. You two youngsters go on without me.'

Captain Kharal needed no help in finding the site of the explosion: black smoke was still drifting around, filled with the acrid post-explosion stench. But he drove more carefully on the approach, his eyes searching the ground for sharp pieces of metal. The explosion had left a large crater in the sand, shattered rock lay everywhere, mixed with shredded vegetation and cracked lumps of baked earth. Of the APC, nothing remained bar a few chunks of mangled metal and many unseen hot shards.

'There's nothing left,' said Tarek quietly, his eyes wide with shock and awe.

'Then consider what one of your devices will do to your end target.'

'Yes. I am.'

They drove back in a silence born of thought and visual impression.

'Impressed Professor?' Malik asked.

'I think I'm seriously impressed, Doctor. The second one is further out?'

'As I said, 16 kilometres away. Let's see whether the transmitter has the range. Go.'

Tarek pressed the green button, pressed 0 then 2; watched the signal fanning out, hold on point and he pressed the red button. This time the wait seemed longer. Tick tock, tick tock, tick … And in the distance a similar black cloud bloomed in the sky above the desert, its malevolent orange heart aflame. And then moments later they heard the booming savage blast of the explosion as it reached their ears.

'Bang!' Tarek exclaimed. He paused, turned to Dr Malik and asked: 'What does a nuclear explosion look like? The Captain said you had one near here.'

'I wasn't here for the tests,' Malik replied, 'but you don't see the detonation. Firstly it would blind you if you looked at one direct and secondly, you don't because the test took place underground.'

'It's just that my sponsors were asking, asked me to ask you, about something a little larger than our NuCans.' Tarek looked south to the smoking desert. 'There was mention of a nuclear warhead. It was Saad al-Kabuli who asked.'

'No,' Dr Malik said with finality. 'I will not supply anyone with a completed nuclear warhead or other similar device. Nor do we have the facilities at Wana to even start.'

'My sponsors don't want you to produce one. They believe that you know where Pakistan's nuclear weaponry is stored; they'd like to know as well.'

'Why?'

'Because they'd like to steal one.'

10 ~ From Deception to Lies, and Back

The Poet's Jasmine that had once draped itself elegantly over the pergola, had grown fat with the years and had adopted a more wanton style. Even so, it provided welcome shade from the heavy heat of the late afternoon sun. Two wicker chairs had been placed at a precise angle of 45 degrees to each other, facing out onto a manicured lawn surrounded by jacaranda trees. On the low table, to the front and between the chairs, Salman placed two cut glass crystal old-fashioned tumblers on cork coasters. He placed one perfectly shaped cube of ice into each glass and poured exactly two fingers of Johnny Walker Black Label whiskey over each cube. Having arranged everything to his satisfaction, he waited as the two men sat down before approaching with the water jug.

'Please, just a little,' said Dr Malik. He watched as Salman poured. 'Enough! Perfect.'

'As usual,' General Mustagh said, pointlessly as his 'usual' dribble of water had already been added.

Silently, the General's manservant, driver, cook and general gofer, placed a bowl of nuts on the table, setting the whiskey bottle and water jug to one side.

'Thank you, Salman. Sometimes that man can be so pompous and pernickety,' he complained behind Salman's receding back, reaching for the bottle to give both glasses a little more strength. 'Cheers,' he said, raising his glass.

'Cheers,' Malik responded.

They sipped their whiskey, smacking their lips in appreciation.

'But I do have to say that Salman's Sindhi fish pulao is beyond excellence. Mouth-wateringly good, Pamir. That was snakehead fish, yar?'

'I have absolutely no bloody idea. It was excellent, I totally agree, but I only tell him something like that perhaps once a month, otherwise his head is getting even bigger. Then God help us all.'

In the back garden of his small European styled mansion just off Lawrence Road, General Pamir Mustagh could relax and

246

allow himself to wear something other than his (ex)uniform with its array of gongs. Since Sami Malik was a friend as well as a colleague-in-arms, he'd dressed down to a simple white cotton kameez salwar. However, being a guest, Dr Malik still felt obliged to wear the statutory white shirt and dark green tie; although since lunch he'd dispensed with the latter.

General Mustagh felt underneath the table and produced a half empty box of Cohiba Espendisos. Taking one cigar out, he neatly clipped off the rounded end, then turned the other end in the flame of a burning taper. Once he was satisfied with the red glowing tip, he mashed the taper out on the ground and sucked wetly, noisily on his cigar. Plumes of smoke jetted from either side of his mouth, bringing with them the fine scent of Havana's pride. Malik shook his head in disgust.

'I can't believe you're still smoking those things, Pamir.'

'They all went well then, the tests,' Mustagh said, ignoring Malik's comment.

'Perfectly, every one. Ahmed Kharal's team outdid themselves and all praise to the Captain himself. A superb job. He's used one transmitter for all four bombs, which makes a lot more sense than using a separate one for each device. Simple really: receiver codes programmed to zero plus numbers. Even if you only used nine, that means that in theory, assuming that all the devices were in range, you could set them off consecutively like a string of firecrackers.'

'What a wonderful vision,' Mustagh commented, blowing a thick smoke ring towards the jasmine above.

'They were tested at a maximum range of 16 kilometres; two at eight and two at sixteen. What is key here is that the second sequence was initiated without direct line of sight between transmitter and device. Admittedly the only barriers were sand dunes, but even so … It suggests that we should run our own trials to see just how far we can push remote detonation. And listen to this: from the work he's done on this project and others, Kharal thinks that there's a way to adapt the technology for use with drones. Of course, that's a way off at the moment but think of the possibilities: once the device is placed, it could be detonated from a location thousands of miles away. And if the device has sleeper capability, my God, we could blow up the future!'

'Presuming we have a client,' said Mustagh dryly. 'I assume therefore that our existing esteemed client, Professor al-Shami, is duly pleased and has confirmed the actual order.'

'Of course. We have agreed on four armed units and two dummies; of the same weight and size but without comms or explosive. Production of those will commence as soon as the next financial instalment has been transferred and confirmed. The Professor was so excited by the tests that I suspect he may have set those wheels in motion already.'

'Excellent. Delivery?'

'Since all the engineering tech's been done, everything's ready to run; plus it's a relatively simple device so essentially it's down to assembly. Bottom line, Captain Kharal can have them done, dusted and delivered in four weeks tops. Agreed point of delivery's the Port of Karachi.'

'So we're talking what? Beginning of November?'

'Yeah.'

'Then we've agreed that the final payment should be made immediately after the first successful detonation, irrespective of target results?'

'That's what we've suggested and has been agreed.'

'And if he doesn't pay?'

'He will. Especially since he knows that we know that he's got three more units to detonate.'

'Point taken. Do we know where they go to from Karachi?'

'Dubai. And then, I suspect, to England.'

As though they both needed to mentally process the information, they sat back and sipped their drinks. Mustagh blew more smoke rings, tried to make the second smaller than its predecessor and blow it through the middle.

'You've got a house in England, haven't you?'

'Mmm, yes in Holland Park. But I don't think they're going to target my house, Pamir.'

'Of course not, but it makes you think, doesn't it?'

'No! What on earth are you talking about?'

'I'm saying,' said Mustagh pacing his words, 'that we need to make absolutely sure that there is no way the British can reverse track the process. All connections, communications, transactions – even the tiniest record or echo needs to be erased. A connection with a British target in British territory is different; it's not the same as selling the odd missile to Talibs in North Waziristan.'

'OK, now you're making sense. Agreed, 100 per cent.'

'On the other hand, since you and Captain Kharal have produced such a fine product, couldn't we sell something similar to someone else?'

'Pamir, it's a one off bespoke product with a silly name. No! Mind you, I can just see the marketing strapline: want to blow up your neighbour's house but don't know how? Now you can, with NuCan!'

General Mustagh sprayed a mouthful of whiskey over the cigar in his hand, his laughter coming out in choking gasps. Doctor Malik giggled. Both men took another swig of whiskey. It took them a while to come down. Then Malik's face took on a more serious aspect. He looked sideways, directly at Mustagh, catching his eye.

'What?'

'Al-Shami expected you to be there, at the Iron Graveyard.'

'Why? You and Kharal had it under control. And didn't you have Bheyrya in tow as well? Presumably he flew you back to Lahore?'

'Yes, we refuelled at Multan. But that's not the issue.'

'Then what is?'

'Apparently, he had a conversation with an old friend of ours – Abdul Saad Mazari.'

'Saad al-Kabuli himself. The Professor is clearly keeping very bad company.'

'He says that he was asked to pass on a request, for information. The request does not just come from al-Kabuli, it comes with the endorsement of the Sheikh. Apparently, they are seeking information on the locations of Pakistan's nuclear weaponry, and for reliable information, they will pay one million dollars.'

'Why?'

'They would like to steal one or two nuclear warheads.'

General Pamir Mustagh roared with laughter; stopped when he saw the expression on the Doctor's face.

'You're serious?'

'Mmm-mm.'

'What would they do with a pair of warheads?' he exclaimed. 'They're not fireworks, Sami; you know, light blue touch-paper and stand well back. As far as I know, al-Qaeda doesn't have many ballistic missiles for handy delivery. They don't have the facilities or the personnel or ...'

Mustagh suddenly realised that Malik wasn't sharing his lightweight dismissal. What he saw was the greyed-out expression of a man looking at shadows. And then he understood.

'Shit!' he muttered, and reached for the Johnny Walker. 'Unless we charged five million dollars, apiece,' he added, and poured.

*****

The sky was blue above the dull beige boxwork of flat-roofed buildings on the other side of the street. The normal suspension of yellow dust absent, thanks to the rare late morning rains. Danny leaned out of the window, thankful for once that the air conditioning had broken down, that he had an excuse to breathe fresh air. It was hot, clean and uncomplicated. He could hear the siren voices in his ear, reminding him of how pleasant it would be to just swim in the sea, play a little matkot in the sand, watch the girls go by, and just chill. He flexed the muscles in his shoulders, feeling the tension unwind and thought of how pleasant it would be to go sailing.

'Danny?'

'Aaron,' he said laconically.

'I've got Major Roberts on VoIP?'

'Yeah, all right.'

Danny dragged himself away from the window, packed the pleasant beach dreams in a mental box and walked across to the screen Aaron had indicated.

'Hey Danny, how's it going out there?'

'Mike, hi, yeah good. Shit, that's a lie. Listen, I meant to touch base a few days ago but I wanted to see how it would all pan out.'

'What?'

'Al-Shami in Pakistan. They lost him pretty much from the get-go. We have a link man at the US Consulate in Karachi, guy named David Bernstein. He was briefed to put a surveillance team of three men onto al-Shami: he put on two. He was told we needed experienced professionals: we get amateurs. Our two comedians get eyes on at Jinnah International where he gets picked up by a big guy in a Suzuki Potohar and taken to the Paradise Hotel in downtown Karachi. So they stake out the hotel all night and nothing. One of them, a man called Ghous, went in to check it out at nine the following morning. Our bird had flown. Ghous found an empty silver Samsonite in the room and that's all.

'So we have no idea where he went after that. However, this guy Ghous had been raving to his buddy at the back, Farrukh, about seeing a couple coming out of the hotel entrance just after seven. He swore they were Lollywood film stars doing their thing in an off piste hotel. According to Ghous, the woman was slim and very elegantly dressed in abaya and, and she was wearing a niqab!'

'That's like a hijab, right?'

'Yes-ish. A niqab isn't just a scarf around the head, it comes with a full veil that covers your face but has a slit for the eyes. My guess is that the woman was al-Shami. So someone arranged for the disguise and then brings him out past the watchers in full view. This was organised by professionals who knew exactly what they were doing. Where the Professor went next is anybody's call. What I can tell you is that he didn't go anywhere near Sindh Madressatul Islam University in Karachi. According to the Uni's diary in Beirut, that's where he said he was going. Checking with Sindh Madressatul, that's a never-heard-of-the-man.'

'Somebody definitely wants to keep him off the radar. Dr Malik?'

'Could be. Al-Shami got back to Beirut this morning on a Kuwait Airways flight. From Lahore. Means the man's been travelling around. But that doesn't mean that he met with Malik. Hey, I'm sorry, we did a bad job.'

'Hey back, it wasn't your fault.'

'Yeah, but it shouldn't have happened. However, we can't turn back the clock. Mike hold on. Yo Aaron?'

Mike had the usual nice view of a wall. And then Danny reappeared.

'Our man works fast. This has probably come through at your end as well but Tracker's just picked it up here. Al-Shami sent an email to Malik just before lunch which reads: Excellent tests! Have transferred the second instalment to your account as agreed. Malik replied an hour ago. Incidentally, I'm talking Beirut slash Tel Aviv times and it's 1600 over here. Even so, it's a quick return. Malik wrote: Thank you, bank has confirmed transfer. Production in hand and Kharal is now saying possibly three weeks. Mike, unless you have any more intel, I think that we need to help ourselves rather than wait for Tracker.'

'You're talking Marina?'

'I'm talking Marina. But this time there won't be any mistakes. She's knows what she's doing and Marina does what she knows very well.'

'Who does she belong to?'

'Mossad. I recruited her myself a couple of years back and she's still mine.'

'That's good enough for me. Run her.'

'You got it. But you called me. Was that just a catch up on Karachi or …?'

'Karachi was the main thing but there were couple of others. The email from someone called Amin with an IP address in London?' Danny nodded. 'OK, Watkins asked Tracker for possible matches and found the same internal IP address in the Poole-Bournemouth area. So Amin's using the same machine but Watkins also thinks that he may be using another email address as well, perhaps a business one. He's got the system doing random searches on Google and playing the numbers with social networks like LinkedIn and Facebook.

'The other point, I don't think that this is remotely connected but I thought you might be interested. You probably remember

Admiral Buller talking about us stopping a biological attack on London's water supply?'

'This is the one where you went swimming for Queen and country?'

'That's the one. We squeezed both of the guys we arrested for any information we could get but neither tube produced much paste. What we did get was that both were al-Shabaab fighters and admitted to supporting al-Qaeda, at least in principle if not fact. And then one of the mentioned someone called al-Kabuli? Any bells?'

'We know him. An al-Qaeda commander and close to the centre.'

'According to one of the Somalis, al-Kabuli was assessing fighters for, as he put it, 'special project training' in Pakistan. In the meantime he, or al-Qaeda (question mark), was funding basic attacks on an ad hoc basis. He thought al-Kabuli was based on some kind of boat, moving between the Med and the Red Sea. It didn't really make sense. But just in case, I thought … well the Pakistan link and all that.'

'The more the intel, the greater the workload. I was just thinking about going to the beach so fuck you very much.' The big open grin gave the lie to the words.

'You're such a sweet man,' Mike observed, grinning back, 'now go talk nicely to Marina.'

'Your wish is my command.' Danny signed out, swivelled his chair to look at his assistant. 'Aaron can you get me …'

'I have Marina on five for you Danny.'

'I love it when you get into my head Aaron.'

He picked up the phone.

*****

The light was starting to fade as they walked along the Corniche, her arm linked through his as though they were a familiar married couple rather than brother and sister. They stopped opposite Raouche's Pigeon Rocks, leaned on the rail, looked out and down. On the near side, the limestone rock faces were a dark white, shadowed by their own bulk. And yet, through the arch a beam of sunshine glowed on the water forming a golden pathway to the land. A few seagulls floated high above them, their wings outstretched and almost motionless as they rode the thermals that rose unseen from the city below. The smell of salt was strong on the air and the light breeze lent a chill. Ayesha shivered slightly, snuggled up to Tarek's warmth.

'You're cold?'

'Mmm-mm.'

'Coffee? Something to eat?'

'Not coffee, it's too late. A glass of wine first, and then something to eat perhaps.'

They turned away from the Corniche, crossed General De Gaulle and turned left up Gibra Nassar a little further down. The lights from La Vieux Colombe were friendly beacons in the haze of dusk, their implied warmth an invite to go in and sit for a while. They found an alcove with a table separating a faded rose banquette from two chairs, similarly upholstered. Ayesha ordered a glass of the vin blanc de la maison; Tarek a sirop de grenadine pétillant. He thought she looked tired; she thought he looked strained.

Tarek had been back from Pakistan almost three weeks but he'd been immersed in work at the university, he'd explained as they walked along the Corniche. While the Director was pleased that Tarek undertook most of the travelling necessary to fulfil the faculty's remit to ensure top budget, he had felt that Tarek needed to spend some actual time at the university. Ayesha told him she understood; it wasn't a big deal. Then he'd told her about Karachi, the tests at the Iron Graveyard in the Kharan Desert and flying back to Lahore with Dr Malik. He hadn't said anything about Saad al-Kabuli even though his sister would probably have remembered the photo in their father's Book of Photographs. He didn't think it was necessary to unduly alarm her.

'So what happens next?' asked Ayesha, taking a sip of her wine. 'When will Alan get the bom ... NuCans as you call them?'

'Dr Malik has already confirmed that Kharal has almost finished and they should be shipped very shortly. In the end it was simpler for them to arrange shipping from Karachi to Jebel

Ali. He said he'd confirm delivery details when they were en route.'

'So they could be on their way already?'

'It's possible. I've warned Amin and he should be flying out to Dubai in the next few days. In turn, he'll have told Alan. Amin will air freight them to the UK, fly back himself, pick them up from the cargo terminal at Heathrow and then hand them over to Alan. Bismillah it will be simple and go without a hitch. Alan will install them as soon as he can but that depends on the ships. There are some things that cannot be planned to the letter. Hopefully, the time to begin will come in mid-November.'

'Have you any idea where the first one might be?'

'No, but there are only a number of possible locations. Not only will I have to be within range, I also need to be able to get away with reasonable ease. And undetected. Anywhere around the Eastern Mediterranean coastline running up from here, past Tripoli, Latakia in Syria and around to Taşucu in Turkey. The ferries give us greater options and so that area also includes Cyprus.'

He paused for a moment to look at his sister but her face showed no emotion.

'The Suez Canal itself is a possibility, from Port Said to Suez and down through Gulf of Suez, maybe as far as Hurghada. Certainly the canal. Further afield, the Gulf of Oman's a possibility, off the coastline around Muscat and perhaps off Salalah. The Persian Gulf should be an obvious choice but my gut tells me it would be too risky: Bahrain, Qatar and the UAE all have far too strong a relationship with the west, especially with America and Great Britain. The Gulf of Aden might make sense but in Yemen, one would be trapped with no real available exits.'

Tarek stopped his monologue to take a breath.

'You haven't considered the rest of the Med or perhaps the Arabian Sea then?'

'No but only … ha, ha, ha. Ayesha, this is serious!'

'I know,' she said, her smile taking away the possible taint of sarcasm. 'Tarek, I was looking for one single idea, not an analysis of the whole region. Until we have details of shipping movements from Amin, we can't make an informed decision.

When we have, we decide; when the moment arrives, we will be there to strike.'

Tarek sighed, said: 'Ayesha, we've been through this, you can't be involved. It's too dangerous, for one ...'

'Puleese, little brother! Think. I have been in more dangerous places this month than you have been in a lifetime. I thought we had agreed that point.'

Any sense of tiredness that might have seemed apparent before had evaporated, burned off by fiery passion and determination. The tired older sister had been replaced by the freedom fighter forged of steel and blood. Tarek held up his hands in surrender, conceding defeat.

'OK, OK. You're right and I apologise. It was a stupid thing to say. But the other problem hasn't gone away: you haven't got a passport Ayesha. And without passport, you can't go anywhere, not officially. And ...' He held up his hand to stop Ayesha interrupting. 'And you need to be able to go anywhere. You can't run under the wire, as it were, like you do when you got to Ramallah or Gaza.'

'Have you finished?'

She produced a pack of Cedars, pulled out a cigarette and lit it with a cheap red plastic lighter.

'Yes,' he said, watching the twin plumes of smoke jet from her nostrils. My sister, the dragon lady, he thought, almost smiling.

From the pocket of her jacket, Ayesha produced a slim burgundy coloured booklet and placed it on the table in front of Tarek. The front was embossed with a gold cedar tree, a line tracing across it to approximate the shape of Lebanon. Arabic script at the top and, using the Roman alphabet, at the bottom it read: Republique Libanaise Passeport. She flipped the pages: the photograph was of her, the names read al-Shami, Ayesha, all the information was correct and it wouldn't expire for another three years.

'My passport, Tarek. A present from friends. Now there is no problem.'

*****

Amin stood on the balcony, leaning over and looking down at the luxury boats that lined the pontoons in the marina below. The whiteness of the boats reflected the sun while the green-blue water absorbed some of that same light, creating a contrast that almost too strong. He and Sophie had bought the two-bedroom apartment in Al Murjan Tower just after it had been completed in 2003, as an investment. Or so they'd thought. It had seemed to make sense since the company warehouse in Jebel Ali Free Zone was just down the road. The location on Dubai Marina was perfect, just off Sheikh Zayed Road which ran from Abu Dhabi right up to Ras al-Khaimah. Not that they'd often been much further than the Barracuda in Ajman and that was rare; bringing alcohol back through Sharjah was risky. Bur Dubai, Deira and the Creek or sometimes down to Abu Dhabi: that had been the extent of their travels. On the whole, being in Dubai had been more about business.

But this wasn't about that type of business; this was personal business, that had to be done but not without risk assessment. After Cambridge, he'd taken the decision to talk to Sophie, and he had. Merde! That had been bad. He remembered how they had sat down in the chairs near the fire. The dogs had been stretched out as though asleep, stupefied by the heat. He'd given Sophie a large drink, had one himself, and then told her the whole story. Of course, she'd heard about what had happened back in '74 but not the bits about revenge and retribution. She'd never heard about the oath taking and could barely believe that it was resurfacing over 30 years later.

'Di donc, tu est vraiment, complètement fou! Merde! Avec le cerveau d'une huître. Va te faire enculer!'

She'd listened, been angry, abusive, angry again and then asked questions. Why? What? How? Where? When? Over and over. Then she'd considered, understood and accepted certain aspects, weighed up the options and they'd agreed terms of engagement.

'Écoutes bien à ce que je dis, cheri. You take delivery of these explosives, you give them to Alan and, maybe, you give Tarek information on the ships. And that's it. Non plus! D'accord?'

'Yes, agreed.'

'If we have to, we will go. It would not be so bad I think, and better than having you in prison for years. So, I agree as well for this, how do say in English, set the bricks in the ground for the strategy for exit.'

'Lay the foundations,' he'd replied.

'But first me,' she'd said with a smile.

Amin smiled at the memory. She might speak an amalgam of English and French but Sophie could twist the words quite fluently. The email had arrived a few days later.

To:
<amateal@aol.com>, <tar10sham991@hotmail.com>,
From: <kilamsmalik@hotmail.com>
Subject: Delivery

Gentlemen
Your consignment will arrive at the Port of Jebel Ali on Wednesday and should immediately be transferred to your warehouse at 1243rd Street at Jebel Ali Free Zone South. In the event of any hold up, please contact Jamal at KaraPak Logistics FZE located at JAFZA South (S124) on 050 456 331964. Please note that the additional smaller unit included in the shipment should be removed before forwarding.
Good luck with your endeavours. We look forward to hearing about you in the near future. M&M

'This is Channel Four on one-oh-four-point-eight FM, the beat of the UAE coming at you on a bright and beautiful Wednesday morning ...'

As the sound of the radio filtered out from the kitchen, Amin turned to listen, waiting for the traffic details.

'It's the beginning of the tenth hour of the day people, and at 10.00 hours it's warming up very nicely out there. Current temperature in Dubai's at a pleasant 29 degrees Celsius and the weatherman says it's going be nice and dry with humidity taking a low, low profile today. Traffic's flowing smoothly on Sheikh Zayed right the way through to the Trade Centre. It's slow going north over Al Garhoud Bridge but it's all sweet running south. Al

258

Maktoum Bridge is running clear in both directions but past the Clock Tower in Deira, they're a lot of unhappy motorists clogging up around Al Rigga Road with a breakdown there. Shindagha Tunnel's moving slowly but constantly. That's where it's at for a five while we take a break for KT Tunstall and Under the Weather. Coming at you from Channel Four on one-oh-four-point-eight FM, the beat of the UAE.'

Amin switched off the radio wincing, wondering for the hundredth time how stations like Channel Four managed to find DJs with an IQ that was probably lower than that of an amoeba. Briefcase in hand, he took the lift down to the second floor of the underground parking levels, picked up the rented Hyundai, drove out and headed for Deira. Sheikh Zayed was as smooth as promised and Al Maktoum Bridge was clear as he drove across and up to the Clock Tower. Heeding the warning, he turned left along Al Maktoum Road as far as Baniyas Square. Threading his way through the back streets, he found a parking place off Old Baladiya Street, not far from Deira Gold Souk and walked the last few hundred yards to a small, modern but discreet shop with a plaque that read Abd al Aetar LLC, Dubai. The door opened easily and Amin stepped into a softly lit air-conditioned room. Niches inset in three of the walls bore elegant glass jars of varying sizes and shapes, containing oils and perfumes Amin assumed.

'Coloured, scented water. Mr Masri?'

'Yes. Mr Mansoor, I assume. And you're right. I was wondering.'

Abdul Mansoor held out a slim hand that was soft to the touch but Amin could feel strength in the fingers. Mansoor inclined his silver-haired head in an additional welcome.

'Please, do sit down,' he said, indicating three large squared armchairs in white and gold brocade.

Amin chose one and lowered himself gingerly down into what felt like an incredibly comfortable box that would defy all attempts to escape. Resting his arms on the arms of the chair meant that his hands were at shoulder height. He leaned forwards, out of the box, towards the coffee table. In contrast, Abdul Mansoor managed to sit in his seat totally naturally, a man in his own environment. He waved his hand towards the walls.

'It's a natural assumption, that these are full of absolute, or even essential, oils but when one considers the value, one might also realise that such a thing would be insane.' He pointed to a nearby spherical glass flagon with a long pointed stopper filled with a liquid tinted a delicate peach. 'That contains about two and half litres of liquid. If, for example that were absolute oil of orris root, the retail value would be in the region of 114,500 American dollars.'

'I take your point,' said Amin, looking at the container with a modicum of respect.

'May I get you some refreshment before we begin?'

'Thank you, but no. Unfortunately I have other engagements.'

'Ah the pressures of business. Then to our business. One moment.'

Mansoor stood up, opened the door at the back of the room and brought in two wooden boxes, each with a leather handle and hinged at the back. The satin sheen of the rich brown wood shone lustrously in the soft light. Laying one on its side, Mansoor opened the lid to reveal six bottles, each one nestling in its own padded space. Each one bore an embossed metallic label. Abdul Mansoor took out the nearest bottle, holding the neck in one hand while the other balanced the body, displaying it for Amin to see as a sommelier with fine wine. Amin read the label out loud.

'Abd al Aetar: Orris Absolue. And this is one litre?'

'Yes, each bottle contains one litre of oil. Since you were not entirely specific about which oils your client needed, I have interpreted your instructions to the best of my ability.' He returned the bottle to its place, then pointed at each one as he ran through the names. 'First the four smaller quantities of absolute oils: orris root, calendula, jasmine and lotus. Then the two essential oils: frankincense and cedarwood.' Mansoor opened the other box. 'And here you have three more litres of frankincense and three of cedarwood. I hope you are satisfied, Mr Masri?'

'That's perfect, Mr Mansoor. I'm sure my clients will be delighted, presuming that the price is proportionately lower than the level of satisfaction.'

The two men smiled at each other, their mouths full of teeth like two dog foxes sizing each other up before fighting for the vixen.

'Of course. I will of course give you an itemised invoice, should you wish. That is $33,516 for the absolute oils and $2,558 for the essential oils, making a total of $36,074. Shall we round it down to $35,000 for good will?'

'Why don't we round that figure down to $33,300? It has a certain numerological ring to it, don't you think?'

'You drive a hard bargain, Mr Masri, and I am but a poor simple man. Bismillah, this will be but the first of many transactions between the two of us, thus I submit to your wishes.'

'Good,' said Amin dryly. 'And the other matter?'

Abdul Mansoor closed and latched the two boxes, putting them side by side on the floor by the table. When he looked at Amin, his expression was somehow harder, perhaps more wolf than fox.

'In this, your instructions have been followed to the letter. My associate only finished his work yesterday evening but he said he is happy with what he has done. That means that the papers that you requested should be perfect.' Once again Mansoor retreated through the door at the back, returning immediately with two thick A4 manila envelopes which he handed to Amin.

'Please look,' he said as he sat back in his seat.

Amin spread the contents of the envelopes in two piles on the table. He looked carefully at each item, shaking his head or pursing his lips, occasionally looking up at Mansoor and nodding. It was almost ten minutes before he'd completed the task and replaced everything in the envelopes.

'Please give your associate my regards and respect. His work is nothing short of exemplary, superb. My thanks to both of you. I believe that your fee for the two sets was $100,000 American?'

Abdul Mansoor nodded: 'Indeed'.

Amin reached for his briefcase, placed it on the table and flipped the catches. The lid slowly lifted to reveal 20 small gold bars and stacks of $100 bills. Amin counted out 19 bars of gold which he placed on the table beside the briefcase and pushed them towards Abdul Mansoor.

'For the papers, gold bullion as agreed. At today's Dubai gold price, each 250 gm bar sits at US$5264.68. Nineteen bars comes to $100,028.92, which means you made a profit on the day.' Amin smiled; Mansoor did not. 'Please check.'

Mansoor checked the gold prices on his phone, did the numbers, smiled and nodded. Amin took out 33 $1000 stacks, pulled three more notes from another stack and passed them all over. Mansoor placed the bars in his own bag, followed those with the stacks of notes, fanning each one beforehand. Amin placed the two envelopes into his briefcase.

'I think that concludes our business for today. Thank you so much for your help.'

Abdul Mansoor was all smiles.

'It was my pleasure Mr Masri. I look forward to our next meeting.' He went to the rear door, called out a name. 'Your car is nearby?'

'Yes, just round the corner.'

'Saif will ... ah Saif, please take Mr Masri's oils to his car,' he said to the boy who appeared through the door.

It took Amin just over an hour to get to the warehouse in Jebel Ali. He parked his car at the side of the building, under the sign that read Marhaba Al Fatah International FZE, next to Gush bin Shabib's scarlet Nissan Navara pickup truck. Leaving his briefcase locked in the boot, Amin carried the two wooden boxes around to the front, nudged open the door and scooted past before it closed. He found Gush checking stock along one of corridors that ran between the high racks of industrial metal shelving. Or to be more accurate, somewhere between the concrete floor and the corrugated iron roof.

'Hey Gush, how are you doing?'

'Amin, my man,' he shouted down from his lofty perch. 'Yeah I'm good. When did you get in?'

'Yesterday late and then this morning I had stuff to do in Deira. Came straight down here afterwards.'

'KaraPak delivered a pallet of what looks like big tins here about an hour ago, addressed to you. Guess you know about that, huh?' Gush descended slowly, standing in the yellow box on the small single scissor powerlift as he talked. 'Tickets say it came from Karachi but there's nothing to say what's in the tins.'

The lift table came to a halt a few feet above ground. Gush dropped off the edge, ignoring the steps, walked over to Amin and enveloped him in a crushing bear bug. As broad as he was tall, in a former life Gush had been a Master Sergeant in the

UAE's Union Defence Force and the Royal Guard Brigade's star wrestler. Ten years down the line from leaving, he'd lost none of his shape or strength. The bald head however had grown shaggy brown locks and the erstwhile clean shaven face was covered by a woolly beard, but that could not hide his smile of delight.

'It's so good to see you, even though you look like shit,' he said, holding Amin by the shoulders and at arms' length. 'Too much good food, filthy alcohol and lack of exercise in my opinion. Let's get you back into training and I'll have you fighting fit in one month.'

'Yeah, and then I'd look like you? No way do I want to look like that!' The reciprocal smile said it all. 'It's good to see you too, Gush. Just don't get out here as often as I'd like, but that could change. Who knows? So where are my tins, as you call them?' he asked, changing tack.

'Over there, by the main roller door. Let's take a look. What's with the wooden suitcases? Let me take one of those. How's the beautiful Sophie, who you don't deserve?'

'As wonderful as ever and she sends her love.'

'You didn't say what's in the boxes.'

'Patience, Gush.'

Amin took a Stanley knife from the shelf by the door and sliced through the heavy duty shrink wrap plastic. Together they peeled and cut away the covering to reveal six shiny steel cylinders, each one clearly numbered on the top. Picking up the one marked 06, Amin twisted the top in an anti-clockwise direction until the lid separated from the body of the cylinder. A few centimetres below the lip was a metal cover with a small handle at its centre to which Amin gave a half turn before that too came away in his hand. And there, in the internal space of the cylinder, was – nothing.

'What the … it's empty!'

'Well spotted Mr Bin Shabib.'

'Amin, forgive me for being totally stupid but why have you bought six empty steel drums?'

'Perfume.'

'Perfume,' Gush repeated, now looking totally bemused.

Amin opened one of the boxes, looked at the contents and removed the bottle of frankincense. Carefully breaking the wax seal on the bottle, he extracted the tight-fitting stopper with some difficulty. But once done, the heady scent filled the air with the smells of pines and dry earth, a hint of citrus fruit perhaps, warmed by an unknown spice.

'Too be accurate, absolute and essential oils that are used to make perfume. This happens to be frankincense.'

He emptied the bottle into the cylinder, holding it upside down and waiting to ensure that every drop was used.

'And since when have we started shipping whatever-you-said oils, in OTT cans?'

'Since Jacques Polge, Chef Parfumeur at Les Parfums Chanel asked Sophie if we could. He designed the containers himself.'

'You are joking?'

'Not at all. It's absolutely true,' said Amin, amazed at his own mendacity. 'I don't understand exactly how they work, but the cylinders allow the oils to somehow mature.'

'OK,' said Gush, 'what do you want me to do?'

He leaned down, reaching out for the nearest cylinder marked '02' and began to lift it from the pallet. Amin pushed his hands gently back.

'I've been given very specific instructions as to how to decant the absolutes, so I'll do this. Can you get on to Emirates SkyCargo. In an ideal world, pick the pallet up this afternoon or tomorrow morning and then it needs to go on a direct flight to London Heathrow. But not before tomorrow morning, I need to get back to the UK, pick up one of our vans and collect it from the Cargo Terminal.'

'Will do,' said Gush and started to walk away. He turned back. 'If you want the valuables protection they'll need to know the approximate value of the cargo Amin.'

'Fifty thousand dollars.'

'For six cans of oil! Man, are we getting into the right business. What's our margin on this stuff?'

'At point of delivery, probably 400 per cent on diluted absolutes. In real terms, it's going sky high,' Amin added, with a knowing grin.

'I like this business!'

Amin watched Gush walk through a door on the other side of the warehouse, en route to the offices. Once he was satisfied that he was alone, he turned his focus on the job in hand. He was pleased to see that Abdul Mansoor had enclosed a magnetic silver coloured name tag for each of the oils. Opening the second box, he took out another bottle of frankincense, broke the wax seal on that one, un-stoppered it and poured the oil on top of the first. He worked methodically, calmly and carefully, starting with the two essential oils. He attached the name tags under the number: frankincense was 06 and 05 contained the cedarwood oil. When he opened the next cylinder in sequence and removed the plate, instead of empty space there was just a slim gap of perhaps two and a half centimetres.

'After that it's several kilos of high explosive.' He shivered involuntarily. 'I'm holding a fucking bomb!'

He opened the bottle of lotus absolute oil, emptied it into number 04 and reaffixed the internal lid. A thick film of oil squeezed up around the edge, quickly covering the metal almost up to the top of the handle. A little more oil than was needed, he thought. A small part of his business brain strived to calculate what the saving would have been if he'd only bought 75cl bottles. He shrugged the irrelevant thoughts into his mental waste bin. The whole task took less than half an hour. He looked at the results: 01 Orris Root; 02 Jasmin; 03 Calendula; 04 Lotus. The four scents of death.

Re-stoppering the empty bottles, he replaced them in the wooden cases, shut them up and stacked them on top of the fragrant cylinders. It was only then that he spotted the plastic pouch stapled to the wood at the far end of the pallet.

'God, I forgot about those!'

Cutting the opaque plastic from the staples, he unwound the bag and looked inside. He removed one of the handsets, stared at it, pushed the on button and watched the small screen light up with an eerie green glow. Then, realising what he was doing and knowing what it was, switched it off again, letting it slip from his fingers onto the floor. He could feel the sweat beading on his forehead.

'Fuck, fuck, fuck!' he said, staring straight ahead and seeing nothing.

The transmitter lay on the ground, a seemingly innocuous rectangular plastic box-like thing that looked remarkably like an old mobile phone. Amin picked it up, checked to see that the fall hadn't cracked the shell and it was fine. It reminded him of one of the Nokias from a few years back, a 1220 perhaps. Placing it carefully back in the pouch with its partner, his fingers touched a slip of paper, pincering and pulling it out.

'Enc: 2 x NuCan transmitters. Identical usage. 01-04 nos correlate with NuCan nos. Identity of each NuCan should be known for successful transmission.

Good luck AK.'

Amin folded the piece of paper and dropped it back into the pouch with the two transmitters, rolled the plastic up again and sealed the opaque plastic sausage with packing tape from the shelf. Footsteps on the concrete; Gush was walking towards him, looking pleased.

'Done,' he said. 'I'll make sure I'm here in good time tomorrow. SkyCargo are picking up at 08.30 in the morning but they haven't got air space until Friday am. That gets in to Heathrow at 12.15 on Friday UK time. You can collect on Friday afternoon or Saturday between 0800 and 1200; after that, it's next week.'

'Perfect. Can we wrap this lot up again?'

'Easier to crate it, Amin. And safer.'

Gush pulled across a heavy plastic box with a similar footprint to the pallet. Within minutes they were done and the box closed with lead security seals.

'Excellent. You're a star Gush. Got time for a beer in the Captain's at the Beach?'

'Of course! In a bar you're less likely to run off after better company.'

'I need to drop into DHL on the way but after ...'

'See what I mean?'

*****

It was extraordinary how much they had in common, Tarek thought. His parents lived in Nabatieh and she'd been born there. She loved Arabic music and had a special fondness for Charbel Rouhana's oud playing; he had the CD 'Mada' with Rouhana playing with Hani Siblini. She was clearly knowledgeable about

266

Islam, had strong views on Shari'ah and obviously wanted to discuss them; he found that so refreshing in a woman. That was where it had started, a couple of days ago, discussing women's rights and Shari'ah on the Green Oval, next to the Bliss Building at the university.

He'd left his car in the car park that abutted the Bliss Street gate and to get there one had to walk past the Green Oval. It was almost as though she'd been waiting for him, the way she just happened to be there. Of course it was a coincidence but all the same, he rather liked the idea of her stalking him. She reminded him that he'd promised to give her some discussion time, once he returned from Pakistan. So he was obviously back, and would now be a good time, she'd asked. He hadn't felt he could say no in the circumstances. She'd been wearing the same jeans as before, the ones that fitted her like a second skin, outlining every little curve and indentation. And she did have very attractive legs. Then there had been the cream silk blouse that contrasted deliciously with her tanned, smooth skin; the buttons undone to reveal the shallow valley between the curves of her breasts.

They'd talked there, sitting on the grass, discussing thoughts, points of law and opinions. A first he'd talked from a position of strength, the learned professor talking to the eager student, but he'd quickly found that she was more than capable of taking a stand against some of the views he'd expressed. It was rare that he found himself defending points of law, least of all with a woman. Then realised, more forcibly than the first fleeting time, how much she reminded him of Ayesha in the way she talked, moved and even looked. And, of course, there been that same cough. At which point he'd found out that she had a distinct fondness for smoking hashish. She produced a joint that they'd naturally shared. And, apart from having a bite to eat in Faysal's snack bar in the old shot-up building next to Al Ghoussainy's mini market, that had been that.

Until tonight. He'd suggested dinner at Le Ragueneau on Maarad Street, DownTown. She'd accepted. At her request, he'd picked her up by the bullet riddled dark metal figures that comprised the Martyrs' Statue on the El Shouhada side. Although it was eight o'clock, the night air was still warm and the sky was a dark blue dome above Beirut, studded with silver.

He remembered seeing her there, by the roadside, wearing a light wrap chiffon dress that ended half way down her calves. Swirling patterns of scarlet and blue. Le Ragueneau's food had been fine but the company was better. They'd talked a lot, laughed, asked questions and given answers. She'd invited herself back to the Mansourieh apartment.

Sitting in the passenger seat, she'd stretched one leg out, keeping the other bent. The fold of chiffon had fallen away, one leg naked to the thigh. She'd rested her left hand lightly on his leg, nails scratching gently, almost abstractedly, at the material. Tarek had found it distracting, disconcerting even, and tried to concentrate on the road ahead. Marina's right hand crept upwards to cup her breast through the thin material; her left hand crept upwards, stroking his erection through his trousers. Tarek heard himself quietly moaning.

Once through the door of the apartment, she'd pushed him against the wall, undone her belt to let the folds of her dress fall apart; undone his belt with nimble fingers and unzipped him to rampant release. She fucked him there first, on the floor in the hallway, riding him with forceful passion that bordered on savagery. And then, in the bedroom, a softer, more indulgent lovemaking that had left him drowsily, gloriously satiated. She'd suggested having a smoke on the balcony, with some music.

Marina rinsed herself quickly under the shower before stepping out, wrapping a towel around her. Leaving the water running, she went into the living room and looked out towards the balcony. Tarek had his back towards her, busy preparing the nargile. Across the room, she could see the light glowing on his laptop, on the desk. Returning to the bedroom, she quickly retrieved her clutch bag and padded out to the laptop. Before lifting the top, she checked that she was hidden. Blind. As she opened it up, the screen came to life; as she hoped, he hadn't signed out. A simple click and she was looking at Tarek's Windows desktop screen.

Taking the small flash drive from her bag, she inserted it into the USB slot on the side of the machine, double clicked on the icon that appeared under My Computer. Marina's eye flicked down the list of files, stopped at de.exe, floated over the name and double clicked again. Another window popped up, with the legend: DemonsEye Keylogger is installing ... Run DemonsEye in background? Yes or No?' Marina clicked, ticking yes. 'Enable autorun.inf ... Yes or No?'

'Yes again,' she whispered.

She watched the system installing the files, watched the names flash up, change and move on.

'Marina? Are you OK?'

'Shit,' she muttered. ''I'm fine,' she called back. 'I'll be there in minute.'

Leaving the system still running, she dashed into the bathroom, turned off the shower and towel dabbed the worst of the remaining water from her skin. Ignoring her underwear, she slipped on the wrap dress and belt, pushed her hair backwards. As soon as she got back to the living room, Marina looked at the blank computer screen, touched the power button to bring it back to life.

'Installation complete. For security, please remove the flash drive. Your computer will restart in 30 seconds.'

'I'm on my way,' she called, removing the flash drive from the USB slot, slipping it back in her bag.

Folding the laptop's screen back onto the keyboard, she threw her bag onto the bedroom floor by the bed, walked back through the living room on her way to the balcony. She paused by the bookcase to look at the handful of framed photographs. One was of two teenage girls, one of whom Marina thought might be Tarek's sister. The other, who knew? She turned it over: nothing. There was another with Tarek and, this time, obviously Ayesha which looked as though it hadn't been taken that long ago. Marina let her eyes linger on the other woman for a moment and wondered what she'd be like in bed. She smiled, replaced the picture and picked a third. Looking even more recent than the others, it showed a group of smiling people standing on a boat. The fourth was of three young boys on a beach somewhere, perhaps further up the coast. The one in middle is Tarek, she guessed and turned the frame over. This one did have an annotation:

Byblos 1973
Ali   Tarek   Amin

She wondered who the other two boys were, and where they were. Still carrying the photograph, she wandered out onto the balcony. Tarek was curled up in his usual wicker chair, his lips wetly fused to the mouthpiece of the pipe. Removing it when she appeared, he smiled at her like a delighted child, stretching out a hand to touch her leg. Adroitly avoiding Tarek's groping hand, she took the hose and sucked deeply on the mouthpiece, dragging the fragrant smoke into her lungs. Handing it back, she looked out over the balcony to the lights of Beirut, breathed the smoke out into the warm night air. She sat down in the other chair, waved the photograph towards him, for him to take.

'That's you in the middle, right?'

'Yes, a long time ago now. That's Ali Abbas on the left, Amin Masri on the right. As kids, we did everything together and then the war came. That broke everything up, but then I guess you remember that?'

'From a distance,' she said, in a minor lapse of concentration. 'Where are they now?'

'In England. Amin is in sort of food distribution and has his own company. Ali works for the government.'

'Really, doing what?'

'Why do you ask?'

'Just curious,' said Marina, backing off fast and cursing her lack of judgement.

She reached over to take the nargile's hose back, curled her lips around the mouthpiece and sucked hard. Standing up, she walked across to stand over Tarek, leaned down and put her lips over his, letting the smoke seep into his mouth from hers. She slipped her hand between his legs, gently fondling.

'I plan to get to know you a lot better,' she said.

*****

Aaron stared at the screen on his left, shaking his head in disbelief. Then looked back to the one directly in front of him. The message had been encrypted as per usual, fed through several relays before it arrived in his inbox. Decoding the message wasn't difficult since he'd been responsible for setting up this particular line of communication to begin with. He reread

Marina's message again before turning his attention to the numbered attachments. Opening up the first, he found himself looking at a photograph of three boys; the second was of two girls; the third was a picture of a group of people taken leaning over the rail of a boat; fourth was an image of two people, clearly brother and sister.

After he'd printed two copies of each one, Aaron went back to the third picture, enlarging it on screen to 200 per cent. Moving the picture upwards to show the lower part of the picture, Aaron looked at the bow of the boat, smiled and printed two copies of that one as well. He went back for the third time to the email itself.

> To: DnA5h&8438bl03%59BVvoH@tormail.net
> From: M8hKn&*x2ju02gHm0069@tormail.net
> Subject: The Best Laid Plans
> Danny/Aaron
> Subject ensnared. DemonsEye should be running on his laptop, sending keylogs to you at this email second. Suspect you will have happy hunting as T has little security. Attached pics (from phone) of framed photos in apartment. 1: left to right in 1973 – Ali Abbas, Tarek al-Shami, Amin Masri. Abbas and Masri both UK based; A works govt (role n/k); M works own company food (?) 2: Taller girl is Ayesha al-Shami, other girl n/k but probably related to one of the other boys in first pic. 3: Tarek al-Shami as now, second from left; others n/k. Perhaps you can identify from background? 4: T&A al-Shami (recent). T relatively soft target but underlying tensions. Will maintain unless you call off.
> Love from M@Lb

Aaron printed two copies of that as well. He turned his attention to the other screen: it showed a window linked to DnA5h&8438bl03%59BVvoH(2)@tormail.net, as Marina had promised. At the top of the panel: DemonsEyeKeyLogger: PC Activity. Underneath it read: Keystrokes 9 with the time and date next to each one, showing the path buried deep in the host system. As he bent to the task, his smile got bigger and bigger.

With a little more work and a little more patience DemonsEye would give him all of Tarek's passwords.

'You are a very, very bad girl, Marina,' he said, not for the first time.

Putting the printout of her email beside his keyboard, Aaron fed the names Amin Masri and Ali Abbas into Tracker's brain for consideration. Within a nanosecond, Tracker made connections: Amin=amateal@aol.com; IP at 34.130.97.12 cb London; breakdown am=amin; at=at; eal=eel (correction); eal=ealing(?) Retry? See: tar10sham991@hotmail.com=connect.

Aaron sat back in his chair for a moment.

'Danny?'

'Yes Aaron,' he said twisting his chair so he could look at his assistant. 'Aaron why are you wearing that idiot grin?'

'Because I think I have al-Shami's friend in Ealing, London whose name is Amin Masri.'

11 ~ Eeny, Meeny, Miny, Moe

The first floor flat on Tring Avenue had been Sophie's idea of a relatively inexpensive pied-à-terre within spitting distance of Marble Arch. A sizeable two-bedroom conversion in a Victorian house, a short 100 yards from the green grass and leafy trees of Ealing Common, it was a steal at £649,950, she'd said. And it really was a useful place to stay when either or both of them needed to stay near London. So it had made sense to collect the Range Rover from the Long Stay car park and go straight there from Heathrow. All things considered, there was little point in driving almost down to Southampton to pick up a company van; he could get all of the cylinders and the boxes in the car. Plus an anonymous black Range Rover was far less memorable than a sign-painted van.

Ealing had been cold and dark when he arrived the previous night. He'd taken a detour to pick up a doner kebab from the place near Uxbridge Road, Topkapi Kebap, he'd told Sophie on the phone. Told her that he was fine, should be back tomorrow afternoon latest and that he loved her. He'd poured himself a beer, warmed up the doner in the microwave and sat down in front of the faux log fire, complete with variable glow and fan heater. Ealing in the morning was cold and light.

By 9.30 Amin was already on the M4, on his way to collect the cylinders from SkyCargo at Heathrow. The text he'd received told him that: 'DocNo:103/77910817; Ref EK00015/388LX01; May be Collected at: U1, dnata City, Northumberland Close, Stanwell TW19 7I'. There was a bit more about required identification and proof of bonding if applicable. A few miles down the road, he took the slip off the motorway, picking up The Parkway. The satnav fed him past Terminal Four and within minutes he was parking by a massive warehouse that shared a site with several other, equally massive warehouses. The door marked Reception seemed to be his only option.

'Yeah mate. What can I do for you today?' said the young man with the shiny bald head, wearing a light grey, short-sleeved polo shirt and a HiViz vest with reflective stripes.

Amin showed him the SMS he'd received on his phone. Your Man took the phone, read the message, punched the numbers on his keyboard, looked at his screen and then looked at Amin.

'You'll be Mr Smelly then,' he said with a grin.

'Sorry,' said Amin, 'what did you say?'

'I said, you're Mr Smelly. Or rather, your crate stinks, mate!'

'Do NOT panic,' said a voice in Amin's head. 'Why NOT?' asked another. 'Oh shit,' Amin muttered. Remembering the adage, attack being the best form of defence, Amin spoke accordingly.

'Excuse me but are you telling me you've broken the lead seals on my consignment without my presence? God help you if anything is missing or damaged. You do realise how valuable that cargo is, since it's stated on the bloody air waybill. I will …'

'Pin your tongue back mate. You're hassling the wrong man. Obviously HMRC waved it through because it's going to a bonded warehouse. You've got the paperwork with you, I take it?'

'Of course.'

'Right, so aviation security in cargo's getting hammered in the press because everyone's worried about bombs in planes right? They've been having a go every now and then since 9/11 in America. But you can't check everything. It's not like passenger bags that you can screen with x-rays. If we screened cargo like that, not only would it take bleeding years of manpower to process one month of cargo but we'd have to take most of it apart with crowbars and claw hammers. Then you would have something to moan about! Last year, almost one million tonnes of cargo came into the UK and most of that came to Heathrow.

'Anyway, one of the security blokes sees that the waybill says 'absolute oils for perfume' but can't see anything through the plastic of the box and the dogs aren't smelling anything either. He thinks that's a bit odd so he gets the cutters, snips through the seals and opens it up to have a butcher's. Gets engulfed in a cloud of pong so strong that he gets all nauseous and has to sit down. After that he just waved it through. Conclusions? It's definitely what you say it is and you're Mr Smelly 'cos something's definitely leaking. But that isn't down to us, mate.'

'Fine,' said Amin, keeping his voice firm, supressing the urge to jump up and down shouting Allahu akbar. 'Thank you. Obviously I'll need to check everything carefully and hopefully it's only a little seepage. Otherwise I'll have to take the matter up with SkyCargo. Where's the crate now?'

'Round the back in the secure zone. I'll open the gate and you drive right in. Red box on the right hand side; but it's not difficult to find, even with the lid back on. Right, papers please mate.'

Ten minutes later, Amin was inside the compound, surrounded by the chain link fencing topped by complementary razor wire. He reversed the Range Rover up to the crate, removed the lid and felt immediate sympathy with the security officer. The commingling of such powerful scents had produced an undiluted perfume haze that was indescribably pungent, complex and totally overwhelming.

'That's awful,' said Amin, wiping tears from his eyes, 'and strong!'

He stacked the two carry boxes to one side of the boot, following those with the cylinders, one at a time. Although the lids had been engineered for a close fit, there were no rubber or other seals to prevent the slight seepage that had occurred. Thrown around in cargo depots, jolted in the hold of the plane, the angle of the plane at take-off and during its descent: Amin presumed that all of them had contributed to the agitation of the liquid causing seepage. By the time he had finished, Amin's hands were as fragrant as the goods he had handled. Each cylinder seemed to have at least a modicum of oil on the metal casing, making them slick and dangerously slippery. Most of him firmly believed that his highly explosive cargo was in safe hibernation; another part screamed at him not to drop one on concrete. Even bears can be woken in winter.

By putting it upside down over the cylinders, there was enough room to add the crate to the boot and the lid fitted neatly down the side. Amin wasn't planning on leaving any trace of the cargo or his visit. As he drove out of the compound, he was glad that the Range Rover didn't have personalised plates. Feeding onto the M25, just before Wraysbury Reservoir, Amin finally allowed himself to breathe as he felt the tension in his body start

275

to ease. He pulled out into the middle lane to overtake a TNT Global Logistics truck, accelerating past at an even 75mph which was safe enough, given the flow of traffic. In the dirt on the back of the truck, someone had scrawled: TNT – always bang on time!

'You and me both,' he said wryly.

A turmoil of grey and black clouds gathered in the sky above as Amin headed south but the threat of rain did not materialise. And despite the dreary road works that trailed down the M3 like slime behind a slug, the traffic kept moving. An hour later, he was parking the Range Rover in the drive next to Sophie's Mercedes. As he got out of the car, she appeared at the front door, naturally flanked by Borak and Jemila. The couple met half way, hugging silently as they stood on the gravel in front of the house. She finally pulled away, laughing.

'Bof,' she said, melodramatically holding her nose. 'You smell as if you are spending all of last night in an American brothel. Eugh.'

'Shouldn't that be French brothel?'

'Mais non. If it was French it would be sophisticated and subtle; this is more cheap, too loud and slutty, I think.'

'Believe me, cheap it is not.'

They smiled at each other, enjoying the brief bit of banter. And then onwards.

'Everything went well then, I hope?'

'I'm here. And so are they,' he said nodding towards the Range Rover.

'Show me,' Sophie said quietly.

Amin opened the back, removed the plastic crate and the lid, putting them on ground. Together they stared at the six oil-satined, shiny cylinders, sitting like alien visitors in the boot that was so often home to the dogs or crammed with shopping bags. These geometric metal shapes that had no link, purpose or relevance to their lives seemed threatening by their very being.

'Which ones are the bombs?'

'They all have numbers on the lids, from one to six. See?' Amin pointed to the nearest, indicating the numeral etched into the metal.

'And number two, this is one?'

'Yes. The first four are all packed with high explosive. Now they are safe, asleep one could say. I sent the radio transmitters to Tarek by courier from Jebel Ali. He might already have received them. He'll use one to send the signals that will detonate the bombs. Without that radio signal – nothing.'

'So this one, this, this and this.' She touched each one in turn. 'And the other two?'

'They're just dummies; full of essential oils.'

'But the bombs. They have oil in too, no?'

'Yes, but only a litre of absolute oil in each one.'

'Putain! Mais ceci, c'était vraiment cher.'

'Yup.'

'What are you going to do with it all?'

'For the moment, pour it back in the bottles. They're in these boxes,' he said pulling them out towards them.

'I will help.'

There was a workbench at the back of the garage where, on the rare occasion that the spirit moved, Amin had attempted to make or fix things. Together they emptied the boot, carried everything there, putting the cylinders carefully on the floor. Amin opened one of the boxes, removed the bottle marked 'Jasmin', found the matching cylinder '02' with 'Jasmin' underneath, and put them both on the bench. Sophie searched the rack above, found a large plastic funnel and placed the spout in the neck of the now opened empty bottle. Amin unscrewed the lid from the cylinder, carefully removed the internal cap, easing it through the film of oil and holding it at an angle to let the viscous liquid run back.

'It would smell nice if it were diluted with other oil. Like this, it is too puissant, too strong.'

'You ready?'

'Oui. Vas y.'

Amin poured very slowly, not wanting the sluggish stream to back up in the funnel. Now and then he paused, when he'd poured a little too much too fast, or when the weight became a strain. Sophie watched the level of oil slowly rising, watched the stream turn to a trickle and finally to a series of last fat droplets. Holding the cylinder now under one arm with difficulty, Amin used a wooden spatula to guide the remaining slicks towards the mouth of the funnel.

'That's it,' he said, letting empty '02-Jasmin' down onto the workbench with a gentle thump. 'We've lost a little.'

'Wait one moment,' said Sophie, disappearing through the door that led from the garage into the kitchen.

She returned a moment later with a large almost full bottle of grapeseed oil.

'They use this grapeseed oil to dilute huiles absolues, so we wash the inside with a little and make a little more for the bottle.'

The thin oil seemed to thicken fractionally as Sophie swished it around the inside with a pastry brush. They topped off and stoppered the bottle of Jasmin, then turned their attention to the next cylinder. Over an hour elapsed before they finished refilling the bottles and washing the inside of the cylinders with grapeseed oil to reclaim the last residues of the oils. And when they'd finished they washed the cylinders with soap and water.

'Enough,' said Amin. He put his arms round his wife. 'Thank you.'

'De rien,' she murmured.

'You smell glorious,' he said.

'You're a liar. And you stink,' she replied.

The application of gel and hot running water under a shower washed off most of the grime and residual oil on their skin, as well as ameliorating the smell. They emerged gently scented, rather than reeking of perfumed oils. Tainted clothes went in the washing machine for a more rigorous form of detoxification. They regrouped in the Orangerie where Amin had fired up a patio heater and turned down the lights. Sophie had found her place on the sofa with a coffee table at her side. Amin handed her a glass of white wine, sat down beside her putting his own on the table.

'You should try to recoup some of the money for this. How much did you pay?'

'Thirty three thousand dollars, for all of them. But remember, I have one hundred thousand in Switzerland that they have paid.'

'Of course, but you have paid for the papers no?'

'Uh-uh. I'll show you those.'

He reached for the briefcase; her hand, gentle on his arm, put him on pause.

'In a moment. Maybe I have an idea for these oils. We should get rid of them now and I think out of the country is best.'

'Of course. If, and it is an if, customs or security decided to do a follow up, for whatever reason, it's better if everything seems as though it's been sold on, as implied. Even if we ignore what they don't know, it's possible that customs might do a check because they're bonded. I haven't got a solution but you, you have? In retrospect, the whole oil idea was bloody stupid.'

'No it had merit, not least because it worked. The bombs of course must be given to Alain; you can phone him in a moment.' She took a sip of wine. 'The bottles of oil, we take to France. Take the ferry to Calais and declare them as imports to customs. They are bonded here and so we use the external transit certificate for there, which you have already. Then we have paper proof that the oils have been imported into France. After we drive down to Marseille and see Papa. Perhaps you remember, he has the small bottling plant near Toulon? They used to bottle drops for the eyes, small ones maybe only five millilitres, and they should still have the proper machines. With this we would have 200 bottles of each absolue and 800 of the essential. Enfin, we brand them as Les Senteurs de Beyrouth; Leena can sell them at Les Goûts. Ça marche?'

'Oh yes Sophie, I think ça marche vachement bien.'

They raised their glasses, clinked, drank and smiled. Amin reached for the briefcase again, flipped the catches, retrieved the two envelopes and tipped the contents onto the table. Sophie flicked through the dark red passport to the page with the photo, then to the page with the UAE resident's visa, checked the health card, driving licence and pushed them all into a pile.

'French? Nice, Monsieur Marechal.'

'Mon plaisir, Madame Marechal.'

'Phone Alain, for Sunday. Maybe Tuesday would be a good day to go to France.'

*****

279

Leigh Delamere Services on the M4 was about half way between Aberdare and Burley. Approximate but near enough. Alan had spotted Amin's Range Rover fairly quickly, parked closer to the Travel Lodge than the Services. There weren't too many other cars close by, but enough to make the exchange seem perfectly normal and not draw attention. He'd imagined a conversation between a brat and parent.

'Mam, did you see that Mam? Over there, that man just gave the other man a box or something. I bet it's drugs Mam.'

'Now don't you be looking at what other people are doing. What's their business, is their business.'

'Mam! He's just given the other man another one. Look Mam. Maybe it's a bomb. Maybe they's terryists.'

'Well I don't know. Maybe it is and maybe they are ...'

Neither man had wanted to linger. Their conversation had been brief and to the point. Amin had mentioned the numbers on the cylinders, the need for correlation with missile numbering, telling Tarek the same, and that Tarek had the triggers. He'd mentioned exit strategies and the need to have one, to watch his back and gave him a key to the Ealing flat, just in case. It had taken a matter of seconds to transfer the cylinders from the Range Rover to the Volvo. And then Alan had driven back to his home near Aberdare, to Megan and Anwen, with four steel cans full of high explosive. Zero one dash Orris Root (Orris for short) he left in the boot; the others were carefully lined up on the floor under a dustsheet at the back of the garage.

Alan looked through his office window, sipping his fourth cup of coffee of the day. He could see the Volvo, just outside, still wet from the early afternoon rain. As the cloud base began to fracture and dissipate, the sun took brash advantage, sending golden spotlights to target the world below. For one brief moment, Alan's car shone in unexpected illumination, in the searching light of a sunbeam. He turned away from the window, walked back to his desk and started to study orders out in line with shipping schedules. After checking the lists several times, he realised that their target ships more or less ordered themselves. Stripping a sheet of paper from the pad, he wrote down the details as he saw them.

1. HMS Gloucester to NATO Operation Active Endeavour out mid-November. At station Limassol, Cyprus end-November.
2. HMS York to NATO Operation Active Endeavour out end-November. Patrol Leb/Syria coastline end-November on.
3. HMS Edinburgh Combined Task Force out end-November. Join at Mina Salman, Bahrain mid-December. Suez Canal anticipated 2/3 December.
4. HMS Manchester Standing Maritime Group 2 out end-November. Cairo early Dec to off Leb/Syria mid-Dec.

Due to the update requirements forwarded by the MoD, all four ships were due to receive their complements of Sea Darts imminently. He checked the manufacturing schedules: both Gloucester and York's orders had already been completed and were in pre-delivery safe storage. His inclination had been to install before completion but now he had no other option. And perhaps that was all to the good, he thought, they would all have been through quality control and signed off. The drawback was that installation would entail removing the bolts around the nosecone and easing that forward without it disengaging. Then take out the gyro-et-al box, replace with the NuCan, slide the nosecone back and re-bolt.

Alan sighed, ran the sequence through his mind and then did it all over again. Each time he searched his mental scans for any problems that could or might arise. His time would be limited and he couldn't afford any mistakes. He hoped that Tarek had remembered to organise the magnetic switch; and that Malik and his team had followed through. If that hadn't been fixed … that was something that Alan really didn't want to think about. He glanced at his watch. The production crews would have already left the factory and most of the office staff would have gone as well. The predictable, reliable and ultimately habituated Steven Lee would provide the necessary information and almost certainly be the last to leave. Within five minutes, was Alan's guess; the tap on the door came in two followed by the opening thereof.

'I'll be off then,' he said. 'Are you staying a while, Alan?'

'Yeah, just a few more things I want to get done today, before I go.'

'If you need any help …' said Steven in that way that silently added: 'but please don't ask'.

'No you're fine, Steven. Go.'

'I thought I might drop into the Rhoswhenallt for a couple on the way, so if you're coming by …'

'I might just do that if there's time.'

Right, I'll be off then,' Steven repeated. 'Want me to tell security you're staying for a bit?'

'Thank you. Goodbye.'

'Right,' said Steven. And left.

Alan waited, watching Steven Lee drive to the gate, saw him talk to the security guard and drive through. Another few minutes. Leaving everything in his office as it normally would be when he was working, Alan walked down the corridor, out through the front door and over to his car. Opening the boot, he lifted the cylinder out, elbowed the boot lid shut and walked back into the building. As long as everything appeared normal, nothing he did would be noticed by security. Inside, he walked back along the corridor to the far end and unlocked the door that led onto the factory floor. He turned right, walking along the side of building until he came to a line of tool racks. Taking a torque wrench and a set of long-nosed sockets to add to his load, he turned back on himself, crossing the factory floor to a pair of electronically controlled broad steel-bound doors, some 20 feet high. He inserted a key in the lock to the right, gave it a half turn and then punched in his code on the keypad above. The familiar whining sound screeched eerily in the abnormally silent space and Alan winced, half expecting some nervy security guard to come rushing into the factory. He walked through the ever widening gap as the lights blazed automatically into life.

HMS Gloucester's Sea Darts were all racked in five flat blocks near the front. Alan checked the serial numbers stencilled on the metal casings with the ones on his list. The numbers were sequential, running upwards from FI60-7998/525 through FI60-7998/545; Alan chose the last missile in the second rack, serial number FI60-7998/533 being in the middle of the sequence and easily accessible.

Retrieving everything from the doorway, where he'd left the tools and cylinder, he started work. The torque wrench and slim socket made easy work of the inset bolts around the head. Easing the cone forwards, he removed the guidance module and picked up its replacement. To his relief, he saw that the magnetic release had been fitted. The cylinder slipped into place without leaping out of his hands, only clamping into place when he pressed the button. Slide the cone back, retighten the bolts and get out fast! Making sure that he hadn't left anything behind, Alan walked to door with the wrench and socket set; and paused.

'For fuck's sake,' he hissed, turning back.

Alan could feel his heart pounding as retraced his steps to collect the guidance module lying alone on the ground next to the missile rack and in full view. He picked it up, shaking his head at his own stupidity. Hit the buttons, turn and take key, hear the closing whine as you walk away and return the tools their allocated places. Leave though door, lock same and breathe while walking back to office.

'Losing your touch, Mr Abbot?' he asked himself quietly. 'First run done.'

He took his time, shutting his computer down and tidying his desk before leaving. Remembering to lock the main door, he got into his Volvo and drove to the security barrier. Nametag Freeman, M. leaned down to look through the window, touched the shiny peak of his hat.

'Working late tonight, Mr Abbot?'

''Fraid so Martin, and probably for the rest of the week, thanks to Her Majesty's Royal Naval cock-up. Brought the next series of delivery dates forward. Such is life. Night, Martin.'

'Good night, Sir. Drive carefully, I heard mention of black ice on the Llwydcoed road if you're going that way.'

As he drove away, Alan felt a sense of calm fatality enclose him like a comfortable old cloak and he sad-smiled at its familiarity. Even though he hadn't done anything quite like it before, arming the Sea Dart, realigning its very purpose and direction, had its roots in the past. It reminded him of the past and a grim smile flitted across his face. It is time for the reckoning, he thought.

He dropped in to the Rhoswhenallt on the way, had a half even though Steven had left. Parked in his usual place outside the house, took the guidance module into the garage and took the second cylinder, Jas he called it, and put it in the boot. Went inside, kissed Megan and Anwen, asked them how their days had been and eaten dinner, after a proper drink. He did all the usual things that he did when he got home after work, and that was fine.

The following evening, Alan repeated the process, waiting until everyone had left before getting 02-Jasmin from the boot. Down the same corridor, through the door onto the factory floor, collecting the same set of tools, opening the same doors to the secure zone. But this time he looked for the missiles due for HMS York, chose serial number FI60-7998/623 and made the switch. On Wednesday, Calendula went into FI60-7999/112 bound for HMS Edinburgh and Lotus was inserted into FI60-7999/139 on Thursday, on its way to HMS Manchester. He phoned Tarek from the car park at Tesco, just off Depot Road in Aberdare.

'Hullo?'

'Tarek, it's Alan.'

'Hey Alan, it's good to hear from you. What's new?'

'They're all done. You're good to go.'

Tarek's wordless response sounded simultaneously like an intake of breath and a long sigh. And then: 'Allahu akbar'.

'No Tarek, Allah might know, but I installed them. And this is isn't about Allah.'

'Yes, I know. It's just that ... you know.'

'No, I don't know Tarek. Listen to me carefully, when you do this, it will be you pushing the buttons or Ayesha, not Allah. You need to remember that.'

'I will but ...'

'No buts. Have you got a pen and paper?'

'A moment.'

Alan could hear the shuffle of papers, something fall on the ground and then white noise.

'Alan? I'm back. OK, tell me.'

'I didn't want to put this in an email just in case. I doubt that anyone's looking but there's no sense in taking chances, as you said yourself; your pay phone will definitely be under the radar. They're all out for delivery next week but the ships won't be in your area until later. I suspect that you'll have to visually identify each one, although the transmitter will obviously search for its target. Just in case they're of use, I'll give you MMSI number for each one and its call sign. The MMSI's Maritime Mobile Service Identity. But you would need access to VHF radio and someone who knows what they're doing. Are you ready?'

'Yeah, go.'

'Number one is HMS Gloucester. She should be leaving Portsmouth in a couple of weeks to join a NATO task force in the Med. Her MMSI's 234595000; call sign GBBF. Her pennant number is D96 and that's painted on the side of the ship.' Alan paused. 'Karma, Tarek. From late November, HMS Gloucester will be based out of Limassol.'

Alan heard the scratching of pen on paper. Then the intake of breath, even more audible this time but with a sibilance that suggested more than one person. And somebody, in the background, said 'Yes' in a distinctive call of triumph. He smiled with assumed recognition.

'Ayesha's there with you, isn't she?'

'Yes, she saw me write the name.'

'Give her my love.'

Alan dictated the rest of the details of each ship from his sheet.

'And that's it,' he said with finality. 'You have the transmitters I hope? Amin said that he'd sent them by courier from Jebel Ali.'

'Yes, they arrived on Monday.'

'Good. Listen, I should go. I was already late before I stopped to phone; Megan will wonder where I am. But one more thing: memorise the information that you've written down and destroy the piece of paper. I'm gone. Good luck, Tarek.'

Before Alan could cut the call, another voice came on the line.

'Ali, it's Ayesha.'

'Hey, beautiful.'

'Thank you.'

'There's nothing to thank for Ayesha, but it's appreciated. You're going to do the first one, aren't you?'

'Yeah. Yeah, I am. For Leena, Faridah and Mama, of course for what happened. But it's also for Halah and you, for all Palestinians. And I'm doing it for me, yes.'

'Be careful.'

'I will. But what are you going to do if … they might trace the bombs back to you, no?'

'I think that's possible, mmm, maybe probable. And the answer is, I don't know. I don't know that I can get away, escape. Leaving Megan and Anwen is not an option. No, I'm still thinking.'

'The clock is ticking Ali.'

'I know.'

'Take care. Love you.'

'You too, Ayesh.'

This time Alan did cut the call, put the phone in his jacket pocket and stared across the tungsten yellow tarmac with its coloured chequerboard of cars. A light rain had begun falling while he'd been on the phone, leaving droplets of water that refracted the light in places, creating tiny rainbows in the darkness. He started the car, drove to the far corner of the car park and stopped underneath the small overhang of branches. Opening the car door, he held the piece of paper over a lighted match, watched the flame take hold and race up towards his fingers. He let it burn and char, holding on to the corner until only that was left and then let it fall to the ground. All that remained were a few sodden ashes and a tiny white triangle of wet paper. Alan closed the door and drove home.

*****

For a change, Helen was hosting the party in her eyrie on the first floor. Admiral Reginald Buller made no bones about the fact that he preferred the library for discussion; at least there he was allowed to smoke. There was a resemblance in so far as the wood panelling, bookshelves and chairs went but that was the limit. Stretching across the front of the Red House having six tall windows that let the light in from the world outside. The paintings on the walls were modernist abstracts full of swirls of bright colours apart from a copy of Escher's lithograph 'Relativity'.

'Everything is right in the wrong places until the wrong places are looked at in the right way. Which reminds one that most of what is wrong is generally in the right place but one tends to look at the overall picture in the wrong way,' Helen liked to say.

The three of them were sitting in comfortably squishy chairs at one end of Helen's office where a large screen was attached to the wall with a direct feed to and from the basement. The view was of a screen within a screen within a screen, going on and on into the virtual distance, getting smaller and smaller. A small camera shot popped up at the bottom of the screen, showing a live view of John Watkins looking uncomfortable.

'Hallo, can you see me?'

'Yes, John,' said Helen, 'where are we?'

'It looks as though Mossad's on the nail with the 'amateal' email address connection. The IP address was in the Ealing area. It took a while but we found a flat in Tring Avenue in Ealing.'

A photograph appeared on the screen of a Victorian house with a flat parking area in front, bordered by a few trees. A smaller photograph appeared towards the top left showing what looked like a shot of an interior.

'It's the flat here,' he said, as a red laser dot circled a window on the first floor. 'The registered owner is one Mrs Sophie Masri of French descent, who is married to Mr Amin Masri. It looks as though Mr Masri has dual nationality as he seems to hold Lebanese and French passports. Major Roberts kindly put one of his chaps on a bit of a stakeout, Tim Grayling,' Watkins said, looking down at his notes. 'Tim kept an eye on the property for a couple of days off and on but there's been no movement. If you look at the inset,' which expanded as he spoke, 'there's no obvious sign of life. I'm pretty certain that's because the Tring Avenue flat's a second home.'

The house photographs were replaced by a picture of a group of people leaning over the side of a boat.

'This was obtained by Ms Marina from Professor Tarek al-Shami's flat in Beirut. I'm not quite sure of the circumstances under which it was obtained but I got the impression that her, umm, methods were slightly umm, unethical. I believe the word is honeytrap.' Watkins' face appeared to have taken on a distinctly pink hue. 'It was taken on her phone after ... I don't think it matters. Zooming in to the background, we took several snapshots to see whether we could match it with any marinas in the south of England for starters. As you can see, the boat's called Sirens' Choice and we checked that with the DVLA's Small Ships Register.'

Not a word was said by the two men and one woman upstairs: Helen and Mike were both making notes while the Admiral stared at the screen and admired what he could see of Sirens' Choice.

'So the upshot is that Sirens' Choice is a Jeanneau 46, powered by twin Volvo Penta 480hp diesel engines. The overall length is 46 feet, ten inches with a standard keel draught ...'

'Watkins, much as I love mucking about in boats and admiring this one, I don't need the bloody specifications,' the Admiral growled. 'Get on with it man.'

'Sorry Sir. We've established that the registered owner of Sirens' Choice is Amin Masri and its normal mooring is at Poole Quay Boat Haven Marina. I'm afraid we can only identify two of the people in the photograph: Tarek al-Shami here,' said Watkins hovering his red dot, 'and Amin Masri, here. We're working on the rest. Moving on from there, hazarding a guess that the Masris probably lived in the area we ran checks and, discovered they live here.' A photograph of the house duly appeared. 'It's between Burley and Bagnum in the New Forest.

'Then we worked on the employment or business fronts. The Masris aren't short of a penny or two by the looks of things and they like spending money. They own a company called International Foods based near Southampton and as far as I can see they're clean as whistles. It's been vetted by the Ministry of Defence at least twice for government supply contracts, that the company won. Vetted again this year under the tendering process for a specific quick reaction supply contract which was awarded only a month or so back.

'Masri's only crime so far is that he's a friend of al-Shami. Mr Spiegel's assistant Aaron is working on obtaining al-Shami's passwords from his computer. Unfortunately, getting those depends on when he happens to type them in on that particular machine. I think that's more or less what I have for you at the moment.'

'Do we know where Masri is at the moment, John?' asked Mike.

'Afraid not, or rather not for certain, Major. Tim Grayling seemed pretty sure that no one was actually living in the Ealing flat, so I'd guess that they're at the house near Bagnum. Cedars' Stand it's called. Strange name for a house, if you ask me.'

'And going back to al-Shami, do we have any more on this NuCan business?'

'Nothing on our side nor, as far as I know, from Tel Aviv.'

'In that case, we'll let you get back to cyberspace. Thanks John.'

Helen switched off the monitor. Not one of them moved, each totally absorbed in his or her own thought processes. Admiral Buller was first to break the silence.

'This NuCan business, Mike. What's your gut feeling?'

'I don't know, Sir. The name's got to be euphemism for something and I'm guessing that something's not good. According to Danny, Dr Sami Malik first appeared on the scene at Kahuta, working with Abdul Qadeer Khan producing highly enriched uranium. It's fairly certain that he was at least present, if not directly involved, when Pakistan tested nukes in May 1998 in the Kharan Desert. Over the years there've been all sorts of rumours flying around about liaisons between Pakistan and China exchanging nuclear technology, nuclear resources being smuggled in from countries like France and Germany. Even, allegedly, from us. Malik was at the heart of all that; he has knowledge, expertise and is probably very greedy.

'I'm not an expert, but I do know that nuclear devices don't just use uranium or plutonium. A high energy explosive like HMX is detonated around a sphere of uranium or plutonium that compresses the atoms. They reach critical mass and initiate a nuclear explosion. As I said, I'm not a physicist let alone a nuclear scientist, but the point I'm making is that Malik almost certainly knows his way around explosives, from TNT to HMX and HEU for nukes.

'Khan has been accused by many people, including his own countrymen, of trying to sell nuclear technology to Iran and

289

Saudi Arabia and probably a few more countries. The chances are that Malik could well have been in the loop. Being lower down the food chain, who's to say that Malik didn't emulate his master and sell explosives or explosive technology to anyone who'd pay? It's also been suggested that Khan tacitly supported, or sympathized with, terrorist groups like al-Qaeda. Again, it's possible that Malik's of the same mind. Sorry, I'm brain storming aloud and not making much sense.'

'Don't worry,' said Admiral Buller, 'but what are you suggesting?'

'I'm not sure.'

'You think this NuCan is a bomb of sorts, don't you Mike?' interjected Helen.

Mike looked at her for a moment, looked at the ceiling and then back again.

'Yes, I think I do. Or rather that's what bothers me, that these NuCans might be bombs. Thinking rationally, however, why would an academic want a bomb? As an academic, his specialities cover Islam and, more importantly, Islamic law; but there's nothing to suggest that al-Shami's a fanatical fundamentalist nutter. Nor is there any evidence that points to a terrorist link.'

Helen opened a folder in front of her, flipped through the various papers, stopped and pulled one piece half way out.

'The emails that Danny flagged up when you talked to him last,' she said. 'From an untraceable tormail account. 'Congratulations, you've been chosen to meet the main man … wait outside with the little bluebird.' That is weird and it might be just spam. And then again, it might not.'

'And if it's not, what? A coded message?'

'Etcetera, etcetera.'

Their pause allowed Admiral Buller to rejoin the conversation.

'If these blasted NuCan things are bombs, what's the target?' he asked. 'Or perhaps that should be – where are the targets? John Watkins said that Masri ran a firm called International Foods and has a reactive contract with the Navy. A contract like that would involve the resupply of ships overseas and potentially supply support to marines on the ground. I think we can safely assume that Masri has a fairly efficient international logistics network.'

He left the subject hanging in the air, a bloated mental piñata waiting for the stick to release the gifts of possible unpalatable conclusions.

'But it's all just bloody hypothesis,' Helen hissed. 'We need more facts.'

'Of course, Masri could be a red herring,' the Admiral said, almost as though it was an afterthought. 'Maybe we're reading the whole NuCan story in the wrong way. Fanciful I know, but think on this. Overtly al-Shami may not have terrorist connections and he may not appear to have fundamentalist leanings, but he is a mullah which, by definition, is someone learned in Islam and Shari'ah. He makes numerous visits to Islamic conferences, madrasas and similar which provide contacts and followers. Do we perhaps have a Mullah al-Shami waiting in the shadows until the moment comes when he takes of his cloak of invisibility?

'Shining that light on the situation, is his association with Sami Malik a key component in a greater plan? We've seen the word NuCan and saying 'new can' as one word, with the emphasis on the first syllable. Maybe there's another way, off the top of my head: take the first three letters and pronounce them as 'nuke', assume the next two letters are anagrammatic and then give them balance. Then you might have: Nuke, the Atomic Nexus. Purely imaginative or plausible fiction? And can we take the risk?'

*****

Weapons Engineer Officer, Lieutenant Commander Christopher 'Kit' Furney leaned over the rail and looked at the two big trucks on the dockside. Big tractor units pulling twelve metre flatbed semi-trailers, boxed in by plasticised canvas over tubular frames; all in olive green. Unadorned, there was no branding, sign painting or logos; not even something scrawled in the dirt on the back or the sides. There was no telephone number to call for sales or help, or even to comment on how well driven the vehicle had been. And yet, to the initiated the trucks screamed missiles, bombs, explosives and weapons of mass destruction. Or, as Kit might have put it over a drink in the pub: tools of the trade. Two other trucks had gone further up the quay to unload at HMS York with, he assumed, a similar load.

He watched as the drivers undid the ties, pulling the canvas back along the frames to reveal their cargoes: ten Sea Dart missiles in under-and-over racks on each semi-trailer as per the tickets. The wharfies moved in with their hoists and pulleys on mobile tractors. It never failed to amaze him how precisely they moved the vehicles, attached the pulleys to each missile in turn, hoisting them gracefully in the air and then lowering them to the ground. Loaded mobile platforms towed away by mobile tractors, disengaging the missile from its companions; reuniting them all tween decks in a separate mechanical dance. It was all done with such practised ease, and Kit admired that in the men.

He watched until they were almost done before turning away from the show, walking in through the nearby door, making his way down to the missile magazines. The last two Sea Darts were coming in as he walked into the cramped space. Kit did a quick head count, making sure that he hadn't been short changed. Twenty asked for, twenty received and all was well. Working quickly and systematically, he visually checked each missile, then the serial numbers on his sheet with those stencilled on the Sea Darts. All present, correct and correlated. He signed off on the paperwork, handed it back to the man and cast an eye around the magazine before leaving. Down here, with the ship at anchor and the engines off, the magazine space was a silent dormitory for the sleeping Sea Darts, each one comfortably tucked up on its own supportive half-tube. As they were, under the low level lighting, the look was more bleached-out bland industrial rather than high-contrast streamlined threatening. Kit hoped he wouldn't have to wake them up in anger in the six-month tour ahead.

HMS Gloucester left Portsmouth on the morning tide two days later, sailing at a sedate regulation-driven speed of ten knots. Crossing the Solent, she cruised down the eastern point of the Isle of Wight past Bembridge and out into the English Channel, gathering speed. Taking an initial bearing of west-southwest, the Gloucester moved up to full speed, churning through the cold grey-green water at a speedy 30 knots. A stiff breeze above sent the massed grey clouds churning in the opposite direction at a similar speed. By mid-evening, Gloucester had rounded the north-western French port of Brest, heading down the outer edge of the Bay of Biscay.

'Biscay, wind in the north, southerly or southwesterly four, increasing five or six,' the weatherman crackled out over the radio. 'In the south, variable, mainly southeasterly, three or four. Sea in the north, slightly moderate, occasionally rough later. In south, slight or moderate.'

'That's not bad so far,' Kit said to Communications and Information Specialist, Lieutenant Commander Patrick Keeley.

Patrick said nothing in return; both men were well aware that if the weather could change, it would, and quickly.

'Gale warnings have been issued at …'

'Here we go,' said Pat. 'Bet you it'll get us in Fitzroy about 0500 tomorrow morning.'

They both glanced at the swirls of colours on the screen beside them.

'Off the northwest coast of Spain past La Coruña, then all the way down past Porto,' he added.

' … Fastnet, Sole and Fitzroy. Fitzroy: southerly gale force eight expected later. Wind: in south, southerly five or six. In north, southerly or southwesterly, five to seven, increasing to gale eight for a time. Sea state: in south moderate, becoming rough in west. In north, moderate or rough, occasionally very rough in west.'

Patrick switched off the radio and said, 'Told you so. That'll slow us down a touch. Eighteen to twenty five feet waves, give or take; those'll get your toys downstairs rolling around a bit.'

Patrick had been off the mark by an hour with the gale really taking its toll by six o'clock. As the Gloucester surfed the big Atlantic swells, Kit was down in the magazine checking schedules ahead of time, not worried about any movement by the Sea Darts, but keeping an eye just in case. Everything had been strapped securely down before the ship had sailed. The grey dawn broke with dark clouds shooting large calibre raindrops from a thousand natural chain guns on the black troughs and white peaks of the ocean below. Kit could hear the clatter of rain on metal above the mechanical sounds of the ship even on the feeder hatch above him in the overhead. On the deck above, the Sea Darts' twin launcher was bolted to the deck, a few feet behind the 4.5 inch 55-calibre Mk Eight naval gun.

By the time HMS Gloucester sailed through the Straits of Gibraltar, at the Spanish Navy's recommended speed of 13 knots 'to avoid whales', the sun was shining with warm beneficence from a cornflower blue sky and the Mediterranean sea ahead was a deep-green blue mirror. And little changed as Gloucester pushed eastwards, almost seeming to skim across the water at 30 knots like some monstrous metal water bug. It took her just under four days to cover the 1,942 odd nautical miles, almost the full length of the Mediterranean if one excluded a final push to Tripoli on the north Lebanese coast. At around 1800 hrs, HMS Gloucester dropped anchor in Akrotiri Harbour at Limassol Port on Cyprus.

*****

They ambled the few hundred yards from the Metropole Hotel on Ifigeneias Street to Limassol Castle and then down to the Old Harbour. They scanned the coloured boards advertising snorkelling in crystal blue waters, fishing for tuna or octopus or simply lazing in the sunshine on a catamaran. Neither fishing nor swimming was on the agenda but a boat trip would suit very well.

'Lie in the arms of the Sea Goddess. Let Aphrodite Cruises' newest catamaran take you on leisurely cruises on the beautiful warm waters around our Cyprus coastline. Our half-day cruise will take you down Lady's Mile Beach and around the Akrotiri Peninsula, into the astonishing clear waters of Episkopi Bay. Here may you swim for some times, maybe with fishes at your feet. Or just lie in the sunshine, on board our wonderful Sea Goddess.'

Ayesha looked at her brother and smiled, a slight questioning look in her eyes.

'I think that will be perfect,' he said, nodding solemnly. 'But on the way back, not out.'

'Of course,' she said, as though there was no other sensible course of action. 'You want to check the ship this evening?'

They'd arrived in Limassol two days before, not knowing exactly when the Gloucester would arrive. There'd been no sign until late this afternoon when they'd seen what was clearly a sleek warship off the coast, heading towards Akrotiri Harbour.

'We should, especially if we're going to do it tomorrow.'

'Yallah!'

The black Mercedes taxi dropped them off on Harbour Road, only a stone's throw from the wharves, warehouses and the ships that lay at anchor in the water. The stern and superstructure of the ship docked at the wharf straight ahead clearly identified it as a warship. As they walked alongside the light grey hull, Ayesha reached out, her fingers splayed, almost as though she wanted to stroke the hard metal. A gangplank angled its way from quayside to gunwales as though inviting all comers on board; the armed sailor standing by on the wharf indicated otherwise. He nodded at them as they walked past, not considering them to be a threat.

As they passed the halfway mark, Tarek pointed at the painted letter and numbers; D96 stood out darkly against the lighter metal. Standing back, he looked up and beyond the rails to the naval gun and the strange stands behind. He let his eyes track along the ship's lines as they walked back, Ayesha's arm linked amiably in his.

'Which ship is this?' he asked the seaman on guard duty.

'HMS Gloucester, Sir.'

'British, yes?' asked Tarek pointing at the flag hanging limply in the warm still air.

'Yessir, Type 42 destroyer in Her Majesty's Royal Navy. Interested in ships I take it?' the man asked politely.

'Warships, in warships. Thank you.'

'I believe the Commander's allowing visitors on board next week, if you're still about.'

'Perhaps, thank you.'

Tarek led Ayesha back towards the road a little more quickly than before, cursing himself for asking the pointless final question. Corporal Robbie Wilson of the Royal Marines narrowed his eyes slightly as he watched them scuttle away down the wharf. Like a pair of crabs, he thought, and then dismissed them from his mind. Another black Mercedes taxi took the al-Shamis back to the Old Port.

In the dark of the night, Ayesha stared blindly at the dull opacity of the ceiling, emotionless but focused. The emotion had been strangled, killed off over the years and she had taken payment for what had happened back then many times over. Most of the men she'd killed had no personality or definition in her memory; they'd been justifiable targets within the parameters of a firefight, casualties of war. But there were a few who fitted the profile of revenge, because of who they were or what they were doing at one specific moment in time. Two, three, maybe more, had etched their faces in a shadowed part of her memory; not as totems or scalps, but because she had killed them coldly and knowingly. They had a right to be remembered. But tomorrow was about shutting the door, finally putting it all in a box, to be locked and filed away in that vast grey archival warehouse of her mind. One ship, one box, al nihaya! The end.

And in the dark of the night, Tarek's mind turned over the fires of insecurity and worry, like a suckling pig on a roasting spit. He thought about every person who he knew, who knew about the project: Malik, Alan (or Ali), Amin, Kharal, Mustagh, Bheyrya, Faisal, al-Kabuli, Ayesha for God's sake. Too many names, too many links that might weaken or be broken. Hah! What about himself? And then about the people who might know but he didn't know. It was the right ship? Of course, of course it was, they'd checked. Tomorrow, on the catamaran with the ridiculous name, would the transmitter work properly and would it connect? What if the catamaran wasn't close enough? But it would be because they'd tested it for up to 16 kilometres. Wasn't that just under ten miles? For God's sake! By a few feet, yes. Tarek finally drifted off into a dreamless sleep of exhaustion.

The Sea Goddess left its mooring in the marina with a handful of people dressed in warm clothes against the morning chill. The sky was its usual peerless blue, unstained by the dirty white blemishes of cumulous or the scuffs of cirrus but the sun had yet to lend its warmth to the elements. Ayesha and Tarek had staked a place on the starboard side of the webbing, ensuring the best possible view of the town and coastline. Past the entrance to Akrotiri Harbour they looked across the sea wall defence, the view angling backwards along the wharves. HMS Gloucester was a dark silhouette, its size disguised by the narrow profile presented as it was with the bow facing towards them. Although something seemed to have changed.

Kit Furney stood on the deck by the rail admiring his handiwork. As planned and arranged, two Sea Darts had been winched from the magazine through the feeder hatch and now sat proudly side by side in the twin launcher. The grey-white nosecones facing towards the sky in readiness for a need that would not arise. They looked good, the part, as people might say, and Kit was pleased because they were his responsibility and he knew they were ready to be fired, if and when needed. And that would be his responsibility too, as and when and if it happened. He looked out to sea, idly taking in the catamaran passing in the open water beyond the harbour wall. No point without sails, he thought, and turned back to his babies.

Nor was there any point in stopping to let people swim, was the thought that went through the Sea Goddess skipper's mind. He took the cat a little further out to sea in the hope that they might see dolphins, tuna, shark or even flying fish. Sylvanos believed in giving people their money's worth and the word of mouth publicity that it provided. Not that the couple on the front of the webbing would be that interested. They'd barely said a word since they'd left the Old Port, just stared at the land. Curious, that fixation; they'd even switched seats to the port side after he turned for home.

'We're going to be heading more less straight for the harbour from where we are,' said Tarek. He pulled the transmitter from his pocket, handed it to his sister.

The Sea Goddess was moving on a slow diagonal, along the hypotenuse of a right-angled triangle, the vertical side taken up by Lady's Mile Beach. Tarek estimated they were within range: the Sea Goddess was 6.9 miles away from HMS Gloucester and closing.

'Go Sister. Allahu akbar,' he whispered into the passing breeze.

Ayesha switched on the transmitter, pressed the green button, dialled 01 on the keypad and watched the bars of the signal fan out. Time seemed to freeze in a limbo of repeating green lines, fanning out over and over again.

'It's not working,' said Tarek, about to reach out for the device.

Then saw the fan lock and flash in a solid block. Ayesha pressed the red button hard, one thumb folded over the other. They stared silently waiting, deaf and dumb but not sightless. First came the smoke, rising up in great black and grey billows that swelled and grew, churning upwards from the superheated air. And then came the explosions, one after the other, harsh deafening roaring blasts that left little to the imagination. Angry orange flames burned at the heart of the fat pillars of smoke; a vision of hell itself, bent on devastation.

'And so it begins,' hissed Tarek, his fist clenched in triumph.

'And for me it ends,' said Ayesha softly, her words carried away on the breeze and unheard by her brother.

Sylvanos gave Akrotiri Harbour a wide berth, taking the Sea Goddess back to her mooring as quickly as possible. Faces frozen in horror were galleried across her twin hulls, all eyes on the smoke and flames that still eclipsed the stricken destroyer. The sounds of sirens laid down a shrill shrieking soundtrack that sang of blood and pain, of screams and death.

12 ~ Death of a Destroyer

'Looks like your hole,' he said somewhat grudgingly as he eyed the other man's ball which was within inches of the fifteenth.

The General Officer Commanding, Administrator of Her Majesty's Sovereign Base Areas of Akrotiri and Dhekelia, Commander of British Forces Cyprus, Air Vice-Marshall Roland Wells was being whitewashed by a mere naval Captain who was barely half his age. On consideration, at least 15 years his junior. Bloody cheek really! After all, the Princess Mary Hospital Golf Club was in his own back yard. In which case, perhaps it was only courteous to let the damn man win; in all fairness, he was, after all, the visitor.

'Probably,' muttered Captain Sam Aitken as he eyed his shot.

Knees bent and slightly apart, thigh and calf muscles naturally flexing, Aitken let the putter swing through using its own weight. The unexpected booming roar of the twin explosions shattered the pregnant silence that naturally enfolds such moments. His wrists twisted reactively as the metal head made contact, flicking the Titleist ProV1 to the left and away from the lip.

'What the bloody hell was that?'

'Sounded like exploding bombs,' said the Air Vice Marshall, his voice grim with experience, 'but it's probably a gas explosion.'

'If it is, it's a pretty big one. Look! Jesus!'

Both men stared at the dark black-grey smoke boiling up over the green horizon of the golf course. The dark clouds billowed upwards, a manmade hellish image of building thunderheads.

'Roland, that's not a gas explosion. Whatever it is, that's burning rubber, paint, maybe metal … Fuck's sake! That could be coming from the harbour.'

Both men started running, leaving clubs and balls lying on the grass behind them. Younger and fitter, Sam Aitken got to the clubhouse a good two minutes ahead of his erstwhile golf partner. By the time that Roland Wells arrived, the Captain had the jeep's engine running.

'Go, go!'

Aitken hit the accelerator and dropped the clutch simultaneously; the knobby tyres bit deep, spinning out sprays of gravel as the jeep shot off towards the road. Wells flipped open his phone, speed dialled RAF Akrotiri's Station Commander.

'Good morning, RAF …'

'Ben, it's Roland. What the blazes is going on in Limassol?'

'It's bad, Sir, Where are you now?'

'We've just left Mary's golf course, we'll be on Flamingo Way in a couple of minutes. We heard what sounded like explosions, saw a lot of smoke in the sky. Sam thought it could be from the harbour.'

'Sam Aitken's with you, I take it?'

'Yes.'

'Go straight to Akrotiri Harbour, don't stop here. There was an explosion on the Gloucester, Sir. As far as we can tell, there were two Sea Darts in the launcher and both detonated.'

'Not being rude Ben, but Sea Darts don't just decide to fucking explode! How bad is it?'

'Sir, what can I tell you? Our fire crews should be down there already working with Limassol teams. Lim fire has sent in two 10,000 litre water bowsers and there's a fireboat in the harbour, waterside. An emergency medical team from Princess Mary left a couple of minutes ago and a couple of ambulances are on their way from Limassol New General. I've just come off the phone from Pat Keeley, Gloucester's comms officer; at the moment they've got four dead and ten wounded. But those figures are likely to rise. At the moment, some parts of the ship are too hot for the firemen.'

'Christ! Poor bastards. OK Ben call Whitehall, get in touch with …'

'Already done, Sir. I spoke to the First Sea Lord's ADC and given him as much information as I can. He's going to inform the Secretary of State.'

'Fine. If there's anything new from London let me know. I'll probably leave Sam at the harbour and come back. Talk later. Bye.' He put the phone back into his pocket. 'I assume you got the gist of that?'

'Yeah,' said Sam Aitken.

It took almost half an hour before they could get to the harbour and several more minutes before they could get anywhere near the Gloucester. Flames still flickered across the mangled blackened metal and acrid smoke was still drifting at ground level. Greasy black smoke that stung your eyes, tasted sour on the tongue and left a black stinking film on clothes and hair. They found Lieutenant Commander Patrick Keeley by the torn remnants of HMS Gloucester's bow. As though ripped away by the fiery hand of a demon from hell, the bow had gone, replaced by a dark metal mouth edged with blackened jagged teeth. Where the naval gun and launcher had been on the foredeck was little more than a molten steaming pit.

'Pat, what in fuck's name happened?' asked Sam. The tone of his voice was a complex blend of emotions: horror, awe, sadness and anger.

Pat Keeley rubbed the filthy heel of one hand in one begrimed eye before looking at his Captain.

'I don't know Sam, I don't fucking know. First thing this morning, Kit got the Sea Darts up in the launcher as planned and he's happy as Larry. Since we docked, he'd got all his toys stored in the vertical magazine ready for operational use and he'd checked everything twice. I was dockside when I heard the explosions. The whole of the front of the ship was one fucking great fireball and somewhere in the middle ...'

His voice tailed off into wordless sorrow. Sam Aitken put his hand on the man's shoulder, squeezed lightly.

'I'm sorry Pat.' He looked up at the empty space where the Sea Darts had been standing to attention in their launcher with the officer by their side. 'Yeah, I'm sorry. Kit Furney was a good friend and a bloody good officer. What a waste. Pat, have you seen a medic?'

'No Sir.'

'Then go and find one. Now.'

He watched Lieutenant Commander Patrick Keeley walk slowly away along the dock towards the emergency vehicles; then turned to Roland Wells.

'I need to sort this mess out. Christ, I hardly know where to start.' He sighed. 'I'm going to start to gather the crew together, get them organised. Can you house them on the base?'

'Goes without saying. I suggest you check with the medical teams, some of your lot may be taken to the new hospital here but some might go to Princess Mary. Depends on who's got the right resources. Mary's been scaled down a lot over the last few years so ... fatalities will almost certainly stay in Limassol. Sam, I don't know what to say ...'

'That's because there isn't anything that can be said. Just get on with it, is what we do isn't it? This wasn't an accident. I don't know how it happened, but it wasn't an accident. Somebody, somehow blew those birds up and I will get those fuckers.'

'There'll be an investigation, of course. I suspect they'll send someone.'

'Yeah, I bet they will,' Sam Aitken said, his voice taught with cynicism.

*****

Mike Roberts took the slip off the M3, drove down the A31 until he found a layby. He checked the number of the last caller and pressed to return the call.

'Hi Helen, What's up?'

'Gloucester's blown up, Mike. HMS Gloucester in Cyprus, about lunchtime.'

'Sorry, I think I must have misheard. Say again.'

'No Mike, you haven't got a hearing problem. Apparently, two Sea Dart missiles exploded on the foredeck of HMS Gloucester.'

Mike listened without speaking as Helen gave him as much detail as she'd been given. The graphic description left little to the imagination but Mike let the word pictures drift away and focused on the unanswered questions.

'The Station Commander at Akrotiri explained the situation to Vice-Admiral Sir Richard Parfitt. He passed it on to the First Sea Lord and the Defence Secretary. It's gone right the way to the top Mike and now it's all over Whitehall. A gag order's been issued to the press and everyone's complied but that's only good for a day or two. There's no way of suppressing the local Cypriot papers without someone screaming in Athens. So it's a sieve waiting to leak and Whitehall wants some answers before the mess is all over the floor. Defence's Permanent Secretary has talked to Sir Reginald and you fly out now!'

'Shit. OK.'

'Where are you now?'

'On the A31, just outside Winchester, on my way to Southampton.'

'Whatever, turn round and go to RAF Brize Norton. It should take you, what, about an hour and a half from there?'

'Give or take, yeah.'

'Fine, I've already got RAF Marham on alert. There'll be a Tornado waiting for you with instructions to fly direct to Akrotiri. On full tanks without ordnance, Akrotiri's within the Tornado's maximum range without refuelling, so the pilot should get you there within about two hours. Perfect, you should be there for a late cup of tea.'

Helen's final comment was meant to be light but the tone of her voice couldn't carry it through.

'They're asking you to start working on this as soon as you get there. And before you say it, I know, it's a crap shoot. Good luck Mike.'

'I'm on my way. Before I go Helen, do me a favour. I was on my way to International Foods, Masri's factory? Thinking about what Admiral Buller said, can you get your hands on a list of everything that Inter Foods has imported within the last couple of months. Get someone to impersonate an inspector from Contracts or Customs. It's a long shot but … just in case there's something out of kilter, offline. You know what I mean.'

'Yes, no worries. Consider it done. I'll talk to them myself, this afternoon.'

'Thanks Helen.'

Reserve Gunner Simmons of 2624 Squadron, on duty at Brize Norton's Control of Entry point, was initially confused by the rugby shirt and jeans. When Mike handed the man his Army identity card, the man's speedy recovery would have delighted his commanding officer. Handing back Mike's ID with alacrity, Reserve Gunner Simmons stood to attention, snapped off a smart salute and raised the barrier.

'Major Roberts, Sir, they're waiting for you on the flightline.'

No stranger to the airfield, Mike knew exactly where to go, heading down towards the control tower on the far side of the main runway. Minutes later he was parking the BMW next to a large hanger, jumping out and running towards the waiting Tornado.

'Afternoon Major. Flight Lieutenant Gary Peters.' The pilot had a ready smile and a firm handshake. 'Ms O'Connor told us XL, so hopefully this should fit,' he said handing Mike a flight suit. 'You've flown Tornadoes before right?'

'A couple of times, yes,' he answered, shrugging on the suit.

'OK, let's go.' Peters handed him a helmet as walked towards the plane. You play rear gunner. Climb aboard.'

Flight Lieutenant Gary Peters taxied to the runway, rolled to a stop, opened the throttle and let the power build. Twenty tonnes of fighter plane gathered speed as it ran down the runway, full afterburners on as it lifted steeply off the ground and shot into the sky.

'Enjoy the ride, Major. We should be landing at Akrotiri in about an hour and a half.' And Peters was as good as word. 'Let me know when you need a lift back,' he said as the Tornado taxied to a halt.

'Thanks for the ride. Are you staying just for me?'

'Those are my orders Major. Right now, you're the most important man in my life.'

The light comment finally drew a grin; he gave Gary the finger as he climbed out of the cockpit. On the ground, he found himself looking at faces that were grim and strained.

'Welcome to RAF Akrotiri, Major. Ben Chalmers, I'm the Station Commander. And this is Captain Sam Aitken.'

Whitehall having sent a direct request to Air Vice-Marshall Wells, the crew from HMS Gloucester had been assembled in the pilot briefing room. When the three men entered, every person in the room turned in one synchronised movement. Their faces were drawn, tired or simply blank, drained of all emotion by the shock of the day's events. Mike explained who he was and why he was there, said he needed to talk to them and any tiny thing that anyone could remember was worth mentioning. Captain Aitken stood at the back, shaking his head as he listened. Finally.

'Major Roberts, I appreciate that you've been sent out here to, shall we say, investigate what happened to the Gloucester today but my crew is tired and in shock. And to be frank, so am I. At the moment, I don't give a flying fuck what Whitehall wants. Please don't patronise us, and don't behave like some pansy policeman with your weaselly 'I understand how hard it is' and 'I'm here to listen'.

'We've lost eleven men and two women today; they were not just valuable and professional crewmembers, they were family. There are fifteen more in hospital and three of those are critical. As for the Gloucester, the dockside's peppered with shards of metal fragments, the deck's still smoking and the bow's bloody disappeared. And you stand there and say you understand? Right.'

'Captain, I …'

'I suggest that we let the crew go now and regroup here at 1100 tomorrow morning. You and I can have a brief conversation now and we'll visit the Gloucester at first light. Crew, dismissed. Tomorrow, 1100 hours, here.'

'Sir,' they said as they filtered out of the room, one by one.

He waited until they were gone, looked Mike Roberts in the eye, calmly without any sign of his former rancour. Smiled an almost sad smile.

'Major, I could do with a drink and, I think I owe you one. That was a bit out of order. Ben?'

'No, I'll stay away tonight, Sam. Catch up with you tomorrow morning. Major Roberts.'

They watched Group Captain Ben Chalmers head towards the office block.

'He's got a lot on his plate as well,' said Sam.

'Captain Aitken, I just wanted to …'

'Off duty, Major. You can call me Sam. Mike?'

'No problem.'

They'd settled at a quiet(er) table in the Akrotiri Arms on Queen Elizabeth Street, overlooking the salt lake. The sun was drifting slowly downwards to the horizon, sending out golden beams across the roseate backs of a thousand flamingos. They sipped their beers in noisy meditation, reflecting the ambient noise. At Sam's request, Mike had told him a little about his own background and Captain Aitken had had the grace to fractionally apologise for some of his former comments. Mike had reversed the conversation to talk about Sam's life on the ocean wave. And then they turned to business.

'Kit Furney was our Weapons Engineer Officer and the Darts were his babies, knew them inside out. Poor bastard wouldn't have known what hit him and there's nothing left. It's bad enough with the others; but at least there's a body to send back home to the family in each case. How do you tell a widow that her husband's been blown into a billion pieces each the size of an atom? And this was murder on a big scale, Mike, cold calculated and planned. Call it an act of terrorism or whatever, but at the end of the day, that's what it boils down to – mass fucking murder.'

'Before you jump down my throat, I'm not disagreeing with you, I'm asking: how do you know it wasn't an accident?'

Sam Aitken picked up his glass, took a long swig and set it back on the table.

'How much do you know about missiles, Mike? I don't mean handheld stuff like RPGs or Javelins; I'm talking bigger missiles like the Sea Dart.'

'Background stuff so assume zero.'

'OK, there is no way that a Sea Dart could self-destruct; there's no mechanism to allow that to happen. The same goes for spontaneous combustion; there's no source of heat or chemical reaction that might generate it or cause a chain reaction. Impact. I can tell you now, they'd didn't bloody fall over and go pop. Firstly, the missiles are brought up automatically from the magazine and secured on the launcher. And Kit would have checked them afterwards. Perhaps more importantly, the Sea Dart's not an impact weapon. You could bang it with a sledgehammer or drop it on its nose and you'd get precisely nothing, (unless the drop was out of a plane, maybe). All of the electronics and guidance systems are packed into the nosecone and detonation is triggered by a proximity fuze. Your fragmentation high explosive warhead explodes before it makes contact with the target and the supersonic shockwave produced shatters the casing etcetera etcetera. End of technical lecture. My problem is that I can't think of a way that anyone could kick them off.'

Sam took another pull at his beer; Mike followed suit and then sat thinking, seemingly staring out over the lake. The odd flamingo stretched its wings and the sound of waders calling could be heard over the waves of voices from the bar.

'Is it possible to remove the nosecone and get at the electronics, Sam?'

'Yes, I'm sure you can. Kit used to talk about checking guidance systems occasionally.'

'Can you take the whole lot out? As a unit?'

'Probably, I don't know. Now you're drilling past my level of technical knowledge. You'd have to ask Kit's 2iC, Robin Beavis, tomorrow. You're thinking that someone tampered with the electronics?'

'Perhaps, or someone replaced the electronics with a bomb of sorts? Can we get into the magazine to have a look at the remaining missiles, is another question.'

'I suspect that won't be a problem. But backtrack. Apart from Kit and Robin, no other crew member would have the necessary expertise, nor would they easily get access to the magazine. Obviously it wasn't Kit and I'm 100 per cent certain it wasn't Robin. So there's a big who and another one, how?'

'Where do the Sea Darts come from?'

'I have absolutely no idea. We requisition them, the MoD orders them and green trucks deliver. I have a feeling that there's a company name stencilled on them with the serial number. With a bit of luck we'll find out tomorrow.'

'Another beer?' asked Mike, already in his feet.

'Why not?' Sam answered with a wry smile. 'Let's face it, I'm not going to be patrolling the Mediterranean tomorrow with Operation Active Endeavour catching terrorists.'

*****

By eight am the light rainfall that had started in the early hours of the morning had more or less stopped but had left a legacy of damp suspension over Limassol. A watery skin clung to every surface, each one coldly clammy to the touch. The cool sea breeze made the 15 degree centigrade temperature feel two degrees colder. As they waited for their taxi outside the Metropole, Ayesha wrapped her arms around her, trying to retain a little warmth. Both of them stared down the empty street, looking for the car. Andreas was only 10 minutes late when he finally arrived and saw no reason to offer an apology. And neither of his passengers asked for one.

'You want to go to Akrotiri Harbour first, as you said yesterday?'

'Yes,' said Tarek. 'to Limassol New Port number one. But we want to go down the east side, past the container sheds to the end.'

'But why?'

'We like to see ships in harbours.'

'Uh-huh. You know, there is a bombed British ship of war on the west side now? It happens only yesterday I think. Very bad. Maybe you want to see that?'

'Maybe. We're interested in military ships as well.'

Andreas looked in his rear view mirror, at the man and the woman in the back seat. She was a dark haired lady, attractive face and with those eyes. Dark velvet pools in which a man could drown; not big enough breasts, he decided. The man was pinched, also dark but in a bad way and weak. Still, there were not so many people in Limassol in November.

'Is €75 each, plus the harbour visit fee of €20, plus €50 for a two people only use of a car for four persons, plus the one way supplement, Limassol to Larnaca International Airport of €50.' He'd been adding it up on a calculator as he spoke, eyes glued to the little screen. Looking up triumphantly, he said, 'Which comes to a total of €270, payable in advance, please.'

'That's absolute extortion!' Ayesha hissed.

'I know,' said Tarek, counting the notes out of his wallet. He handed them to Andreas through the gap between the front seats. 'Let's go.'

The roads were clear and it took less than ten minutes to get to the east side port gate. Taxis being a familiar sight, even around the commercial port areas, no one stopped Andreas driving down the jetty to the very end. He stopped the car side on to the dockside, giving his fares a clear view across Akrotiri Harbour. He shrugged his head in the direction of the destroyer destroyed.

'The British ship of war I told you about. It's a mess. I don't think it will go very far.'

Tarek wound down the blurred rain-wet window for a clearer view. Ayesha leaned on his shoulder, looking past him and out through the open window.

'It's still afloat,' said Tarek, switching into Arabic. 'I thought there would be nothing left, that it would be blown apart. They told me how powerful the explosive was that was being used, and I saw it shatter a tank, obliterate an armoured personnel carrier and leave nothing. I don't understand.'

From the far side of the harbour, HMS Gloucester was a scorched blackened hulk. Her bows had ripped away from the foredeck that was torn apart with jagged gashes scarring her sides. The superstructure to the fore had been torn backwards, ripped open as easily as the lid on a can of sardines, leaving jagged fingers, black knives that reached upwards in failure. But despite those explosive depredations, the Gloucester was indeed still afloat.

'They have paid what they owe,' Ayesha finally replied in the same language. 'I think there will have been those who lost their lives here, others who were hurt and the ship, that is also hurt. We have hit back for all the reasons we talked about and the debt to us has been paid. To Palestine and the Palestinians, maybe not. But that may not be our fight at the end.'

'There are three more bombs on three more ships. Once those are detonated, then it is finished, for us Ayesha.'

'Maybe. We will see how the wind blows in the weeks to come. We should go Tarek. Someone will notice the car if we stay much longer.'

'You're right.' Switching back to English. 'Thank you. I think we should go.'

'No problem,' said Andreas, switching on the engine.

Turning the car around, he drove back up the dock and through the town, then headed east on the main road to Larnaca. He dropped them off outside the terminal and watched them walk away without even a piece of hand luggage between them. It wasn't his business, he thought, but they were certainly a strange pair. He shrugged. They hadn't complained about the fare, so why should he care? Andreas picked up the main road and headed for home.

*****

On the other side of the harbour, shadowed by the mangled ship, the three men walked up the gangplank that had been set to the stern. Sam Aitken led the way forward, walking as far as he could towards what used to be the bow of the Gloucester. They stood on the buckled plates of the deck, facing backwards across the charred mass of metal, wire, cable and shattered plexiglass.

'What a mess!'

'It could have been a lot worse, Major,' Lieutenant Robin Beavis commented.

'I'm sure, but explain.'

'The Sea Darts were mounted side by side on the launcher on deck at an angle of approximately 45 degrees. But there were two separate explosions, so I'm assuming that one was triggered somehow, exploded and detonated the second missile. Because they were deck mounted, the energy of the warheads was to an extent dissipated by the lack of containment and the trajectory of fragmentation followed the 45-degree angle of incidence.' Robin Beavis noted the lack of comprehension. 'Draw a mental 180 degree vertical line through the warhead and you'll understand why most of the bows are missing and why the explosion took out the bridge. Follow the plane of rotation around that opposing 45 degrees and you'll find fragments of shattered metal embedded in everything. Of course, the shockwaves would also have had forward motion and that's the part where energy loss would have been greatest.'

'I think I understand all that,' said Mike, 'if that's the case, what happened to the deck?'

'Simple. The Sea Dart uses a kerosene-powered ramjet engine and a solid fuel booster for initial acceleration. Igniting gallons of kerosene in conjunction with explosive solid fuel will give you one hell of a hot fire. Pretty well melt the deck from under your feet. And that's what we've got.'

'OK, I've got that. I know I asked you this last night Sam, but bear with me on the same question for Robin. Could it have just been a faulty missile? Some weird electronic spark, shorted out, connected up badly, anything?'

'Nope, absolutely not. The Sea Dart has a safety catch, like a lot of weapons, to ensure that it doesn't go off at the wrong time. The safing and arming device is there to ensure that the missile won't detonate until it's reached the target. On the Dart, that's the proximity fuze: a device that will only send a signal to the detonator when it senses that it's close enough to do the maximum amount of damage. Underline the word proximity; with a frag-HE warhead, you want close not contact. The detonator can only do it's job if it gets the thumbs up from the proxy fuze and gentlemen, that ain't going to happen if the Sea Dart's bowing in the breeze on the foredeck.'

'Would it be possible to somehow make the fuze believe that the missile was closing on a target? A sort of virtual reality system on a timer?'

'Honestly, Sir? No.'

'In that case Lieutenant, in your opinion, what's the explanation?'

'An additional explosive device, somehow inserted and remotely detonated.'

'Can you elaborate?'

'I'll try Major, but without looking properly, I can't be sure. The forensics guys may be able to find out more but with this amount of damage, even they're going to be looking for needles. Some form of explosive was used to detonate the train and given the extent of the damage here, I'm guessing the secondary explosive was seriously powerful in its own right. It wasn't trying to be clever and trick the fuze. Oh no, whoever designed this decided to use raw power to blow the fucker up! Excuse the language, Sir.'

Mike shook his head in dismissal; Sam grinned.

'In turn, that would have to be triggered somehow, probably using a transmitter to send an electrical signal that was strong and hot enough to spark it all off. The thing is, Sir, usually the transmitter has to be reasonably close, within a few miles at the outside.'

311

The three of them looked at each other, all trying to digest the information, the possibilities and the implications. The raucous calls of seagulls, water slapping on the hull, distant traffic and the hum of a crane hoisting a container on the eastern dock. In the absence of speech, the sounds of the harbour flooded back but did little to disturb the men's thought processes.

'Can we get to the magazine, Robin?'

'I think so, Sir. Follow me.'

Lieutenant Beavis led them almost halfway to the stern before turning in through an open door. Down a ladder and along a passageway that led through several more doors before they reached the magazine. Robin pulled up the dogs and it opened, but not without complaint.

'It's even twisted the metal down here,' he muttered.

The fetid air inside the magazine smelled of overheated metal, ozone and smoke. Light filtered in through ragged slits in the deckhead, beams saturated with a suspension of dust. The Sea Darts stood as pale sentinels in the tainted dimness, mute reminders of violent despatch.

'The lights are out.' He found a torch on a rack. 'OK, what do you want to do?'

'Check the serial numbers.'

Crouching down by the nearest missile, Robin shone the torch on the stencilled number near the base. Mike pulled a notebook from his pocket.

'Gimme that one.'

'FI60-7998/526,' said Sam, reading while Robin held the light steady.

'Next?'

'FI60-7998/529.'

'Can you get around the side, Sam? Give me a couple from there?'

'FI60-7998/538,'

'Yep. And another?'

'FI60-7998/539.'

'Can you see anything higher?'

'Yeah,' hissed Sam as he squeezed into the gap. 'Give me the torch, Robin? OK, you've got FI60-7998/442. That's as far as I can get, bulkhead's pushed in too far.' He eased backwards. 'They're all from the same company: Forbes Industries.'

'The ones that went up have to have been in the middle of the sequence somewhere,' said Mike. 'Not that it matters what the numbers were; they're obviously all part of the same batch. Robin, you suggested that explosive might have been inserted? If they were, where might they have been?'

'It's got to be somewhere at the top. From the bottom up you've got the Chow solid-fuel booster, Odin ramjet and kerosene, explosive train ... I'd have to go for under the nosecone with the electronics. Or instead of the electronics.'

'Can we get one off? Just to have a look?'

'You're not thinking that there's another sabotaged missile, are you Mike?' Sam asked nervously.

'No. At the moment I'm just trying to get the options but another one on the same ship wouldn't make sense. What worries me is that there's another one on another ship. Or even ships!'

'Jesus!' said Robin.

'Yeah, we could do with a hand,' said Sam.

'A cone?' Mike reminded.

'We can try?'

Among the tools on the rack, Robin managed to find a torque wrench and a socket that fitted.

'Shit!'

'What?'

'We can't reach the cones when they're in the magazine; they're too tall. And we can't take them down without power.'

'You know what?' said Mike, 'I don't think it's that important. If you think it has to be under the nose, that's good enough for me. Let's go topside, I'm toasting down here.'

The sun had broken through while they'd been in the magazine but the air was still cool. Mike gulped it down appreciatively, glad to be out of the enclosed space. They drove back to RAF Akrotiri without talking, each one letting his mind chill after the intensity of the Gloucester. As Robin pulled in to a parking slot, Mike recognised the building: they were next to the briefing room. He looked at his watch and sighed.

'You'd forgotten?'

'Yeah, momentarily.'

'Debrief in five Mike. Let's go. To be honest, I doubt that anyone will have much to add. It all happened so fast and a lot of them were on shore leave, nowhere near the Gloucester.' Sam paused and turned to look directly at Mike. 'Do me a favour Mike? Keep it brief? If I think about it, the only people who might have something to say are either in hospital and or in the morgue. I still can't believe it.' He looked away, towards the sea, not wanting Mike to see the tears in his eyes. When he spoke again, the words were choked, painful and full of emotion. 'Jesus Mike, Kit must have been right by the Darts. Pete, Jenny … eight others died when the bridge was taken out. Thirteen lives, just snuffed out in a matter of seconds. And there may be more. When I checked this morning, we've still got three on the critical list.

'Robin clearly thinks it was sabotage, a bomb, and so do you. Catch the bastards Mike, and tell me if I can help.' He cleared his throat, rubbed his eyes with heels of his hands, got the control back into his voice. 'Let's go.'

Captain Sam Aitken turned on his heel, opened the door and walked down the short corridor to the briefing room. As he walked in, the crew were on their feet, every man and woman saluting. Their grim, sad, concerned, fearful and loyal faces all turned towards him in solidarity. He saluted them back, his face reflecting those very same emotions. And Mike stood there, sharing their emotions but feeling like an outsider looking in from the outside. He felt Robin slip past to find his place among the crew.

'Sit down, please,' Sam said, dispensing with the usual formalities. 'We've just come back from the Gloucester, Major Roberts, Robin and I. At this point, we're not in a position to say categorically what happened yesterday, but I will tell you that we think that it was, almost certainly, an act of terrorism. I know that we're all thinking about the friends who didn't make it but here and now isn't the time to grieve. We need to find answers. If anybody can think of anything you might have seen, or heard, tell us. It doesn't have to be now; you might remember something later.'

He looked at the sea of blank faces looking back at him, wishing that someone knew something. Nothing. He wasn't surprised.

'As of now, everyone's on shore leave; there's nothing that we can do until the forensic boys have finished and they're not due out until this afternoon. Pat, you're obviously point on communications, so you'll need to stay close.'

The communications officer nodded. 'Yes, Captain.'

'The rest of you, please stay in touch with Pat for updates. That's it, dismissed. Pat, let me catch up with you here at, say 1400?'

'Fine.'

As the crew trailed out through the door, one man lagged behind. Corporal Robbie Wilson, the last man in the line stopped in front of Captain Sam Aitken and snapped off a smart salute.

'Sir, if I could have a quick word with you and Major Roberts. It's probably nothing at all but I just thought …'

He let the sentence die.

'Of course, Corporal, you never know.'

'I was on guard duty, the evening before last when this couple comes wandering down the dockside. They're staring at the Gloucester, almost as though they're looking for something. They wandered past, going towards the bows, but didn't get that far. He points at the pennant number painted on the hull, then they both look up, above the railings to the 55-cal and the launcher. Of course, Lieutenant Commander Furney (God rest his soul), he hadn't put up the Darts at that point. Anyway, after a bit they come walking back up, and they stop.

'The gent asks me which ship it was, I said HMS Gloucester and that it was a destroyer. I thought they were just really interested, you know how some people are? So I asked him if he was interested in ships – and this is the weird bit – he said, yeah, but only warships. But when I told him about you, Captain Aitken, Sir, perhaps letting visitors on board next week he didn't seem that chuffed. Sort of nodded and said, perhaps they would and off they went. Didn't think about it after. I mean, you don't do you. Sir.'

'Did they talk to each other?' asked Mike.

315

'Not a lot, Sir. Just a few words now and then. There was a bit of talk when they were down by the pennant number and then when they walked off. Not that I understood anything; my Arabic's pretty rubbish. Shoo-krarn, if that's how you say it; that's about my limit.'

'Shukran,' said Mike, automatically correcting the corporal's pronunciation. 'But you're sure it was Arabic?'

'Yes, Major. I did two tours in Iraq and worked with a lot of ragheads but everything was in English, or through an interpreter. Stupid I suppose but never got the chance to learn the language. But yeah, it was definitely Arabic they were speaking, although it was different to the way the Iraqis talk.'

'Meaning?'

'On our first tour, we spent a lot of time patrolling the Syrian border 'cos a lot of insurgents were coming through. It wasn't porous, Sir, it had more holes than a fucking sieve. Sorry, Sir.' Mike shook his head in dismissal and Robbie Wilson continued. 'Yeah, so we also had a lot of dealings with the Syrians. And that was closer. Yeah, the couple on the dock, their Arabic was definitely more like the Syrians speak it; there's a different tone or whatever.'

'Can you describe them, Corporal?'

'I think so. They were quite similar, could easily have been related. Cousins, maybe even brother and sister. Both had dark, probably black hair; his was short normal cut and hers, just off the shoulder. It was the eyes that got me 'cos they were almost black as well, but shiny, intense. She was a stunner, in an Arabic way, if you know what I mean, high cheekbones and pouty lips. And not a bad figure from what I could see. Quite slim, about five nine, tight jeans, light floppy jumper. He was taller, probably closing in on six feet, clean shaven with a bit of a pinched face. I'm guessing older than her. The light wasn't all that good by then.'

'What you're really saying, Robbie,' said Sam Aitken with a grin, 'is that you checked out the eye candy and ignored the wrapper.'

'If you say so, Sir,' Robbie Wilson replied, returning his Captain's grin.

'But you'd recognise them again,' Sam continued.

'I think so, Captain.'

'Anything else you want to add, Corporal?'

'Can't think of anything, Major Roberts. Apart from, I hope you find the bastards who did this and fuck 'em up badly.'

'I hope so too, Corporal Wilson. And thank you.'

*****

A light breeze ruffled the sea of red-brown reeds, sending ripples across to the water's edge. Current flowed against countercurrent causing little eddies in the seeming liquid grasses. A great egret stalked arrogantly through the reed beds, its startlingly white feathers in stark contrast to the environment. On the far side of Akrotiri Salt Lake the massed flamingos formed a ragged pink carpet that seemed to run up to the waved lines of the Troodos Massif that loomed much further away in the distance.

Away from the base, somewhere off the road between Akrotiri Village and the bars of Lady's Mile Beach, the only noises were the sounds of the birds and susurration of the breeze in the reeds. Sitting there on his own, his mind skipped along the coastline to skirt Episkopi Bay to Pissouri Beach. Other bombs at another time, over thirty years ago. Seemed like a lifetime ago. It was a lifetime ago. And yet he could still see the gut wrenching horror, hear the screams and taste the bile. They never did catch the people responsible for those atrocities. Much later he'd found out that initially three Palestinians had been accused of the bombings but they'd been released after questioning. There were no case details on file, he'd been told. It had been closed and there was nothing else in the archives. Mike knew that something was missing, some part of the picture that had been erased, permanently. Now it was too late to find out.

'That's not going to happen this time,' he murmured into the breeze.

For a moment his thoughts turned back to the Gloucester and her crew. And then pushed them away. Mike let the events of the previous 24 hours sift themselves in the back of his mind. He inhaled the salt in the air, enjoying the tingling sensation in his nose and thought of Ellie back in the bright lights of Chiswick. Thinking he might call home, just in case she was in, he brought his phone to life. No signal. Mike wasn't surprised. But someone had left a message. He clicked through to the list.

'Call me.'

Never one to waste words, Helen had sent at 11.50, when he and Sam had been talking to Corporal Wilson. Time now: 14.30 hrs. Reluctantly, Mike scrambled to his feet and started walking back to the road. Obviously, he was not going to get any reception until he was within RAF Akrotiri's perimeter fence. It took half an hour for him to reach the junction of Konstantinou kai Elenis and Flamingo Way; which meant he was only around half way if he was going back to the briefing room. Seven minutes later Mike was standing at RAF Akrotiri's checkpoint and once through, he checked his phone again. Still no signal. He went back to the checkpoint.

'Sorry Sir, the only place you'll get a signal on the base with a mobile would be in the air terminal. Go to the Station HQ off Canberra Drive.'

Another half an hour elapsed before Mike Roberts walked through the door at SHQ and another 15 minutes before he could find someone who could direct him to a phone he could use. He perched on a seat still warm from the female warrant officer's rather large behind and swivelled as he waited.

'Mike, I assume that's you?'

'Finally, yes. Hi Helen. I only just picked up your message. It's been somewhat hellish out here, as I'm sure you can imagine.'

'That bad?'

'Yes. Thirteen dead, three still in intensive care in Limassol General and 12 more injured. And several of those are still in hospital under observation. As for HMS Gloucester, she may not have been sunk but she's not going anywhere fast. A naval architect or engineer might be able to say she's worth a refit but I'd guess her next port of call will be the Turkish shipbreaking yards in Aliaga. Perfect, that's only about 500 nautical miles round the corner in the Aegean.'

'Ouch.'

'Yeah, big ouch.'

'Mike, the Admiral's had the MoD, the Foreign Office and even bloody Downing Street on the phone. The PM's obviously,

318

overtly, concerned about loss of life, sadness for the families dee dah, dee dah. Whitehall simply want information that they can spin positively to the press. And they're pissed off because the gagging order is still in place but know that some of the internationals are mining intel from their contacts. Der Spiegel, Le Monde, Washington Post and Corriere della Sera are apparently the main frontrunners; which means that the heavyweights over here are getting very antsy. Which means: give me something they can play with, Mike. Pretty please.'

Slowly and carefully, Mike gave Helen the timeline and a rundown of the physical investigations that the three of them had carried out on HMS Gloucester. He recounted Robin Beavis' explanations, their considerations and then gave her their conclusions.

'The forensics team was due in this afternoon; I haven't seen them but they will have arrived. Beavis clearly knows what he's talking about and I agree, somebody, somehow inserted an explosive device into a Sea Dart missile without anyone fucking noticing! Unbelievable but, that's what it looks like. However, you definitely do not want to tell the press about that part unless you want mass career suicide on your conscience. After that, we've got precious little.'

'The Darts were made by a company called Forbes Industries. It's as good a place to start looking.'

'OK we'll get on to that. Anything else?'

'It's unlikely but …'

Helen listened to Mike retell what Corporal Robbie Wilson had told them at the end of the meeting that wasn't. She asked a few questions, checked a few details and then there was a long pause.

'Mike, bear with this, OK?'

'Yeah,' he curiously with a hint of caution.

'Where are you?'

'Cyprus.'

'Nearest mainland countries?'

'Working clockwise: Turkey to the north, east from the north, Syria, Lebanon, Israel, Egypt … Christ! Lebanon! No, that's too much of a coincidence.'

'Is it Mike? Is it?' All she could hear was his breathing, softly inhaling and exhaling. 'Which makes my news more acutely important. Amin Musa just happens to have, 'gone on an extended holiday with his wife' according to Henry Perkins, the Works Manager at International Foods. Mike?'

'Damn!'

'Since I sent you off to Cyprus, I thought it only fair to make the run to Southampton.'

'What did you tell Perkins?'

'That I worked for the MoD, (which is not too far from the truth) and that my visit was a snap inspection. Actually Perkins didn't seem that surprised and was perfectly happy to comply with anything that I asked him to do. If there is anything going on, I'm fairly certain that he's not involved. Fortunately, all imports and exports are all inputted into a searchable database that's comprehensively categorised. And bless him, Henry Perkins helped work through the last couple of months' records.'

'God, how long were you there for?'

'Most of the day, and yes of course it was tedious,' she said, picking up the implication. 'Everything was totally straightforward apart from one small group of items which was handled personally by Amin Masri. According to the digitized records Masri imported four litres of absolute oils and eight litres of essential oils. They were purchased in Dubai, sent by air freight to Heathrow where he collected them personally.'

'Helen, you've lost me. Masri's company deals with food, like tinned goods as well as fresh. What's the big deal with a few litres of oil?'

'Idiot, we're not talking cooking oil. These oils are keystone elements for perfumes like Chanel, Dior, Dolce and Gabanna?'

'And?'

'Mike, you're being irritatingly obtuse. Why would a food company import perfume oils? And please don't suggest they're for his wife. We're talking about oils with a market value of around US$80,000. However, the oils don't stay in the country, they're exported to France within days of them arriving at Heathrow. From what Henry Perkins said, Mr and Mrs Masri took them over to France in person. The paperwork lists two wooden boxes each containing six litre bottles of perfume oils.

320

But there's no point of delivery because they took them in themselves and because they're both French passport holders. So we lose sight of the bottles after they leave Calais. There are connections in Paris and Marseille, but who knows.

'This is where it gets even more interesting. Inter Foods has a subsidiary in Jebel Ali near Dubai called Marhaba Al Fatah International FZE and I managed to speak to a guy there called Gush bin Shabib. I asked if Masri was there: negative. Said I was from Chanel in Paris, chasing up an order for bottles of perfume oils that should have come from Marhaba. He said that they should have arrived in steel containers because Masri had transferred the oils from the bottles into them before freighting. According to Shabib, Masri had said something about the oils maturing better. And here's the bit you'll hate the most. Shabib said that the tins, as he called them, had arrived on a pallet separately, before Masri turned up with his oils. The pallet came into Jebel Ali as a part-container load on a ship from Karachi.'

'Jesus! So somewhere in between Heathrow and Calais the steel tins, or containers have disappeared?'

'You've got it, Sherlock.' There was no smile in the words; Helen's voice was grim. 'After the Masris returned from France, they told Henry that they were going on holiday, as said, and so they've disappeared as well. There's no sign at the house in Hampshire or the flat in Ealing.'

'Any ideas?'

'My guess is Dubai. As well as the business in Jebel Ali, they've got an apartment in the Al Murjan Tower next to Dubai Marina. But it's only a guess, Mike.'

'Helen, you've been in this business a lot longer than me. If you say it's a guess, I'm guessing you're in the ballpark. I assume John's got Tracker working on airport departures?'

'Yes, Border Control records. There are bloody millions of them! Heathrow's obviously the most likely but there are a lot of other airports to play with. He's doing the ports as well for what it's worth.'

'Can you get Tim to poke around Cedars' Stand, a little sensitive breaking and entering since the Masris are away? I'm thinking outbuildings, garages; anywhere there's space and tools. I suppose even the kitchen's possible.'

'It's a long shot, but can do. When are you back?'

'I'm thinking tomorrow morning. I don't want to keep my taxi waiting too long.'

'Too right. From memory, the lowest estimated cost of a Tornado flight works out at £35,000 per hour; I have no idea of the standing cost. Get back soon.'

'Ouch! OK, I'm gone.'

Mike stared at the phone for less than a minute before dialling the office number in Tel Aviv.

'Please, say your name, slowly and clearly,' said the robotic female voice.

'Mike Roberts.'

'Thank you. Now, say the name, of the person, with whom, you wish to speak.'

'Danny Spiegel.'

'Thank you. Please give, the reason, for your call, by choosing from, the following options: emergency, security, active service, political, religion or personnel.'

'Oh for God's sake.'

'I'm sorry, I didn't understand, that choice. Please choose again.'

'Emergency.'

'Thank you. Please say, or key in, your telephone number, including country, and area codes.'

Mike peered at telephone base on the desk, searching desperately for a number, still holding the phone to his ear. Nothing. He could see the warrant officer on the other side of the office and was about to wave.

'I'm sorry, I didn't understand, that choice. Please try again later.'

And all Mike could hear was a continuous tone. He scrolled down the contacts list on his mobile for Danny's direct line. Mildly cursing himself for not thinking of it before. He punched the numbers out on the landline keypad, listened to it ringing.

'It's Danny,' said the now familiar voice.

'I hate your phone system.'

'Yeah? You're meant to. I hear you have a little problem over on the island. I take it you are on Cyprus, Mike.'

322

'Bad news always travels First Class. Yeah, I'm here, based at RAF Akrotiri. I need a couple of favours but first ...'

Once again, Mike ran through all of the things that had happened since he'd arrived. The physical examination of the ship, his discussions with Sam Aitken and Robin Beavis, Robbie Wilson's account of the couple on the dock. And then went through his subsequent conversation with Helen O'Connor. Danny Spiegel listened silently, without interruption, but Mike could hear the scratch of pen on paper.

'So what do you need?' he said, finally speaking.

'Have you got a recent photograph of Tarek al-Shami?'

'Several, but trust me, a lot of them you don't want to scc. Marina sent them. Yeah, we've got a mug shot on file but the best one is the pic of Tarek with Ayesha that she sent over. You want copies there?'

'Please.'

'You at the Station HQ, I'm guessing?'

'Yeah.'

'Aaron, Mike Roberts nee ...' Danny's voice drifted off as he turned to talk to his assistant. 'On its way in two. Done. Next?'

'You have people in Dubai, don't you?'

'The Bedouin have a saying: the more lovely the camel, the greater number of fleas. Let me guess, you want me to see if I can find Mr Masri and shake him for answers?'

'Well, yes.'

'It'll be my pleasure, and I'll deal with it personally. You going to come out to play when we have him?'

'Hopefully.'

'Excellent. By the way, why didn't you phone on your mobile?'

'There's no signal on the base, apart from a small area in the airport terminal.'

Mike could hear the Mossad agent laughing loudly, telling Aaron and the laughter peeling across the room.

'I love it! That is soooo British.'

*****

Al Quoz was hot, dusty and dirty as one might expect of a vast rambling industrial estate. As well a new battery, his car seemed to have gathered several layers of grime and a scratch on the passenger door. Not that it mattered. The second hand white Range Rover was not quite as new as the one at home in England but it had been cheap and, on the whole, in good order. He thought that he'd probably been overcharged but, in the big picture, it didn't matter.

'God, it's hot,' he said looking up at the grey-blue dome of the sky.

He thought of Sophie lazing on the balcony and then of a long glass of iced water. Perhaps something stronger later. Reaching the car, he unlocked it with the remote, climbed into the driver's seat and switched on the ignition. And then felt a heavy hand on his shoulder.

'How nice to finally meet you,' said Danny Spiegel.

13 ~ Pandora's Box

Double Explosion on British Warship Kills Fourteen

Cyprus: A little after midday on Monday, a double explosion occurred on HMS Gloucester, anchored in Akrotiri Harbour, Limassol. Information sourced by Cyprus Mail has revealed that the crew sustained 13 fatalities. Of the three crew members initially placed in Limassol Hospital's intensive care unit, one has since died, bringing the death total to 14; although out of intensive care, the other two still remain in hospital under observation. A further 12 crew members sustained a variety of injuries, ranging from cuts and burns to respiratory problems caused by smoke inhalation.

A Type 42 destroyer in the British Royal Navy, the Gloucester was visiting Limassol on its way to join NATO's Operation Active Endeavour. Sister ship HMS York is already on her way from Portsmouth in the United Kingdom, also intended to join the fleet of international warships deployed in the Mediterranean. Initiated in support of the United States after 9/11, Active Endeavour is NATO's only article 5 operation on anti-terrorism.

A spokesperson from the British Forces HQ at Episkopi in the Western Sovereign Base Area told Cyprus Mail that two missiles fitted to the launcher on the foredeck of the destroyer had exploded.

Speaking to Cyprus Mail direct, he said: 'Our initial investigations indicate that the detonations may have been caused by additional explosives possibly inserted elsewhere and triggered remotely. If that is the case, the aggressor would have been within a few miles on land or out at sea. We would welcome any information from the public in respect of a person (or persons) who they might have seen behaving strangely on Monday or indeed Sunday and Tuesday. However, I would emphasise that investigations are at a very early stage and we cannot rule out the possibility that the explosions were due to other causes.'

The officer was unable to amplify on what 'other causes' could be considered. He said that he thought it extremely unlikely that this could happen again, saying that this was clearly a 'one off'. As the ship was at anchor in the harbour, there had never been any danger to members of the public.

In an open letter, the British Prime Minister condemned the [possible] attack as the 'cowardly act of those who seek to instil terror' and that 'murder is murder whatever colour it's painted'. Sending his condolences to the bereaved families and crew, he swore to 'hunt down the perpetrators of this vile and heinous crime, and bring them to justice'.

British forensics specialists continue to analyse the scene and the debris for possible clues as to the methodology and the identity of the bomber(s). The bodies of the deceased crew members will be flown back to Brize Norton, England, in the next few days. Thus far, no group has claimed responsibility for this act of terrorism.

Rear-Admiral Sir Reginald Buller threw the piece of paper onto the coffee table and sucked furiously on his pipe for a moment.

Smoke gathered above his head as storm clouds form before the thunder rolls across the sky.

'And this was published this morning, on Cyprus?'

'Yes. And it's been syndicated internationally, which means that it's appeared in most of the key papers either in toto or a clipped version.'

'Bugger! Whoever the bloody man is who opened his mouth needs his tongue torn out at the root. Explosives inserted in missiles and triggered remotely! Even if it is true, it's too bloody early to say anything. But now, for some reason, we've taken a leap into the land of imagination and surmise; a British destroyer has been the victim of a successful attack by terrorists. Fact. Just in case the notional terrorists didn't know, HMS York is on its way. And apparently that rabid moron in Downing Street who's meant to be leading the country has taken it all in and given it gravitas. Did the bloody man actually say all that in an open letter, Helen?'

'Apparently he did. Someone on Cyprus, presumably our spokesperson rolled it all past the Foreign Office yesterday afternoon, they kicked it over to Number Ten and the gentlemen of spin did the rest. I suspect the PM just signed off on it.'

'And nobody contacted us?' the Admiral spluttered. 'Why do we bloody bother, for Christ's sake? Rhetorical question.'

'I know.'

'I'll phone the buggers later; have a very loud word in their ears. Where's Mike Roberts? Didn't he say that he was coming back today?'

'That's what he said,' said Helen with a sigh, shaking her head, 'but I wouldn't be surprised if plans changed after this.'

'Why?'

'Cats and bags spring to mind.'

*****

After cruising 28 October Avenue, Christodoulou Chatzipavlou and Spyrou Araouzou Streets for over an hour, Andreas was bored, tired and irritable. Parking on the pavement outside the newsagents, he walked into Michaelides shop, bought a pack of Marlboro Red cigarettes, a copy of the Cyprus Mail and two lotto tickets that Tomas sold for Speranza. They grunted a few words at each other as Tomas organised the purchases and extracted the money from Andreas. They moaned about the humidity, the lack of tourists and the traffic, discussed the possibility that Aris Limassol FC could be relegated to the Second Division next season and whether goalkeeper Michalis Kokkinos was responsible for the team's eighth position in the league table. As ever, everything normal.

He drove back down to the Promenade that ran along the seafront, parked the car in the shade of the palms of Molos Park and switched off the engine. Winding down the window, Andreas tapped a cigarette from the already open pack, lit it with the cheap plastic lighter that Tomas had given him and blew smoke into the humid haze. He watched a young couple saunter through the trees, hand in hand, oblivious to his presence. Then picked up the paper, intending to read sports pages; but it was the front page splash that stopped him turning.

A full colour image of the front and side of HMS Gloucester dominated the top half of the page, clearly showing the damage to the bow and the absence of the bridge. The photograph could only have been taken from a boat on the water in the harbour. Or with a long lens, from the jetty on the far side of the harbour, Andreas thought. In fact, possibly from the very place that he'd taken the pinched man and the dark lady with the come-to-bed eyes. One of them could almost have taken the picture, he thought, but neither had a camera and the light was all wrong.

His eyes wandered through the picture for a while before reading the text underneath. Andreas read the words slowly, his lips moving silently with every one as though praying. He wasn't sure how to pronounce the word 'heinous' and didn't know quite what it meant, but he knew it was bad. When he'd taken the two foreigners to see the ship he hadn't really thought how bad it had been, that people had been killed. Mother of God! Fourteen people! Jesus, the two foreigners. They could be linked; they could have been responsible for this. As Andreas reread the piece, the video replayed on the screen of his mind. The couple waiting outside the Metropole, getting in the car, the woman looking cold, both dark and unsmiling. The man's voice played out against the memorised reflection in the rear view mirror of the car.

'... to Limassol New Port number one ... down the east side, past the container sheds to the end ...We like to see ships in harbours ... interested in military ships ...'

Once again, he saw them both staring through the open window, across the harbour to the ruined ship. She'd been leaning on his shoulder, so her head had been lower than his; a perfect double portrait in monochrome from a strip of old film stock. Neither saying a word, just breathing in harmony, staring in synchrony. And then the whispering, in what sounded like Levantine Arabic, Lebanese or Syrian maybe. It was like putting a mental jigsaw puzzle together without having all of the pieces, not knowing what the final picture might look like and not really wanting to see.

Andreas dropped the paper unopened on the passenger seat, looked out of the window into the middle distance seeing nothing apart from reruns as the video looped in his head. The pair had been strange, that was sure, and the writing said they needed information. About anything strange, or rather anyone behaving strangely. As a rule he kept well away from policemen, avoiding confrontation and conversation. He could hear his mother quoting proverbs:

'Don't sprout where you haven't been planted, Andreas. If you join the dance circle Andreas, you must dance!'

But this was different. Snapping open his mobile phone, Andreas dialled the telephone number printed in the box at the bottom of the front page of the newspaper.

*****

Abdul Saad Mazari [al-Kabuli] stood with his feet apart, unconsciously moving with the soft rhythm of the dhow's gentle rolling in the warm waters of Alexandria's East Harbour. A warm breeze brought the scents of the city on its wings; the earthy smell of baking bread with dark undertones of heady coffee, a hint of diesel oil and the pungency of rotting vegetables. And all of those, seasoned liberally with the tang of salt and the aroma of raw fish that had overstayed its welcome.

The Sea Wind had dropped anchor the night before, when the light was fading, and the cityscape that encircled the bay had been a blurred panorama of beige-grey shadowed blocks. In the early morning sunshine, the lines of the Citadel were etched into a clear blue sky, the eastern walls of the old fort enjoying the golden warmth. Beyond the fragments of traffic on El-Gaish Road, the elegant minaret and four large domes in arabesque of the cream-colored Abu al-Abbas al-Mursi mosque glowed in a mellow haze. While on land the city sprawled away into the dusty beige distance, the Sea Wind's tanned brown timbers and physical size stood in sharp relief among a shoal of smaller boats. Blue, yellow, red or green, they were strewn across the harbour as though they were coloured beads, haphazardly cast by divine hand.

Among the clamour of seagulls and the rippling gurgles of wavelets on boat hulls, the tenor buzz of powerful outboard engines took the lead in the morning's unpractised symphony. The slim speedboat skimmed across the bay, brushing the water with violent grace, leaving an angry wake of white foam. As it approached the dhow, Naseem cut the engines and allowed the craft to drift alongside. Leaving the mooring of the boat to the crew member beside him, he climbed aboard the Sea Wind with the ease of a cat leaping onto a high wall. The canvas walls of the canopy had been rolled up earlier, allowing him to walk more easily to the foredeck.

'What we heard on the radio? It is true. It took a little while, but I found a copy of the Cyprus Mail on a newsstand near the fish market, so it smells a little,' he said apologetically as he held out the newspaper.

Al-Kabuli rested the paper on the broad wooden rail, his hands resting on the edges to hold them down. He looked at the photograph for a long time before speaking.

'The ship's badly damaged but I suspect a lot could be salvaged. Too much damage for it to go anywhere though.' He smiled. 'They have done well, al-Shami and his friends. Unlucky for them that the missiles were on deck, not below in the magazine. Masha'allah. Next time, insha'allah.'

Naseem said nothing, remaining silent as his master read through the report below the photograph. Al-Kabuli nodded thoughtfully as he scanned through the text and then reread it from the top.

'Fourteen dead is not so bad,' he said. 'It says that another warship, this HMS York, is on its way to join the NATO operation of arrogant water policemen. Maybe this York is al-Shami's second target?'

'It could be, Sayyid. There is no indication that York will also dock at Cyprus; reports say that she will be patrolling the East Mediterranean coastline crescent from Turkish Antalya to Cairo in the south.'

'Which would mean sailing past Syria, Lebanon and onwards. Perhaps al-Shami thinks that he can detonate this one from his balcony at home,' al-Kabuli said with a wry smile.

'That would be impossible Sayyid,' observed Naseem seriously.

'I know, but the thought amuses nevertheless. But the bomb could be triggered from land, no?'

'No, I am sure. We know that the mobile triggers supplied by Dr Malik have been tested successfully to a distance of 16 kilometres and maybe that could be extended a little but …'

'You're thinking of territorial waters? The Zionist shit-eaters are in and out of there like mosquitoes.'

'Of course, Sayyid,' said Naseem patiently. 'But the NATO ships obey the United Nations convention and will not enter territorial waters. Those extend from the low water line out into the coastal belt for twelve nautical miles. And that equates to over 22 kilometres. Assuming the next target is HMS York, al-Shami will have to be at least seven kilometres out at sea to be sure he's in range. And that's assuming the York is sailing on the edge.'

'In that case, perhaps the good Professor needs a helping hand. Where is he now?'

'I think he is in Beirut. Nothing different has come through.'

'The sister, Ayesha?'

'With him, Sayyid. Not all the time, but she often stays at the apartment in Mansourieh.'

'Contact Faisal. Tell him to contact al-Shami, arrange another meeting here, on Rih Albahr. His sister also should be here. If we average around 18 knots, we can easily be off Beirut within 24 hours. And after the York, we will see what is to be done.'

'Your wish, Sayyid,' said Naseem, bowing his head just a fraction before striding off down the deck.

'And then which should it be?' al-Kabuli whispered in the sea air. 'The Professor or the woman?'

*****

Sami Malik sipped black tea from a bone china cup decorated with roses: large white blossoms on the outside against a pink background and a scattering of smaller pink blooms on the inside painted on pristine white. He smacked his lips together making an unattractive wet sucking noise and placed the cup gently on the gold-rimmed pink saucer. The vintage set, made by Royal Doulton of Stoke-on-Trent, England, had been imported by his mother some 70 years earlier, before he'd even been born. It had always been there, in use when he was growing up in Islamabad and then later in Lahore. There had been a few breakages over the years but most of the set was still intact and he was really rather fond of it all. And, for some bizarre reason, he was amused by the fact that the china contained at least 30 per cent of cow bone with the possible inclusion of human material.

He took another appreciative sip before turning back to the copy of the Wall Street Journal on the sofa beside him. The front page devoted most of its space to the Democrats seizing control of both houses of Congress in the United States. George Dubya Bush had grudgingly agreed to work with the enemy and accepted the resignation of dastardly Defence Secretary, Donald Rumsfeld. Malik grinned; as long as America kept sending the multimillion dollar handouts to Pakistan, and it would, who cared what happened in that corrupt cesspit of western politics. He turned the page and his grin broadened.

'Cyprus: Fourteen Killed in Terrorist Attack on British Warship,' read the headline. 'Two Sea Dart missiles sited on the foredeck of a destroyer in the British Royal Navy exploded without warning ... experts believe that HMS Gloucester was sabotaged and that an additional explosive device may have been installed in one or both of the missiles ... were detonated by remote radio signal ... no-one has claimed responsibility ...'

Malik read the short report all the way through twice before reaching for his mobile. Listened to the phone ringing at the other end, heard the General pick up and grunt his name.

'A very good morning to you Pamir.'

'Why is it a good morning?' General Mustagh asked grumpily. 'I find no reason for such an observation. It is hot and humid and my air conditioning has broken down, I have run out of cigars and my second wife is demanding a new car because my first wife has just replaced hers. So what part of the morning is good?'

'The part that says we should be receiving the sum of US$500,000 within the next few days. Have you see the papers this morning?'

'No. Has al-Shami been successful?'

'I think so, no, I'm certain, because it all fits. When we were at the Wana facility, remember, he talked of hitting a ship, specifically a destroyer. So listen.'

Malik read the report out loud, slowly and distinctly. He could hear the General's heavy breathing in his ear as though he was physically next to him.

'So he didn't manage to sink the ship?'

'No, but that is the twisting of fate. In the final analysis, he was successful. So the first bomb plus the first ship equals half a million American dollars, isn't it?'

'Excellent, I can tell my second wife that she can have a new car, as long as it's one of those cheap little Indicas made by Tata. You are sure that this is him, Sami?'

'Absolutely. There are too many coincidences: the ship, even down to the type, the location and its proximity, the way the bombs were detonated. Yes, I'm sure. And I will contact him this afternoon with a request for payment.'

'Are there any more, how shall I say, projects in the pipeline?'

'No, not really but that can change.'

'I've thought about al-Kabuli's request, you know, the one about ... I think we should consider it. Five million each is probably too steep but five between us wouldn't be so bad.'

'No Pamir.'

'Think about it Sami, just think about it.'
'I will, but the answer will still be no. Maybe.'

*****

The news is always bad, she thought, looking at the array of papers on the vendor's stall, beside the trash magazines full of no-talent celebrity trivia. The Daily Star's lead always seemed to be about assassination, betrayal, corruption, murder and today was no different. The assassination of a cabinet minister was shocking in its own right and while the people mourned, there was always that imperative to find someone to blame. The media and the government pointed the finger of accusation towards Damascus but many in Beirut held America and Israel responsible. In the end, did it matter? Dead was dead. She bought a copy, folded it neatly and tucked the newspaper under her arm before heading for the Café de Prague on Makdisi in Hamra.

Marina found a table by the window, within sight of the door, ordered a cup of proper Lebanese coffee with cardamom and a finger of baklava. The rich bitter taste of the dark liquid contrasted so well with the sticky honeyed sweetness of the baklava making the whole process a distinctly sensual experience. It was hard to resist but she stopped herself gorging, wanting the sensory anticipation of the next blended mouthful. Licking the sweet stickiness from her fingers was a vital element in the indulgence that was almost erotic in its practise.

Wiping her fingers on her jeans, Marina thumbed idly through the pages, scanning the headlines without really taking in the content. She was half way through the paper before something told her to go backwards, a subliminal flash of relevance. Slowly turning the pages, her eyes flickering across the newsprint, she was pulled up by a small headline over a short double column: 'Bomb Kills 14 on British Warship in Cyprus'. Two missiles exploded, detonated remotely by someone who was either on the island or offshore but nearby. Marina tried to work out why she'd been drawn to the piece. True, Cyprus wasn't that far away, only about 45 minutes by air, but in itself that was irrelevant. The fact that it was a British warship? She didn't trust the British: they were arrogant liars who excused historical facts by forgetting them. But it wasn't that. Then history reminded her.

'Al-Shami?' she muttered quietly to herself. Her mouth twitched her lips into a brief moue. 'Maybe.'

Opening the flap of dark green leather sling bag that lay on her hip, Marina took a small notebook and a pen. Flipping open the hard top, she began making notes.

> TaS & AaS – Palestinian/Lebanese (Syrian anteceds?)
> Father Najib – PLO, PFLP & Hezbollah connect
> AaS – active PFLP/PLO fighter. Involvement in both Intifadas almost certain
> Family – hatred Israel; UK same same – historical blame; anti US support
> TaS – overt connect with Pak nuke scientist S Malik + visits to Pak x 3 known
> TaS – Pic at Byblos '73 – childhood friends now in UK. All three have Palestinian anteceds. Amin Masri in food distribution; Ali Abbas in government – role n/k. What?
> TaS not in boat pic ∴ he took pic. AM & AA prob in image
> Why were they all together?
> Compare boat images w Byblos for similarity
> Is it poss that TaS respons for Gloucester bomb? Yes
> Who else involved? AaS – Yes. AM & AA – probably; need to find both
> First – Tarek al-Shami

Closing the notebook, Marina stared through the window, considering her options. It was all hypothesis and, on paper at least, it seemed to make sense. But there was nothing concrete, no evidence to back up her theories, to tell Danny and Aaron. On the other hand, if she was right, she needed to get to Tarek al-Shami quickly. And possibly the sister, Ayesha. There was too much that she didn't know.

335

Finishing her coffee and baklava, with slightly more haste than normal, she gathered up her newspaper, put the notebook and pen in her sling bag and left the money on the table. She waved goodbye to the server as she walked out onto Makdisi. It was a short seven minute walk from Café de Prague to Marina's apartment in Ras Beirut. There was a certain irony in the fact that her way home took her onto Bliss, only a short distance from Tarek's office, and past Faysal's where they'd snacked before going to Mansourieh. Marina hadn't told him where she lived and, at this stage had no intention of doing so; her imperative was to get back to his apartment.

Her home was a two-bedroom apartment on the first floor in one of the older blocks in Ras Beirut. On the corner of the building, long windows ran around the ninety degree angle providing her living room with wonderful ever-changing light. In the early morning, the cool blue sunshine streamed in through the eastern aspect, warming slowly as the sun moved around through the day. But Marina loved it most, when the sun dipped down in the afternoon, bathing the room in that glorious golden glow. Sitting on the balcony with a glass of wine watching the sun set over the sea, its final shafts crossing almost horizontally across the water; blue-green water to gold to blue-green until it met the blue-blue sky. Sheer joy.

The room was velvet warm as Marina strode towards an old oak writing table, tucked away to one side but perfectly illuminated by the ambient light. Pulling out the swivel chair to allow her to look at the view, at least obliquely, she took out her phone and pulled up the text screen, keyed in Tarek's number.

'Are you back in Beirut?'

Slow spinning back to the desk, she put down the phone, opened her laptop and brought it to life. She checked her normal email while she waited: nothing but rubbish or messages that could wait. Starring a couple of them, including an invitation to dinner at the US Embassy about 16 kilometres up the coast in Dbayeh, she closed Gmail and Firefox, switching to Tor. Her phone pinged softly.

'Hey Marina! Good to hear from you. Yes, back in Beirut. How r you?'

'Good, but missing my tutor,' Marina texted by return.

'How does dinner sound?'

'Wonderful. And then Mansourieh.'

'Done. Can't wait. Pick you up at eight?'

'Yup, outside Faysal's xxx.'

'No problem. C U xxx.'

Marina shut the messaging system and smiled. Using the cable Aaron had sent her, Marina plugged her phone into the USB socket on the side of her laptop and opened Tor on her screen. Clicked on F-Call, click on Encrypt, open contacts list, scroll down to D&A@Moss and click. Aaron had sent her the link to the programme he'd designed only a few weeks before, told her how to install it and they'd tested the connection; this was the first time that she'd used it properly. The sound seeping from the computer's speakers sounded more like the snores of a large dozing bee than a ringtone. And then the bee woke up and switched on his webcam. Aaron's moon face came into focus against the vanilla backdrop of the wall.

'Hallo beautiful Marina. What's up?'

'Hi back Aaron, looking good yourself. Is the handsome Daniel in the room or out playing with the lions?'

'Man's out of the country on Emirates' Roads. What do you need?'

'You've seen the papers, about the bombing in Cyprus?'

'Yeah, we've read about 15 different versions so far in almost as many languages.'

'I think the bomber might be Tarek al-Shami.'

'OK. Go on.'

Marina opened her notebook, reading out loud what she'd written down in the Café de Prague and adding a few more thoughts. The view on her screen was filled with the top of Aaron's head as he made notes. He looked up when it was clear that she'd finished.

'We're on to most of that,' he said slowly, glancing down at his own scribbles. 'I'm not sure that Ali Abbas has been followed up by the Brits but I can push that. Might do a composite of those images,' he mused, talking to himself rather than her. 'OK, hold fire for a couple of minutes.'

Silence filled her ears as Aaron's face disappeared and Marina was left with the view of the wall.

'Aaron? Aaron,' she said more loudly. Nothing but the wall. 'Shit!'

Aaron reappeared briefly, holding a mobile to his ear, held up three fingers and then disappeared again. Marina swivelled her chair, looked through the window across the Corniche below, to the sea and the sky. A single grey-white stack of cotton wool cumulus was the only blemish on the otherwise untainted canvas of rough blue-green oils of the sea and the cornflower blue watercolour of the sky. Despite the heat of the sun-warmed room, a cold shiver slithered over her shoulders and down her back. All alone, with no else to ameliorate her interpretation, the innocent formation looked exactly like the mushroom cloud after a nuclear explosion, She was glad when it started to break up a second later; even gladder when she heard Aaron's voice.

'Yo Marina! Come in lady!'

'Hey, you're the one who went away, klutz!' she retorted, swivelling back to the screen.'

'I've just spoken to Danny. The Professor is looking like numero uno on our list. There's still stuff to pull together but, yeah, we think al-Shami could be the point man. He said to keep your eyes open for anything that could be a trigger device: a small radio transceiver, some kind of hinky looking mobile phone. The thought is that if we're all right, Gloucester is only the first ship on the wish list, so any hint of names would be good. The Brits have this really weird thing of naming them after cities like Birmingham, Sheffield, Edinburgh etcetera. Photograph anything you see and send. Stick with him as close as you can but be careful Marina. Danny's cautious about pulling al-Shami in Beirut for the obvious political reasons; the international media would feast on something like that. If you can get him out of Lebanon, that would be excellent but I'm guessing it's a bit early for happy holidays?'

'I think so, but we'll see. He's in Beirut, I texted him before I called you, meeting for dinner and then back to Mansourieh.'

'Cool. Danny said to tell you, 'feel free to screw your brains out as long as you get us the goodies'.'

'Tell him, fuck you very much; you're just so sweet for telling me Aaron.'

Flipping the finger, she gave him a big smile and cut the call. Aaron watched her face fade from his screen, the sardonic smile seeming to last the longest, reminding him of the Cheshire cat in Alice's Adventures in Wonderland.

*****

Group Captain Ben Chalmers, the Station Commander had lent Mike Roberts his office for a while, just so he could answer the phone, have some space to talk to people and even interview one or two. Since the Cyprus Mail had gone to press, there'd been weirdos and cranks coming out of the woodwork.

At least two had said that they'd been responsible for explosions. One claimed he was a practitioner of pyrokinesis, had concentrated his mind and directed a powerful mental flame to rid the world of the deadly weapons on board HMS Gloucester. Unfortunately he had not anticipated the collateral damage, regretted the loss of life and felt the need to confess! Another said that his voices had spoken of evil demons living on board, shown him visions of the creatures of the dark and told him to destroy the ship. He failed to explain exactly how he achieved his mission beyond saying that he had detonated the warheads by touch in a dream!

There had been plenty more, along the lines of greater powers ridding the world of the machinery of war: sightings of fiery angels in the heavens, powerful spirits from the astral world, manifesting themselves outside their plane of existence. But there were also those who thought they might have seen something strange, unusual, and thought perhaps they ought to mention it, just in case. And those ranged from an observation of Chinese tourists practising tai chi on a beach near Paphos to 'a man carrying a large box'; at least he'd been seen near the marina in Limassol. There was a knock on the door and Mike let out an involuntary sigh.

'Come in.'

Warrant Officer Susie Hartwood loomed in the doorway, managing to fill most of the space sideways if not quite to the top. She wore a distinct frown tinged with a good measure of distaste as though she just trodden in something particularly repugnant.

'Major Roberts, Sir. There's a taxi driver outside called Andreas Panayiotou; I've checked his papers. He says he spoke to you this morning, that you asked him to come to the base,' she said almost accusingly. 'Stinks of cigarette smoke and he's pretty scruffy,' she added in a loud stage whisper.

He looked at his notes: Panayiotou was the last one on a very short list, apart from Robbie Wilson who was due in … Mike glanced at the time … 20 minutes.

'Send him in please, Warrant. Corporal Wilson should be coming in as well fairly shortly. I'll see him as soon as I've finished with your taxi driver.'

'He's not mine Major!' Managing to rotate herself in the doorway, she presented her broad rear view that was worse than the front when assessed on size. 'Major Roberts will see you now,' she bawled, stepping three paces forward and turning sideways to allow the rancid little man to pass.

Andreas walked through the doorway, his eyes firmly fixed on Mike Roberts, avoiding even a glance at Susie Hartwood's fearsome voluminous bosoms. He shook the outstretched hand and sat down on the chair in front of the desk as requested. Mike shuffled the small pile of glossy photographs; one of the base photographers had printed them up for him after Aaron had sent them through. Another Warrant Officer, the RAF snapper had raised an eyebrow or two when he saw the couple of extras that Danny had thrown into the mix. Those had not been included in the pile on the desk.

'Thank you for coming in Mr Panayiotou.'

'No problem, Sir. I feel it is my duty as a proud Cypriot, that such things should not happen in my country and if I can be of assistance …' Andreas held out both arms, the palms of his hands upturned towards the ceiling, and shrugged.

'Mr Panayiotou, could you tell me again about the people you drove to the harbour that morning.'

'Sure, I picked them up from outside the Metropole Hotel on Ifigeneias in Limassol about 15 minutes after eight o'clock, maybe it was two or three minutes later. They complain because they say I am more than ten minutes late. It's nothing. This is a man and a woman, both with dark hair and almost black eyes. Hers were big eyes, very attractive, a beautiful woman maybe; but him, he has weasel eyes, sly and he has a pinched face. But they pay well. I charge for the trip to the harbour, then to the airport at Larnaca and supplement for one-way ride. The woman she mutters but he pays.'

Andreas did another one of those things with his arms again and the shrug.

'How much did you charge them?'

'That was €270, for everything.'

'You charged them €270 to take them to Larnaca!' said Mike with disbelief. 'And they paid?'

'And a side trip to Akrotiri Harbour. Sure.'

'But that's extortionate!' Mike expostulated, without thinking.

'Is business,' Andreas argued. 'Plus, I am not liking them so much, so it costs more. Anyway, they paid so …'

Mike shook his head in disbelief, and then started to wonder.

'So they asked you take them to the harbour,' said Mike, encouraging the taxi driver. 'Can you remember what they said?'

'I told them that about the damaged ship. He says, we like to see ships and we like warships. I took them right to the end, where they could see across the water to the broken one. Up to then, they're saying nothing but then they are looking and talking, but in Arabic, from Lebanon or Syria I think.'

'You don't speak Arabic?'

'No, but I meet many people from Lebanon and Syria when they come here, many times. During the fighting they come and afterwards, but also for holidays. So I know a few words but not enough to speak, to understand.'

'And then?'

'Then, he tells me enough, we go. I drive them to the airport in Larnaca and then I drive home.'

Mike pushed the photograph of Tarek and Ayesha al-Shami across the desk to the man. Looked him in the eyes.

'Do you recognise these people?'

Andreas briefly looked down at the photograph and then back up to Mike.

'Sure, this is them for sure.'

'Take another look, Mr Panayiotou. I need to be certain.'

Andreas shrugged his trademark shrug, looked down at the photograph and studied it for a little longer this time.

'It's them for sure,' Andreas said confidently. 'I remember thinking, she would be even more beautiful if she had bigger breasts. And that pinched face of his. Yeah, no problem, I'm sure.'

He slipped the photograph back across the table to Mike.

'Is all I can tell you. But you will not mention my name to anyone?'

Taking the lead, Mike stood and Andreas followed suit.

'Absolutely not. This conversation is totally confidential and anonymous. The details of what you've told me will be shared with my colleagues; your name will not. My thanks Mr Panayiotou, you've been extremely helpful.'

Mike walked to the door, opened it and let the taxi driver walk out into the main office. On the far side, Corporal Wilson was waiting patiently in a chair; Mike nodded to the man and Wilson stood up.

'Warrant Officer Hartwood will escort you out, Mr Panayiotou, Thank you again for your time and valuable assistance. Goodbye.'

He'd only just started walking away, but Andreas paused, turned on his heel and walked back the few feet he'd travelled.

'If you catch them, might there be some reward for helping you today? I'm just asking, in case, and then to say that then I would be happy for you to remember my name.'

'It's unlikely, but possible. If there is any such reward, I will ensure that you're contacted.'

'Thank you, Sir.'

Mike watch the man scuttle across the office towards Warrant Officer Susie Hartwood and her voluminous bosoms and shook his head. Robbie Wilson walked smartly across the office towards Mike, in the opposite direction to Andreas Panayiotou. The difference in the bearing and demeanour of the two men was remarkable in its contrast. When Corporal Robbie Wilson stamped his way to attention and snapped off that same smart salute from the day before, it was duly noted by the senior officer.

342

'Corporal Wilson, good to see you again,' Mike said with a welcoming smile, 'please, sit down.'

'Thank you Sir.'

'This shouldn't take too long. I'm hoping we can ID the man and woman you talked to by the Gloucester. Cast your mind back to the couple, try to see them on the dockside. According to what you told me before,' he said, glancing at his notes, 'they looked as though they could be brother and sister. Your recollection of the woman was quite detailed: intense, almost black, shiny eyes, high cheekbones and pouty lips. 'She was a stunner, in an Arabic way,' were the words you used. Slim, tight jeans and floppy jumper – you clearly got a good look.'

'Er, yes, Sir. And I'll stick by what I said, she was a stunner.'

'No problem. Going on to the man, we're a bit shorter on detail. You said he was around six feet, clean shaven with 'a bit of a pinched face'. And you thought he looked the elder of the two?'

'Yes, Sir. It was as much his manner as how he looked. There was something, I dunno, teacherish about him? Rather serious, if you know what I mean. She looked as though she might be fun if the mood was right. I don't mean that badly, Sir, she wasn't tarty or anything, just that I'm guessing she probably had a really nice smile. He didn't look as though he'd had a laugh since he was a kid. I dunno, probably talking rubbish on that one, Sir.'

Taking the same photograph off the pile that he'd shown to Andreas Panayiotou, Mike slipped it across desk to Robbie Wilson. Carefully picking the picture up from the table, the Royal Marine held it an angle with his fingertips and stared intently at that frozen moment of two happy people. Mike waited patiently for the man to speak.

'It's definitely them, Sir. Her, I'd recognise anywhere because she was so striking. And I'd recognise him too, but especially with her. Surprised he can bleeding smile though, not that it makes him look any younger.'

'You also said that the light wasn't so good by the time you talked to them. Take another look.'

'Sir.'

Robbie Wilson dutifully studied the pair in the image for a few moments more, the skin of his forehead wrinkling slightly with the effort of concentration. Finally, he put the photograph back on the desk, nodded and slid it across to Mike Roberts.

'There's no doubt in mind, Sir,' he said, looking directly at the Major. 'It's definitely them that was on the dock, one hundred per cent. You know who they are, don't you Sir?'

'We know who the people are Corporal. We don't know for sure that they're responsible.'

'Sorry, Sir, I wasn't suggesting anything ...' He tailed off lamely, not sure of his ground.

'At ease Marine, if it is them, we're not going to let them get away.' Mike's smile was honest and open. 'By the way, you were wrong, she's seven years older than him. On the other hand they are brother and sister and he's a university professor. Two out of three's not bad.'

Corporal Robbie Wilson returned the Major's smile with a grin that was almost shy.

'Who'd have bloody thought it? A professor? So what's his beef?'

Mike ignored the questions.

'Thank you Corp, I think we're done.'

'Sir,' the man said as he stood up and away from the chair. 'I'd like to say something before I go, if that's all right?'

'Go ahead.'

'Well, with the Gloucester out of action for the duration, Sir, it looks like our lot's going to be stood down and sent back to England for a while. Just thinking, if you're building a team to sort it, I'd be proud to be in with a shout, Sir.'

I could do a lot worse, Mike thought, looking at the man in front of him.

'I'll keep you in mind, Corporal Wilson, I'll keep you in mind.'

'Thank you, Sir.'

Again with the snappy salute, the young Royal Marine turned on his heel and strode out of the office. Mike watched him leave, mulling over everything that the man had said. As Robbie Wilson disappeared from his line of view, Mike turned his focus back to the pictures on his desk. Flipping open his mobile, he scrolled down to Danny's cell number, picked up the handset from the phone on the Station Commander's desk and dialled. He listened to the dialling tone, heard it click into message mode, listened to the synthesised voice announcing that the owner of the mobile was unable to pick up and to please leave a message after the tone. The flat single note that indicates you're speaking to an inanimate machine.

'Danny boy, ring me at Akrotiri SHQ on the Station Commander's extension. I've got two positive IDs on the brother and sister pic. Get back to me as soon as.'

The phone rang five minutes later.

*****

Everything was unrelieved, unblemished, untainted, white. The door, walls and floor were the white of the chalk cliffs near Dover on a day when the air was dense with a suspension of rain. The ceiling had the gloss of the sour white belly of a dead fish, with just a hint of rotting ochre lent by the light filtering through the line of Perspex panels that ran from one side of the room to the other. The wooden bed was painted white, the sheets and blankets, the deathly white of shrouds, their very dampness adding the scent of the grave. Even the bucket in the corner that they'd given him to relieve himself was painted matt fucking white!

They'd brought him back here when the black man had told them to, after the man's phone had rung, flipped onto voicemail and he'd checked who'd called. Amin sat on the thin kapok mattress on the low unsprung bed, his elbows resting uncomfortably on his raised knees, his head in his hands. His upper lip was painfully fat with bruising, the split above his left incisor slowly seeping blood. The cut over his right eye, on the bone at the top of the eye socket, had stopped bleeding; now the blood was a thick dark coagulation weighing down the dense hair of his eyebrow. He tried to work it out, to make sense of what had happened.

The black man had been in his car when he picked it up at the dustblown fleapit of a garage on Al Quoz. Amin remembered the heavy confidence of the hand on his shoulder coming from behind. He'd said something: how nice to finally meet you ...

345

'... I've heard so much about you and your friends. Or should I say friend, since I really don't know anything about the other one.'

Amin had tried to twist in his seat to get a look at the intruder in the back seat. The hand held his shoulder down, pulling it firmly against the back of the seat and Amin was limited to turning his head sideways. Most of his aggressor's face was hidden in the shadow of the curved peak of a black baseball cap and the lower part of the face that was showing was deeply tanned. Given his line of view, Amin's focus took in a well muscled, and equally tanned, arm that disappeared into the sleeve of a black t-shirt. He tried to release himself from the man's grip but to no avail.

'Who the hell are you?' he'd asked angrily, still struggling.

'You don't want to leave so fast Mr Masri. Or should I call you Amin. Nah, just Masri will do. Masri, yes. About leaving, no not a good idea. You see we have so much to talk about you and I.'

'Who the fuck are you? What the fuck do you want.'

'Tsk, tsk, given your excellent standard of education, and in la belle France, I would have expected better. What do I want? To converse, discuss and elicit information. As to who I am? Mmmm, probably your darkest, blackest nightmare.'

And then the lights had gone out. Using the inside of his forearm, Danny had hit Amin hard on the right hand side of his neck, quickly and efficiently delivering a brachial plexus stun. No one would have seen anything in that dusty godforsaken corner of Al Quoz. Nobody was stupid enough to walk in the heat of the sun that blazed down on the burned dessicated ground and reflected dazzling stilettoes of light from glazed windows and shiny metal frames. Calmly getting out of the back seat, Danny had opened the passenger door in the front, dragged Amin onto it from the driver's side and slipped plasticuffs over his wrists, pulling the ties until the loops fitted snugly. And then fastened Amin's seatbelt to ensure that it would be more difficult for him to move if he revived rather than any sense of duty of care.

Shutting the door, Danny had clambered into the driver's seat, fired up the engine and driven out towards the edge of the sprawling industrial estate. Turning south on Al Khail Road, he drove for a few minutes before taking Umm Suqeim Street. He parked in the drive of a large but non-descript house on an unremarkable street in Al Barsha. He looked across at Amin who was starting to come around, albeit not quite able to focus on his surroundings. Danny sounded the horn once with immediate results: two men appeared from the back of the building to help the only slightly struggling Amin out of the car. They put him in the white room, cut off the plasticuffs roughly with a pair of gardening secateurs and left him alone.

They'd come back for him three hours later. Ignoring his questions, they had silently and firmly escorted him down a long hallway, opened the door and pushed him into the room beyond. Sunlight streamed through the glazed doors on the far side of the room that looked out over the mirrored surface of the water in a large swimming pool. The water was a dark lagoon, tiled in a mosaic of deep green, the colour of the jungle as darkness falls or the dangerous fruits of a Serrano pepper bush. On the edge of the pool, what looked like a large wooden kitchen chair with armrests stood facing the sun. His chair.

The legs were fastened to the paving stones by a simple heavy duty hasp and staple arrangement and the arms were accessorized with sturdy, well-oiled leather straps. His escorts manhandled him into the chair, cinched the straps over the lower part of each forearm. Amin sat there silently waiting; shouting and screaming was clearly a waste of time. The sun was still high on its trajectory through the sky, the air hot and humid; within a matter of minutes, Amin could feel the sweat beading on his forehead, his shirt sticking to his skin and his groin itching with the heat of his trousers. He looked up as he heard the noise of a chair being pulled across the stones.

'So, good afternoon Amin,' said Danny sitting down in a canvas backed director's chair. 'I thought that using Amin might be a little more friendly. I hope you've had a good rest and you're ready to talk.'

'You fucking bastard,' Amin spluttered, 'who the fuck do you think you are? You can't just …'

The sentence was split in perfect synchrony with his upper lip. The backhanded blow from one of the escort's fists effectively stopped speech and brought immediate pain. Amin could feel the blood beginning to flow sluggishly, searched tentatively with his tongue and brought the copper taste into his mouth.

'As you see, I think I can do whatever I want, in answer to your unfinished question. Let me introduce you, although you've already met physically. On your right is Mean, on your left, Nasty, and as you've probably guessed, they both do their jobs very well. By the way, I hope your neck doesn't hurt too much; I think I might have hit you a little hard.'

'What do you want?' It hurt to speak.

'Information. I want you to sing like a canary.' Danny dropped the friendly, jokey tone. 'Let's start. Tell me about the shipment of canisters that you received from Karachi, that was delivered to Marhaba Al Fatah International, your warehouse on Jebel Ali.'

'I have absolutely no idea what you're talking about.'

Danny nodded. Mean clenched his fist and backhanded Amin across the circumference of his left eye, breaking the skin at the top of the orbit.

'Jesus!'

'Is a dead prophet,' Danny finished. 'Let's start again shall we Masri? Perhaps I should have explained the rules. If I know you're lying, one of them will hurt you. If you don't answer my questions, one of them will hurt you. Oh, I forgot, I do have someone keeping an eye on the lovely Sophie, making sure that we know where she is all the time that you're our guest.'

'You bastard!'

'That's the second time you've called me names. But, I won't hold it against you. The canisters Masri.'

'They were specially made to transport oils for perfumes to be sold in France. It was a new line I was trying out for the business. I had them made cheaply in Pakistan, had them delivered here, filled with the oils that I bought in Dubai for the purpose and air freighted them back to the UK. I then took them personally to France and sold them. And that's it.'

'Masri, Masri. I am so disappointed in you. But I'll let you have that one for free. Perhaps I should try a slightly different angle. That you put oils into the cylinders that you received and freighted them back home, I accept. However, after that, you decanted the oils into bottles, probably the ones that they occupied originally, and you took the bottles to France. But what did you do with the canisters? Mmm, you call them NuCans; isn't that a bit of a strange name for an oil tin? And why would an Islamic scholar be involved in such a business? I refer of course to your old friend, Professor Tarek al-Shami?'

Danny watched Amin Masri carefully, noting the increasing pallor of his skin despite the heat. The split in the man's lip was opening, spreading like a rotting peach; the cut over his eye wasn't so much of a problem although Masri would be sporting a fine black one within 24 hours.

'I gave four of the canisters to an acquaintance. You're right, it was an idea that didn't work out, which is why we put the oils back in the original bottles. I was told by French perfumers that the oils would mature in the NuCans, it was their idea, in fact they gave the whole idea to begin with. I've still got two NuCans at home, you can check, send someone down to look. They're in the garage, at the back I think, and it should be open.'

It had all come out in flood of words and Danny thought there probably was a grain of truth in there, somewhere.

'My associate thinks that they actually contain explosives.'

'That's ridiculous. Listen, I distribute food, wet and dry goods, you obviously know that. What do I know about explosives? As you say, Tarek's an academic, a scholar; so what would he know about explosives? Nothing. Tarek was involved in the perfume oil deal because he needed money and he knew a manufacturer in Pakistan who could make these NuCans, as Tarek called them, cheaply. I put up the money for the purchase of the oils and the containers; he was going to get a cut of the profits once I'd sold the oils. Look, check the other two in the garage at Cedars' Stand, at the house in Hampshire.'

'This acquaintance you gave the other four to, who is he?'

'I don't know, he's a scrap metal dealer in Southampton, not far from the factory. I don't know his name. I might have met him at some Chamber of Commerce lunch or business meeting. I mentioned the containers, he said he'd take them off my hands. He told me that they weren't worth anything, said that kind of steel went for less than a pound a kilo, so he gave me fifty pounds cash for the four. And that's the truth.'

'So why keep two?'

'I don't know, really. I thought we might use them at home, even if we used them as plant pots or something. Anyway, the guy only really wanted to take four.'

'You and al-Shami were friends as kids, yes?'

'Yeah, we grew up together in Beirut.'

'There were three of you weren't there? That grew up together.'

'I'm not sure what you mean.'

Danny sighed and took the photograph from an envelope by his side. He held it up by the top edge, leaning forwards so Amin could clearly see the image of three small boys on a beach. Danny's focus was on Amin's eyes.

'It says on the back that it was taken in Byblos in 1973; you're on the right, al-Shami's in the middle and on the left ...'

The persistent ringtone of his mobile broke the concentration of the sentence; he glanced down at the caller number, recognised the international code for Cyprus. Danny let it run: if it was Mike, he'd leave a message, and if it was Mike it had to be important.

'Yeah, the one on the left is someone called Ali. Remember him, your buddy in Byblos? What's his surname, Masri? And where is he now?'

'Ali Abbas. I do remember him. Where did you get the picture?'

'So Ali Abbas made up the trio in 1973, but where is he now?'

'God, I haven't seen him in years. My family moved to Paris in 1976 and I haven't seen him since then. I think he and his family stayed in Beirut, but they were tough days in Lebanon and who knows what happened to them.'

'OK, we're done for the moment. We can get back to this later. Take him back to the room, give him something to eat, and some water. And Jacob, put some antiseptic on his lip; the little shit won't be able to talk otherwise.'

He waited until they'd taken Amin away before calling the Cyprus number.

'Hey Mike, good to hear you. I was talking to our house guest, Amin Masri, when you rang. He says the canisters weren't bombs and he's still got two in the garage at home in England to prove it. What does a scholar and a businessman know about bombs he says. But what are they doing talking to a big player like Malik? By tomorrow, Masri'll be talking very quickly and truthfully.'

'You've seen the papers, the reports on the bombing?'

'Yeah, but there's nothing new ...'

'There is Danny. As said, I've got two positive IDs on al-Shami and his sister: one before the bombing on the dock by a Royal Marine who spoke to them; the other's from a taxi driver who took them down to the other side of the harbour so they could look at their fucking handiwork before taking them to Larnaca airport! Ask Masri what he thinks about that.'

'Trust me, I will. I spoke to Aaron earlier, with Marina on another line and she's been doing some thinking. Marina's planning to stay very close to al-Shami, find out as much as she can and try to find whatever he used to trigger the bombs. She also mentioned the third boy in the picture, Ali Abbas. Has anyone done a search on him yet?'

'Only Tracker. Nothing on an 'Ali Abbas' in the UK comes up on the radar.'

'He works for the government but we don't know what he does or where he's working. Masri swears he hasn't spoken to him in years; I think he's lying. We think he's in the picture of people on the boat. Aaron's working on a comp at the moment, doing a comparison of faces between those in the Byblos pic and the ones on the boat.'

'Abbas is the bomb maker, isn't he? Danny, Abbas doesn't work for the government, he works for the company that makes the fucking missiles!'

'OK, I'll take care of Mr Masri. I'm guessing he'll spill his guts within 24 hours. There's no need for you to be here. I'll let you know as soon as I do. And you?'

'I'm riding the tornado, Danny, storm chasing.'

14 ~ Moves on the Chess Board

Tarek smiled as he reread the short thread of messages and wondered what Marina would be wearing that evening, how she would look. Snapshots floated in his head behind his eyes, jumbled images of her on the Oval Green, across the table at Faysal nibbling on spinach fatayer, laughing at the juice running down her lip, leaning back in the car. The time for indulgence and pleasure would come later, he told himself, pushed the images from his mind. Tarek slipped the phone into the back pocket of his chinos, leaned on the balcony railings, looked out across the jigsaw puzzle of Beirut to the sea beyond. On the big canvas, the view was a watercolour in low contrast: the soft browns, green and beige of the land and cityscape drawing a ragged line across the bottom of the blue-green water fading to the horizon.

Somewhere out there, not too far away, Saad al-Kabuli was standing on the Sea Wind, perhaps even looking towards Mount Lebanon and his apartment in Mansourieh. Perhaps al-Kabuli was thinking about him even as Tarek was thinking of the al-Qaeda commander. Tomorrow was another day, but one that could well change the future. His gaze moved to the southwest, looking into the distance as though he might actually see the other ship. He imagined it would be much the same as the one before but this time it would be moving. At the moment the oceanic panorama was unburdened by either warship or dhow, carrying only a few pleasure craft close to the shore and what might be an oil tanker, breaking the horizon's soft line between sea and sky.

He went inside, padding quietly across the floor in bare feet, poured a glass of iced water and took it with him to his laptop. Bringing the screen back to life, Tarek opened up his mailboxes.

> To: Professor al-Shami <talshami@gmail.com>
> From: QQ <ag49iut8zxg68so3@tormail.net>
> Subject: TimeToGo

Pop went the weasel! Congratulations again! The Main Man is in Town Tomorrow. You're going on a boat trip to pop another weasel that has just paddled past Benghazi. Excited? It will be here in less than 24 hours and this is your **One Day Only Offer**. And there's the Bonus: we'll be collecting You and Big Sister Tomorrow Morning. That's at Eight; we won't be L8. It's Party Time and we plan to make it go with a BanG! Don't forget to bring that **Special Mobile**.

Tarek read the email carefully, at least three times, working his way though the cryptic message. The email was totally clear on one point: someone would be picking them up in the morning on the direct orders of al-Kabuli. The Sea Wind was equipped with marine VHF radio equipment and maybe it was possible to follow the movements of other ships. Whatever the truth of the matter, the message implied that HMS York was on a course that would take it northwards, parallel with the East Mediterranean coastline. But why was it necessary to take a boat trip? And why did al-Kabuli want Ayesha to be there as well? Perhaps because he knew that she'd been with him in Limassol and that she'd been sleeping at the Mansourieh apartment since they'd been back. Only Allah and a few other people knew what she did during the day.

Tarek clicked on the reply icon and typed, 'Fine'. The thought struck him a nanosecond before he hit the send key: he assumed that Marina would be staying overnight as before. Damn! What difference would it make? He added, 'I have a friend, a woman, who may be staying overnight. I assume that you would have no objection to giving her a lift to Beirut on the way tomorrow? Please let me know asap. Thanks. And clicked the send icon. Text Marina and Ayesha.

> 'Ayesha, sponsors want a meeting 2morrow with both of us. Pick up from here at 8! Hope U R OK with this.'

Send. Then Marina.

> 'U there lovely?'

353

Putting the phone on the table by the side of the computer, he scrolled down to the next email to be dealt with; one of those rerouted from his Hotmail account.

To: <tar10sham991@hotmail.com>
From: <kilamsmalik@hotmail.com>
Subject: Congratulations & Payment

My dear Professor
I believe that congratulations are in order. As the old mantra runs – actions speak louder than words: yours have spread across the globe thanks to the power of the media. Certainly, this would appear to be your first success – Strike One, as the Americans would say.
Which brings me to the next point, ie the process of final remuneration as agreed. Please would you therefore transfer the sum of US$500,000 at your earliest possible convenience to complete our transactions. I look forward to receiving confirmation from the bank.
In the meantime, allow me to say that it has been a pleasure doing business with you and we look forward to serving you should you require assistance in the future.
Your humble servant SM

Tarek shrugged, his incipient smile tinged with the slightest of sneers. Malik and Mustagh were little more than financial sinkholes with contacts and a degree of muscle. Although he had to concede that the product supplied had thus far proved to be very effective and the money was indeed due.

To: Franz Honegger <frhonegger.dir@krieggessner.com>
From: <tar10sham991@hotmail.com>
Subject: Transfer

Dear Herr Honegger
A/c CH10 00250 00A1076332795
As per previous instructions, please now transfer the amount of US$500,000 to A/c CH10 00250 00A1297470476. Thank you for your assistance. TaS

As Tarek clicked on the send icon, he heard the familiar soft ping from his phone. Bringing it to life, he smiled when he saw Marina's name come up on the screen.

'Hey you, I'm here now. What's up?'

'Nothing that changes tonight. But just been called to a meeting in the morning and car picks up at 8am, so early start.'

'That leaves plenty of time to play in the moonlight. It's cool.'

'Nice image. We can drop you off in Beirut on the way thru.'

'No problem. Think of me till later.'

'Can't stop thinking. Dinner at my favourite, La Paillote?'

'Love it. CU.'

Tarek turned back to the larger screen of his laptop, satisfied that that minor problem had been solved. There were already responses to his previously sent emails. The two word reply from Faisal simply said: 'No problem'. The other was from Krieg Gessner, the bank in Zurich.

> To: <tar10sham991@hotmail.com>
> From: Franz Honegger <frhonegger.dir@krieggessner.com>
> Subject: Re: Transfer
>
> Dear Professor al-Shami
>
> Thank you for your email in respect of your requested transfer which has been effected as per your instructions. Therefore, the sum of US$500,000 has been transferred from your nominated account to that of a/c 1297470476 as of immediate. In addition, I have advised the client by email to confirm the payment.
>
> However, your email pre-empted my email to you with confirmation of payments made. As per instructions from our client/your financier, I have transferred the sum of US$100,000 to a/c 1076332795 in respect of first completion. Please be advised that I have also paid similar sums into your two colleagues' accounts as agreed

by our client/your financier. In turn, they have both been advised of their individual payments by separate emails.

If I can be of further assistance at this stage, please do not hesitate to contact me.

With all my best wishes
Yours sincerely
Franz Honegger
Exec Director, Non-resident Private Banking

There was still plenty of money in his account from the first payment he'd received: to date he'd only spent around eighteen thousand. It was comforting to know that there was over $180,000 in his Zurich account; even better to have a Platinum Krieg Gessner Visa debit card to access the account at most ATMs around the world. The 'NuCan Project' (as Tarek still liked to think of it), wasn't about the money but the money provided some security.

There was always the chance that someone would get to Amin or Alan, they'd break under questioning and draw a map that would lead straight to Beirut. At the end of the day, Amin had been the delivery boy and his information was limited, although knowing the other two conspirators was a good starting point for anyone on their trail. As a captive, Alan was a far more dangerous prospect: he knew how the NuCans had been installed, which ships carried them and the sequence of destruction. Becoming a hunted fugitive was a distinct possibility and Tarek wanted to be at least reasonably comfortable in exile. But that also depended on leaving before he was caught.

He'd seen the picture in the Daily Star, read the report at least four times, searching for any indication that they had any leads. There was nothing; it was bland and empty. Had Amin and Alan seen reports, he wondered. Tarek knew that the international media had covered the explosions and deaths in Limassol, referring to it as 'a story'. Some story, he thought. In some ways, he wished he could explain, give the world reasons, the rationale behind Operation NuCan. In the end the glory would go to al-Qaeda, they would claim the responsibility, make threats and demands to which the West would never accede. But the aim of terrorism is to terrorise and plant fear into the minds of infidels around the world. Tarek pondered the idea of emailing his friends, to check that they were fine. And if he didn't receive any answers, what would that prove? Nothing. Tomorrow would be another day of vengeance; tonight would be just for pleasure.

*****

'Praise be to Allah, Lord of the world, prayer and peace be upon Muhammad our prophet and upon those who follow his guidance. These words of mine are firstly for the peoples of Britain, but should also serve as a warning to those in America, their vassal dogs in Israel and all those who seek to oppress Muslims, destroying our homes, murdering our men and raping our women.

'The destruction of HMS Gloucester is one part of the retribution for the injustices perpetrated by the British government against Muslims and Islam in the name of the British people. Together with America, Britain has invaded the Islamic countries of Iraq and Afghanistan in the name of freedom! But you do not know what freedom means. The intentional killing of innocent women and children is a deliberate policy. Your promised freedom and democracy begins with lies and intolerance; it is given with bombs, missiles and guns. For you, resistance is simple terrorism. We have witnessed the oppression and tyranny by Israel against our people in Palestine and Lebanon, supported by money and weapons supplied by Britain and America. The world saw the violent predations of Israel upon those whose only crime was to exist, and the world did nothing. Is defending oneself and punishing the aggressor in kind, objectionable terrorism? If it is such, then it is unavoidable for us.'

Helen pressed the pause button, freezing the picture on screen. The familiar long face topped by a white turban and extended by the dark beard with its greying centrepiece reminiscent of a dirty skunk's tail, lips curled in mid-rant. As ever, one finger pointed heavenwards, emphasising his point.

'There's a lot more, in the same vein before he gets to the point,' she said, lifting her cup of coffee. She took a sip before continuing. 'The tape was syndicated by al Jazeera as per usual; their people claim it's bin Laden's voice but we're not so sure. John Watkins has been playing around with it, running voice recognition and behavioural biometrics that apparently help to identify the speaker. Don't ask him, Mike; he'll get terribly excited at your interest, start wittering on about frequency estimation, hidden Markov and Gaussian mixture models. You won't understand a word and you'll be bored out of your tree within seconds.

'Bottom line? The Watkins Conclusion says that someone has done a very good job on a video-editing suite, cutting and splicing different bits of visual tape together, giving it that authentic shaded blur. Then the voice-over's laid down on the visuals, re-edited, smoothed out and bingo, our old friend Osama threatening the infidels with doom and damnation. But of course, Watkins could be wrong.'

'At the end of the day it doesn't matter, does it?'

'Yes and no. Nobody's really sure where bin Laden is, or even if he's alive. You might remember the letter the Americans intercepted, sent by Atiya Abd al-Rahman to al-Zarqawi?'

'Yeah, that put bin Laden somewhere in Waziristan.'

'Uh huh. It would make sense: it shares the Afghan border, gives him a total of over 11,000 square kilometres in which to hide in a region that is mainly mountainous. Plus, his kindly hosts belong to that unlovely group of people, Tehrik-i-Taliban, which has been known to offer him a cave over his head and close protection. That's the most likely possibility, although he could be elsewhere in Pakistan. There have been rumours that he died in the Kashmiri earthquake, of typhoid somewhere in Pakistan and of kidney failure in Iran. To plagiarise Mark Twain: the reports of bin Laden's death have been greatly exaggerated.

'But here's the rub, Mike, if the voice isn't bin Laden's, whose is it? Given our concerns about the region and the vulnerability of Pakistan's nuclear armaments, shouldn't we be worrying about an al-Qaeda affiliate or commander whose face is not so well known? Someone only just below the top echelon of the hierarchy with that implied level of authority who can move relatively freely, rather than their erstwhile leader who's living in a bloody cave. I think you'll see what I mean.'

Helen leaned forward, hit the play button and then the slow fast forward. They watched it spooling through for a few seconds until Helen stopped it and touched play.

'I think he finishes ranting about here.'

'.. you should beware. After her cubs have been slaughtered, does not the lioness have the right to attack the killer? Thus shall it be with you. As there are four winds, so shall we destroy one British ship for each one. The second will be greater than the first and will not be stayed; but even the great west wind will listen to those who will bow to its might and bend. Once again, we call upon Britain, America and their allies to withdraw all troops from Afghanistan and Iraq by the spring of next year. But that commitment must be given immediately in an open statement that we will honour and trust.

'In addition, we demand that sanctions be imposed on the aggressive Israeli invaders; that all financial and material support be ceased, that they be forcibly persuaded if necessary to return those lands in the West Bank and the Gaza Strip to the Palestinian nation which should be recognised as an independent state with its own sovereignty. Israel must also be forced to cease all aggression against Lebanon and allow free movement by Lebanese Palestinians between that country and their lands. We ask that these processes are agreed by the UN Security Council and acted on immediately.

'If Britain, America and their allies are not prepared to accede to these reasonable requests, al-Qaeda will have no alternative but to pursue its own policy of protection and defence. In this scenario, the remaining ships will also be destroyed, wherever they may be. In the months to come, such elemental fires that are within the grasp of men shall rain down upon you, consuming homes and citizens, men, women and children without distinction. Allah is our Guardian and Helper and he shows us the way but you have neither belief nor guidance. All peace be upon him who follows that guidance.'

The screen went blank and Helen turned off the wall-mounted screen. Neither spoke: Mike simply stunned into silence, Helen waiting for his response.

'Jesus! They don't want much then.'

'Give me some comments, Mike, without thinking about it too hard. I want reactions.'

'Uh, it's hard to take it all in but … OK, al-Qaeda is claiming responsibility for the Gloucester but I still believe that al-Shami pressed the button. If that's true, he's being bankrolled and authorised from the very top, by this guy,' said Mike, nodding towards the screen. 'Then we're looking at the probability of another ship being blown out of the water and a lot more people being killed. The chances of stopping that in time are remote: we have absolutely no idea which ship is next on their agenda. I believe we're closing in but we could be talking several days before we hit the wicket and that could be a day too late. Fucking bastards!'

He ran the fingers of both hands through his hair, the frustration and anger engraved on his face, glinting in steely eyes.

'There's no way that Whitehall will consider any of the demands, so it's a race against time for all of the ships. I presume the Admiral's talked to Whitehall?'

'He's been on the phone to one mandarin or another most of the day and he's even more irascible than ever. 'Join me in the library for a council of war once the Major's seen the blasted video', he said to me before you arrived. For a moment, go back to the reactions. What about the last bit? How do you read his apocalyptical vision of elemental fires?'

Helen looked at him, seeing the understanding in his eyes and waiting for him verbalise the thought.

'They've actually got a plan to get their hands on some kind of nuclear material, bomb, warhead. I don't know. That's the only thing it can mean. And the most obvious place, with the greatest vulnerability and where al-Qaeda has superlative access is – Pakistan.'

'Yeah, we think so too, Mike,' Helen said quietly. 'Listen there's a lot more talking to do today, so we need to go down and join Admiral Buller in the library. If we can cut our way through the thunderheads of smoke clouding the room. If ever there was a day to give him some slack, it's today.'

They found the visibility in the library remarkably clear, enough to see the detailed scrolling on the ceiling rose and Rear

Admiral, Sir Reginald Buller's scowl in all its magnificence. Sitting in his usual favourite wing-backed leather Chesterfield, he was leaning over the coffee table, preparing what appeared to be his first pipe for some time. Carefully tamping down the load of Borkum Riff with his thumb, he put the stem between his lips and went through the delicate ritual of lighting the tobacco with a long kitchen match. He peered at them wordlessly through the rise and fall of flame, the first wisps of smoke rising towards the ceiling. For a few seconds he sat there smoking, building a tower of billowing smoke, a pall of cumulo-borkum hanging above his head.

'First bloody smoke I've had all day' he said, looking accusingly at the newcomers. 'Haven't had a moment to myself: the Whitehall hens have been pecking each other to death trying to apportion blame, telling me to get this bloody mess sorted out for them. Not asking, telling! The slimy little man in Number Ten says that it's awful, that his best friend George is really rather upset and that French Jack is waving a Gallic finger, threatening a nuclear strike against any country that sponsors terrorism that might affect La Belle France. Which, I would remind you, is what he said earlier in the year and still forgotten that it's totally irrelevant! And where have you been when I need you? Amusing yourself playing pilot in a bloody Tornado!'

'I have to confess, I did actually fly it some of the way, Sir. Did a couple of barrel rolls, one rolling scissors and a defensive spiral, finishing off with Pugachev's Cobra over GCHQ in Cheltenham, Sir.'

'Sarcastic young upstart,' the Admiral snorted, blowing twin streams of smoke from his nostrils in imitation of an angry dragon. He smiled benignly, and in a softer tone: 'Welcome back Mike. This is a bloody mess. You've seen the video I take it?'

'Yes, Admiral.'

'On gut reaction, Mike's comments were the same as ours,' Helen said, stepping in before Mike could continue. 'Agreed. It sounds as though al-Qaeda's desire to acquire a nuclear weapon has given birth to at least a basic plan and the most likely market for that is in Pakistan.'

'You realise that there's no way the PM's going to even consider the demands, despite the danger of losing three more

361

ships and their crews?' the Admiral asked rhetorically, looking at Mike. 'He spouts out the tired old clichéd arguments of not negotiating with terrorists and not being held to ransom, parroting the Americans. Utter rubbish, we've negotiated with terrorists for bloody years; it depends on one's definition of terrorist and terrorism. The problem with al-Qaeda and other groups of similar ilk is that their demands are so grandiose that there is nothing to negotiate.'

Admiral Buller paused to take breath or perhaps to inhale a prodigious amount of smoke before jetting it vertically upwards to increase the volume of the cloud formation above.

'Therefore,' he continued, 'negotiation isn't actually an option and curbing Pakistan's vulnerabilities is not today's concern. Helen?'

Walking over to the two cardboard boxes stacked by the door, Helen lifted one with some effort and carried it across to the men. She placed it carefully on the coffee table, opened the cardboard leaves at the top.

'Amin Masri wasn't lying about the two containers in his garage,' she said, addressing Mike. 'Tim didn't find anything else of interest at Cedars' Stand but at least found these, as promised, and brought them back to London. They're identical,' she said, nodding towards the other box. Take it out, have a look.' She noticed the raised eyebrow and grinned. 'We're not that stupid Mike. They've been checked and dusted for prints. Forensics only picked up two sets of prints but they have no matches. I'm guessing they belong to Masri and his wife; I've passed on a message through Aaron for Danny to get actuals for comparison.'

Standing, Mike lifted the cylinder from the box, held it out in front of him, rotating it slowly in his hands and then rocking it gently from side to side.

'Some kind of light steel alloy?'

'Not too far off the mark, Major Roberts. According to the forensics team, they're made of maraging steel. Apparently that's an age-hardened iron-nickel alloy with additives, in this case cobalt and molybdenum. Aerospace uses it for various bits on planes, tooling, gears and, curiously, missile casings.'

'And who would use maraging steel cylinders for transporting perfume oils? Quite. The weird thing about it is the balance. At a guess,' he said hefting the container for a second, 'it's about eight or nine kilos but all the weight is in the bottom.'

Sitting down, he balanced the container on his knees and tried to unscrew the top. In less than three revolutions it came away in his hand. His nose starting twitching involuntarily, sniffing the fragrance that still lingered, despite the Masri's efforts.

'You can still smell the oil.'

Helen leaned forwards, her nose searching the air like a hunting dog on point. Then looked at the top of the lid for confirmation.

'Mmm, that's the one that held cedarwood; the other's frankincense.'

Mike lifted the internal cover out of the cylinder, placed that on the table and turned the whole thing on it's side, putting one hand inside and the other on the base. He tried to gauge its thickness by sight and feel, then replaced it back on the table.

'I'd say the base is a good six centimetres thick and almost certainly solid. If it was simply meant to be a container, why would you need it to be bottom weighted? Masri said he sold the other four for scrap metal. I think he's lying. If we're right about al-Shami and Malik, one container full of high explosive was in the missile on HMS Gloucester and there are three more on three other ships. For some bizarre reason, they had these made at the same time to be used as dummies? In God's name, why?'

'Just in case they were stopped in transit? Maybe Masri thought that if the containers were queried at Heathrow, he could pick up one of the dummies and innocently show them that the cylinders simply contained oil. And look, here's another innocuous container. I can't think of another reason.'

'It's all rather weak,' said the Admiral, throwing his thoughts into the pool, 'this perfume business smacks of poor planning. However, I take it that you think these ones are visually identical to the more explosive variety?'

'Yes, Sir,' Helen and Mike answered simultaneously.

'And you think that Masri gave the other four cylinders packed with explosive to someone else? Probably this chap Ali Abbas?'

'It's possible,' said Helen slowly. 'We think that the missiles were probably sabotaged somewhere during the manufacturing process, the guidance systems modules replaced with these explosive devices. Company's called Forbes Industrial based in South Wales; the MoD's been dealing with them for years. According to the Defence Vetting Agency (which carries out the checks on military and civilian staff for Whitehall), company employees have to undergo developed vetting. The CEO took time out to remind me that developed vetting is required for Forbes personnel because they handle top secret materials. Patronising cow! Following MoD guidelines, personnel go through DV security clearance prior to employment, reviewed every seven years. She also said that spot checks are routinely carried out during those seven year periods. Like hell! I doubt whether she'd have any records to back up what she said; spots don't feature in MoD guidelines. And the rule with most of these agencies is: look at the minimum, find corners to cut.

'OK, may be that's a bit harsh but this needle hunting is so frustrating and prats like her don't help. To be fair, the DVA has a good reputation in the industry but most of that's based on meeting performance targets, percentages, management, financial reports. You never hear about them catching the bad guy with his trousers down!

'Back to Forbes Industries. The company's based in the Cynon Valley area of Rhhondda Cynon Taf near Aberdare in Wales, so they're pretty much out of the way and hidden. Easy access, however, to the M4 which is a little over 16 miles and then it's a straight run east. On average, Forbes employs around 860 people across the board. Some 60 per cent are actively involved in production, ranging from the guys on the basic production line to the design engineers. The name Ali Abbas doesn't appear on the register, we have no bloody idea where he might be or what connection he has with Forbes or any member of staff! Or indeed, if the name's just a ringer. Curiously, the guy who more or less runs the place shares the same initials: name's Alan Abbot.

'Abbot's been with Forbes for around 19 years. He did a BSc in Mechanical Engineering at Birmingham Uni and worked as an intern with Forbes for the practical aspects; the filling in the sandwich. When he graduated with first class honours, Forbes snapped him up, gave him a fulltime position and put him through a double Masters at Cranfield. Abbot was marked for the top job from the day he left Birmingham for good. Married a local girl called Megan; one kid, a daughter named Anwen. Perfect employee, ideal husband and loving father. Happy families. The only slightly odd thing is that there's no paper trail before he's at Birmingham University. On the other hand, we know he lived in some hovel in Sparbrook in the inner city, so maybe it's not so surprising. Nobody kept records of the poor buggers in areas like that, least of all the slum landlords.'

'Has anyone talked to Alan Abbot?'

'Not yet. Short time and shorter fuses, I'm afraid.'

'I'll phone him when we're done, hopefully make an appointment to have an informal chat and then drive down tomorrow morning.'

'And if he's our saboteur?'

'Point taken, I'll go quietly tomorrow.'

'Any news from Danny?'

'Not since I spoke to him last. At that time he said he was in talks with Amin Masri and expected him to share information some time today. Looks as though it's taking a little longer than expected.'

A cough that came from somewhere near the library doors broke into the moment's silence. Initially the three looked at each other expectantly; a second discreet cough drew their focus. John Watkins was standing in the doorway.

'I have Mr Spiegel on video link, it's urgent he says. Shall I patch it through to your wall screen Ms O'Connor?'

'Please, John. And tell him we're on our way. One sometimes wonders whether Mossad has us bugged,' she added, and stalked out towards the stairs.

By the time Admiral Buller and Mike arrived, the screen was already switched on with Danny's head and shoulders framed by a few palm fronds stamped on a blue sky. He smiled as he watched the latecomers arrange themselves in the semicircle of chairs.

'Helen's always the fastest mover, right? Good afternoon Admiral, Mike. As you probably gathered, talking to Amin Masri took a little longer than expected. But no matter. I'll get straight to it since I know that you're going to want to run as soon as you hear this stuff. Aaron enlarged the boat picture to get portraits, then overlaid those with the kids faces from the beach picture. He ran the originals and the comps side by side through face recognition and image comparison software.'

Expanded copies of the two photographs appeared on the screen, the boys on the beach at Byblos to the left, the happy people on Sirens' Choice to the right. Danny's voice came in from behind.

'Ironically, one mirrors the other, at two ends of a timeline that spans 33 years, I think. So running left to right in the Byblos shot, you have Ali Abbas, Tarek al-Shami and Amin Masri. On Sirens' Choice, the running is pretty much the same, except the names are slightly different. Al-Shami is still in the middle with Masri to his right but the guy on the left is Alan Abbot. The woman and the girl by her side are wife Megan and daughter Anwen. By the looks on your faces, you can fill in a gap?'

'You're sure the name's Alan Abbot, Danny?'

'Yes Mike. We showed him the newspaper reports on the Gloucester, told him about the sightings of the al-Shamis in Limassol, let him look at the composites … hey, we basically told him everything that we knew. Perhaps with a few embellishments. According to Masri, Ali Abbas changed his name by deed poll to Alan Abbot when he went to Britain with his father, in the late 70s he thinks. And here's the kicker, going by antecedents all three men are Palestinian. Today and officially, al-Shami's Lebanese, Masri French and Abbas/Abbot, English; but in 1973, they would have all been classified as Palestinian. So before I go on, what are you all thinking?'

'Literally a minute before you called we were talking about Alan Abbot and Forbes Industries, the company he works for,' Helen explained. 'There's no record of an Ali Abbas in their records, we thought that as Abbot runs the factory, he might be a good starting point. Mike was planning to have an informal chat with him tomorrow. Jesus!'

'Still a dead prophet,' Danny muttered out of habit. 'Masri finally admitted that he imported the bombs, that they were outwardly identical to the cylinders you guys have. You picked them up from Cedars' Stand, right?'

'Yes,' Mike responded. 'Did he say what he did with them?'

'Sure. He says that he met Abbot at Leigh Delamere service station on the M4, gave them to him there. Masri claimed that he didn't know the name of the company where Abbot works nor what he actually did. And wait for this, he maintains that he didn't know that they were bombs and had no idea that there was a plan to blow up your ships! In turn, that means he's not fingering al-Shami for pressing the button. You gotta admit it, the guy has balls. At the moment. I was planning on disabusing him of the silly idea that he lacked knowledge.'

'Bloody hell,' said the Admiral, 'you've certainly managed your questions rather well. We'll get Abbot arrested, take him up to Paddington Green and have a long chat.'

'No offence, Admiral Buller but you need to lift this guy from his house in the early hours, take him somewhere dark and squeeze him hard. Abbot knows the types of missiles, names of the ships and the kill sequence; you need to know all that like yesterday. Fuck Paddington Green and long chats.'

'It's not really how we do things in England …'

'My apologies Admiral, but that's bollocks, Sir! Mike, tell him.'

'Danny's right, Sir. This has to be a covert operation and it should be tonight.'

Danny's oversized eyes stared at the Admiral from the screen with a hint of disbelief sparking in his expression. In Helen's office in the Red House, Helen and Mike looked at Admiral Buller with bated breath, not saying a word.

'I suppose you're right,' the Admiral finally said, almost grudgingly. 'But God help us all if this thing leaks in any way.'

'It won't Admiral,' Mike told him confidently. 'We'll take him to Bwthyn Llwyd near Pen y Fan. It's a stone cottage in the middle of nowhere that's sometimes used as a safe house. If we lift Abbot at four am, we can be there by five. Hopefully, he'll spill his guts fairly quickly. The sooner we get him to talk, the sooner we can save ships and lives. Take him to Paddington Green and some idiot in Whitehall will scream press release; you might as well wrap him in cotton wool for a few days. And we haven't got that sort of time.'

'Fine. I'll leave it to you to organise. But keep it tidy.'

Danny was nodding approvingly on screen.

'Way to go, Bro. You want me to keep the pressure on Masri or parcel him up and send him home?' he asked.

Mike looked at Admiral Buller, who looked at Helen, who looked at the two men. Ever the tactician, the choice was tacitly left to her.

'What condition is Masri in, Danny? He's capable of travelling, I assume, but is he likely to draw much attention?'

'Helen, I am desolated that you should think that I would hurt ...' He changed tack immediately, seeing the flinty look and the hard line of her mouth. 'He's fine to travel and he doesn't look too bad. He's got a cut over one black eye and a split lip but that's not so bad. Those were handed out at the beginning just to make him realise we were serious. They've been medicated, so apply a little makeup and he'll pass muster. There're a few more dents but they're not visible.'

'What about the wife? Sophie?'

'Nate's been keeping her company. She's knows what's happening, she's scared for Amin Masri but she's a tough little lady and really loyal. Defends him like a wild cat and would physically defend herself if anyone had tried anything. Not that they have,' Danny added hastily. 'Her story correlates with his in so far as he told her what was going down just before he went to Dubai. That's all she knows. She's safe, unharmed and basically under house arrest.'

'Of course send them back,' Helen said decisively, 'but separately. Put Masri on the earliest direct flight you can and we'll pick him up at Heathrow. He's not going to do anything stupid if he knows that Sophie's still under guard at the apartment. Let us have a few days to talk to him and get a statement without duress. Don't look at me like that, Danny, you know what I mean.' The face on the screen dispensed with the mock wounded look and grinned. 'And he's more likely to do that quickly if Sophie's in your tender care in Dubai. Can you do that, please?'

'No problem.'

'When we're done, we'll let you know and then send her back, again on a direct flight. Since there's no point in charging her, we'll simply take her home, probably to Cedars' Stand.'

'That's fine. I'll leave Nate in charge of her for the period. Other things to do and places to go. Let Aaron know when you're ready and he'll tip off Nate. Getting back to the identity of the triggerman, Marina thinks it's al-Shami and the rest of us think it might be al-Shami. It is possible, maybe even logical, that the person who actually detonated the bomb in Cyprus was someone totally different, perhaps from al-Qaeda; the al-Shamis went in to watch. What's not in question is that Tarek al-Shami made all the arrangements from organising finance to manufacture. Marina's planning to shadow him closely for as long as she can, without raising any suspicions. And we're talking very closely. We can't send a team into Beirut and get them out again without a lot of noise, not too mention instigating an international crisis.' Danny paused, looked at three people in the office in London individually, gazing at each one in turn. 'So here's the question: do you want me authorize Marina to take him out if she has the opportunity and a clear exit?'

The only sound in the room was the ticking of a grandfather clock, counting the seconds with sonorous old metal tones, its pendulum hidden behind the polished oak door. Tick tock, tick tock, tick tock. Helen O'Connor looked towards the light of the windows, frowning with concentrated thought, perhaps hoping for enlightenment. Major Mike Roberts stared stoically back at the inscrutable warrior's face on screen, understanding but uncomfortable with the principle. Rear Admiral Sir Reginald Buller looked up at the ceiling as though asking the gods for guidance, then looked back at the screen and stroked his neatly trimmed beard. Clearly the final decision was his.

'We're talking assassination, Daniel, are we not?'

'Yes, Sir, we are.'

'Yes.'

That one single word crashed through the expectant stasis as a rock through a pane of glass. It screamed finality, a sentence pronounced in letters that seemed to be almost tangible in their weight.

'It's imperative that she finds the trigger mechanism first, the remote, and destroys it and any others. Or she has to be absolutely certain, in her own mind, of definite intent and capability. Either/or – kill him.'

*****

Marina watched the final radiant sliver of the sun's golden orb disappear into the sea as she sipped a glass of wine on her balcony. The heat of the day was slowly waning and what had been a cornflower sky was gaining depth, becoming a darker, richer blue. She liked that contrast, welcomed the velvet feeling of warm night falling after the hot, bright light of the day. A waxing crescent moon was imperceptibly making its honeyed journey through the heavens, throwing a rippling band of light diagonally across the water. Even the sounds of the city became softer at this time of day: the strangled desperate noises of traffic became a languid rhythmic hum, the angry shouts of exasperation and haste gave way to more amiable conversation. And she was looking forward to dinner and sex. The soft ping of her phone gently pierced the fabric of her reverie.

Turning away from the sky and ocean, Marina walked inside, to the table where she'd left her phone. She brought the screen to life and read the single new text.

'Search as said, then queen takes bishop. Endgame. Take care xx'

Just to make sure, Marina read the text again, shrugged and typed: Understood, fine. Putting the phone back on the table, she took her glass back to the doorway to the balcony and stared out into the dusky evening.

'What a shame,' she said quietly. 'I was just beginning to enjoy myself.'

Finishing her wine, Marina walked back through the living room and into the bedroom. She had at least forty minutes before she needed to leave. Opening the sliding door to the wardrobe, she ran her eyes critically across the clothes on their hangars. Her fingers flipped through them, considering and discounting, finally deciding on a light merino wool burgundy dress. Stripping off jeans and blouse, she stood in front of the full-length mirror, appraised what she saw and approved. The dress fitted her like an old friend, curving down her body in a comfortable rather than clinging way. A reasonably revealing cleavage at the top, the dress stopped mid-thigh at its lowest point. Marina sat down on the edge of the bed, watching the dress ride up her thighs. It had the right effect. She added sheer black hold up stockings, small garnet earrings and assessed the overall effect. A pair of strappy sandals would complete the ensemble.

In the kitchen she hesitated, poured herself another half glass of wine, took it into the living room and sat down at the table. She picked up the phone, holding it in one hand she tapped the bottom on the table as she pondered the thought that had occurred to her a few moments earlier. Security? Insurance? Reopening the recent thread, she keyed in a new message.

'Insurance for U & me. Locator is ON as of now. Follow?!'

Send. Danny's response came a minute later.

'Of course. Aaron tracking. Premonition?'

'Not a prémonition, just cautious.'

'Any serious concerns, abort. I mean it.'

'I know. Thanks for thinking.'

Marina stopped the thread and shut her phone. She felt calmer knowing that they knew where she was, they would know if something wrong happened, even though they wouldn't be able to help in a crisis. She hadn't lied, it wasn't a premonition, it was more of a slight prickling sensation, an awareness. The fact that Tarek had a meeting in the morning was not surprising; that he was being chauffeur driven was simply – strange. All the more reason to be prepared. Picking up her favoured sling bag, Marina slipped her forefinger into the solid metal ring standing proud of the top corner at the back of the bag. A little tug was all it took to seat the handle of the karambit knife in her fist, the razor sharp curved blade hooking out forwards from below. The claw of Hanuman, crafted in Indonesia, was Marina's favourite weapon for self-defence. She looked almost fondly at the light shining on the dull metal before slipping it smoothly back into the oiled scabbard.

Leaving the bag on the bed, she returned to the wardrobe, this time ignoring the racks of clothes, pushing them to one side.

Pulling away the heavy black curtain at the back revealed a tall metal cupboard, bolted to the wall. Marina punched in the security code on the keypad, twisted the handle and opened the door. Not touching any of the arms in the lower part of the tall rack, from the top shelf she took out a Baby Glock 26 9mm semiautomatic pistol and a box of ammunition. She sat down on the bed, removed the ten round clip and emptied out the bullets one by one. Two short. She reloaded the clip, pushed it back into place and put the gun on the bed. A spare clip, emptied and reloaded, was added to the pile; a short but effective suppressor screwed into the threaded barrel. She returned the box of bullets to the cupboard and pushed the door shut. The Glock and spare clip went into her bag, secured to a rigid side panel with quick release straps.

Marina stepped into her sandals, fastened the little straps in the tiny buckles, hung the sling bag crossways over her body from her left shoulder. She walked back to the mirror to take a last look of appraisal and nodded approvingly.

'Let's go play' she said to her reflection.

Ten minutes later, Marina walked into La Paillote and spotted Tarek at a table by the window looking out over the shadowed waves, lit by the moon and the amber lights on the sea wall. They embraced as friends do when they meet in public, he complimented her on the way she looked and pulled a chair out for her like a true gentleman. He eased the chair underneath her as she sat down, then walked around to other side of the table, sat down opposite her and gazed like an adoring puppy with a large sloppy grin on his face. Marina pushed the table away from the window, shifting her chair around to be at right angles to him rather than opposite. He was clearly surprised at the manoeuvre until he felt her softly stroking his leg under the cover of the drapes of the tablecloth.

She ordered six oysters and the crispy shrimps with spicy sauce; he ordered creamy crab followed by the sea bass in salt. A bottle of still water as well, and a bottle of the Kefraya Blancs de Blancs. They chattered over the olives and flatbreads about trivia. He picked at his crab, his attention focused on the way that she sucked the oysters from the half shell, slowly and sensuously, the touch of Tabasco reddening her lips. She asked him where he'd been; Cyprus he said, without thinking. When she asked whether he'd gone on his own, he truthfully replied that he been on the island with his sister. A family affair, she'd asked, licking her lips; he'd blushed and stammered protestations. They moved on to the shrimp and sea bass, away from the dangerous waters of Cyprus. While his eyes flickered sideways, gorging on the hinted curve of her breasts peaking out from the edge of the soft material of her dress, she wondered idly whether she would have to kill him tonight or whether it would wait a little longer.

The food was delicious, the wine superb and the ambience, warmly comfortable. They didn't hurry, enjoying each other's company: the conversation, the laughter, innuendos, the innocent covert fondling and occasional overt hand-holding. Lingering over coffee for a moment longer before Tarek paid the bill and left to fetch the car. When he got back, he walked around to the passenger side and opened the door for Marina who slid smoothly into the seat. He watched as she raised her knees slightly as she reached for the seat belt, looking downwards as the hem rose up beyond the tops of her black hold ups, revealing a few centimetres of suntanned satin skin. He caught a glimpse of rose coloured lace and averted his gaze like a naughty school boy caught in the act, scuttling around to the other side of the car and scrabbling his way into his seat.

Once out of the city, the ride pleasurably mimicked the previous drive back to the apartment. Slipping slightly down in her seat pushed her hemline even further up, revealing rose coloured knickers cut high at the sides. At the top the dress had opened further to show the edges of a matching rose coloured bra. Her right hand crept underneath the scalloped lace edge to enclose her breast while her right hand alighted gently on Tarek's trouser leg, moving smoothly upwards to the bulge in his trousers. He was clearly trying to concentrate on the road ahead but was having difficulty and was almost relieved when she took her hand out of her dress. Delighted and alarmed when she started to caress herself through her knickers, synchronising her strokes with the ones she was now applying to him. By the time they reached his parking space, their breathing was distinctly ragged with pent up lust.

As he unlocked the door, her arm crept around his waist, pulling him against her groin. She slipped past, taking his arm and leading him into the bedroom. Turning him towards her she held his arms to his sides for a moment, kissed him hard on the mouth, then looked into his eyes to make sure he understood. Nimble fingers unbuttoned his shirt, slipped it over his shoulders and away from his arms. His belt was undone and he heard the sound of the zip, as much as feeling it being pulled down. Hands reached into his pants, and he felt her lips encircling his erection. His hands reached for her breast but were gently brushed away. As her moist warm sucking mouth did its work, she could feel his legs starting to give way and pushed him onto the bed.

As he lay on the bed naked, she stood at the end, pulled the dress over her head and dropped it onto the carpet. She undid her bra, provocatively easing it off each breast in turn, then squeezing them together, pinching the nipples. And lastly the rose lace knickers were slipped down her legs and kicked off leaving her standing naked apart from the black hold ups. Climbing slowly across the bed she straddled his thighs, lowered herself just enough that the lips of her vagina touched the head of his penis; took it in her hand and rubbed it against her clitoris for what seemed like eternity before sinking down, taking the whole length inside her. Rising and falling, her hands gripping her calves, head thrown backwards, her body taut with sexual energy; him, rising up to meet her as she sank down, gripping her buttocks to pull himself even further inside her.

They made love once again before they were totally sated, lying naked side by side on the crumpled sheets, sweat beading on both their bodies, glittering diamonds in the moonlight. Tarek turned to look at Marina, his eyes running down the contours of her body, across the perfect breasts, the flat stomach and lean muscled legs, hardly believing that it had all happened. She noticed him looking and smiled with perhaps a tiny hint of sadness in her eyes. Leaning over, she put her hand gently on his face, ran it down the side and blew him an air kiss before turning back. And together they drifted off to sleep, both happy in that moment.

Neither of them heard the key in the lock of the front door, heard it open and then softly close. Nor did they hear the connecting door between the two bedrooms open, or the soft padding of feet across the carpet. Ayesha stood at the end of the bed, looking at the two slumbering forms lying close together but not quite touching. The combined smells of perfume, sweat and semen lingered in the air, an olfactory echo of what had taken place earlier. She walked round to the woman's side of the bed to take a closer look at her brother's lover, her curiosity stemming from the need to be suspicious and cautious. As she ran her eyes over the woman's body, there was no lascivious glint in her eyes, no prurient interest, just cold appraisal.

Ayesha scanned the lean taut muscles that ran across the shoulders and down the arms. She noted the strong legs with muscled thighs and trim calves. The stomach was flat and hard, the muscles clearly defined. This obvious level of fitness was not achieved by going to the gym once or twice a week, she thought, it was the result of possibly years of military training. The woman's sling bag was right next to the bed, within her reach, which in itself was not surprising but … Ayesha carefully picked it up from the floor, alert to any sign of movement, and took it into the next room. Walking across to the window for a little more light, she soundlessly opened the bag, felt inside and smiled grimly at the moon.

*****

Ed turned off the lights about half a mile from the cottage, driving slowly and carefully in the dim light. What little there was came from the dull scimitar of a moon already sinking down past the apex of its nightly arc. Both sides of the single lane road were lined with trees and bushes that formed an additional barrier but none of that caused him much concern. After some of the roads he had driven down in Baghdad heading up an SAS team, this was a walk in the park for Captain Ed Clarkson. He stopped the black Range Rover at the t-junction, leaving the 4.2 litre V8 supercharged engine purring quietly.

From the outside, it looked like any other luxury SUV from the Land Rover stable but the inside had none of the whistles and bells of a Chelsea Tractor. The stripped back interior more closely resembled that of a rally car with bucket seats in the front and the back, roll bars and small fire extinguishers bracketed on either side. Polished walnut, leather and chrome had been replaced with black plastic, dark grey breathable fabric and painted steel. Communications equipment had been installed where one would normally expect to see an expensive sound system.

The four men in the vehicle were dressed identically in one-piece black assault suits and each carried a 9mm Sig Sauer P228 pistol with a 20 round magazine. None of them expected to have to use their guns. Pulling a black balaclava over his head, Ed checked that the three other men had done the same, then looked at the man in the passenger seat.

'Ready, gentlemen?' asked Major Mike Roberts.

'Sir,' the other three chorused.

'Let's go collect the bastard.'

Ed turned left, driving at a crawl to minimise the noise of the already dampened engine. As they got closer, he blipped the accelerator for a mini burst of power, killed the engine and allowed the Range Rover to coast to the garden wall at the side of the cottage. The two troopers in the rear soundlessly flowed onto the tarmac, one linking up with Ed, the other with Mike. One pair slipped over the wall heading for the back door; the second worked its way round to the front. It was barely a minute before Ed and Mike were inside, leaving the two troopers outside to cover the windows. Nothing stirred. They checked each room before meeting at the bottom of the stairs. Mike looked at Ed, touched the pistol holstered on his belt; the other man nodded, withdrawing his Sig and checking the safety was on. With Mike in the lead, they moved carefully up the stairs, testing each step for creaks before putting their whole weight on any one. They split off on the landing, listening outside the doors for aural evidence of occupation. Ed raised his hand to catch Mike's attention, tapping the air with one finger towards the door at the end of the landing. Giving the thumbs up, Mike walked back along the landing, withdrawing his own gun at the same time. He nodded towards a side door half way down, held his hand flat at shoulder height and pointed to his eyes. Ed nodded. They turned to face the door, calmly opened it and walked inside.

Leaving Ed by the entrance, Mike walked to the bottom of the bed and then around to the side. Holding the pistol in both hands, he pushed the barrel into the man's cheek with just enough force to jar him awake. Alan Abbot involuntarily turned his head in the direction of the gun, cutting the skin over his cheekbone on the cold metal.

'What the fuck … who the fuck are you?' he asked, peering into the gloom.

'Is that a nice way to greet new friends?' asked Mike, this time pushing the gun barrel against the recumbent man's forehead. 'We have friends in Whitehall who'd like you to tell us about bombs and missiles. Get out of bed shithead, you're under arrest. Lights' he added, glancing at Ed.

Soft lighting suffused the room from five downlighters embedded in the ceiling, changing to a bright glare as Ed turned up the dimmer.

'You want to talk about the factory? I'm not allowed to talk about my work,' said Alan, blinking in the brightness.

'Oh my God! Alan!'

Megan stared wide-eyed with fright and horror at the two men in black holding guns. She clutched his arm, squeezing into his side for protection. Then her gaze switched away from the two men in the room to a point somewhere beyond the door. Catching the look, Ed swivelled like a dancer on the balls of his feet, to find himself looking at a teenage girl in a nightdress. Her hands covered her open mouth to stifle the scream that was trying to escape, her eyes even wider than her mother's. Their eyes locked and Anwen did scream, emitting a shrill howl of fear and panic as Ed caught her by the arm. He pulled her from the landing into the room as a ferret drags a rabbit through a warren. Keeping the momentum, she flung herself on the bed with her parents.

'We have quorum, I believe. Alan Abbot, I'm arresting you under the Terrorism Act of 2006. Now get out of the fucking bed and dress. We're going on a ride. Stay where you are, both of you,' Mike said, addressing mother and daughter. 'We have no intention of harming either you or Anwen, Mrs Abbot.' He could see the shock register on her face when he used their names, a creeping fear of the unknown, of what her husband might have done. 'As they say in press releases, your husband will be helping us with our enquiries.'

'But what has he done?' Megan asked, her voice hushed and tremulous.

'I can't talk about it, I'm afraid. Someone will be in touch with you in due course.'

As he watched Alan Abbot finish dressing, sitting on the edge of the bed lacing up his shoes, Mike wondered at the man's calmness. He had an air of resignation that was almost dignified in its stoicism, an acceptance of fate but with no sense of guilt or apology. After the initial shock of finding armed faceless men in his bedroom, he'd said nothing more, shown no weakness or fear. He'd kissed his wife and daughter, told them he loved them and hoped that he'd see them soon. His back was straight and his head held high as he walked out onto the landing. Mike wondered how long it would be before Alan Abbot revealed Ali Abbas and talked. He wondered what it would take to make Abbas give them the information they so desperately needed. And prayed that Marina could stop Tarek al-Shami.

They escorted him down the stairs, fed him into the car to the middle seat, to be flanked by the two troopers. Alan looked out through the glass, up to the window and those sad silhouettes. He prayed to Allah that they would be safe, that he would see them again insha'allah, and stifled the anguish of loss that was already dripping into his heart. Then mentally closing the shutters on his emotions, he started to think and plan.

*****

Over three and a half thousand miles away in Mansourieh, the darkness of night was beginning to fade. In the cool blue-tinged twilight of the early morning that filtered in through the half-opened curtains, Marina was standing on the carpet by the bed, already wearing the previously discarded underwear. Unzipping the side pocket of the sling bag, she retrieved her mobile and from the main pocket, the supressed Baby Glock. She looked across the bed at Tarek's sleeping form and softly cleared her throat. The rhythmic soughing of his breathing never faltered and the only movements, the rise and fall of his chest.

She walked out into the living room and headed for the table with the laptop. Assuming that Aaron had probably hacked it, she ignored the computer to concentrate on more physical items. She sifted quickly through the papers on the side, glancing at each one in turn. Carefully opening the two drawers, she poked her way through the mundane assortment of paper clips, pens, a stapler, a stack of business cards. Nothing. She ran her fingers lightly across the pad of paper, paused, and then repeated the movement. The indentations were faint but definitely there, as though he had written something down with a ballpoint pen or rollerball, then stripped off the top two sheets. Tearing off the top sheet, she folded it into a small square and tucked it into the top of her knickers.

The shelves were more complicated and deeper in shadow; using her mobile as a makeshift torch, she searched in front and behind books, the backs of photographs and even decorative statuettes. A carved wooden box with mother of pearl inlay on the lid was filled with lumps of cannabis resin and a plastic bag of grass. Marina searched the room for over half an hour before she gave up, deciding that it was time. She padded back into the bedroom, slipped the mobile back into her bag and walked around to Tarek's side of the bed. Nothing had changed, not his breathing or the movements of his chest, but from this angle she could see the beatific smile on his face. She smiled back lifted the Glock with two hands, pointed the gun at his head, flipped off the safety and pulled the trigger. The hammer fell on the empty chamber with a dull snap.

'They don't work without bullets bitch.'

Marina's head shot up to find Ayesha, dressed in jeans and a t-shirt pointing a gun that looked to be a good match to her own, the suppressor adding to the similarity. The only sound was Ayesha's laughter as she let a stream of bullets rain from her hand onto the sheets. With the speed of a cobra, Marina leaped over the corner of the bed in offensive attack. Ayesha calmly shot her in the arm as she landed; Marina had not even noticed the low cough of the gun. Knocked to the ground, she nursed her wounded right arm with her left, gritting her teeth against the burning pain.

'You fucking Palestinian piece of shit.'

Ayesha kicked the wounded arm hard with the outside edge of her foot.

'Marina? What's going on? Ayesha?'

Half awake, Tarek leaned up on his elbows and peered over the end of the bed. Marina looked back at him from her seat on the carpet, her face contorted with pain.

'Tarek help me,' she said, trying to be appealing. 'Your sister's insane. She just fucking shot me in the arm. Get the gun.' Her voice had become shriller and angrier. 'Take her fucking gun and kill the bitch, Tarek,' she screamed.

Another kick to her wounded arm silenced her voice, sending agonising knives of pain into all the shattered nerves.

'She tried to kill you Tarek,' said Ayesha. She leaned down to retrieve Marina's pistol and threw it on the sheet in front of her brother. 'With this. I found it in her handbag last night and unloaded the magazine. Earlier this morning she rummaged through your desk, all the shelves etcetera, etcetera and found nothing.'

She glanced back to Marina, leaned down again her hand outstretched towards the woman on the floor. Marina smashed the hand away with her good arm; Ayesha slapped her hard in the face, then reached down and pulled the square of paper from her knickers. 'Except this.' Unfolding the paper she held it up to the light, trying to read the indentations. 'Which might be a list of ships. Or might not. Why not come with us to blow up HMS York? She's a fucking Israeli spy, Tarek.'

Ayesha shot Marina in the other arm with surgical precision.

15 ~ Damage Limitation

Monochrome grey twilight had given way to a pale blue dawn, coloured by the rising sun's golden tint, as yet to share its innate warmth. Blue morning light, cold and harsh, has no kindness or feeling but a sharpness that brightens highlights and darkens shadows. But where those early rays touch kindred colours in that spectrum of reds and browns to yellow, they may lend a glow that is almost ethereal.

In that light, some colour had returned to the drawn skin of her face and her shoulders took on an almost bronzed tint. A tattoo of red rings decorated the top of each arm where rough tourniquets had been applied to slow the bleeding. Below that the colour appeared to have leached out of both arms that rested on the brown satin legs that just caught a hint of the morning glow. Her wounds had been bandaged with functional grey military field dressings, her ankles secured to the upright chair with white cable ties. They provided stark contrast to the delicate rose coloured lace bra and knickers that were her only clothing. The result was a strangely surreal picture of a semi-naked woman, blending sensuality with violent abuse, sitting sideways in a frame of drab normality.

From the relative safety of the living room, Tarek stared out at his erstwhile lover barely understanding what had happened. The raw nerve endings of his emotions rubbed against each other as though each was trying to inflict more damage and confusion. There was an abyss of immediate loss: of unlikely friendship found, better sex than he'd ever experienced and perhaps even love. Already he missed the electricity of her touch, the satin feel of her skin under his fingers, the taste of her lips and liquid tongue. He could still hear the warm melody of her laughter and see the fond and gentle mockery in her eyes. But anger stood on the edge of the abyss with the bow of betrayal and a quiver full of lies.

'For fuck's sake Tarek, stop feeling so fucking sorry for yourself!' Ayesha's voice was harsh and unforgiving but also confidently commanding. 'Leave the bitch to think about her lifestyle; you need to pack some clothes.'

Tarek didn't recognise this woman who looked so much like his sister. He remembered the cold look in her eyes when she'd shot Marina for the second time, as though dispatching some kind of rodent; the way she'd kicked her wounded arm with calculated cruelty, untempered by remorse. He watched Ayesha drag her out of the room by her legs, through the living room and out onto the balcony. She'd made him lift Marina onto the chair, hold her there while she concentrated on tying tourniquets and leg restraints. And once all that was done, Ayesha had tended her with gentle care, carefully cleaning the wounds, disinfecting and bandaging them up with practised skill. Even injecting two ampoules of morphine to absorb the pain when it kicked in properly.

'Tarek! Faisal and Naseem will be here in one hour; they will not want to keep Abdul Saad waiting. You have to pack a bag with a change of clothes and a warm jacket. Naseem told me we may be away for a while. Perhaps even for a month.'

Tarek stared at his sister, once again wondering how well he really knew her, or what she did.

'How do you know all this?' he asked, suspicion adding sibilance to his voice.

'I called him earlier to tell him about her,' she said, nodding towards the balcony.

'What I meant,' he said through gritted teeth, 'was how do you know Naseem? How is it that you have his phone number?'

'The simple answer is: he gave it to me Tarek. I've known Faisal and Naseem for quite a while; we met shortly after you went to England to meet Ali and Amin.'

'But they're al-Qaeda members!' Tarek blurted out, 'You called them 'Wahhabi fanatics who believe that all non-Muslims should be killed'. I remember it clearly, and agree, that this was about Palestine and Palest ...'

'Be quiet Tarek, and listen,' she said curtly. 'I told you at the time, I wanted to be involved as long as the bombings were not carried out in the name of Islam, or on the irrational whim of a stoned imam of some fanatical religious faction. But I needed to be sure and you didn't convince me that you knew all the facts.' She paused, seeing the look on his face. 'Don't give me that wounded-look shit. You're an academic who had a plan. What did you expect? It wasn't difficult to track Faisal down; he's a gofer for al-Qaeda, acts as a linkman with Hezbollah and has connections with the PLO. If you're plugged in, he's an easy man to find because he wants information that he can sell. Faisal introduced me to Naseem who in turn, introduced me to Abdul Saad al-Kabuli. And he did convince me.

'Tarek, he's called al-Kabuli because he's an Afghan and comes from Kabul. His links with al-Qaeda go back to when he was with the mujahideen fighting the Soviets. So yes, he's an al-Qaeda commander but his primary allegiance is to Afghanistan. He's demanded the evacuation of Western troops from Afghanistan and Iraq, sanctions on Israel and Palestinian sovereignty. In many ways we share the same ambitions. I trust him. And I like him: he's intelligent, single-minded and he's got a great sense of humour.'

The normal balance of things had been turned upside down. Tarek shook his head from side to side as though that might clear the fog of unreality that clouded his mind.

'That's why you weren't surprised when you got my text, isn't it? Because you knew about it before I did. I suppose you're sleeping with him as well!'

'Abdul Saad is Afghan and proud of his heritage; he's true to his country and his faith. So the answer is no and nor will it happen. Is guilt suddenly raising its ugly head from your sea of lust brother? With all your moralising and pompous lecturing, you forgot your beloved religion as soon as that one dropped her knickers.'

Ayesha looked at Tarek's face that was red with anger or perhaps embarrassment; she doubted that shame flickered anywhere in her brother's mind. She shook her head in mild despair.

'I'm so-so-sorry,' he stuttered. 'I didn't mean … it's just that … Everything happened so fast. One minute it was all wonderful and then, you just shot her! I can't believe she's a spy. Why would she make love to me like that?'

'Tarek, you're beginning to whine, and you're about to make me vomit. She didn't make love, she fucked you brainless and then, like some humanoid praying mantis, she was going to kill you. How many normal people go round with a silenced loaded gun and a spare clip of ammunition? Who searches through someone's house in the dark, using a mobile phone to provide just enough light to see but not to be noticed? And then there was this vicious little toy, tucked away in her bag.'

Pulling the knife from its leather sheath, she put her forefinger through the ring at the top of the white bone handle and let it hang in the air. The sharp curved blade glinted in the morning light that had started to chase away the shadows. She turned her hand, allowing the handle to fall naturally into the palm, closing her fingers comfortably round the carved bone. With the speed and fluidity of a striking rattlesnake, she swung her steel clawed fist in a wide horizontal arc, the needle tip only centimetres from Tarek's stomach. He blanched and she laughed, but there was no humour in the sound.

'A little closer brother and your guts would be spilling across the floor.' Ayesha slipped the blade back into its sheath and pushed it into her belt. 'Now forget the bitch and fucking pack!'

Quailing from Ayesha's long tirade, Tarek walked towards the bedroom but turned back to face her before entering.

'Where are we going? You said it might be for a month; the message simply said a boat ride.'

'A long boat ride. You know, you were right and I was wrong and Abdul Saad agrees with you: one is not enough. Today we send HMS York to hell, then sail south through the canal to Suez and the Red Sea. Our plan, Sayyid al-Kabuli's plan,' she said, correcting herself and carefully adding the honorific, 'is to head for the Strait of Hormuz. We anchor in one of the bays to the north of the Musandam Peninsula and we wait. Abdul Saad believes that we can pick off the next one, HMS Edinburgh, if we get the timing right, just after it passes Musandam on its way to Bahrain. If need be we can run across the Strait to Qeshm; once we're Iranian waters, they cannot follow.'

'And then what?'

'If, if we have to go to Iran, then we will have to make our way by land, but that is not the plan. Abdul Saad is sure that with the dhow, we can leave unnoticed and we sail for Gwadar in Balochistan. From there I'm not sure, he mentioned going to Lahore. Enough, you have ten minutes.'

Tarek walked slowly into the bedroom, retrieved a flight bag from the wardrobe and began to pack. With no idea what to take or comprehension of what was happening, he packed in a state of abstraction barely aware of what he was putting into the bag. Ayesha packed both guns and the spare magazine in her kitbag, added a box of 9mm ammunition and Marina's mobile. She walked out onto the balcony to check the woman, to see if she was awake, noted the flicker of eyes and returned inside. Marina stared calmly straight ahead, aware of the other woman's presence but refusing to give her the pleasure of turning her head in subservient acknowledgement. Her mind was spinning slowly, assessing, thinking and planning.

Earlier she'd cursed herself for assuming that it would just be the two of them in the house. It should have been as it was before; but that was an hour ago. Thanks to the morphine, the pain in her arms was more of a dull ache but the damaged muscles allowed little movement and even less strength. But there was nothing wrong with her basic faculties such as hearing and speech; and she had heard plenty. But morphine is a soft, hazy comforter and their words had sounded clear but far away. She blinked. What use was information when it lay stored in your head? There would be a way, had to be. She felt something sharp touch her cheek, remaining still until the light pressure was removed.

Ayesha stepped around the chair to face Marina, the karambit reversed in her hand so that the claw was curving upwards. In her other hand she carried a light cotton garment, a woman's white djellaba.

'You can't come without clothes and this will cover you for the journey. I've had it for years, it's Moroccan. So, I'm going to free your legs and help you put it on but if you try anything, I will cut you with your little knife.' Ayesha turned her face to let Marina see the old scar that might have faded with the years but still snaked clearly down the side of her face. 'Like this, but worse.' She reached out to touch Marina's cheek with the steel point, pressing just hard enough to let a tiny drop of blood bead on her skin. 'You understand?'

'I get the point,' she said, with a thin smile.

385

Strangely, Ayesha returned the smile, almost wishing that things could have been otherwise. Kneeling down she cut the cable ties and rubbed life back into the ankles with her free hand. She helped Marina stand, eased the sleeves of the djellaba over her arms, carefully pulling it upwards and over her shoulders. She fitted the small button knots through the loops down the front of the beautifully embroidered coat.

'You know, I wish we could have met under other circumstances,' Marina said quietly.

They heard the sound of a car. Ayesha said nothing, taking her by her arm and keeping the karambit clearly in view.

'Yallah!' she commanded, now pushing Marina from behind.

They put Marina in the back seat of Faisal's car, locked between Ayesha and Naseem. Tarek sat in the passenger seat, unable to look at the three people behind. Faisal glanced pointedly in his rear view mirror, flicking his eyes from Marina to Naseem.

'It's fine, she's not going anywhere Faisal.'

He nodded, switched on the ignition and headed down the hill. Rather than taking the main road into Beirut, Faisal took them through the vanilla high-rise residential towers of suburban Dekwaneh along silent sterile roads. The green trees and landscaped emptiness gave way to the maze of narrow streets of Bourj Hammoud, or as some call it, Little Armenia. Home to Armenians, Kurds, Shiites, Syrians, Ethiopians and more, Bourj Hamoud was a vibrant, bustling machine that kept the knife to the whetstone and its eyes on the blade's edge. No one noticed or commented on the unremarkable car as it passed through. No one spoke inside the car, each one either watching the world as it went by the window or silently thinking.

Faisal fed onto Charles Hellou Avenue heading west, running parallel to the coastline. As before with the taxi, that first time when Tarek had met al-Kabuli, Faisal turned in towards the old St Georges Hotel, turning left again following the line of the marina as it curved round the bay. Drove the car to the end of the jetty, turning in at an angle to face across the marina. In the clear light of the early morning, the usual glare of the yachts and power launches was rendered to a flat bone white; the painted wooden hulls of the smaller boats seemed dingy and faded. The oily water was no longer exotically iridescent but a slickly flat, matt black undulating surface. A chill salt wind was blowing in from the sea, breaking on the masts and stays of the yachts; the sound like the laments of unseen mourners in the sky.

This time there was no waiting. The slim speedboat was already hugging the dockside, its powerful engines at rumbling idle in contrast to the vibrato cries of the stays. Naseem pulled gently but insistently at Marina's arm, easing her out of the car and onto the tarmac outside. Without complaint, she allowed herself to be guided and helped into the boat. When Ayesha dropped lightly into the boat from the quay, Naseem imperceptibly nodded his approval; when Tarek clambered down heavily, he frowned. Visually checking that all was in order, the coxswain eased the throttle open and guided the boat smoothly to the entrance. Left on the quayside by the car, Faisal watched them disappear beyond the sea defence of piled concrete blocks, heard the roar of the engines as the throttle was opened wide and turned back to the car.

The Rih Albahr was less than two kilometres out at sea, gently rolling in the swell with her anchor still on the sea floor. As the coxswain expertly came alongside, Naseem tied mooring lines fore and aft to rings fixed on the hull. Helping Marina to her feet, he led her to the side, put his hands around her waist and lifted her into the air as though she weighed no more than a baby. The pain arced across her shoulders and arms as two pairs of rough hands slipped underneath her armpits, lifting her over the gunwale with one swift, coordinated movement. Naseem and Ayesha followed, now like two cats leaping lightly onto a wall, sharing the moment and then alighting soundlessly on the deck. And as before, Tarek was left to drag himself up the short ladder like a sloth not quite ready for a vertical climb.

The canvas sidewalls of the long deck canopy had been pulled down and secured to the deck. Inside all was the same: the long floor sofas stretched out on the rug-covered deck either side of the low well-worn wooden table, the cushions propped up against the bulwarks through the canvas walls. Al-Kabuli was sitting in his seat below the window of the bridge, scanning a maritime map of the Eastern Mediterranean. As the group appeared at the

387

end of the canopy and moved towards him, al-Kabuli looked up from his work.

'Good, you have arrived; so now it is time to leave.' The sound of a powered windlass raising the anchor from the seabed echoed a response to the implied command, accompanied by the rasping clanking of the chain as the links passed over the gypsy wheel. Al-Kabuli nodded his head in approval. 'Thank you Hassan. Take her west past Al-Manara for 16 kilometres then set a course for 193 degrees south by west. Make sure that Mohammed keeps his eye on the radar; HMS York may be in a group of two or three ships. But there may be more than one group. We have to identify York visually to ensure that she is in range. With visibility as it is, sightline to the horizon should be around eight kilometres. Tell me when you have sightings.'

'Of course Sayyid.'

'Naseem, bring them closer.'

As the four approached, Al-Kabuli indicated the men to sit on his right and the women to the left.

'I am glad to see brother and sister together today, and both alive. And you, tell me you name?' he asked Marina.

She looked at him with unwavering eyes but said nothing.

'Your name,' he repeated, but no words came in return. 'You should know, I estimate that it will be perhaps over two hours before we meet the York. I think it will probably be somewhere between Sidon and Tyre but it might be further. So we have plenty of time to talk and enjoy each other's company. Your arms are bleeding.'

Bright red stains had blossomed on the white sleeves of the borrowed djellaba. A consequence perhaps of the squeeze in the back seat of Faisal's car and, more probably, the way she'd been hauled up onto the deck of the ship. Marina glanced down at her arms and then back to al-Kabuli, understanding the implied threat.

'Marina.'

'Marina what?'

'El-Aoun.'

'That's a Lebanese name.'

'Of course, I'm Lebanese.'

'Ayesha thinks you're an Israeli spy.'

'I'm not a spy!'

'And I am not stupid. You carry a silenced gun and a knife, you search for information or something else in the house, and Ayesha tells me you know krav maga fighting moves. It's unlikely you would learn an Israeli military self-defence and attack system in Beirut. Let us concentrate on the truth.'

'I met Tarek, I thought he was handsome, intelligent and fun. Why would I spy on him? And I carry the gun and knife for protection. I'm alone in Beirut, I have no one to protect me.'

'Naseem, please go sit with our guest.'

Rising without the help of his hands, Naseem stepped over the table and slipped down beside Marina.

'Ayesha, please hold Marina's shoulders. Marina, if you do not answer honestly your journey with us will be painful. Naseem will start to break your fingers. Let me give you an example. Naseem.'

The man's fingers wrapped around the woman's wrist like a vice, forcing her hand down on the table, holding it there. He prised the little finger of her left hand from the wood, pushing it slowly backward beyond the point of return. It broke with a dull snap like a slim dry twig, twisted away at an unnatural angle. She grimaced at the sudden pain.

'I am sorry that we have to do this,' said al-Kabuli, holding out his arms, palms turned upwards. 'But what should I do? You must help me Marina El-Aoun who is only in love and is not a spy. So, let us try again.'

As the Sea Wind sailed south, al-Kabuli's brutal interrogation continued. Naseem broke another finger before Marina started to weave a story that combined truth with fiction. Yes, she was technically an Israeli but not Jewish or Zionist, she told him. She was born in Haifa, lived with her parents who were Druze; her father referred to himself as an Israeli Druze and supported the State, sometimes saying that he was a non-Jewish patriot. She was 18 when she was conscripted into the IDF, Marina told him; it was where she learned the techniques of krav maga, how to shoot and use a knife. But she never shared her parents' views nor their pro-Israeli beliefs.

After serving her two years in the IDF, she headed for Lebanon, crossed the border near Marwahin. Marina told him that she'd worked her up through the country with the help of Lebanese Druze to join the fight in Beirut. Like them she was in favour of pan-Arabism and the Palestinian resistance, she said, fought the Lebanese Front alongside fighters of the PLO in the civil war. She fought with the militias who supported the Druze Progressive Socialist Party, with the PLO and the Syrians who backed them, in the Mountain War in the Chouf District. And when it all finished, she stayed in Beirut, made her home there, she said.

The questions were unceasing, backwards and forwards between the past and the present. The only voices to be heard were those of Abdul Saad al-Kabuli and Marina El-Aoun. Against the accusation that she was a spy, she wove a tapestry of dissimulation and deceit. She swore that she had lost her mind to Tarek, was desperate to find something to hold over him, to keep him for herself. Al-Kabuli seemed to find that last part particularly humorous but when he stopped laughing, he invited Naseem to break yet another of Marina's slender fingers.

'Sayyid, we have three ships on the radar, to the south.'

'How far Hassan?'

'Mohammed believes it is 18 kilometres but it will not be so long before we have a visual contact since we are travelling in opposing directions.'

'Of course. Ladies and gentlemen, let us go to look at the grand NATO ships that protect us on lawless seas.'

Picking up a pair of large green rubberised Steiner M2080 military binoculars from beside his seat, al-Kabuli rose and walked beyond the canopy to the rail near the bow. Ayesha and Naseem followed, each one lightly holding one of Marina's arms as she walked with them. Tarek followed in their wake, his face still ashen with disbelief at what he had witnessed within the space of a few hours. The line of five looked to the southwest, across an undulating blue-green sea to a faded blue sky in which a golden sun held reign. They waited silently, expectantly in the strong salty fresh breeze, five sets of eyes scanning the horizon for tiny grey rectangles.

'Sayyid, two ships over there.'

Naseem was pointing across the bow to the far horizon where two barely perceptible grey shapes had appeared. Training the powerful binoculars on the broad area, al-Kabuli quickly located the pair of warships. Sailing northwards along the Lebanese coastline, their course was running parallel to the Sea Wind's southerly route. He scanned along the hull of the first of the two destroyers and found the pennant number D561; then as the boat slipped through the water, the name Francesco Mimbelli, painted near the stern. The Italian flag fluttered proudly above in the wind driven by the ship's own velocity. Al-Kabuli shifted to the second ship, saw the brave Union Jack flying from the short jackstaff on the bow, the pair of Sea Darts mounted on the twin launcher on the foredeck and the pennant number D98 painted clearly on the hull.

'HMS York I believe,' he said quietly. 'Professor, the stage is yours.'

Tarek stared at the two ships in the distance, so far away. It hadn't been like this in Cyprus, where he and Ayesha had seen the Gloucester. He'd seen the missiles and the ship from the quay, almost close enough to touch. He remembered Ayesha stretching out her hand towards the grey metal, talking to the marine on guard duty and even seeing one or two sailors on deck. That had all made it personal, allowed him to focus on revenge on a defined clear target. But this wasn't personal, these tiny grey blocks moving along the horizon meant nothing, had no identity or even clear form. Tarek suddenly felt alone, isolated in his thoughts and hardly aware of the people around him. Their voices seemed muffled, white noise in his ears.

'Professor.'

'Tarek, do it now!'

'Don't do it Tarek! It's murder!'

He felt a hand in his pocket lifting the transmitter out; without looking or thinking, he swung his arm outwards, his fist clenched. It met hard stomach muscles that easily absorbed the backward punch.

'No!' he screamed as the device clattered on the deck.

Undisturbed by her brother's wild and feeble assault, Ayesha bent down to retrieve the small black mobile look-a-like, stepping away from Tarek. She glanced back to assess the situation: Naseem had a firm hold on Marina while al-Kabuli himself had both his hands locked on Tarek's shoulders. She turned to look outwards, across the expanse of grey-green water under the now overcast dull sky. By feel, she pressed the power button and then looked down at the small screen; keyed in 02 and watched the fanning signal searching for its hidden mate. Time on pause, in limbo. Until it stopped and locked on. Drawing a slight breath, Ayesha mashed her thumb down on the red button and looked up.

Apart from the soft slapping of the bow wave, the whispering of the swell and the rough hum of the engines, the world was silent. Nothing for an interminable fraction of a second. Then a little puff of grey smoke on the horizon, that rapidly grew in form and volume. The sound of the first explosion followed almost immediately: a roaring, blasting bang that assailed both body and eardrums. The spumes of grey-white smoke and grey-green sea that mixed together in the air above the stricken destroyer were soon overtaken by oily billows of blackened smoke with a angry core of red-gold flames. More explosions followed, hard on the heels of the first as other Sea Darts detonated in the fierce heat of the hellish conflagration. Within minutes all that could be seen of HMS York was the thin line of the hull below an ever growing, towering mass of black-grey smoke lined with dark fires.

They stood silently on the deck of the Rih Albahr, the group of five near the bow and the crew strung out along the gunwales to the stern. They could hear the sharp staccato fire of ammunition detonating, a rapid snare drum to the loud bass notes of greater explosions. But they couldn't hear the screams of the wounded and the dying, the shriek of torn hot metal or the fierce thunder of the burning flames. Nor could they see the molten steel, shattered bodies or the rivers of steaming blood.

'Sayyid, we should go,' Naseem advised.

Al-Kabuli nodded, signalled to Hassan. As the dhow came up to full speed, the view of the burning ship disappeared behind them and no one looked back.

'Ayesha, bring your sad pathetic brother. We should sit down, take some refreshment and talk. Today's work is finished and you should be proud of what you have done. I am proud of what you have done. Come.' He turned as though to walk back under the canopy to his seat, then stopped and turned. 'Keep hold of the Professor. Naseem, get rid of the woman.'

'Sayyid.'

Every muscle instantly responding, Naseem casually gripped Marina's waist with both hands, lifted her up above the railing and threw her overboard. Her screams of outrage and shock were silenced in the foam of Rih Albahr's bow wave and the Mediterranean swells.

*****

He'd switched the headlights back on when they'd left the cottage, aware of the fact that time really was of the essence. Heavy shadowed clouds had spread across the sky in an uneven ceiling that obscured both stars and moon making the depth of darkness almost palpable. It had started drizzling somewhere between Llwyn-on Reservoir and the tiny village of Nant Ddu, making him switch the windscreen wipers on intermittently. Nevertheless Ed Clarkson had made good time, driving quickly and expertly on the all but empty roads of the Brecon Beacons.

Bwthyn Llwyd stood on its own, a few miles from Pen y Fan itself, down a stony track only negotiable with a four-wheel drive vehicle. Perhaps three hundred years old, the stone cottage was not built for modern times or those people used to such refinements as central heating, insulation or double-glazing. When they'd arrived, it had been cold, wet, dark and uninviting. One of the troopers had built a fire in the iron grate that stood in the massive hearth that dominated what passed for a living room. The other fired up the ancient Aga in the kitchen beyond. But they put Alan Abbot in the only other room on the ground floor.

In another century it might have been a byre for a few cattle but now it served as an isolation cell. Rising to the full height of the two-storey house, wooden timbers and planks formed the high ceiling above which were only roof slates and the sky. The small window at one end was boarded and nailed firmly shut. The larger one at the other end boasted an iron grille instead of glass allowing free entry to the wind and rain. Otherwise only dark grey granite walls surrounded the basic furnishings in the room: a heavy wooden table that might have once graced a kitchen, three wooden chairs and a low slatted wooden bed. Alan lay on his back on the thick white cotton sheet that covered the thin mattress and wondered how long it would be before they started.

Dark night began to slowly fade a long 90 minutes later, giving way to a dim grey twilight, opaque with heavy drizzle. Sitting on the broad window ledge, he stared out into the murk lightened by sporadic swirls of white mist floating like angel hair on unseen breaths of air. What might have been a wall, perhaps a farm building or a tractor, all became abstract forms where lines and forms blurred. Occasional brushstrokes of dim semi-colours: the dull grey-green that might have been grass or a dark dirty speckled reddish-brown memory of ancient machinery long since turned to rust. The watered down colours served to ameliorate the drabness of the unknown outside. Another hour or so went past before he heard the door open and the sound of boots on the stone floor but he didn't turn.

'You want to be called Alan, Ali or arsehole? Personally I don't actually give a shit what you want, but it's only polite to ask. In the same way as, it's only polite to look at someone when they're talking to you.'

Alan swivelled off the window ledge to put both feet on the ground, turning to look at the speaker. The voice was the same as the one he'd heard in their bedroom, the one who'd told him he was being arrested but that man hadn't had a face. Mike was still wearing the black assault suit but the balaclava was gone. He looked him in the eye, searched his face for clues as to his personality or for weakness but found no obvious vulnerability. The brown flop of hair might be an affectation but the face was strong, determined, professionally confident and unreadable. He stood up to mirror the stance of the man in front of him.

'Alan will do just fine,' he said. 'And you? What do I call you?'

'Major will do. Let's sit.'

Alan shrugged, following Mike's example who'd pulled up a chair and sat down. The rasp and crunch of something heavy being rattled across stone materialised in the doorway as Ed Clarkson dragging a gas heater into the room.

'As usual it's colder than a witch's tit in here, you might need this later. If we let you.'

Mike made no introduction but waited until Ed was seated before starting the questions.

'Let's begin with the easy stuff. Tell me exactly why you want to blow up the Royal Navy's ships? I mean, you've got to have a bloody good reason for wanting to blow up a destroyer and murder hundreds of innocent people. So what's your reason? I want to understand.'

'Why would I want to blow up destroyers, Major? I run a factory that supplies the armed forces, including the Royal Navy, with arms such as missiles and rockets. Blowing up ships would be self-limiting, losing the company money and putting my livelihood into jeopardy. Not to mention the possibility of being thrown into prison for a very long time. As well as my job with Forbes, I have a wonderful family and a very pleasant lifestyle; why on earth would I want to throw all that away? Major, I have no motive.'

'You've obviously read about the bombing of HMS Gloucester in Cyprus?'

'Of course. An awful atrocity carried out by al-Qaeda and I feel so sorry for the families of those who died. But exactly what has that to do with me?'

'Fourteen people died on that ship. They had careers with a future, just like you; some of them had families, just like you. But for some reason, you and your friends decided to blow them off the face of the fucking earth! And I want to know why.'

Mike glared at him as though he could get a confession or extract information, simply by force of will. Alan held his gaze.

'I did not kill the crew nor did I blow up the Gloucester, Major. I haven't been out of the country.'

Reaching out for the envelope that Ed had brought with him, Mike pulled out a small stack of photographs. Pushed them across to Alan's side of the table and fanned them out.

'These were taken on the Gloucester a few days after the explosion. That's the foredeck where the Sea Darts were mounted on the launcher, including the one you sabotaged. The heat melted the deck but fortunately that didn't detonate any of the missiles still in the magazine. Small blessing for us; bit of a bummer for you I'd say.'

'Major, I cannot ...'

'Shut the fuck up until I've finished! This one was taken from what was left of the bow; what you're looking at is the mangled burned remains of the bridge and several fine officers. The next one shows some of the missiles left in the magazine and that one's a close-up. Recognise the markings? Those missiles came from your factory; we've double-checked the serial numbers. And this one,' Mike said, picking up a separate photograph from his pile, 'is a picture taken at Cedars' Stand of a dummy bomb. I believe you called them NuCans.'

'Major, I have absolutely no idea what you're talking about.'

Mike Roberts leaned towards him over the table, grabbed a handful of shirt and yanked Alan forwards.

'If you don't tell me what I want to know of your own free fucking will, I will bury you so deep that you'll be climbing upwards to hell!' Mike threw him backwards with intended force, the momentum sending Alan's body onto the back of the chair; the imbalance accelerated the motion, slamming his head and shoulders into the wall behind.

Spitting involuntary expletives, Alan felt the back of his head and his hand came away bloody.

'You're out of line, Major. As far as I know, beating someone up who you've arrested on some specious charge is against the law and gross contravention of human rights. It's illegal. You can't just try to beat information out …'

Mike's right hand shot across the table in a narrow arc, the back slamming against the side of Alan's face.

'Oh I think I can, Abbot, I really think I can. There are no cameras or microphones in Bwthyn Llwyd and the people here won't talk, will you Captain?'

'About what Major?'

'My point, I think. Listen carefully Abbot because I have a very short fuse and I'm in a hurry. Colleagues of mine caught up with your mate Amin Masri with his lovely wife Sophie in Dubai. He sang like a nightingale before he was sent back to the UK. He's sitting in a cell somewhere and, I believe, his wife's been allowed to go back to Cedars' Stand. We'll talk about you, Megan and Anwen later.' Mike pushed across another photograph. 'I'm sure you recognise Masri and his wife. After all, the three of you did spend some time with them on his boat together. What was it called? Sirens' Choice if I remember rightly. And the other guy, Tarek al-Shami, he was there too. Three old friends together. Just like Byblos in '73, last century when you were kids.

'Where was I? Oh yeah, according to Masri, al-Shami organised the bomb production with Dr Malik in Pakistan, Masri imported them ready perfumed, got rid of the smell and delivered them to you at Leigh Delamere. Presumably you then ...'

A knock on the door was followed by one of the troopers coming straight in without waiting.

'Sir, I'm really sorry to interrupt but apparently this is urgent. Admiral Buller's on the satphone and he needs to talk to you now.'

'Shit. Captain, run the rest of it past Abbot.'

Shutting the door behind him, Mike followed Jamie through into the kitchen, picked up the Iridium satphone from the table and went over to the stable door on the far side. Leaning out through the open top half for reception, he lifted the phone to his ear.

'Yes Admiral, it's Mike Roberts Sir.'

'Mike, the bastards have blown up HMS York off the coast of South Lebanon.'

'Sir, we've got low cloud cover and heavy drizzle down here. Did you say that ...'

'The bastards blew up the York in the Eastern Med,' Buller said, completing the sentence. 'Sounds as though it was probably south of Tyre, latitude-wise not far from the Israeli border.'

'Christ!' Mike swore softly. 'When did it happen?'

'Less than an hour ago, York was following an Italian destroyer, the Francesco Mimbelli, 13.5 nautical miles off the coastline so they were keeping in international waters. Mimbelli was a reasonable distance ahead, has some damage to its stern but minor. Captain Agostini put out a mayday call as well as calling it in to both NATO operations in Brussels and Maritime Command Headquarters at Northwood.'

'How many ... the York must have been carrying a crew of what, 270 including officers?'

'A full complement of 287, but God alone knows how many are still alive. HMS York was sunk, Mike, totally destroyed by multiple explosions. The Francesco Mimbelli has picked up a few survivors and two Israeli patrol boats that were in the area have joined the search. Plus three fishing boats out of Sidon. That's all we know at the moment. There's nothing we can do to help the poor buggers but we have to prevent any more attacks. Your chap told me that you lifted Alan Abbot this morning and you've got him there?'

'Yes, I'd already started questioning him when you called.'

'Mike, I can't overstate how vital it is that we stop this carnage. We need the names and locations of the other ships now. You're sure he knows?'

'I can't be 100 per cent certain but, yeah, I'm sure he knows. In the end, Masri was totally clear that he delivered four explosive devices. Abbot has the knowledge, expertise and access. There's nobody else in the frame.'

Mike could hear the Admiral breathing, carefully considering his next words.

'Get that information Mike. I don't care if you have to surgically excise it from his bloody brain, make him talk.'

'As soon as I can Admiral. I'll call you later with an update Sir.'

'Good luck Major.'

Mike stared out into the swirls of mist that had started to dissipate in the strengthening light. Drizzle had turned to soft rain, falling from the blanket of grey-white cloud that the day had thrown over the landscape. A creamy brown shape lolloped across the yard, paused to scent the air with neck outstretched and nose quivering, before moving off into the long wet green grass. Mike smiled sadly, letting that immediate rush of anger fly away into the mist, wishing the rabbit would come back and make him smile some more. Turning back into the warmth of the kitchen, he walked across the living room to the closed door on the opposite side. Opening the door without knocking, Mike walked inside to stand by the window, looking out through the glass and the black rusted bars of the grille.

'Barely an hour ago, HMS York was blown up about 25 kilometres off the Lebanese coast. She was carrying a crew of 287 men and women, every one of them committed to preventing terrorism. They were there to enhance maritime security in the

Med, there to help protect the peace. But most of them aren't alive any more because you and your friends murdered them in cold blood!'

His voice rising with emotion as the anger tried to return, Mike turned to look at the man sitting opposite Ed Clarkson. In that moment he didn't see Alan Abbot the intelligent British engineer with a Masters from Cranfield; he saw Ali Abbas, a rabid Palestinian terrorist with fanatical eyes, black with hatred. As Mike walked towards him, Alan jackknifed upwards, leaving his chair clattering on the floor. Presenting Mike with a three quarter view of his body, he stood calmly poised, awaiting the potential confrontation. Ed was on his feet a split second later. And the three men froze in a tableau of pent up aggression, each assessing the possible chains of reaction. While the two main protagonists stared at each other, Ed looked from one to the other, unsure of how to support his superior and simultaneously prevent deadly chaos.

'There is no point in violence here,' Alan said, speaking directly to Mike. 'I will fight until one of us kills the other and I accept that it is likely that I will be the one to die. Masha'Allah. But then you achieve nothing but revenge. You learn nothing. In a way, you and I are similar: you want revenge for what you see as the inexplicable, callous murders of hundreds of your colleagues in the Navy. Tarek, Amin and I vowed to take personal revenge for an atrocity perpetrated by members of the British Royal Navy over 30 years ago; and I sought to avenge the persecution and oppression of Palestine and the Palestinians.'

'Trust me, you and I are not the same in any way, shape or form,' Mike snarled. 'In my book, you're a murderer and a fucking terrorist. And if I'm hearing correctly you've just admitted you are.'

'No I did not; but wait for one moment. In 1974 my father, mother and I went on a holiday to Cyprus with the al-Shamis and Masris. Our first day was spent on a beach near Paphos. We swam and splashed each other in the sea, played football on the beach, boys against girls. I remember it was a sunny day and very hot. There was a lot of laughter and everyone was happy. On our way back to Limassol, we were stopped by a military road block and after that the laughing stopped. There had been two bombs on a beach near the British base at Akrotiri and I think many servicemen and women were killed. The soldiers arrested my father and Tarek's and Amin's on suspicion of carrying out terrorist attacks. Do you know why Major? Because we were Palestinians, Lebanese, we were therefore automatically assumed to be connected to at least one terrorist organisation. What paranoid ill-informed xenophobic bullshit!

'The rest of us were taken away separately, forced to stay in a filthy apartment in a disused barracks block and the door guarded by two armed sailors. Later that night those two armed sailors unlocked the door and came in with more sailors. In their drunken blind anger, they blamed us all for what happened on that beach. There was no question in their minds as to our collective guilt. Tarek's mother and sister, Amin's mother and sister: all four of them were raped over and over again. We were powerless against grown men with guns; had to watch it all happen, unable to do anything. Not that we were excluded from the numerous punches and kicks.

'Even though my father and the other two were totally exonerated, there was no apology for the initial wrongful arrest. Not was there more than a whispered hasty apology for the rapes. As far as I'm aware, the filthy gutter sailors were never caught and I suspect that the news of the rapes was supressed. I was only nine at the time but I remember it all with too much clarity. Are you surprised that we wanted to avenge our families?'

'No. But taking revenge by killing and maiming innocent people is not ...'

'The right way to do things?' Alan laughed bitterly. 'What could three kids do about it back then? The Royal Navy must be held accountable and take responsibility for the crimes that their sailors committed. And it is ...'

'You little piece of shit! Fuck your father and your mother! I don't know who detonated the bombs but I do know that I was on Pissouri Beach when the bastards went off,' Mike spat. 'I heard the screams, the cries for help, saw the dead and wounded. And I saw my own mother lying in the sand with half of her left arm blown off. I think of that day every time I see her. What about my fucking revenge? I was only six but I haven't spent the rest of my life full of hate and planning revenge. You can't kill shadows

Abbas. What you and your friends have done has resulted in mass murder by carrying out acts of terrorism.'

'How strange that we were both there, almost within sight of each other, at the same moments in time. I am truly sorry for you and your mother. Mine was murdered by a missile attack in Beirut, in the civil war. Maybe the British supplied the weapon, maybe the Americans, but I cannot apportion blame on supposition. However, you clearly aren't listening carefully. I was talking of revenge not terrorism. It's a curious truth that when just a few people seek revenge, they're called terrorists; when governments seek revenge or take sides, they call themselves liberators. But I suggest we don't waste time philosophising.' Turning his back on Mike, Alan leaned down to pick up his fallen chair and carefully set it down on all four legs. 'After the news of HMS York, I believe it's time to talk. Please.' He waved towards the chairs on the other side of the table, eyes flicking from one soldier to another. Not one of the three sat down but Mike moved closer towards Alan.

'You're good at talking, aren't you? Let me make myself very clear. At the moment every muscle in my body wants to help my hands tear you apart and the way I'm feeling right now, I might just do that anyway. But I need information first. So sit the fuck down and talk, without the philosophy, before I lose my temper and start removing your bodily parts to assist your memory.'

Mike hit Alan in the chest with a short jab from the heel of his hand; hard enough to send the man crashing back down on his chair.

'Mother fucker!' he gasped. 'Listen ...'

'No you listen. Then you imitate Masri, and sing like a fucking nightingale.'

Mike sat down facing him while Ed stayed standing.

'OK, let's cut to the chase. Do you admit to sabotaging missiles with explosive devices, knowing that they would be delivered to Royal Navy ships?'

'Yes. Or more accurately, I'm telling you that I installed explosive devices in four Sea Dart missiles which were delivered to four separate ships. Major, please let me stop this measured line of questioning which could go on for hours. So far, bombs have been detonated on two ships: the first did not shake the world or really get the media's attention. The sinking of HMS York will. After all these years, I believe that our families have been avenged, which is a personal and perhaps selfish matter.

'I'm sure you've seen the video given to Al Jazeera after the bombing of the Gloucester. Of course, the Sheikh claims that al-Qaeda is responsible but remember his explicit demands: for Western forces to leave Afghanistan and Iraq, sanctions on Israel, free passage for Palestinians and Palestinian sovereignty. What happened to HMS York will have global coverage and bring those issues firmly back into the limelight. Again, I believe that sinking another ship would not further those causes beyond this point.'

The room fell silent as Alan stopped talking, letting Mike and Ed digest what they'd heard. Not wanting to talk out of turn, Ed looked questioningly at Mike, a hint of a frown wrinkling around his eyes.

'Go ahead,' Mike said with a shrug.

'You're saying that al-Qaeda funded everything?'

'I didn't, but yes, al-Qaeda funded the operation.'

'Where's Tarek al-Shami?'

'I have absolutely no idea. Do you?'

'No,' replied Ed. And stopped his questions.

Mike studied the man and, not for the first time, wondered at his calm. Abbot was an academic technician, an engineer, and yet he had the balance, awareness and mindset of a soldier or fighter.

'What do you want Abbot?'

'Freedom Major, just as you want freedom; only the details are variable. I want guaranteed safe passage out of the country for my family and I. And the same thing for Amin and Sophie. Five lives to save more than six hundred would seem a fair deal, Major.'

Ed couldn't stop a grin creasing his mouth and raised his eyes in amazement. Mike narrowed his eyes, staring at Alan who looked back without blinking.

'You're insane,' Mike said quietly. 'Or possibly very clever. But Whitehall will never agree; it goes against all the spin, about not negotiating with terrorists.'

'I think you'll find that you're wrong. Whitehall will not be negotiating with al-Qaeda which is naturally perceived as being responsible for the atrocities. Thanks to the resourcefulness and actions of the intelligence services et al, the destruction of two more ships will have been averted and hundreds of lives saved. Triumph over adversity and the global war on terror continues unabated. Hurrah. Apart from a very small number of people, nobody will hear of our very confidential agreement. We will leave the country and that will be the end of the affair. I suspect Whitehall will consider it to be a compromise born of necessity which in turn spawns a grudging win-win result.'

Mike found himself almost admiring the man's Machiavellian thought process.

'You haven't said what we get in return?'

'Simply information. The names of the two ships and their assumed locations. Where the devices are installed, how to safely remove them and deactivate the trigger mechanisms. Naturally we would be under house arrest, perhaps at one location, until both ships have been made safe. Once that's been achieved, we will be allowed to leave. Escorted from the country, if you like.'

'How do you know you can trust us? Why don't I tell you that's fine and you give us all the information; once it's all done and dusted, we lock you and Amin into Broadmoor for the duration? Or however long you last.'

The smile on Alan Abbot's face was honest and perhaps even a little conciliatory. He shrugged his shoulders, looked Major Mike Roberts in the eye.

'Because at this level of security, I trust you to honour the agreements made below the radar of the media. Naturally, I expect the final arrangements to be discussed in London and not in a cold damp room in a stone cottage buried somewhere in the wilderness.'

'Abbot, words rarely fail me but on this occasion, I'm struggling. You're an unbelievable cunt, but one has to admire the balls on you.' Mike sighed and shook his head. 'You want some coffee?'

'Please. Black with no sugar.'

'Ed?'

'Tea please, Major, thanks.'

'I'll get Jamie onto it while I call the Admiral.'

All so polite and almost normal, he thought as he walked out and back to the kitchen. Asking Jamie to make coffee and tea was a natural request. He picked up the Iridium satphone from the table, taking it over to the stable door. The rain had stopped and a few rays of sunshine were burning through the gossamer veil of mist, silvered gold on white. A spider's web stretched delicately across the dark green thorns of the gorse bush by the wall, it's exquisite tracery heavy with beads of dew that shone as bright diamonds in the ethereal light. Its simple beauty so vulnerable and transitory, constructed with malice and intent by the industrious arachnid, it could be torn down by a touch of the hairs on a passing rabbit's tail. Closing his mind to nature's brutal irony and more potential philosophising, he dialled Admiral Buller's encrypted direct number.

'Mike?'

'Yes, Admiral. Abbot's going for a deal.'

'Bloody hell! You're serious?'

'Yes Sir. And I think it's a genuine offer.'

The Admiral did not interrupt verbally during Mike's tale of the standoff in the small room and what Alan had said. The occasional grunt, snort and snarl might have been expected from the bellicose ex-mariner but even those were muted. Even Abbot's demand that the deal had to be done with the Admiral himself in London provoked little more than a soft curse. When Mike had finished, he waited patiently for Admiral Buller's response and could almost hear the man's mental machine running at full power.

'How long have we got to play with, Mike? Has he given you anything at all?'

'Based on the York's location when she was sunk, Abbot says we have a maximum of five days to deactivate the bombs before we're in the next danger time zone. That much he has told us, but until we agree to his side of the bargain we get nothing more.'

Another short silence. Mike could hear the sound of a bird's beak tapping somewhere on the wall, as though marking the seconds as they slowly ticked by.

'From what you've said, and what you haven't, you think that this is the best way forward, Major.'

'Personally I'd like to slowly cut the bastard up into little pieces and feed them to the dogs, Sir. I don't like it but cutting a deal is going to be our fastest way of getting to those bombs. I didn't expect it but Abbot's a tough bastard and he wouldn't break easily. By the looks of it, at some time in the past he's been used to street fighting. Squeezing information out of him by force could take a long time; longer than we can afford.'

'That's what I thought you'd say, Mike. And you think he's honest?'

'Yeah, I do. It's the way he said the bit about trusting us because of the unique circumstances. And there's something else … I think this was planned. He knew the chances of everything tracking back to him were high and this was clearly his best exit strategy. It's ironic that the turning point came today: the sinking of the York achieved his key objectives, we'd already lifted him and the rest becomes history.'

'I see what you mean. OK, bring him to London today. How long will it take you?'

'Should be around four hours, Sir. Where do you want him?'

'Take him to Kentish Town, the house on Montpellier Grove. Mrs Ellis will be there when you arrive; I'll be there at four. Tell Abbot he has a deal. With a little clarification on the details, to be negotiated on both sides, I suspect.'

'Yes, Sir.'

'Don't wait, leave now Mike.'

And the phone went dead.

'Yes, Sir,' he murmured.

He was slotting the satphone into its sling when Jamie came back into the kitchen carrying an armful of wet logs.

'Drop those, we're on our way. Where's Will?'

'Checking the perimeter, Major.'

'OK. Pull him back in; then shut everything down. We haven't been here. Half an hour max.'

'Yes, Sir.' And the man was gone.

Mike walked across the living room and opened the door to two pairs of questioning eyes. He turned to look at Alan Abbot and nodded slightly.

'You've got your deal, Abbot. We're on our way within half an hour so take a piss now if you need one; I'm not planning on too many stops on the road.'

'Thank you, Major.'

'Don't thank me, Abbot. I sponsored the idea with the Admiral because I reckon it's the fastest way of getting you to talk. Believe me, if I thought I could get it faster in a more physical way, you'd be leaking blood all over the floor.'

'You have such a way with words, Major.'

'Sarcastic shit! Move out.'

'Incidentally, where exactly are we moving to?'

'One of our secure houses in London; you get to stay there free of charge until we're done. Admiral Buller is meeting us there this afternoon. OK we're done, so let's wind this up. Stay with him Ed, I need to change into civvies.'

Once again in the driver's seat, Ed took them cross country until he joined the single track road just south of Abercybafon. On a sunny day in spring or summer, it would have been a pretty drive but now the fields were flat and dull, the trees starkly bare without their leafy clothing. The still waters of Talybont Reservoir, so often a mirror for blue skies with candy floss clouds, was a dull gunmetal surface darkly relieved by shadow lines from above. Grey clouds had once again obscured the light, closing the cracks where the sun had slipped through before. There was almost a collective sigh of relief when they joined the A40 at Llansantffraed and Ed could pick up speed.

They joined the M4 at Newport for the dreary monotonous run past Bristol and eastwards towards London. It was over three hours before Ed was turning right on Countess Road onto Montpellier Grove. Rather fine Victorian terraced houses lined the street on either side, each with its own little flight of steps running up to the front door. Once rather downmarket, many had been bought up by investors who'd seen the potential in their proximity to the centre of London. Most had been converted into apartments that sold for £200,000 and more. Alan Abbot's new temporary home had been bought back in the 60s when Kentish Town hadn't been on so many people's wish list.

Mike led the group of four between whitewashed stone walls to the navy blue varnished door set slightly back from the faux whitewashed squared-off pillars and their rectangle of the flattened portico. Pushing the bell button to the side resulted in a metallic clamour from inside and the door opening to reveal a portly matron of a certain age with iron-grey hair and an unsmiling face.

'It's been a while Michael Roberts. Sir Reginald said you were on your way, bringing trouble as ever.'

'Yes Mrs E, and you're as beautifully sunny and cheerful as ever.'

She tried very hard to scowl at him but failed, a friendly smile creasing her naturally forbidding face.

'It's good to see you,' she said in low voice that only Mike could hear. 'Come in now, all of you.'

Mrs Ellis stood back, holding the door out of the way, as they walked quickly inside, along the short corridor. In the wider space beyond, they stood waiting for her directions.

'Sir Reginald's coming soon I believe. He said you and your man Abbot should wait for him in the drawing room, at the back.' She opened a door on the far side to reveal yet another corridor. 'You know where to go, Major.' Turning to the remaining three: 'you boys can come with me to the kitchen. Sure you could do with a cup of tea while you're waiting.'

Mike stood in the bay window, looking out onto the high walled garden at the rear of the house. The trimmed lawn stretched out to the baseline of the wall in all directions, studded with tall plane trees around the edge. At the back, a shed that might once have been creosote dark brown had faded with age and was now more a milky grey; but still sturdy and firmly locked with a heavy padlock. He wondered idly whether it contained anything more than a lawnmower and a handful of garden tools. Hearing movement from behind, he flicked his eyes sideways, searching for Alan's reflection on the glass of the windowpane. And found the reflection looking back at him. Silence prevailed but they didn't have long to wait.

Ten minutes later Mrs Ellis opened the door to let Admiral Buller and Helen O'Connor into the room. The Admiral grunted a greeting in Mike's general direction, vaguely included Alan and sat down in one of the utilitarian but functional armchairs. Helen smiled at Mike and looked piercingly at Alan before sitting on a hard-backed upright chair by his side. Producing a notebook and pen from a capacious brown leather handbag, she crossed her legs and waited.

'I want to get this done quickly. I take it you're Alan Abbot?'

'And you're Rear Admiral Sir Reginald Buller; I've seen photos of you on several occasions.'

Curbing his irritation at the man's perceived impertinence, the Admiral continued.

'You're here and unharmed because Major Roberts believes that it's the quickest way to stop further damage to crews and ships. In return for giving us all the details of the bombs, you would like us to let you, your family and the Masris wander off into the bloody sunset. That more or less sum it up?'

'Yes, Sir.'

Fractionally pacified by the more respectful form of address, Admiral Buller became slightly less bullish.

'Then I'm sure you'll understand that we can't have you waiting at home in comfort or chatting to your mates at the local about how you pulled one over on Her Majesty's intelligence services. Tell him the rules of the game if you would, Helen.'

'Of course, Admiral.' She looked Alan directly in the eyes and held the contact. 'There are immutable conditions attached to our acceptance of your proposal covering the period up to your departure from the UK and others concerning your future status and that of your family.

'There can be no consideration of any form of house arrest as you call it, with Megan and Anwen in Wales. Naturally that will also apply to Amin Masri who will be transferred here from prison. He's been kept in a segregation unit since he arrived back in the UK, so I'm sure he'll appreciate the company,' she added wryly. 'Until we can be certain that the threat has been eliminated, you will both remain here without any contact with your families or anyone else in the outside world. You will not be allowed access to the internet, telephones, television or newspapers; in effect you are in total media quarantine. Mrs Ellis will ensure that you are adequately fed and watered. The two troopers who escorted you here from Wales will continue to babysit for the duration. Any information or requests on either side will generally be transmitted through them. Any questions so far?'

'Only one, Madam. I would request that a message be passed to my wife to assure her that I am safe and anticipate seeing her in the near future. A similar message should also go to Sophie Masri. I am sure that you will tell them that we are helping the government with its enquiries,' Alan said, delivering his own wry riposte.

'Conditional on the fact that they do not speak of the matter to anyone at all. Something that we will be sure to impress on them; any leak on their part will be regarded as a breach of our agreement.'

'Accepted.'

'When all of this is done and dusted, you'll be allowed to leave the country with them if they so wish and vice versa. As far as we're concerned, neither Megan nor Anwen had any knowledge of your plans and as British citizens would therefore be allowed to remain in the country. Your current passport has been cancelled as of today; you will be issued with a new passport prior to your departure with eight months validity. That will allow you to travel to any country that you choose, provided that you are issued with a visa if necessary. I would add at this point that for the purposes of international agencies we will not black code you for entry. However, should you attempt to re-enter the UK or one of its protectorates, you will be refused entry.

'Putting it in a nutshell without the woolly words Abbot, once you're out of here you're an exile. That means you're on your own. As a farewell bonus, we'll pay for the flights and any visas, you get a personal escort to the airport and we make damn sure that you're on the plane. There're probably a few more little things that I haven't mentioned but we can make those up as we need to. Any more questions? Comments?'

'I'll work on them while I enjoy your gracious hospitality. Oh but one while it occurs to me: do you know when Amin is arriving?'

'Some time tonight. We'll probably ease him out around two tomorrow morning. Are you done?'

'Yes.'

409

'Then it's your turn to talk.'

Helen raised her pen above her pad and looked at him expectantly. As Alan Abbot talked, she wrote down his words verbatim, the hieroglyphics of her shorthand marching across the paper. She wrote down Admiral Buller's questions and Alan Abbot's answers, made a note of Major Roberts' comments and Abbot's replies. She listened to what each man said, took down every detail and even annotated the text with her own observations when they paused for breath. It wasn't until everyone had else had run out of things to say that Helen finally spoke.

'Are you done?' she asked Alan, who nodded his reply. 'Admiral? Major?' Both men replied in the affirmative. 'Gentlemen, Mr Abbot has given us clear instructions in respect of the retrieval and deactivation of the bombs themselves. Unless there are any objections, I do not believe it's necessary to go over those again. Obviously I will run the instructions past him again before sending them out to the Weapon Engineer Officers. However, I suggest that I summarise the key points of the assessed and imminent dangers.'

The three men were silent and attentive, their eyes firmly fixed on the woman in the room. Helen's eyes swept across each on in turn and seeing no dissent, continued.

'Very well. The intended third target is HMS Edinburgh en route to Bahrain, expected there latest in mid-December. However, she's expected to get to Port Said at the beginning of the month. The Suez Canal could be considered as a possible kill zone if al-Shami is land based. Considering the terrain, logical points would be the built up areas of El-Qantara or Ismailia; easy to slip away unnoticed. That would have the additional effect of bringing all shipping in the canal to a standstill. On the other hand, sinking Edinburgh in the Strait of Hormuz would be a massive coup for al-Qaeda. Imagine the media coverage and comment if a British ship is taken out on the Combined Task Force's doorstep, the dragon's lair. If I was directing the operation, that would definitely be my choice.

'Target number four is HMS Manchester due to join the Standing Maritime Group off Cairo at the beginning of December. After that she's to take up her duties which initially mean sailing up the coastline in the wake of HMS York. Which might indicate a copycat hit. We've already worked out that al-Shami has to have been on some sort of boat when he detonated the bomb on the York because of the range of the transmitter. Therefore the same would apply to a hit on HMS Manchester and the Edinburgh if they went for the Strait of Hormuz option.'

Helen paused, perhaps wondering if any of the others had come to the same conclusion. She found no indication of horrified enlightenment.

'It is possible, even likely,' she said, releasing the words in measured cadence, 'that Edinburgh and Manchester are sailing in convoy. If that is the case, my guess is that they are already in the Mediterranean sailing east. And if I were al-Shami, I'd opt for the even greater coup than the Hormuz scenario; imagine sinking two ships at the same time with all Cairo to watch.'

Helen let her words sink in, watching the looks of appalled realisation blossom on the men's faces. Her final words fell like hot shards of metal into freezing water.

'We do not have the luxury of a five day window; we may have as little as 48 hours before the ships are within al-Shami's strike range. Perhaps even less.'

16 ~ Triangulation

Ayesha looked up at the dark blue dome of night, shimmering with the silver-white diamonds of a million stars scattered carelessly across the sky. The moon was a slender crescent of creamy white, curving round the dark side in new birth. She let her gaze drift slowly downwards until it met the blurred line of the horizon. The sea was a blackened sheet of molten glass, cleft in two by the moon's slim beam and broken by the inky silhouettes of ships at anchor. The requisite triangle of immigration lights, one red over two white, glowed above the featureless shapes like fireflies in the darkness. Ayesha did not have to look upwards to see that very same glow at the unseen tip of the mast.

She lay on one of the sofas on deck, enjoying the light breeze that whispered through the open sides rolled up on either side of the canopy. Four Hurricane storm lanterns shed soft light across the tables near the bridge, lending a ghostly aura to al-Kabuli's face as he smoked a nargile. The sweet smoke that wafted gently on the breeze had the scent of orange blossom without the cloying thread of cannabis resin that tainted Tarek's mix. Her brother sat on his own, on a cushion near the bow and away from the rest of them. He'd said little since the woman had been thrown overboard and Abdul Saad's caustic words afterwards.

Naseem and Haroun were talking softly in resonant liquidity that lulled the senses. Ayesha rested her head against the pillow of her kitbag, just listening to their voices against the background hum of the city. Port Said: the town that never sleeps. A rich tenor voice began singing a low lilting lament, adding another melody to the air. Although she couldn't understand the Pashto words, she could appreciate the beauty and emotion of the song. Ayesha wondered which one of the crew was singing and allowed herself to lightly doze. It would be at least another two hours before they moved.

Even though the dhow was technically too small, a little-bigger-than-small bribe had got Rih Albahr an early place on the first convoy to leave Port Said for the slow drift down to Suez. Including the wait in Great Bitter Lake, it would take at least 14 hours before they slipped into the Gulf of Suez. Compared to the leviathans that were assembled in the North Anchorage, the Rih Albahr was but a breath of sea wind as her name proclaimed. When they got to Ismailia, another bribe would be offered and the dhow could slip past the high-stacked containers and supertankers heavy with petroleum.

Within minutes those sirens of sleep overcame Ayesha's self-allowed doze. The symphony of shouted orders, ships' engines and creaking ropes brought her back to life over two hours later. A glance at her watch confirmed they were on the move; at 01.36 hours, the slow process of moving the ships into place had been under way for over half an hour. For a while she watched the crew prepare the ship, saw the coils of rope that had snaked wetly over the side, heard the rasp of the chain as the anchor was winched up from the seabed. Then another lull came as they waited to take the fourth place in the convoy. Enlivened by her sleep, she remembered something that she'd forgotten to do earlier, subsumed as it had been in the drama of the day.

Reaching into her kit bag, she pulled out Marina's mobile and brought it to life. The woman hadn't had the opportunity to switch the phone off or switch on any locks. Ayesha started probing into the other woman's mobile life. The mail system was locked, asked for a password and when none was forthcoming, faded out. She didn't waste her time trying to guess what the password might be; the possible permutations were endless. Certain that Marina had taken photographs with her phone, Ayesha opened the media folder, and found nothing.

'Bitch! She wiped them,' Ayesha muttered to herself. 'Messages.'

She clicked across to the appropriately marked icon and clicked. The file opened without a problem, offering a choice of received, sent and missed messages. Received displayed only two message threads: the most recent started by someone called Danny; the earlier one, by Tarek.

'U there lovely?'

She looked across at the dimly lit figure by the bow, shaking her head with a mixture of disbelief and despair. Reading through the rest of the thread merely raised her eyebrows higher. Abdul Saad was right, she thought, her brother was pathetic. That reality irritated her more than she'd have expected. It added to her jaundiced feelings about her brother and Ayesha couldn't accept his fraudulent self-deception. A sort of Jekyll and Hyde thing. By day he was a Professor, an Islamic scholar expatiating on the Qur'an and the Hadith for the benefit of lesser mortals. As the evening drew near, the mosque of his mind locked its doors and hot asinine lust ran through his veins. The phrase cunt-struck came to mind. Ayesha spat into the scuppers to rid her mouth of the foul taste that accompanied her thoughts.

The more recent of the two threads sounded an alarm bell in her head, drowning out her previous thoughts. The first line was a cryptic message sent to Marina.

'Search as said, then queen takes bishop. Endgame. Take care xx.'

Ayesha stared at the line for several seconds, a frown wrinkling her forehead and turning down the corners of her mouth. It didn't take long to work out that the woman was 'queen' and Tarek was 'bishop'. Checkmate. She'd been ordered to assassinate him by this 'Danny'. And the two kisses: another lover or someone altogether more menacing? What followed added at least one more alarm bell to the clamour in her head.

'... Locator is ON as of now. Follow?! ... Of course. Aaron tracking.'

'Fuck, fuck, fuck!' she hissed, staring at the little mobile device with supreme hate.

Going back to the main screen, she studied the little boxes carefully, then smiled and clicked on the icon with the silhouette of a dancing gypsy. It reminded her of the French cigarettes, Gitanes; the blue and white design used on the box. How simple and accurate: GPS lurking at the heart of the wandering gypsy. The list presented on screen was short and each item had only two options: on or off, positive or negative.

Gypsy connection: ON
GPS sats: Connected
Tracking: ON
Gypsy boost: ON
Audio: OFF

Ayesha clicked on each one, cutting the satellite connection and turning the other items to the off position. Breathing a sigh of relief, she returned to the main screen and pulled up the phone's sparse contacts list. There was no entry for Danny, but there was one for D&A; D for Danny and A for Aaron. How cosy. Naturally she didn't recognise the number but Ayesha knew the international dialling code very well: +972, the code for Israel; 3, the area code for Tel Aviv. Discounting the other lover scenario, that could only mean one of two organisations – IDF or Mossad – and neither were welcome to join her on the cruise to Musandam. Marina's mobile would just have to stay in Egyptian waters. Languidly getting to her feet, Ayesha turned to lean over the gunwale and dropped the phone into the sea. She heard the distinctive plop, saw it disappear beneath the surface, on its way to the seabed.

Some 255 kilometres away as the crow flies, the duty officer in Aaron's office was laboriously updating the evening's log after a long telephone conversation with an agent in Mumbai. It was complicated, Nariman House in Colaba run by Rivka and Gavriel as a Chabad House, a synagogue and a Jewish outreach centre. Or one might say, a drop-in centre for young Israelis on their way to and from partying in chilled out places like Goa. Then it went on to young Israelis being used as virgin drug mules, duped by the smuggling organisations in Mumbai and that Nariman House was a happy hunting ground for recruits. Not that it was difficult because most of them were too stoned to ask any questions or too stupid, and stoned, to think. Fuck's sake! What was he meant to do about it, sitting in an office in Tel Aviv. Like Mossad would be interested anyway. He didn't think. But the report still had to be typed up for the log. Shit!

So Duty Officer Lev Rabinovich didn't notice when the little green flashing bead on Tracker's main mapping screen went dark. He didn't see the light in Port Said's harbour disappear and Lev couldn't log an accurate time when he noticed its absence almost two hours later.

*****

The message had come from the First Sea Lord himself, succinct and to the point. The Captain was appraised that a branch of the intelligence services had ascertained that the Edinburgh was carrying a Trojan horse. Explicitly, an explosive device similar to the ones detonated on HMS Gloucester and York.

'Imperative that it is found, removed and destroyed. This exercise should be effected in deep water, at least 20 nautical miles from land. Be aware: indications are that previous detonations were triggered from a small commercial vessel or a leisure boat.'

The detailed information and instruction sheet that had followed immediately afterwards brought reality into sharp relief. It had not been the easiest task to give to his Weapons Engineer Officer even though he and his team were the only people for the job.

Trespassing into Egypt's territorial waters was not an option for an armed British destroyer. And Captain Henry Powell was not in the mood to get into an argument with some irritating raghead in a uniform with attitude, commanding a blasted patrol boat. Although it had occurred to him that it might have been a little more comfortable being closer to land if it all went pear-shaped. Thus the Edinburgh was approximately 145 nautical miles northwest of Alexandria and 90 odd nautical miles south of the line drawn between Crete and Cyprus. That placed them in the middle of the Levantine Basin with over 2000 metres of seawater underneath, according to the ship's sonar. At dead slow ahead, HMS Edinburgh was moving sluggishly through the water at a bare two knots. On any normal day Henry Powell would have been champing at the bit, wanting to get a move on with the engines pushing the old girl onwards with at least 22 knots. But it wasn't a normal day.

Flanked by two other officers, Henry Powell stood on the bridge gazing over the great empty expanse of water, scanning his horizon for even the tiniest of dots that might indicate another ship. Two specialist technicians, two ratings, the Communications and Information Systems Engineer were behind him; each one totally focused on the screens and instruments in front of them. Earth, sea and air were monitored in sectors, models and fractals with every available sensor. While

416

temperature gauges kept a tally of the heat levels in certain key sections of the ship, the fourth element of fire was not something that anyone wanted to consider. But all emotional thinking was with the team three decks below.

The missiles in the vertical magazine directly underneath the twin launcher on deck were already there when the ship had left port. Weapons Engineer Officer, Lieutenant Commander Charlie Balfour had checked the details and serial numbers twice with his second in command, Warrant Officer Jake Peters. The cheat sheet from the Admiralty had clearly stated that 'the sabotaged missile should be in the batch delivered from Forbes to the vessel immediately before leaving port'. The pair were standing on the brightly lit deck below, with two Able Rate weapons system technicians waiting patiently for their instructions.

'It's the word 'should' that I don't like.'

'Yeah, I know what you mean but that's what the man said. And reading between the lines, I'm guessing that the bastard who gave them the information to begin with had a hand in planting the device.'

'Point taken.'

Charlie Balfour and Jake Peters had been working together for over 18 months and developed a mutual trust and respect. Below decks in their world of weaponry, they worked on a first name basis.

'OK guys, let's do this.'

The three men and one woman team moved into a semicircle around the magazine with its 20 deadly sentinels pointing upwards. Suzie low on the floor, reading the serial numbers off the plates illuminated by Alec's torch. Charlie marked the numbers off on the sheet on his clipboard; Jake repeated to confirm. It took less than a few minutes.

'Alec, you're with me; Suzie, work with Jake,' said Charlie. 'We'll take the first sequence, so that's FI60-7999/100 to110. Jake and Suzie, start at FI60-7999/111. Anybody sees anything out of the ordinary, sing out loud. Once identified, we all work on the same programme.'

'Yes Sir,' all three voices snapped out in unison.

As Jake and Suzie moved out of sight around the other side of the magazine, Charlie and Alec moved the small gantry in to the stack; close enough to serial number FI60-7999/100 that they could hug the damn thing, Charlie thought.

'OK, we undo bolts at the bottom of the nosecone, ease it up and have a look. Take it easy, we go slow and smooth.'

Alec nodded as Charlie handed him one of the two torque wrenches in the tool rack attached to the side of the cage. The heat was oppressive in the enclosed space, exacerbated by the lights and the air seemed to thicken with hot apprehension. Charlie could feel the sweat beading on his forehead, damp patches darkening his shirt underneath his arms. He noticed the same visual evidence on Alec as the technician started to undo the first bolt. Fitting the socket over another of the inset bolts, Charlie applied firm, consistent pressure to the torque handle, easing off when he felt that slight shift. Hearing the rasp of the ratchet as he pulled back, he then reapplied the pressure.

'I'm done, Sir.'

'Good man, likewise. OK, hands on and ease it up.'

Four hands gripped the nosecone at four points, slowly easing it vertically upwards. Charlie shifted his grip crablike down the sides of the cone until he could slide his fingers underneath the edge, tipping the whole backwards at a slight angle. Alec responded by feel, automatically accommodating the slight shift in weight and taking the strain accordingly. Inside, everything was as expected or perhaps hoped for: the dark grey-pink of the guidance module, dull and drab in its comfortable familiarity.

'It's not this one,' Charlie said, and heard Alec exhale. 'I know it's difficult, but breathe man. OK, let's put it back together again.'

Between them they eased the nosecone back on to its seating flange, finger tightened the bolts before cranking them in with the wrenches. They could hear the sound of Jake's gantry being shifted along the stack, wheels loud on the metal floor. Charlie and Alec were a few seconds behind.

'It's not a race you know,' Charlie shouted, trying to lighten the tension that lay heavily in the air.

'You're just getting slow in your old age, mate,' Jake shouted back.

Charlie and Alec moved their gantry to the next missile, fitted the socket heads to the first bolts and applied the torque. Until the sound of Jake's voice stopped them at the half turn.

'Charlie! Charlie, I think we've found the fucker.' Despite all his experience and skill, his voice had a distinct tremor. 'We've got a single steel cylinder that's taking all the space that the guidance modules did together. Suzie's got the weight but it would be nice if you two could get your arses round here!'

Alec began to retighten the bolts on FI60-7999/101; Charlie nodded.

'Do the rest and then follow me round. I'm on my way,' he shouted, dropping off the gantry and onto the floor.

He found Suzie frozen in position, neck and arm muscles tensed, strain clear on her usually impish face. Between the three of them, they moved the nosecone back to the vertical, its weight now distributed across three pairs of hands.

'Alec!'

'On my way now, Sir.'

Rapid footsteps echoed as the technician trotted quickly around the stack. At Charlie's direction, he took the officer's place, allowing him to take his first proper look at a NuCan. Not that he'd ever heard it called that or ever would. At first he tried to ease it out from the missile casing, assuming it had been simply slotted in to the Sea Dart.

'Magnetic release and lock, Charlie,' Jake reminded him.

Charlie nodded, his eyes speedily locating the button, one finger pressing lightly down. A green light flashed. Slipping his hands as far as he could into the narrow space, he found the cylinder slipped out as easily as any well-oiled part of a precision built machine. Holding it carefully with both hands, he backed down off the gantry and stood there waiting like a child with a birthday present. But the look on his face was not one of joy; professionalism seasoned with caution and the salt of anger might be more accurate. And there he stood until the other three had finished bolting the nosecone back into place.

'What's the plan?' asked Jake.

'According to the sheet, we won't be able to get the receiver off the side of the casing. Instructions are for a controlled explosion.'

In the workshop on the deck above, next door to the upper magazine, Charlie put the innocuous-looking cylinder on a stainless steel bench. Unscrewing the top as per instructions, he removed the inside lid to reveal the shallow cavity beneath.

'Damn thing smells of some kind of perfume,' Jake said with some surprise. 'What's that about?'

'Who knows, Jake, who knows anything about what's really going on?'

Noticing the rectangular box on the side, he took a closer look, peering at the black plastic shell.

'I reckon that's the receiver. Tempting to just rip it off, or ease it off with the help of a cold chisel and a lump hammer.'

'You want to try, feel free but do it in your own back garden. Man at the top says blow it up and the sooner we do that, the sooner I'm a happy bunny again.'

Charlie called the bridge, asked for Captain Powell. The familiar voice was on immediately.

'Charlie, you found it I hear. Thank Christ for that.'

'Third one tried Captain. News as ever travels fast.'

'What do you need?'

'Are the comms boys reporting any traffic Captain, because we have to detonate this baby on the water?'

'We're clear for over 17 nautical miles Charlie. Since we're more less in the middle of the Med, speaking north south, we're well away from the main shipping lanes. Therefore, reading your mind, there are no ships of any sort within close enough range to detonate your bomb. So?'

'I need one of the RIBs manned by a couple of seamen and four buoys. It's got to be a surface detonation; we can't risk it on the seabed.'

'Understood. Ready when you are Charlie. How long do you need?'

'Enough time to stick detonators into a couple of packs of PE-4 and wire in a timer. The bloody thing's got a screw top; we just pop the plastic inside and replace the lid.'

Within half an hour, Charlie was in a RIB, equipped as requested with a Lead Hand at the wheel and an Able Rate by his side. Speeding through the light chop, all he could think was:

'Please God, let me get this mother into the water and us back to the ship to watch the show'.

'How far, Sir?'

'About a mile will be fine.' Noticing the slight look of alarm on the man's face, he added, 'Most of the force will be dissipated by the water. It'll make for a good water spout though.'

Nevertheless, Lead Hand Mike Kellerman made absolutely sure that he took the RIB one good nautical mile rather than the cheaper land version. Easing the throttle back, he looked over his shoulder at Charlie with a questioning look. Clocking the thumbs up, he swivelled round in his seat. He watched as the ship's senior Weapons Engineer Officer unscrewed the top of his steel can and reached in to set the timer. A knot formed in his stomach as the Lieutenant Commander carefully replaced the lid and placed the whole thing in a rope net. 'Come on, come on,' the voice screamed in his head. As Able Rate Terry Shaw lent a helping, but slightly shaking, pair of hands to tie the net onto the buoys in the boat, a similar voice was screaming in his head as well. The three of them gingerly lifted the ungainly contraption over the side of the RIB and let it slip gently into the water.

'We're done, let's go Lead.'

Mike Kellerman needed no encouragement.

'Thank Christ for that,' he muttered under his breath, as he eased the boat away from the bomb submerged between the bright orange coloured buoys. 'How long's the timer set for Sir?' he asked nervously.

'Twenty minutes, Lead.'

'Fuck's sake,' muttered Kellerman.

Charlie grinned as the man pushed the throttle lever up to maximum, taking the RIB flying back in the direction of HMS Edinburgh at a speed of 25 knots. It took no more than five minutes before both RIB and men were back on deck. Over the next ten minutes most of the crew had lined up on the port side, standing in silence as they waited. Every man and woman silently thanked the gods for their escape; each one honestly believing that they'd been aware of the extent of the danger. They had no idea. Charlie glanced at his watch: two minutes.

Under a bright yellow sun in a cobalt sky, a patch of sea turned black and red and white-gold, a boiling angry churn of water spreading outwards with spittle on its lips. The small burping bang of the exploding plastic gave way to a deep blast that seemed to grow in immensity as a thick column of rotating grey-black water reached upwards like an inverted tornado. Inside that column was a tongue of red-gold flame that must have come from the black throat of hell itself. It was a ghastly vision of deadly energy unleashed; the shock and horror etched on every face whose eyes watched the explosion.

As the colour faded and rage left the water's surface, that column of smoke hung in the midday sky as a grim reminder of what might have been. Then they did understand, as they stood motionless in that terrible silence of which they themselves were a part. And then that in turn was broken by the sound of someone clapping. Then another and another and another. The whole crew was applauding the man who stood on the bridge beside Captain Henry Powell.

'You did it Charlie. Thank Christ, you did it.'

*****

Rear-Admiral Sir Reginald Buller was standing in the bay window of the library with his back to the glass. The yellow-orange glow from the street lamps outside mantled his head and shoulders, lending him a strange kind of cosmic aura. Even his personal clouds of smoke seemed to be tinged with gold; white spumes drifting upwards as he exhaled to be transformed by the hand of the unseen alchemist. The sound of high heels on the wooden steps of the stairs drew his attention to the doorway and Helen's entrance, a smile to his face.

'You look like a rather avuncular wizard, pleased with his own magic, Reggie. And why not?' She walked to the drinks trolley, poured two fingers of Lagavulin from the decanter into two crystal tumblers. 'Mike should be here in about ten minutes, or less,' she said, handing him one of the glasses. 'I managed to catch him as he was leaving Montpellier Grove; spot check on security apparently, now that Masri's there as well as Abbot. Sláinte.'

'Cheers.' He clinked his glass against hers, sipped, savouring the peaty tang of the whisky on his tongue. 'I take it you didn't mention anything?'

'Not on an open line, no.'

They heard the soft pop of the lock, heard Mike's footsteps on the stone flags and the door click shut again. Helen poured another glass of whisky and held it out to him as he walked into the library.

'We're celebrating?' Mike asked. 'Thank you,' he added,' taking the tumbler.

'The First Sea Lord was on the phone about an hour ago. Sir Philip informed me that he's received confirmation from the Captains of both HMS Edinburgh and HMS Manchester that the EDs in their respective Sea Darts have been removed and safely destroyed.'

'That's absolutely bloody brilliant,' Mike exclaimed, 'thank Christ for that.'

'Pretty much what Captain Powell said on the bridge of the Edinburgh after he'd seen the thing exploding. Even in the sea, apparently horrendously powerful. We know only too well what one did to the York. Poor buggers.' Admiral Buller paused for second, then shrugged away the thoughts of anger and sadness. 'But thank Christ, the gods or whoever indeed. And you, young Michael. Sir Philip specifically asked me to thank you for a job well done, and your correct call on Abbot's bargaining. He was as good as his word, I'll give him that, and of course we'll honour the deal. At least getting rid of the pair of them will save the Prison Service an estimated £80,000 per annum. But we'll let the bastards stew for a few more days. Whitehall want to keep the news under the covers for a bit until they sort how to spin it.' The Admiral snorted his disgust with a billow of smoke, then raised his glass. 'To lives saved and lost,' he said, and lifted his glass to his lips as he heard his toast's double echo.

Leaving his place by the window, the Admiral sat down in his Chesterfield and waved Helen and Mike to follow suit.

'Who knows whether Helen was right about al-Shami going for a double hit, but it was certainly a bloody close shave. Tell him, Helen.'

'Danny called from Tel Aviv, a couple of hours ago. Obviously as soon as we heard about the York, we realised his agent in Beirut hadn't been successful. Damn right, someone clearly got to her first. Aaron was tracking her using the GPS signal from her phone and could see she was somewhere offshore but couldn't get a proper constant fix. The last time he checked was mid-evening, before the night duty officer came on. At that point, it looked as though she was heading towards Port Said. The signal disappeared entirely sometime between midnight and two in the morning. And they could have been heading west towards HMS York and Manchester.'

'If they did, they didn't make it in time. Bloody hell! That would have been close. Are the distances doable?'

'Yes.'

'Ouch. So no idea about Marina?'

'Fortunately, the answer's yes. She was lucky. According to Danny, a couple of Israeli patrol boats were not that far away when the York blew. One of their guys spotted her in the water as they were on their way to help if they could. She was barely alive, mainly due to water inhalation caused by the fact that she couldn't have been able to do much more than doggie paddle.'

'She couldn't swim?' asked Mike, the surprise clear in both tone and expression.

'Being shot in both arms and having several broken fingers does make breast stroke a tad difficult,' she answered drily. 'She's alive and obviously able to talk. The IDF took her to Bnai Zion Medical Centre in Haifa and she asked them to contact Mossad. They thought she was raving but did it anyway just in case. Aaron picked up on it. That's all we know. Danny's going up there to see her this evening so we might have more tomorrow.

'But whoever dumped her in the sea, kept her phone as far as Port Said. At which point it either ran out of juice or someone realised that it was sending out a GPS signal and turned it off. We're assuming that al-Shami was on the boat, but since she was sleeping with him it isn't very likely that he was the one who shot her. Not that it really matters now. Although it would be nice if we could hurt him somehow. Who knows where the boat's going now. For all we know, it's still waiting somewhere off the Egyptian coast.'

'Al-Shami isn't near the top of anyone's priority list now the ships have been secured,' the Admiral interjected. 'As said, Whitehall want the whole thing hushed up. That includes the Admiralty, the MoD as a whole, Foreign Office, the lot.' Attempting a parody of a television newsreader, he said: 'In a co-ordinated effort with international agencies, Britain's intelligence services managed to track down the terrorist cell responsible for these atrocities and stop them in their tracks'. Vanilla reporting. The trade agreed with Alan Abbot will be buried for a hundred years and even the slightest allusion made in writing by anyone will be redacted. End of story. Next!

'For a few moments, we can bask in the knowledge that we've succeeded in stopping this load of bastards in finishing the job.' He paused to concentrate on his Lagavulin for one or two sips. Instinctively, the other two shared the moment, drinking in silence. Staring at his now empty glass, the Admiral gave Helen what he hoped was his most endearing smile. 'Be a darling and give us all another small one.'

'How could I refuse, seeing such a leer from an old seadog?' she said, grinning.

Uncoiling her long legs, she rose from her chair and neatly plucked the empty tumbler from his hand.

'Mike?'

'Why not?' he replied, throwing down the last dregs and holding out his glass.

Making the most of the brief hiatus, Admiral Buller bent to the arduous task of refilling his pipe.

'You do realise you're on borrowed time Admiral? I think the ban on smoking in offices comes into effect in July next year,' Mike said mischievously.

'This isn't a bloody office and we don't officially exist. So tell me, exactly how does your blasted law affect me? Stealing the line from Scrooge: bah humbug!'

'Naturally he's not bothered about us because we don't exist either,' remarked Helen returning with three refreshed tumblers.

Conspicuously ignoring them both, Admiral Buller leaned back in his chair and took his time. After obscuring himself behind a veil of smoke for a full minute, the clouds finally parted to reveal a beatific smile on his bearded face.

'So,' he said, snapping back to business. 'Apart from the obvious tragic aspects, the fallout pervading Whitehall derives from that blasted video from Al Jazeera. Of course, nobody even stopped to consider the speaker's demands. Incidentally, consensus among UK analysts is that it's definitely not Bin Laden's voice. In their opinion, that's supported by anomalies in the text: in particular, the emphasis on western withdrawal from Afghanistan and Iraq, and on the Palestinian issues. A genuine Bin Laden speech would be laced with religious issues and references to Islam. Is what they say.

'What concerns people the most is the bit about elemental fires. In camera, we all concur with the belief that it's a reference to a nuclear warhead or similar. And we're back to the same country – Pakistan.'

'Which is exactly what we said after the speech,' Mike said. 'In terms of vulnerability and lack of nuclear security, Pakistan obviously takes first place. It's one of those subjects that's gnawed at, over and over again. It's like chewing gum: when all the flavour's gone, we spit it out. Pakistan has always said it will join the Nuclear Non-Proliferation Treaty if India will and that's not going to happen. The States gets overtly pally with India, as Bush did earlier in the year, happily agreeing to sell civilian nuclear material. Meanwhile, on the other side of the Line of Control, they're pumping in millions of dollars to sustain the lifestyles of a few Pakistani Generals and their friends. Fuck's sake, Admiral, a few Whitehall mandarins expressing their concerns over a rant on a video is not exactly going to change the programme. Sorry Sir, rant over.'

'Thank you for that erudite summation, Major Roberts.' The heavy sarcasm was accompanied by a broad smile of mockery. 'This time it's serious Mike. Of course Edinburgh and York were military targets but their destruction has sent a wake-up call that's reverberating from the Thames to Whitehall and Number Ten. No it's not a parallel to 9/11, but the memory of the London bombings is still very raw; compounded, they're a potent call to action. The image of a nuclear version of 7/7 doesn't bear thinking about. Behind closed doors, it's been accepted that we have to do something to at least limit Pakistan's nuclear vulnerability. In an ideal world, I'd be saying eliminate all exposure, but that would be naïve.

'Getting to the point, we've been asked to attend a meeting at the Foreign Office tomorrow morning at 10.00 hours. We, being all the three of us, I suggest gathering here at eight thirty.'

'Do we know who else will be there?'

'Sir Angus McFadden, the Permanent Under Secretary for Foreign Affairs,' Helen said, picking up the question. 'Brigadier Stephen Carson, the Director Special Forces; Brendan Horton, Minister for Security and Counter-Terrorism, from the Home Office; and Jamie Heathcote from the Secret Intelligence Service, attached to Counter Proliferation.'

'That sounds like a COBRA meeting.'

'That's because it is, but in a different building, and we're only joining the party for the second half. I suspect this isn't the first meeting on the subject and that it's already been decided that we should be asked to tackle the problem. Who knows, but I think we'll find out.'

*****

A grey mist hung over the Thames, creeping across the Embankment and drifting into the nearby streets in wispy filaments. The chill air felt damp and clammy, undisturbed by even the slightest of breezes. Traffic was already building up to the rush hour peak but every car, truck and motorbike had dipped headlights warming the coughing exhaust fumes of the vehicle in front. The streetlamps were still on when Helen keyed herself in to the Red House, walked across the hall and up the stairs to her office. Fifteen minutes later, she was sitting at her desk with a cup of coffee and waiting for her computer to awake from its slumber. Her intercom buzzed softly, the light flashing next to the name, John Watkins.

'Good morning, John. You are the early bird. No duty mole on shift underground?'

'Morning, Miss O'Connor. There was, is an operative still here but there were one or two things I wanted to get done before the day really started to get complicated.'

'Let me guess, you were hoping to get home a little early to catch some of the Ashes action from Adelaide. Confess Mr Watkins!'

Helen could hear the man giggle nervously and almost see his face redden.

'Actually, yes. I didn't know you were a cricket fan, Miss.'

'Actually, I'm not. But I am aware. Enjoy. You buzzed?'

'Mr Spiegel called a few minutes before you arrived. Wanted to speak to Admiral Buller, you or the Major, as he put it – when one of you turned up. He said he'd spoken to Marina. Shall I get him on screen for you Ms O'Connor?'

'Give me five minutes.'

Taking her coffee, she walked down the length of the room, flickering through the thin light and shadows as she passed the line of long windows, interrupted by panels of wall. Switching on the screen, Helen made herself comfortable on the sofa directly in front. As light slowly bloomed on the screen, she crossed her legs, adjusted her blouse and sipped her coffee.

'Good Morning, Daniel,' she said to the tanned handsome smiling face on the screen. 'To what do I owe the pleasure of this early morning call?'

'Helen, you're a vision of delight and I couldn't resist the impulse. Anyway, ten o'clock is hardly early, is it?'

'It is if you're in London talking Tel Aviv time. Do me a favour; turn the web cam to the view from your window.' Sun-kissed beige walls and blue sky appeared momentarily, before Danny flipped the web cam back to himself. 'Bastard. It's cold, grey and damp over here.'

'So come and live with me forever in the sunshine,' he said, smiling lasciviously.

'Is this about Marina, Danny?'

The smile faded out, a more serious expression taking its place.

'Yeah. Bnai Zion have got her in a private room on her own. I went up there yesterday evening; got there about 19.00 on our time.'

'Obvious question, but how is she?'

'Pissed off and angry with herself more than anything else. She was sure that she'd be alone with Tarek al-Shami for the

428

whole night. After they'd finished playing and he's asleep, Marina goes hunting. The sister turns up, shoots her in both arms and then patches her up. Weird. Amazingly, both bullets went straight through muscle without directly hitting bone, although the left humerus was slightly chipped. The surgeon actually managed to find the bone chip, cleaned out and dressed both wounds. Bad trauma to tissues but she's a tough little lady and she'll recover.

'The broken fingers came later in the day. A guy called Naseem broke several of her knuckles and that's painful. Surgeon's pinned them, strapped them up and then it's a waiting game till the fractures heal. They've got her on a glucose drip, morphine and antibiotics. She's a mess but she'll live. And little Marina says she wants to stay in the game because she wants payback!'

'We all make mistakes sometimes; and sometimes mistakes can be fatal. This time Marina was lucky,' Helen said, somewhat coolly. 'I assume that there's a little more than just the 'poor little girl' story?'

'Yeah,' he said, looking at Helen with slightly different eyes. 'You don't take any prisoners, do you Ms O'Connor?' Danny didn't wait for an answer. 'OK. After patching her up, Ayesha tied Marina to a chair on the balcony. She says that she was obviously in pain, but swears that she was totally lucid and could hear them talking in the living room. The kingpin in the equation is Abdul Saad Mazari aka al-Kabuli.'

'The al-Qaeda commander the Somalis talked about to Mike?'

'One and the same. He's clearly been the conduit for the funding from al-Qaeda, with the authority to transfer funds. Without her brother knowing, Ayesha's been getting cozy with al-Kabuli and two of his men. One of those is Al-Kabuli's second-in-command Naseem, who is also his enforcer and advisor. The other is simply a foot soldier-come-gofer called Faisal, based in Beirut but unimportant. They collected the al-Shamis and Marina; took them to a boat of some sort. It might have been some kind of dhow, but she's not sure. According to Marina, triggering the explosion on the York from the boat was pre-planned.

'Back to the conversation in the apartment, Marina is sure that after finishing the York, they planned to sail through the Suez Canal and the Red Sea to the Gulf of Aden. Ayesha mentioned something about the Musandam Peninsula and the Strait of Hormuz but Marina couldn't catch the detail. She is certain that they were heading for Pakistan, possibly via Iran. She admits that she might have been a little muzzy by then.'

'That could make sense,' Helen said slowly. 'HMS Edinburgh is due to join the Combined Task Force in Mina Salman in a few days. Were any other names mentioned?'

'Gwadar – which is on the coast and close to the border with Iran – and Lahore. It doesn't make a lot of sense but maybe you guys can tie it in with other intelligence. Let me know. And that's about it. I'm sorry there's not more.'

'Hey, don't worry.' Helen looked at the somewhat dispirited face on the screen. 'Christ, I can be an insensitive bitch sometimes!' Now the face was simply startled. 'The whole programme here has moved on to focus on Pakistan because the other two ships are safe.'

He listened carefully as Helen updated him with the news, starting with the information 'extracted' from Alan Abbot. She omitted the part about Alan Abbot bartering that information in return for three one-way tickets out of the country. Nor did Danny ask for the details.

'... and since there were only four bombs, thank God, that's pretty much the end of that bloody mess. But since seeing al-Qaeda's video after HMS Gloucester, Whitehall's gone into panic mode over Pakistan's nuclear vulnerability. They have a vision of a huge terrorist demon carrying an oversized Kalashnikov in one hand and a nuclear warhead in the other. We have a meeting with them in about an hour.' She paused, looked him straight in the eyes. 'And Danny, I'm sorry for the cheap 'little girl' line. It was neither fair nor necessary: so, I'm sorry.'

'Apology accepted. Just that there's history and ... enough said. That's really good news; I'm guessing the bombs were found just in time. But I don't think the performance is quite over as the players are still on the stage. Aaron's fairly certain that the voiceover on the tape is al-Kabuli which would mean that he's the man on the hunt for nukes. Interestingly enough, it wasn't

Tarek al-Shami who detonated the explosion on the York, it was big sister Ayesha. I'm guessing al-Kabuli's team building: putting Ayesha with Naseem to work as a double act and planning to use Tarek somewhere as a pawn. But at the moment, that's simply an hypothesis.'

'Thanks Danny, for everything. Listen, I have to go. I suspect we'll be catching up later this afternoon. Take care.'

'You too' he said.

Helen's screen went blank and she could hear the sound of voices in the hall below.

'Helen?' Then a little louder. 'Helen!'

'I should remind you that I'm not actually deaf,' she called down from the top of the stairs. 'Very smart,' she remarked, observing Mike's change of garb.

Given the nature of the meeting and its attendees, he'd eschewed his normal sartorial elegance, dispensing with polo shirt and jeans. Instead he sported dark blue chinos, a navy blazer and white shirt complete with regimental tie.

'Couldn't quite make the suit then, Mike?'

'Damn right. Too bloody uncomfortable. Morning Helen.'

Daylight had finally arrived outside but without any real enthusiasm. The early morning mist had dispersed, giving way to light drizzle that drained slowly from the white-grey muslin sky above. Tiny droplets of moisture had already covered their shoulders in the few seconds it took them to get into the chauffeur-driven statutory black Jaguar XJ8 sedan. Mike took the passenger seat next to the driver in deference to age and seniority, he said; a comment that earned him abuse from Helen and the Admiral. As the car threaded its way through St John Smith's Square, staggering over Victoria Street towards Horse Guards Road, Helen ran through her conversation with Danny. No analysis or conclusions; only the details.

'Do you think you were wrong with your idea of the double hit?'

'It doesn't matter Mike. They'll have gone through the canal anyway if they're heading for Pakistan. The only difference between the two possibilities is the time of realisation. If they already know that we've found the bombs, they'll head straight for Gwadar or another port. If they don't, they'll find out when they try to hit Edinburgh. And that could be anywhere along the route from Port Said to Bahrain. Just because they're on a boat now, doesn't mean to say that they'll stay on the boat or switch from one to another.'

'Yeah, but you have to agree Helen, it is a bit of a coincidence that al-Kabuli's going to Pakistan at the same time as we're taking a closer look.'

'It's not a coincidence, Mike, it's a logical bloody progression,' she snapped.

Mike raised a mental eyebrow, shrugged and turned back to look through the drizzle spattering the glass of the windscreen. Admiral Buller looked sideways at the woman sitting next to him who was staring through the blurred window at the passing facades of Whitehall's ivory castles.

'Spit it out, woman,' he said softly. 'What's rattled your cage?'

'I'm not sure, Reg,' she replied, equally softly. 'I think ... there are too many loose wires that I think are still sparking. The al-Kabuli circus that's somewhere out there, probably in the Red Sea by now, is surfing towards Pakistan on a marketing wave of success. They've shown they can destroy British ships with seeming impunity; that's a big unique selling point for recruitment, it's a thunderous rallying cry. It'll bolster support from the converted and convince the waverers; which in turn means assistance from militant groups all over Pakistan. All we know about their whereabouts is that they're on some boat that might look a bit like a fucking dhow in thousands of square miles of sea. And I wonder how many other dhow-like boats there are out there.

'We're about to go into a meeting to politely listen to theories on how we might limit the exposure of Pakistan's nuclear weaponry. I'm sure they'll suggest a chat in Islamabad with the Prime Minister over an early gin and tonic at the Secretariat. Share our concerns and persuade him to let us take all his warheads and put them in safe storage for a while. In the meantime, we forget about the very real danger of al-Kabuli searching for the weakest link in the nuclear fence. We can't lose that thread Admiral,' she said, reverting back to official-speak.

'Somewhere in all this, there is a lead, a connection, and so far I haven't managed to put it together.'

'You will,' he said confidently, 'you usually do.'

'Thank you.'

The car left King Charles Street, turning under the arch and through into the quadrangle beyond. Stopping close to a set of stone steps on the far side, the chauffeur got out, opened the rear door for Admiral Buller and waited patiently. Lesser mortals were not offered the same courtesy. A security guard at the top barred their way until the Admiral showed him his pass. Stone steps became marble-floored corridors that led past marble columns beneath intricately carved plaster ceilings. Marble turned to stone again and carvings disappeared as they walked down yet another corridor. Another security guard looked back from the other end, waiting for them to approach. Checked all three passes, opened the heavy wood panelled door beside him and stood back to allow them past. Across small anteroom, a double set of doors. Admiral Buller strode across, knocked lightly, opened both doors with a flourish and walked inside.

'Good morning, Sir Reginald, punctual as ever I see.'

'Sarcasm is but a stream of foul water over a strong duck's back. Morning Angus.'

Despite the grandiose doors, the room was surprisingly small, drab and windowless; dominated by a wooden conference table with six seats on either side and one more at either end. As Chair of the meeting, Sir Angus was sitting at the head of the table at the far end, under a bank of blank screens. Admiral Buller took the opposite seat, Helen to his right and Mike to the left. The seats between were an empty divide as though between two warring parties.

'Good morning,' Sir Angus said, nodding first to Helen and then Mike. 'Thank you for coming. Just in case you don't know them, running around from my left: Brigadier Stephen Carson, Brendan Horton from the Home Office and Jamie Heathcote from SIS with specific responsibility within Counter Proliferation.'

'Ms Helen O'Connor and Major Mike Roberts,' the Admiral countered. 'You may not know them personally but I'm aware that you have all been duly briefed on their respective backgrounds.'

'Let me be the first to offer my congratulations,' said Brigadier Carson. 'Thank God you managed to stop them when you did. Two ships were embarrassing; four would have been disastrous, not to mention making us an international laughing stock. I hear young Captain Clarkson and his boys were of some use with the bomb chap at Forbes?'

'Yes Sir, extremely,' answered Mike.

'Thought so. Ed Clarkson has been brought to our attention on more than one occasion. Should think you'll be needing him and a few more troopers on the next operation.'

'Sir?'

'I think it should also be said that failures on the part of the intelligence services allowed this whole mess to unfold to the point where we did lose two ships,' Brendan Horton cavilled. 'It was only by the grace of God that fatalities on the Gloucester were as low as they were.'

'For God's sake, don't start with all that shit again Brendan,' Jamie Heathcote countered. 'The Home Office may oversee things and pretend it's co-ordinating security operations but you never actually get your fingers dirty, do you? Abbot was a sleeper for over 20 bloody years and was unattached. And before you apportion blame and point the finger at SIS agents, al-Shami was basically an academic who had a nodding acquaintance with a few listed groups, essentially through his father. Low risk and not worth surveillance for years.'

Sir Angus raised his hand in an attempt to bring the room to order.

'Enough!' spoken in a stentorian voice had more effect. 'Your petty bickering is wasting my time and achieves nothing.' He looked down the table towards the Admiral. 'I'm sure that you, Ms O'Connor and the Major do not need any reminding of the situations that currently exist in Pakistan, Afghanistan and the Tribal Areas in between. However, one must focus on a few key details. In Afghanistan, NATO is fighting an asymmetric war complicated by tribal rivalries, dubious loyalties and fuelled by massive corruption. In my opinion it's a war that we're unlikely to win and be able to leave the country cleanly.

'Pakistan is a hotbed of groups and factions: Tehrik-i-Taliban, Lashkar-e-Toiba, Jaish-e-Mohammed etcetera. Allegedly the country plays host to over 40 terrorist and extremist groups, including al-Qaeda which has affiliations with others, notably both the Afghani Taliban and Tehrik-i-Taliban. Al-Qaeda has professed its nuclear ambitions on several occasions but most recently on the video released after the Cyprus disaster. But national and trans-national groups have also looked greedily at obtaining nuclear warheads. The difference between ambition and desire is only marked by the range: whereas al-Qaeda's view is global, most of the others have a much more parochial outlook. Given Pakistan's nuclear vulnerability and lack of security, the temptation is tantalisingly and realistically within reach. A conclusion that I am sure you have come to yourselves. And it's imperative that some of the holes in the dyke must be plugged.

'On a different level, we have to consider international diplomacy and Great Britain's relationships with other countries. Naturally we have to consider Pakistan, but we also have to think of the United States, India and Russia. In other words, we have to tread very carefully and quietly on and with whatever we decide to do. In principle, we think that probably the best way forward would be to persuade Pakistan that it might be a good idea to move and store some of their nuclear weapons, somewhere rather more secure.'

'Angus, if I heard you correctly, you suggested that we tell the Prime Minister and probably a few Generals that their security isn't up to speed. Then warn them that in all probability, al-Qaeda and/or the Taliban are likely to exploit those weaknesses and steal a nuke. Just in case they haven't realised, that could lead to Islamabad being vaporised and possibly kick off World War Three. And then suggest that we help them shift a few to safer ground? That about sum it up?'

'You make it sound so bloody patronising, Reg! But yes, that is basically what we do have in mind.'

'And exactly where is safer ground?'

'Obviously at the moment, I don't know,' Angus retorted, sounding more than little frayed at the edges. 'That's something that would have to be discussed with them.'

'I thought the Americans had some gung-ho bang-bang plan.'

435

'Jamie?' Angus asked pleadingly. The man nodded.

'In the event of a nuclear weapon being seized by insurgents, the Joint Special Operations Command initiates what it calls a 'render-safe' mission. Basically they send in the SEALs or Delta Force to retrieve and immobilise the weapon. In the event of a larger scale action such as a coup by al-Qaeda, God help us all, the operation gets scaled up beyond the capacity of JSOC and would be led by US Central Command. They call that a disablement campaign; I call it the foothills of Mount Armageddon.

'Apart from that aspect, the obvious downside to the whole spectrum of JSOC's plans is that they're reactive. In addition, its commander has been quoted as saying that US units will not enter Pakistan except under extreme circumstances and with the government's permission, which it has the right to deny! Therefore, what we're suggesting are pre-emptive, preventative measures to be carried out with Britain's support.'

Mike tentatively raised his hand; Sir Angus nodded.

'Can you quantify the number and types of nuclear weapons? And do you know their locations, Mr Heathcote?'

'I'll be honest Major, our information is limited by circumstances and lack of clarity on the part of the Pakistan government. As far as we know it has approximately 95 nuclear weapons, plus or minus ten, but has the fissile capacity to double that figure. Some of those are buried underground or in hardened bunker facilities, probably near air bases; those we're not so concerned about. It's all the other ones that are based on road mobile launcher systems, bearing in mind that all of Pakistan's missiles are road mobile. Ironically, since JSOC's containment plans leaked out, they think the Americans are planning to steal nukes. The result has been that the Pakistanis have been moving warheads in unmarked commercial vans.

'Officials from their MoD have said that all weapons are stored demated; in other words the warheads are kept separately from both fissile cores and launchers. Apart from the few that aren't! We know that there are always a few missiles ready to go, just in case. What we do accept is that all their missiles are aimed at Indian targets. It would be impossible for us to secure Pakistan's complete nuclear arsenal. But if we could secure the garrisons which hold road-mobile missile launchers, the world would be one hell of a safer place.'

'And locations?' Mike prompted.

'Sorry. Yes, we've identified three. The Sargodha Garrison which is about 140 kilometres north of Faisalabad; Pano Aqil Garrison near Sukkur in Sindh Province; and the Khuzdar Garrison in Balochistan.'

'Thank you.'

'And what exactly are these 'pre-emptive, preventative measures' of yours, Heathcote?' asked Admiral Buller, retrieving the verbal baton. 'It all sounds rather vague if you ask me.'

'As I said, that's because we don't have all the information at our fingertips. We can't be seen to be snooping around, poking our noses around garrisons and air bases looking for nuclear warheads. That would give the Pakistanis a perfect excuse to arrest our people as spies!'

'Isn't that what you are?'

'That's a cheap jibe, Reggie,' said Angus. 'You know what he means.'

'Of course I bloody well do. I'm just waiting for you to get to the point rather than fannying around at the edges of the problem.'

'Fine. Having talked about the matter at length, we would like Major Roberts to go to Pakistan to assess the situation on the ground. The British High Commissioner to the Islamic Republic of Pakistan is Sir Bartholomew Jinks, based in Islamabad. Been out there for a few years now and knows the country well. I understand that he gets on rather well with the Prime Minister; apparently they share a love of cricket. Bart's sound, with a lot of experience and plenty of common sense. He'll facilitate a meeting with Prime Minister Asif and accompany you to the Secretariat. Don't worry, you'll have plenty of time to discuss battle plans with Bart beforehand. I suspect it'll be at least a couple of days before Asif will grant an audience; that's how it usually is with these people.

'He will be able to give you all the current background information you need and introduce you to the other key players. The Strategic Plans Division Force is the group responsible for protecting Pakistan's nuclear and strategic weaponry; currently headed up by Lieutenant General Ikram Bhutt. But he won't be the only one. I should think Asif will have at least two more Generals on the platform plus someone from Inter-Services Intelligence. The ultimate aim of the visit is to persuade Asif and his cohorts of the absolute necessity of reducing nuclear vulnerabilities by removing their road-mobile missiles to a totally secure location. In my opinion, that's likely to be in deep underground silos. Naturally, Great Britain will assist once the necessary assets have been identified, whether material and/or personnel. I think that pretty much covers it. Since this is an official request Admiral Buller, I take it you're happy for Major Roberts to undertake this task, bearing in mind that he will be going under the aegis of the Foreign Office, albeit under your control?'

'Of course, Angus. That goes without saying.'

'Major Roberts, do you have any reservations? Or any questions?'

'No, Sir Angus. I would however like to say that I'm honoured that you feel that I'm the right person for this particular job. In the first instance, I would have thought it's more of a diplomatic role.'

'Which is why you'll be working directly with Sir Bartholomew. Overtly you're being seconded to the High Commission as the Military Attaché. Therefore you're officially in an advisory role at the highest level. One might offer congratulations but please, don't feel honoured.'

'You devious old bastard!' exclaimed Admiral Buller, grinning with amusement.

'Thank you for the compliment, Reggie. Unless there's anything else, I think that we're done for the day. My people will make the travel arrangements and I'll talk to Bart Jinks in Islamabad. We'll let you have all the information this afternoon.'

Sir Angus collected up the papers in front of him, in readiness to leave. The men about him began to follow suit.

'Sir Angus, there is one more item which I do believe is vitally important.'

Helen's clear strong voice stopped them all in their tracks and each one sank back down in his chair, more than one with a sigh of resignation.

'Of course, Ms O'Connor. Please.'

'Thank you, Sir Angus. While I appreciate the importance of sending Major Roberts to Islamabad for talks, there is the very real danger that an al-Qaeda commander is on his way back to Pakistan with the specific intent of obtaining a nuclear device. We have reasonable intelligence that Abdul Saad al-Kabuli is travelling to Lahore as we speak, following his direct involvement in the destruction of HMS York. I believe that Mike's brief should be expanded to allow him ...'

'Ms O'Connor,' he interrupted, sounding wearily impatient, 'al-Kabuli is where? The Red Sea? Gulf of Aden? It doesn't matter. Now that the bombs have been dealt with, neither the Edinburgh or Manchester are at any risk of being blown up by al-Shami or his sponsors. Indeed, it's always possible that the hunted becomes the hunter, since HMS Edinburgh should be hard on the heels of the bloody dhow, or whatever it is, by now. That would be a coup! Al-Kabuli has still got a long way to go before he can even consider looking for his nuclear Grail. That's why we're doing what we're doing. Good morning, lady and gentlemen.'

'Sir,' Helen said, falling silent as she watched Sir Angus McFadden stand and walk past the table towards them.

He paused briefly before he left the room.

'Thank you all for coming this morning. Major Roberts, good luck. Reggie, Ms O'Connor.'

Brigadier Stephen Carson, Brendan Horton and Jamie Heathcote: they all wished Mike luck as they filed past and nodded politely to Helen and the Admiral. Helen remained silent as the three of them found their way back through the warren of corridors and staircases. The Jaguar was waiting for them in the quadrangle, its engine already purring quietly. The driver pulled out and underneath the arch, back toward the Red House.

'Sami Malik lives in Lahore, doesn't he?'

'Indeed he does, Admiral,' replied Helen.

'Then I think we should add Lahore to your itinerary, Major Roberts, don't you think?'

'I think that would make sense. After all, Sargodha has to be seen and that's less than 200 kilometres away. And I hear that

Lahore is the cultural capital of the country. How could I miss that?'

*****

Dwarfed by the vast oil tankers and container ships, the Rih Albahr slipped easily through the lines, her small size allowing her to follow a more flexible route. In the shadows of the towering dark walls of sheet metal and rivets, the temperature dropped by at least three degrees. Away from that slow moving line of darkness, the sun shone brightly in a cloudless sky, glittering on the blue waters of the Red Sea. The warm breeze carried the strong taste of salt, drawn from the heavy saline waters below, and had the grit of sand on its wings.

Abdul Saad al-Kabuli looked over the starboard bow toward the islands looming in the distance. His eyes flickered over the charts on the table, tapping his forefinger on his planned route.

'Hassan, that should be the beginning of the Dahlak Archipelago by my reckoning. How long do you think until we get to Bab el-Mandab?'

'At this speed, possibly 15 hours, Sayyid.'

'Can we get past this line before we reach the choke point?'

'If I squeeze out a few more knots, I think yes.'

'Good.'

Al-Kabuli looked back at the chart. At its widest point, the Red Sea was a little over 220 kilometres. At Bab el-Mandab, the strait connecting the Red Sea to the Gulf of Aden was only 30 kilometres across, divided in two by the island of Perim. He knew that the notorious bottleneck could hold them up for hours if they were badly positioned. But he had faith in his own maritime skills and those of Hassan. He settled back in his chair to watch the pair sparring on the foredeck. With Naseem as her teacher, Ayesha could become just as dangerously lethal. She already had that same lithe fluidity of movement, supreme control and a natural sense of precise timing. Techniques and moves could be taught and learned; her ability was innate. Al-Kabuli smiled as he saw her catch Naseem off guard with a blow from her elbow. They will make a good team, he thought.

440

Turning away from the two fighters, he looked across at Tarek al-Shami who was sitting on a sofa by the gunwales. Although he was holding a sheet of paper in his hands, his eyes were closed as he silently mouthed words and sentences, not looking at the writing on page.

'Professor, are you ready to make our film for Doctor Malik and General Mustagh?'

'Yes, Sayyid.'

'Perhaps you should give me a flavour beforehand. Begin.'

Tarek al-Shami cleared his throat and began to recite.

'To whom it may concern and is interested in my words, by the grace of Allah, my name is Tarek al-Shami. Although I conceived the great plan to ...

'A little more work is needed on the text and your presentation. I need to believe your confession and enjoy your denunciations.'

Al-Kabuli threw back his head and bellowed with laughter.

17 ~ In a Gentleman's Game

Emirates Flight No 2 from London Heathrow touched down at Dubai International at 00.40 hours. Despite the unholy time and the three hour wait for his onward flight, it was a relief to get off the plane. Late booking and little availability on a busy flight had allowed little choice; with no room to manoeuvre, he'd been squeezed towards the aisle by the sheer girth of an obese elderly lady with halitosis who was sitting in the window seat. The onward flight to Islamabad differed only in the detail: on flight 612 he was twinned with a distinctly odoriferous gentleman in a heavy serge suit who snored. In spite of his undesirable and unchosen companions, Mike Roberts slept remarkably well. He awoke instinctively when his body sensed that the plane was descending, confirmed by the double thump of the landing gear locking down.

By the time he'd negotiated immigration, customs and the mayhem of the baggage reclaim hall, any refreshment that his sleep had provided had been eroded below emotional ground level. Mike fought his way through the piles of tricoloured plastic bales tied with string and trolleys stacked with suitcases like land-based micro-container ships. Elbowed by impatient suits, pushed by angular men in panicked haste and kneed by elegant women in smart dresses with expressions that denied liability, he was relieved to see a single Caucasian in a lightweight cotton jacket towering over the assembled pack of Asian men dressed collectively in white salwar kameez.

'Richard Watts, British High Commissioner's Office,' the man said as Mike finally emerged. 'I'm assuming Major Mike Roberts?'

'And you'd be assuming right, Mr Watts, but I answer better to Mike.'

'Rick,' the other man replied, holding out his hand.

His handshake was firmly confident; Mike reciprocated and smiled.

'Come on, let's get you out of this ghastly mortal version of Hades.'

They walked out of the terminal into a chill wind that blew up the road towards them. Dust devils rose spasmodically from the dry ground, adding grit to air that brought the smells of jet fuel, cooking oil and spices. Rick led them to a dust-beige Toyota Hilux that was probably dark green and once had been new. Dents and scratches bore testament to a life of hard use.

'Climb in,' said Rick, grinning at Mike's obvious surprise. 'Admit it, you expected a black Merc with diplomatic plates.' He grinned again when Mike nodded, looking slightly shamefaced. 'Those cars are for when you want to be seen or have to be seen: official occasions such as dreary ambassadorial dinners and pointless ministerial conferences. We drag them out for genuine VIPs and some whose aspirations to VIP-dom need to be pandered to or encouraged.'

He switched on the engine and drove out of the car park to pick up Airport Road.

'This ruined old beast has a beating heart under the bonnet that, touch wood, hasn't let me down yet. Ten years old and still firing on all cylinders as though she was a youngster. But the main thing is that her looks don't draw any attention, which is just the way I like it to be.'

Rick steered the Toyota onto the slip road to join the Expressway.

'Islamabad's a strange place in many ways. One has that weird feeling that modern Islamabad was prefabricated in the 60s in some foreign factory, then beamed down to slot in next to Rawalpindi. A sort of time zone contrast installation dreamed up by some astral sculptor-come-architect. Look at almost any other city in Pakistan, possibly the world, and you'll find that each one has a heart, a central hub from which everything else radiates. Not Islamabad. Pakistan's capital is more of a sprawling middle-class wealth-driven suburb studded with 'centres', plural: there's the Convention Centre, Allergy Centre, the Information Centre, di-dah di-dah. You get my point.'

Rick hammered his foot down on the brakes as an ancient battered Mercedes swerved across the front of the Toyota on a determined diagonal.

'Which brings me back to why I have this old girl,' he said, accelerating up to speed. 'If you last a tour out here without having a bash or two, you've either been bloody lucky or you didn't drive! Nobody understands the meaning of lane control, the point of traffic lights and has no concept of braking distances or viable spaces in traffic. Actually, it's rather fun. Security bods say don't drive outside the city – technically it's banned – but the hills are just a little too tempting sometimes.'

'Presumably security concerns feature fairly high on the agenda in Islamabad,' said Mike, squeezing the sentence into the brief pause left as Rick hauled the steering wheel around to avoid hitting the car in front.

'Absolutely,' Rick replied, throwing the truck back into the nearside lane. 'Most of the time people bumble along in the daily grind and the dangers fade into the background, despite the constant security checks. But that's the danger; people become complacent, get lulled into that sense of false security. And then something happens. A lot of the people who work in the Diplomatic Enclave tend to take the shuttles. Think like a terrorist for a moment. What better target could there be for a roadside bomb than a van full of foreigners? So, I stick with my faithful Hilux and fade into the background.'

For a while both men were silent: Rick Watts negotiating his way through the early morning traffic; Mike Roberts taking in the buildings that flanked the Expressway. He leaned forward to look past Rick at the forested folds of hills that rose fleetingly out of the sea of dappled brick, concrete and trees; a wild green whale ascending above the constructs of mere mankind.

'Shakarparian,' explained Rick. 'Most of the year, it's a great place to go for walks or have picnics without leaving the city. But that's also where they have the Parade Ground. Either side of Pakistan Day the place is locked down with the parade itself taking place on 23 March. It's what amounts to being Independence Day for them, commemorating the Lahore Resolution of 1940 and the transition to an Islamic Republic in 1956, on the same date 16 years apart. It's a massive parade when the government trots out everlasting columns of troops from all three sectors of the armed forces. They have jets tearing up the sky, a ceremonial fly past, tanks chomping up the tarmac. Then of course there's the mandatory display of explosive might with rockets on trucks and missiles on launchers. Pakistan's power show didn't happen this year because of the earthquakes. At the end of the day, nature's always more powerful than man.'

'True, but nature doesn't discriminate when it spits out a tsunami or an earthquake. Mother Earth doesn't aim to punish or take revenge or murder because of what somebody else believes.'

'Considering all the damage that we do to her, maybe that's exactly what she's doing; it's payback for man's crimes against the environment. As for bombs and missiles, few of those differentiate between what the sender would call a legitimate target and civilians. The Americans have it nicely tied down: where the missile strikes, terrorists are legitimate targets and civilians, collateral damage.'

Mike grinned at the man in the driver's seat and forked two fingers to ward off the evil eye.

'Lord preserve me, I'm sitting next to a tree hugger!' he said tremulously, in mock horror.

'Nope, I'm simply of the opinion that one should consider cause and effect, and factor those into the equation. The situation in Pakistan is a complex conundrum, full of conflicting opposites that frequently conspire with each other against foreigners. And the foreigners happily collude, while following their own agendas.'

'Beware the philosopher diplomat for he speaks with forked tongue.'

The joint wave of laughter took a while to subside. Towards the end of Faisal Avenue, Rick turned right along Margalla Avenue and right again on Street 14A, running through a dense copse of evergreens. The residential area beyond boasted palatial houses and villas tucked in side by side but with walls or fences dividing garden from patio. The High Commissioner's private residence was a rather fine ochre coloured two-storey villa with a red-tiled roof, surrounded by lush green gardens to the sides and rear. Stopping the car in front of the gilded cast iron gates, they waited as a camera on top of the razor-wired wall peered down at the car. The gates swung slowly open, dragging across the gravelled drive in noisy rattle. As the pair walked across the deep bed of stones, the front door of the house opened to reveal a trim grey-haired, bare-footed man in a white short-sleeved shirt and burgundy trousers.

'You managed to dig him out from the airport, Richard. Good man. Major Roberts, welcome to Islamabad. Come in. Leave your bags by the door, Moheem will take them to your room. Follow me.' With that, Britain's High Commissioner to Pakistan padded off along the corridor, his feet making slight smacking noises on the marble floor. Coming to a small hall, he led them up a marble staircase bounded by wrought iron railings topped by polished wood banisters. Once on the second floor, he led them out through an open door onto a wide verandah with white painted railings that encircled the house. A white linen tablecloth covered a large square table, already laid with cutlery, water glasses and napkins. Finally pausing, he turned to look at Mike and shook his hand.

'Sit down, both of you. No need for introductions since we all know who we are. I thought we'd have a spot of breakfast first since I doubt you had very much on the plane. They usually serve such awful stuff anyway.'

A willowy young woman, perhaps in her early twenties, appeared from the far end of the verandah. The emerald green kameez was unadorned save a little gold embroidery around the high neckline; the matching salwar below, plain. Walking towards them with unconscious sinuosity, she stood out against the darker green of the garden's evergreen spiky foliage. She stopped a few yards away, put her hands together and bowed very slightly, her eyes focused on the three men.

'Namaste,' she said, looking directly at Mike Roberts.

He smiled at the woman and responded instinctively, mirroring her gesture.

'This is the lovely Hina,' Sir Bart said, addressing Mike. 'She and her husband Moheem take care of the house and me in that order. Apart from being terribly organised, clever and beautiful, Hina's also an outstanding cook. I heartily recommend her omelettes. Major?'

'Sounds wonderful, Sir.'

Sir Bart rattled off several sentences in fluent Pashto to which Hina answered with single words, short phrases or a wiggle of the head.

'You like chillis?'

'Yes, Sir.'

'Sterling,' said Sir Bart, and ran out a few more words in Pashto before she turned and left. 'You're staying here at the Residence while you're in Islamabad. Several reasons: we have six bedrooms and since I only use one of them, there's plenty of space. Hina and Moheem have their own separate quarters. I think it would be wise if we kept you out of the High Commission offices in the Diplomatic Enclave, away from prying questions from nosey people. Not that I don't think you can hold your own Major; rather that I don't trust all of them not to flap their lips in the wrong ears. Plus it will be far easier to have discussions in confidence here rather than in one of the offices. I think you'll find it a lot more comfortable and the food is definitely a lot better. Speaking of which ...'

Placing a large white plate in front of each of the men, Hina dexterously lifted out three perfectly folded omelettes from a hot metal bowl. From a small ceramic dish, she took pinches of freshly cut coriander, sprinkling a little of the herb on each one. Visually attractive, the combined aroma of the constituent parts was sublime. Lightly sautéed onions and chopped chilli with a hint of cumin and perhaps a shade of turmeric, blended into the lightest of eggs carefully cooked in a smear of ghee. Mike forked up a small mouthful.

'This smells divine and tastes, absolutely heavenly,' he gushed.

Hina rewarded him with sunny smile as she added a plate of roti to the table. She poured black tea into white china cups with gold rims, placing a sliver of green lime on each saucer. A dish of freshly prepared fruit – segments of pink grapefruit, orange mandarins and sweet oranges – completed the service, complementing the display and adding a tart zing to the already aromatic air.

'Doesn't matter what time of day it is, I always love being up here. Those are the Margalla Hills over there,' Sir Bart said, pointing to the range of dark green forested hills a mere stone's throw away. 'Mainly coniferous trees, which is why it's so green all the time but a decent percentage of flowering deciduous ones as well. Glorious birdsong at this time of day and cackling jackals at night with a few screeching rhesus monkeys to fill in the gaps.

'Folklore has it that Margalla stems from a mix of Persian and Pashto meaning the abode of snakes. Not surprisingly, there are a lot of them in the hills but only three that are poisonous. Russell's vipers, cobras and kraits. Some people call the blue krait the half-minute killer because of the extreme toxicity of its venom. Not that the krait's actually blue, more a shiny brown-black with white bands. This time of year the snakes tend to stay up in the hills but we quite often get them down here in the rainy season. That's July-August, just in case you were worried. On the whole they don't bother us and Moheem's not a bad snake catcher when the need arises.'

Sir Bart polished off the remnants of his omelette with a sigh of pleasure and wiped his plate clean with a scrap of roti. Glancing at Mike's similarly empty plate, he pushed the fruit dish in his direction.

'Have some, they're delicious. Particularly the kinnows,' he said, pointing at some deep orange segments. 'I'm told they're a highly prized hybridized mandarin that's grown mainly in the Punjab. These come from the Sargodha region, about 242 kilometres south. Usually we don't get any until late December or early January.'

Limiting himself to a few pieces of fruit, Sir Bart sipped his tea thoughtfully, chewed occasionally and watched Mike Roberts tucking in to a goodly pile of citrus segments. Throughout his career, first in the army with the Royal Dragoon Guards and subsequently with the Diplomatic Service, Sir Bartholomew Jinks had assessed men of all ranks and positions; those assessments were rarely wrong. He told himself that it was far too early to say, but young Major Roberts came with impeccable references and a fine track record. And Bart Jinks had a good gut feeling about the officer at his table, enthusiastically attacking a pile of fruit.

'Must have some coffee,' he said out loud. 'Too much blasted tea.'

As though he'd been speaking on an intercom, Hina materialised only a few moments later to clear the table. As she gathered up the empty dishes, she acknowledged the compliments with smile and a nod.

'How many coffee?' she asked haltingly.

Only Rick demurred. Hina reappeared with two cups of strong black coffee and a small jug of cream within minutes. Sir Bart added a little cream, sipped the hot liquid through the cold and smacked his lips with satisfaction. Producing a small black cheroot, he placed it between his lips and lit it with a cheap plastic lighter. He blew a stream of toxic smoke into the air above his head.

'I've known Angus McFadden, vaguely off and on since he was a snotty-nosed brat at Winchester, a year below me if I remember rightly. The headmaster was a strange chap called Desmond Lee; very tall with an odd way of speaking. Thought that English Literature was 'weak' and that teachers who taught the subject were probably subversive. I digress, although mirroring Lee and reading Classics probably enabled Angus' mindset. He's always been convinced that he has the ability to dissect complex problems, quickly analyse and come up with the perfect solution. He gave me the bones and cartilage of your objectives in Islamabad. But I prefer to hear it from the bright dog on point rather than the blind handler. So, in your own words Major Roberts, I'd like you to tell me why you're here and what you hope to achieve.'

Mike Robert's mind went into overdrive, trying to understand exactly what Jinks was asking, what he was looking for beyond what he'd heard from Angus McFadden.

'My brief from Sir Angus is to assess where the vulnerabilities are in Pakistan's nuclear security. Identify and plug them, if possible, by moving those particular weapons to a more secure location. It's been suggested that I aim to visit the three key sites which are thought to be the most vulnerable. That would be my first objective. After that, to discuss the options with the Prime Minister, Lieutenant General Ikram Bhutt and other advisors who might be involved.'

Mike paused to look at the two men, Rick Watts to his left and Bart Jinks on the other side of the table. At first sight, the High Commissioner's face was unremarkable, almost bland, until one looked into the hard blue-grey marbled eyes. Incisive and interrogatory, his gaze was hard and direct. Neither Watts nor Jinks said a word, simply waiting for Mike to continue. And he knew that they knew there was far more to say than the regurgitation of a few nebulous ideas.

'I do realise that any success in that arena can only be damage limitation rather than a complete security solution. However, my colleagues and I are more concerned about what we believe to be an imminent danger that could result in a nuclear warhead or material being seized by terrorists.'

'Before you continue Major, your colleagues in this instance are Rear Admiral Sir Reginald Buller and Ms Helen O'Connor?'

'Yes, Sir.'

'Angus mentioned that they were at the meeting. Go on.'

Mike ran through the chronology of the sabotaged ships uninterrupted; the questions started when he began to detail what he knew about key individuals. Jinks asked for a verbal audit on the NuCan devices that conclusively implicated both Doctor Sami Malik and General Pamir Mustagh. Watts asked for more evidential detail on Abdul Saad al-Kabuli's role and seemed especially interested in the perceived areligious bias. When the interaction finally slowed to a halt, Sir Bart called for more coffee and lit another cheroot.

'So you believe that al-Kabuli is going to Lahore to see Sami Malik? Why?'

'That actually does make sense, Sir,' Rick Watts interjected. 'Malik has comprehensive knowledge about the nuclear programme as a whole and, more specifically, knows how to put them together and pull them apart. Without someone like Sami Malik, al-Kabuli might be able to steal a warhead but without knowing how to exploit its potential, it's just a useless lump of metal.'

'Even Malik wouldn't help someone like al-Kabuli with nuclear weapons,' Jinks remonstrated. 'I suspect he's fairly certain that he's safe from reprisals in respect of al-Shami's operation: there's no bi-lateral extradition treaty between the UK and Pakistan. Pamir Mustagh may be technically retired but he's still a senior executive member in the hierarchy of the Strategic Plans Division Force and is well placed in the powerhouse coterie of Generals. Mustagh could protect Malik anyway, to a degree, but I'm sure that the two of them spread a little of the largesse received from al-Qaeda. If he plays nuclear games with al-Kabuli, he'll have no protection, anywhere.'

'But he might play along if he was threatened?'

'Devil and the deep blue, Major. Capital punishment is legal in Pakistan and the authorities have no compunction in applying the death penalty. Sixty people have been executed this year in the Punjab alone and historically, Islamabad is part of the Punjab. If Malik aids al-Kabuli without success, he has a chance of surviving. Success would almost certainly result in a show trial and execution if he were caught; if not, I doubt whether al-Kabuli would keep him alive longer than was necessary. On the other hand, he'd be killed if he refused or tortured until he changed his mind. Whichever way you look at it, Sami Malik's up shit creek without a paddle. However, let's assume that your theory about al-Kabuli's planned visit is right, what's your plan, Major?'

'I'm hoping to persuade the Prime Minister to place Malik under house arrest.'

Mike's statement floated onto the table between them as though it was written on papyrus in Egyptian hieroglyphics. Confusion was palpable.

'My aim is to convince them that Doctor Malik could be as much of an international embarrassment and liability as Abdul Qadeer Khan. If the Americans caught a whisper of the fact that Malik was selling nuclear technology to rogue states that would be enough to shut him down in the same way as Khan. There's a direct connection since Malik not only worked under him at Kahuta, he was an integral part of research and development. Malik's taken the programme one step further by manufacturing explosive devices (and other types of munitions) and selling those to rogue end users. In our case, the end use resulted in the destruction of two ships and massive loss of life. That puts him firmly on the books as a freelance terrorist who doesn't care who the buyer is or how they plan to use his products.'

'Sorry, I still don't get the point.'

'Sami Malik's the tethered goat waiting for the tiger. At best it stops there; at worst, al-Kabuli or someone else collects Malik and takes him shopping for nukes. Either way, we stop them all.'

'Who exactly is 'we', Major Roberts?' Sir Bartholomew queried.

'I thought it might be useful to bring a cricket team out from Hereford. Of course there'd be one or two coaches as well, with me included in the line-up. If Malik's under house arrest, I'm guessing his guards' only remit will be to prevent him wandering off on his own. But we'll be waiting. Might even get the odd match in with the Army boys.'

'It has merit,' Sir Bart said slowly. 'I think the UK Trade and Investment Office in Lahore could be persuaded to stump up some accommodation. But let's go back to the original plan, or should I say, Angus' non-plan. In principle I agree that security might be improved. You might find this strange Major but to a certain extent, I do also agree with Ikram Bhutt when he defends the safety of the nuclear programme. Much of it is a uniquely Pakistani way of dealing with the problems; and there is more than just one from the Generals' point of view. The Americans are in a tailspin, in the belief that nuclear warheads are being transported around the country in commercial vehicles without escorts. Poppycock! Parts belonging to nuclear weapons – unarmed warheads, nuclear pits or fissile cores of the things, plutonium and uranium elements – are apparently often transported in commercial vehicles because they blend in with all the other traffic. That's more to hide nuclear movements from the Americans rather than jihadis or terrorists. The best place to hide is often in plain view. That ring any bells with you, Major?'

'From a long way back, Sir,' Mike answered, smiling at the memory the line conjured.

'There's no military escort or big warning sign because that would give the game away. Get your nukes here, type of thing. Fully armed nuclear weapons on transporter erector launchers aren't driven around in full view; the ones you see in parades are obviously unarmed. So the key factor here is that individual parts are transported independently; on their own, they're useless to anyone who might try to steal something even if they knew which truck to hit. Therefore, keeping with Pakistani logic, the most vulnerable points would be at commonly known garrisons like Sargodha; which is precisely why they have 'maximum and impenetrable security' as Bhutt likes to say.

'However, a covert initiative to improve security at key sites might be welcomed. Some information could be leaked to the

452

Americans after the fact, which would pacify them enough to at least ensure the continued flow of dollars. Omitting the details of new locations would serve to infuriate but not change. While Afghanistan remains as volatile as it is, the US needs Pakistan as a back door.'

'London suggested moving the warheads from the garrisons at Sargodha, Pano Aqil and Khuzdar. In an ideal world, I should visit each one but will they let me?'

'Dear boy, as the Military Attaché to the British High Commission to Pakistan, they will be absolutely delighted to give you the guided tour; of all three facilities if you wish. It gives them the opportunity to parade their nuclear power and demonstrate that maximum, impenetrable security.'

'Can we do it more covertly? I understand that a team of Inspectors is arriving this week from the International Atomic Energy Agency. Is there any possibility of piggy-backing as one of them?'

'Afraid not Major, unless you want to visit power stations. The IAEA has a Safeguarding Agreement in place with Pakistan but that only extends as far as the use of nuclear power for peaceful activities. Until India signs up to the Non-Proliferation Treaty, Pakistan isn't going to play either. That stalemate isn't going to be resolved for quite a while yet. But you don't need to look that closely. I suggest going to one, Sargodha. It's the biggest, probably the most vulnerable of the three, and it's the closest to Lahore. If you're right about al-Kabuli and Malik, that's where they'll go shopping.

'I'll set up a meeting with the Prime Minister and certainly Lieutenant General Ikram Bhutt. I suspect that at least one or two of the other Generals will be involved and one of those could well be Pamir Mustagh. Are you planning to denounce him as well as Malik?'

'I hadn't decided ...'

'It might be prudent to hold back on General Mustagh. If he thinks he's not in line for house arrest and punishment, I suspect he'll be in the vanguard of those wanting to bring Doctor Malik to his knees. And we definitely wouldn't want the Doctor forewarned of his position in the great game.'

*****

The drab rocky hills of Masirah Island were a minor visual relief after the beige-brown monotony of the earlier Omani coastline. Sandy off-white strips of beach wound their way through the jagged rocks to aquamarine waters that lapped so kindly in return. But where the water deepened to become a rich marine blue, patches of bright aquamarine warned of the dangers below. Held up by invisible fingers of coral, the wrecks and skeletons of boats were displayed as trophies, a reminder of how treacherous the waters could be if one got too close to land. Heeding those warnings of sight and memory, Hassan sailed clear of the island to the west, keeping a course that would take the Rih Albahr parallel to the coast for some 153 more nautical miles before they reached Al Hadd on the northeast spike of Oman.

Keeping just outside the limit of Oman's territorial waters, the Rih Albahr pushed through the light chop at precisely 20 knots, throwing up a small white bow wave, spitting spindrift into the warm air. As was becoming their custom, Ayesha and Naseem were training together on the foredeck, maintaining a drum concerto of percussive thuds and grunts. Al-Kabuli and Haroun were in quiet conversation in their usual place near the bridge, occasionally pausing to watch the controlled violence of athletics near the bow. Tarek sat on one of the low sofas, his head resting against on a cushion, idly watching the distant coastline go by. The murmur of voices from below was like a thousand small stones moving hither and thither with the flow of water.

Out to sea, around an arc of some 240 degrees the dark blue undulating Arabian Sea stretched out to the horizon. On that vast ever-moving liquid canvas, the huge oil tankers seemed as toys while stacked containers on the low decks of their long ships painted patchwork quilts of colour. The light rusty pastels of commercial fishing boats added a few more matt dabs among the glitter spawned by the many reflections of sunlight. Once in a while a small pod of dolphins might appear but little else relieved the monotony. Until a new ship appeared on Mohammed's radar to the south, sailing on a parallel course to the Rih Albahr but at a far greater speed.

Travelling at approximately 28 knots, the ship would overhaul them in just over an hour and the distance between them, assuming the current course would be between six and seven nautical miles. A super yacht was unlikely to be cruising at that speed, but it was possible if it was being delivered to a client in Dubai or Abu Dhabi. Omani customs or fisheries launches would be too far from any home base to be so far down the coastline. Which left only one possibility and that was a naval ship.

The international call sign reading gave GBBE; the Maritime Mobile Service Identity number, 234590000. The first three digits of the MMSI number told him the vessel was British, but short of radioing the ship and asking, he had no way of finding out its identity. Then he remembered the list that Sayyid al-Kabuli had taken from al-Shami after the York had been destroyed, with the details of the British destroyers.

'Hassan, you have al-Shami's list of English ships?'

'You have seen something?' he asked, extracting the now scruffy sheet of paper from the map case.

'I have an MMSI of 234590000 on a ship about nine nautical miles south on the same bearing, sailing at 28 knots.'

'It's the third one, called HMS Edinburgh. Will our courses converge, Mohammed?'

'At the moment there is no sign of them closing the gap between us. On my calculations, it will pass us in maybe 55 minutes, minimum six nautical miles east.'

Al-Kabuli received the news clearly since it was called loudly through the open window on the bridge as Hassan leaned sideways while maintaining contact with the ship's wheel. It filtered through Tarek's reverie, paused Ayesha and Naseem's exertions. Anticipating the call to counsel, the latter two walked back along the deck towards the bridge, sitting down on a sofa close enough to be addressed, far enough to not be intrusive.

'She is earlier than we expected. If the Edinburgh maintains her current speed she will pass through the Strait of Hormuz a long time before us. Hassan, how far do you estimate it is to Musandam?'

'Almost 455 nautical miles, Sayyid.'

'Haroun, you're the mathematician.'

For a few seconds the Bookkeeper tapped numbers into a calculator.

'They will be ten hours ahead of us by the time we reach Kumzar. As they sail through the Strait, we will have just passed Muscat. There is no way that we can catch up unless they stop for some reason. And that is not likely. We must assume that they will go directly to Mina Salman.'

'Then it would be out of range and we cannot risk following her to Bahrain. Which means we try to destroy her now, or we abandon and move on. Naseem, what do you think?'

'That we try now, Sayyid. We do not know whether the British have discovered the remaining two bombs but I think that maybe they have. If we try to detonate and nothing happens, we will know for certain; but if the ship is destroyed, then we will have one more success. Either way, going back to strike the fourth ship in the Mediterranean Sea is not an option for us. And there is one more thing: it is possible that they are hunting for us, for the Rih Albahr. I do not think that is the case, but if it is we do not want to turn towards them and show our face.'

Haroun tapped more numbers into his calculator.

'Assuming that Edinburgh's course runs parallel to ours at a distance of six nautical miles, plus or minus one half, she will be at optimum range when the two ships are aligned. She should be in range for approximately 15 minutes either side of that point but at the limit of the transmitter's range at both ends of the spectrum.'

'You agree with Naseem, that we should try with the transmitter?'

'We have nothing to lose by trying Abdul Saad, and information is knowledge. I do not think I am mistaken: there is no way that the British or any other agency could identify the Rih Albahr or connect her with you, me or the organisation. Even the purchase was carried out on instructions that passed through some five levels of persons. If the transmitter does not work, we must assume that instructions as to where the bombs were and how they should be removed were extracted from the source. They will know the names of Amin Masri and Tarek al-Shami as well as Ali Abbas, or Alan Abbot as he calls himself. They will not know where we are now but they will be watching for any little mistake.

'Ironically if the transmitter works, we show our hand and our approximate location. But it will take time for them to mobilise and their ships will be looking for one unknown fish in a shoal of many. Whatever happens, we should sail straight to Gwadar from here, then by sea or road to Karachi. Driving would add 133 kilometres to the journey but it would be faster.'

Haroun took a breath, poised to continue but was stopped by al-Kabuli's upheld hand.

'The details of that will wait until later, my friend. Ayesha, I have not as yet asked you for your thoughts. Please.'

Recognising his request as a token of his esteem and his acceptance of her at this ad hoc council-of-war, she coloured slightly with appreciation. Ayesha knew that it was highly unusual for a woman to be allowed sit on such a council, let alone be asked for her opinion, in the complex patriarchal social systems of the region. She bowed her head to hide the feelings that might have expressed themselves, overtly giving obeisance to al-Kabuli.

'I too would agree that it makes sense to at least try to destroy one more ship. If it is as Haroun believes, Amin and Ali will have told the British all they know and we will need to be cautious wherever we are. But perhaps we will be successful once more, masha'allah. In this case, I would suggest that Haroun's advice to sail directly to Gwadar was amended; it is what they would expect us to do. We would be better concealed by sailing up the eastern side of the peninsula and crossing the Strait to Qeshm. Rih Albahr would easily pass for a commercial Iranian dhow. But I understand that it would make the journey much longer and perhaps lose too much time.'

'Then we are of an accord in respect of the Edinburgh,' said al-Kabuli. 'Hassan, where is she now?'

A muffled conversation from the bridge sent unintelligible noises to the gathering on deck.

'The Edinburgh will be in direct alignment with us in 12 minutes and the distance between us has closed to just under four nautical miles. She's maintaining a new parallel course without further convergence, Sayyid. You should have visual contact on the horizon in a couple of minutes. The ship is well within range now.'

'Ayesha, the transmitter.'

'Am I not to be consulted?' said a slightly distant and petulant voice.

'No Professor al-Shami, you lost that right several days ago. But I'll allow a brief comment,' al-Kabuli added with magnanimous condescension.

'I don't believe that Amin and Alan have betrayed us. We took an oath, vowed to avenge what happened to our families and they have played their parts. I believe that the NuCan is still in the missile on that ship and that when the signal is sent it will trigger another explosion. If Ayesha still wants another blood payment, so be it, but I believe that the debt has been paid. Marina's torture and death was needless barbarity; even now I do not believe she was …'

Al-Kabuli's slow handclap brought Tarek's speech to a halt.

'You never fail to amaze me Professor. You clearly missed your vocation: you really should have been an actor, a thespian specialising in melodramas. Revenge as a specific was simply a new opening in our fight for the cause, the struggle against invaders and oppressors. I do believe that our fight in Afghanistan, Iraq and for all Palestinians is right and just. You lost reality in a conflicting cocktail of religious academia and hedonism, stirred with the olive of a single bitter memory. No matter, you still have a part to play in the great game.'

He turned to Ayesha and looked at the transmitter, held loosely in her left hand.

'It is your right, if you so wish,' he said, the question implicit in his tone.

She nodded, gave a grim smile that conveyed both intent and calm confidence.

'Look to the east, I think that must be the Edinburgh on the horizon now,' cried Naseem.

Picking up his binoculars, al-Kabuli quickly found the grey silhouette in his sights and confirmed Naseem's supposition. Without losing his focus, he told Ayesha to begin. She turned the transmitter to on, pressed the green button, keyed in zero three, pushed the red button and watched the familiar green fan searching for its mate. After almost a minute the fan froze, turned orange and faded to black. Ayesha tried again, with the same result.

'Nothing,' she said.

'Try the other number, just in case the devices were the other way around.'

She pressed the green button again to bring the transmitter back to life: keyed zero four, mashed the red button and watched the fan searching, seizing, turning orange and fading to black. Ayesha repeated the sequence again to no avail, then switched off and started again from the beginning. Nothing.

'You were wrong Professor, and Haroun was right: Abbas gave the British the information they needed to save the other two ships. I suspect he traded the information for freedom for him and his family. Perhaps Masri and his wife were included as well. It would make sense and, in his position, I might have done the same. Perhaps for different reasons; one cannot fight the war from inside a prison cell.'

Plucking the now useless transmitter from Ayesha's hand, al-Kabuli threw it overboard and watched it disappear.

'Hassan, set course for Karachi. When do you estimate we will arrive?'

'In just under 24 hours, insha'allah.'

'Excellent. It's time to raise the stakes.'

*****

A slate blue sky leaked warm grey drizzle over Islamabad, blurring details of tiling, colour and contrast to drab whitewashed blankness.The Prime Minister's Secretariat at 44000 Constitution Avenue looked lack-lustre and tired. Lines of blind windows, framed by darkened archways or stark boxes, sheltered between the innumerable turrets that seemed to rise from every possible position. Those octagonal guardians stood silent and faceless, gazing invisibly from between the slim columns, under stone hats that reminded Mike Roberts of creamy pith helmets.

Moheem stopped the black Toyota Land Cruiser in front of the double wrought iron gates under an arch in the same style. A large enamelled boss was inset into each gate bearing the national colours of a white crescent and star on a dark green background. Neither of the armed guards flanking the gates moved a muscle, but a junior officer appeared by the side of the car. Despite the fact that he clearly recognised both the High Commissioner and Rick Watts, he insisted on seeing their identity papers. He studied each one as though trying to scan it with his eyes; compared photograph with actual face no less than three times per person. Finally satisfied, he saluted smartly, disappeared into his guard cave and the gates swung slowly open.

Leaving Moheem to park the car, the three men walked up the steps to the front entrance and into a cool marbled atrium. They were greeted by more guards and uniformed officials wielding handheld body scanners in front of two arches of walk-through metal detectors. Very politely but firmly, one official told them that each man would have to be properly identified, assessed and checked for anything that might be used to cause physical damage before entering the Secretariat proper. Despite Sir Bartholomew's protestations, the man insisted and requested their papers once again. He stopped immediately at the sound of what sounded like a torrent of abuse in Urdu. A clatter of shoes on the marble floor as a wiry besuited man wearing glasses and a large frown walked towards them as fast as his legs could carry him.

'Sir Bartholomew, I am mortified not to have been here when you arrived,' he said in a voice that had clearly been honed at an English public school.

He snapped out a few more sentences in Urdu at the squirming officials who immediately opened the barriers. They bowed obsequiously without looking up as the British High Commissioner to Pakistan walked through, followed by Major Mike Roberts and Special ADC to the High Commissioner, Rick Watts.

'Javed Khan,' Rick whispered to Mike as they walked past the bowed heads. 'Khan's the Prime Minister's Personal Assistant, Secretary and self-appointed fixer. Knows Asif's mind better than the Prime Minister himself and, some say, often makes Asif's mind up for him. About as trustworthy as a blue krait and allegedly, sometimes as lethal, but an extremely useful friend if he's on your side.'

'Ah, here we are,' Sir Bartholomew observed, breaking his half started conversation with Javed Khan when Mike and Rick arrived a few seconds later. 'Rick Watts you already know, naturally. However, I'm delighted to introduce our Special Military Attaché Major Mike Roberts on secondment from SAF in London.'

As though by magic, Khan materialised immediately in front of Mike with his hand extended.

'Javed Khan, the Prime Minister's Personal Assistant. I'm delighted to meet you Major Roberts.'

'Likewise, Mr Khan,' Mike responded, shaking the other man's hand.

The handshake was firm, the skin dry smooth and the nails perfectly manicured.

'Please gentlemen, follow me,' he said, walking towards the broad staircase that curved upwards to the left, onto the first floor. 'Sir Bartholomew mentioned that you're attached to SAF? I don't think I've heard of that agency. Please, do enlighten me, Major.'

'It's an acronym …'

'Aren't they always? People seem to feel it necessary to use a bloody acronym for everything under the sun. I have this terrible vision of people talking acronymically without using one single whole word. Imagine, CYPPTS at the dinner table instead of could you please pass the salt. And think of all the misunderstandings that might arise? My apologies, Major, I have to confess to being something of an acronymaphobe. You were about to say.'

'I sympathise but sometimes the full version really isn't that interesting. Special Arc Force. We're a small element in the broad spectrum of Britain's intelligence services.'

'Aha, so you are a spy, Major Roberts?' Khan asked, turning to look directly at Mike.

'No. But perhaps you might call me a facilitator.'

Javed Khan held his focus, checking Mike's expression for disingenuity or mockery. Finding none, he roared with laughter.

'Perhaps unwitting, but touché anyway. I believe someone may have been speaking out of turn. No matter. It is my privilege at times to perform the same role for Prime Minister Asif.'

461

Khan paused at the top of the staircase, waiting for Sir Bartholomew and Rick to catch up, before leading the way down a wide corridor lined with ornately carved marble niches and faux arches. Stopping at double doors made of polished walnut, he knocked twice with his knuckles before opening both in grandiose movement. Stepping aside to let his guests into the wood-panelled room beyond, he closed the doors behind them.

A lead crystal cut glass Waterford bowl filled with fresh flower heads floating on water adorned the glass-topped coffee table. Sitting on an antique Persian carpet, it formed the centrepiece of a space bounded by a rose-pink sofa with gilded edging down the sides and four matching armchairs. Wan light spread softly through the tall arched windows beyond that looked out onto the gardens below. The man standing in front of the sofa was clearly Prime Minister Asif; his familiar face had been replicated on vast posters that covered walls as well as frequently appearing in news broadcasts and print.

Clean-shaven with light grey hair combed over to one side, he was wearing a dark blue woollen suit that might have been made in Italy. The emerald green tie was shot through with silver threads, contrasting with the pristine white shirt. Mike thought the man looked tired, the fatigue showing in the colour of his skin and the bags underneath his eyes. But those eyes were still alert and the smile seemed genuinely welcoming. Perhaps that was one of the lesser weapons in a politician's armoury, a small voice posited cynically.

The other two men were both in uniform but there the resemblance ended. By the looks of the gongs that hung around his neck and decorated most of the left hand side of his beige uniform jacket, Mike guessed a rank General or higher. He couldn't quite read the name on the right hand side underneath the paratrooper's wings. Given the slack fatty jowls, panda eyes and the large belly that flopped over his belt, it was a fair assumption that it had been a while since the General had jumped out of a plane.

Dressed in light brown-green camouflage fatigues and polished army boots, the other one looked fit and used to active service. The ribbons on his chest were limited to three discreet bars but by the pips on his shoulders, his rank was not far below that of a General. Shaded by the peak of a baseball cap laden with gold braid and dark glasses hiding the man's eyes, his was a difficult face to read. The only other feature was a thin hard mouth edged by a thick black pencil moustache. Mike thought back to the meeting in Whitehall and concluded it was Lieutenant General Ikram Bhutt.

'Good morning, Sir Bartholomew, Mr Watts and, I believe, Major Roberts. For the sake of the Major, let me introduce General Pamir Mustagh who is the titular head of the National Command Authority and, under that banner, leads the Employment Control Committee which is responsible for developing our policies for the deployment and use of nuclear weapons. On my left, Lieutenant General Ikram Bhutt, the Director-General of the Strategic Plans Division which is responsible for nuclear security. He too has a role within the National Command Authority as a senior member of the Development Control Committee which deals with the technical development of weapons and their command-control systems.'

Each man acknowledged his introduction with a stiff formal bow towards the British contingent. But in both cases, the men kept their eyes focused on the visitors just in case something untoward occurred.

'Good morning gentlemen,' Sir Bartholomew responded, maintaining the cordial tenor of communications. 'And thank you Prime Minister for the introductions. Clearly I do not need to introduce Major Roberts as Mr Khan has already indicated by implication, you have already been briefed on his background and role. But perhaps I should explain ...'

'My dear High Commissioner, I do think that we should all sit down and take some tea before dealing with this tedious business. Please,' he added, walking across to an old-fashioned bell pull on the wall near the doors.

They conversed politely on inconsequentialities as they waited for the tea to arrive. The high levels of humidity for the time of year, the stupidity of fast bowlers Shoaib Akhtar and Mohammad Asif taking nandrolone to enhance their performance, and whether England had done better than Pakistan in the ICC Champions Trophy. When the tea boy arrived, the aromatic liquid was served with just a touch of milk in rose decorated scalloped porcelain cups on matching saucers. Naturally accompanied by an array of biscuits artistically displayed on a matching plate. As the conversation slowed and the levels of tea descended, Prime Minister Asif decided to open talks on more serious subjects.

'I believe that you wish to dredge up the bones of concern over the perceived parlous state of Pakistan's nuclear security for the umpteenth time, High Commissioner. However Javed said you wished to offer some positive suggestions with which Britain would be prepared to assist. I might suggest that you have forgotten one of your own British proverbs, Sir Bartholomew: whose house is of glass, must not throw stones at another. To date, our security has been tested but not breached; yours I believe has been found to be sadly faulty in recent days. However, please accept my profound condolences on your country's terrible losses.'

Biting down hard on the desire to be extremely rude to the Prime Minister, Bart Jinks simply acknowledged the final remark with a nod and a shrug.

'Without intelligence, there was no way that we could have prevented either of the tragedies. The man who planted the bombs in the missiles had been living in Britain for over 20 years, had top-level security clearance and a senior position with a key supplier to the Ministry of Defence. It's thanks to Major Roberts, his colleagues and contacts in the other agencies that he was arrested. The information that he provided enabled us to save the two other ships that he and his accomplices had planned to destroy. I assume you've seen the video given to and screened by Al Jazeera after the Gloucester's destruction in Cyprus?' Registering the nods of confirmation, he continued. 'Then you'll be aware of the 'elemental fires' line. Given the high levels of proscribed terrorist organizations in Pakistan and our concerns over security, Whitehall was keen to assist your country to help ensure that a nuclear weapon does not fall into their hands.'

'Let me allay your fears, Your Excellency.'

Ikram Bhutt leaned out of his chair towards Sir Bartholomew, his head and chest jutting pugnaciously outwards, reminiscent of a fighting cockerel. He then proceeded to repeat almost word for word what Bart Jinks had told Mike over breakfast two days before. He spoke of high levels of security especially on air bases, of hardened surface facilities and deep underground storage. The Lieutenant General explained the way in which nuclear weapons were stored demated, divided into the three component parts: delivery systems, fissile cores and warheads that would need to be reassembled before they could be fired.

'We enforce tight operational security measures to the point that no one person knows the location of every single nuclear warhead in Pakistan. That information is compartmentalized first between the army and the air force and then by region. Each location can be linked if and when necessary. What allows us to function collectively in this unique way is that every one of our warheads is targeted on India. Nowhere else.

'And finally, we operate a Two-Fisted-Authority Protocol; the Americans call their system PAL – Permissive Action Link – our TFAP works in a similar way. Arming and firing any one nuclear warhead, however deployed, requires codes from two separate people. That principle applies from the top to the bottom of the system, from the President's command to the man who carries out the final action. No aspect of the process can be activated unless coded by two authorised parties and all the codes are controlled by a computerised management system. That extends to the nuclear warheads themselves: they will only arm themselves on receiving a specific arming signal that's uniquely generated outside the missile or bomb. Every nuclear weapon in Pakistan can only be made operational through TFAP and each one is equipped with the code management system. In my opinion, Your Excellency, gentlemen, it would be easier to conduct brain surgery with a knife and fork while blindfolded than successfully hack TFAP and operate the embedded systems.'

Ikram Bhutt spread his arms with palms facing upwards, shrugged, a smile of satisfaction curling his mouth. His was the facial expression of a man who completely believes that his words are irrefutable, anticipating and annihilating any possible argument. Rewarding himself with a Nankhatai zafrani khoya biscuit from the plate, he relaxed back into his seat and nibbled.

'Lieutenant General Bhutt, if we could go back to the storage of the demated weaponry,' said Mike Roberts, breaking into the sound vacuum. 'Am I right in saying that at any one location, although the missiles are demated, all three elements are stored in the same building?'

'Yes, and no, Major. Although they are in the same building, the various elements are segregated. The delivery systems, the missiles, or rockets if you prefer, are stored in an area comparable to an aircraft hangar, to allow easy access for technicians to work and be able to quickly bring in TELs, the transporter erector launchers. The warheads are racked in a separate secure area within the same building, as are their fissile cores. Personally I prefer the name nuclear pit, it reminds me of mangoes. All access is single coded entry apart from the pit storeroom which is keyed and coded, but also single entry.'

'So actual access is not tied in to the TFAP protocol.'

'No, that would not be necessary. Javed Khan mentioned that you have brought a suggestion from your Whitehall to enhance our security. May I ask what it is?'

Mike Roberts remained silent for a few seconds, considering whether Sir Angus McFadden's suggestion was even worth mentioning given what he had heard from Ikram Bhutt. In the final analysis, it was worth mentioning even if all it did was allow Mike to move on to the more important issue of al-Kabuli. Deep breath.

'Sir Angus McFadden, the Permanent Under Secretary for Foreign Affairs, and his advisors have considered possible vulnerabilities and believe that it would make sense to move the weapons at the garrisons to more secure locations. In their view, the garrisons at Sargodha, Pano Aqil and Khuzdar are the weakest links in the chain of security.'

'And where exactly does Sir Angus McFadden propose that we store them? Somewhere in Scotland perhaps?'

'My apologies Lieutenant General if I sounded patronising. We sincerely do want to help, in any way we can, to minimise exposure to possible terrorist activity. We are ... I am sure that you are better equipped to judge where best to store the warheads, presumably underground, and the location is of course your choice. Secrecy and anonymity being a concern, I would be happy to organise an SAS squad to come out to Pakistan to help with transportation and security. And I would personally take command of the squad.'

Lieutenant General Bhutt removed his mirrored glasses to reveal dark brown eyes that gleamed in shadowed sockets. It reminded Mike of a fox he'd once seen in the woods, its eyes glittering in the moonlight. And Ikram Bhutt seemed to be looking at him just as the fox had looked at the rabbit before making his lethal move.

'I do believe that you are sincere, Major Roberts,' Bhutt said, the cadence of his voice measured, 'and I shall consider your offer of an SAS squad. Sir Angus' idea of moving warheads or missiles is neither necessary or, in truth, very practical. Clearly he has little actual knowledge of nuclear weapons. Let me use the Shaheen-II as an example. The missile itself weighs 25,000 kilos, is 17.5 metres long and has a diameter of 1.5 metres. Moving several at any one time could not be done with any sort of secrecy; moving them one by one, ridiculous. The nuclear warhead alone weighs 700 kilos; again, transporting those is impracticable en masse, requiring not just muscle but also equipment such as hoists and cradles.

'But the suggestion does bring other thoughts to the fore. My first thought is that I take you to visit Sargodha Garrison and then you will have a better understanding of our security measures. Perhaps when we have finished here, Major?'

'Of course,' said Mike, finding himself suddenly on the back foot. 'I'd be delighted.'

'Another thought. Although moving the missiles or warheads makes no sense, shifting the nuclear pits may have some merit. That too will make a little more sense when we are at Sargodha and you can see what I am talking about. I think there will be plenty more to discuss.'

A combined belch-cough drew their attention to the so far silent General Pamir Mustagh. He raised one digit in the air to call his listeners to attention.

'I have listened to this exchange of thoughts with interest,' he said, not hiding the intended barb. 'But I do wonder exactly what benefit might be gained for Pakistan by these measures.' The sentence was clearly rhetorical since he moved on without pause. 'As Chairman of the Employment Control Committee, under the overarching umbrella of the National Command Authority, I am aware of the developments considered in our use and deployment of nuclear weapons. One of those is to upgrade our Khalid class submarines to accept and deploy the Babur cruise missile. Perhaps Great Britain would consider assisting Pakistan in that endeavour, as part of your country's overall policy of concern, Sir Bartholomew?'

'I can't make any promises, General Mustagh, but I would be happy to lay your request on the negotiating table in London. However, Major Roberts does have a more immediate nuclear security concern which we believe needs our immediate and joint attention. Returning to your earlier comments in respect of the Royal Navy's ships, this is directly connected. Major Roberts, if you would take the stand.'

As Mike Roberts gave the three Pakistani officials the basic mechanics of the plot to blow up the four naval destroyers, they listened impassively. The news that it was funded by al-Qaeda with al-Kabuli's authorisation raised the odd eyebrow but aroused little surprise. That the explosive devices were designed and constructed at a facility in Pakistan, overseen by one of the country's pre-eminent nuclear physicist engineers engendered a range of emotional outbursts. Disbelief, derision, anger, disgust, shock all co-existed in words and expression.

'I assume that you have proof of your accusation, Major Roberts?' Prime Minister Asif asked coldly.

'Yes Sir.' Mike passed him a slim dark red A4 card pocket folder, marked: Restricted Access – SAF Operational Use. 'You'll find copies of emails exchanged between Professor Tarek al-Shami and Doctor Sami Malik. There are annotated details of al-Shami's visits to Pakistan and the UK over the last year and copies of those bank statements we have been able to source to date. There's a copy of AA's confession with comprehensive details of meetings between the conspirators. In it he specifically names Doctor Malik and al-Kabuli in relation to manufacture and funding respectively. I'm afraid that the document has been redacted for the sake of British security; those names that have Pakistan connections have been left untouched.'

'Naturally we will have to go through these papers very carefully before we decide on their veracity, Major Roberts. If your allegations had any foundation, this would be a matter of grave national concern and the offences would exceed those of which AQ Khan has been accused. If we feel that it is a matter that we should take further, and it is a very large if, Major Roberts, we will investigate it with care, precision and determination. Make no mistake, Pakistan takes this form of betrayal extremely seriously and any such miscreant will indeed feel the full weight of the law and justice system. But Javed has indicated that there is something else that you wish to add.'

'Yes, Prime Minister. We believe that Abdul Saad al-Kabuli is currently on his way to Lahore with the intent of somehow persuading Doctor Malik to assist him in his objective of obtaining a nuclear device or weapon of sorts. Probably from the garrison at Sargodha.'

'And you can supply evidence to support this theory also, Major Roberts?'

'No, Sir. But we believe that the pieces of the puzzle all fit together. Al-Kabuli knows that Malik supplied the bombs to al-Shami; blackmail could work quite well. Other options would be bribery or torture and al-Kabuli's no stranger to either of those. We presume that Malik has the necessary access codes and we know he can reassemble nuclear weapons. It makes entire sense, Sir, doesn't it?'

There was a long pause as Prime Minister Asif stared at Mike Roberts as though he was a strange alien being in the form of a dung beetle. Asif steepled his fingers underneath his chin while propping himself up on the arm of the sofa with one elbow.

'To be frank, Major, this is complete conjecture based on a foundation of assumption and beliefs. Without actual evidential material how am I meant to believe in your beliefs? Assuming for one moment, that I do consider your theories to be indicative of a genuine threat, what would you ask of me?'

'I would ask you to place Doctor Malik under house arrest and use him as bait for al-Kabuli. Then I would propose that my squad and I would scoop them all up when they're all chatting cosily together. Sir.'

'Mmmm. I can only say that we will examine the contents of your file and discuss the matter over the next few days. Something of this magnitude should be given full consideration and time. I realise that you have concerns of immediacy but as far as I can see, al-Kabuli is probably still on this dhow in the Gulf of Aden or Arabian Sea. Dhows have a habit of travelling rather slowly, Major Roberts. We will meet again once we have made our decision, or earlier if we feel we need further input from you. I think you have a flight to catch.'

Prime Minister Asif stood up, indicating that the meeting had come to an end. The others followed suit.

'Gentlemen, thank you all for your contributions this morning. A pleasure as always, Sir Bartholomew. Mr Watts. General Mustagh, Javed, if you would accompany me to my office. Enjoy your visit to Sargodha, Major Roberts.'

After leaving the meeting room, the various groups of men parted company, overtly amicably. Mike Roberts followed Ikram Bhutt through the marbled corridors of the Prime Minister's Secretariat, eventually popping out at the back of the building. For a few moments, he wasn't quite sure that his eyes were working correctly. In the middle of what normally served as a car park for some of the officials working in the building was a Bell AH-1 HueyCobra attack helicopter, its twin-bladed rotor already turning lazily in the late morning sunshine that had finally broken through.

'Surely you didn't think we were driving, Major?' Bhutt said, with a broad grin. 'Climb aboard.'

Ejecting the young Pilot Officer from the flight captain's seat, he strapped himself in and began running through his instrument checks as Mike settled into the cockpit's second slot. Mirrored glasses back in place under his flight helmet, Bhutt checked to see that his passenger was properly secured and similarly helmeted. Feeding in the power, Ikram Bhutt took the Cobra up to a hover and stepped on the microphone foot switch.

'Good to go?'

'Yes, Sir,' Mike responded, giving the thumbs up as reinforcement.

Bhutt grinned, increased the collective and twisted the throttle, sending the Cobra screaming up into the sky over Islamabad. The journey that should have taken almost an hour, lasted barely forty minutes. Five hours later, Bhutt flew him back in similar style, dropping him off at the Pakistan Air Force base at Islamabad

International. An Army driver ferried him to the High Commissioner's house. Minutes later Mike was sitting outside with Bart Jinks on the second floor verandah sipping a welcome gin and tonic.

'More or less as he said really,' Mike told him. 'To all intents and purposes, everything is secure. The storage for the missiles and warheads is exactly as he described. Transporter erector launchers are parked up in a separate building. His nuclear pits as he calls them are tiny, or rather much smaller than I expected. Quite a few of them are only a little larger than a cricket ball. Makes you wonder how the bloody things can do so much damage. Each one's in a cage in its own steel container within another steel container and they're not that big either. Anyway, more of all that tomorrow.'

'Absolutely, I'm sure there's a lot more to tell.'

'Oh yes, Bhutt gave me the nod to fly the squad out to Lahore.'

'Did he now? Interesting. By the way, you told Asif that the confession was redacted. I take it therefore that Mustagh's name doesn't appear?'

'You take it correctly, Sir Bartholomew. That's it with today. Must admit though, I do wonder where al-Kabuli really is right now.'

As they sat drinking their glasses of gin and tonic on the verandah in Islamabad, the unremarkable Rih Albahr was sailing quietly into the Port of Karachi.

471

18 ~ Convergence

A soft damp blanket of cloud covered the top of the Margalla Hills, shedding white curls and tendrils of mist that slipped down as angel hair across lush green shoulders and into shadowed valleys. The mid-morning warmth of some 18 degrees Celsius without any breeze made sitting on the verandah a pleasant place to wait for something to happen. But without a mandate or even promise of one, he found the process of helpless waiting, frustrating. It had been two days since Mike Roberts had flown to Sargodha with Ikram Bhutt who had implied that bringing over a team was a good idea. But as yet, that hadn't been confirmed. Nor had there been any message from the Prime Minister's Secretariat to indicate that they had come to a decision on, or even considered the Sami Malik file. As he sipped his third cup of coffee of the morning, Mike wondered how much longer they would take decide on either item.

Of course it wasn't long in the political diplomatic way of things, but he was neither politician nor diplomat. Mike was used to evaluating a situation quickly and carefully, assessing the risk/gain factors, making a decision and taking action as appropriate. He didn't understand a rationale that allowed the toxic combination of prevarication and procrastination. Reporting back to London the day before, which was therefore only a day after the meeting, he made those very comments. Only to have Helen tell him to cool his jets. Where did that one come from?

Apart from updating Helen and Admiral Buller on the status quo in Islamabad, he'd put in a request for an 11-man SAS squad headed up by Captain Ed Clarkson with the guys from the Welsh run, Jamie Kirton and Will Leese, to be included. Mike got the answer back in exactly eight minutes: squad was organised and ready to go. When he had raised the subject of equipment such as 12 silenced 9mm Sig Sauer P228 pistols with two 20 round magazines for each one, he was told – no problem.

'The status of the diplomatic bag allowing the United Kingdom to send any damn thing it likes to her embassies or high commissions is enshrined in the 1961 Vienna Convention on Diplomatic Relations,' Helen had said. 'Ed Clarkson and friends are on standby waiting for you to call it, Mike. He knows what you all need and that'll fly out with them as diplomatic baggage. At the moment I'm looking at putting them on a flight via Muscat, singleton seats on separate bookings. They're regular daily flights and we can push them on under various official guises. But they're next day flights, Mike. Or we can send them out to Lahore now and you're covered immediately. What do you want to do?'

'Leave it for 24 hours. I'll call you,' he'd said.

Now as the back end of those 24 hours was ticking down, Mike was waiting impatiently for midday on Islamabad time. If Helen were being true to form, she'd have just distilled her first cup of caffeine; he was considering indulging in a pre-lunch iced bottle of Murree's Special Strong Brew. As he glanced down to check his watch, he heard footsteps on the stairs, followed by Sir Bartholomew appearing on the verandah.

'Morning, Major. Sorry to have had to leave you on your own for so long; a few papers that required my personal signature according to Rick. I'm sure that Hina's been taking good care of you in the meantime.'

'She has, Sir Bartholomew, thank you. I've had a very pleasant time sitting on your verandah and watching the view while Hina's been treating me to another divine breakfast and copious amounts of exceptional coffee.'

'Don't praise her too much or Moheem will be demanding more money. Actually, poor souls aren't paid enough as it is but one can't buck the going rate too much because it upsets the status quo. More coffee?'

'I think I've probably exceeded the recommended coffee intake by about 200 per cent, so I'll say no, thank you. I've been thinking over what Helen O'Connor said to me yesterday, about bringing out the squad now? So if I could use the phone in your study again, Sir Bartholomew, I'd be grateful.'

'Of course, but actually I left the High Commission earlier than I expected because I had a call from Javed Khan this morning. I'm sure you remember him from our meeting at the Secretariat.'

'Yes. Rick hissed some details at me as we were going through security. Said Khan knew the Prime Minister better than the man himself and that Khan was – as dangerous as a blue krait but could be a good friend.'

'Master Watts being a little simplistic perhaps, but not too far off the mark in some ways. Javed Khan should not be underestimated, as some have found out to their serious detriment. Khan is a highly intelligent and clever … arranger of things. He has an uncanny intuitive capacity for spotting people's weaknesses and strengths; some would add, manipulating them as a puppet master his marionettes. On the whole I think that's too harsh; I don't see him as some dark Machiavellian vizier. Perhaps the best analogy would be to call him a grand patriotic chess master who plays every game as it best serves Pakistan. The codicil to the analogy is that he also believes that he knows what is best for Pakistan. If you accept those principles, then you begin to understand what makes Javed Khan tick. And perhaps you realize why Rick's oft quoted lines about kraits and friends are far too simple for such a very complex man.

'That might have been a touch prolix but I think worthwhile since we'll be talking to him in around …' Bart Jinks glanced at his watch, 'fifteen minutes. Rather short notice I'm afraid, but I suspect you'll be pleased with the outcomes of the discussion. Khan usually works independently at the outset but his network of contacts is legendary. If Javed Khan wants something to happen, it usually does. He was very keen to talk to you as soon as possible and specific on the conversation being here rather than at the Secretariat or the High Commission.'

'I hope so,' Mike said, feeling a fraction more positive than he had earlier. 'Lovely as it is sitting here, it's so frustrating not being able to do anything practical.'

'You could always ask Moheem if he wants a hand in the garden,' Bart Jinks said, a slight smirk flittering across his lips.

'Of course, if you'd like …'

'Joke, Major. If you suggested anything like that to Moheem, he'd be totally mortified, thinking that you were criticizing his work. Excuse me for one moment.'

Sir Bartholomew disappeared through the doorway and down the stairs, returning only a few moments later with a large plate of biscuits.

'Sort of de rigueur when one has this type of meeting,' he said, plonking the plate on the table.

The sound of tyres crunching on the deep gravel at the front of the villa against the loud purr of an expensive car engine announced his arrival. Then silence, followed by more gentle footfalls on the stones and the muffled exchange of greetings at the door. Two sets of feet on the marble stairs. Balancing a tray with three highball glasses and a large jug of opaque whitish liquid, Hina came out onto the verandah with Javed Khan close behind.

'Please do not get up gentlemen,' said Khan, slipping past her to take a seat at the table. 'Sir Bart, Major Roberts, thank you for seeing me so quickly.'

He paused, watching Hina as she filled three glasses almost to the brims and placed one in front of each man.

'Shikanjvi, yah?'

She bobbed her head in acknowledgement. Without waiting for the other two men, Khan grasped his glass, sipped tentatively at first and then took a long drink, smacking his lips in appreciation after swallowing.

'Wah wa! Marvellous. Pakistani lemonade,' he said in English, addressing his words to Mike Roberts. 'It's quite delicious and very refreshing.'

Hina smiled her thanks for his compliments and topped up his glass before vanishing in the shadows of the stairwell.

'If she can cook as well as she makes shikanjvi, you're a very lucky man, Sir Bart.'

'She can and I am, Javed, so don't try to steal her.'

'Don't worry, I wouldn't dare. My wife would automatically assume the worst if I brought such a talented, attractive girl into the house. Mahruhk would probably put poison in my food, murder me and blame the girl,' Khan added, his voice bubbling with laughter.'

'You're right, this is lovely,' Mike exclaimed, breaking into the exchange. 'What's in it?'

'Water, fresh lime and lemon juice,' answered Sir Bart, ticking the ingredients off on his fingers, 'ginger, cumin, salt, black pepper and saffron ice cubes. I'm afraid the quantities and balance of ingredients is a Hina-brand secret which she won't even give to me!'

They sipped their drinks and chewed on biscuits as Khan rummaged through some standard questions for a while, but each one with a slight kink. How did Mike like Pakistan, and which of his senses would he say was most stimulated? Was he married and how did he view polygamy? How many children did he have, which one was his favourite and why? Mike had the strangest feeling of undergoing an audio permutation on the Rorschach test in which the abstracts were disguised in cloaks of normality. He could almost hear the sizzle of hot mental analysis producing Khanesque psychological interpretations. When the change of lines came on the train of Khan's questions, the switch was made brutally quickly with no warning.

'At the meeting the other day, you said that AA's confession had been redacted. Although Doctor Malik's name occurs mainly on its own, there are several cases where it is conjoined with another; that second name has been redacted in each instance. I would like you to tell me the name obscured by secure black ink.'

'I'm afraid that I don't have the authority to reveal ...'

Javed Khan shook his head, simultaneously waving an index finger from side to side in synchronised rejection of the unfinished sentence.

'If we are to work with each other my friend, there must be some elements of trust, yah? Therefore, as tokens of my very good faith, I will tell you that I do believe the evidence of my eyes and agree that Sami Malik organised the manufacture of the bombs for a large sum of money. I am also inclined to agree with your hypothesis that Abdul Saad al-Kabuli is intent on purloining something nuclear from one of our bases. Whether that intent includes Doctor Malik's dubious services, who knows? I agree it may be a possibility but since Pakistan has in excess of 1,800 nuclear physicists and technicians, there could be an element of doubt. Quid pro quo, Major Roberts?'

He saw Mike's eyes flick towards Bart Jinks, saw the latter's minute shrug and divined both knowledge and indecision. Neither of the two men spoke, almost as though they were trying to communicate telepathically.

'Let me attempt to release you from your state of quandary, Major Roberts. I believe that the redacted name is that of General Pamir Mustagh. I would be grateful if you would confirm my suspicion.'

Mike searched the man's face for any sign of guile and found none. Javed Khan's gaze was direct without being aggressive, his eyes unblinking. There were no minute involuntary twitching facial muscles that so often betray people's nerves. And his body language spoke of a person who was calm, relaxed and confident. Decision made.

'Yes,' he said finally. 'As General Mustagh heads up the National Command Authority, we were certain that he was bound to be at any nuclear weapon related meeting. Obviously we wanted to avoid Doctor Malik being alerted and thought that by redacting the General's name, he would assume that we had no information to connect him to the deal with al-Shami.'

'Pamir Mustagh may not be the sharpest knife in the drawer but nor is he stupid. It's perfectly possible that he has drawn the same conclusion as me, specifically because he has been working in partnership with Malik. However, by implication, you're suggesting that because he hasn't been named in conjunction with the Doctor, he'll say nothing and hang Malik out to dry. Did you know that they both live in Lahore, Major Roberts?'

'No Sir, I did not.'

'Thank you for confirming my assessment, Major; I do like verification and it's always so satisfying to be proved right.'

Khan drained his glass, reached across the table for the jug and poured himself another. Took a biscuit from the plate and nibbled at the edge like a mouse with a fragment of stolen chocolate.

'From what you said earlier, about working together, Javed,' said Bart Jinks, over the sound of crunching teeth, 'you have something in mind?'

'Absolutely. Could we possibly have another jug of this wonderful lemonade?'

'Of course,' he responded, immediately disappearing down the staircase in search of the lovely Hina. Finishing his biscuit, Khan then spent his time carefully mining crumbs from his teeth with the bright green ends of a mint-flavoured toothpick.

'Have I missed anything?' asked Sir Bart, returning to his seat and placing a refreshed jug of lemonade on the table.

'I was waiting for you to return, since I think you should both hear what I have to say. Firstly, Ikram Bhutt and I have discussed the idea of moving nuclear material to a more secure location. Combine your principle with his close focus and the idea has merit. In other words, we move all fissile material to a secure location. Without those balls of uranium and plutonium, the warheads are big metal bullets full of high explosive; big enough to cause localized damage but not nuclear. As you have now seen Major Roberts ... do you mind if I call you Mike, Major? The full appellation in all cases becomes rather tedious, don't you think?'

'Of course, Mr Khan.'

'Javed please. As I was saying, you have seen the size of the nuclear pits and their containers. As far as I am aware, not one of them weighs more than 100 kilograms. In terms of size, the drums are around 70 centimetres high with a diameter of approximately 50 centimetres. Ikram has calculated that we could transfer the containers with one flight per location with a maximum of three helicopters per flight. That of course includes flight crews and troopers.'

'Mr Kh ... Javed, you said helicopters? Wouldn't it make more sense if you used a transporter; one of the air force's C130 Hercules?'

'As sensible as that might sound Mike, the Hueys are faster, more manoeuvrable and, more importantly, they can land in places that a Hercules cannot.'

'Wait a minute, you're talking about Bell UH-1 Hueys? Is the US still making those guys?'

'Not any more but they're still very much in service here and a few other countries. In Pakistan, they're used as utility craft rather than attack helicopters. For that we have HueyCobras, like the one you flew in with Ikram. So we will be using Bell UH-1H Iroquois helicopters, each one carrying up to 14 containers, two pilots and between four and six troopers depending on how many aircraft are necessary. We plan to supply the helicopters with pilots; you will supply the troopers. By using your SAS team to transport and secure the loads, we have excellent protection and security without any possibility of new locations being leaked. You and your men will not be told where they are taking the containers; any GPS or other tracking signals will be automatically blocked by onboard jammers. Incidentally, Ikram will be flying the lead helicopter.'

'I'm happy with that. The squad's on standby so I should be able to get the men on a flight tonight, but is that to Lahore or here?'

'Islamabad. Initially it will be easier to co-ordinate the operation from here. I assume that they will be arriving individually. Let me have the flight details as soon as you know, together with a list of names; I will arrange for five taxis to collect the men. The drivers will be waiting in the arrivals hall. For their short time in Islamabad, they will have rooms in a very nice hotel that is not more than a few minutes walk from here. It is also close to Faisal Mosque which is a major tourist attraction in Islamabad, so they will not look out of place or unusual on the streets.'

'Some equipment will be travelling with them in the diplomatic bag. I don't know how ...'

'One of the drivers from the Diplomatic Enclave will collect it from the airport,' Sir Bart interrupted. 'I'll organize the collection so that it can be delivered here rather than to the offices. Fairly standard practice for a lot of things sent over here – delivered direct to the recipient.'

'If they leave today, your men should arrive tomorrow afternoon,' said Khan, taking back command of the conversation. 'If that is the case, there can be a briefing with Ikram on the following morning and then you go. There are some changes that I should mention in passing, Mike. You now have four garrisons to clear: Sargodha, Khuzdar, Akro and Pano Aqil. We decided to add Akro in Sindh Province, just north of Hyderabad, because of its proximity to the border. Also, due to distance and other factors, you will stop at Dera Ghazi Khan; it is possible that there will be a collection there as well. We anticipate that the entire run should take no more than three days.

'After Pano Aqil, you fly to Lahore which be your final stop, and there you will turn your attention to the business of Messrs Malik, Mustagh and al-Kabuli. You see, I believe that you're

479

correct in your assessment: I think Abdul Saad is on his way to see Doctor Malik. If General Mustagh gets caught in the crossfire, so be it; otherwise we will sweep him up in the aftermath. Again, we will arrange a base for you in Lahore and two Hueys will stay, as will Lieutenant General Bhutt and the other pilots. It is highly unusual for Ikram to be so personally involved but the nature of both operations is too secret to delegate any other part of the line of command. In addition, if the Lahore end plays out as I suspect, the media will give the story a very high profile unless it's suppressed by the ISI. As the Director-General of the Strategic Plans Division, they will either hold Ikram accountable for the failure or praise him for the success of the operation.

'Given that yours was the initial approach, I will take your acceptance of and agreement to all that I have said as tacit. For my part, I would like to thank you personally for your assistance Mike and, I suppose, I should extend that thanks to her Britannic Majesty's government, Sir Bart. Other than that, are there any questions?'

'Only one at this stage Javed, and it's more of a statement really' said Mike. 'Apart from the security element, we're more or less providing simple muscle moving the nuclear containers. Ikram Bhutt is obviously in a control and command role during that period. When it comes to Lahore and dealing with the situation on the ground, I need to take that role and make the calls. I need to know that Ikram Bhutt's going to be cool with that.'

'I do not envisage any problem with the change of control and command, as you outline. Both Ikram and I have nothing but respect for the British SAS, which I am sure is reciprocated in respect of our own Special Service Group. When all this is done, I can arrange a visit to their base at Tarbela if you wish. With Ikram at the controls, it's a little over one hour from Lahore in a Cobra.'

'Thank you, Javed, I'll bear it in mind. But if there is any argument over command, the Lieutenant General and I need to have a talk like now.'

'There won't be a problem, you have my personal guarantee. Now gentlemen, I think I have taken up more than enough of your time.' Pushing his chair back, Javed Khan stood up and quickly finished the dregs of his lemonade. 'Sir Bart, thank you for your hospitality as ever and Mike, please phone me as soon as you have flight details. Or any questions that come to mind.' A gilt-edged business card appeared in his hand. 'Please phone my mobile at any time of day or night, Major Mike,' he said, passing the card over. 'I look forward to our successful association.'

'I'll see you out Javed,' Sir Bart said as he walked with him to the stairs. 'Before you came I was thinking about what General Mustagh was asking, about upgrading your subs to carry Babur cruise missiles? As I said at the time, I'll have to talk to Whitehall about that. Sea-based missiles would of course give Pakistan another orientation in relation to India and I suddenly wondered if you would be interested ...'

The rest of the sentence was lost as the High Commissioner and Javed Khan walked out of range in the hall below. For a moment, Mike idly wondered what Sir Bart was talking about and how the sentence might have ended. Then his mind turned back to the job in hand. Pouring the remaining lemonade from the jug into his glass, he started mulling over all that the man had said.

'Game on,' he said quietly to the bird eyeballing him from the branch of a nearby tree. He raised his glass in its direction.

'Caw,' said the crow hoarsely and flew off toward the Margalla Hills.

*****

They'd left the Rih Albahr berthed at the Port of Karachi in the capable hands of Hassan's second in command, Mohammed. Al-Kabuli and Naseem had collected two 4x4 dusty red Toyota Hiluxs, from somewhere outside the dock area and brought them back to the mooring. It was while they were away that the men appeared from the lower deck where they'd been bunking with the crew. Ayesha had wondered about the voices that sang in the night a few days earlier, and to whom they belonged. All Naseem had told her was that they were fighters from Somalia, members of a new organisation named al-Shabaab. Translated from Arabic that meant young or youth. He'd helped Sayyid train them for this operation in Pakistan.

Chronologically the ten men were young, but their eyes and expressions told a different story. Hard eyes that had seen too much shone darkly in drawn faces, rich brown skin pulled taught over high cheekbones. Apart from two who wore short trimmed beards, they were clean-shaven but none of them laughed or even smiled. Dressed in loose variously coloured shirts and baggy trousers rolled up to just below the knees, they all wore sandals or walked barefoot. Now they sat in the backs of the two trucks, five to each Hilux, a keffiyeh wrapped around every head and face against the wind-driven dust. Only their eyes showed through the narrow slits in the cloth masks. After three days on the road, each man was a uniform colour, covered with a brown-grey film of greasy dust. But not one man had complained.

There was little conversation on the road; the noise of the engines combined with the wind that rushed through the windows when open, or the grinding whine of the ailing air conditioning, prevented any normal discourse. The fertile plains around Mirpur Khas, Sanghar and Nawabshah had been rich with colour and heavy with sweet smells. Lush green fields, vast stands of sugarcane, ranked orchards of mangoes and banana trees – all had been left behind as the trucks passed the desert wetlands and lakes of Deh Akro, turning right on Thar Road. Little more than a wide track, it led north through the edges of the Thar Desert itself.

Often covered with sand, the road stretched away ahead of them in an undulating snake that seemed to fade away in the distant dusty haze. An arid sand and scrub landscape spread out on either side: dull yellow-green tangles of grasses grew between angry dark green tamarix bushes on stony ground. Occasional wiry acacia and kandi trees stood like solitary guards on Thar's open prison. Sometimes in the distance to the east, great sand dunes rose from the desert floor ever-shifting and changing with the winds.

A few kilometres south of Sorah, Hassan and Naseem synchronised the satnavs in the two vehicles, compared waypoints as they planned the route northeast using finite tracks. Letting a measure of air out of the tyres, they lowered the pressure to allow the trucks to be driven easily and safely across the sand itself. Leaving the Thar Road behind them, they headed up along what was little more than a narrow depression in the sand, only defined by its soft edges. For over four hours, the two trucks drove in convoy across the desert sands, well away from the towns and small cities. The air was hot and dry, carrying a suspension of dust that crept into every possible orifice, irritating eye and grating in throat. Drinking water was rationed to sips rather than cups. Even though each truck carried two 20-litre jerrycans, that only allowed three litres per person for the journey through the desert.

By the time they crossed the border from Sindh into Punjab province, dusk was beginning to fall and al-Kabuli called a halt. Some 37 kilometres southeast of Sadiqabad, they made camp just within sight of the electrified fencing and concertina wire of the Line of Control between India and Pakistan. India's border fence was a wavy stippled strip of shadow along the horizon, splitting country from country and sky from land. As darkness fell, two al-Shabaabis dug a firepit in the sand and built a fire of sticks and desert detritus. The temperature plummeted from the earlier high of 32 degrees Celsius to a chill 16 and the group huddled around the flames eating a spare meal of strips of air cured salted lamb, roti and dried fruits.

'How far to Muridke from here, Hassan?' asked al-Kabuli, looking at a laminated detailed topographical map of the Punjab.

'I would estimate another 1,000 kilometres, Sayyid, unless we take some of the more main roads. If we stay with this route, we keep away from densely populated areas, but it will take us another two, maybe three days.'

'Your figures correlate with mine. With the al-Shababis in the back, it makes sense to stay away from the towns; we do not want to draw the attention of the military or the police. In the countryside, the Somalis might pass as dark-skinned Sindhis, especially if they keep their faces down and do not speak. They may get some strange looks but they will not cause alarm. To stay in the background, we keep to our route and there is no need to be in a hurry. The wise man walks around the lake to get to the far side; the fool rushes into the water and drowns, believing that the fastest route was straight ahead.'

'There is only one full jerrycan of petrol left, Sayyid, so we must stop soon. There is a station on the Gari Road near Khanpur, about 70 kilometres from here and we can stop there. I think this is best. Then from there we drive east into the Thar as far as the old fort at Derawar.' Hassan leaned towards al-Kabuli, indicating the route with his finger. 'From there, northeast until we leave the desert here, near Hasilpur.'

'This is good, Hassan. Haroun, my friend, you have the list of equipment being supplied by Lashkar-e-Taiba?'

Haroun carefully extracted the document from a side pocket of the ever-present briefcase and handed it to al-Kabuli.

'Don't let it blow away in the wind, Abdul, if you have lost your own, it is the only copy we have.'

'Yah, mine is safe but unmarked; yours has the agreed items marked off.'

He scanned the short list carefully, noting the agreed number of 14 AK47s, each supplied with two 30 round magazines and a total of 840 rounds of 7.62mm ammunition. One refurbished Russian RPG7 rocket launcher supplied with six high explosive anti-tank warheads and one pair of heavy-duty cable cutters. There were a few more minor items but al-Kabuli's eyes dropped to the amounts of money written at the bottom.

'We have paid them for all of this, Haroun?'

'Only half of the money requested.'

'Good. His prices seem high. Four hundred and ten dollars for each Kalashnikov including the extra magazines? Two months ago that would have been $285. For 840 rounds, $4,200 now would have been $840 then! It's extortion.'

'According to Bilal, prices at the markets in Darra Adamkhel have soared over the last few months. Apparently the dealers in the Federally Administered Tribal Areas blame the Afghan government for the de-weaponisation campaign that was instigated by America a few years ago. People were persuaded to sell their guns and that's led to the current shortage. Anyway, these are Russian guns Abdul. The Iranian ones were cheaper but not so reliable, he said. What to do?'

'That's bullshit! Negotiate with the bastard. Carving price comparisons on his back might help him change his mind.

Motherfucker. We'll argue after we see the goods. Everything will be there?'

'He has everything now, at the base in Nangal Saday about five kilometres north of Muridke. Consider this Abdul: what we are paying Bilal for all the equipment and the use of his men is a fraction of what we paid for al-Shami's operation. Imagine, if we are successful, even his prices will be a bargain; if we fail this time, we can afford to try many more times.'

Al-Kabuli threw his head back, bellowing with delighted laughter and handed the piece of paper back to his bookkeeper. Still gurgling with laughter, he turned to Naseem and Ayesha.

'We all go to Nangal Saday and stay there for two days. Naseem, you and I will bring the two groups together, Bilal's jihadis and the al-Shababis, and teach them to understand their roles: wolves and mules respectively. Ayesha, Haroun will give you a map of the area in and around Lahore, and the floor plans of the house and gardens. We need plans for entry, securing the house and three exit strategies.' Turning away to look at Tarek, he continued, 'When we are ready, you Professor will come with us to pay a visit on Sami Malik. Together we will persuade him to take us on a guided tour of the nuclear facilities at Sargodha.'

Once again his laughter rang out, crashing through the immense silence of the desert.

*****

They'd arrived the previous day, fairly early in the afternoon, drifting out into the arrivals hall in dribs and drabs. Dressed in an assortment of jeans, cargos, polo shirts, tees and loose cotton jackets, they fitted in pretty well with the traveller-come-tourist profile. Some were clean-shaven but most sported designer stubble and every one wore dark glasses from the get go. Even their luggage seemed haphazard and undefined; well-worn old rucksacks next to one or two scuffed hard-shell Samsonites adjacent to a stained green canvas holdall with leather handles and a canvas shoulder sling. The rest were clearly stitched on the same workbench. Second-hand or simply age-worn, they were carried, dragged or pulled along by lean looking men with lazy manners and sloppy demeanour. Ages? Anywhere from mid-twenties to early-thirties or more.

Before dawn, they'd left the hotel in ones and twos, following directions to the house on Street 14A that Mike Roberts had given them in the Kabul Restaurant over skewers of grilled lamb the night before. Push the button in the wall, speak quietly with your mouth close to the microphone obscured by the grille, slip in through the gate when the electronic lock clicks open. Already kitted up, Mike had been there too, directing them to the clothes and equipment that had been sent through in the Diplomatic Bag.

They knew without asking what they were expected to take from the array. Combat fatigues without insignia, boots, fire-resistant close-fitting balaclava the colour of burned wood and a 9mm Sig Sauer P228 was standard for all. Mike was already carrying a Heckler and Koch MP5SD supressed submachine gun; Ed Clarkson, Jamie Kirton and Will Leese picked up the other three. Several more collected sawn-off Remington 870 shotguns but the two HK417s with 20-inch accurized barrels fell naturally into the hands of the squad's two snipers, Mark Fallon and Kim Reagan. On the gravel in front of the house, a white minibus with white curtained windows and the words 'Pakistan Tourism' printed on either side in large green letters. It took exactly half an hour to travel from Street 14A to PAF Base Chaklala at Islamabad International.

In the early morning light filtering through the blinds into the briefing room, one might have been forgiven for thinking these were different men from the ones that had arrived on the Omani flight from Muscat. It wasn't simply the common dress of lightweight camouflaged combat fatigues and laced hitop desert army boots. These men were alert, bright eyed, well-muscled and obviously very fit. Even though they were sitting casually on waiting-room plastic chairs coloured neon orange, each one was an oiled and coiled steel spring requiring only the slightest touch to release the hidden power and energy. Experts in their field, in perfect control of mind and body, they sat chatting idly to each other as they waited.

All conversation ceased, heads turning expectantly, as the door opened and Ikram Bhutt walked to the front of the room. His immediate companion was a tall barrel-chested man with a

486

face that might have been hewn from a walnut tree. Hooded eyes, the colour of dark flints, looked out from above a hooked nose that angled down to a neatly trimmed beard and moustache. Two other men followed them through the door but stood to one side near the wall. All four men wore flight suits with the insignia of Pakistan's Special Services Wing.

'Good morning, gentlemen. My name is Lieutenant General Ikram Bhutt and I'm the one who has final responsibility for the security of nuclear weaponry in particular. So I am grateful to Major Roberts for bringing you to Pakistan to assist with these vital operations and possibly save my butt.' He paused to allow the polite snickers of amusement from floor and smiled his appreciation. 'It is always a pleasure to work with our colleagues from the British SAS. On my right is Major Bheyrya of the Special Services Wing; he will be joint second in command with Major Roberts. As ever, I must take first command of the operation. Major Bheyrya and I will be the commander pilots flying you over the next two or three days, together with Lieutenants Parwaz and Raj,' he said, indicating the two men by the wall, 'who will be flying the third helicopter. In the first instance ...'

Mike Roberts tuned out as Ikram Bhutt continued in a similarly protracted way, giving the men a verbal blueprint for an operational model that would apply at each garrison. Pushing aside one of the blinds, he looked through the glass to the concrete apron slowly warming as the sun rose. His eyes wandered through the view from the right but stopped at around 45 degrees through the arc and grinned at the sight of the three helicopters sitting near a fixed wing runway like monstrous metal bugs with large Perspex eyes. Picking up on a detail in Bhutt's wordflow, Mike dropped the blind back and turned forward to listen.

'... without protective latex gloves. Boxes of gloves have already been placed on board for your use in handling the containers. This, you understand, is to protect the equipment rather than you. According to our physicists, even if you were to handle the nuclear pits themselves with your bare hands there is no danger of radiation contamination. Apparently, they just feel rather warm but I would prefer it if none of you decided to find out the truth of that.'

Mike shook his head as another ripple of polite laughter trickled across the room. He listened as Ikram Bhutt trudged verbally onwards, covering the security of information in respect of location and post-operation downloading, of the ban on the use of mobile phones and any other tracking devices. Then told them about the jamming devices operating on both helicopters! Etcetera, etcetera. Mike was relieved when Bhutt called for questions and received none.

'Major Roberts, if you would like to fly as co-pilot with Major Bheyrya for a while? Bheyrya?'

'No problem, Sir. Major Roberts?'

Mike shook the extended vicelike hand and almost winced.

'Delighted, Major.'

'Captain Clarkson, you will be flying with me. To the aircraft then, gentlemen,' Ikram Bhutt commanded, with a distinct hint of melodrama.

As the company walked across the tarmac to the helicopters, more than a few British eyebrows went skywards. Mike listened to the soft rush of whispers, grinning all the way to the flightline.

'You have gotta be kidding me!'

'Are you seeing what I am seeing?'

'Tell me that isn't a Huey, Kim.'

'That isn't a Huey, Mark.'

'Man, the last time I saw one of those was at the American war crimes exhibition in Ho Chi Minh City a few years ago. Damn thing was parked on the grass outside.'

'Nah, in a rerun of that old film, Apocalypse Now. Made back in '79 I think, with Marlon Brando.'

'Shit, we weren't even born then! How old are these mothers?'

'About 20 years old,' answered Bheyrya who had overheard the question, 'and still going strong.'

Ikram Bhutt split the squad into two units, dividing the men equally between the lead helicopters. With great originality, he called them Alpha and Bravo fireteams, oblivious to the irony but he did have the sense of balance: the snipers and the guys with the MP5s were split to allow even firepower in both teams. As the troopers clattered onto the metal floor in the main cabin, Mike pulled himself up into the Huey, slipped his right leg round the cyclic and dropped onto the mesh of the co-pilot's seat.

Bheyrya was already in, pulling his shoulder straps down to snap the metal tongues into the buckle on his lap strap. He watched as Mike did the same, helmeted up and checked the radio link. Mike gave him the thumbs up and Bheyrya clicked the trigger switch on his collective to fire up the engine. He watched his dials carefully for any sign of overheating as the big rotor blades began to slowly turn, getting faster and faster with each rotation. As the needle dropped back from the potential red danger zone into cool green, he waved at the fireman on the ground outside. Twisting the throttle a little more, Bheyrya fed more power into the Lycoming T53-L-11 turboshaft engine, raised the collective and took the helicopter off the ground. Feeding in a little more power, he nudged the cyclic forward and the Huey followed the motion. Within minutes, all three helicopters were up and flying due south in a line that was three dark birds in a blue sky.

At an altitude of 5,000 feet, the flight settled down to a cruising speed of 109 knots. Mike looked down through the Perspex bubble beneath his feet to the ground below. From above it looked as though someone had spread a vast camouflage blanket across the ground; a used old stained throw, holed and torn in many places. Irregular rectangles of dull green, baked earth brown and dust grey that indicated some form of cultivation or husbandry. Deep ravines that fell to thin threads of dark streams and dark splashes of brown-black rock were ravages on what seemed a dreary agrarian canvas.

'The Pothohar Plateau,' observed Bheyrya, nodding down towards the land below. 'The land is slowly dying but they still try to make a living by growing things like wheat and barley. By the Indus River to the west or further south, near the Sawan River, they can grow crops like tobacco or melons but here, no. Here in the middle we have oil and gas. Apparently we have about 52 trillion cubic feet of gas left underneath the ground and 850 million barrels of oil. The oil barons say it's not enough to make a decent profit in the long term. Fuck them and their mothers.'

'How far to Sarghoda?'

'From here? Thirty, thirty five minutes, I think. You are in a hurry?'

'Yea, sort of.'

'And why?'

'I'd like to get this whole nuclear moving thing done as fast as possible and then get to Lahore.' Mike changed the subject, not knowing how much Major Bheyrya knew about the Lahore end of the operation. 'So, if it's not a rude question, how come you're called Major Bheyrya but your name tag says Bangash?'

'Because Bangash is my family name. But everyone knows me by the other name; Bheyrya is an Urdu word which means wolf in English. They call me wolf, like the lone wolf, because they say I hunt alone. We are both majors, so just call me Bheyrya; I have forgotten my original given name. And you?'

'Mike.'

'You said you wanted to get this part of the operation finished quickly. You're worried about al-Kabuli getting to Doctor Malik before we do?'

'You know about that?'

'Of course, otherwise you would have another pilot. Doctor Malik was becoming something of a concern to certain parties and I was instructed to look into the matter. It was thought that he was being a little incautious in his dealings with some people in other countries, and becoming a little too greedy. I was tasked with discreet covert investigation without alarming either the good Doctor or his associate. After official representatives made the appropriate introductions, I began to work for him on a when-needed basis as his pilot and, occasionally, provide close protection. One of the early tasks was to fly a man from Karachi to the Iron Graveyard in the Kharan Desert. The Graveyard's generally used as a weapons-testing site for missiles and rockets. It's not far from Chagai where they carried out the nuclear tests in the late 90s. The guy who I took there was called Tarek al-Shami; later in the day, I flew him to Lahore with Sami Malik.'

Mike turned to look at Bheyrya and found the man already looking at him.

'Are you telling me that you knew about al-Shami's plans and did fuck all? Is that what you're saying.'

490

'No Mike, nobody knew anything about al-Shami or his plans until it all fell into place a few days ago when you arrived. You were the one who made the connections between Malik, al-Shami and al-Kabuli. The National Command Authority assessed the tests organised by Malik for al-Shami and decided that since they were for static high explosive devices, it was not worth following their end use. General Mustagh apparently voiced the opinion that since al-Shami was Lebanese/Palestinian, they were probably destined for Israeli targets. Since Pakistan shares Iran's view of Israel, nobody gave a shit. Continued surveillance on Malik was felt to be necessary but not continuous. I don't know exactly what you said to them at the Secretariat but you definitely left a tiger in the room.'

'Yeah, it all makes sense. Shit, I'm sorry I jumped down your throat Bheyrya.'

'No problem, you thought you had reason.'

Neither of them spoke for a while: one concentrating on flying, the other looking down again through the Perspex. A rocky stone vista of harsh brown hills thinly clad in green gauzy mantles of trees, wrinkled and creased by time immemorial. Unforgiving stone folded down to a thick sluggish line that slithered sinuously through the fields like a lethargic grey snake.

'The hills we have just flown over are called the Salt Range. The salt mines of Khewra produce mountains of rock salt, 98 per cent pure, they claim. Down there, you can see the Jhelum River. In twelve more minutes we will be landing in Sargodha. Bhutt will have phoned ahead to the garrison and warned them of our arrival. Don't be surprised when you find the place deserted and the main hangar doors open and waiting. Parwaz and Raj will land their bird right inside; we let them through between us and Bhutt, then land immediately outside.'

Bheyrya lowered the collective, taking them slowly down in perfect formation with Green Leader in front and Green Three to the rear. Increasing the helicopter's forward speed, Bheyrya moved them up to position them next to the Huey in front. Mike glanced to his left to find himself looking at the grinning face of Ikram Bhutt. It actually looked as though the man was enjoying himself. Sargodha's hangars suddenly loomed below, only a few hundred yards away. The reversed diamond formation broke apart as Bhutt and Bheyrya split off in opposite directions and Green Three flew straight through the middle. Angled at a perfectly judged decline with its forward speed slowing every second, Parwaz brought the Huey down to a hover barely five feet off the ground and smoothly nudged it through the open doors. The other two looped back on themselves, stopped mid-air and softly dropped their skids down on the concrete among the dense clouds of dust pulled up by the rotors' downdraught.

'Fucking hell,' Mike exclaimed in awe.

Bheyrya looked at him and grinned as he cut the power. Mike eased off his helmet, unhooked the seat straps, pulled on his balaclava and picking up his MP5SD, jumped out of the machine onto the concrete. Alpha and Bravo were already on the floor, and moving. Leaving the helicopters guarded by the two snipers plus Jamie and Will with their MP5SDs, Mike joined the pack of men following Ikram Bhutt into the warehouse. He fell in step with Ed Clarkson, the two of them forming another buffer of protection to the rear.

Although the helicopter had been shut down, the inertia of the rotor blades was such that they were still rotating at a slow blur. Inside the huge hangar, the hallmark thumping wop-wop-wop-wop sound of the blades was eerily loud. A transporter erector launcher was parked at the end of the hangar, to the right of the Huey, pre-loaded with a missile that must have been at least 16 metres long and well over a metre in diameter. Looking at the headless missile, Mike felt as though he was seeing it the kind of museum that Billy had been referring to on the apron in Islamabad. He wasn't the only one to have stopped; the removal men from both fireteams had paused to look at the monster.

'That gentlemen is a Shaheen Two, medium-range ballistic missile with an operational range of 2,000 kilometres,' Ikram Bhutt informed them proudly. 'It weighs 25,000 kilograms and takes a payload off a variable 700 kilogram load depending on whether we use a conventional high explosive warhead or the nuclear version. Now, we must get on,' he added turning towards the other end of the building.

'TMI,' Ed muttered, falling in step with Mike.

'What?'

'Too much information.'

'Right.'

'Do keep up with the times, Major Roberts.'

'Cheeky sod.'

The Lieutenant General led them down to the other end of the hangar to the bare wall that was only relieved by a huge steel roller door, some 20 feet high and as wide as a double car garage. Bhutt walked to panel fitted to the wall to the right of the door and beckoned Mike across.

'When we were here before, I did not have time to show you our entry security systems.'

Bhutt pulled down the metal panel to reveal a card reader slot, a numerical keypad and what looked like a camera. Producing a rectangle of plastic, the size of a credit card, he slipped it into the slot and punched in a long sequence of numbers on the keypad. A brief message flashed up on a small screen and he moved fractionally to ensure that he was looking exactly into the lens. As soon as a green light flashed on the screen, the system spat out his card and the sound of heavy lifting machinery grinding into action filled the air as it took the strain. Slowly but surely, the heavy metal door started to clatter and clank upwards, groaning as though in terminal pain.

'Biometric recognition, Major Roberts. The card carries my personal details that have to be authenticated with a numerical sequence. The machine then asks me to either look at the lens or to place my fingers on the plate below,' he said, pointing to the mirror-like glass. 'The system uses both iris and/or fingerprint recognition which must correlate with the information on the card. If there is any inconsistency, the door will not open, an alarm will sound at the security gate and in the Garrison guardhouse.'

As the door rolled upwards onto its hidden spindle, banks of lights in the ceiling came to life, bathing the space behind in bright white light. Dull grey ranks of warheads lay in cradles, carefully numbered and racked, filed in a system of planned-for destruction by type, weight and missile matching. Ikram Bhutt did not linger, leading them along the wide lane that ran through the middle of the lines of stark weaponry. Ghauri-I, Shaheen-II, Ghaznavi, Hatf-I … Mike read the names off in his head and counted at least nine different types of missile match.

The door in the far wall was clearly made of steel, reminding Mike of the door of a vault that he'd once seen in a London bank. Even from the outside it looked heavy and solid. Fitted with a double handle to the left to pull the door open once unlocked, it was equipped with finger/palm recognition pads as well as numerical dials. Mike was grateful that this time Ikram Bhutt failed to give him a lecture on the security devices. Instead the man concentrated on opening the door that quickly swung open to reveal a caged area with racked steel containers on either side. Between them stood two mobile trolleys with electric hoists.

Mike and Ed stood guard by the door as the six troopers, working in pairs, loaded the containers onto the trolley beds. They quickly assessed that each trolley had capacity for only three of the nuclear pit containers; shifting the loaded trolleys on their steel castors confirmed that they needed three men on each to push and pull. In total it took seven runs to clear the room of the containers and their deadly cargo.

At the beginning a distinct frisson of nervous electricity sparked across the men as the containers were hoisted onto the corrugated metal deck of Green Three. Somehow the sound of a steel box containing the core element of a nuclear warhead, rattling across the metal ribs in clear view was horribly chilling. Time and men seemed to freeze, waiting for the inevitable blinding moment of boosted nuclear fission. But all they heard was the sound of metal rattling on metal and the blood pulsing in their ears.

As the Bravo fireteam clambered back into the helicopter, Mike watched their backs and then hauled himself into the co-pilot's seat. Peeling off the balaclava, he ran his hands through his hair before easing his head into the flying helmet.

'We're done,' he said, strapping himself back into the safety harness.

'First the collection, now the delivery,' Bheyrya said with a wry smile on his lips. 'Maybe there's a business plan here somewhere. Nukex: moving your pits to where you want them.'

Bheyrya fired up the engine on the Huey, listening to the high-pitched whine of the starter motor as it strained to turn 48 feet of rotor blades above their heads. He looked up through the Perspex canopy as the big blades spun up to the blur of operational revolutions. On the ground, Lieutenant Raj stood watching Green Three as Parwaz eased the now loaded machine back onto the apron, pushed the button on the wall to lower the main hangar door and reclaimed his seat. They waited for Ikram Bhutt to give them the signal to go.

'What other security is there, out here, outside the hangar?'

'The double security fence runs right the way round the perimeter of the concrete surround. What you have is two rows of welded mesh fencing which is electrified and topped by razor wire. The 20-metre gap between the fences is mined, which means that there is only way in and out of the compound by land. The concrete apron around the hangar is a uniform 300 yards wide and has pressure sensors running underneath. Those are switched on and off at the security gate or by someone using an authorised card, such as the one that Bhutt would have used to access the main hangar.'

'What's in the other part of the hangar?'

'Most of the actual delivery systems, the missiles and the launchers. Workshops, stores and offices. That's about it.'

'What about the gate?'

'Two armed guards and one officer as standard. Everyone has to provide verifiable authority to enter or be accompanied by someone with that authority. There's only a standard pole barrier at eye level but they have controllable crocodile teeth barriers on the ground. Those spikes are strong enough and big enough to stop a loaded truck. Going in they obviously flatten down but if you want to get out, they can only be lowered from the gatehouse. The only vulnerability is from the air; so the hangars were built with reinforced concrete double panels with a tungsten steel core. The place is pretty much impregnable.'

'Yeah? Would that stop you trying if you fancied the idea?'

'Hell no!' said Bheyrya. 'But I can think of better places to break into than Sargodha. Personally, I like the idea of Fort Knox just for the challenge.'

'Old ideas Bheyrya. Nothing more interesting?' Mike asked, as both of them started laughing.

'We're leaving,' he said, dropping the conversation as he turned to flying.

Static crackled from the radio and he changed frequency.

'This is Green Leader. Bracket Green Three with Green Two taking rear.'

'Green Leader, this is Green Two, taking rear.'

The three Hueys formed up in the same line formation that had been used on the flight to Sargodha but this time Bheyrya and Mike were the last in line, behind the nuclear laden Huey.

'So where are we going?'

'You know I can't tell you that.'

'Why not? If you said Bagwahdelta or whatever, I still wouldn't have clue.'

'In that case why ask the question?'

'It's called conversation, Bheyrya.'

'Sisterfucker,' he said with a grin.

'Now that's not polite,' Mike replied, grinning back at the man.

The compass told Mike that they were flying southeast but he was sure that they'd been flying northwest earlier. Staring at the rocky ground below that changed from grey to green to brown, bisected by wavy grey-blue lines or black-brown ravines didn't help. It was like navigating a route by colour without having a key. Mike suspected that Bhutt was flying them in circles specifically to confuse. After half an hour in the air, they started to descend towards a broad flat area abutting a rock face cut into the hillside. Another compound surrounded by a double row of wire fencing but this one had no break for an entrance. Outside the wire, there were signs that there once had been an access road, but that hadn't been used for some time. The three helicopters landed more or less simultaneously, each one churning up it's own personal dust storm. As before, the fireteams deplaned, taking up their allocated positions as instructed while Ikram Bhutt approached the large iron doors fixed into the rock.

About 12 feet high, the doors seemed old, either carved in some strange way or more probably, pitted with rust. Under the layer of whitish dust that covered everything in sight, they seemed a sickly shade of pink. From his hand movements, it looked as though the Lieutenant General was ringing the bell, then stood back and waited. It reminded Mike of the scene from the film of Lord of the Rings when Gandalf was trying to open the Elven gate. Or so he remembered it.

After several minutes of waiting, the doors swung outwards with a grating sound that indicated limited use. A slim man stood in the doorway dressed in a light grey one-piece overall with a hood affair that effectively covered his face. He had a brief conversation with Ikram Bhutt before walking back down the tunnel lit by the series of bright LED lights tracking along the roof. A few more minutes went by before Mike heard what sounded like several small four-stroke engines, getting louder as they drew closer. Four all-terrain-vehicles appeared one after the other, ridden by four men in the same type of overalls as the first. One look at the rutted stony uneven ground in the tunnel told the story of why the ATVs with their big knobby tyres were being used. Each one pulled a six feet long, high-sided trailer similarly equipped.

Reversing the process, in a matter of minutes the troopers had unloaded the containers and transferred them to the waiting trailers. It would be one simple run instead of the seven it had taken to transfer them at Sargodha. As soon as the trailers were loaded, the riders drove back down the tunnel, quickly disappearing from sight. The iron doors closed behind them, resealing the entrance. Mike knew that asking questions was a fruitless exercise but couldn't resist the urge.

'Excuse me Sir, I just wondered where those guys are actually taking the pits?'

'Under the hills and far away, Major,' replied Ikram Bhutt, wearing that same irritating, childish smile as he had before when he thought he'd said something witty. 'A secure and secret place underground where no-one will find them,' he added, rubbing his hands.

A video clip of Gollum suddenly switched on Mike's head and he had difficulty in supressing his laughter.

'In addition, they will be totally hidden from the American spy planes. Do not be concerned Major Roberts, the nuclear pits will be absolutely safe but accessible in the event that Pakistan needs to deploy them. I hope that will never happen in my lifetime but we need to be alert and not allow ourselves to become complacent. We are done here and so we go on to Dera Ghazi Khan.'

Bhutt raised his arm in the air, forefinger extended, and described several circles. Crank up – a signal that everyone understood even if they didn't know its origin. As the teams reboarded the helicopters, the pilots fired up the engines. Having stayed in his seat, Bheyrya was ahead of the game; by the time that Mike got to the aircraft, the blades were already a blur, filling the air with a storm of pink-white dusty particles. The balaclava protected most of his face but he could feel the grit in his mouth, getting into his eyes, and gratefully hauled himself into his seat away from the shitstorm. It wasn't until they were airborne that Mike unconsciously licked his lips and tasted salt. Salt! He looked down through the bubble to the dwindling manmade plateau ringed by wire, the raw rock face of the cut hillside and remembered the pink-dusted iron doors.

'Khewra's Himalayan salt is pink!' the voice in his head exclaimed.

Mike almost laughed at the simplicity of the idea. Instead of securing the nuclear material in a Russian matryoshka of rooms, they'd buried it in the mines under the hills of the Salt Range.

'Under the hills and far away indeed, Lieutenant General,' he said aloud, a wry smile curling his lip.

'Sorry?'

'Nothing Bheyrya, an idea made me smile. How far to Dera wherever?'

'Dera Ghazi Khan. A little over 180 kilometres. It should take us an hour and a half, but we have new instructions to head straight on to Khuzdar which is another 450 plus kilometres. We'll have to stop at DG Khan to refuel but that's all. Doing the maths, we should get to Khuzdar in just under four hours. Then we pick up from there, drop, fly straight on to Akro and stay there overnight.'

'Whoa, sounds like somebody up the chain's pushing buttons.'

'Right at the top, Mike.'

'Wake me up when we get there.'

Mike watched the Punjab pass by 5,000 feet below. For a while it was a faded green patchwork quilt, sewn together with rough brown thread; threadbare in many places where brown earth showed through. Then the transition to the rough white-brown expanse of the Thal Desert; from the air, a featureless arid wasteland. Mike snoozed in the winter sunlight, bored after watching the drab desertscape for 15 minutes or more. The flight landed briefly at DG Khan airport, some 15 kilometres southwest of the city. There was little to see on the ground apart from the refuelling rig on the truck and the small white terminal with little pointed domes on top of four white boxes. The traffic control tower sticking up in the middle did rather spoil the overall image.

Refuelled, Ikram Bhutt took the flight southwest, flying high above the range of Sulaiman Mountains. From creamy white through chocolate brown to greenish black, the mountains displayed every imaginable shade of that spectrum. A sea in stasis turned to stone, leaving ripples and folds of solid rock. Deep troughs and peaks, patches of dark green forest, arid plateaus and deep ravines, ever-changing and yet unchanged for millennia. But after an hour or so, Mike's fascination had dulled to a leaden tedium and he was glad when they began to descend towards Khuzdar.

The layout of the facility at Khuzdar was remarkably similar to Sargodha's: the same single entry, double wire mined fencing, the broad apron with the hangars in the centre. Only the detail changed fractionally and it took the teams less than forty minutes to remove and load the nuclear pit containers into Parwaz's Huey. Even the destination was similar to the one in the Salt Range. This time, Bhutt didn't bother to try and confuse his passengers.

The flight time was perhaps ten minutes and the landing zone a small plateau ringed with mountain peaks, only accessible by helicopter. A wire fence was unnecessary and even the door had been dispensed with on this occasion. Landing caused little to no dust: the ground was compacted and hard, almost frozen. An icy wind blew silently through the rocks, biting any naked skin with bitter teeth. A few yards inside the mouth of the open tunnel, the men found sleds with heavy ropes attached to enable them to be pulled along the slick ground. Loading the containers onto the sleds, they followed Ikram Butt along the tunnel using head-mounted lamps for lighting. Every now and then, they passed darkened entrances which clearly led into natural caves or spaces arduously hewn by hand. Perhaps four hundred yards into the system, Bhutt stopped by another entrance blocked in by a heavy wooden door. Producing a large iron key, he unlocked it and opened the way into a small storeroom. It took over an hour to transfer the containers and carefully stack them in pairs.

'Bheyrya, was that for real out there?' Mike asked, as they lifted out of the plateau and set course for Akro, just north of Hyderabad. 'I mean you all think that that's more secure than underground or whatever?'

'Sure. Firstly, it is underground. Not far but far enough that Bhutt's favourite spy planes can't see anything. Two, unless you knew where they were, you would never find that plateau again in a million years. Trust me, if you were to try to find that same plateau only one hour after we have left, you could not. There are thousands of them in these mountains. Three it puts the nukepits ten minutes away by helicopter; we have fast easy access.'

'You're all insane! The first lot you put into a salt mine and the second into some kind of deserted Stone Age commune.'

'I thought you'd put that one together. Pretty obvious, but you won't remember that one either. Particularly when you have no idea where the technicians put them. Underground, Khewra covers an area of over 45 square miles on the main level alone with more than 40 kilometres of tunnels. And those are the publicly known figures. Pakistani logic: it requires complex asymmetrical thinking and is rarely understood by westerners less blessed with understanding than ourselves.'

'I give up. How long to Akro?'

'An hour. Maybe a bit more. Hey smile. Look at it this way, that's two done and two to go. Tomorrow morning we'll already be on site. Do that, then Pano Aqil and we'll be in Lahore by mid-afternoon. Chill out, hit the town and crash out. After that, we find out which way everyone's playing the game. Did I tell you, they've got a couple of Rangers watching Sami Malik's house?'

'No you didn't. That's good. At least someone's keeping an eye.'

'Maybe. I didn't tell you who ordered the surveillance.'

'This I have to hear. Who?'

'General Pamir Mustagh.'

'Genius.'

The moon rose and set, leaving the sun to work the sky for another day. Akro and Pano Aqil followed similar patterns to the previous two and although the end locations used were less dramatic, they were somewhat unusual. In both instances, the containers were taken underground to strongrooms protected by biometric security systems. Akro's containers were removed and taken to a location near the Sukkur Barrage, not far from Pano Aqil; the tunnels ran under the great Indus River. But the Pano Aqil containers' new resting place was far more prosaic than any of the other three. Simply added to those already stored at PAF Base Rafiqui at Shorkot, it was almost as though the Generals had run out of novel ideas. Ironically, the transfer at Rafiqui had taken the longest, complicated by the lack of understanding of the need to evacuate the facility. It had been another long day and it was almost five before they left. Lahore beckoned.

*****

Dressed in black t-shirts, jeans and trainers, Naseem and Ayesha were barely visible, standing in the space between the high wall and a line of white siris trees. A waxing gibbous moon was already high in the clear night sky but only served to darken the shadows around them. They threw small grappling hooks onto the top of the wall and pulled the light ropes taut before walking up the brickwork to the top. Supporting themselves with one arm, they threw felt pads over the sharp fragments of glass that studded the concrete coping before climbing on top. From there it was simple to reverse the grappling hooks, flip the ropes and slide down the other side. A quick jerk released their grip on the wall.

They walked soundlessly across the grass to the ornately framed glazed doors that led into the darkened kitchen and breakfast room. Producing a thin flexible piece of mica sheeting, Naseem eased it between the door and frame, bringing it down to the latch, pushing it carefully down and back towards him. Hearing the latch click open, he pulled the handle down and pushed the door quietly away from him. There was just enough

501

light for them to negotiate their way to the archway on the other side of the room. They paused listening patiently for the sounds of the house to give them direction. The mellow tones of a woman's voice singing a haunting ghazal drew them to a door along a short corridor. Pausing once more, they could also hear a man trying to hum to the music. Naseem winced, recognising the singer as Munni Begum, and detesting the man for his crass efforts. He motioned to Ayesha, walking his fingers in the air, pointing back to the kitchen and then held up two static fingers. She nodded; he slipped away. Ayesha counted off the seconds, as she had done many times before; she opened the door on the 121st second.

Doctor Sami Malik was sitting on a sofa, sipping a gin and tonic, happily humming tunelessly. He'd neither heard nor seen Ayesha, but he clearly saw Naseem as the man walked from behind the curtains that had been drawn across the doors between drawing room and garden. His first reaction was one of shock; his second was one of rage at the intrusion and the violation of his private space.

'Who are you? And how dare you come into my house unasked?'

Naseem hit him hard enough to stop him talking. Then held one finger up to his lips.

'Abdul Saad al-Kabuli will be here very soon Doctor Malik. Then you can talk. Ayesha, go.'

She stepped cautiously into the hallway, checking for the smallest flicker of light or whisper of movement. Easing the knife from its sheath on her belt, Ayesha walked slowly along the marble floor, her feet rising and falling in precise movements to avoid the usual shriek of rubber against slick stone. Stopping at the front door to listen again, she could hear someone inhaling, pausing, then exhaling. Malik's driver/personal bodyguard was smoking a cigarette in the driveway. The door was open, the latch locked back. With her shoulders against the wall, she gently kicked the bottom of the door to make it swing open.

Her next movements were a blur of speed and brutal action. In less than a second, Ayesha was behind the man, yanking his head harshly backwards with a fistful of his hair. Her other hand drew the razor sharp edge of the knife swiftly across the man's throat, cut through jugular and carotid, arteries and veins. Letting his body drop to the ground as Naseem had shown her, she stepped quickly away from the initial fountains of blood that soon dropped to a slow carmine flow. She didn't have long to wait to hear the dyspeptic grumbling of the expected ageing Suzuki SJ-410 at the gate. Ayesha leaned inside the door and pushed the button to open the wooden gates.

Al-Kabuli stepped out of the passenger side of the vehicle once Tarek had parked it beside Doctor Malik's green Landcruiser. He glanced at the corpse on the ground and nodded approvingly to Ayesha before leading the way into the house. In the drawing room, he sat down in an armchair looking directly across at Sami Malik, leaving Tarek standing beside him. Ayesha brought up the rear, closing the door behind her.

'My apologies for the rather sudden intrusion Doctor, but there is a certain necessity for secrecy and, perhaps the element of surprise.'

Malik looked unsure of himself, his eyes flickering from one unwanted visitor to the other as a moth is drawn to the flames. His glances at the door were duly noted.

'Unfortunately, it's unlikely that anyone will come to your assistance. Ayesha met your friend in the drive and sadly cut his life short, literally and permanently.'

What little blood there had been in Malik's face seemed to drain away, leaving him as white as a ghost. On the other hand, his expression was set, determined and angry.

'Some time ago, the Professor mentioned to you that I wished to obtain a nuclear warhead. I was disappointed that you didn't have the courtesy to respond. You did receive that message, did you not?'

Malik nodded, unable to speak.

'The time for me to obtain that weapon is now, Doctor, and you are going to help me get it.'

'I cannot, will not help you,' Malik stuttered. 'You don't realise the immense danger of using nuclear weaponry, not just the immediate destruction but the lasting contamination of radiation. Using such a weapon would have a domino effect that could race around the world in hours. Nuclear weapons are not meant to be used – the world understood that after Hiroshima and

503

Nagasaki – they're bargaining chips, tools of gamesmanship on the inter ...'

'Please do not lecture me on a subject I fully understand. You will accompany us to Sargodha, where you will let us in to the hangars where they keep the warheads. We will then take one or two and leave. Later you will show me the best way to exploit the weapon without a launcher. I have a team of armed men waiting for us with two vehicles near the facility. They will provide protection if necessary and, more importantly, muscle.'

'Sayyid al-Kabuli, you don't understand.' Malik saw the man's mouth open to release more words. 'Please, hear me out. The smallest warhead at Sargodha weighs 500 kilos; that's basically high explosive and metal. Each one needs nuclear fissile material to work in the form of a pit or ball that has to be inserted into the warhead. But even if you do that, the systems will not let you arm the warhead. You would be wasting your time.'

'Stop Doctor. This nuclear pit or whatever you call it, is how big?'

'Anywhere between the size of a cricket ball to a volley ball. But ...'

'Tell me, if we obtained one of these balls, you could build a device such as the ones you made for the Professor. With the ball at its centre, that device would be nuclear, yes?'

'Yes, but ...'

'No buts; buts always mean no, and that is not an option.' Al-Kabuli threw a square jewel case on the table between them. 'That is a copy of a DVD recorded by Professor Tarek al-Shami on which he confesses his crimes against Great Britain. As part of that confession, he gives very precise details of all his discussions and meetings with you in Lebanon and Pakistan. He also mentions the way you bragged about your dealings with countries including Iran and North Korea. If you do not comply with my wishes, I have two options. One of those is to disable you and deliver copies of the DVD to the Secretariat and the British High Commission in Islamabad. The other option would be to kill you but I feel that would be self-defeating.

'Naturally, I would prefer you to come to Sargodha willingly and, with that in mind, I will give you my proposal. You will help us gain entry to the hangars and any rooms within; I know that you have clearance and can do that. Get past the card readers and the biometric machines. For that alone, I will pay you $500,000 American; another $500,000 will be payable on the delivery of a nuclear device which you will construct. In addition, we will ensure that you have new papers and a new identity.'

In Malik's Toyota Land Cruiser with Naseem at the wheel, it took them a little over two hours to drive the 200 kilometres to Sargodha. The two Hiluxs were waiting behind a deserted petrol station on the Lahore-Sargodha Road, not far from the old flourmill. It took another 23 minutes before they could stop near enough to the facility. Leaving the Hiluxs out of sight, Naseem drove the Land Cruiser sedately up the driveway to the gatehouse. Once there, he immediately got out of the car and walked around to open the door for Malik. The two guards stood waiting, each cradling a Kalasnikov in his arms.

'I think we've met before,' Malik said confidently. 'Doctor Malik from Khan Research Laboratories in Kahuta. I realise that it is rather late but the Prime Minister himself asked me to show these gentlemen and lady around the facility before they return to Islamabad tomorrow morning.'

'Your papers and card please, Doctor.'

'Of course.'

Seeing everything was in hand, the second guard walked past them to the car to check its occupants. He didn't notice the cough of Naseem's silenced Glock or his colleague's grunt of surprise as the bullet burned a hole through his chest to his heart. He died just as quickly when Ayesha shot him in the head through the open window. At the same time, Naseem walked calmly into the gatehouse and shot the officer at his desk. While Malik fed his biometric card into the reader, Naseem flicked his torch on and off, shining the beam out into the darkness towards the road. Hassan and Haroun drove the trucks up the drive, following the Land Cruiser to the main hangar doors.

They waited as the huge doors rumbled slowly upwards and the hangar filled with light. Then drove the trucks to the far end where Malik had the roller door clanking upwards in less than two minutes. The smile on al-Kabuli's face stretched from ear to ear as he took in the brightly lit view of some twenty plus potentially lethal warheads. He walked down the aisle as a bridegroom before his wedding, touching the cold metal warheads on either side. At the end, he stopped, turned and waited for Malik to catch him up.

'Ayesha, Naseem. Take four of the men to the front of the hangar and position them as you think best. Those four,' he said, pointing at the group of armed al-Shabab fighters. 'Give the RPG launcher to one but make sure he knows how to use it.' He watched the five men and one woman walk back towards the entrance for a moment. 'Take the Land Cruiser and one of the trucks back to the entrance just in case,' he added, shouting at them. 'So Doctor, introduce me to the nuclear age.'

*****

Lieutenant General Ikram Bhutt's Green Flight was 109 kilometres from Lahore when the call came through on his Thuraya satphone. After what had been a long two days, both squad and pilots were tired, dirty and looking forward to a decent meal. Several of the troopers had voiced their need for cold beers. Mike stared at the horizon, splitting his view into two halves. Below the line, the world was a graduated patchy dark black-brown with only the barest hint of green, fading up to a pastel beige at the line. Above the line, where pastel meets pastel, the palest of cornflower blues growing to a deeper and richer colour until seamlessly joining heaven's blue-black dome.

'This is Green Leader to Green Flight. Divert to Sargodha Nuclear Missile Facility as of immediate at maximum speed. Repeat, divert to Sargodha as of immediate at maximum speed.'

The radio crackled in anticipation of confirmations.

'Green Three, divert confirmed.'

'Green Two, copy and confirmed.'

As if it were one machine, the flight banked left, changing course to head north-northwest and accelerating. Ikram Bhutt pushed their speed up to 117 knots at an altitude of 4,000 feet. The radio crackled with static again.

'Green Leader to Green Two.'

'Green Leader, we have you.'

'Major Roberts, to bring you up to speed. Surveillance on Doctor Malik's house reported in one hour ago. Said Malik was visited by unknown parties and driven off in his car. Destination unknown. They left a diesel 4x4 Suzuki in the drive and a man down with his throat cut. Instruction from Shadow is check Sargodha.'

'Jesus, why the fuck didn't anyone follow?'

'Pass. Shadow also passed a message on to you personally. Reads: White Commander take control, good luck. When we're on the floor, Major, it's all yours.'

'Thank you Sir.'

Mike clicked off and pressed his footswitch.

'Bheyrya, can I speak to Alpha over the radio?'

'No, but you can talk to Captain Clarkson.'

Bheyrya turned the dial to another frequency. 'Try that one.'

'Alpha One, Ed do you copy?'

'Alpha Bravo, you have me. Go Mike.'

'We have to assume that al-Kabuli's on the floor and inside the hangar. He'll be protecting the front end across the arc of 180 degrees. I doubt that he'll have sweepers out on the edges. Firepower's going to be too hot to go in by the front door, so get Bhutt to drop you off back right. Drop off back right, you copy?'

'Yes Sir, I copy.'

'We go left. Snipers go wide by the fence, MP5S at one and two with shotguns in between. If it takes off Ed, stay alive and do what's necessary. Update on visual. Out.'

Mike swivelled round in his seat to look through the gap at the five men behind. There was little chance of talking to all of them over the noise of the engine, rotors and constant clattering metal of the helicopter. Kim Reagan was the closest.

'Kim, can you hear me?' asked Mike, bellowing over the cacophonous symphony.

'Yes, Sir, just.'

Kim scooted closer as Mike gave him a mirror plan of the one that he'd given to Ed Clarkson.

'Back left and sweep. Windscreen wipers.'

'You got it. Pass it on to the rest Kim, please.'

'Sir.'

Mike sat back in his seat.

'Of course, they might not be there,' he said, looking over to Bheyrya.

'They'll be there. You know it and so do I. What we don't know is what weapons they have. I doubt they'll have Stingers but I'm guessing one, maybe two RPG launchers with anti-tank grenades. Make sure your guys are strapped in if there are. You want to go down back left?'

'Yeah, I'd like to have a sniper in the air as well but we're short on that front.'

'Aren't you the lucky person?'

Bheyrya reached around the back of his seat and produced a grey semi-automatic rifle with a folding stock and a telescopic sight fitted. He passed it over to Mike who stared first at the gun and then at him. 'Russian 7.62mm Dragunov SVDS. Ten round magazine, fully loaded. Enjoy.'

Mike grinned happily as he went to work, reminding himself of the mechanics of a gun he'd shot a few times but a while back.

'Yeah, but isn't there too much vibration to be accurate?'

'Freehand, yes. But there's a rubber sling attached to the door arch which works like suspension and stabilises the gun. They used to have a machine gun attached back in the day.'

'Cowboys,' Mike snorted. 'How long?'

'Fifteen minutes for eyes on.'

'Thank God we moved the containers in time. This is just too close for words.'

'Tell me about it. But Shadow doesn't want them wandering off with a warhead either. Who's to know that it's not armed and lethal when they see pictures of al-Kabuli next to one in the news?'

'Good point. By the way, who the hell is Shadow when he's at home?'

Bheyrya grinned. 'You'll get it if you think hard enough.'

Mike flexed his fingers and shoulder muscles, breathing deeply as he stared through the Perspex as though urging the Huey to go faster. The moonlight cast a yellow glow over the blurred ground below, doing little more than deepen shadows and pick out highlights. As Ikram Bhutt took the flight down to 1,000 feet, he could see the dotted lights of houses and the occasional car headlights.

'Green Leader. We have eyes on target. Green Three take middle and high; Green Two take left on fan approach. Copy.'

'Green Three on middle and fan.'

'Green Two, copy and right.'

'Good luck gentlemen.'

The glare from the open door of the hangar was a bright beacon up ahead, shedding light onto the concrete apron. The three helicopters changed formation as they descended, now flying side by side with Green Three elevated in the middle. The descent seemed to have gained speed and they were close enough to see the vehicles in the entrance and figures on the ground. Looking down, Mike spotted a man on the left hand side pointing what looked like a big stick in their direction.

'Incoming RPG at seven o'clock,' he bellowed.

The rocket motor ignited a millisecond later, the grenade arcing towards them trailing orange flame. Bheyra flared hard to the left, turning the Huey on its side to avoid the impact and the grenade flew harmlessly past. Levelling out, he took the helicopter in a circle as they watched the other two Hueys sink down towards the back of the hangars. Heard the door open behind him and dropped down towards the man with the launcher. Heard the subdued thuds of Jamie's MP5 as he sent careful shots downwards but the man had pulled back into the hangar. A sharp staccato rattle of angry shots as someone sprayed bullets upwards from a Kalashnikov on full-auto and tic-tic sounds as one or two hit home.

Bheyrya pulled up again out of range, flew in a long loop across the hangar and back again, coming in low towards the rear fence. He raised the pitch of the rotors just enough to leapfrog the wire, dropping the Huey on the concrete behind the left hand corner of hangar. As Bravo jumped onto the ground, both Mike and Bheyrya undid their harnesses. The pilot leaned over and picked up the Dragunov.

'Nobody shoots at my helicopter without paying,' he said, grinning madly.

'Welcome aboard Major.'

They could hear exchange of fire from the far corner of the building and Mike waved the line forward at a trot. Working his way round to the front, he could see four men with AK47s, firing sporadically towards the right hand side of the building. Jamie and Mike both opened fire, shooting in a deadly burst that cut all four men down. The man with the RPG launcher appeared, pointing the weapon but didn't have time to pull the trigger. The dull heavy muffled thump of the Dragunov came from just above Mike's head and he saw the man fall.

'Nice shooting Bheyrya.'

'Thank you. It was my pleasure to serve.'

As Bravo worked its way along the front of the hangar, they could see Alpha closing in on the other side. Sprays of bullets flew from the inside of the building, forcing them back. Then the sound of an engine being fired up. The red Hilux flew out of the entrance with three al-Shababis crouching in the bed, firing randomly backwards as the truck hurtled towards the gatehouse.

'Fuck,' said Will as he was thrown back against wall. 'That hurts!'

'Where are you hit?'

'Flesh wound, Sir. Left bicep. I'll be fine.'

'Freddie, check it,' ordered Mike.

He turned back just in time to see the Hilux hit the crocodile teeth at about sixty kilometres per hour. The metal spikes bit hard and deep into the tyres, holding the front end fast and kicking the back end off the ground. The three men in the back were thrown out onto the ground; the driver had gone through the windscreen.

'Time to clean up,' said Mike, walking carefully forwards.

In the sudden quiet, the Land Cruiser's engine seemed loud as it shot from the doorway and headed for the exit. It braked hard and stopped when the driver realised the way out was blocked. All four doors flew open as the occupants poured out onto the ground. Ayesha and Naseem hit the ground on their fronts, both holding handguns. Al-Kabuli stood up using a door as a shield on one side; Haroun and Hassan on the other. But not a shot was fired. It was patently clear to them which side had the greater firepower.

'Ed, take the lads and round those bastards up, carefully.'

In a scene worthy of some old western or war movie, the two fireteams walked towards the Land Cruiser with their guns pointed towards the opposite group. Al-Kabuli and friends simply waited, laying their guns in the dust.

Mike and Bheyrya walked carefully into the hangar, senses and instinct on high alert for possible danger. The big building was silent apart from the sound of a man breathing heavily. They didn't find them until they reached the end of the line of warheads. One man was propped up against the open door of the room that had once contained the nuclear pit containers. Doctor Sami Malik was sitting in a pool of blood, his head sagging forwards, breathing hoarsely.

'Christ, they've shot off both kneecaps,' whispered Mike.

They found the body of Tarek al-Shami, a few yards away. Shot twice in the head at point blank range, he was lying on his back with his arms folded on his chest, a DVD jewel case in his hand.

19 ~ Endgame

Rear Admiral Sir Reginald Buller looked through the glass at the grey drizzle that was creeping down the windowpane. Somehow that didn't bother him one bit. If anything he was positively cheerful as he stood there blowing smoke rings at the drops of water as though he could trap them. He viewed it as a metaphysical game of horseshoes. The door in the hall clicked open in the hall and he heard Helen's high heels on the staircase beating a tattoo as she almost ran down. Walking to the open doors of the library, he was just in time to see her kiss Major Mike Robertson on both cheeks.

'Put her down Major, she'll eat you alive,' he said, as he joined them on the stone flags. 'Welcome back Mike, and congratulations on a job well done.' The Admiral pumped Mike's hand at least four times before adding, 'I think a celebratory drink is in order.' Taking them both by one arm, he walked them into the library. 'Sit.'

Suspended in a wrought iron stand, a silvery ice-bucket bedewed with condensation stood waiting beside the desk. Buller withdrew a bottle of Dom Perignon 1998, removed the foil and carefully eased off the wire cage around the cork. Rocking the cork slowly from side to side, he watched as the pressure pushed it ever upwards, leaving the neck of the bottle with satisfyingly loud pop. He filled three champagne flutes, passed two to Helen and Mike and raised his own in a toast.

'To Colonel Mike Roberts.'

'Sorry?' said Mike, questioningly.

'Of course, I haven't told you yet have I? You've moved up a rank on recommendation from the Foreign Office, which I naturally endorsed. So, congratulations, Colonel!'

Helen echoed the toast and all three took a decent sip or two, including Mike effectively toasting himself.

'Prestige and more money my boy. Nothing else changes apart from greater expectations. Glad to be back I'd guess. I'm sure Eleanor was pleased to see you.'

'Yeah, although it started with few tears and slapping me hard on the cheek. After that she was fine. You know the deal.'

'Absolutely. Anyway, a mixed bag of messages and feedback has floated in while you've been lazing around with your lovely wife. The Prime Minister's Secretariat in Islamabad has been in direct contact with Angus McFadden at the FO, in the shape of the Prime Minister's Personal Assistant, a Mr Javed Khan.'

'Interesting man. I met him at Sir Bartholomew's house.'

'I'll come back to Bart Jinks in a moment. Prime Minister Asif has sent his personal thanks to you and your team for your help; praised the professional and skilled way in which you tackled the various problems. Apparently Asif was appalled to find that two of his senior people were 'complicit in crimes against Pakistan which appear to amount to treachery in certain instances'. Allegedly his words.'

'So what's happened to Malik and Mustagh?'

'Doctor Malik is still in hospital, recovering and waiting to see whether they can operate on his legs. I thought bloody knee-capping went out with the Troubles in Ireland. Technically, he's under house arrest, as is General Mustagh. Asif's talking show trials but there are plenty of people who think they'll stay under house arrest for a few years until they're forgotten. After that, simply retired or even fed back into the machine; it's happened before.

'But there's more, and I don't think you're going to like this part. According to official reports, al-Kabuli and four others were being transported by van to the Central Jail in Rawalpindi with a police escort from Lahore, where you handed them over. Somewhere near a town called Jhelum, the convoy was attacked and all five prisoners escaped with the help of their rescuers. Officially, there are no actual leads and everyone from al-Qaeda through Lashkar-e-Taiba to the Pakistani Taliban has been blamed. No group has claimed responsibility. Chaps with our SIS are pointing the finger at Pakistan's ISI, suggesting that they want al-Kabuli back in the Federally Administered Tribal Areas to maintain the balance. Al-Kabuli acts as a lodestone for the mujahideen fighting in Afghanistan and Kashmir. Yes, I know,' Buller said, looking at Mike's grim expression.

'What the fuck's the point Sir?'

'In this case, the points plural, are that you managed to shift nuclear material in the nick of time which therefore did not fall into al-Kabuli's hands. By handing over Malik and Mustagh to the authorities, you put them out of business, possibly permanently. As a bonus, Tarek al-Shami's dead and we do have his confession on video to prove we were right. Saves a hell of a lot of money. Look at the achievements, Mike, we'll get al-Kabuli another day. Rather ironic that al-Shami's sister has joined him.'

A few more sips of champagne were necessary before he continued.

'This will make you smile. According to Bart Jinks, General Mustagh suggested we upgrade Pakistan's submarines to enable them to carry cruise missiles. That gave Jinks an idea which he suggested to Khan: that one of the most secure places to store nuclear material would be out at sea. Khan loved the idea, mainly because he had a vision of a mobile floating platform with missiles constantly pointing at India, creating a second nuclear front. I'm told that he clapped his hands and referred to – a nuclear sandwich. The upshot is that wily old Bartholomew sold HMS Invulnerable to Pakistan for almost £2.5 million. Already decommissioned, the MoD was about to sell it for scrap to Gemi Söküm for £1.8 million and off it would have gone to Aliaga in Turkey to be made into razor blades. Cunning old bastard's now negotiating a deal to refit the ship as well!'

Mike shook his head in amazement.

'I thought there was something in the wind when Khan left the house. Sir Bart started saying something about shipping but I missed most of it. Bloody hell, what an idea!'

The Admiral refilled their glasses, sat down in his favourite Chesterfield and lit his pipe. For a while they sipped their champagne and chatted amiably over lighter matters.

'So that's that one over and done with,' Buller said, changing the subject from gundogs. 'There's a rumour that al-Qaeda's developing a stronghold in the Wakhan Corridor in northeast Afghanistan, sort of stuck between the Pamir Mountains and the Karakorams. You've done a touch of climbing before Mike, how d'you fancy an all expenses paid trip up there to have a look?

Lethal Memories ~ the Authors

Of Afghani-English descent, **Jamil Sherjan** was educated in the United Kingdom and after leaving school was commissioned into the 3rd Battalion, the Parachute Regiment. He saw active service in Cyprus and Jordan, chasing terrorists, revolutionaries and insurgents. Subsequently he ran several companies in London. During that period he was engaged in covert activities in tandem with British intelligence agencies. Now retired, Jamil lives in Kent with his wife Angela; his focus on writing in between watching cricket and rugby matches.

Rob Flemming worked as a Senior Reporter/Photographer for the national newspaper, Khaleej Times in Dubai, regional newspapers in the UK and has written for numerous international magazines. His coverage has included conflicts in Lebanon, gold mining in Tajikistan, falconry in Pakistan and security issues in the oilfields of Iran. With particular interests in geopolitics and global cultures, his work has taken him to many countries across the globe. Rob lives in Gloucestershire but his writing and photography work continues wherever he may be in the world.

For more information on Jamil Sherjan, Rob Flemming and Lethal Memories, visit:

https://lensandpenpublishing.co.uk